D1276993

THE LOVELOCK VERSION

By the same author

The New Zealanders
Summer Fires and Winter Country
Among the Cinders
This Summer's Dolphin
Strangers and Journeys

THE LOVELOCK VERSION

Maurice Shadbolt

ST. MARTIN'S PRESS
NEW YORK

Copyright © 1981 by Maurice Shadbolt
For information, write: St. Martin's Press,
175 Fifth Avenue, New York, N.Y. 10010
Manufactured in the United States of America

Library of Congress Cataloging in Publication Data

Shadbolt, Maurice.
The Lovelock version.

I. Title.
PR9639.3.S5L6 1981 823 81-8720
ISBN 0-312-49953-1 AACR2

10 9 8 7 6 5 4 3 2 1

First Edition

To the memory of Pine Taiapa,
gratefully:
Kia mate ururoa, kei mate wheke.
Haere, Pine.

and with love to Bridget, Sean, Brendan,
Tui, Daniel, Brigid and everyone
else around.

Tell us why you wept so bitterly . . .
That was wrought by the gods, who
measured the life thread of these
men so that their fate might become
a poem . . .

—HOMER

Author's Note

Acknowledgements are due to Donald K. Oates, of the Windmill Press, for permission to reprint passages from *The Lives of Lovelock Junction* (1968), the first attempt at a comprehensive account of the Lovelock family, and without which this version would not have been possible; and to Kevin Ireland, holder of copyright, for permission to reprint portions of Iris Lovelock's verse from his book *My Great-Aunt and the Muse* (Randolph House, 1977). Likewise to those later members of the Lovelock family who could be persuaded to assist with this version, and whose desire for anonymity has been respected; and to Mrs Phillipa Goodyear, of the New Zealand College for Psychic Studies, for her most material help in locating the original Lovelocks. Otherwise reference to almost everyone, living or dead, is more or less intended.

Auckland–London 1976–79

Lovelock Junction: Remains of remote town founded with nineteenth century utopian fervour up Porangi River. No road; difficult water access only. Much mystery about settlement's origin; said largely to be work of sometime gold-seeker, Herman Lovelock, who arrived here with family when then Maori-populated region was still war-torn and perilous in late 1860s. Economic base appears to have been timber milling, mining of indifferent quality coal (beware shafts) and farming a little upriver at Spanish Creek; also suggestion of local ironsands being exploited. Only one derelict house left standing of many. Overgrown graves tell of lonely lives lived here: some short, some stunningly long. Crumbled shell of once vast Lovelock mansion, something of architectural legend in its time, of interest for connoisseurs of ruins: little else now to be discerned under high tides of blackberry, honeysuckle, convolvulus, secondary forest growth. Plateau setting offers superb vistas. Last known inhabitants left 1920s after debris-laden flood ended easy water access. Lower part of settlement, called Dixtown, scene of celebrated and bitterly contested labour struggle 1898–99. Birthplace of once legendary early-century operatic soprano Felicity Lovelock (1874–19??). More recently site of short-lived commune under leadership of distinguished poet Hillary Lovelock, descendant of founder Herman, who has written of river's solitude in recent verse. Prison-escaper Frank Lovelock (whose relationship to founders evident but obscure) dramatically arrested here by police posse ending long 1970s manhunt. Perhaps most piquant mystery of all is ghost-town's name: Lovelock Junction does not junction with anything, never has, never could: there is little but rugged and roadless wilderness in any direction (see *Porangi River*).

Porangi River: One of New Zealand's largest loveliest least-known rivers (174.6 kilometres long) with abundant wild scenery. Flows into North Taranaki Bight, after circuitous route from volcanic region, between sister rivers Awakino and Tongaporutu. (Often confused – though should not be – with Mokau River nearby, which has not dissimilar history.) Pioneering began here early; now abandoned. 1920s flood left waterway debris-choked: now unnavigable by all but small boats. Journey recommended only for adventurous and skilful jet-boaters (beware snags) or cautious canoeists. Has been, sometimes still is, known by other names: one whimsical Maori version is *Miminui* or 'big urine'. Those dwelling in holiday-fishing community about river mouth tend to shy off traditional name: *porangi*, origin perhaps in legend, means mad or idiot. Upriver are pioneer remnants (see *Lovelock Junction*).

—*The Shell Guide to New Zealand*
(revised version, 1979)

Part One

The way was hard, but we were bold
And all our days became as gold

—Iris Lovelock

One

Vanity, the angel said. Waste and vanity.

That, later, seemed the main message.

The confrontation with the angel, crucial in the Lovelock legend, came on an otherwise undistinguished January day in 1864. The oral record of the incident suggests that Herman Lovelock had suffered no encounters with angels, or congress with demons, prior to that day. Moreover, he was a man with no profound religious passion, no murderous metaphysical despairs. On the surface of things, and God only knows we must deal with the surface of things, his rough-cast character made it all the more unlikely that he should have been selected to receive shimmering if sometimes shopsoiled wisdom from the half-human creature who stood before him on that warm January evening. Let us suppose, for convenience, that Herman drew a demoralizing ticket in some transcendental lottery.

For angel there was. Legend admits no plausible qualification, no alternative explanation. Herman Lovelock, for example, was never more than mildly given to the drink. Nor to unreliable fancies. An upright thirty-five years old, a level-headed husband and father of three, a much voyaged veteran of goldfields across a great part of the globe, someone until then of substantial disappointments and tiny triumphs, he was nevertheless an unembittered and practical man who had no problem in persuading himself to get on with life as presented to him young among the meadows and markets and quaysides of his native Devon, and later among the diggers and diggings of California, Victoria and uninhabited Otago.

The day of the angel marks the divide in his life. He was never the same thereafter. Haunted? Hardly. Ghosts haunt. Angels instruct. And Herman Lovelock's part was to construct – well, yes, construct a kind of life in which a measure of grace might enter. Many of us would be similarly shaken, given his almost unimaginable and largely original circumstance. Many of us might likewise look skyward with the traditionally pathetic plea: 'Why me, O Lord, why me?'

More than a conventional shock to the psyche. Rather, a sword in the soul. With a festering wound thereafter. That is how we might try to see it: if we can swallow his angel, we can inhabit his skin. If not?

If not, then the question is how not: how anyone can survive this life without a suspicion of conspicuous sorcery. Apart from which only an angel, or some close equivalent, makes possible the telling of this tale. The existence of unseen, unknown stars has been deduced from the behaviour of other heavenly bodies; the existence of an angel might be deduced from the behaviour of the earthly Lovelocks, above all Herman. Otherwise legend is left with a dizzying black hole; the last thing we need. So, for God's sake, give Herman his angel. Swallow it whole. And, look, here we are, walking within his boots, in his muddy moleskins and flannel shirt, under his broad brimmed rowdy hat, in this fading twilight of January 16, 1864. Mark this too: we share his content, his fresh satisfactions. His family, recently fetched from Australia, now dwell with him in the one-room hut his blistering hands shaped from the schist and shale of the bleak Otago plateau; his two adventurous younger brothers have likewise late arrived, from Devon, plunging into the Pacific to join his search for gold as eventually profit-sharing partners on stark terrain in a strange new country. Of which more later: it is not yet a character in this chronicle, and far from obsessional in Herman Lovelock's life: let it live primitive on the wheel a little longer, rather than harden prematurely in history's kiln.

With Herman, then, we breathe the evening air. Beyond the snow-rimmed mountain ranges to the west the last of a spectacular sunset rages. The tussock brushes our boots as we walk; we leave a distinct sound of crunching shingle in our wake. The hut and tents of the small miners' camp, lit yellow with outdoor firelight, diminish behind; there is a child's voice, a woman's reply, and a whinny of a horse. And we rise to a high point, a hill of sorts, where we can consider the sunset light as it perishes upon the corrugated plain below. Grateful for the first chill of night, after the desert heat of the day, we sit comfortable on rock recently glacial. A clay pipe, a plug of tobacco; what more can we want? Herman, we see, as we weave through the corridors of his consciousness, isn't without poetry; he needs no instruction in the techniques of terrestrial meditation. This world, mark you, is best contemplated on a full stomach, which we and Herman have after a hungry winter, blizzard and flood, and a treacherous white spring which left him a bag of bones; he was, then, a man more in need of red meat than a miracle. Also there is no denying that a man is mightily receptive to the world, even among alien mountains, when the gathering of gold has gone well. The last cruel rain of spring ripped through the thin skin of earth, on Herman's claim, to leave colour literally gleaming on the hillsides. A gift? Rather a prize well won. In humanity's great nineteenth-century grab for gold, the Lovelocks have not been left wanting; Herman and his brothers have had a heady harvest. So we sit with him, on that Otago hillock, with the glimmer of orange light on a distant lake, a ripple of red on even more distant snows, and no sense of life as other than intoxicant; or possibly hallucinogen.

If the narrative pauses unpardonably here, it is possibly from compassion: we are prolonging Herman's last moment of peace. All is lucid as the light leaves the silent land; every darkening prospect pleases; and the stars grow dense in the sky. Well, then.

Herman, by rights, should rise from that rock now, and walk home to his camp again; he should call quits to this vigil. Can't he see his wife waiting, his children too? Can't he see his brothers, still fresh from Devon, are just as dependent? Can't he see that the world has no further need of his wonder? Can't he see, in short, that he is pushing his luck? We – the unfathomed future – try to warn him now: 'Herman, look, you've got a lot going for you. Can't you see where it's at? You're young still. You face a future, for once, with pockets full. Listen. Listen to reason. Go. Go now.'

He shivers suddenly: a tremor of precognition, or just the cooling of the night? Either way, it doesn't serve to shift him from that rock and leave the Lovelocks minus legend, minus most meaning; and this narrative prematurely emptied of purpose.

All right: so we have to do the angel after all. First perhaps as a vague light, high and hovering in the sky, with bluish tinge; something another century might see as a flying saucer ready to disgorge a platoon of little green men with a foolproof plan to postpone Armageddon. Herman's eyes, ours too, widen with interest as the light descends. Then that radiance slowly settles, solidifies, upon our surprised sight. And lo, we have our angel at last.

Behold, be not afraid.

Who the hell wouldn't be? He only wanted a walk to smoke his pipe in peace. Never in his life has he had much use for mystery. Yet his first panic passes, nevertheless, as he considers the angel.

Who, truth be told, the unusual lighting effect excluded, is really no more than a crabby old clerk with wings. And an ill-fitted, spasmodically incandescent halo. It is possible to sense impatience with an eternity spent as merely a message boy. Notes rustle.

Herman Lovelock?

The same, Herman answers at length.
Behold, the angel announces, you have been chosen.
Herman might well ask: For what? And by whom? And why me?
In fact he asks none of these questions. His throat is an abyss down which unspoken syllables tinkle.
All is vanity, the angel says with a wince of distaste. All is waste and vanity. All.
There is a brief pause, with notes furtively consulted, allowing Herman an intervention: You sure, he asks, you got the right man?
It seems relevance should first be established, above all accurate identity. He sees no profit in passing himself off as a willing victim.
But he merely prompts the angel to take the curt tone of prosecuting counsel.
Your name is Herman Lovelock? Your occupation is that of gold digger? Your current abode is in Dead Man's Gully, on the Otago goldfields, in southern New Zealand?
Yes, yes, yes, Herman agrees. But—
So what of your soul? the angel demands austerely.
This is an unpromising line of approach to Herman, his character considered. Also problems of bodily need have lately preoccupied him to the exclusion of concern for the soul. He feels unfairly harrassed. Just when he seems to have found content for the first time, having earned it hard besides, something like this has to turn up. Just his luck.
Soul? he says, helpless.
Is it not true, the angel asks, that you have wasted youth and strength pursuing yellow metal?
Waste? queries Herman. It brings a damn fair price.
At what cost? To the soul?
I have a wife, Herman objects. Children to feed.
His problem, the angel's unyielding expression suggests. For he – or it – seems determined to allow him no fig-leaf in this flinty Eden where few men, if any, have walked before. Even Dead Man's Gully is a name no more than three months old, since thaw uncovered a lone, lost and anonymous prospector whom Herman buried.
Keep to the point, the angel insists.
It is the blasted point, Herman argues.
Consider gold, proposes the angel.
Herman considers it, as suggested, with some satisfaction.
So what is it? the angel asks after further perusal of notes.
You tell me, Herman sighs. It looks to me like you got all the answers there.
Vanity, the angel insists. Waste. It neither toils nor does it spin.

It what? I see. Is that my fault? Who made it?
No matter. Consider nectar.
Consider what?
Nectar. The nectar of the flower kingdom. And bees.
Herman considers both nectar and bees with mystification.
Nectar exists, the angel asserts, but to draw bees to the flower. Similarly there is gold in a land but to draw people. Like you.
Herman has to concede a possible parallel.
What, the angel asks, hypothetically, would you make of a bee which never flew home to the hive to make honey? But wasted life, and life's purpose, in vain pursuit of nectar, no more?
A queer bee, Herman agrees, and then gets the point. But you're talking of me.
Indeed, says the angel with triumph.
Look, Herman protests. I know I'm making money, not honey. God knows, though, I just do my blasted best.
The creature is now pure contempt: Consider yourself.
Herman tries honourably, and fails. Who wouldn't?
Given a new land, the angel goes on, what do you do? When you have nectar enough for the taking, what is it you continue to do?
Shovel, Herman suggests helpfully. You can't say sweating over a shovel doesn't keep me out of harm's way. I have no idle hands for the devil to use.
Shovel? the angel mocks. You grovel. You still grovel for gold. It is not what you, Herman Lovelock, were born for. Think on that.
I am thinking all right, Herman replies. And the first thing I am thinking is that it's time to head home to the camp.
It is most likely the onset of a fever. Either that or the monotony of shovelling and sluicing and panning has played merry hell with his brain. But no rational hypothesis, it appears, has power to put the apparition to flight. It obstinately and luminously lingers before him. Perhaps the confounded place is haunted: he should have known better, maybe, than to burrow into a depression he casually called Dead Man's Gully, possibly confirming some curse upon it.
Too late, the angel declares.
Quite correctly. Our hindsight has been no help at all. We may also soon find Herman's skin a substantial hindrance unless we leap free. There. Done. A near thing. Who wants to be caught implausibly arguing with an angel in AD 1864? In any case a dispassionate view of events, from this point, is more desirable than inhabiting Herman.
To seek gold for itself, the angel resumes, is no adult way for a grown man to behave. For whom shall it profit, in the generations of men? Will

it make for grace, for wisdom? Shall it leave your children one with creation?

Hell's bells, says Herman. Why pick on me?

Because you are here, the angel answers.

Herman Lovelock, then: a virgin Everest which the holy spirit lusts to deflower. Or worse. All the same, he is not easily to be gelded by God, if this is the case.

And only half alive, the angel adds. Only half alive in this life.

There are other poor sods of whom the same might be said, objects Herman.

But they are not you, Herman Lovelock. Not you.

No?

No. You have been chosen. I come to deliver your mission. Your destiny. Your destiny here.

Here?

Here. In this land, no less.

Bloody hell, says Herman, which is no more than truth; he remembers the purgatorial miseries of winter, and snow, and floods filled with the corpses of drowned diggers; he is fresh from a day roasting in a trench as hot as the devil's own oven. Here? This bloody business is quite out of hand. His destiny can be delivered elsewhere, preferably in Devon, when he gets back. He has never lived in landscape more murderous. Or Godless, for that matter. There is but one mission for a man in his right mind to embrace here. Gold, and getting out fast.

Henceforth, suggests the angel, you shall have done with gold. You shall lead others to grace. Your name shall be sung, shall be honoured, in the human family.

Herman, reeling, feels it pertinent to ask: Why? What for?

Man must learn how to live, explains the angel. A new land is a new chance. There is little time to lose.

How long?

Maybe a century, the angel replies. Maybe a few decades more, but not much.

Good God, says Herman. By then I'll be dead.

Quite, agrees the angel. But think of your seed. Your sons, your heirs, and those who come after. Think. Take it from me, there's chaos abroad, with still more to come.

Bugger me, says Herman, appalled. I reckon enough is enough.

You take my point, the angel misunderstands smugly. Now I suggest you get on with it fast.

With what?

The light suffusing the angel begins to flicker, to grow faint, rather to the apparition's alarm.

With what? Herman persists.

The angel manages, dimly, to gasp: Use your imagination. All will be, Herman Lovelock, as you choose.

Choose? Me?

Choose, the angel agrees vaguely.

For the creature now appears essentially preoccupied with its own problems. Something is radically wrong. The light flutters, the wings twitch feebly; perhaps a divine energy crisis.

You've shown me no damn credentials, says Herman. How in hell do I know who you are?

Choose, argues the angel, who is now shrinking fast and soon far away. Choose.

Lo: the frustratingly ephemeral creature has flown. Behold: Herman is left bulkily earthbound on the hillock, with nothing but darkness, and the light of his distant encampment.

Henceforth the paranormal will never have so ambitious or ambiguous a place in Herman's story. Which is no help at all; the damage is done. The tale is recorded here with reluctance, also in fairness to family legend. Take it or leave it. The sceptic, in any case, can swiftly dismiss it as dream; doctors might characterize the vision as a discharging lesion of the occipital cortex, diagnosing Herman as potentially epileptic; spiritualists might explain the apparition as a playful elemental presence, of the kind which upsets an otherwise instructive seance, or perhaps as the deceased digger of Dead Man's Gully giving vent to goldless despairs; the psychic researcher will request evidence which might stand in a court of law, and in its absence will announce that there is no case to answer; Jungian psychologists might talk of manifestations of the collective subconscious, and Freudians guess at buried Oedipal guilts.

Considering such confusion, we had best make do with the angel and get Herman home. Not to the green and generously wooded Dart Valley of Devon, which is at the moment his deepest desire. Realism allows him but a few hundred barren yards of ground back to his camp. Nothing there shall be untoward, or disturbing. His children will be sleeping; his exhausted brothers too. His wife will be welcoming. He might even sleep, and wake in the morning much the same man. Nevertheless, daylight's sweat will nourish doubt, and the intimations of destiny the angel planted; and nourish this narrative too.

For the following day, or the day after that, it hardly matters when,

Herman finds occasion to rise to his full height – perceptibly more than six feet – from the dehydrated alluvial debris of Dead Man's Gully, from his graceless grovelling for gold, and announce: 'This, by God, is no adult way for grown men to behave.'

With that, he slams down his pan, before sight of his astonished brothers; never did a cymbal sound with greater emphasis.

'Tell me different,' he challenges.

They cannot.

Two

In the circumstances, brevity is preferable to padding this narrative with speculation. We have too far to travel.

Once possessed of a theme best left to theologians, Herman, as absurdly and marvellously human as any of us, has to shape it as his own: insufficient to shelve the embryonic idea and wait for it to find form, or desirably to wither. 'Gold,' he pronounces, 'is for the feeble minded.' Almost daring fortune to do its worst. And since Herman heaved himself free of a family of distinctly frayed fortune in the first place, this is no meagre challenge, emphatically not on a claim so rich. The claim isn't called a Homeward Bounder for nothing; it has first-class steamer passages printed from peg to peg. It has been Herman's intention, since he took ship from Torquay to California fifteen years before, to gather up enough gold to make his family substantial upon his return to his Devon hearth, a prodigal with bullion, saviour of the Lovelock line. It has been no part of his intention to make more than temporary camp in any new country, most of which are only good for fools of amateur farmers anyway; never to settle for longer than gold lasts, or at least longer than dietary deficiency becomes acute; never to do more than pad his pockets for that return as a man of means capable of reclaiming a family estate, replenishing a lost domain. No. Never. Now, a heartbeat or two from consummation, ambition fails him. Not nerve: ambition. The mineral to which he has given his life is a base metal after all – such is the perverse alchemy of the angel – to the point of being unworthy of the world: certainly of human aspiration. But if this is the case, where is the adult way for a grown man to behave?

From this point, for our own sake and Herman's, we must see him as a man not to be seduced by trivialities. By simplicities, perhaps. There is certainly nothing tawdry in Herman's stance, crashed gold pan at his feet, towering manly beneath ice-moulded mountains. Here is one to win wild applause from the heavens.

Wait, though.

For one thing, he is looking at eroded hogsback and treeless highland, the lofty and barbarous landscape about him, as if he has just woken from dream. Where is he? Who is he? And why?

Questions not exclusively the curse of the Lovelock line. Who and why shall remain unanswered; the angel has short-changed him there. Mankind must evidently be kept in business. The who and why, in crazed shout or hoarse whisper, shall continue to be the real music of men in this world.

The where? That is answerable, just.

For latter-day Herman landscape has been of two kinds. Landscape where gold is, landscape where it is not. Other categories are inconvenient. California, Victoria, Otago, veined or grained with gold, merge as one. Countries are irrelevant appendages. The appendage of this place is called New Zealand, if Herman remembers the name right. He recalls a settlement of sorts where his boat berthed. Dunedin. A misty hole filled with muddy Scotsmen. Cattle and burnt-off bush. Expensive whisky and sharp shopkeepers. Herman paused there only to buy some boots before hiking upland. And food, at a right rare price too. That is all Herman has seen of the country. That, and these mountains. There must be more to it, God knows, than diabolic wastes to be endured only for gold; why else expend an angel upon it? True that men of Herman's complexion are late-comers here. The place appears to be no more than two or three punitively tall islands distributed upon uncongenial seas. A certain amount of geography has impressed itself upon him by way of bucking cargo boat, thorny foothills, vociferous rivers, and pitiless mountain passes. History, if any, has yet to reveal itself underfoot.

Not that he needs it in a conventional sense; not when embarked on carving his own. Herman, who has never gone much on the Bible, locates a decrepit copy in the camp, and gives himself to concentrated search for clues to his condition. Before long he has Ecclesiastes haunting his head: he communes with his own heart, saying, Lo, I am come to great estate and have gotten more wisdom than all they that have been before me . . .

And Herman, God help him, God save the Lovelocks, now gives his heart to know wisdom, and to know madness and folly.

Grief?

Well, yes. For in much wisdom, sayeth the prophet, is much grief; and he that increaseth knowledge increaseth grief.

Herman shall have his share. He may not increaseth knowledge greatly; but as sure as hell he is about to increaseth grief.

*

With Herman in apparent brainstorm, it might be tactful to consider his camp. His wife Sarah, a shy dark Welsh girl met and married in Australia, is still a bewildered bride for all their three children; Herman is a happening in her life which she is still at pains to comprehend. She loves him, since this is expected of her, and other people's expectations are all she has ever had to call her own. When she weeps, it is always in corners, unseen. As a cook, and she is never much else, she already has a creditable range of improvizations with mutton and mouldy potatoes. As a mother, she has three sons who have survived; testimony enough to her competence. As a wife, she is still surprised by this muscular man who sighs so fervently upon her slight body: is this weak, lost stranger her Herman? She is flattered and dizzied by his evident need of her. But she carries water from the river, looks up at the sky, and tries to remember the words of an unusually evocative hymn she heard once. They will never quite come, though she can taste them inaudibly on her tongue. Impromptu prayers arrive easier. God must have mercy, in the end; that much she knows. And on her children. On Herman too. On them all. Otherwise, why this? Only when she weeps is the otherwise overwhelming in Sarah's life.

The three children? They are too young, Benjamin, Ernest, and Luke, to contemplate at length: six, four and two years respectively. Nor with any confidence in their future; it might soon be surmised that they have none. In any case they will recall next to nothing of these difficult days. Victims of lightning strike sometimes suffer loss of memory.

Finally, before we return to that brainstorm, we need to note Herman's two brothers, Richard and James. They alone, of a half-score of Lovelock sons in far Devon, acknowledged Herman's call to the latest goldfield in the Pacific. Richard is as big and heavy as Herman, at times as handsome, though flawed by a flabbiness about the lips: he can kill a sheep quick, and knows what gold is about. It is about money. Money asks no questions, and nor does Richard. He has a shrewd countryman's eye on the wealth they have begun to win, and is already sure no bugger left behind in Devon is going to benefit. Herman can go home a hero. Richard has no such aspiration. He will go home rich, envied, and the toast of Totnes when it suits him. The apathetic Lovelocks left in Devon will never ride easy on Richard's back. He cannot imagine not returning, since to this point Herman hasn't. In Herman Richard has rediscovered a father. Their mutual father perished of brandy and bitterness while the death-watch beetle industriously ticked through the Elizabethan beams of a falling family home; a picture inclement enough, especially financially, to spur Richard downriver to Dartmouth, then from port to port, in pursuit of the first Pacific-bound boat when Herman's call came.

Then there is James. The youngest of the Lovelock sons. Slender, wispily bearded, brown with the goldfields summer, and but a babe when last seen by Herman. When he called for brothers to follow, he didn't bargain on this gentle boy, with barely more than the clothes he stood in, in steerage with Richard. The fiddle he carried seemed inauspicious. Herman has nevertheless done his best to make James more functional. He has persuaded James to see that enlightenment comes best at the business end of a long-handled shovel; that there is poetry in swinging a pick. True that he can still fiddle a day away if rain drives them to shelter. But Herman and an arid summer ensure that days to fiddle away are few. Then there is the matter of his art. James fell into the wandering hands of a pederast schoolmaster when younger: a gifted drunk who taught him to draw. Sketchbooks pillowed James's head in steerage. Now they reside in his bachelor tent. He has drawn their camp, and other camps nearby. When he takes packhorses to the nearest canvastown to fetch provisions, he draws there too. He has even sold an unsigned selection of these drawings to a passing stranger. This selection is to be discovered dusty in a Dunedin basement a century later. When exhibited, they will be described as an unique record of early Otago goldfield life – 'vibrant,' said *The Otago Daily Times* critic, 'with the truth of lonely lives in harsh landscape . . . the hills skeined with the thin smoke of campfires.' They are to fetch up finally in the Arrowtown museum – Arrowtown being one of those Otago goldtowns described by buggy-riding tourist Anthony Trollope as evolving from canvas to corrugated iron ('it does not make picturesque houses,' he said), finally to wood. At which point it solidified under a sea of sycamores to strike a pleasing pose for the Instamatics and Polaroids of this century's tourists. The tiny museum houses all that is left of the Lovelocks in Otago. Lately published in modest portfolio ('nothing is known of the artist or his origins,' says the museum note) James Lovelock's drawings show Herman, Sarah, Richard and the three children as they were in their camp before their lives were blown elsewhere, leaves in an unworldly wind.

There they all are, forever, young in a wild land. Herman feeding gold-bearing gravel down a long tom. Richard panning the residue. Sarah cooking. Benjamin, Ernest and Luke like tiny exclamation marks among the tents and rounded hilltops of Otago; such punctuations will proliferate.

God's mercy. We must leave them there.

*

The truth, then. Not all in this narrative is speculation. Much is translation of the oral record. Some is interpretation of the written. Finally, and here we tread aberrant terrain, some is derived from apparently reliable report of Herman beyond the grave; he was not, such evidence suggests, a man to be confined by any bloody wooden box. (James, yes, and Richard have had more meagre say, which means they have failed to outshout Herman down the available channel of communication.) It is to that especially resonant voice from the less than distant dead that we owe knowledge of the resurrection of James's drawings, for example. They were sighted in the Arrowtown museum only last summer; exactly where Herman, or some capricious impersonator of the man, predicted they would be found. Make what you will of that.

The Lovelocks, then, do they live? Never, mercifully, this narrator's problem. But yes. If you like. If you must know. Yes. They do. They live. This life, this unfinished fable, this scriptless dream, and too untidy by far, is also too short for elegant sport with the spurious; and too intricate for truth. So we have this fool's game we call fiction: fables within fable, dreams within dream. Finished. Scripted. Tidy transactions with the probable. But what if all is improbable? Besides, who dreams the dreamer? Who dreams this narrator dreaming Herman dreaming the angel?

It seems we are back in business.

Three

Richard stares. James shades his eyes against the sun.

'Gold,' Herman repeats, 'is for the feeble minded.'

'So what,' Richard asks, 'are you trying to tell us?'

'Just that. It is time to give this childishness away.'

Now Richard is incredulous. 'Give it away? Gold?'

'We will leave here honourable men. All three.'

'Please God,' Richard prays, 'leave me feeble minded.'

'Henceforth,' announces Herman, already distinctly taking angelic tone, 'we shall behave as adult, grown men. What is gold, after all?'

They wait, Richard and James, for Herman to tell them.

'Mother's milk,' Herman suggests. 'In new lands such as this, mother's milk. Where new children suckle the land. No more. We have had our time at the teat. Now enough is enough. Infancy is over; we must wean ourselves.'

'The sun,' Richard says sidelong to James. 'This blasted sun. The heat. Gone to his head. See it in his eyes.'

True that Herman's eyes burn. But he ignores Richard's commentary. 'Otherwise,' he goes on, 'infancy is forever. And whom shall infancy profit?'

'Bugger me,' says Richard. 'Herman, do I hear right? James, do you hear what I hear? Here we are, dragged around the world, both of us, for what? For him to tell us, the moment money comes in, that we don't need the gold. If I hear right, I am out of my mind. Or he is out of his. I'll tell you whom infancy profits, Herman. Me.'

Herman is nevermore to be tempted by the venial. 'We have,' he informs them, 'large things to do with our lives.'

'Like what?' Richard asks.

An answer is still skirmishing for a form in Herman's head; he makes no reply.

'James,' asks Richard, 'are you listening to all this?'

James nods.

'Then say something, man.'

'I am,' replies James, 'interested in what Herman has to say.'

'Interested?'

'In what he means.'

'And you know what he means?'

'No,' James confesses. 'Not yet.'

'That makes two of us. All I can see is, Herman is now too proud to pick up gold. And don't see fit to tell us why.'

'He is trying,' James decides, with compassion.

For Herman has gone into mental retreat. If he hears his kin, he gives no sign. His gaze is beyond them, upon distant mountains. Those old pagan pathways to the sky still make eloquent offering to the imagination. One or two hundred miles north, that summer afternoon, a short dark sheepman by name of Samuel Butler, having done with the day's shearing and played himself out on his grand piano, is meditating upon the same mountains. His imagination is finding its way past rock and river, eventually and satirically to inhabit Erewhon. Herman's condition, on the other hand, is substantially lyrical: he sees, if mistily, somewhere fit for Lovelocks to live. An elsewhere, still unknown. No Erewhon.

'What is it, Herman?' Richard asks. 'What is it you want? To go back?'

'Back?' says Herman vaguely.

'To Devon.'

'Devon?'

'Pardon us for being alive,' Richard says. 'We just want to know what you are thinking. Is it too much to ask?'

'Ask what?'

Richard kicks at a stone in ill humour. This saves him from kicking Herman in ill humour. Bad enough to live in crisis. Worse not to know the nature of that crisis. Richard is a man blind in a blizzard of possibilities. So is Herman, though that isn't clear yet.

'Ask if we're going back,' Richard explains. 'Is it too much to ask?'

'There is no going back,' Herman announces. 'Man must go forward.'

Not more than a day or two earlier, though Richard can hardly bring himself to believe it now, he had an elder brother who spoke with some sanity. And who offered no pronouncements on the nature of man. Who took gold as it came. Life as lived.

'The plan was always to go back,' Richard protests. 'Always.' He pauses. 'So what is new?'

Fortunately for all concerned, under a common-sense summer sky, Herman does not propose astral interference – nor even a querulous and often uninformative angel – as answer. He can but convey to his kin that life as lived, gold as gathered, is insufficient for such as they. The rest will reveal itself. Doubt that, and he might doubt all.

'What is new,' Herman answers, 'is that I have eyes to see.'

'Favour us, for God's sake, with what you see,' Richard insists.

Herman blinks. Shades his eyes yet again. Visionaries late to their vocation are seldom deterred by momentary loss of vision. And sometimes visions are literal to the eye.

'I see mountains,' Herman announces. 'Many mountains.'

So his brothers share his westward gaze. And contemplate mountains. Many mountains.

Herman's confidence climbs.

'Beyond those mountains,' he continues, 'is land. Empty land. Land which knows nothing of man.'

This knowledge does not derive from vision. Herman has been told so by an itinerant on the Otago fields who once roved that western, mountain-shielded side of the South Island and failed to find colour there. 'There is nothing over there,' this haunted and toothless itinerant said into his whisky. 'Nothing. No human face in ten weeks' walking. And no gold.' This last is reassuring, for Herman's purpose.

'Consider,' says Herman now, surprising himself with that which his voice discovers, 'what man might make of such territory. Consider what we might make of it. Consider.'

If Herman pauses, it is palpably because he has only just begun to consider it himself: in flying so outlandish a kite he has to be more than a panoramic breathing space ahead of his brothers. So he strains to see what the mountains might still tell him. Otago goldfields historian Vincent Pyke, writing twenty years later, will see these mountains as a mote upon the eye of the earlier diggers: he will explain the eventual desertion of the Otago diggings in 1865 as due to 'the very natural curiosity confessedly felt to ascertain the nature of the country beyond the snow-clad ranges . . . '

Thus, as we shall see, Herman is only a year ahead of his time. But that alas can be left till later; no need to confuse this narrative now. Enough for us to know that Herman is now thinking something like a minute ahead of his brothers. Richard has ceased looking westward in despair. James, on the other hand, is not yet past seeing romance in unknown peaks.

'We have been as the blind,' Herman declares with considered provocation. The theme, besides, offers opportunity for further improvization. 'We have been men made blind by Mammon's gleam.'

'What of Devon?' Richard asks.

'Devon?'

'Where we belong. Remember?'

'The future shall see it,' Herman predicts, 'as where we began. Not where we end.' With eloquence leading him by the hand, Herman suddenly and magnificently senses where he has arrived: he suffers his brothers the reminder of the Lord's bidding to Abraham.

Richard, rather bitterly, confesses to needing more specific reminder. He is disposed to believe that the Bible, as sabbath soporific, is best seen and not heard.

It is his good fortune, then, that Herman yet again has the unkempt camp Bible in hand: it is never to be found far from him now. Herman quotes: Get thee out of thy country, and from thy kindred, and from thy father's house, unto a land that I will shew thee. And I will make of thee a great nation, and I will bless thee, and make thy name great; and thou shalt be a blessing . . .

'Let me get this right,' Richard intervenes. 'Because of what God gabbled to some old Jew, you want to make the Lovelocks a great nation?'

'A great name,' Herman suggests, more modestly. 'A blessing.'

'By God,' announces Richard, 'then I am in a dream. Pinch me, James. It isn't real. I wish to wake. Today I am a gold digger. Tomorrow I am a nation. A great name. All things holy.'

But Herman is still travelling; any precedent is pearl of great price. 'Beyond those mountains,' he tells his two listeners, 'is our chance to begin. What does mankind most want?'

'This nation needs tobacco,' Richard proposes. 'We're down to our last plug. And dare I speak of good gold in this ground crying out for deliverance?'

'Mankind most wants progress,' Herman answers to his own satisfaction.

'Progress?' Richard objects. 'You call walking off a profitable claim progress?'

'Progress,' Herman says, now with a fertile noun to father more nouns, 'is coal – an honourable, god-given substance. Timber too. Iron. All those things, more, might be to the west. Who shall know?'

'Who wants to know?' asks Richard.

'Let it be written,' suggests Herman, 'that the Lovelocks ventured.' Coal, timber and iron now make an ungainly dance with God in his head. How and why, heaven knows: of such incongruity is prophecy often shaped. Let us see Herman as human, merely a man of his time. If the refashioning of foreskins seemed a covenant to prehistoric Abraham, why not coal, timber and iron to nineteenth-century Herman? Gold is the devil's gaudy lure in man's long darkness. Coal, timber and iron are of the light. That light, in his time, is called progress.

'Herman,' announces Richard, 'you are out of hand.' To James he adds, 'We must put him to bed.'

'I cannot see how that will help,' James observes sanely. 'Herman must have his say.'

'He has had enough to say.'

'Clearly,' James goes on diffidently, 'Herman has much on his mind.'

'He has madness on his mind.'

They talk as if Herman is not present. In other than a physical sense, of course, he is not; his mind's eye is moving mountains aside; his actual gaze doesn't waver from due west by the compass. Brotherly babble is neither here nor there.

'Something has happened to Herman,' James concludes presently. 'The least we can do is listen, with sympathy. It may all pass; who knows?'

One hesitates to terminate this curious family cameo; but narrative by nature is addicted to the notion of progress too. Such conversation cannot go anywhere. All the sympathy in the world will not help toward understanding Herman. True that his elevated tone will pass; his derivative eloquence will become provisionally and earthily his own. That will make Herman at least a more intelligible burden to his brothers. But next morning late-sleeping Herman will wake as if his departure from the goldfields is accomplished fact; his imagination is already crossing mountains. Naturally he will be irritated to find that everything is as before, that Richard and James are energetic out on the claim already, that Sarah is baking damper bread on the outdoor fire, that Benjamin, Ernest and Luke are squalling merrily through the Otago morning.

Sarah has not been perceptibly gripped by Herman's news that they are departing the goldfields, which is all he has so far seen fit to tell her. The prospect of moving camp yet again occasions her no surprise. Since she shipped with her parents away from the dusty slate valleys of Snowdonia, Sarah's life has been a tapestry of struck tents and broken camps. In any case she has never been able to imagine dwelling long in a place with the name of Dead Man's Gully. 'All I would like is a home,' she tells Herman.

'You shall have it,' he now promises to excess.

Now, dark and sweaty over the bread, she hears Herman's long howl from within the hut. That howl paralyses the children at play. It makes Richard and James pause on the claim, lift their heads and look at each other. Neither has heard a howl like it. Sarah races into the hut. Herman is merely pulling a shirt over his shoulders. And rediscovering the disparate detail of human existence: clothes, boots, a full bladder and empty stomach, wife, children, brothers. Detail sufficient to suffocate any vision. Having made himself audible, perhaps even in heaven, he feels considerably refreshed.

'What is it?' asks Sarah.

'We get on with it,' he answers.

He does. He begins the battle with detail. He rides to the nearest tent town to sell off gold, buy packhorses and provisions. He tells Sarah to pack small. He has his problems, of course. Richard at first refuses to desert the claim, and appeals to James also to stand fast; James appears to waver, though in truth he is only being thoughtful, and at length allows it to be known that he is going with Herman. 'Why?' demands Richard. 'Are you mad too?'

'No,' insists James. 'But I am interested.'

'In what?'

'In what happens.'

'What can happen?'

'That is my interest,' James answers. 'No one can know. Anything can.'

'You will be sorry,' Richard promises.

'That is possible too.'

James has no pecuniary grief; he is in search of the currency of the sublime. If anything is likely to make him sorry, it is more the thought that he might never see the marshes, rivers and moors of Devon again. But there is more sorrow in the prospect of not seeing Sarah again. Virginal James has been in love with Herman's shy wife since he first sighted her. It is a hopeless thing, but love has no need of hope. Nor of gold. He will follow Herman and Sarah.

'Look what you are doing to us,' Richard tells Herman. 'We are falling apart.'

It is no use. Richard hurls himself upon the claim with fresh ferocity while the Otago era of the Lovelocks ends around him. The others are busy preparing and packing. Richard already feels alone in this desolate place; he imagines winter without Herman, Sarah and James; he begins to panic. Perhaps, after all, the gold is growing thin on the claim. Perhaps, after all, Herman knows something Richard does not know. And perhaps Richard will miss out.

Next day, when the others are ready to ride, Richard is visibly if irritably ready too. They begin, with the creak of harness, the clatter of saucepans, the muffled dissonance of children, to move slowly towards the mountains. The Otago sun heats shadeless valleys.

Where are they riding? Beyond the mountains is land. Herman at least has that right. It has largely been left alone by man. He has that right too. What he has not considered is that there may be compelling reason for leaving it alone. Where there is not black rain forest, there is swamp. Where there is not swamp, there is black rain forest. French voyager Jules de Blosseville, in a prospectus for the place, called it 'one long solitude, with forbidding sky, frequent tempests, and impenetrable forests'. That Gallic lyricism has been tempered by feverish and foot-sore Anglo-Saxons. The first white man unwise enough to attempt a traverse of the coast recorded in his journal on March 21, 1847: 'Rain continuing, dietary shorter, strength decreasing, spirits falling, prospects fearful.'

There is something else material to their journey. On that January day when Herman announced his westward move two Maoris beyond the mountains found an interesting rock in the Hohonu River. It was solid *pounamu* – also called greenstone, or New Zealand jade, the hardest material ever worked by neolithic man, and certainly the most attractive. Maoris on that bleak coast were few, mostly dislocated survivors of slaughtered or enslaved tribes who had taken sanctuary in uncoveted wilderness. Their one advantage has always been that the rivers of their region were studded with *pounamu*, precious for weapons and adornments, useful for barter and to buy survival from more powerful tribes. Naturally these two Maoris, lately baptized Simon and Samuel, were delighted by their discovery. With limbs of trees they levered the boulder from the bed of the river. When muddy water cleared from the cavity left by the boulder, there was a distinct gleam of coarse gold. Simon and Samuel knew about gold. It was, so to speak, the *pounamu* of the white man. They had observed wasted and fretful whites seeking such stuff. On the other hand they had not met many white men nor seen the point in gold. They were far more interested in the demonstrably beautiful boulder of *pounamu* they had won from the river. Their problem was how to break up so big a boulder and get it, piece by piece, down to the coast for commercial purposes. So they hiked down-river and reported in to their chief Tarapuhi, mentioning the gold almost as afterthought, and with Tarapuhi set off to the nearest trading post to fetch drills and a heavy iron hammer to break up the boulder. At the trading post Tarapuhi explained his business with the boulder and, never one to leave a success story unfinished, considerately drew the storekeeper's attention to the gleam in the river Simon and Samuel had seen. It was just the news two eavesdropping white men needed.

It is certainly not news that Herman needs as he heads the little horseback column of Lovelocks out of Otago, toward the mountains, toward that coast, toward an adult way for grown men to behave.

Four

No printed account has done justice to the journey. Nor, for sanity's sake, can this one. It is treated as peripheral apocrypha in Philip Temple's *Trails of New Zealand's Wild Westland* (Little Akaloa Press, 1974). In connection with the rugged Haast region, between Otago and Westland, mountaineer Temple says '. . . there is also a dubious oral tradition of a large family group, with young children, adventuring through this area at a time when it was still considered too hazardous by many hardy explorers. Contemporary records are, however, virtually silent on the subject; and to historian and mountaineer, a century later, it seems a most improbable trek.' It is dealt with as unreliably in the inadequate centennial publication *The Lives of Lovelock Junction* by Maurice Shadbolt (Windmill Press, 1968), an indifferently researched booklet hastily and dutifully produced by an ill-defined Lovelock descendant, and about which Herman has apparently had much robust criticism to make from his roost in the beyond. The cartographically incurious and pitifully cautious author refers merely to 'an epic journey overland', no more, leaving the impression of likely adjectival extravagance. In his scholarly essay *The Happy Havens: Utopian Adventures in the Antipodes* (Harrybrooke House, 1956) E. H. McCormick, in a paragraph or two given to Lovelock origins, mentions travel of 'some apparent magnitude' and 'evidently involving great vicissitudes' but otherwise frankly confesses himself at a loss in accounting for the early movements of the family: in this respect he has something in common with the Lovelocks themselves, as might be seen. There is another cryptic account in *New Zealand Ghost Towns: A Pictorial Record*, by Dick Scott (Southern Cross Books, 1975). Scott, whose primary interest is elsewhere, refers to Herman harshly as 'the fanatical founder of a fast forgotten town' who led his family on 'a miraculous and little-known long march across mountain and river, through immense and menacing wilderness', looking for a place to plant his colours. For the rest, Scott's atmospheric prose is concerned with winds whining through the derelict doorways of Lovelock Junction, river waters lapping at fallen jetties; and that is no help to us here, with Herman still a hellish long way from Lovelock Junction.

'How long?' asks Richard.

'Ten days,' Herman estimates.

Months later his answer will still be ten days. If creation encompassed seven days, including one for rest, mountains might prudently be crossed in ten. Also Herman is not inclined to make provision for rest.

They have no maps. There are none. Goldfield gossip tells of an Austrian explorer who found his way through. So far, perhaps slow to recover, he has composed no map for the enlightenment of his species.

Left-over January is largely occupied with relinquishing Otago. They pass the solitary tents and tiny towns of diggers who have pushed excitably inland. These skeletal men dig literally for their lives on any riverside with suspicion of colour. Tucker claims, not Homeward Bounders; and tucker is the poorest mutton money can buy. Graves are free, and frequently dug. Nothing, in short, contrives to divert Herman from his course. They soon ride in a land of lake and canyon and reverberant alpine torrents; all sawtooth terrain with spiky scrub. Seeking low country, Herman leads his column into precipitous cul de sacs too often for comfort, and Richard's patience. Vast slides of shingle slow their horses. Crevasse and complaint alike persuade Herman to see virtue in pushing boldly skyward, sometimes into cloud, up stony ridges and across fissured plateaus.

He does not press the pace, though often tempted. At times, in this warm weather, they seem something of a picnic party. They camp, for a time, along lakesides. They feast on wild duck as relief from salt beef. The extremely scenic silences grow still more pertinent. They are well in sight of the mountain wall ahead. Day by day that wall shows itself to greater advantage. The lakes fill with the reflections of those increasingly lucid peaks.

In February they find the mountains undisguised. Between one hill and another the desert disappears. God has never drawn a line more precise. Here is dry tussock country. There is damp forest. No preliminary. Beyond the damp forest the mountains untidily mass. They shut out half the sky.

Richard reins in. 'There?' he says. 'We go in there?'

'Where else?' asks Herman.

He calls a halt, nevertheless, in order to comprehend the most influential sight, and they camp short of the forest. Richard explores tomorrow's route, vanishing into the dark vegetation. The children fetch scrap wood for a fire. Smoke soon rises; so do tents. Sarah, fanning the flame, fears that their provisions may not last. James, after tuning his fiddle, and offering the afternoon a jaunty air, finally settles for sketching their last Otago vista. Crag and lake take on queer peace, perhaps premature nostalgia, as he looks down valley; he prefers to keep tomorrow's mountains to his rear. Herman fills his pipe, lights it, and walks contemplative circles around the camp.

Richard returns to communicate his findings. He conveys grime and facial anguish. Words are more difficult.

'So?' Herman demands.

'Those aren't Devon woods in there,' Richard announces. 'Nothing like. Nothing like anything, except jungle maybe. It goes on and on. And nothing above. No sky. Just trees. Ferns. Creepers. Fungus. Growing up and up. A man cannot see further than five paces. I am lucky to get back. Herman, there is all that ahead. Not to speak of mountains.'

'Then,' argues Herman, 'we shall not speak of mountains. One thing at a time.'

'We could still turn back,' Richard pleads.

Herman seems not to hear. Next day they leave the sky. The forest is all that Richard promised. Trees. Ferns. Creepers. Mud underfoot. Gloom. True that birds bell somewhere above them. Otherwise they hear only the formidable roar of wild rivers, and then sound more unfamiliar, energetic vibrations. Herman half-heartedly tries to persuade the party that it is the sea; that they are close to the other side of the island. But the truth is soon apparent: avalanches are beginning to boom about them. It is impossible to ride horseback. They lead their horses. All but little Luke, slung in an improvized sidesaddle cradle. An hour earns a hundred yards. The forest floor is a mosaic of moss, filmy fern, slimy rock, rotting logs and leaves. Fungus flourishes as long as God's beard. Horses slither and stumble. Humans too.

March is mostly mountains, more forest; April is indistinguishable. Often, weeks later, they find their own campsites again. They are travelling in circles, more often in triangles; these geometric unravellings give Richard in particular ample cause for grievance. They name places as they pass, and pass again. Buggeration Gully. Purgatory Peaks. Catastrophe Creek. Sarah's fear for their provisions is well founded. They are soon down to their last few handfuls of flour and oatmeal. Richard's rifle blasts birds from the bush. Otherwise pickings are lean. Sometimes, and typically at the point where they think they have located a flaw in the maze, they find themselves frustrated at the brink of a great ravine, where a generous river tumbles. They begin again, seeking a new way west. Any other point of the compass causes Herman to be contankerous. In any case even return east would now present a problem, if they tried. They do not try. Herman still leads. Man must go forward. Progress is all. Nevertheless, valley after valley is crammed with crashing waters. They lose two horses when Herman tries to urge them, against their better instinct, across a flooded stream. They almost lose Herman. While he holds most tentatively to a slippery rock, shouting at stunned Richard to throw a rope, the horses speed downstream in a liverish torrent, dying what men now style the New Zealand death. Richard throws a rope. Herman does not die the New Zealand death. He is fated to prove this labyrinthine journey possible. Minus, however, his mildewed Bible. That has been lost, along with assorted implements, downstream with the horses. So Herman, when he needs recourse to scriptural precedent, has to make the most of memory. Memory is fallible, Herman is human, and his interim revisions are environmentally instructive. The tale of Noah takes a surprising turn; he drowns. Abraham's agony becomes starker still; God fails His cue, and a son is sacrificed. Jonah's whale has lockjaw. The loaves and fishes make a miser's meal for four. And Lazarus suffers a fatal relapse. There now appears to be an eleventh commandment, hitherto unsuspected by scholars: Thou shalt obey thy elder brother, whose heartbeat shall be as thy own, and honour him that thy days may be long upon the land which God hath given thee.

Later, when Herman rediscovers the Authorized Bible, he will find it an unsatisfying, often disillusioning document; a rag bag of received wisdom contrived by those who have suffered no useful revelation. Herman's version, begat of the wilds, is seamless. There is no tautology, no ambiguity. It is precise. In essence, every parable suggests Herman right. And Richard, for argument's sake, wrong. Not only Richard. Also God's self-appointed spokesmen, past and present; he sees priests as bred to their trade like bricklayers, wilfully walling up the imagination with dogmas of human imperfectibility, for fear they might go out of business; peddlers of the puny. Thus it might be observed that, theologically at least, the challenge of mountain and forest concentrates Herman's mind magnificently; the Authorized Bible, and its orthodox interpreters, will have no honoured place in Herman's house hereafter. It is perhaps to the point, however, that his current problem is topographical rather than theological. The lives of the Lovelocks, whether or not their elder brother is obeyed, do not promise to be long upon this lethal heartland. The trees grow taller, the mountains more immense, the wild rivers wider. May brings rain sufficient to fell a man into the mud within four paces, and June brings blizzards. They camp in a cave. A fire burns at the mouth of the cave. The flesh of birds, and sometimes eels, is their sustenance. Often, in the long nights, Herman dreams of finding the sea. It is just over a green grassy hill. He climbs this hill, his heart thudding, with the insistent sound of the sea filling his ears. Then it is there below him. Sunlit. Elegant and empty. He darts down the hill, his limbs light and singing, and wades into the warm waves. Balboa reborn. The virginal world a rich chorus. All about are fertile fields and sanely arranged woods; a good green land, altogether edible. The feast ends. Herman wakes to the bleak cave, the fire ever smoky with wet wood, the hungry horses, the roaring rain outside. So Herman's howl is heard again. It is heard often in these mountains. But the acoustics of the cave do it justice. The others merely note another of Herman's reverberant nightmares, and struggle for sleep again in the first grey light. By now the children are thin and subdued. And Sarah is sickening. Gentle James tends her with all the love he will ever show Sarah. Husband Herman gives himself, in his waking hours, to reconnaissance of the terrain, so far as rain and snow permit, trying to determine their next move out of the mountains, when and if weather clears. It is a perilous occupation. He sinks out of sight in snowdrifts, hurtles hundreds of feet down mountainside on the seat of tattering trousers. The mountains remain unmoved. When mist clears, which is seldom, they bulk white with snowfield and glacier, then more snowfield and glacier, their tops too tall to be seen.

The business of Christian men with these heathen heights should be brief. The mountains not only decline brevity; they refuse to reveal themselves as a mere means to Herman's end. They are, they begin to insist with frosty emphasis, the end. Here, now, shall the Lovelocks finish – fodder for the newsmen of the 1970s who report a curious find of human bones in a cave where a tramping party has taken shelter. But that is in Time B. Time C, for interest's sake, has them turning back successfully to Otago in April, and eventually taking ship to Devon from the port of Dunedin. Herman will prosper modestly as a merchant; Richard will perish in a public-house brawl; Sarah will live to be a great-grandmother; and pre-Raphaelite James will become an intimate of Dante Gabriel Rossetti. Time D likewise has its moments. The Lovelocks grow monumentally rich on the Otago goldfields, in the absence of angels, but end badly; they are soon after shipwrecked on a subantarctic island where Richard is found, a hollow-eyed and skin-clad hermit, a lone survivor, twenty years later. Meanwhile, Time A marches through July, which is best forgotten, into August. Marvellously, all are still alive, even the horses despite their bloat from feeding on forest leaves. Late in that month mists lift sufficiently for Herman to glimpse a possible new way west. Initially this route demands the felling of giant trees across a deep river, thus creating a firm bridge for the party. Since the trees do not always fall where they should, this enterprise engages Herman, Richard and James into September. Their axes give out a tiny, alien sound under the alps. The trees fall too short, fall too far. The three seek other sites. There is an early thaw. The glaciers above groan and rumble; waterfalls, where none existed before, storm down the dank valleys. Their bridge, near done, is found to be under fifteen feet of floodwater.

James, in that cave, dreams too; and of gypsies. This isn't by chance. He once ran off with gypsies to Dorset, until hunger and homesickness – along with prospects of a prolonged whipping – overtook him just outside Lyme Regis. There he earned a few shillings, more than enough to fill his belly for the journey home, hunting up fossils on Ware cliffs for a geologist with a fine Georgian residence in Silver Street. This most congenial man confided in James his belief that all the wisdom of creation might be found in a fossil. Now James dreams this geologist as an aged gypsy, all intricate wrinkles and yellow teeth, in the campfire's light; he is trying to strike an obscure bargain for James's soul with something – perhaps just a fossil, God knows, or all the world's wisdom – wrapped small in red velvet. About the campfire, hungrily watching, are gypsy women with sensual eyes and extremely full lips. Tambourines sound, and stringed instruments. The congenial geologist turned unkempt gypsy begins to laugh with great passion and peel away the red velvet from his mysterious package. The women, for some reason now naked, circle closer, all eager to participate. They bear away the red velvet by the yard. Yard after yard; it seems the package is just lush packing. Some women, all satin flesh, sigh about James. The clashing tambourines become tumult in his ears. The old gypsy laughs ever more violently. Then the gypsy women tug James from his clothes, wondering at his manhood, while his soul leaps in his flesh. But he begins to understand that, for some queerly carnal purpose, the women are now binding him tight in the endlessly unfurling red velvet. He struggles, helpless, and feels himself shrinking. He has become the package. He is the mystery. Then he takes leave of the dream tambourines for grumbling glaciers, drumming waterfalls, booming rivers.

Richard, when not blasting birds, felling trees, does not dream perceptibly; he merely wonders, in his waking hours, why he was born a Lovelock. And how he ever came to inhabit this hell. If ever a man needed an angel to make sense of his days, or gypsies to colour his dreams, it is Richard; but that is life's notorious injustice, perhaps God's perplexing plan. He grows still more tense with the passing of time in these mountains. He fossicks stealthily for colour in the more approachable stream beds, but fails to find more than drenched feet. It might much intrigue him to know that to the north diggers are pushing through more negotiable alpine passes at the rate of two hundred a month, soon two thousand a month, in consequence of the coarse gold sighted by the Maoris Simon and Samuel. So far as Richard knows, they are travelling away from a gold rush, not toward one. We shall not excite Richard, nor dismay Herman.

Ailing Sarah has the mystical sensation that her children are stealing her strength to survive. She accepts this peacefully; it relieves her of responsibility, of all maternal guilt. Though thin, they still look distinctly durable. Even little Luke has learned to suck the marrow from the bones of birds roasted on the fire. She is still sure that Herman will save them; that there is a future, a home that will be hers, beyond dark trees and white torrents. James? When he kneels before her with concern, she begins to see something she would prefer not to see in his eyes. So, on the whole, she doesn't.

Late September brings a slow settling of the floodwater; their bridge rises, with a clutter of debris, above the rapids. Herman announces that they will travel high, following the melting snow, in search of a place where the peaks will part. So days later they gasp out of the tangled valleys, above the treeline, into icy air; they steer their horses along stony mountainside, among patches of dirty snow, boulders battered by avalanche.

The peaks do part. They sight, at last, a horizon rimmed with sea. Between mountainside and sea are more clammy valleys. So they drive down into dark forest again, following the rivers. In the deep valleys cataracts upstage their parent peaks with histrionic virtuosity; water falls from high in silky threads and convulsive tangle. At times the saturated Lovelocks have to lead their horses along slimy terraces set within strident curtains of water. Chasm, precipice and prodigal water-course restrain even James from introspection; he nurses sagging Sarah and her mount to safety time and again. The rivers become one; it widens to the sea. Then there is the sea.

Herman guides his horse down the dunes, through tidal walls of whitened driftwood. There is, after all, more sea than he cares to consider; it seems he can have nothing here by halves. Destiny is still as close as a Cornish oyster. Warm waters, fertile fields, pleasant woods? All is black rock, sterile sands, chill spray, toppling towers of water. Sea and sand sprawl north and south, backed by dark forest, until lost in fine marine mists. A few jaundiced gulls wheel high. The din numbs.

They prepare camp between dunes and forest. Richard goes off with his rifle. James quests for shellfish along the shore, for food and bait. Scrambling around a headland, he looks down on huts. Rooftops. Crude chimneys. A village. A mirage, perhaps, or miracle. He calls the others. They descend, marvelling, to the village.

But the quiet of the place soon commands them. There is no human face at any door. Underfoot are weeds and wild potatoes. The place is less a village than a random clutter of ill-crafted dwellings. Some have now fallen. Others are conserved by tight creeper. Spiders have spun dense webs within. Rats scatter. Near the huts is a collection of crosses; a graveyard. An inscription scraped with a nail on a rotting slab of wood tells them a tale of a sealing gang set down on this shore, then forgotten, fifty years earlier. James, in search of a roof still tolerable, finds a hut set apart. Inside is a sight surely designed to haunt him until his terminal hour. The last sealer sits at a plank table; creeper has found its way through crevices in the hut to entwine rib cage, climb vertebrae, and surface through the orifices of his skull. Upon the table is an iron plate, from which the apparition doubtless partook of its last meal, and a rat-nibbled journal. In this journal James reads of an ex-convict crew, recruited by stealth in Sydney by a lawless ship's master, and shipped away in darkness from the penal colony they were forbidden to leave. They were promised tropical seas in search of sandalwood. Instead they were given intemperate southern waters, and left expendably on this wild shore to slaughter and skin seals; ship and skipper were never seen again. Their worthless forty thousand sealskins rotted away. Death called upon these redundant men in many forms. Some drowned. Some were crushed by falling trees. Some died of vexation. Some fell to killing each other with indiscriminate passion. Two were taken off for cannibal feast by Maoris from the forest depths. One built himself a boat, launching himself toward sunset and Australia in his old age, and surely perished. The wobbly writing in the journal is the work of one Alexander Crimmins, in another life a London clerk who purloined his master's money; toward the end he thinks the year might be 1836. They have been there since 1812. 'Will there ever be a fellow mortal,' he wonders alone at the end, 'to know our sad and terrible story? Please pray for the repose of our souls, for surely none have earned peace more.'

Awed James cannot resist that plea; he drops to his knees among rat filth and sunless creeper and prays unsparingly for the souls of Alexander Crimmins and his companions. His own fears, his sorrow for

Sarah, are but tinder to his piety; he weeps for commonplace humankind, and in deepening fervour sees all mortal yearning as one. He seems to rise from that floor, with one last compassionate look at skeletal Crimmins, a man enriched; he hopes Herman will never see him as just a boy again.

The others, meanwhile, have found two relatively weatherproof huts in which to camp; Herman and Richard are busy with external repairs while Sarah struggles to excavate the interiors. She finds, among buckles, chains, pots and other assorted metalware, a discoloured bronze crucifix. It seems an omen. Men of a Christian kind have sanctified this place; they may survive. She strings the crucifix about little Luke's neck, and instructs him never to lose it. James is quiet about his own discovery, but that night is visited by the gaunt spirit of Alexander Crimmins, who has much difficulty conveying what he means, since his skull is still tongueless. But his metacarpal gestures are eloquent, his finger joints finally lacing in supplication. Next day, unknown to the rest of the party, James delivers truant bones to the sealers' graveyard, and repeats his prayer. Alexander Crimmins, aside from a visit fleshed and hirsute to express his gratitude, does not disturb James again.

Herman sees something like happiness around him. The shore, however bleak, is a relief. The malign heights are behind. They all still live. James hooks fat fish from the tidal shallows. Richard shoots and skins a seal which, lately returned to this coast, thought the long massacre of the southern seas finished. Also it is October and the weather is warmer. Sarah, sitting in the fitful sunlight, appears to improve in health. She and Herman, for once on this journey, have some marital privacy, their own hut; her husband, though still a mystery, at least howls much less and seems more her own. The children no longer need her strength. They fatten on their own account, even little Luke with that lucky crucifix about his neck. Sometimes now Sarah is seen to smile. Lovesick James, in consequence, too. For the children, all is adventure; they manufacture games with the sealers' junk, the corroded knives, the rusty muskets, and keep their uncles company when they fish. Richard finds more stray seals to kill, and cures their skins to make warm garments. James locates edible berries in the forest, strange herbs which he heroically eats first before risking them on others; he pounds out a rather muddy-tasting paste from fernroot, a recipe found in Alexander Crimmins' journal.

The horizon remains empty; perhaps no sail is ever seen there. Herman knows this is not the place, that their comfort can only be temporary in November's tepid sun; there is a world elsewhere to win, where grown men can behave in an adult way. He sees no promise of coal and iron here, though the trees are tall. They must march northward. Sunward. Wilderness has whitened his beard; his skin has the parchment hue becoming to prophets.

'When?' asks Richard, who has begun to bicker less with his stomach full.

'While the sap is rising,' Herman insists. Nature's legislation is not to be taken lightly; spring is apparent.

The forest fills with floral surprises as they labour north. There are cascades of white clematis, trees wreathed with red-blooming vines. The foliage is noisy with unfamiliar birds, chorally mating. Many have forgotten how to fly; parrots with functionless wings prattle all but underfoot. Of four-legged creatures the forest has none; creation has been content with feather rather than fur. But on one riverside they do meet the kumi, a terrifying lizard purely of Maori mythology, which naturalists say never existed, but which nevertheless advances upon them with six slithering legs, cruel jaws, and glowing eyes. Richard gives it both barrels of his shotgun. The kumi, which does not know that it is purely mythological, and thereby immortal, with nothing to fear from Richard's gun, flees forever into the forest. The mortally shaken Lovelocks do not understand that this encounter is apocryphal, that the monster is a zoological improbability, a hallucination at best, a psychic residue or telepathic impression, and Richard is ready to release both barrels again for some time thereafter. To tell Richard in old age that he has never looked into those burning reptilian eyes, while his gun roared, will be distinctly perilous, leading perhaps to the production of a shotgun pointed at whoever proposes his account less than authentic. A shade more plausibly, at least for posterity, they also meet a moa, which is not mythological, merely decades extinct, the most dinosaurine feathered thing ever known, house-tall and harmless. This ungainly giraffe of a bird, browsing among leaves and berries, has never been appraised of the extinction of its species. Richard with one accurate shot makes it ornithological history. The Lovelocks feed richly on its flesh for three days thereafter, oblivious to the fact that such fare is uncommon, and indeed utterly unlikely in late 1864, and that they are imposing still more strain upon the credibility of this narrative; they will even, when later told they must be mistaken, continue to insist that the avian apparition was the best bloody fowl on which they ever feasted; they will still salivate with the memory of that mistake.

Meanwhile they have more argument with rivers. These have to be crossed again and again. Some are forded at the coast when tides are low. They raft themselves precariously across others. Often they must wait until muddy floods fall. They lose two more horses and eat a third. They follow the coast when they can, force their way through forest when they must. Sealskin binds their feet as leather boots rot away. They pass glaciers, trampling extravagantly through treefern almost to the sea, sights at which men more receptive might marvel. The Lovelocks hardly lift their eyes. Apart from Herman, whose gaze is ahead: he has begun glimpsing open land, more and more of it, valleys, plains, closer day by day.

It is not incumbent upon this narrative to negotiate more of the forest alongside the Lovelocks. Sufficient to say that Herman, for once, has it right: that there is more open country to come along that darkly curving coast between ocean and alp. But we are not altogether delivered from particulars. On a late summer day they look down on a wide river; yet another. This one, however, is unique in their recent experience. For one thing, it is filled with ships. Some are in fact shipwrecks, slowly shattering on a sand bar, turning turtle on the tides. Others are moored to a makeshift wharf, and several stand off to sea awaiting a berth. There are tents. There are shacks and shops rising; they can hear saws and hammers. There is the smoke of many fires. All this, and rather more, in the land where Herman has led them, promising no human face in a ten week walk.

There can be no mistake; they are about to become citizens of a gold rush town. Herman looks heavenward. Richard charitably assumes that this is what Herman had in mind all along, the sly sod, and that they have merely arrived a little late. James, once past the surprising poetry of human endeavour on this shore, looks sidelong at shrunken Sarah and feels a chill. Benjamin and Ernest gambol bravely down towards the town, and soon little Luke leaps after them, crying for them to wait.

The first face to cross their path is familiar. A rough diamond of a digger, known in Otago, and apparently just off a ship, a swag on his back and heading inland.

'By Jesus,' he says, 'you lot look like you been walking.'

'You might say that,' James agrees amicably.

The man is more impressed by Herman's response. The howl hurries him uphill; he never once looks back at the Lovelocks.

Otherwise, by way of footpath and ferry, they proceed peacefully into the town.

Five

Hokitika, for that is the name of the place where they have arrived, does not especially embrace the overlanding Lovelocks; it is busy about its own legend. 'Like a dream to see a large town spring up as it were by magic,' pens a journalist rather laboriously as the Lovelocks limp past his door, 'and there are some here as witness to the fact that San Francisco itself did not rise so fast, nor Melbourne, nor any other town that grew on gold, with wealth to be won beyond all Solomon's measure. I am writing from a site destined to be seen, a century hence, in the heart of one of the world's wonder cities.' (For the record, he is writing from a riverbank site where seagulls a century hence shall be seen picking at refuse.) The journalist, a nervous young man who nibbles his fingernails, especially since each line pays only a penny, observes the passing Lovelocks and locates more to say. 'By land and sea they come, the streets a babble of languages, Italian and German, Swedish and Greek, men of all kinds and creeds. Only this minute I noted an exhausted family group, unusual in this town still mostly of men, arrived from heaven knows where to make their fortune. The gold fever is in their pinched, pitiable faces; there is no mistaking it. The same fever which makes for weekly shipwreck upon the river shoals as the diggers pour in. It fairly astonishes the few Maoris here, who never saw the like before; they think the diggers brought by the devil, which sometimes seems not an unreasonable supposition. What devil, for example, drives those poor wretches who have just passed me by?' Feeling his copy still insufficiently coloured, and meditation on the Lovelocks in particular worth a penny or two more, the journalist adds: 'How will it all end for them? With golden dream fulfilled, or embittering disappointment? The mind reels. In this unbelievable bedlam all is still possible; the high and humble are born anew and equal in a gold rush town. What, I repeat, will become of them?'

A pertinent and eminently repeatable question. For the new-born

Lovelocks, reeling in more than a mental fashion, and less than equal to the occasion, the unbelievable bedlam is at that moment unravelling the best part of a mile of hotels, shops, banks, and dwellings. Butchers and bootmakers, jewellers and lawyers, barbers and apothecaries, are already offering goods and services, sometimes still painting their signs. Between buildings are the stumps, often the trunks, of trees lately felled. Wagons lurch along the lengthening street with loads of furniture and produce; there are sheep and cattle being driven to the yards. At corners there are crowds of conversational men, sometimes so dense that the Lovelocks must elbow their way through, dragging their last skinny horses. Their enfeebled arrival does not pass unnoticed, though largely by way of fertile silences; comment would be unkind. Their archetypal trek, with which tradition can make free, and historians and mountaineers now reliably cut dead, is all but over. Not their trials.

The highly coloured hotel facades are dizzying, making it difficult to pick and choose: the Robbie Burns or the Rory O'More, the Ballarat or the Old Bendigo, the Shotover or the Scandinavian. All might be immaterial, a mirage about to dissolve into dunes, trees and swamp again. Richard left less tenuously convinced of reality by the smell of civilized red steak issuing from the Cafe de France. Little Luke cries loudly; he has forgotten people, and finds all frightening. James sees painted nymphs of the pavement, with parasols and bright costumes, and averts his eyes weakly. Sarah wishes only to desist from having to place one foot before another. Faint, near dropping, she clings to James.

Herman, most fortunately, can still hold them together. 'Here,' he announces, at the Maison Marie, since they are outside its door; and he prefers the name decidedly to that of the El Dorado, across the way. Also the Maison Marie seems to offer beds along with booze, which is more than can be said for most. 'Mother of God,' says the proprietress, one Marie Louise Regan, late of the Victorian fields, taking little Luke up into her ample arms. 'What can a poor lady like me do for the likes of you?'

Herman, who sees no lady, nevertheless knows exactly what she can do for the likes of the Lovelocks; they walk with no impediment into Marie Louise's life.

Hokitika becomes their home. Herman has to share in the madness of man again, if not succumb to it; he has no choice. Conceivably it is God's game to give him no choice, to test his survival in civilization as well as wilderness. For Sarah is dying. A drunken physician says so. Sarah knows so. James thinks to deny it so long as there is breath in his own body, love in his soul. It is no swift business, rather a slow erosion of flesh, and there is the physician to be paid daily; the man insists on cash, with a bonus of Marie Louise's booze upon departure from her establishment. Otago's gold can only go so far. They must serve their time at the teat again. After Richard rides into the moist hinterland, rummaging about rock and silt with manifest optimism and finally and jubilantly staking a claim, Herman joins him on the site with some suffocation of soul; he works with Richard most of the week, then returns to his invalid wife. James is left at the Maison Marie to care for the children, nurse Sarah, and play fiddle or piano for Marie Louise's customers. Marie Louise does her best to comfort lacklustre James by way of her kitchen. She is a cook of no mean quality; her loin of lamb Lyonnaise and sweetbreads Soubise have been legend on three goldfields. Anecdote relates her murkily to royalty, and her regal manner goes far to confirm it. Fact does not fall too far short. Certainly her father, as chef, was one who had gratified the gluttony of Napoleon, not to speak of a Czar or two when left behind on the retreat from Moscow. Conceived by way of a willing kitchenmaid, Marie Louise was reared so as to be no disgrace to her famous father; nor has she been since in matters culinary. For immediate purposes, however, James sees an unnervingly vivid woman with a loud laugh whose kindnesses discomfort him in some way he does not wish to consider. She demonstrably does not discomfort Herman, Richard, or other men who grow noisy in her bar. She has buried two Irish husbands in California and Victoria; they have bequeathed her a distinctly Dublin tartness of tongue which combines queerly with a silky Gallic volubility in the interests of commerce. She is generous in buying rounds of rum for celebrating customers, but debtors and brawlers frequently feel the sharp edge of her Parisian boots; she suffers no interference with joie de vivre. Which is hardly what the Lovelocks bring into her life, most conspicuously with Sarah perishing beneath her roof, but they nevertheless satisfy some maternal lack. If she has no family of her own, it is not for want of effort, as two extinct husbands testify. She helps James with Sarah, bathing that thin body, changing nightdress and soiled sheets, and weeps often. She feeds and spoils the Lovelock children as her own, not least little Luke, for whom she finds it difficult to disguise great love. By way of return, the Lovelock men help add rooms to the rear of her hotel, to provide for the crowds still arriving clamorous in Hokitika. Herman and Richard also serve behind the bar when they ride to town; both can deal efficiently with brawls. Less muscular James, when finished with fiddle and piano for the night, hastens up the stairs to see the children are asleep, then sits in Sarah's room, often all night. She seldom speaks, unless out of dream or delirium. He sometimes holds her feeble hand. He sometimes prays. He sometimes contemplates taking his own life at the moment of Sarah's death: the prospect of such a dark wedding, free of flesh, also of sin, stirs him strangely. Marie Louise cannot conceal dismay when she finds James dozing in Sarah's room long past dawn. She does her best to convey to James that his condition is far from healthy. He is young; he has his life ahead. For his part, he prefers not to comprehend. So her grief begins to go to James rather than Sarah. She will have peace soon. James has no such prospect, and besides is thinning too, for all her nutritional enterprise. Marie Louise begins to pray that Sarah will perish fast so that James will survive. She alone knows of James's clandestine drama. Others under her roof, the children, Herman and Richard when they come to town, are altogether unaware. James is James, has always been, for some reason. It isn't so much that Herman lacks a husband's grief, or is heartless in neglect of Sarah; rather that thought and deed have demands on him elsewhere, and that he has to hold family and future together while Sarah succumbs. If pressed, he would possibly confess himself grateful that James gives Sarah so much of his attention, and mean no more.

While Sarah diminishes, Hokitika flourishes. Soon there are sixty-seven hotels. Also skating rinks, skittle alleys, bagatelle tables, shooting ranges, billiard rooms. And concert halls with gymnasts, minstrels, ventriloquists, magicians, balladeers.

But the greatest wonder is the weather: it is more than rumour promised. It can rain for three months without perceptible diminution. Then there is a day's pause, as if for a drawing of breath, and it rains for a month or two more. Skeletal shipwrecks sometimes sail like hallucinations up the main street on a flood tide. Unlike hallucinations, however, the wrecks remain high and dry. Bloating bodies, drunks capsized in the night, float in the lake-like puddles of the town, and sometimes Benjamin and Ernest boat there. Storms take buildings apart with impressive method and distribute debris half a mile inland. When the rain retreats at last, and a lukewarm sun shines, there is the stench of rotting refuse, and worse, the offal of slaughtermen, the excrement of the town.

Some sink into incurable fevers. Some cut their throats. Herman, having survived landslip and near suffocation in mud out on the goldfields, urges his horse over the soggy road into Hokitika and knows there is no mistaking hell. The parasols and painted faces of the pavement nymphs, abroad again, are as parasite flora on a cesspit. Others can call it civilization.

'It is no place for a grown woman,' he informs Marie Louise, who is never slow with solace, nor with rum. A burgeoning bank balance is her own comfort in the rain and premature rot of this rackety town.

'What of grown men?' she asks affectionately. She doesn't yet wholly understand that Herman is haunted by knowledge that the world must be other; that the measure of man is not in gold, but preferably in timber, coal and iron. On the goldfields Herman goes disguised as a man merely about the business of filling his pockets fast. It is an effective disguise. He is filling his pockets fast. The substance he despises showers into his hands from mountain crevice and creek, wherever he hikes. Richard is impressed by this infallible capacity to find gold where others fail. He isn't alone. Diggers break camp when they hear of Herman Lovelock on the move again, and follow fast, pulling their packhorses along rough ridges, through dangerous rivers, desperate lest they lose sight of him; he is never responsible for a duffer rush. The secret is simple. Wherever Herman finds himself powerfully oppressed, wherever distaste rises like bile in his mouth, there gold shall be found. Since it is best to get on with it, for the sake of suffering Sarah and the children stranded in Hokitika, not to think of hopeless James, he tells Richard to make camp and cook food. Then Herman pans bitterly for his first pennyweights of gold, and wishes the world other.

So what of grown men?

'There is no hope,' Herman answers, 'when circumstances do not permit. Maybe the truth of circumstances is that they never permit. Think of what men might be.'

'I think of what the buggers are,' says Marie Louise.

'Which is what I mean,' Herman explains, warming with the rum. 'They are creatures of circumstance.'

'If they weren't,' observes Marie Louise, 'I should be out of business.'

'If man is never to be more than something made of circumstances, then he is never to be more than nothing much.' This is something Herman has contemplated with increasing conviction. Not least since he found himself less reliant on scriptural revelation, now long down-river. 'Man is meant to be at war with circumstances. Otherwise there is no point.'

'Man is going to die,' says Marie Louise. 'That is a circumstance, if ever I heard of one. Or what sort of circumstance did you have in mind?'

'The world,' replies Herman heavily, 'or God.'

'You mean you want a war with God?' asks Marie Louise with mock alarm. 'I'm thinking you're a wilder one than I thought, and no mistake.'

While Herman tries to determine the accuracy or otherwise of this diagnosis, circumstances suggest to Marie Louise that he needs a second rum. She has never had a more curious customer, nor met a digger depressed by gold before. Better for her financial future if she were less fascinated. But she is. There is no finer figure of a man on all this coast. With dying Sarah, pitiful James, handsome Herman, and Luke always lingering at her skirt, Marie Louise not only tends to turn to rum; she also reaches for laudanum as her nights lengthen.

Richard, always indisposed to release his grip on a good claim, rides to town only on Herman's insistence. That is often when Herman requires solitude. Also when there is gold to be delivered to a banker by way of Marie Louise; and provisions to be packed back. Richard is an irritation to Herman. His brother has no large talk. No small talk either, unless of gold. He sleeps, eats, and gathers gold. Herman is distressed when he sees his own existence as all but indistinguishable. One discernible difference is that Herman washes, even in the worst weather. Richard is impatient with human hygiene. Every daylight hour can deliver up more gold. He also breaks wind foully, and gives himself to prolonged excavation of his nostrils with filthy fingers. Richard's absences can be a source of content.

With gold in his saddlebags, Richard becomes nervous on these rides to town. There has been talk of bushrangers; diggers have vanished. Convicts loosed from Australia are said to be seeking prey. He is always grateful for first sight of Hokitika, and a bellyful of rum. Then he stops shaking.

Riding back to the claim is better. Then he has no gold to lose; only their provisions and, perhaps, his life in a river. On one ride he falls in with two other men, fresh to the goldfields. Both are bushily sideburned and thickly moustached, and amiable about most things, though they look as if they have been living rough. They have, it seems, suffered the goldfields of Otago and Victoria too; and are much interested in news of prospering diggers hereabouts. Richard, who pleads poverty on such occasions, contributes diversionary advice. One of the two, a baldish man named Burgess, with alert eyes and wry smile, is surprisingly well-spoken, considering his companion Kelly's low-born Irish whine. An odd pair, they appear, the longer Richard rides beside them. Kelly does not seem in any sense the servant of Burgess, though it is clear that Burgess does most of the thinking and almost all the talking for the two. And he begins to talk too much, in his gentlemanly manner, for Richard's mental peace. Gentlemen, in his experience, want more than they say. Burgess needs more than goldfield anecdote.

Locating a wish to ride alone, Richard invents a deviation from the main diggers' route into the mountainside fields, parting company with the strangers and offering them oatmeal to keep them going meantime. They accept this with some hesitation, and a look or two at each other; and Richard leads his horses off into the thickest available vegetation. There he tethers them and he steals back to see if Burgess and Kelly are following. He has almost satisfied himself that they are not when he hears violent cries. Eventually, after pushing through undergrowth and wading through swamp, he comes upon an unappealing scene. Burgess and Kelly are butchering a digger in a lonely camp. Kelly holds the protesting man down while Burgess cuts his throat. There is another digger, already dispatched, nearby. Trying to comprehend this extraordinary sight, also attempting to persuade his leaden legs that they were made for motion, Richard stands exposed at the forest edge. 'Hold him down, man,' Burgess is shouting at Kelly. 'Keep your mind on the job. Hold the bugger down.' Squeamish Kelly, unable quite to contemplate the business upon which they are engaged, looks up and sees startled Richard at the very moment that Burgess, after several slashes, locates the digger's jugular. Kelly calls out. Burgess spins about with bloody knife. His staccato roar looses Richard from paralysis. Richard leaps back into the trees, but into swampy ground. All nightmare; sludge sucks at his feet as murderous Burgess and his knife attempt to engage with his neck. Kelly is yelping at the rear. Sounds suggest that Burgess has slipped, and that clumsy Kelly has fallen over him. While the two disentangle, with Burgess's oaths filling the forest, Richard gains five yards, then perhaps ten, on to firm ground and thicker vegetation; he crashes across a creek, reels over some rocks, forces his way up a ridge dense with fern. But the cries of Burgess and Kelly are still close; the day is fluently shaping as Richard's last. They are running him to ground, a pig in a hunt. He has one advantage, not much more, over a pig. Elevation. When he sees a suitable tree, with low enough limbs, he gives himself to climbing it with more tenacity than technique. He hurls himself higher, branch after branch, with increasing expertise; his breath comes in huge sobs. He can hear Burgess and Kelly hoarse with frustration below, blundering back and forward, and baffled. 'We should have done for him in the first place,' Burgess is shouting. 'But he had no gold,' Kelly replies. 'Gold or no gold, we should have done for him,' Burgess blusters. 'He knows everything now.' He curses Kelly vilely. Kelly begins to weep, much as he will when sentenced to hang alongside Burgess for more massacre within the year. 'What will become of us?' he asks with justifiable premonition. 'You're just Dublin dung,' says Burgess with contempt. 'Shut your whimpering. He's here somewhere.' 'Where?' asks Kelly pathetically. 'Anywhere,' answers Burgess. 'Up a tree, for all we know.'

Richard, faint, tries for greater grip upon the topmost portion of the tree; a thin branch cracks underfoot. 'Up this tree, as a matter of fact,' Burgess cries with joy. 'We've got the bugger now. All we do is shake him out like a ripe apple.' Burgess is optimistic; the tree is four hundred years old and its trunk more than a few feet thick. Upon further consideration, Burgess says, 'Go on, you go up and get him.' 'Me?' Kelly replies. 'With the knife,' says Burgess. 'Mother of God,' says Kelly. 'Up there? I got no head for heights.' 'You've got no head for anything,' Burgess claims. 'Why do I bother with you?' 'Because you love me,' Kelly proposes. 'You said so yesterday.' 'That was yesterday,' Burgess insists. 'This is today. Go up and get him.' 'Why me?' Kelly pleads. 'Because I have to do all the killing,' Burgess announces brusquely. 'It's time you learnt the trade.' 'Not now,' Kelly suggests. 'Later. Don't send me up there. It's a big tree. And he's a big bugger. I could break my neck.' 'You'll have it broken anyway,' Burgess observes, 'if you don't get your Irish arse up there.' Kelly, whose brother's neck has not long been fractured inefficiently on an Australian gallows, weeps again with even less moderation. 'You don't love me,' he tells Burgess. 'No one does. Only my mother.' 'Fuck your mother then,' Burgess says. 'Don't you say that,' Kelly cries with vehemence. 'Don't you ever say that.'

Astonished Richard hears verbal skirmishing turn to physical violence at the foot of the tree; Kelly has evidently dashed his fist into Burgess's face, and from the thumping and sobbing it soon seems that Kelly is getting the worst of it. Richard appears reprieved. Please God, he prays, let them leave me alone. This prayer is shortly answered, if perversely; the cries and grunts of the two bushrangers, as they roll into undergrowth and fall through fern, suffer an insidious change in character. Crude oaths turn into lewd endearments. Nothing could be more calculated to degrade Richard's dying hour, or give him less peace before he meets his maker. He has to listen; he has no choice. To attempt blocking his ears, for decency's sake, would be to make his position more precarious upon the tree; he needs both hands to hold himself steady. Nor can he haul himself higher, away from it all. One mercy is that their lust is not of long duration. Richard is certainly left alone, if in consternation, while it lasts; he sees virtue in making his prayers more precise. For their renewed affection frees them to contemplate Richard without pity.

'We could chop the tree down,' Kelly decides. Burgess snorts. 'It would take all day,' he says. 'All night too. We've got that camp back there to clean out and those two buggers to be buried quick. We can't lose time getting rid of this one. Talk sense.' 'I can't go up there,' Kelly snivels. 'Honest I can't. It'll be the death of me.' 'I heard you the first time,' Burgess sighs. 'All right. I'll do it myself.'

Richard braces himself as Burgess begins to climb the tree; the one thing in his favour, since God knows Richard needs something in his favour, is that he is at the top of the tree. Presently he is able to observe Burgess, knife between teeth, rising through foliage. 'I'll join with you,' Richard proposes. 'I'll ride with you. I won't say I ever saw what you did.' 'So you won't, will you?' Burgess says. 'No,' Richard promises. 'Never.' Burgess's eyes flicker over Richard's face. 'In that case,' he says with some charm, 'you won't mind me making sure, will you?' 'Making sure of what?' Richard stutters. 'Making sure you never say anything,' Burgess answers softly. 'Why don't you come down so we can do it all clean? With no fuss at all?' He is really quite persuasive; Richard has to remind himself that Burgess is actually making a proposition to cut his throat. 'You can have all my provisions,' Richard offers. 'As for gold, I can get all you want. I'll lead you to my brother Herman. If you leave me alone.'

Burgess continues to climb, all the while concentrating his gaze on Richard. 'Go on,' he urges. 'You interest me. Tell me more. Tell me as much as you like.' Burgess believes his infinite capacity for evil fascinates people, makes them feel the world worthless if such evil exists, prepared to make their lives forfeit. Indeed it often does. Nevertheless he has the wrong man. Insensitive Richard has no desire to depart this world because it is blemished by a bad bugger called Burgess. After calculating the inconvenience of an amputated ankle, he plants his boot in the bushranger's face rather than succumb to a flawed universe. Not once but several times, with growing satisfaction. Burgess loses his knife, one or two teeth, finally his grip on the tree. Foliage breaks most of his fall, also Kelly, almost crushed at the foot of the tree. Unaccustomed to finding his capacity for evil frustrated, Burgess now appears to see injustice inherent in the criminal condition; he deals curtly with Kelly's consolations.

'Listen,' he roars up the tree at Richard. 'Listen with care. We can still get you. Only a matter of time. But we won't. We'll let you live. But if you say one word, one word to anyone about what you've seen, we'll be back to get you. Even if we've gone to the gallows we'll be back. That's a promise. Understand? One word and you'll never be safe. Never sleep easy. Never have peace. Understand?'

Richard understands: it is not a pronouncement replete with ambiguity anyway. This time, at least, Burgess has judged his man well. Richard shivers, triumph short-lived.

'We'll fry your balls for breakfast,' Burgess promises, 'then ease out your guts sweet and slow. Then we'll skin you, all the while with you looking, until we're ready to razor off your nose, trim your limbs with an axe, and burn out your eyes. Isn't that right, Kelly? We'll keep in practice so we can do it right when the time comes. Don't think you'll ever escape us. We'd be back from the grave. Nothing would stop us. Or save you. Nothing.'

Richard, fragile again, remains a further forty-eight hours up the tree, until certain that Burgess and Kelly have quit the vicinity. After a second sleepless night filled with slow rain, he finds his way feebly back to the horses, then home to Herman on their claim. His only remaining facial colour resides in his bloodshot eyes. Herman wonders if the cause of his brother's condition, and his long absence, isn't perhaps a woman in Hokitika; but that hardly accounts for Richard's hysterical insistence on sleeping and eating with a loaded shotgun hugged to himself. He is reluctant, for some time, to surrender it for a shovel. Herman cannot know that Richard is all the while having his balls fried, his guts eased out sweet and slow, by bushrangers who vow to find gallows and grave no handicap should he say a word about them. The mere twitch of a bird in the bush might herald the beginning of the business; or the hoot of an owl in the night. So he doesn't say a word, not to Herman or to the patrolling constable who calls at their claim with news of missing diggers nearby. 'We got our suspicions,' he explains. 'We picked up a couple of felons, gallows bait both, down the way. One called Burgess, alias Hill when it suits him. The other called Kelly, alias Noon when he's drinking. Just out of prison for armed robbery in Otago. But we got nothing to prove they've been round here. And no bodies neither. You got no news?'

Herman can't help. Nor Richard, who is shovelling shingle into a cradle with extreme concentration.

'Well, watch yourselves,' warns the constable.

Superfluous advice for Richard, who has just visited death upon another dozen diggers, at conservative reckoning, before Burgess and Kelly are caught. Their victims shall have much to tell Richard in his more turbulent dreams. He will wake with fright and disgust and assuage his conscience, insofar as it can now be detected, with the growing conviction that most men are worth little in this life. With no respect left for himself, he will thereafter seek such respect in the eyes of others. One thing Richard knows. Riches win respect. He now goes after gold with great passion as a means to that end, not as an end in itself, and Herman will have less curiosity about Richard's condition. Also less reason for complaint about his brother's hircine habits. Richard begins cleaning himself assiduously, even when the climate is at its most chilly, night and morning; he now has a carbolic reek. Herman can continue to presume that the wonder has been worked by a woman; that perhaps Richard needs his loaded shotgun near to protect himself from jealous rival or cuckolded husband. So shall Richard secrete his treetop terror; no one literally, metaphorically, or even ectoplasmically, will fry his balls for breakfast. Never.

Herman, in any case, has circumstances to consider. His might make him the envy of many; certainly of the men on the goldfields who at best earn enough to subsidize their sad encounters with soiled doves in the bars and brothels of Hokitika. This must be discounted. Gold will purchase no cure for Sarah's condition, nor his own discontent. The way through the wilderness has left Sarah interminably dying, Benjamin and Ernest young gold town ruffians. Nor is Luke, all considered, likely to remain Marie Louise's innocent little lamb. James is not to be taken into serious account. Richard is something to be suffered in the greasy murk of the forest. So much for circumstances. An unequal contest. His howls are judged by Richard to be the one great hazard of living alongside Herman. Perhaps, on the credit side, such expressions of concern keep bushrangers at bay. Richard is not to understand that Herman in truth is holding circumstances at bay.

Marie Louise is something else again. She cannot be kept at bay. Not as months pass, then more than a year. Herman, mourning Sarah, is nevertheless a man. Likewise mourning, Marie Louise is a woman and there is no nevertheless..Mutual affection cannot be denied, nor finally resisted, though seldom to be seen beyond a bedroom sometimes shared. Reason – not to speak of twentieth-century narrative – baulks at excluding carnal detail. His acceptance of Marie Louise's comfort can by convention be construed as infidelity to a long-dying wife. Flesh, loneliness and compassion, not necessarily in that sequence, compose their own conventions. When Herman is in weekend residence, and the hotel is at last quiet for the night, she journeys softly to his room by way of sleeping children, surviving Sarah, and dozing James. Candle in hand, she often hears alpine rains on the roof, wind whining in from the south, the booming of surf out on the sand bar, with some shrinking of soul; the brisk and gregarious businesswoman is banished. The candle lights her small shy way through the great cold and dark of the world. True that less cosmic sounds also keep her company: the boozy snores of some deep-sleeping digger with a bed for the night, the giggle of one of her girls with a good paying client. She arrives at Herman's room with relief, undresses shivering, and takes her place beside him. Nothing is said. Nothing acknowledged. What can be?

Marie Louise is not the first of her sex, nor certainly the last, to find terra incognita a stimulus to intimacy. She knows from experience that mystery usually leads to grief, often by way of disillusion in the beds of bad bastards. Herman might be mad, but he isn't bad, or no more than most born with masculine genitalia; his beauty resides in the fact that he continues to baffle. He is a man addicted to the notion – and she has been overly familiar with a few of the kind before – that he has a date elsewhere with destiny, and that his horse has gone lame. Unlike Herman, however, others of that description haven't felt hobbled by affluence; they have been crippled by penury, and only rich in complaint. In that respect, Herman is more than mystery. Rather, pure magic. Which may make for grief as great as that in the bed of any bad bastard, but who is to know?

So it isn't altogether from avarice that she talks to Herman of money. It is on a par with the warming bouillabaisse she prepares when he arrives cold and damp from the claim. A way of conveying her love, otherwise unspoken, and to relieve him of care. 'Money in the bank is lazy money,' she declares. 'You must make it work for you. Nothing lasts. Not even money, if neglected. Think of old age.'

'I think of precious little else,' he informs her. 'I shall have nothing to show for it other than holes in the hills.'

'You talk as if cursed.'

'It becomes my impression.'

'I can make the curse less apparent if you will give me your trust.'

'You have that already,' he insists.

He is after all a man who values peace, to think thoughts now more morose than visionary, and there is no virtue in being nagged. The upshot is that Marie Louise thereafter manages his money, and proceeds with buying up Hokitika apace, including a fourteen hundred seat opera house with gas chandeliers, reading and billiard rooms, jewelled and ringleted waitresses, and dress circle seats at six shillings. She and Herman have a private box there, when she fills him with sufficient rum to suffer entertainment. He also comes into ownership of the Shakespeare Casino, though he is not aware of this, and nor is Richard, who has lately become a familiar figure there.

Even a moderately indifferent bystander in Hokitika of 1866 could not fail to be impressed by Richard's determination to play the role of epic shit. More than a century later there is still little the most ingenious narrative can do to dignify a shit. True that it can make an attractive technical exercise; but Richard, for the most part, will lead no narrator into temptation. Compassion cannot be carried further than to suggest that, for all his industry and aptitude, he will have reason to die disappointed, his full excremental potential still unexplored, remembered at best as a miserable turd. So much for sympathy, in search of which we have had to confuse chronology and plunder the produce of the future; for the present we must contemplate his exceptional early promise.

He now has his own money. He is no longer content to have Herman bank it on his behalf, which has been the situation since joining Herman on the Otago fields; he is also no longer just the lacklustre young brother of Herman Lovelock, long-haired, filthy and smelly on the claim. He asserts his right to be heard on his own account. Certainly to be seen. No more in clay-yellowed moleskin trousers, American boots, flannel shirt and cape crudely cut from a blanket, the digger's uniform, but in black velvet waistcoat, silk neck tie, and kid gloves. Also in the matter of appearances, he contrives to pick his nose more fastidiously, fart with discretion. He has discovered that money alone does not bring the respect he needs. The display of money does. He becomes conspicuous at social and sporting functions. He is there the day that the butcher and baker attempt to hammer in each other's heads for one hundred and seventy-five rounds over four bloody hours, and backs the winner; he is an equally successful investor in the barmaids' fifty yard sprint, and his winnings purchase him a place in the bed of the victor in that event, a lanky and drawling auburn-haired girl from Melbourne who yawns and slides off to sleep before Richard can consummate a memorable day. That doesn't deter him from betting on the whaleboat and skiff races on the Hokitika River, or from taking his place on the bridge of the wrecked brig *Montezuma* which serves as grandstand for horse races on the beach; he sees his selections head the field in the Westland Handicap, Butcher's Purse, Barman's Bonanza, and Pack Saddle Scurry. Richard, in short, is suddenly a young gallant about town, a cut above, say, the likes of the Tipperary Boys, who tend to bash each other with bottles. The fact that he is a Lovelock, the legendary Herman's brother, certainly loses him no reputation, and indeed makes him eminently desirable company for some, the recipient of sidelong stares and then introductory handshakes in such gaming palaces as the Shakespeare, or the Casino de Venice, where the bagatelle tables, roulette wheels and affluent barmaids are always busy; and where Richard, fresh back from the latest Lovelock claim, is seen unburdening himself of bundles of new banknotes. Gambling ceases merely to be a socially acceptable activity in which he should be seen to be engaged, for the sake of respect; Richard begins to relish the tingling anxieties and orgasmic relief of a winning streak on the tables. He feels so primally fulfilled, after such encounters, that it is he who now often falls celibately asleep when bedded beside auburn-haired ladies after the casinos shut for the sabbath, which has lately arrived in Hokitika, along with temperance and improvement societies, a sign of regression and likely harbinger of depression in any good gold town. Of course there are losing streaks too, God knows unfairly, but Richard is financially well enough endowed to buy the relief and respect he compulsively needs in at least one win by the end of the night; he is intimate with triumph, if not necessarily his bedmate, and never really needs to tally how much Lovelock money might now be contributing to Hokitika's inflation. It should also be observed that Richard soon smokes cheroots and drinks bourbon, and above all deals poker hands from a deftly shuffled pack of cards, in the company of some of the more distinguished and disappointed swindlers and speculators of the town, men who have clung to bullion's bandwagons by their yellowing fingernails since '49 in California, and have still notably failed to found personal fortunes.

Let us be fair about one thing. Richard is not excessively simple-minded. This narrative has already passed over protestations from Herman in the spirit world, vehemently insisting that we correct the record, especially in respect of Marie Louise; we cannot risk reproaches from the shade of Richard too. To suggest that he has no native cunning might be to test the flashpoint of his patience in the hereafter. With no illusion about his own need in life now, he is immune, for the most part, to the illusions offered by others: the fictions which human beings parade in place of their own personalities. Richard knows there is a scrawny, filthy and potentially treacherous boy trapped under the velvet and silk of every man he meets. So it happens that the first time Ira Dix tries to play Richard false in a poker game, Richard rather recklessly – considering the ivory-handled Colt revolver Dix is known to carry under an armpit – reaches across the table to recover the two aces which his fellow gambler has elegantly if inefficiently concealed in the folds of a monogrammed handkerchief up his sleeve.

Ira Dix is a man with extraordinarily small and humourless eyes. The smallness is genetic; the humourlessness environmental. By now, considering his crooked delight in his craft, the energy and enterprise he has expended in gold towns too many to count, he should be living it up large in his native St Louis. Inexplicably, he isn't. He senses himself near the last throw of the dice. True that a good gambler knows that the last throw may make sense of his life. But Ira has grown impatient with his gifts rather than continue to cultivate them; his problem has become the haunting one of genius without talent. He sups the flat beer in the bottom of the barrel when a hick kid catches him out in Hokitika.

All the same, he is no mean sight. He wears a broad-brimmed black hat low over his head, a Mexican silver chain about his neck, and the corners of his mouth, under his huge black-dyed moustache, give off a professionally menacing twitch. Though rumour says it was his wont back in the West, in crisis, he doesn't reach for his revolver. Instead he concentrates those small humourless eyes on Richard.

'Very good,' he says. 'I tell you for a true fact that was very, very good.'

Richard could not have been more surprised, or relieved, all things considered.

'Yes,' Ira continues. 'Very, very good. I tell you for a true fact I like to place a new partner on test. I respect a man like yourself who has eyes to see, and can keep a game clean.'

This is, of course, implausible as an explanation of that which has just transpired across the table. Greying Ira once had more ingenious ways of winning himself from a hole. But he has, for a true fact, spoken the magic word. Richard still needs all the respect he can get, and Ira Dix is offering it explicitly with a leering movement of the lips which might be mistaken for a smile. Ira is down to the rock-bottom belief that survival is all: the world, who knows, might soon be fresh out of goldfields, and St Louis is a long way home from Hokitika in steerage. There might be more than one way to skin a cat, especially one which insists, like Richard more or less from that moment, on eating out of Ira's hand; Ira is gratified by how well his wit has worked. Other things being unequal, as other things catastrophically are for Ira, it seems guile is still his real stake when the chips are down.

From that night Ira and Richard are companions in the casinos and hotels of Hokitika. If Ira loses, it is largely Lovelock money; if he wins, Richard may be observed reaping an agreed percentage of the profit. But Richard's real profit is spiritual rather than financial; he has a sense of profound well-being in the company of a man of the world. And Richard has refurbished Ira's faith in himself. They need each other.

Concerning complaints from the other side, something must be said, if only to cleanse these pages of a controversial subject. Herman (posthumous Herman, that is) appears to think – and here one must allow for the known difficulties of transmission, misunderstanding on the part of the medium involved, misinterpretation of his vernacular vocabulary – that thus far he appears here as an especially pious pain in the arse. Can't the twentieth century, he asks, do better by him? In reply to which only one plea is possible: what the hell more can be done, short of transferring this narrative tragically to Time B, leaving the Lovelocks' yellowing bones in some lost cave, with a man who makes himself miserable by discovering gold in immoderate measure? A man, moreover, who in consequence of a confusing consultation with an angel now has a dying wife, one brother an apprentice wastrel, the other an aspirant write-off, three children as good as strangers, and an unmentionable love life? And a man who isn't happy about owning half of Hokitika, about his huge stake in the San Francisco of the South Seas?

Nevertheless a promise has been made, in the interests of balance, to print Herman's considered revisions. Nothing coherent has yet come through. Not unless one takes as true record those obscenities which have been passed on with obvious embarrassment by the medium concerned. They suggest, at least provisionally, that as a pain in the arse Herman is not altogether as pious as he might appear.

James? All we need to know about James, for the moment, can fit into a footnote. When other things allow, and other things mostly allow, he still sits in a dim room with Sarah. He seems to be withering away with his virginal will to die. God knows, or ought to, that there is enough grief in this world without dwelling longer on James. Besides, villainy always makes for better copy than virtue.

About the gaming tables of Hokitika it comes to pass that Ira Dix and Richard Lovelock encounter the idea of the Travelling Hydrostatic Suction Gold Miner and Amalgamator. This marvellous machine, as explained by its designer and promoter, will win all the alluvial wealth of the coast, indeed most of the gold of the globe, in a matter of weeks. Moving on mighty wheels, powered by steam boilers, the appliance would perambulate over the toughest terrain, sucking up gold wherever concealed, drawing up the metal through chambers where mercury sodium amalgam would do the work of sifting impurities, and through further chambers where a set of retorts would turn the dust into pure metal, finally into solid ingots. It would work, that is, in the manner of a modern harvester on a wheatfield; its owners would follow behind, gathering up the ingots as they spit from the rumbling rear of the Travelling Hydrostatic Suction Gold Miner and Amalgamator. Further refinements are conceivable: the machine might eventually be persuaded, for example, to invoice the ingots for dispatch to a gold hungry world, and eliminate the need for middle men.

It is not given to many to share the labour pains of revolutionary new technology. The gathering of gold – the wearisome digging, sluicing, washing – has changed little in the memory of men living, and indeed only in minor detail since Pliny documented it in Spain twenty centuries earlier. Ira Dix and Richard Lovelock observe the chance of their lives: all past gambles appear petty. They draw the designer into a prolonged and drunken game of poker, and when he is sufficiently and considerably in their debt, they place a prepared document before him to sign. This gives them the right to ninety per cent of the profits accruing from manufacture and use of the Travelling Hydrostatic Suction Gold Miner and Amalgamator. The designer is to receive a royalty of ten per cent, contingent upon his continued collaboration with the project.

'I will buy and sell St Louis,' announces Ira.

'Why St Louis?' asks Richard, who does not understand sentimentality.

'Why not?' asks Ira, and then to demonstrate that ambition is not altogether absent, adds: 'After that, New York. London. Paris.'

'What would be left for me?' Richard also lacks much geography.

'Africa,' suggests Ira. 'The continent of the future.'

Richard is not impressed. 'I wouldn't mind Paris,' he says wistfully. For one thing, he knows it not to be inhabited by homicidal black men.

'You wouldn't know what to do with Paris,' Ira insists. 'You need some feeling for the finer things. Nevertheless,' he goes on, shuffling the deck again, 'we shall play for Paris. And much as I feel myself too old for the challenge, I am prepared to take Africa on an I.O.U. should it come to that.'

While they play for the world, first for Paris (Ira's on a flush) and finally for China (Richard's on a paltry pair of tens), the designer sleeps at their feet in dipsomanic despair. The triumphant pair, however, have an irritant problem with morning's light. The Travelling Hydrostatic Suction Gold Miner and Amalgamator does not yet exist. It is still a rough drawing in a Hokitika back shed. To surmount this problem, they drag the designer, his legs dangling limp between them, to the shed. There they instruct him to get on with reshaping the world to their satisfaction.

The designer, whose name is Norman Strout, for all that it matters now, is understandably upset by their impatience. He protests, in enfeebled fashion, that he needs money. Materials. Manpower. But most of all money to get his invention on the road. Ira and Richard look at each other with dismay. This is an unforeseen hazard. There is another more sobering. Norman Strout, the effort of protest undoing him, falls in a faint and is in delirium for five days. Ira nurses him, with profound attention to his every need, while Richard returns to the Lovelock claim to continue earning the money for capital development they plainly require. Ira concludes, as Strout teeters feverishly between life and death, that the man might be suffering more from diminution of rights in his enriching machine than from, say, a fatal brain lesion. When he mentions adjusting the designer's share to twenty per cent there is perceptible improvement in Strout's condition. At twenty-five per cent his eyes flutter open feebly. At thirty-three and a third per cent he is suddenly on his feet and they are in business again. Strout may take India, but what the hell.

Richard sees industry in the shed when he rides back to Hokitika. This industry consists mainly of Strout going over his drawings with Ira, explaining the complexity, and ingenuity, of the crucial retort system within the apparatus, while Ira looks on with small blank uncomprehending eyes. Then there is the matter of the system of steel rods, still to be developed in detail, which will probe and loosen the earth in advance of the machine, thereby allowing alluvial gold to be sucked up with ease and released from surrounding impurities by means of mercury sodium amalgam. The beauty of the arrangement resides in the fact that steam boilers will do all the work, and man none, apart from giving stopcocks attention and of course harvesting the ingots as they fall. 'All we do,' explains Strout in jubilation, 'is set it rolling on the bosom of mother earth, and follow behind.' Not a vision to be discarded lightly.

Meanwhile, though the Travelling Hydrostatic Suction Gold Miner and Amalgamator may well suck up all the gold from Hokitika to the Himalayas, it sucks up much Lovelock money. Strout, for example, needs £500 worth of steel rods, many of which he rejects on grounds of poor quality, to perfect his system. He needs £1,000 worth of plate to ensure safe boilers; again he seems unnecessarily adventurous with Richard's money, since much of this plate is left to rust in long grass under the rains of Hokitika. Retorts shipped from Sydney prove too small for the tasks Strout has in mind, and he orders more at great expense. Richard's bank account is best not examined. A revolving whalebone brush turning on a flywheel, to dust off dry impurities, also causes much anguish. No less than fifty versions are needed before the revolving whalebone brush revolves, and the flywheel flies. Meantime much whale pillage crunches underfoot and flywheels of diverse dimension are discarded outside the shed. Pistons by the score pose mysteries to Strout too. Dozens of drums of mercury sodium amalgam begin to bulk in the shed. Then the shed itself becomes the problem. It is soon too small as the Travelling Hydrostatic Suction Gold Miner and Amalgamator begins to rise to heroic dimension. The roof has to be raised, and the distance between the walls widened, again and then again, until the shed is no longer a shed, but as sizable a factory as any

Hokitika has to show, with a labour force of five sweating within, excluding Ira and Strout. By this time, let a clean breast be made, Richard is broke. The enterprise survives solely on what Richard can wrest from the Lovelock claim. His brother and partner Herman's striking if surly gifts save Strout's marvel from stillbirth. Even so, fiscal midwifery remains urgent until Ira and Richard, acting inspirationally as one in their desperation, have freak success on the gaming tables; it seems to presage larger triumph to come. An armed guard is placed nightly on the prototype miracle as it nears final and fascinating form. All concerned are sworn to secrecy in a solemn ceremony at which Ira's ivory-handled Colt prominently figures. There is really no need for this. All the workmen involved, even Richard and Ira when they climb within, are baffled by the labyrinths of boilers, chambers, hot-air distributors, pistons, pipes, flywheels, troughs of mercury amalgam, revolving brushes and retorts which have begun to grace the cavernous interior of the Strout treasure dome; none could duplicate the arrangement from memory, not even Strout himself, essentially an intuitive designer, proceeding from problem to problem as imagination moves him. More than once he disembowels the increasingly corpulent beast, greatly to the pain of the onlookers, in his pursuit of perfection; such modifications mean, of course, more delay. And more, much more of all the money Richard and Ira, and particularly Richard, can muster. Of their sacrifice, and patience, it is perhaps superfluous to speak; mankind's profane perfection always demands a due. Within a twelve month of winning their two-thirds share in a project virtually to print money, Ira and Richard learn from Norman that, at last, the machine is near ready. It is time, in truth, to place their cards on the table before rumour-ridden Hokitika.

They cannily choose March 17, 1867, for the unveiling: St Patrick's Day, a holiday, with all the Fenians abroad and green beer spilling over every bar. Ira hires blessings from both a priest and a Protestant clergyman to give the event tone, and as an afterthought, to allow God no get-out, the rabbi from the Tancred Street synagogue. Richard tries to drum up a diggers' band to give some temporal colour to the occasion, and in the process, since Hokitika owns no diggers' band yet, has to invent one: he finds a man, for example, who can produce a reasonable rhythm on an empty carbide container, another with capacity for a jew's harp, still another with a swanee whistle, a fourth who knows the lagerphone, a fifth, sixth and seventh with knowledge of the bones, the saxolin, and finally and magnificently the accordion. He buys red shirts, black bandanas, white moleskins and blue bowyangs as uniform for these motley musicians. To keep cost down, Richard dispenses with the concept of conductor: melody, not harmony, is the need. He makes only one rule beforehand: they must play the same tune. Richard's creation of March 17, 1867, will be long remembered: because of tales told it will be resurrected in the twentieth century, long after gold rush days, and called the Kokatahi Band, still at last report conductorless and trying to play the same tune at the one time, and now regarded as a nation's cultural treasure. So much for Richard's immortality; now for Norman Strout's.

Hokitika's population on that day is 7,101, with an estimated 5,406 souls on the surrounding fields. Or 12,507 in all. Some 12,501 witness the unveiling, or rather the demolition of the shed surrounding the Strout-Dix-Lovelock Patent Travelling Hydrostatic Suction Gold Miner and Amalgamator. Three of the half-dozen known absentees are Lovelocks. Sarah, on her deathbed, and James, beside her deathbed; also Herman, out on his claim, oblivious to the entire affair, though Richard has informed him often enough by way of the more irritating background noise which Richard is prone to supply when working beside Herman. Otherwise Hokitika is empty, with every hotel shut down, every casino silent, hospital beds vacated and police cells flung open, the Fenians ceasing to fight and even the jewelled and ringleted waitresses from the opera house, usually aloof, joining the crowd on the outskirts of town. To demonstrate the remarkable potential of the Strout invention Richard has liberally salted a field beyond the shed with the finest Lovelock alluvial gold. The crowd understandably, especially given the insobriety of St Patrick's Day, is kept at a distance from the field and, even more understandably, from the mysterious shed. Last-minute sabotage still seems all too possible. The stern editor of *The Hokitika Evening Star* has already done his best to encourage Luddites: 'Science,' he has warned his readers rather prophetically, given the optimistic tenor of his times, 'may yet become a ravaging and ravenous monster out of the control of man. This machine may well be a symbol of things to come. If rumour has it right, and there is seldom smoke without fire, these goldfields might be emptied of every last particle of wealth overnight – and, who knows, in the dead of night. One hopes, perhaps vainly, that reason shall prevail. In both colonial and local interest, indeed, one must pray that it shall.'

Reason is demonstrably not prevailing in the impatient crowd outside Hokitika. Nor is prayer, though the priest, Protestant clergyman and the rabbi are arranged in their appointed places. Rum and bad whisky, in picturesquely labelled bottles passed from hand to hand, prevail far more prominently. The atonal diggers' band, at least harmonious in colourful costume, still disparately searches for an identifiable tune to play. The sound – of jew's harp against swanee whistle, of lagerphone anticipated by saxolin, fleshed with a composition for accordion to the approximate beat of the bones and the carbide drum – is distinctly unusual, even appealing in an enigmatic way, with a certain measure of melancholy; it produces a shivering silence in the souls of some of the more sober and sensitive, and they look up at the grainy rain-forested hills, the shiny alps beyond, becoming conscious of life's brevity and seeing all human endeavour as an ephemeral frolic between one world and the next. They shall not be suffered any disillusion on March 17, 1867. Also, that day may at least throw light on Aeschylus's ancient proposition, that the gods are best asked for nothing excessive.

'Right,' says Ira. 'Let's go for broke.'

He fires his revolver in the air as signal. Ten workmen take the shed apart. They knock out pegs, haul on ropes. The corrugated iron roof flies off first, tearing apart and tumbling to the ground with a series of dull detonations, while nearby spectators flee. Then the walls begin to quiver, to crumple and collapse outward as noisily. Such is this initial spectacle that first sight of the Strout-Dix-Lovelock contribution to goldfield science could easily be anti-climax.

It isn't. The rather fundamentalist Protestant clergyman falls prematurely to his knees. The priest fingers his rosary and finds himself whispering the last rites for the dying. The rabbi fondles his beard while his eyes fill with Old Testament awe. The diggers' band is conspicuously silent; there is no conductor to tell the seven to strike up again, and it is doubtful whether even a baton-wielding Gargantua or Goliath could more than momentarily hold their attention, much less persuade music from their sagging jaws or paralytic fingers. The spines of an estimated five hundred auburn barmaids tingle. Bottles of bad whisky fall. Some, seeing an unmistakable harbinger of delirium tremens, swear off the drink forever or anyway the day. The hush of a history-making moment even infects the children, their minds already engaged in processing and printing a memory for their own children, and their children's children, thousands of yellowing psychic photographs for sceptical posterity. These mental portraits, alas, or maybe mercifully, are all posterity will possess. The one physical photographer there for the occasion, hidden under a huge hood above his tripod, will later swear that no image could be made prisoner on his plates, though he exposes all of a dozen once he overcomes his fright.

Profanities aside, Marie Louise is first in the multitude to offer a coherent comment, one of passable profundity, given her earthy delight in the practical conveniences of her century. 'This,' she says, holding

Luke tight, 'is the end of civilization as we know it.' Words worthy indeed of her beloved Herman, from whom she has doubtless picked up a depressively prophetic tip or two.

There it stands anyway: the industrial revolution's first triumph in fresh antipodean fields, ravishingly vast and complex, immensely menacing, something which could well carry men to the moon and cause no further surprise. And everywhere sprouting heads of steam with malevolent hiss. Norman Strout, leaving nothing to chance, has fired the burners beforehand.

Ira Dix leaves nothing to chance either. Still with revolver, now useful to encourage spiritual conviction and the finer things thereof for a true fact, he persuades the clergy closer to the abundantly articulate work of the devil. When it appears their feet can approach no further, he obliges them to get about their business, brooking no delay. Norman Strout's blackening and mildly frowning face is sometimes to be observed surfacing from the steam; his finely tuned ear tells him of a possibly imperfect stop-cock.

Nor does Richard neglect the diggers' band. As the captive clergy flee one by one for freedom, he insists that the bandsmen demonstrate their diverse virtuosity with the tunes of 'Gold is a Great Friend of the Masses' and other well-loved goldfield ditties. Their sound – especially the increasingly dolorous beat of the unsteady carbide drummer – is sometimes heard above the sighing, rumbling crowd. Children bicker like wild birds of the forest again, daring each other to defy death and dart closer to the machine, and into the steam. Prominent among them are Benjamin and Ernest Lovelock, still immaturely eight and six years old respectively, and now finding the life of action a sight more interesting than precocity and recent experience have encouraged them to suppose. More passive and tender Luke, huge eyes shining, is lifted high by Marie Louise. The jewelled and ringleted opera house waitresses, and the five hundred auburn barmaids, mortal fascination overcoming fear, all rustle and surge forward, as sibilant as surf on an exotically lonely shore.

'Stand back,' shouts Ira, with another revolver shot for emphasis. At the most charitable, it might be said that he is merely ringmaster, using a whipcrack to command attention; Norman Strout is actually the man in the lion's den, whenever seen, which isn't often, as he ducks and dives among levers and gauges, rapt in the song of several hundred straining horsepower. The lyrics will last him a lifetime, more than adequate consolation for many lesser disappointments.

'Ready, Richard?' Ira calls. Richard is. He strides forward to take his place of honour beside Ira. Behind, the sound of the diggers' band trails off, though the artiste on the jew's harp seems determined to pursue his solo until entirely satisfied.

'Norman?'

Norman agrees, if with some lingering reluctance to part with the more inspirational preliminaries, that the Strout-Dix-Lovelock Patent Travelling Hydrostatic Suction Gold Miner and Amalgamator is indeed ready to roll.

'So be it, for a true fact,' says Ira solemnly, with his meticulous sense of theatre. He raises his revolver yet again, fires, and perforates a passing hawk. The tumbling corpse complements rather than confuses the scenario.

There is no histrionic tension lost in Norman Strout's increasingly passionate reading of his role either. For half a minute, which seems about that much of a month, he swings manfully – then in something approaching an epileptic fit of frustration – on a master lever which will set all, at last, in motion.

Nothing happens. In the ensuing human silence adulation is diluted by a public jeer or two.

He swings the lever yet again.

Then everything happens. It is as if Norman has freed several score thunderstorms. The machine remains shuddering and stationary for an indecisive moment, as though baffled briefly by its existence, making a metaphysical inquiry of the world into which it has been born, and then with loud anguish lurches from the ruins of the womb where it has been gestating for only marginally more than the conventional human span. It roars and screams and squeals, spinning off sparks like lightning flashes, cloaking itself in cataracts of steam as pistons pump, boilers bubble, and its visionary retort system begins to blaze. Its savoir faire is soon undeniable. For finally, and most fantastically, it reverberantly unfurls that spellbinding system of sharp steel rods designed to loosen and recover the riches buried in the bosom of mother earth as it rolls around the world. These rods, however, do not behave precisely as Norman proposed, though they display much energy as they revolve and slash. They make no contact with the earth; their bravura is confined to creating currents of air. The angle of approach needs adjustment, a deficiency which Norman discovers too late for repair, since those mighty wheels are moving and he is greatly occupied with leaping clear. Essentially the effect is that of a condensed cavalry charge, all lances and swords bristling brightly in a rare burst of Hokitika sunlight, before a monstrous and ungainly forerunner of a modern tank, one which could have concluded the battles of Balaclava or Gettysburg in a matter of minutes.

Which is to make no idle narrative point. Materially the facts are these: Norman, never one to compromise quality, has given his undivided attention to the implicit stresses and strains within his design, and indeed has often shown uncanny if not infallible instinct for exactly where such stress and strain is likely to strike, and place the entire enterprise in peril; he has given less attention to, for example, steering. And to the consequent and certainly more literal peril of the Strout-Dix-Lovelock Patent Travelling Hydrostatic Suction Gold Miner and Amalgamator having to locate its own direction without recourse to human artifice. The direction which it happens to be taking, partly due to the uneven nature of the terrain on which it has been deployed, is towards 12,501 people of Hokitika and surrounding districts. The impression produced by that remarkable system of spinning steel rods is one of imminent massacre. Five hundred auburn barmaids, and three dozen jewelled and ringleted waitresses, scream as one woman. The carbide drum, not to speak of the drunken drummer, is near trampled flat by resonant feet as the flight begins. Herman Lovelock, lonely out on his distant claim, at first hears the commotion as a curious auditory effect produced by some shrill alpine wind, conceivably backed by avalanche of uncommon substance; and then wonders if it might not be some hallucinatory message of coming chaos impinging upon his consciousness, a herald of the hells to be harvested by grown men who do not behave in an adult way. Thus rationalized, the sound soon seems to diminish.

Nothing else has. The true miracle of those effervescent minutes in the history of Hokitika is that all 12,501 survive, with not even a near fatality in the riotous scramble for safety. Bruises and abrasions are many, but there is no laceration directly due to those stabbing steel rods, nor anyone sucked hydrostatically into the bowels of the machine, to be removed of earthly impurities by means of mercury sodium amalgam, and then passed through the fires of the retort system for the pure metal of their souls to be excreted as immortal ingots from the rear. Ira and Richard, clear of the crowd anyway, are fast – and first – to find safe ground. There they are shortly joined by a singed and tattered Norman Strout, who is already well into planning an improved directional device, with foolproof reinforcement.

For the crowd there is consolation. The Strout-Dix-Lovelock horror, still moving at surprising speed, given its bulk, efficiently locates an unsuspected braking system within its interior; and thereupon shivers to a stop. There, while some yards short of the excitable crowd, Norman's creation produces yet another surprise. It begins, at first with delicate little dance, all points and pirouettes, and at length with unnervingly lusty waltz, to break up. Pistons protest; boilers burst; retorts erupt volcanically with dazzling flashes of fire. The steel rods whirr their lethal last, then droop pathetically, leaving the rape of mother earth unaccomplished. Ira sees his proprietorial dreams of St Louis and Paris shrivel. Richard watches China follow Africa down the drain. Norman, by contrast, has a perverse if passing moment of pride: he recognizes, as even God must do at times, that any creation of integrity has the right to an autonomous character. As rivets pop like firecrackers, steel plate booms into the air and bowls away on an invisible wind. Finally there is explosive internal collapse; within one wondrous minute the machine reveals itself as no more than smoking debris and melted metal. Coup de théâtre has, after all, become coup manqué. The Hokitika crowd, flattened by the force of the shock waves meantime, begins to rise, to stir, to offer gratitude to a merciful God, and otherwise to express itself most colourfully.

Norman Strout, Ira Dix and Richard Lovelock are nowhere to be seen, and have not been since toward termination of the danse macabre; when Richard concluded the time appropriate to cut their lucky. They are in fact making considerable progress into dense vegetation beyond the town, expressing themselves in tones of agitation when they find breath to speak. 'It'll be a lynching,' Ira insists, familiar with the menace disenchanted men in the mass can present, once having suffered a noose uncomfortably about his neck before the sheriff arrived, and twice having been tarred and feathered out of town. Between gasps Norman Strout explains to his unresponsive companions that he believes their difficulty to have been a design problem, primarily, likely with the retort system having bottlenecked the energy inherent in the Strout-Dix-Lovelock enterprise; he appears, insofar as he can be understood, to be dismissing the disaster as a temporary inconvenience. Richard, the least articulate of the three, is presently displaying his remarkable proficiency as a tree-climber, thus offering much inspiration to his companions still clumsily struggling up lower limbs; Richard is preoccupied with the thought that his life might become a limbo of treetops. Less contemplatively, he understands that they face a cold and comfortless winter in the forest unless Christian charity tempers the ugly mood of the town.

This fear proves superfluous. As sounds of anguish subside, one digger is distinctly heard shouting to another, 'By Jesus, Jock, that field out there is still fully of bloody gold.'

From that point the Strout-Dix-Lovelock spectacle becomes no more than a piquant, if somewhat poignant, folk memory. Hokitika is witness to the shortest lived, certainly most concentrated gold rush chronicled in the South Pacific. There is none of the ceremony of staking out claims. The field fast seethes with swinging shovels, flashing pans and rocking cradles, and human beings in ecstatic mass. Barmaids, no doubt apocryphally, are reported as having been seen carrying off gold by the bucket. Children, with equal exaggeration, are said to have founded family fortunes. The truth of the matter – facts are usually unkind to such endearing and durable legends – is that the more experienced diggers make the most profitable haul, and in distinctly swift time, thereby enabling themselves to get on with celebrating St Patrick's Day in more conventional and spectacularly spendthrift way; Hokitika is quite thunderous by nightfall, with liquor abundant in consequence of Lovelock gold, and Richard lavishly the toast of the town after all. Norman, Ira and Richard, meanwhile, are making their muddy way back from their autumnal forest sanctuary, all but forgotten and, so far as anyone remembers, forgiven. St Patrick's Day will never seem the same again, confides one digger to a particularly bosomy barmaid, just before a Fenian pushes a fist into his face with no especial malice. When that fight finishes to mutual satisfaction, the digger continues explaining to the barmaid that Norman, Ira and Richard should be put on the town payroll for the further edification, enrichment and entertainment of Hokitika. Such public spirit convinces him that the community has a future; it might yet play more than second fiddle to San Francisco.

We need not pursue such iridescent rationalizations of the day further. Far more to our purpose that Rabbinical tradition tells of one indestructible bone in the human body, the Luz, located imprecisely but nonetheless immortally, the nucleus about which resurrected flesh will form. Flesh, rotting or resurrected, shall not concern us. Spirit shall. No mortal endeavour of meaning is destroyed easily either, and it need not wait upon the last trump to bring forth its fruit. Folklore the Strout-Dix-Lovelock folly may become, to be passed from fathers to thousands of marvelling sons, but because of one footloose and fancy-free son, who travels far and at length finds himself a post-impressionist artist in Paris, it will trickle like a tributary into the glutted mainstream of twentieth-century art: specifically, it will encourage the iconoclasts in love with the suicide of several art forms (as well as, more enhancingly, by way of another branch of the tale, seeding the heroic fantasies of the late W. Heath Robinson). In yet another Indian summer of civilization, the 'sixties of the century which has most recently come to our attention, learned scholars, cultivated critics, and literary gentlemen of jaded appetite will gather solemnly in New York to watch a large and superficially complex work of sculpture – and possibly, for all aesthetic purpose, the entire art form of sculpture – inventively self-destruct. Unnecessary to add that in essence this enterprise, though attributed to a typical contemporary merchant of the grotesque called Tinguely, for all that the name matters now, shall be weedily derivative of Norman Strout's masterwork. (Norman in affairs notionally utilitarian also has diverse motor vehicles, several aircraft, and more than one malfunctioning nuclear plant to his posthumous credit.)

The end of civilization as we know it? All prophets, not least Marie Louise, can be a shade premature. To put it more modestly, March 17, 1867, is only the end of hope as Ira Dix and Richard Lovelock have lately known it. Norman Strout is last seen looking for another back shed.

Six

Sarah does die. Two years, ten months and fourteen days after their arrival in Hokitika her bed is empty, and her coffin briefly resident on a trestle in Marie Louise's bar. The coroner's verdict on her passing is his familiar one, sufficient to most post mortems on the goldfields: it is, he pronounces, a visitation from God. In connection with Whom, it has to be added, there is some argument concerning Sarah's last coherent wish: that is, to have a preacher of the same persuasion as her family chapel in distant Blaenau Ffestiniog conduct her funeral service. Marie Louise prevails over Herman's contempt for ecclesiastical tradesmen, earthbound all. Sarah's wish is respected. Hokitika now has a plumed hearse of great splendour, drawn by dark horses, to carry the coffin to a now near replete hillside cemetery, where black tree-stumps rot among rain-stained headstones. James, after all, has not taken his own life at the moment of Sarah's death, which eluded him while he dozed, but that does not make him an any more willing participant in this narrative. Love and grief have long enfeebled him; his flesh is thin and transparent, and his eyes pale and ghostly. As the coffin bumps down into the clay, he does move forward weakly, in a formal attempt to share the grave with Sarah. Top-hatted Herman and Richard think his feet are merely losing their grip in the graveside mud and unimaginatively insist on holding him upright. Others, and there are not many others, think him the worse for drink. Dark-dressed Benjamin and Ernest do not grieve with conviction; their mother has too long been a waxy and wasting stranger in the gloom of an upstairs bedroom. Little Luke, in lace collar, weeps mainly because Marie Louise is sobbing with considerable commotion beside him, which frightens. Also there is a wrinkled man with curious collar reading words from a large black book. His father is making noisy interruptions, perhaps because the wrinkled man cannot read well, and all this shouting unnerves Luke too. At length, marvellously, there is silence. The shadow of a vast bird seems to pass over the mourners. They look up. There is no bird. The alps, with fresh snow, rise sharp in the sun. Herman begins to shovel clods of sticky clay upon the coffin, and Sarah is one at last with the otherwise of life.

There is a wake. James has no heart for the fiddle, without which no true wake is complete. In view of his personal condition, however, he is excused more than token attendance. He plays but one melancholic air, receives the ceremonial silver, and absents himself swiftly. While noise begins to surge from the bar below, he falls upon his bachelor bed, death's discarded lover, attempting to embrace sleep as second best mistress. He bitterly wishes one sign from Sarah, just one, that she has known all along of his love. But his sleep, slow to arrive, is dreamless.

Herman, among the mourners who have multiplied in number since Marie Louise opened the bar again, appears equally unhaunted. He may now be a man less captive of circumstance, but there is thus far no positive evidence that he comprehends his new situation; possibly it has been too long coming. He also retires early, leaving Richard blind drunk and babbling at the bar. Richard, since the catastrophic feast of St Patrick, is often blind drunk and babbling at a great many bars, sometimes with Ira, sometimes not, since he is no longer so particular about the company he keeps, nor the way he dresses, well knowing the apparent devotion of many companions to be a snare and delusion, designed to part a Lovelock from Lovelock gold. Richard, through the long and reliably wet winter, has been both trying to repair his fortune, with Herman's help, and to pay off many distracting debts in consequence of his investment in Norman Strout. So far he has succeeded only in paying off debts, though there is still a Sydney bill or two to settle, or conceivably to evade. Richard is not conceiving much at the moment, apart from a venomous hangover. Insofar as he can be comprehended, he is communicating to those malt worms still upright at the bar that the world, despite appearances, still hasn't heard the last of him. Nor, such is our luck, have we. On the other hand it has to be conceded that his ex parte version of recent events can touch the hearts of some, especially when glasses stand empty on the bar. Richard is not even to be distracted by gladiatorial combat about him, which Marie Louise has to quell alone.

She closes down the Maison Marie some time after midnight, when the last maudlin drinkers have located the door with her assistance. As her staff whisks away shattered chairs and broken bottles, she rather miserably surveys a scene with the polish of confirmed prosperity: giant mirrors, grand piano, brass railings, bright spittoons, and the finest quality sawdust on the floor to soak up blood and booze. All hers, for what that is worth. Business, once booming, has become less remunerative. Hokitika now has one hundred and two hotels; she sees superfluity looming. Personally too. Once she hoped that Herman's money, well managed, would hold him down in Hokitika. This no longer seems likely. The San Francisco of the South, never notable for its summers anyway, has just suffered its first frost. Sarah's decease has coincided with the departure of a hundred or two diggers for more paradisial fields. Rumours run down Revell Street that the Chinese are coming to clean up the goldfields: another ill wind by any measure, since industrious Orientals are always in at the death of any good gold town.

Sighing, she pillows Richard's snoring head, and decides to leave him approximately where he has fallen, between the slop buckets behind the bar. As her staff departs, she extinguishes the gas chandeliers, and then wearily traipses with her candle to the children's bedroom to see they are safe. She ruffles their motherless heads lightly, kissing them on the cheek, tucking down their blankets, and gives a last large hug to Luke. With Sarah's death, Marie Louise feels more menaced. She can now imagine the Lovelocks leaving, as Herman has often and heavily hinted might happen when circumstances were on his side again. Marie Louise is forced to take circumstances seriously for the first time in her life. So she begins, carrying her candle down a hotel corridor, to weep with some passion. She cannot live without little Luke. He is as good as her own. He is her own. Also there is her love for Herman, if it can be acknowledged now, and her fears for James. The two widowers, in fact: the one of the flesh, the other of the spirit. Frisking as a little girl in lacy things, Marie Louise dreamed of golden princes. She has made do with whiskery men who wrestle into her body to still their strange torments, and has even encouraged them in such torments: none golden, none regal, and mostly drunk. She has made a modest best of so unsatisfactory a situation. Life, as her first lovably wiry husband told her, is a ride on a rainbow. When you look down, there's nothing there, and no one. The trick, he insisted until the day she buried him, the trick is to ride the rainbow while it lasts, and never look down. Marie Louise, with renewed determination, rides her rainbow by candlelight to Herman's door.

There it ends. When she lifts the latch, and silently eases the door open, she is able to observe Herman's fine figure in trousers, shirt, and braces. His back is half turned to her. His shirt sleeves are rolled above his wrists and he is holding a candle of his own. His left hand forces the flame of the candle against the palm of his right hand, which is beginning to blacken and blister. He does not flinch, or cry out, though his breathing is loud.

'My God,' says Marie Louise.

'Get out, woman,' he hisses; his teeth are gritted. 'Leave me tonight.'

He does not even turn. His left hand does not tremble. His right hand remains hostage to the flame.

She departs as instructed, never having heard Herman so vehement. Beyond his closed door she tells herself not to weep again. She does weep again. Marie Louise suffers a not uncommon if paradoxical human infirmity; she needs to be needed, desirably with passion. That is the mood in which, a little later, she comes to find herself in perplexity at a second bedroom door. Though at this point she is still not aware of it, and thus mercifully spared the implications, she and James, but James especially, are about to burn themselves on a more metaphoric flame. James wakes from his dreamless sleep to confront, for the first time in his life, the wealth of a woman's flesh against his body, albeit agitated. This, of course, appears to be the sign he has sought from Sarah, and who is to say it is not? Mysterious are the ways of God, and murkier are the ways of womankind. Not merely of Marie Louise, who was bound for Herman's bed that night of mourning; but perhaps of the shade of Sarah too, spiritually calling such shots as Herman's private and presumably penitential incineration of his hand upon her passing. Marie Louise, later, doubtless by way of rationalization, may retrieve a memory of ghostly wind gusting her, quite helpless, towards James. There they are anyway, Marie Louise surprisingly soon naked and James still impeded by nightshirt, crushed together in a narrow bed which becomes as an axis upon which the world, certainly for James, begins slowly to whirl. His weak mouth, with some encouragement, finds its way to Marie Louise's impressive breasts; seldom has a suckling infant been more gainfully nourished. Purpose seeps through the long abandoned maze of his manhood; at length it spirals inflammably to his head. He sucks at Marie Louise, at her magnificent flesh, with greedy giddy gulps. Mother of God, Marie Louise asks herself in fright and pleasure, what have I begun? But James has barely begun. He understands the tumult of those dream tambourines in his ears for the first time; his body unfurls from the finest gypsy red velvet, a bending bow about to loose the arrows of Eros. Meanwhile his manhood wakes as a dragon from a dark lair. Marie Louise cannot quite cope, understandably enough, since James seems at her from a dozen directions at once. Her sensations are sufficient to nourish fears for her sanity; something so exquisite seems damning this side of paradise. God, in giving her so many-limbed a lover, might well be preparing her perversely for punishment. She does not comprehend that she is only the recipient of riches stored in the soul of James; that she has tapped a dam and reaped a deluge; nevertheless she allows herself to delight in drowning. James knows, if he now knows anything, which is quite questionable, that his feelings have finally found a language to speak; he is as a dumb savage who has marvellously located, in the miracle of a lightning flash, the tongue of his tribe. And now cannot stop stuttering his joy. He becomes a barbed anchor which he needs to hook in the harbour of womankind before his soul can ride serenely at rest. Down, down he plunges.

'My God,' Marie Louise at last has a chance to gasp, likely an hour or two later.

It seems it can only end in her extinction. Arsonist James is burning out her body with incandescent shocks of ecstasy; she will surely be cinders by morning. Sheets shred, the mattress is soon beyond salvage, and before long the bed also is debris. Furthermore there is some reason to fear for the continued stability of the Maison Marie. Nothing distracts James. Nothing. Perhaps daylight will shape deliverance; her will is water. Dear God, she recalls, I only wanted to console the poor sad boy, to ride the rainbow a little way at most, and where am I now?

She is under the thunderous thighs of James. She senses the demonic at work. No matter. She all but dissolves again upon the rippling rainbow's arch, and believes she will never cease to be airborne.

That belief proves ill founded, at length, when the poor sad boy, with one vague grunt, the nearest to a word he has spoken all night, suddenly sleeps. Considerably sobered, fearing that he might soon wake refreshed, Marie Louise gathers her garments and flees the room. She is startled to see that the world still exists intact, that the morning has the identifiable colour of other mornings, that birds sing recognizably the same songs.

Bleary and bruised at breakfast, Marie Louise is even more astonished to see James downstairs bright-eyed at eight. His brothers make for indifferent contrast. Richard emits low moans from his makeshift bed behind the bar and presently arrives at the table humourless with alcohol poisoning. Bleak Herman has a bandaged hand. Aside from serene James, a man who appears to have found his vocation, the gathering is an uninspired spectacle. Immensely sated Marie Louise dare not seek James's eye lest lust, in diverse manifestation, blast breakfast apart. The children, already fed, run about in the sodden garden beyond the dining-room window; she wishes herself with them, and especially with pure-eyed Luke.

'Well,' Herman says finally. 'There's the end to it.'

No one asks about his bandaged hand. No one but Marie Louise will ever know.

Richard, apparently recovering, announces that he is off back to the claim. Is Herman coming?

'Where?' Herman asks, slow to hear.

'To the claim,' Richard explains.

'I said there's the end to it.'

'To what?'

'Gold,' says Herman. 'Grovelling.'

'Sweet Jesus,' Richard replies. 'Here we go again. I thought that was all past.'

'Sarah is past,' Herman says sombrely. 'No more.'

'You have children,' Richard observes. 'Three, all told. Three motherless children now. Think of them. They won't say thanks for quitting a good goldfield.'

'Children never say thanks anyway,' Herman insists, with some truth.

'James,' asks Richard, 'what do you think?'

'I think Herman is right,' James answers. 'Gold isn't everything. There is more to life.'

Marie Louise fears the conviction in his voice; she shifts uneasily in her chair.

'Like what, pray tell?' Richard demands.

'Like life itself,' James explains, 'and love.'

Marie Louise is all but undone. She knows she can never survive such a night again. There are limits. There are practical things. There are customers to please, meals to be cooked. And there is little Luke, out there in the garden, with his sunny smile. She shivers. And there is Herman, not least.

'What,' Richard challenges James with scorn, 'would you know of love?'

'Dear God,' Marie Louise sighs. 'You boys mustn't bicker. Not this morning.'

'Nothing,' James amiably confesses. 'I know nothing of love, Richard. Who of us do? That is its charm. That is its mystery.'

Marie Louise, though a maid is nearby, finds it expedient to bustle dishes away from the breakfast table.

'Maybe,' Richard says, as she departs, 'brother Herman has more mountains for us to climb, if only he can enlighten us. True labours of love, with damn small profit. Perhaps he might privilege us with a thought or two. Herman?'

Marie Louise hears no more. In her pantry, cloistered among her copper pans, she is close to confused tears. Then she realizes, first with relief, finally with perverse dismay, that James has given her no attention at the breakfast table. His rekindled interest in life and love is extremely indiscriminate. He has not so much as attempted to bring her evasive eyes to perilous rest upon his face. That might, of course, be the act of a discreet gentleman. It might also be the behaviour of an apprentice rake, cultivating indifference to bedmates. Or might he not remember? Her breast flutters with inexplicable pains; she tries to concentrate altogether on Herman when she shows her face at the breakfast table again. This time she is ignored by all. Drama sputters; voices are loud.

Richard pushes up from the table in disgust, burdened by hangover and Herman. 'North?' he is saying. 'Why north? There are just Maoris up there. Savages. Wars. Men roasting on cannibal cooking fires.'

'There is also land of more congenial nature,' Herman argues. 'Empty land. A place to begin.'

'Begin what? More madness? I never saw much wrong in going home to Devon anyway. Talk of that, and you talk more sense.'

'Not now.'

'Why not?'

'My Sarah is buried here.'

'Must we share her grave?'

'It cannot all have been for nothing; her suffering seems the seal. Now we have a covenant with this country.'

'By God,' says Richard. 'He is away again.'

'No country belongs to anyone,' Herman finishes, 'until there is a death. Now we have our death. And a country.'

'You'll be the death of us all,' predicts Richard. 'Last time it was mountains. Next time, Maoris. And no Hokitika to save us. No gold. Just a cannibal cooking fire.'

Richard stalks from the room. Soon after, the three still at breakfast hear him thud away on his horse. James appears least concerned, and fortunately presents no menacing distraction to Marie Louise. He has a dreamy smile, a vacant face, in some world of his own.

'You mean it?' she asks Herman most tentatively. 'You mean you are leaving Hokitika?'

'I mean everything,' Herman answers. 'Have I ever not? Circumstances closed the door on us here. Now the door, with death, stands open.'

It is all that Marie Louise fears. She does not see herself sharing that open doorway, death or no death, hand in hand with Herman. And she is confused, still quite moist with the memory of James.

It seems, later, that her first task must be to clear that confusion. A golden prince, if long awaited, is nevertheless too much of a good thing; best that he be banished with the frilly fancies of girlhood. Or so she tells herself, attempting realism, through most of that melancholy day. Also realistically, though not without heartburn, she takes it upon herself to tell Sydney Sal and Melbourne Liz, two long-legged ladies in her employ, that there is a strange unproven rumour in Hokitika that James Lovelock is more than he limply seems to be; that he possesses a formidably physical gift. For good and sufficient reasons, Sal and Liz find it difficult to respond to this rumour.

'That sad sack,' says Sal.

'Pull my other tit,' says Liz.

'I mention it only as a matter of possible interest,' Marie Louise explains clumsily. 'Where there's smoke, there's fire. The way I heard it, there's a lot of fire. Who knows?'

The tale is so improbable it is bound to travel. Marie Louise, sick in some part of herself, becomes busy at the bar. By noon, the rumour reaches Marie Louise herself, by way of an impressionable and bosomy girl, also in her employ, named California Kate.

'You think it's true?' asks Kate.

'I've heard of stranger things,' Marie Louise allows judiciously.

'He's just a bit of a boy, really.' Kate is wistful.

'They're the dangerous ones,' Marie Louise warns from relatively recent experience. 'The quiet ones.'

This notion evidently appeals greatly to Kate; she giggles away to dispense drink to prosperous customers at the other end of the bar. Marie Louise, feeling faint, decides she is suffering a fever bred of Hokitika's muddy streets and smelly swamps; she might well join Sarah on that hillside cemetery soon, the effort of disengaging from James her undoing, dear God.

Ballarat Gert, a fat and compassionate girl, is next with the news. 'The things they say,' she tells Marie Louise, 'about our poor dear James. You wouldn't believe the like.'

Upstairs, creeping quietly past the bedroom belonging to James, then closing the door swiftly upon her own, Marie Louise doses herself with laudanum and wishes an end to the day. Luke finds her sobbing on her bed. 'What's wrong?' he asks, bewildered. Unable to understand herself, or her role in the cruel comedy in which she has been cast, she takes the child in her arms. Soon, his head on her breast, little Luke begins to sob in sympathy.

Despairing Richard does not ride directly to the claim. Feeling the need to lift himself with liquor, also to win some consoling word, he calls on Ira Dix in a mildewed back room of the Rory O'More. Ira's genius now largely resides in the fact that he can surface moderately immaculate from dank walls, empty bottles, lively fleas and odorous blankets. Ira, feeling the cold, also his age, is in bed when Richard arrives, breakfasting on brandy dregs.

'The bugger's going,' Richard confides. 'The bugger's determined to go. All right for him. He's rich; he's got gold enough to last a lifetime. More. Me, I'm not worth much more than what I stand up in.'

Ira isn't much interested in Richard's condition. Herman's, however, is another matter. 'What do you reckon he's worth?' he asks casually.

'Who cares?' Richard shrugs, utterly dispirited. 'And what difference does it make anyway?'

'All the difference, for a true fact.' Ira is disinclined to suffer frustration where monetary intelligence is concerned. 'You must have some idea. Capital assets. Stocks. Shares. The like.'

'He plays it close to his chest. Marie Louise would know. Probably better than he does. And she's not telling.'

'Unjust, of course,' Ira announces. He watches Richard closely.

'What is?'

'The way the world's wealth is distributed. I've been seeking to remedy the situation all my life.' Ira's pose as southpaw socialist is not meant to be particularly convincing; he is looking for avarice in Richard's eye, and soon observing it with satisfaction. 'It has, so to speak, been my vocation to see that money circulates. Herman's money, sadly, isn't circulating. It is accumulating. Which is unfair for the rest of us. Especially unfair, I might add, for younger brothers.'

Richard seems prepared, quite soon, to see wisdom in this pronouncement. Ira's eyes are also creative. There is a silence of some length. Then Richard stands.

'If you think there's some easy way to get at Herman's gold,' he declares, 'then you're going to wait a long while for the maggot to bite. Forget it. For a start, there's Marie Louise. She's got her hooks into Herman. Nothing I can put my finger on. But I'm no fool.'

'Indeed,' Ira agrees sagely. 'But you need a man with ideas. Meaning me. I should deem it a privilege, for a true fact, to help with your problem.'

Richard rides off to the claim. Ira marks down the morning as the most satisfactory for some time; he might make it home to St Louis yet. He dresses in his last presentable black suit, not too frayed at the cuffs and only a little shiny at the elbows, suitably adjusts his hat and silver chain, and saunters out into the streets of Hokitika in search of ideas.

Marie Louise wakes with little Luke purely and peacefully asleep on her breast. It seems possible that she can cope with purity and peace again. What she cannot cope with – perhaps it is the laudanum, God knows – is the sight of Sarah, in her muddy grave wrappings, and with the faint phosphorescence of decay, standing silent at the foot of the bed.

'Please,' Marie Louise says, though it is not clear to whom.

The apparition doesn't shift. Sarah's eyes are large, dark and gentle. There is no accusation in them.

Nevertheless Marie Louise feels obliged to make apology: 'I have only ever done my best. I'm not to blame for the way the world is. Or the way men and women are.'

Sarah, still silent, shows no interest in this extensive item of justification.

'You want to know how it all happened?' Marie Louise persists.

Sarah, at length, shakes her head.

'You mean you know everything?'

Sarah nods. At least communication of some sort has been established.

'Then why are you here?' Marie Louise asks. 'To haunt me all my days?'

Sarah shakes her head again.

'Then why?' Marie Louise demands. 'Why come back?'

Marie Louise understands Sarah to say: To give you comfort. To give you courage.'

'Comfort?' Marie Louise says. 'Courage? For what?'

Little Luke, thank God, sleeps through it all.

'For what?' Marie Louise repeats, with rising panic. 'Comfort and courage for what?'

Sarah's eyes, in some anguish, rest for a time on Luke. Marie Louise struggles to comprehend the message; it isn't plain.

'For what?' she pleads.

No matter, Sarah seems to say, though her lips still fail to move.

'You want me to get on with marrying Herman?'

Sarah nods.

'That's up to him, now,' Marie Louise points out.

And you, Sarah appears to say with compassion, before drawing together her grave garment, as if afflicted with sudden chill; she looks her troubled last on Luke, and vanishes from the room. The sweetish smell of Sarah's present residence remains for some time.

James, resuming his menial tasks in the Maison Marie, meets California Kate by chance upon the stair.

'Why,' says Kate, 'you are a stranger, James. I don't believe I've seen you in daylight for months.'

'Then here I am,' announces James, with uncharacteristic certainty.

'I do believe you've grown a treat,' Kate declares.

'I finished my growing years ago,' James asserts.

'But you're so tall,' Kate insists. 'You're really quite a man.'

'Things of that nature,' James argues, with self-evident truth, 'are generally in the eye of the beholder.'

'You're worth beholding.' Kate has a shameless gaze.

'Is there something you want?' James feels obliged to inquire.

'Why, yes. I do believe there might be.' Kate, with a quick flicker of tongue, moistens her lips; she becomes occupationally soft-eyed.

Ira Dix, still dawdling through Hokitika at dusk, from desultory casino to half-empty hotel, finds not so much an idea as a face. A familiar face. It floats past him in the growing gloom of Revell Street. Ira stops, turns. The other man has stopped similarly. It can't be. Then it is, for a true fact. Ira hasn't seen that scarred, craggily handsome face since '49 in California, in circumstances saddening to recall. Bully. Bully Hayes, now largely hidden behind a bulky brown beard. A name now notorious across the Pacific, from the Marianas to the Marquesas, a connoisseur of evil and poet of the treacherous, buccaneer, blackbirder, gun-runner, girl-stealer and wife-murderer. What the hell is Hayes doing in Hokitika, skulking among the facades of a gold town where the armed constabulary would like to have his guts for garters?

They close with each other. They consider each other.

'Ira, isn't it?' Hayes says. 'California.'

'A long time, Bully,' Ira suggests.

'Bully?' Hayes looks about with mock surprise. 'I know none by the name of Bully. You're mistaken, friend. The name is Harry Hall, master of the schooner *Lotus*.'

'Whatever you say, Bully. But I bet Harry Hall's only got the one good ear.'

'Quiet,' Hayes proposes with a murderous hiss. Ira was present at the card table when Bully's sleeve was pinned down with a bowie knife. Cards constituting a royal flush were then, in a strained atmosphere, shaken loose from his apparel. To spare their community another noisy necktie social, the miners then proceeded to lop off Hayes' ear with the same sharp bowie knife, and enthusiastically boot his backside beyond town limits. Ira left town that night too, riding in a different direction, rather fast. It may have been his biggest mistake. Had he partnered with Hayes back in '49, he too might have found infamy and fortune upon the Pacific, though not without some seasickness, from which Ira suffers severely.

Ira can observe that Bully now wears his locks long to conceal that missing ear. Most advisably; it is too well known a tale. When Bully turned up briefly on the Otago goldfields three years before – Ira, alas, having missed his colleague there, and missed his chance again – a barber was bribed with a five pound note to crop Bully's hair short and expose the unbecoming residue of that Californian inconvenience. To celebrate, a hostelry produced a libellous playlet called 'The Barbarous Barber'. In consequence, Bully fled the fields with bandaged head, but not without reasonably satisfying revenge. He took to sea again with the most beautiful girl in Otago, sweet Rosie Buckingham, songstress of the Provincial hotel; her ill-used body was washed ashore within months.

'Is there somewhere,' Hayes asks, 'where we can talk?'

Ira gives Bully entry to his room at the back of the Rory O'More. 'Just temporary,' he explains.

'The pong isn't,' Hayes says. 'This the best you can do?'

'I got prospects, Bully.'

'You need them,' Bully observes.

'The great days are over,' Ira says defensively. 'I could have bought and sold St Louis. It's just, for a true fact, that I played one hand too many.'

Bully of course has heard of such hardship before. Men like Ira, with insufficient sense of vocation, never set the world alight. They can be useful only as means to an end. Ira, for example, might be functional in the matter of information. Bully flushes coin from a pocket, and drops it into Ira's shaky palm. 'Go get a bottle or two of the best,' he instructs. When Ira returns, Bully finds the booze efficiently reducing his depression in that smelly candlelit grotto.

'I'm looking for cargo,' he confesses to Ira. 'Pickings. This is a good gold town. There must be something on. I got an empty ship.'

'What run are you on now, Bully?'

'Run?'

'From where to where?'

'I see no virtue in becoming a creature of habit. I like to leave life to chance.'

'But you must have come from somewhere. Be going somewhere.'

'In such matters,' Bully says, 'I prefer to think of myself as in the hands of my Maker. It would be impertinent of me to propose Him a schedule. Apart from which, there's sods in most Pacific ports who seem to want my hide.'

'I did hear,' Ira goes on, 'that you been running guns to the Maoris north of here.'

'We have had certain business transactions,' Bully concedes. 'I ask only a fair return on my capital.'

'As I hear it, them guns have been killing white men in the wars.'

'That right?'

'The guns which fire, that is. There's some Maoris want your head in a basket.'

'I'll take that into account when setting a course. The fact is, old friend, I spend too long on the sea to keep abreast of current events. Know something, Ira? There are times in the deeps of night, out on the dark Pacific, when I have to ask myself what it's all about. Life, I mean. Life's rich tapestry. The colourful passing parade of mankind. You ever think about it?'

'When I see a plus in it,' Ira admits. 'Mostly it's minus. The parade's gone past.'

'I never allow myself to forget that there is much forever beyond our mortal comprehension. We just have to get on with making the most of our talents within our allotted span.'

'I was talking about the gun-running, Bully.'

'And I was inviting you to partake of a wider vision of human affairs.'

'So how come you're here with an empty ship?'

'I had problems with the cargo moving about in mid-ocean. Alas, I arrived without it.

'What kind of cargo?'

'A score of Chinese on their way to Hokitika. After leaving port it transpired that they were deeply dissatisfied with the accommodation provided, the sanitary arrangements, and the food. They also charged my crew with thieving. I did my best to cope with their complaints, even to the extent of arranging security, personally, for their curios and such. What more could I do? Finally they found themselves greatly desirous of leaving my ship.'

'In mid-ocean?'

'In mid-ocean. They preferred, surprising as it may seem, to swim.'

Ira feels a small chill. Then seasickness.

'There are some,' Bully continues, 'who claim to comprehend the divine in a grain of sand. I wish them well. The rest of us have to get on with it. Speaking of which, you don't know anyone in the market for Chinese curios here?'

'If I did?'

'Ten per cent,' Bully offers.

'There could be a curse,' Ira suggests.

'On what?'

'On anyone handling those things. Now.'

Ira possibly has more substance than Bully suspected. 'Twenty per cent,' he proposes.

'Cut me in at twenty-five, and we have a deal.'

'Right,' Bully says. 'Now tell me about Hokitika. And the prospects here. Who's got money?'

Ira has no difficulty in recalling to mind the dilemma of his dear friend Richard Lovelock.

California Kate, that evening, has urgent news for Ballarat Gert. She likewise, still later that evening, has tidings for Sydney Sal and Melbourne Liz. There are soon complaints from customers on the lower level of the Maison Marie about the paucity of girls to serve and entertain. Also about the pronounced lack of music, with the piano stool vacant; the place is as merry as a morgue. Belatedly investigating these expressions of concern, which at length reach her loudly while she mopes among copper pans in her pantry again, Marie Louise climbs upstairs with reluctance. The madness she finds is, of course, of her own making. Nevertheless it is not officially to be countenanced; nor can her mixed feelings be denied. There is a gathering of girls, mostly her own, but one or two from a neighbouring establishment already, tittering and preening outside the bedroom belonging to James. Fortunately she is not without words which seem adequate to the occasion; Herman has enhanced her vocabulary. 'This,' she cries, creating panic and flight as she rushes among them, 'is no adult way for grown women to behave.'

As for the girl, or girls, in residence with James, Marie Louise would sooner not see. She doesn't throw his door wide; she simply makes a businesslike rap upon a panel.

'Soon,' James promises from within. There is some desperation in his tone.

'Soon be damned,' she shouts. 'You earn your keep here making music on the piano. Not melodies in bed.'

She thunders away, shocked and shaky, wholly in daze. Mother of God, she asks, pray for me.

Herman, who has been hidden in his room most of the day, opens his door; the commotion has made him curious.

'What is it?' he asks.

'I think you'd sooner not know,' she replies.

'James?' he suggests.

'The boy has a problem,' she confesses.

'A problem?'

'Of a physical kind. Uncommonly physical.'

'You mean he is sick.'

'Of desire.'

'He's of an age,' Herman observes vaguely. 'Time has a cure.'

'Yes,' Marie Louise agrees. 'Death.'

She sobs suddenly, and finds security against Herman's solid shoulder. 'What is happening to us?' she asks. 'What is going to happen?'

'There,' says Herman, surprised and gentle, leading her into his room. 'What is all this? First wild talk of James. Now tears. Tell me, woman.'

'I love you,' she reveals with pain. 'I know it is not done for respectable women to say. But there. I am not a picture of respectability.'

'Curious you should raise the subject,' Herman says.

'Curious?' Marie Louise has never felt more deflated.

'I have been thinking thoughts, making lists. It's been another long day.'

'No longer than mine,' she argues. And then feels weak. 'What lists?'

'Of that which must be done. I have been interested to see, for example, where imperatives intersect.'

'Imperatives? Intersect?' She feels near hysteria again. 'What is this to me?'

'There is one interesting intersection, where all things converge. Circumstances are unmistakable. Your name needs changing. Better Marie Louise Lovelock than Marie Louise Regan.'

Fortuitously, Marie Louise faints with relief in Herman's arms. She wakes to find herself inhabiting his bed officially for the first time, and mere days from her wedding. Meanwhile, as the night moves on, other imperatives intersect more shamelessly outside James Lovelock's door; the curious queue does not diminish. In exhaustion and increasing delirium, though still anxious to honour his masculine obligations, James finds himself lost in a world of sighing flesh as lonely as he began; the dance of life momentarily leaves him indifferent. In that moment, toward dawn, he falls asleep. Despite the ministrations of several deeply disturbed and evidently unfulfilled ladies, he doesn't rally. They creep out one by one into the cold Hokitika morning.

*

Historians will wrongly attribute Hokitika's decline from Pacific metropolis to a sleepy reef of seaside dwellings as due to the ebb of alluvial gold, the departure of diggers. The truth is that the town will never really recover from the lurch as the Lovelock money decamps; the shock to the communal psyche, the flight of confidence, is to be calamitous. The town is to wilt within months, despite much undiscovered gold in hill and river. There will be reason for a Hokitika editor to lament, as he packs his own bags, that 'little has been done to turn the magnificent revenues to profitable and reproductive purposes', more or less pointing the finger at Herman, though James Lovelock's reproductive enterprise appears to escape his attention.

The wedding of Marie Louise and Herman heralds the end: 'an agreeably handsome occasion,' according to a journalist present, 'designed to temper the hard realities of colonial life.' Herman has to concede a priest to Marie Louise, provided only the bugger keeps to Latin, a language in which he isn't competent to conduct an argument. The temporal health of the couple is blessed with bumpers of French champagne. *Gigot de Porc aux Pistaches* and *Filet de Boeuf en Croûte* are among the more conspicuous items on the immense menu Marie Louise has personally arranged. Jimmy the Slogger has arrived down from the diggings, Liverpool Bill, Gentleman George, and Yankee Dan; there is no well-known name missing. There are Maori men in polished boots and white collars, their wives in bright crinolines, smoking clay pipes. The bagatelle tables and bowling alleys of the town are emptied. The crowd is dense about the Maison Marie.

A disgruntled and soon drunken Richard Lovelock is there, of course. So too, stealthy on the fringe of the celebration, are Ira Dix and Bully Hayes. Ira has had small success in selling off Bully's Asian objets d'art; some diggers dispute their authenticity, having not unreasonable doubts about the middle man, and Ira can hardly produce Bully to prove that he is, for once, in legitimate business. It is enough to turn a crook to crime. Between them Ira and Bully now share some desperation in the matter of plundering Hokitika pockets. Their intention is to collide with Richard while his legs last. A greasy pig chase, suddenly at the centre of the celebration, with men sprawling and champagne spilling and stylish girls wailing with laughter, provides the two with sufficient confusion to keep Bully anonymous; they grab Richard, not before time, and half-carry him clear of the throng. Then they settle him into the conveniently quiet roulette room of the Harp of Erin. Ira opens the conversation with a superficially disinterested inquiry into the health of Richard's brother Herman.

'Why should I care?' Richard says. 'Now the bugger's married again he's pulling out. With him gone, I got no future.'

'Richard,' Ira says, with appropriate gravity, 'it may surprise you, but I tell you for a true fact you have friends. Right here. We have been giving your future considerable thought.'

'Who is we?' asks Richard.

'Why, me and my much valued partner here. Harry Hall, master mariner and trader, of the schooner *Lotus*. Off watch some call him Bully.' Ira is not one to leave a pièce de résistance unremarked.

'Who?' Richard slumps forward, elbow unable to support his head, and peers at the pair through half-closed lids. 'Who'd you say?'

'I said some call him Bully,' Ira repeats with patience.

'Bully? Bully Hayes?' Richard's eyes are suddenly wide. He sits upright and sober.

'Not so loud,' Ira says nervously.

'I'm not in Hokitika,' Bully explains pleasantly. 'Anyone who says I am is likely lying. Or about to meet with a mishap.'

Richard sits very still.

'We have a proposition,' Ira continues, 'concerning Herman. And that fortune which you helped found. Bully here is familiar with the northern coasts of this country, and with many Maori tribesmen. He believes that, as Harry Hall, he can convince Herman that there is land up there on which your brother can settle comfortably with his kin among friendly Maoris.'

'What is that to me?' challenges Richard.

'All plus. Who would inherit Herman's fortune in the regrettable event that the said gentleman suffered, let us say, a fatal mishap? While sailing north, let us suppose, upon the schooner *Lotus*?'

'I'd be last in a long line. There's Marie Louise, now he's married her. James. The children. Maybe me, somewhere along the line. I wouldn't count on it. I don't know how the law works.'

'Then it seems the tragedy would need to be even starker,' Ira suggests.

'What the hell are you talking about?' asks Richard, never bright at the best of times; today is demonstrably not the best of times, other than for the celebrants of marriage at the Maison Marie.

'You plainly would need to be sole survivor,' Bully points out.

'Of what?'

'Of the disaster at sea, perhaps a small shipwreck, maybe an overturned dinghy, in which your nearest and dearest perished.'

'My God,' says Richard. 'What do you think I am?' True that he feels a flicker of fine feeling. But his outrage, for Ira and Bully, falls just short of convincing.

'We are thinking,' says Bully, 'of what you might be. As rich and as well-appointed a young man as any to be found in this colony.'
'It'd be all over quick,' Ira promises fervently.
'Humanely,' adds Bully.
'They'd never know a thing.'
'Nor would you.'
Richard comprehends the enormity of the proposition at last. 'You are asking me,' he announces, 'to be a murderer.'
'Not exactly,' Bully argues with charm.
'There'd be nothing personal in it, you understand,' Ira insists. 'We also understand your distress would be shattering, for a time. Rest assured that Bully, with his vast experience, manages these matters with much delicacy.'
'Death is but a lottery,' Bully observes. 'If we don't fix the figures, someone else will. Apart from which, it is well known that these things are fated to happen all the time at sea. It is just a matter of arranging an introduction to fate. Who can really quarrel with that?'
It seems Richard still can. 'You can't ask me to be a murderer,' he appeals hoarsely. 'Not of my brothers. Not of a woman. And especially not of small children. Think of little Luke. Poor little Luke. My God.'
He begins to weep rather extravagantly.
'Come now,' Ira says. 'We understand.'
'There is,' Bully agrees, 'a natural nobility in grief. Who can deny that? But you seem, friend, a trifle premature.'
'Couldn't we,' pleads Richard, 'leave little Luke out of it?'
Ira and Bully look at each other with small surprise and much satisfaction. It is over but for little Luke.
'Much as I hate to press the point at this juncture,' Bully says with compassion, 'it has to be all or nothing.'
'Imagine the tiny fellow struggling to survive, in this strange country, as an orphan,' Ira suggests. 'I tell you for a true fact it doesn't bear thinking about. Especially not if the law were disposed to consider him heir to his father's fortune. Think on that, if you will.'
'Life is a tragic affair,' Bully allows, placing a hand on Richard's still heaving shoulders. 'Who would deny it? And what is the point? Heaven knows how we struggle on through this vale of melancholy.'
'But little Luke,' Richard protests, choking.
'Suffer little children,' Bully agrees.
'You could stay below deck,' Ira says practically.
Richard is soon persuaded to dry his passionate tears.

*

Two other details before the day is put to rest. Herman is seen distinctly to smile, for the first time in some years, at the wedding celebration. James, once formalities have finished, is not seen at all; nor, from time to time, are some of Hokitika's loveliest ladies.

Seven

Enough to say that, through Richard's not entirely unskilful arranging, Herman soon encounters Harry Hall, skipper of the schooner *Lotus*, while still inclined to give human nature the benefit of the doubt, a probable consequence of his recently having been so resplendent a bridegroom. This Hall fellow, though something of a fast Yankee talker, has an impressive proposal to put to Herman. He is familiar, it appears, with most harbours and rivers to the north of this country. More to the point, he is also intimate with the diverse Maori tribes to the north, knowing which are still warring, which are only lethargically lethal, and which are more or less at peace, welcoming whites on to their territory. It is all, to say the least, and God knows the least is all he can say, a confoundedly complex picture. It becomes even less lucid as Hall freely and considerately offers more information on the subject, at times of a totally terrifying nature: missionaries and militiamen alike, for example, have lately been disembowelled and decapitated, and had their hearts publicly eaten, their eyeballs devoured as delicacies, by Maoris imbued with the stern dietary spirit of the new Hau Hau faith; certain forests and shores in the north bristle with death, while elsewhere all is idyll. To make his way safely, Herman needs a guide of stamina and perception. Particularly in the acquisition of land, Hall makes clear. Even peaceful Maoris are known of late to run amok when a land-buyer appears. Tact and gratuities to certain chiefs are necessary. Herman seeks to clear up any preconceptions the other may have about his quest. He is not, he explains, enamoured of land as an end in itself. He is interested in human progress. Land, and desirably timber, coal and iron, can have utilitarian function in the matter of liberating the species. Hall's eyes grow vacant as Herman enlarges. 'There's a lot of progress around these days,' Hall agrees experimentally, hoping he has kept track. 'I'm all for it, myself, in moderation.' This intervention turns Herman toward expansion of the thought that a new land implies opportunity for men to live in a new way, honourably and adult. This in turn leads to consideration of the nature of man, his likely role in the universe, and the frustrations of circumstance. An hour or two later, a dazed Hall begins to feel he will never get the greenhorn aboard his boat. Another hour or two later he begins wondering whether it would be worth it anyway. Herman, on the whole, is gratified by having found so sympathetic a listener. Just when deeply depressed Hayes alias Hall, unused to playing so passive a part, sees his existence as an increasingly cheerless gambol to the grave, Herman takes a deep breath and halts his discourse: it seems, for some reason, that he might have finished. Lest this not be the case, Hayes alias Hall rises swiftly. 'I'll be in port a day or two longer,' he says. 'Let me know if you need me.' Despite his better instinct he adds, 'I'm all yours.'

To be liberated from Hokitika, Herman, of course, does need Hayes. There is no narrative profit in listing the business transactions of the next few days, largely in company with Marie Louise, which are to leave Hokitika living quaintly on its memories well before time. The agreeable surprise for Herman in this period is that Richard, for all his earlier objections, indeed downright vehemence about not departing Hokitika, now has unsuspected enthusiasm for the enterprise. Herman has reason to assume that he has successfully uncovered, perhaps with chance word, a vein of idealism in his brother; no one now more keenly embraces the notion of an honourable adult future in the north. As for James, the less said the better. As even Herman cannot fail to see, the boy is transparently the victim of too long a sojourn in the incontinent circumstances of Hokitika. Worse, despite his depleted appearance, he can still plainly persuade others to rekindle his fever; fluttering females surround James whenever he shows himself beyond his bedroom door, which is seldom. Marie Louise is moving on none too soon; the Maison Marie is headed for bankruptcy with the girls quite uncontrollable.

There is, as might well have been forecast, a climate of feminine tears on the dockside that misty spring morning when the Lovelocks manage their worldly goods aboard *Lotus*, and then line the schooner's rail to farewell Hokitika.

'Where are we going?' asks Luke.

'You'll see,' answers Marie Louise, who is still far from clear.

'Will we be happy?'

'Very,' she promises.

'Always?'

'Always, my love.'

Nearby, Richard grows uncomfortable as eavesdropper on this conversation. He moves away, looking for Bully. But Bully isn't showing himself on deck yet; he could be recognized by some malicious individual in the dockside crowd at the last moment, and is not disposed to be hostage to ill fortune and the armed constabulary. Ira is also established below, braced for seasickness, but confident the suffering to come will be worth a more than mediocre share of St Louis, for a true fact. There is no plus in a trivial percentage of the Lovelock fortune. Once the Lovelocks are lost at sea, all but grieving Richard, he and Bully will move on to stage two of the operation. Which means splitting the entire fortune fifty-fifty, ridding themselves of Richard when convenient; anyway just as soon as he has signed away his inheritance. There is a stage three in the operation, though Ira isn't aware of this yet. In stage three Bully disposes of Ira, as is his custom, somewhere at sea and many thousand miles short of St Louis.

Meanwhile, with stage one proceeding as planned, and stages two and three no real problem, Bully Hayes should be a happy man. He is not a happy man. Since arrival in Hokitika, and particularly since conversation with Herman unloosed his familiar depressions, as altruists and idealists always do, Bully has been afflicted night after sweaty night by the same ferocious dream. He is aboard a boat. It may or may not be *Lotus*; he cannot for comfort be certain. He is being pursued about the deck by a tall figure, with shadowy face, bent on vengeance of unspecified nature; the figure is going through menacing motions with an iron boom-crutch. Bully doesn't doubt that he is dreaming the hour, and approximate manner, of his own death. What isn't clear is whether this event is ten minutes or ten years away; nor is it apparent who his assassin is to be, since the figure is always impossible of recognition. All he knows is his terror as the boom-crutch finally crashes into his brain; he wakes with huge scream, trembling in his cramped cabin, all the world indifferent to his death. In short, the skipper of *Lotus* has begun to suffer the near impotence of nervous breakdown; there is little help available to him anywhere in the nineteenth century, certainly not in Hokitika. Huddled over a worn and faded chart of the New Zealand coast, trying to plot a course for *Lotus*, and a place to sink the Lovelocks tragically, he flinches from decisions: he might, after all, be deciding the time and place of his own demise.

Until now, in a career never notably ineffective, the nervous tension of new ventures, that rewarding tingle in the gut, has distracted him from depression: indeed that has been the point of new ventures, possibly the point of piracy. A depressive knows the world is against him; the best antidote to depression is to embrace the fact, and have the world hot on one's heels, with the consequent triumphs and thrills of evasion. Now, however, Bully Hayes finds himself inexplicably nerveless. Near the coup to crown his career, the tingle in his gut is missing; he has only the dread of his premonitory dream. Is gaunt Herman Lovelock, for example, to be his killer? If not Herman, who? And when, where? His hand shakes too much to make any useful mark on the map. He reaches for rum, and once again postpones decision. True that this timid, tormented creature little resembles the blustering Bully Hayes of popular Pacific tales, the terror of the tropics, the gangster of the goldfields. Even pirates, for better or worse, can never be perfectly in character.

The Lovelocks, unaware of their many reprieves already that morning, watch as mooring ropes are cast off and *Lotus* begins to slip quietly downriver on a tame ebb tide. The cries of farewell from the shore, the shrill sobs of Ballarat Gert, are soon tempered by mist. Soon James, already suffering withdrawal symptoms, and sickening again, is the only one looking back toward Hokitika, and a lost carnal heaven. The others look toward the open sea, and futures yet to be found, as *Lotus* feels the first force of the ocean over the sand bar, and then under sail heels into its northward run. A giant shaven-headed African, with rings of gold in his ears, rears cool at the wheel.

A brisk following southerly speeds them up the coast. Bully Hayes hides from Herman, still finding rum a convenient anaesthetic for his condition, leaving the helm to the huge negro. Within a day or two, as to be expected in these waters, storm arrives with rising wind and sea under a blackening sky. Sail is shortened by crewmen, until now rather furtive, who surface red-eyed, roaring and cursing, while Hayes takes over the wheel. Herman, determined to miss nothing, remains on deck after dispatching his family below; he believes in getting value for his passage money, and is not disappointed. He rejoices in the rain on his face, the blast of spray on the wind, the walls of water over which they ride, all deliverance; he feels, for the first time in years, his own man again, though there is now Marie Louise to be taken into account. Soon all sail is reefed but for a slender jib; Hayes and his negro mate together hold the wheel as waves bash over the bow, as *Lotus* pitches and yaws. As the sea grows still more inclement, seething about Herman's boots as he grips a stay for support, a corner of canvas flaps up from a shrouded shape on the foredeck; he is given a glimpse of a small, highly polished cannon. Herman seldom finds food for thought without making it a feast. A peaceful trading schooner, pottering from one safe port to another, doesn't customarily carry cannon. Herman is about to make allowances, remembering the skipper's stress on the menace of certain

Maori tribes in the north, when he is given more to contemplate. The wind is whipping the skipper's long hair high as he engages in brutal battle with the wheel. The skipper, it seems, lacks a left ear.

At length Herman goes below, and not merely to see how his kin are suffering out the storm. The children are bedded tight in their bunks. Marie Louise rests haggard in hers. Richard vomits into a wooden bucket. Bruised James has collapsed limp on coils of rope, the last bliss of Hokitika banished. Ira Dix, supercargo of whom Herman should have been suspicious before, is gently moaning, much as he has since *Lotus* left its mooring; Richard has explained the presence of this aged and transparent rogue rather unsatisfactorily. That is, as an old friend of the skippers compassionately being carried north to pick up a passage home and die in St Louis. Given his current condition, immediate burial at sea might be the more merciful.

Herman kicks him. Ira finds more grief to express. His joyless eyes at length reveal themselves. So does something else. Herman has dislodged Ira's bedding to interesting effect. A rather splendid revolver now protrudes from under a pillow.

'I'd like,' says Herman, 'a little illumination.'

'Illumination?' Uttering the word is all but Ira's undoing again. He closes his mouth. Also his eyes.

'So let there be light,' Herman suggests, 'in the matter of our skipper being minus his left ear.'

There is no light. Ira seems to be shrivelling.

'I appear to be getting the message,' Herman adds, 'that his real name might be Bully Hayes. A name not noted for honourable and honest endeavour. What do you say to that?'

Ira has nothing to say to that. With a sense of fortune about to deliver yet another unfair blow, in the region of his overtaxed solar plexus, he attempts an expression of shocked virtue. Then he knows that it is all up. With the boat into even more sickening roll, fresh bile in his mouth, he sees no plus. Let it be all up.

'I have this notion,' Herman continues, 'that his intentions might not be of the kindliest of these parts. I see that you're not without concern for your personal well-being either. In the circumstances, for the general good, I shall relieve you of that revolver.'

'Revolver?' says Ira weakly.

Too late. Herman has helped himself and gone.

The storm passes. The sea settles. The mist rises. The North Island is a serene shadow to starboard. The battered voyagers view a tall and symmetrical mountain, bright with snow, a splendid beacon of deliverance above green land. The Lovelocks, children and adults, linger at the rail. All but Herman. Herman watches Hayes. As a skipper still stricken by the storm, Hayes offers a convincing performance in high key. *Lotus* is taking water through its timbers; crewmen work the pumps. The situation may well be serious. It is not for Herman to judge. He takes up stance slightly behind Hayes at the helm. The schooner responds sluggishly to the wheel. That much is clear. It is less clear what Hayes has in mind when he says, 'It looks like we aren't going to make it much further. We may have to abandon ship.'

Herman has nothing to say.

'We'll take a run,' Hayes announces, 'closer to the coast.'

Herman still has no opinion to offer.

With providence agreeably on his side again, the storm, a leaky ship, a genuine pretext to unload the Lovelocks, Hayes feels freshly in command of his life, if not entirely of *Lotus*. Still, he has harboured vessels less seaworthy before. That doesn't disturb him. He knows the territory north of the mountain. Tribesmen there still war with the whites. They are wholly Hau Hau in this vicinity, cannibals with Biblical colouring, and ceremonies of vengeful Old Testament hue: all eye for eye, and tooth for tooth. None more terrifyingly than the tribesmen of the Tutaekuri. Even Hayes has flinched from dealings with the Tutaekuri: less on grounds of propriety than because of the likelihood of parting with more of his anatomy than eyes or teeth. He envisages delivering the Lovelocks into a decrepit dinghy off the Porangi River, heartland of the Tutaekuri. In the unlikely event that their dinghy survives the surf on the sand bar at the river entrance, they will find the Tutaekuri welcoming them ashore; they cannot hope for more than one miracle. Fate could have no more reliable reinforcement than the Tutaekuri. The problem with this plan is sparing Richard Lovelock and Ira Dix for future reference. Perhaps they can be placed in a separate and safer dinghy, and instructed to turn back before striking the sand bar. Hayes is still filling in the fine detail of his plan when he becomes aware that Herman has no conversation at all.

'I think we'll keep the Porangi in mind,' Hayes observes. 'Those heads, over there, to the north. If we take more water, at least we got a convenient river.'

Herman is silent.

'Did I hear you mention Maoris?' Hayes asks.

Herman hasn't mentioned Maoris.

'Basically they're misunderstood,' Hayes informs him. 'Even, I might add, much maligned. Especially on this coast. Who's to say they don't have a genuine grievance or two? What they need most is a sympathetic ear.'

The words are ill chosen, in a surgical sense. Hayes has the uneasy impression that even with one to spare Herman isn't partial to providing an organ of hearing; he has all the animation of a mausoleum while Hayes works the wheel and shouts commands.

As they tack toward the coast, then shape their course to its contour, the dark headlands of the Porangi begin to rise from a fine fog of spray. North and south are hills greened comprehensively with forest. The beaches below are vast and dark, rimmed with foam; and close enough for those on deck to hear the sea drumming.

Toward nightfall they are hove-to off the Porangi. *Lotus* still takes water. Hayes, with Herman quiet if attentive beside him, orders boats lowered.

'The way things are,' explains Hayes, 'I can't guarantee your safety. I can arrange a partial refund of your passage money, naturally.'

Herman doesn't contest this as other than fair and reasonable. On the other hand, he still says nothing at all. Hayes takes a large breath.

'I suggest,' he continues, 'that you try to get ashore while it's still light. I'll arrange for your goods, chattels and items of monetary value to follow. We'll try to sail *Lotus* in tomorrow. It may founder, meantime. That's a risk me and my men will have to take.'

Hayes is hardly finished before he becomes aware of an unmistakably metallic pressure slightly behind his one intact ear. At length, with relief, Hayes realizes that it is merely a revolver Herman is holding; his imagination had been making cruel play with the boom-crutch promised by nightmare. He has survived the wrong end of revolvers before.

'I have another suggestion, Mr Hayes,' Herman reveals. 'Call your men on deck. All of them. Then instruct them to take the boats. You too.'

James, Richard and Ira, then Marie Louise and the children, arrive surprised on deck. Hayes, with Herman's gun at his head, is telling his men to abandon ship.

'It'll sink under you,' Hayes promises Herman. 'Who's to sail her? Your lot? Never.'

It is, for a moment, an effective filibuster. Herman, ambushed again by circumstance, needs time to consider the hindrance of having no crew. Hayes isn't without hope of a comfortable compromise. That is, until Herman howls. Neither Hayes nor his crewmen have heard the lycanthropic like before. He is transfixed. He sees Herman as a man more than likely to run amok with a boom-crutch if he finds a firearm frustrating. His men, much less preoccupied with visionary menace, take tangibly to the boats.

Richard studies the situation with some intensity, and finds no difficulty in concluding that his future is healthiest with Herman. Nor does Ira. They move toward Herman as one. James is already at Herman's shoulder. Marie Louise has the children gathered tight.

Though weak of limb at the helm, Hayes still has some last vocal energy. 'You'll never—' he begins.

Herman howls again—

That ends it. A humiliated Hayes, worsted for the first time on the lucrative New Zealand coast, scrambles across the deck and vanishes over the side of the schooner to join his likely doomed crew. Actually, kindly currents are to carry them south, to stagger ashore on sand in the vicinity of the European settlement of New Plymouth, days later, where they steal a more functional craft and Hayes farewells New Zealand, takes to the tropics, and in the largely congenial course of time keeps his rendezvous with an iron boom-crutch. In the few years left to him, Hayes, when taunted, plausibly disclaims all knowledge of a stolen schooner named *Lotus*, abandoned off the Porangi in late 1867; he says he was never there that year, nor familiar with a family by name of Lovelock. Certainly no crewmen live to contradict him. His blacker moods, observers note, are often brought on by howling dogs, which he shoots on sight. By one of those coincidences more often found in the rich seams of fact than in the fool's gold of fiction (since iron pyrites affords no excess) his last craft, from which he falls to the sharks, is also to be called *Lotus*. Which does suggest that even destiny can stutter.

Meanwhile, the Lovelocks have a problem on their landsmen's hands in the sensitive shape of a foundering vessel. Minus Hayes and his men, they are lost. Night is near. There is surf of especially spectacular nature between ship and presumably safe river mouth. Imagination has enough to mine without taking the possible temper of the tribe ashore into account. With death by drowning so credible a prospect, Herman now regrets his perhaps unduly emphatic dispersal of those with sea-going skills. On his instruction Marie Louise leads the children below. He takes the helm speculatively. He orders James, Richard and Ira to ease the sheets, and give sail an airing, by way of nautical experiment. Though sick with fright in differing degrees, the three attempt to do as they are told, with indifferent degrees of success. Among other things Ira is struck down by a swinging boom. Richard, in a tangle of rope, topples down an open hatch. James all but takes flight as he tries to recapture an unleashed sail. Wheel and deck contrive to toss Herman to one side. The marvel is that *Lotus*, with lurches, and an unhappy creak of timbers, does find a course, albeit unplanned; the four battered men flatten themselves on the deck as tide in full flow takes them broadside into the surf of the sand bar.

As dusk softens the shore, watchful tribesmen of the Tutaekuri, arranged on every vantage point, find it difficult to believe their impending good fortune. The priests of the Hau Hau faith have prophesied that, in the fullness of time, their enemies would be delivered into their hands. Other prophecies of those priests – such as that strict adherence to the tenets of their faith would produce warriors impervious to bayonet and bullet – have been incapacitatingly inaccurate. But the arrival of *Lotus* suggests a turn in war's tide. As the schooner swerves through the surf it seems to herald divine triumph; who but Jehovah could be preserving it as prize for their persistence?

The four on the deck, finding the vessel in wonderfully calm water, rise to rejoice. Then the event assembling itself ashore tends to terminate celebration. The colourful character of the occasion cannot be denied: the tribesmen, growing in number, are clad in blankets of bold hue, in bullet-holed redcoat jackets, sometimes in tartan kilts. This rippling mosaic is made the more piquant by elaborate facial tattoos. All are armed with shotgun or musket or tomahawk, also with more traditional if still efficient tools of the warrior's trade, clubs of stone and bone, polished and carved staves feathered at their sharp points. They hymn the arrival of *Lotus* with rhythmic chants and a stamping of feet; tongues protrude and eyeballs roll in collective satisfaction. The intent of this activity is not of a kind to leave an onlooker guessing. Herman and James, Richard and Ira, have much to consider as *Lotus* forges ashore at last, hull and keel crunching into shingle and sand.

Protest appears inappropriate. Likewise Ira's gun, which if fired could only signal massacre. Anyway it is fast souvenired from Herman's limp grip. The Hau Hau make *Lotus* their own, leaping aboard, swarming across the deck, revealing a cornucopia of ribald menace. The four men are pinioned. Marie Louise and the boys are fetched up from below. Disappointment appears general that so few are to be found. They are manhandled down to the shore, marched along a beach. Benjamin and Ernest whimper, Luke sobs unashamed. Ahead, the captives can see the fires of a Maori village in the growing dark. 'Is there no hope?' asks Marie Louise. Herman considers answer superfluous. The ferocious cries about them, laced with mocking laughter, are best not embellished.

As they near the village, and presumably their last hour, another party approaches. At the centre of this group, lit by flickering reed torches, is a tall old man of chiefly demeanour; his companions walk slightly apart from him, to convey their respect. Though as tattooed as his fellow tribesmen, two features of his appearance are of some surprise. His English garments may be motley and faded, but he has a fine and extremely clean cravat. He also has a monocle.

Leaning toward the Lovelock party, he says, apparently apropos of their situation, 'How perfectly extraordinary. And how very damned regrettable.'

In all lands there is considerable lore concerning lost tribes: people, that is, who after defeat in battle or some natural catastrophe, slipped away into the wilds, never again to be beheld by other human eyes. Of the lost and all but forgotten Tutaekuri there is little such lore. Nor is there much reliable in the historic record. Indeed there is room for the reasonable suspicion of a conspiratorial attempt to expunge the tribe from the Pacific's annals. This is all the more remarkable in that they did not slip away into some misty inland forest fastness, there to become poignant legend. They vanished, seemingly, where they stood. At one moment they were visible; the next they were not. Still more remarkable, though many modern Maoris can still trace their *whakapapa*, or genealogies, back ten centuries to the time when their ancestors beached their great ocean-going canoes in New Zealand, none claims descent from any Tutaekuri tribesman. The mystery is dealt with in a pamphlet, published privately in 1899 by the Reverend Clive Malmanche, called *Who Were the Tutaekuri?*, from which much of the material in this passage is drawn; this suggests that tales of the Tutaekuri were still troubling men's minds at the turn of the century. After purveying them with relish, dwelling at times on revolting physical detail, Malmanche dismisses most as unlikely horror stories, and finally attempts, for our continued comfort, to deny that the Tutaekuri existed at all; he offers the proposition that they were fairy-tale ogres of the morbid Maori imagination. The most charitable thing to be said is that Malmanche, who was defrocked for irregular sexual practices some six years after publication, was likely pursuing sado-masochistic concerns, in the not uncommon Victorian manner, under the pretence of scholarship. His dismissal of the Tutaekuri can be attributed to a fit of remorse after his having gratified those concerns.

In truth, there is little mystery. It is, for example, understandable that no early European explorer, crossing Tutaekuri territory, wrote of their quainter customs. All potential chroniclers failed to survive their intimacy with those customs. Also understandable that no modern Maori recalls a Tutaekuri connection in his *whakapapa*. None would want to. The Tutaekuri, moreover, were not of the material from which poignant legends are made. In matters of treachery, cruelty and general bestiality they had a record rivalling only that of European man. They didn't merely, like other Maori tribes, practise cannibalism; they invented it. Malmanche, rather romantically, sees them as the vehicle of original sin, the pagan serpent in the serene South Sea garden of New Zealand. One tradition says that their delight in human flesh was discovered on the long Pacific voyage to New Zealand. Other Polynesian voyagers sustained themselves, on the long weeks and perhaps months out of Tahiti and Rarotonga and Raiatea, with dried fish and vegetables and by killing pigs, dogs and rats which they carried aboard. When such sustenance went, they starved. Not the Tutaekuri. Nephews began to devour their uncles, and sons their fathers. Thus amply provided with protein, they arrived in New Zealand fitter and sturdier than other tribes who had made the great voyage. Naturally they early dominated those other tribes. In a land with a paucity of mammalian flesh, they in fact treated those other tribes as beasts pastured for slaughter. Such is the vicious way of the world, their enemies, for survival, were obliged to acquire a taste for their fellow humans; in time they were sufficiently nourished to resist Tutaekuri incursions. As Polynesian voyagers spread across the empty land, the Tutaekuri remained pariahs, as their very name suggests (*tutae*=faeces, *kuri*=dog); it derived from the substance with which the Tutaekuri smeared themselves liberally before battle, in order to make themselves the more unappetizing to their enemies. Contamination alone did not ensure safety. At the mouth of the Porangi River they founded a topographically useful tribal enclave, with advantageous views of the wild coast, also razor-ridged hills and mountains and near impenetrable forest protectively to their rear. Yet why, when the Tutaekuri were regarded with such distaste, did this relatively tiny tribe survive long at all? There is the rub. They were magnificent as allies when larger tribes warred; they were crucial to preservation of the balance of terror. If the Ngati-Maniapoto, for example, were attempting to exact *utu*, or vengeance, from the Atiawa, then an alliance with the detested Tutaekuri was a precondition of triumph. Similarly the Atiawa found the loathsome Tutaekuri invaluable in later reprisals against the Ngati-Maniapoto. The phenomenon is familiar enough internationally.

It was with first European contact, however, that the Tutaekuri shone briefly again; they met men after their own heart. Europeans had muskets which made slaughter far more efficient if, at times, marginally less satisfying. The old ways were shown to be a mere cottage craft. A thousand enemies could be left dead or dying in one inspiring and industrious afternoon: the work of weeks, otherwise. In exchange for muskets, the Europeans wished dried human heads for sale on the Sydney and London markets. They were fastidious, however, about quality; the heads, to have reasonable market value, had to be tattooed in the especially intricate chiefly way. The paramount chief of the Tutaekuri at this time, a *rangatira* by name of Tarawhiro, conducted the preliminary negotiations. He saw no large problem in producing suitable heads, though the only ones in possession of the Tutaekuri were those of revered ancestors dried and smoked to keep their murderous memory green. He ordered himself surrounded by slaves, men often of high rank who had been made captive during war waged by the Tutaekuri in the recent past. Moving among these slaves with the English skipper, Tarawhiro drew attention to the remarkably fine tattoos which frequently distinguished their features. As the slaves began to tremble with premonition of their fate, Tarawhiro said to the skipper, 'Just pick out the ones you want.'

The skipper won the respect and affection of Tarawhiro by choosing a dozen well-tattooed slaves with no delay. It was clear he knew his business, and wasn't content with an inferior product. After Tarawhiro ordered immediate decapitation of the slaves, and preparation of their heads in the traditional Tutaekuri way, the skipper observed, 'It's just a pity there aren't more.'

Tarawhiro saw this as no problem either. He dispatched the surviving slaves to the hut of the tribe's master tattooer. There their heads could be more delicately engraved to European satisfaction before removal from their bodies.

As trade took on, the immediate stock of slaves was depleted. But with muskets multiplying in the hands of Tutaekuri warriors, war parties ranged wider in search of raw material for processing in the Tutaekuri way. When tattooed, prisoners would be presented for the approval of the English skipper before the beheading and baking, the curing by smoke, and the careful packaging of the heads for display in the salons of London and Boston. A Tutaekuri dried head fetched far more on the fashionable market than those crudely produced by other tribes; it was by definition a superior product. Attention was given, for example, to the diet of prisoners while being tattooed, and before termination of their lives; they were firm rounded heads, never thin and haggard. After decapitation all trace of terror was gently smoothed from their facial expressions; they seemed in pleasant repose. As business grew still brisker, and the reputation of the Tutaekuri grew, the English skipper became sole representative of a prominent Mayfair buyer named Thomas Pringle who regularly wrote letters to *The Times* denouncing the woolly humanitarians who sought to suppress dealing in dried heads: he pointed out that such suppression would run counter to traditional British policies on free trade and, moreover, lead to loss of employment opportunities for the natives of the South Pacific.

Tarawhiro, by this time a vicarious captain of industry, often had difficulty in believing the extent of the bonanza; there were soon five muskets for every Tutaekuri warrior. He began bartering off the surplus to inland tribes in return for prisoners in good condition, thus streamlining the entire operation and allowing him to divert his work force to the building of more extensive smokehouses. He was puzzled briefly by a passing missionary who, after arranging purchase of a half-dozen heads at wholesale price, said in the course of attempting to convert Tarawhiro to Christianity that his tribe should desist from their labours on every seventh day. Tarawhiro pointed out that his people would be bored out of their minds. Otherwise he was much impressed by the good mercantile sense of the British; he resolved to send a son to the far lands of the white man to acquire more *mohiotanga*, or knowledge, and perhaps some of the *mana* of the white man too. In this way, the Tutaekuri might well steal a march on other Maori tribes; the Tutaekuri could, in fact, resume their rightful position of power in the land, putting inferiors in their place, and dealing out justice tempered with commercial wisdom. Europeans on the other hand would find the Tutaekuri reasonably sensitive to their needs, provided they made no attempt to disturb immemorial tribal ways. As a hint of the limits to his patience in this respect, Tarawhiro arranged the dried head of the missionary – who chanced to pass again, and seemed likely to make a habit of the thing – above his carved rangatira's whare. Soon after, Tarawhiro called his son Uretika to him. Uretika to this point had been something of a disappointment to his father. There was a lack in the boy. He had no drive; no capacity for imaginative improvization in the matter of dispatching enemies, for example. His features were a shade too fine, almost feminine, and his eyes tended to wander from the large concerns of the tribe. He was sometimes to be seen spinning tops and flying kites with children when he could have been usefully employed inflicting pain upon prisoners specifically spared for that purpose.

Telling his son to draw close, Tarawhiro dwelt for some time on the boy's limitations. Finally he suggested that all was not lost. Uretika now had a chance to show himself a true Tutaekuri, and perhaps make a great mark on the world. He was to go where no Tutaekuri had gone before, as a tribal scout travelling oceans and continents, and then returning with all manner of *mohiotanga* to give his people fresh fibre in the difficult times surely ahead, as more Europeans sailed the South

Pacific. In the new era, the Tutaekuri were not to be *he hiore hume*, as a dog with its tail between its legs. Possessed of more intricate methods of cruelty and new means of massacre – which he understood Europeans to have in abundance – the Tutaekuri would have enough growl and bite to police all the South Pacific at some profit to itself.

Uretika was appalled by the prospect, though he tactfully refrained from saying so to his father. He had no wish to be a lonely scout in the larger world of the white man; no wish to leave home at all. He thought it more than likely that he would be slain or enslaved once out of sight of the Porangi River. He was astute enough to recognize that his tribe was little loved; why should white men show him any more mercy than Maoris of rival tribes? Also he found the dried head trade faintly disagreeable, even if economically desirable, and unbecoming to a man of high rank. Why should he be shown respect? Nevertheless, as was inevitable, he bowed to his father's wish, found himself lodged in the English skipper's vessel, and taken to London. There he was fitted out as an English gentleman by Mr Thomas Pringle of Mayfair, the dried-head buyer who had prospered greatly through his exclusive connection with the Tutaekuri and now felt it a matter of honour, as well as in his long-term interests, to do the right thing by young, bewildered Uretika. Uretika learned to sit upright in a Regency chair, rather than on the floor, and how to manage silver knife and fork without damage to his person. He soon had a decided taste for roast beef and Madeira wine. This tattooed and handsome 'Crown Prince of the Notorious Tootaykoory Tribe', as the London press styled him, was feted by English society. He was at the centre of many a select dinner party; at country houses he learned how to hunt quail, and to ride a horse behind hounds baying after a fox. Though all this had its compensations, especially and avidly female, Uretika began to find it taxing. Trying to keep faith with his father, and search out that which might give his tribe new strength and purpose in an uncertain century, he went to the Tower of London to survey the technology of torture on display there; and left feeling faint. At Newgate he found it impossible to sit through the clumsy procedures of public hangings, particularly of juveniles, which his host felt instructive. According to a newspaper correspondent, one often accused of considerably colouring the facts, Uretika was frankly appalled by such wastage of fresh flesh; and looked about vainly for ovens. A military tattoo, with bagpipes and bright kilts, left him unmoved; it was all ceremony and no slaughter. At all events Uretika was soon seen walking London streets and parks in a mood of melancholy. His elocution lessons no longer aroused him; he recited such texts as the Lord's Prayer, the Creed, the Thirty-Nine Articles, and the Ten

Commandments in lacklustre manner. He felt he had failed his father in this strange cold land, and found himself longing for the simpler life of his tribesmen again, for the sunset upon the Pacific, the ferny forests of the Tutaekuri, the peaceful tidal ebb and flow of Porangi. When snow fell, and rivers froze, he was sometimes observed apathetically attempting to skate on the Serpentine. Try as he might, he could not find it an enlightening pastime. The Porangi would have to be persuaded to freeze over, in any case, if he were to try taking skates home to his father.

At this point, when all seemed lost, Mr Thomas Pringle took it upon himself to offer discourse, before a blazing log fire during the long winter evenings, on the finer pleasures of Art, Science and Philosophy. With sullen reluctance, then dawning wonder, Uretika began to realize that he was within reach, at last, of the more arcane lore of the European. Among the Tutaekuri sacred lore had been the prerogative of the *tohunga*, the priests of the tribe. Until now Uretika had never quite acknowledged his thirst to see behind the brutish business of human existence. Here, in the household of Mr Thomas Pringle, he was able to slake that thirst freely. There was more to mana than muskets. Wasn't it his duty to seek out, to explore, to adventure? Was that not his father's wish? By winter's end he was reading Tacitus and Cicero in the original. The following year he went up to Oxford.

Time passed in triumphant dream; Oxford was all drifting enchantment. For anonymity's sake, and as befitting a future *rangatira*, he changed his name royally to George. His tutors, besides, found his native nomenclature too awkward to handle. However, these splendid fellows took even his tattooing for granted quite soon. A number of eminent English portraitists chanced upon him there, during those years of delight, and their paintings show a grave and elegant young man usually with a classical text in hand: the noble savage with cloisters and academic spires beyond, and green English fields, rivers and flowers. They might have been devastated to learn that this picturesque young savage was far from just decorative in his Oxford function, that he was in fact composing an acerbic critique of Christianity, developing the arguments of Plotinus, Porphyry of Tyre, Iamblichus, and Julian the Apostate; and that he had caused the faith of at least two of his tutors to crumble. Never at a loss in mustering irrefutably logical argument, for precise and telling reference or for wickedly witty aside, George was a popular scholar, respected not least for his ferocity; he suffered no fools, and identified the meretricious sooner than most.

It sometimes seemed to George that this idyll was too good to be true. It was. One winter day, after scoring most satisfyingly in a session with his favourite tutor, he received a letter from Mr Thomas Pringle instructing him to return to London urgently. Mr Pringle was grim, grey and cold. The dried head trade had suffered a steep and displeasing decline. It wasn't so much that the misguided humanitarians were having their way. There had, quite simply, been over-production; and prices reflected the fact that too many torsos had been made headless in recent time. A Tutaekuri head now fetched only three guineas in London as against thirty or forty in the boom years. There was also a message from old Tarawhiro asking his son to return home. George watched Mr Pringle peel pound notes, fresh from the Bank of England, rather grudgingly off a large roll. 'There's your passage money,' said his former kindly mentor. 'You know your way down to the docks.' With a few pathetic bundles of books constituting virtually all his baggage, the once feted Crown Prince of the Tootaykoory made his way miserably to Tilbury in search of a ship, shivering in sleet and then his last English snow.

Four months later, after the Atlantic and Pacific had done their worst, George arrived back on the Porangi to find his tribe in equally pitiable condition. Nothing had been done to diversify exports. Unlike other Maoris, the Tutaekuri had never given much thought to flax, timber or vegetables for the flourishing Australian colonies. Tarawhiro, who could once wither brave men with a glance, had lost heart altogether; he was a thin, weak, trembling old man. 'The rainbow is pale,' he announced. 'The time draws near to converse with my ancestors.' It was the worst of news. George would now have the hopeless Tutaekuri in his care. That night a kingfisher flew out of the forest and settled on Tarawhiro's whare; no mistaking that message. In the morning the old *rangatira* was dead.

For a time the new and unwilling *rangatira* shared the apathy of his tribe. To overcome it, and to win time to consider future strategies, he began building a house. At first, with the unskilled labour force at his disposal, he tried to persuade his dwelling to rise as an approximate replica of Mr Thomas Pringle's two-level Georgian town house. Where memory failed him, he made do. Mostly he made do. Sometimes the design, seemingly from inner need, tried to strike off in directions of its own; and was not easily to be contained. To curb it finally, also to keep the more and more ungainly structure together, he threw a colonial veranda around three sides of the dwelling, leaving the rear to an informal lean-to where pigs and chickens could be killed, prepared or plucked, along with other work of menial nature. In total the house wasn't in the manner, say, of an English country house, a compromise between pomp and privacy; it had no pomp and much privacy. He provided more room for his library than for retainers, and before long was to rid himself of intimate retainers altogether. Also in pursuit of privacy, he resolved to take no wives, breed no heir. When not preoccupied with the leather-bound volumes in his handsome library, he could rove his sunny veranda, observing and when essential guiding the affairs of the Tutaekuri, though with a rather more distant gaze. His longing for London and Oxford was not to be stilled by his new responsibilities, nor by painfully passing time. Slaves fled homeward through the forests; the smokehouses fell into ruin; muskets grew rusty. George wistfully observed European sails, growing in number, passing the Porangi by; the coastline of the Tutaekuri was marked unhealthy on the charts of most mariners. His sense of spiritual exile became the more acute in this civilized oasis. He dreamed of leafy lanes and Oxford spires when he should have been considering, for example, the exact nature of a new alliance with the Ngati-Maniapoto.

Fortunately he retrieved himself just in time. The grumbles of the old men, largely concerning his unobtrusive leadership, became ominous; it was openly said that George – and why George and not Uretika? – had brought weakness, not wisdom, to his people. Politics, as is well known, is the art of the possible. Much as George might want long-term to see his people peacefully prosperous citizens of an ideal authoritarian Platonic society, it was not something to be contrived overnight. In the short-term the spirit of his people had to be refreshed; all George had at hand was Tutaekuri tradition. This was regrettable as a means to an end, but the Tutaekuri had not only to be seen as terrible; they had to be terrible in truth again. Otherwise rival tribes, recalling old grievances, might take advantage of their disarray. That summer, as soon as the kumara was harvested, he ordered and led an attack on the nearest tribe. His choice was ideal. The community raided had lately had its will to resist weakened by the presence of Galilean missionaries, rather ignorant men who knew little of literature beyond the Bible, and who provided George with no enlightening conversation at all before he had them put to death for appearances' sake. The old men of the tribe were well pleased; there was no further mutinous talk. Indeed it was said that George, son of Tarawhiro, would be long remembered for his ruthlessness. There was some truth in this. As he watched villages burn and slain enemies blaze, he found La Rochefoucauld's maxim greatly sustaining: It is less dangerous to treat most men badly than to treat them too well. Precisely because his heart wasn't in warfare, he made an even more pitiless *rangatira* than Tarawhiro, or any other of the past, in his haste to get the killing done with scant standing on ceremony. The less ceremony, something to which his people were prone, the sooner he was back in his library.

Then, just as the Tutaekuri seemed on the point of prospering as before, they were ambushed again. More and more Maori tribes succumbed to Christianity, announcing their desire to produce corn, build mills, hammer swords into ploughshares and turn the other cheek. This made for an impossible situation. Even the Tutaekuri could not wage war satisfyingly with such insipid tribes; where was the triumph, the true grace of conquest? For two or three dull decades, then, the Tutaekuri lived off their reputation and little else, sulking at the mouth of the Porangi, seldom venturing far outside tribal territory, welcoming no white man, strangers even to their fellow Maoris. George, still pondering on the paradoxes implicit in ends and means, went into even deeper retreat, rarely seen outside his house and sometimes unrecognized by children. In his library the limpid truths of existence still eluded him. The more he considered history, contemplated philosophy, and cultivated an understanding of literature, the more unreliable humanity began to seem.

Such was still his condition when emissaries from neighbouring tribes began calling again. For a long time, and understandably, these tribes had wished to forget the Tutaekuri. Now the Tutaekuri were necessary again, in the traditional way, as allies. White men, it seemed, were no longer content with Maori souls; they wanted Maori land too. And these other tribes were falling back fast before British bullet and bayonet, mortar and cannon. Their cornfields were razed, their orchards black ruin, their mills shattered. Almost at the last, they remembered the Tutaekuri. With the emissaries came the Hau Hau faith. Using his critical eye, George saw this faith as a tissue of ecclesiastical and millennial nonsense, derived from despair, and tailored by wishful thinking: something compounded eccentrically from Christian doctrine, yet acknowledging only the Jewish sabbath, and identifying the Maori as God's chosen people; Abraham and Moses, in this version, might well both have been tattooed. The rest, the finer points of theology aside, was murderous and martial, almost the pure milk of Tutaekuri tradition. White men had to be driven mercilessly into the sea. Heads were to be taken again, not even babes in arms spared; cannibalism was solemnized. In return, ships sent by the gods – or by Jehovah presiding over a pagan pantheon – would bear other-worldly riches and wisdom to the Hau Hau. George, with some sense of doom, had no choice but to assent to propagation of this faith, since the young Tutaekuri were already dancing feverishly about the flag-decorated *niu* pole of the Hau Hau. He had grown too tired, too confused, to care. He retreated to his library and the verses of Mr Alexander Pope. The war burned on. The young marched away to fight, chanting their Hau Hau incantations, rapt in the promises of the Hau Hau priests. The consequent death and destruction, one mercy, was mostly at a distance; George and the Porangi were spared. Sometimes a British gunboat stood offshore and fired an inaccurate shot or two. The British seemed agreed that there was no profit in a military transaction with the Tutaekuri. In this they were largely mistaken. The warriors of the tribe were mainly elsewhere, and anyway thinning in number; the remainder could have been overwhelmed in a morning of brisk battle. In fact, with little effort and insignificant loss, they might still make the Tutaekuri no more. But the ferocious reputation of the tribe remains sufficient to deter the British. They never come. No one comes. That is, until the schooner *Lotus* skids over the sand bar, and glides into the calm Porangi, offering up the Lovelocks and Ira Dix on a day late in 1867.

George is woken from a long afternoon doze with the news of the schooner's imminent arrival. He is irritated at being woken. He has been dreaming in especially satisfying fashion of a summer stroll along the verdant banks of the River Cherwell, with Magdalen Tower rising nobly in view. Such dreams do not come often now, as he ages, and are to be treasured. The one discordant feature of this dream was that his father, Tarawhiro, appeared to him in the midst of Oxford; the old man, greenstone *mere* in one hand, musket in the other, was showing great grief. He said, 'It has to end. You must do it.' 'What?' George asks. 'What must I do?' For answer someone shakes him awake in the gloom of his room and informs him of the approach of the Lovelocks. Still trying to make sense of his dream, George struggles with the summons from the waking world. At first he does not take news of the schooner seriously. His people tend to be too impressionable. By the time he has persuaded his legs into trousers, pulled on a jacket, adjusted his cravat and located his monocle, the plunder of the schooner has begun and the *pakeha* captives are being marched along the shore. The clamour is intense. With faint heart, George divines that decisions shall shortly be expected of him: concerning the division of the plunder, for example, and the fate of the prisoners. He no longer has appetite for decisions. In recent time he has observed the world running itself impeccably without any intervention on his part. He wishes the schooner, and the woeful *pakeha*, elsewhere. However they are not elsewhere. They are here, advancing toward him. And he toward them.

He raises a hand until his tribesmen reduce the tempo, and then the volume, of their deafening cries; and embarks upon the essential preliminaries of the conversation with the captives. Fortunately, unlike many of their kind, they speak intelligible English. He has feared further difficulties if they did not; certainly a prolonging of affairs. It appears that they have suffered considerable misfortune. George takes this as a plea for compassion.

'You must understand,' he says, 'that you place me in a deucedly awkward position.'

'What of ours?' replies the largest male among the captives, evidently leader, certainly spokesman. 'What of our circumstances?'

'Precisely,' George explains. 'You must understand that my people need pride in themselves. They cannot be seen as kindly. Should you be spared, the reputation of my tribe could be finally in ruin. As things are, morale couldn't be worse. Not that I can blame the Hau Hau for everything. Who doesn't run a war without superstition? In your land, as I recall, it is called patriotism. Disagreeable as it may appear, the Hau Hau ethic makes no provision for your continued existence.'

'You're talking,' the argumentative spokesman answers, 'of my wife. My children. Of an atrocity.'

'Atrocities are generally in the eye of the beholder,' George suggests. 'However I quite agree that killing is a vulgar affair. On the other hand, as Corneille so aptly observed, violence is just where kindness is vain. The problem, as always, is determining where its application is for the greater good. Splitting hairs will get us nowhere, for the moment, so long as my people are of a mind to split skulls. I propose therefore that you relax with what hospitality I can provide, in my humble if quite commodious accommodation.'

'You mean,' challenges the spokesman, 'while the ovens are prepared?'

'Who talks of ovens? Understand that my tribe is full of the heat of the moment. With less heat, we might have more light. Who knows?'

Eight

To set the scene further: the Porangi River, as it exists in the nineteenth century, and little longer, is no rational and trivial tract of water. It is literally a lunatic river, which isn't to say it is short on schizophrenic charms. At the very first, it is formed from the fluids of fire and ice in the shaky centre of the land, among erupting volcanoes which whiten with winter; sulphurous pools and thawing snows send its tributaries tinkling through rock and tussock until its waters mass headily in fern and forest. At that point its abnormality becomes assertive. It streaks manically across level terrain, and dawdles depressively down steep limestone canyons. At times, with apparent paranoia, it simply removes itself from view, presumably underground. At other times it attempts to share its dangerous delusion that it can travel uphill. It psychotically zig-zags. It wanders off wilfully into waterfalls, when a lazy curve about a mountain would be more to the point. Suffering identity crisis, it divides and subdivides only to become, rather theatrically, a psychopathic torrent in tantrum again. Then it makes a slyly convincing effort to conceal past aberrations and flows with catatonic calm. Finally, if reluctantly, it finds its way to the sea to fatten neurotically upon gross tidal flow. Its treacherous mouth, once shoals are survived, is a modest harbour backed by dark and bulky sandhills. Maori tradition, which explains all, and begins at the end, tells that the sand was blackened by the hot breath of a *taniwha*, or sea dragon, in frantic search for a lost mate; it had reason to believe that its beloved had been seized by especially sinister demons who dwelled in the fiery interior. Maddened by loss, this great *taniwha* battled its way inland, thrusting aside hill and mountain, until in exhaustion it could travel no further, though almost in sight of those pyrotechnic mountains in which the fire demons dwelled. Still crazed with desire and grief, the vast creature wept, wedged forever far from the sea. Tears filled the canyons it had carved; the Porangi began to flow.

Geography and mythology, given their situation, are on the outer margin of Lovelock family concerns. All the same, it is with their arrival on the Porangi that the more verifiable history of the family begins. Certainly the shedding of light on the subject of their survival occupies George greatly for weeks, months, finally a year or two. With some inspiration he explains his extended interrogation of the captives as necessary in order to determine whether they are, in fact, messengers from an outer world bearing wealth and wisdom, as promised in Hau Hau doctrine. The shedding of light involves depleting barrels of surely god-given rum lifted from *Lotus*.

In that wayward and often pernicious publication, *The Lives of Lovelock Junction*, the fatigued chronicler muses: 'That the Lovelocks should have survived their landing among Maoris then energetically at war with whites speaks volumes for Herman Lovelock's sense of tact, hitherto not often in evidence.' The authority for this speculative conclusion is apparently an item in *The Maoriland Settler* of June 4, 1868, a periodical edited by a red-bearded and retired English colonel who often genially declared himself in favour of exterminating all coloured peoples: 'Intelligence has reached us of a forlorn family of Europeans being held captive, and possibly hostage, by Hau Hau rebels on the western coast of the North Island. Little hope is held for their succour. Nevertheless it is regarded as odd that this unfortunate family should have survived their perilous situation thus far. Could it be that this presumably Christian family are persuading the devilish rebels to repent? Could it be that these savages have grown fearful of the just retribution to come? No explanation is so far forthcoming, and there is unlikely to be one until this war is prosecuted more vigorously, and with all the firepower at the colony's command mercilessly administered.'

Volumes for Herman's sense of tact, then? Nonsense. Their survival speaks a large library for the many meals Marie Louise is obliged to prepare in consequence of George allowing it to be known that, after a merry visit or two to France in his youth, he is much enamoured of the cuisine of that country, notably *langouste* either *en brochettes* or *de l'île Sainte Marguerite*, and *palombes à la Béarnaise*. Marie Louise is hindered mightily by the lack of certain ingredients for the success of such dishes, though the local equivalents of *palombes* are produced plump and flapping from the forest, and *langouste* fat and wriggling from the sea, by George's retainers. In the end, however, her improvizations are quite to George's taste, since his memory of the originals has long faded upon his palate anyway. After a time she even finds herself doing fancy things with the fat white grubs which are fetched from rotten logs; they make a perfectly adequate shrimp substitute in *crevettes à la Provençal*. As word of these remarkable dishes spreads through the tribe, and then the mesmerizing taste, it does begin to seem that *rangatira* George might have had some perception, after all, in recognizing the Lovelocks as bearers of other-worldly wisdom. When about the business of cooking, Marie Louise is plainly a woman bewitched. She is, true, often demented. Of all the fates she has foreseen for herself, serving as cook and housekeeper to a vague, bookish and monocled Maori chief is not one. Herman is little help in this continuing, and fast expanding, culinary crisis. He seldom seems to hear the crashing of copper pans, announcing her despairs, as he contemplates humanity and smokes a pipe or two with a mug of rum in George's company. It has to be conceded that the controversies which rent the late classical world in the time of Constantine are not overly familiar to Herman; nor has he much considered the likely authorship of *Iliad* or *Odyssey*, the splendour and complexity of Pindar's odes, or the development of drama in the hands of such as Aeschylus and Sophocles. Nevertheless he finds this no obstacle in elaborating his large concern for the human condition, as he has observed it of late, and proposing its amelioration by way of making war on circumstances. It is perhaps unnecessary to note that their conversations are mainly in monologue form. There are times when Herman imagines George genuinely to have been listening. There are times when George imagines Herman genuinely to have been listening. Superfluous to add that these conversational encounters are for both men most enlightening and deeply satisfying.

Herman, besides, now has reason to conclude that destiny has delivered him to the Porangi. Looking for something to signify that their arrival and survival are auspicious, he finds one beyond his most robust expectation. Iron, nothing less, and literally underfoot. It is patently the mineral which colours the sand dunes darkly about the mouth of the Porangi; those dunes which march murkily north and south, quite as far as he can see from his currently confined situation. Above the dunes rise hills rich in tall timber trees. Now only coal is needed to complete the foreseen trinity. Circumstances may at last have begun to cringe and come over to his side. There are times when his optimism is ill concealed; he can hardly believe the Lovelocks so capriciously and immediately favoured by fortune.

Richard and Ira Dix, on the other hand, have considerable reason to believe the Porangi no plus at all. While Herman, Marie Louise, James and the children are guests of George, Richard and Ira are assigned the role of *pakeha*-Maoris, white warriors, in the fighting force which the Tutaekuri contributes to the Hau Hau campaign in other parts of the island. George is impatient with their protests. He sternly gives them to understand that their conscription is necessary, and can be seen as a sacrifice for the greater good of their group; he is anticipating the grumbles which might arise among his people should all the Lovelocks and Ira be seen indolent about the Porangi, a much too visible burden on an already tattered tribe. To pacify the Tutaekuri, Richard and Ira are sent to war. Richard is given a carbine and tomahawk, and choleric Ira an ineffective shotgun and a rusty Afghan knife. After a turn or two about the *niu* pole, to get them into a sufficiently ferocious frame of mind, they are marched away into the forest. There they are instructed in how to travel by stealth; to wade through water and leave no mark in the wilderness. They learn to savour the pith of fern, to make the most of nutritive mosses and fungus and insects of the forest. They wrestle their way over steep mountain ranges, crash through infinitely receding curtains of creeper, flounder across miles of mud and swamp. They labour on fortifications which more often than not are deserted the day after completion. It is all comfortless confusion. Fast ageing Ira has never felt more remote from St Louis. Richard, obliged frequently to support his feeble companion, cannot quite bring himself to discard the old man on the interminable journeys they undertake, though the act could be construed as kindness. There would then be no one to whom he could confide his bitter conviction that he was born for better things. He has begun to see symmetries in his suffering unsuspected before; these symmetries suggest, among other things, that life has long had it in for him. Not that he sees death as a desirable alternative. They spring ambushes; they survive ambushes. When gunfire begins to boom about them, with scorched leaves drifting down from the trees, Richard goes to ground with fervour, dragging bewildered and dilatory Ira beside him. Surrender is not to be contemplated. The Imperial troops do not take prisoners; they prefer Hau Hau heads, on which there is a bounty paid personally by their godly general, and the heads of Richard and Ira would likely be as profitable as any. The Hau Hau, on the other hand, souvenir hearts, slit swiftly from hot flesh while battle crashes and flashes about them. But not from mercenary motive. The Hau Hau chief, a weathered warrior and flamboyant orator named Titokowaru, whose ugly loss of an eye earlier in the wars gives him an appearance of great conviction, pays no bounty on *pakeha* organs; the hearts are singed with wax matches, to propitiate the martial gods, and so the consequent smoke may indicate which way the winds of war are blowing.

Marching forever through slime and forest, meeting up with allied Hau Hau parties, Richard and Ira encounter other white warriors with whom they seek to commiserate. But these men know the business they are about; they are deserters, onetime Imperial soldiers, who now find killing more congenial on the Hau Hau side. Unkempt among them is an embittered Irishman named Charlie Kane who imagines every soldier of the Queen he tomahawks is one less potential oppressor of his distant native land. An aspirant anthropologist, he is of the belief that Maoris are merely sunburned Irishmen who voyaged into the Pacific to escape the persecutions of Cromwell. His largest ambition is to ship a party of his Hau Hau companions back to County Wicklow to show his confused fellow countrymen how to fight. Meanwhile he is liberating Ireland, in his lonely fashion, in the forests of the South Sea. Or so he confides as he plays a cool game of poker with Ira's muddied deck of cards. He cannot arouse their enthusiasm for his cause; Richard and Ira wish only their own liberation. Also, with a run of luck rare for an Irishman, he cleans them right out of their last tobacco, for which they play in lieu of money. This does little for the long-term morale of Richard and Ira. Nor does the fact that, soon after, Kane makes no return from a furtive mission with a party of Hau Hau scouts sent to observe the construction of a British blockhouse. They learn that companionship in the Hau Hau ranks is a speculative and likely short-lived affair. It appears Kane was quietly tomahawked when his thirst for British blood began agitating him too audibly in his patrol's place of concealment. Thus it comes to pass that no Hau Hau play a picturesque part in the Irish Easter uprising of 1916.

Another queer customer in their company is Kimble Bent, a Yankee but also a half-breed Musqua Indian; he departed the army after twenty-five lashes too many on the punishment triangles in the regimental parade ground, and finds the Hau Hau less abrasive to serve. For one thing, he has been rewarded for faithful service with two Maori wives. The first is old and ugly. The second, by way of promotion, is young and lovely. Her Majesty's 57th Foot Regiment never offered such rapid advancement. When not quietening his wives, who follow him bickering from camp to camp in the forest, this scarred and taciturn hawk of war is occupied as armourer. He repairs rifles and manufactures Hau Hau cartridges from unexploded British grenades, tugging out the fuses with his teeth. Taking pity on the pair, Bent warms them with rum and tobacco, loot from a recent raid on a European settlement. He also invites Ira to join him as apprentice armourer, which should keep him moderately far from the fighting. If he knew of Ira's luck as a gambler, he might have hesitated to let him loose upon gunpowder. He can win no such reprieve, however, for young and able-bodied Richard. Bent often broods, pessimistic about survival; he has seen it all before with the Musqua. 'The British are sending in more troops,' he announces. 'They are even sending Von Tempsky.'

'Von who?' says Richard nervously.

'Tempsky. Don't worry. You'll get the name right soon enough. He might be the last thing you see in this life.'

From Bent's account it appears that this Von Tempsky is the man most to be feared on the British side. A former German fusilier, he tested his talent for massacre upon dissident citizens of Nicaragua and Mexico before arriving in New Zealand to further his fortunes and pronounce the wars unprofessionally humane. Among his innovations has been the butchering of Maori women with the bayonet when their warrior husbands have fled. In retaliation, along with responses of rather more ingenuity, the Maoris have ceased supplying beleaguered British outposts with ammunition to ensure a fair fight. For on the Maori side too chivalrous dilettantes are disappearing, or dead; only the Hau Hau are now adequate to the occasion. Or such is Bent's view. Von Tempsky has to be given credit for making the wars more productive of corpses. Dapper and dashing, with huge moustache and goatee beard, he is usually to be seen with swinging sword where battle is most bloody; or, in the aftermath, coolly crouched on some conspicuous knoll, with stray bullets still whining about, composing delicate watercolours of the scene of slaughter. He has never been so much as grazed; he seems more than mortal. Lately imprisoned for protest against incompetent commanders, especially those who take prisoners, he has been called to the colours again to finish the Hau Hau. 'Some say he has the devil in him,' Bent says. 'Me, I think he's the real thing. Not just a son of Satan. Satan himself.'

Richard is impressed by this unusual intelligence. For a time he just festers. With slight success he tries to persuade himself that he might as well lose his life to a manic Prussian as to some boozy British private by chance bullet. Then distaste for his own destruction overwhelms him. He conceives a deal with the devil. When next in the forest on a scouting mission, he will lose his companions, make for a British blockhouse, and take Von Tempsky into his confidence, especially in respect of the site of the Hau Hau camp. This of course will be rough on Ira, when the camp is stormed, but it is well known that war always takes a quota of innocent bystanders. It will doubtless also be difficult for his kin, back on the Porangi, when his change of heart becomes known to the Tutaekuri there. If they perish, he hopes they will remember with compassion that his plight has also been distressing.

The plan succeeds. When next on patrol, he finds his way alone from the forest, is made captive by a cross-eyed and confused British sentry on his own insistence, and taken threadbare and skeletal before Von Tempsky. The man looks, in every detail, the goateed Lucifer whom

Kimble Bent promised: swarthy, curly haired, forage cap cocked at careless angle, revolver and bowie knife at his belt, a red silk scarf tossed dramatically about his neck. His killer's eyes, at first glittering, empty of interest as Richard embarks upon a recitation of his miseries. Von Tempsky slams his fist upon his rough-sawn desk. 'The point, man,' he says. 'The point.'

'You won't shoot me?' Richard asks.

'Not at the moment,' Von Tempsky promises unconvincingly.

With much prompting, because of his continuing tendency to digress into the marginalia of his months with the Hau Hau, Richard finally delivers to Von Tempsky all the information which that ruthless soldier deems necessary.

'All right,' he says briskly. 'You can go.'

'Go?' Richard says, baffled. 'Go where?'

'Back to your camp, man. Where else?'

Richard is appalled. 'You can't send me back there. Not now.'

'True,' Von Tempsky admits. 'I can't send you all the way. I can provide you with armed escort only as far as the edge of the forest. After that, it's up to you.'

'They'll kill me,' Richard protests.

'Then consider that we might too. In the vicinity of this blockhouse your life's worth nothing. You're a Hau Hau, a renegade white, by your own admission. And we don't have cells here. Prisoners, if any, get buried outside the blockhouse.' Von Tempsky takes his revolver from his holster and places it on his desk.

'You're threatening me,' Richard concludes with disbelief.

'You have,' Von Tempsky judges, 'a rare gift for the obvious.'

'I've told you how I came to be with the Hau Hau.'

'My memory isn't what it was,' Von Tempsky confesses vaguely. 'It's been a long war.'

'I'm a Christian,' Richard recalls.

'Who isn't?' Von Tempsky says wearily.

'A fellow human being.'

'We all have problems,' Von Tempsky agrees.

Richard at last sees the devil undisguised, the brimstone bright in the Prussian's black eyes. His heart seems to have ceased its function; his knees are reluctant to continue supporting his trunk.

'You'll be the death of me,' he insists.

'Very likely.' Von Tempsky begins, in an abstracted way, to sift through regimental papers. 'The flesh is frail.'

'You wouldn't like an innocent man on your conscience.'

'Even in peace, and God knows I've suffered enough of that, I find conscience inconvenient. If you're talking of yourself, I don't find guilt an intolerable risk.'

'But you can't send me back.'

'I can. Look, man, I've enough fools in my force without debate with a Hau Hau cretin too. Your chief Titokowaru isn't an idiot. Otherwise I'd have had his heathen old hide before now. If you're not back in camp tonight, he's going to be suspicious. Rightly so. He'll see betrayal, and move camp before morning, before we can get there.'

'But I'll be in camp when you attack.'

'Such is my hope. I thought I'd made it plain.'

'Your men could kill me too.'

'So wear a white bandage on your head. I'll instruct my men to spare you. You can tell Titokowaru that you had a fight in the forest today.' Von Tempsky rises, draws his bowie knife, and notches Richard's forehead. As blood spurts, the meticulous Prussian adds, 'There. That should do it. I can also arrange a bullet wound in a fleshy part of your leg to make your tale more convincing.'

Richard demurs. 'You sure I'll be safe?'

'Consider it this way, if you will,' Von Tempsky begins. Then he stops, startled. He gazes at Richard as if seeing him for the first time.

Richard is unnerved. 'Consider what?' he asks.

'Consider this.' Von Tempsky's voice has become untypically low; he is still looking at Richard with large concentration. 'An honourable death on the battlefield is a gift of God compared with the slower death which comes to us all.'

'What of a dishonourable death?' Richard asks. 'Whose gift is that?'

Then Richard realizes there is only one answer to that question. Anyway it appears the devil isn't of a mind for more martial theology. He has regained his equilibrium, and his impatience.

'On your way, man,' he says curtly. 'And be quick. I might even, if pressed, say God speed.'

Not that he shakes hands. He looks down at his desk as Richard is led out.

Late that night a bloodied Richard is observed staggering back to the fires of the Hau Hau camp. Sentries pinion him and take him to Titokowaru. Richard is wild-eyed enough, also sufficiently enfeebled with fright, for his tale of a heroic and lonely melee with the British in the forest to carry conviction. After meditation Titokowaru pronounces Richard's life spared; nevertheless he instructs his warriors to pay particular attention to this potential *pakeha* turncoat should he wander far in future. With a sigh for the mixed fortunes of men, Titokowaru then goes off to consult his *atua*, his gods, in the small sacred hut set aside for that purpose. Richard, meanwhile, obtains some relatively clean white material from Kimble Bent and bandages his head as conspicuously as he can. Then he tries to sleep. But his twitching, itchy body allows his spirit no release. Warriors likewise toss and heave restlessly around him, sometimes moaning sweatily in nightmare; owls cry mournfully from the trees. Contemplation tells him that Von Tempsky is to be as trusted as little as terrifying one-eyed Titokowaru. An order to spare a man with bandaged head, even if given, is likely to be overlooked when bayonets begin work. Besides, after battle is under way, there could be many men with bandaged heads. Insomnia further informs him that he is better off with the devil he knows. That established, he decides on pretending a prophetic dream of a Von Tempsky attack on the morrow, and making sure the message gets to Titokowaru. Portents, dreams, are grist to the Maori mill; such a warning cannot miss its mark. He climbs across cluttered Maori bodies, and finds the hut where Kimble Bent sleeps cushioned between his competitive wives. Bent at first is baffled by Richard's fervently conveyed intelligence of the immediate future. Sleepily sceptical, he suggests the dream is a consequence of the damage done to Richard's head. But Richard's detail is disturbingly impressive. 'Von Tempsky was at the head of the attack,' Richard says. 'He had a hellish laugh. A revolver and bowie knife in his belt. A red silk scarf flying round his neck. And his black curls blew in the wind.' Despite the loud complaints from his woken wives, the superstitions of Bent's Indian ancestors have larger authority; perhaps the matter is not to be taken lightly. He has slight respect for Richard's precognitive powers, but he also knows that spirits can convey their messages in unworthy vessels: 'A leaking canoe is better than none,' his Musqua mother told him. At length he races to tell Titokowaru of Richard's dream.

In chill dawn light Titokowaru calls the warriors in the camp together. He has, he informs them, spent all evening in consultation with his *atua*, in his sacred hut. The gods have warned him well; they have delivered him a dream of Von Tempsky's coming. The Prussian wore a red scarf. His black curls blew. 'Friends,' Titokowaru advises, 'be on your guard. Be birds of many sharp ears, fish of many fast fins. For today is evil, a day of danger. A black cloud of peril approaches, with Von Tempsky as the thunder and lightning at its heart. Beware the deluge. Make haste that today Von Tempsky be delivered to his Christian hell. Be as invisible as insects of the forest trees. Tonight our enemy will be as food for the birds of the air and beasts of the field, and for me.' This last is a ritual promise, for Titokowaru is notoriously prone to stomach disorders, avoids fatty foods, and personally cries off the cannibalism he encourages with the plea that his *mana*, rather than his digestive juices, might be impaired by consumption of social inferiors. After yet again recalling the detail of the fictitious dream he has purloined from Richard, Titokowaru raises his ceremonial *taiaha* high. The red parrot feathers at the spear-tip flutter. 'The north-east breeze is blowing,' he declares. 'The winds of heaven are ours.' Richard is buffeted in a storm of chanting and stamping as the war dances grow wilder. Sweat streams. Techniques of decapitation and disembowelment are enacted and sung. Thus refreshed and inspired, the warriors are dispatched to wait in the forest for the British force. Some climb into hollow trunks and cut loopholes for their firearms; others climb trees about the camp with their muskets loaded. Richard, loth to climb trees despite his considerable experience, prefers to crouch in a creek bed, covering the approach to the camp. The day may well be pregnant with evil, as Titokowaru proposes; but the labour pains are longer than envisaged. Cramped warriors above and around Richard begin to complain of the wait, of the time the inconsiderate British are taking, and eventually fall into tactical and theological dispute by way of lightening the slow hours. Richard does not participate in the esoteric gossip. But he is often to be seen rather tensely adjusting the white bandage about his head, for what it is worth.

Then, in late afternoon, there are loud voices. Oaths. Shots. Nervously Richard bites fresh cartridges for his carbine, and places percussion caps in his mouth ready for use. To his dismay, however, he feels excruciatingly painful pressure in the vicinity of his lower bowel, which immediately presents him with the problem of engaging in battle with his trousers in disagreeable condition. His companions in arms cannot conceal their disgust, or their contempt for his disregard for the rules of battlefield sanitation, as he swiftly unbuckles and unbuttons and disposes of the problem just to their rear. By this time Von Tempsky's voice is unmistakable, shouting commands in the growing uproar: 'Don't cluster. Spread out. Skirmishing order. Take cover.' Too late. The British, still stiff and bewildered, tumble out from the trees into the small clearing before Richard; they are unwilling to comprehend that they are about to die. Immaculately leading is Von Tempsky. His sword flashes in the fitful sunlight. Lacerating bullets fly from the foliage. The punctured soldiers sag one by one and slump limp among rotten logs. Richard finds no small pleasure in Von Tempsky's frustration. Then he realizes that, for his future well-being with the Hau Hau, he must be seen to play some convincing part in this war too; and that, further, there has never in the war been a larger part than that which is now his to play. Who knows but that the devil may be mortal? And something, someone, that none need fear? With the devil dead, God could give it away and go out of business; virtue would be a glut on the market. Not that this consideration is finally uppermost in Richard's mind. Rather impurely and maliciously he prefers to recall the humiliation he suffered at the Prussian's hands. Scrambling into a bed of bracken for a clear shot, he takes careful aim with his carbine. Von Tempsky, still coming on, is at a distance of no more than a dozen yards. Never will Richard's life seem quite so luminous again. He is bent, after all, on delivering a gift of God with tolerable accuracy. At that moment the eyes of the two men meet across the pointed barrel. It seems that there has been some secret understanding between them all along. That Von Tempsky has recognized Richard as a bearer of gifts, and returned him to his proper place so that history can proceed as planned. The rifle reverberates. Von Tempsky teeters. His sword falls like the lifeless limb of a tree. Then the tree itself topples, with a slight flutter of red silk. Surprisingly soon Von Tempsky is just another mound of fallen flesh among many; the devil is destroyed with all his men.

Lowering his carbine with awe, Richard envisages himself honoured by the Hau Hau, eventually usurping Titokowaru as commander: he sees himself handsome and tall at the head of long unwinding columns of warriors, the great Hau Hau host, as he completes his conquest of the land before agreeing to his coronation: Richard I, Emperor of Maoriland. (Perversely, not even Time Z provides for a South Pacific court akin to Caligula's.) He is recalled to his uncomfortable bed of bracken by Hau Hau cries, chants and prayers rising eerily in the aftermath of carnage. To complete it, warriors dash out from the trees and hack here and there with tomahawks. All shamelessly claim credit for the killing of Von Tempsky; they bicker over the souveniring of his sword, until Titokowaru takes it, and then squabble for the honour of carrying the corpse. Dismayed Richard surfaces late from the bracken to find history hurtling past him; he has missed the train again. To underline it, a bird, startled to a great height by the sounds of battle, showers shit upon his face. He spits out percussion caps and trudges back to the stockade, in the wake of the corpse-carriers, and attempts consolation in a prolonged game of patience with Ira's deck of cards. For once, there is not even flavour in cheating himself. The ceremonial of the Hau Hau triumph passes him by too, the mighty funeral pyre on which most British bodies burn with Von Tempsky, the dances, the speeches, the songs, the prayers, the festive dismembering of several prime militiamen for the ovens, the dogs barking in the bedlam, and finally the feast of fresh meat delicately textured with fern-tips and wild convolvulus, served with a rich gravy on a bed of sweet potato. Ira doesn't like to see a partner go without; he arrives with flax containers of food for both. Richard eats in abstracted fashion, intestinal hunger being the least of his lost appetites. Ira is soon troubled by Richard's continuing silence, and sullen appearance; the boy is far too susceptible to gloom.

'Know something?' he says. 'I think I'm getting back my taste for life after all.'

This tactlessly timed confession leads Richard to consider the nature of the victuals with which he has been furnished. For a time, until hysteria and superstition subside, he sits perfectly still. Then he continues eating.

The Porangi is not altogether as peaceful as distant Richard, surviving battle after battle, might wishfully surmise. The problem is James. On Herman's plea he has been spared service with the Hau Hau. So James has continued energetically in the service of womankind; he has been endeavouring to dilute the fickle blood of the Tutaekuri in earnest collaboration with most of the maidens, all the widows, and too many wives of the tribe. The women are reluctant to let James out of their sight. Others are less impressed by the tenacious nature of this *pakeha* performance. George is confronted by deputations from the tribe's few remaining fit males. They demand death and very specific mutilation for James. George, as is lately his way, flinches from so harsh a decision.

'I'm sorry,' he tells Herman. 'But we have to do something about that boy.'

'Like what?' Herman asks.

'Like getting him out of the way. Upriver, perhaps.'

'Upriver? What's up there?'

'Wilderness,' George announces. 'Trees. Birds. Precious little more. As solitude goes, it could hardly be bettered.'

Marie Louise overhears this suggestion with alarm. Her affection for James, with the passing of pain, and despite her now distinctly qualified happiness with Herman, has again become motherly. 'You can't send James out into the wilderness,' she cries. 'He'll never survive alone. Never.'

'It's regrettable,' George agrees, since most things are. 'But exile, after all, is a traditional means of mercy in human societies. I fail to see him ripening into respectable maturity at this end of the Porangi anyway. Unless, that is, he can be persuaded to see moderation as virtue.'

Even Marie Louise has to concede that as an unrealistic prospect.

'There it is,' George sighs. 'In any case, he won't necessarily be alone up there. Others have been sent upriver in the past; they may provide him with companionship of a minimal kind. Who knows?'

'You don't seem to,' Marie Louise observes tartly.

'For the most part, they never trouble us again,' George points out. 'Unless, of course, a body washes down. In which case we insist on a decent burial. Mostly we've forgotten who they are.'

'My God,' says Marie Louise. 'Herman, do you hear what he is saying?'

'If James is lucky, for example,' George goes on, 'he may locate a certain *tohunga* of our tribe living in sullen seclusion somewhere along the river. We had to exile him up there a decade or two ago. This priest, you see, had become depressingly persistent about a certain piece of prophecy.'

'Like what?' Herman asks, his interest taken, as often, by prophetic periphera.

'Concerning the mad *taniwha*, the sea monster, which supposedly shaped our river. He insisted that its heart still beats up there, somewhere inland, and that the creature will return to the ocean with an infernal rush in the course of time, carrying all before it. People in its path – he predicted many – will perish by the score. The trouble with these fellows is that they take our pagan tales too literally. He began to get our people in a panic. Nothing for it, in the end, but to get him out of the way.'

'What has this to do with our poor James?' Marie Louise demands, with some justice.

'It is not unreasonable to suggest,' George observes, 'that he has been causing some panic among our tribe too. I am given to understand that the ladies detected in error sometimes plead that they have been lured and led astray by his musical gift – a likely story, of course, but the fact is that soon no warrior is going to feel his sexual life is complete without a fiddle. In times of war, that is a luxury they can ill afford. This settlement could burn while they most unharmoniously attempt to tickle feminine fancies. No. For James's own sake too he must be left to his own devices for a time. In any case, if these stories concerning his prowess are true, his most conspicuous device has earned some introspection. A sad affair, sex. Sophocles, you know, was asked in old age if he regretted the loss of sexual desire. His answer, I recall, was that he was glad to have a madman off his back. James may yet thank us for sending him upriver.'

Marie Louise's scepticism is plain.

'It could,' Herman concedes, since he discernibly has no choice but to look on the bright side, 'be the making of the boy.'

'Or the breaking,' Marie Louise argues.

At that moment Luke skips in to see if dinner is ready; Marie Louise sweeps the boy up into her arms and begins to sob in confusion. If James is to be torn from her table, who next? She fears losing Luke.

Next day natural justice is visited upon James. Still more than a little bemused by the proceedings, and unwilling to take it all seriously, anyway so long as sexual saturation lasts, he sees river exile as a bit of a lark; he packs his fiddle and a few books of poetry, most of suitably pastoral nature, to fill his lonelier hours. He is set aboard a small canoe, given a paddle, provided with dried fish and kumara to see him through his first days, also some ammunition and a rifle in suspect shape, an axe and assorted other tools; and told, in short, to get lost. For an illusory moment it could be the haunting scene at the Hokitika waterfront all over again. There are the same shameless wails, the feminine tears: maidens, widows and wives are quite unrestrained. The difference is that stern Herman and stricken Marie Louise also wave farewell, with Benjamin, Ernest and Luke weeping too, though they don't understand just why. Beyond this group, and *rangatira* George also attempting to convey sympathy, several frustrated males of the Tutaekuri flourish keen-edged implements of agriculture and war. For the first time James sees the affair as less than a lark; he might need to offer up more than a mea culpa if he attempts to return downriver. Meanwhile, the prevalent masculine mood serves as a spur. He begins paddling up the Porangi, seldom pausing to look back, trying to parry the thrust of tide and cut of current; he has to concentrate as his craft lurches from left to right, north to south, in the grip of the capacious river. His shoulders soon ache; sweat bursts from his brow; his hands fast blister. As effort mounts, and the mixed cries of farewell fade upon his ear, he is far from of a mind to contemplate the likely wonders of the wilderness ahead.

Panic passes, and two or three days. Great gorges grow around him. Realms of forest unravel. He begins to accept the rhythm of the river. Birds tinkle and twang in the overhanging trees as wide waters give way to narrower. Startled shags soar from the riverside reeds. Ducks depart in storms of shining spray. Herons float out of the forest and sometimes share his course. Golden blossoms burgeon among grotesquely tall treefern. There are queer spires of limestone, with ranges of mysterious mountains beyond, thinly misted in the morning light. Sometimes rain silvers his journey; he camps in dry caverns. Evenings bring incandescent sunsets. More and more lost, in a land ever larger, he is often bedevilled by awe, inattentive to navigation; he is jolted from reverie by his canoe banging over boulders streamered with silken slime, and steers none too soon into safer water. At length he lets his craft nudge a pale beach, framed with leaf and freaked with light, and judges the site as pleasing a place as any to set his life down. Birds chime in the ecclesiastical calm. He drags the canoe clear of the water, empties it of possessions, finds his fiddle and gives the afternoon a gay gypsy air. The birds seem impressed; at least they are silent. Finally he slumps among fern, the heat and exertion of the journey overcoming him, and sleeps under a canopy of green. Later he wakes to the muttering river, and less agreeably to light rain moistening his face; he begins, without much method, and no very clear plan, to build a waterproof dwelling. This task takes all his energy and imagination for some days to come. The foundations offer frustration; the walls, when persuaded vertical, resist the fitting of crude rafters; the untidy thatch of the roof tries to flee to freedom with the first wind.

It would be extravagant to pretend that even with his hut functionally if shakily shaped, James still finds all idyll. The psalmist might put it this way: 'By the rivers of Babylon, there we sat down, yea, we wept, when we remembered Zion. We hanged our harps upon the willows in the midst thereof.' Substitute the Porangi for Babylon, Devon for Zion, fiddle for harp, and God knows what alien trees for willows, and the picture is all but perfect. Also outcast James wears the willow of mourning in more ways than one. Abrupt loss of erotic ecstasy is more than most can cope with comfortably; for much of his first month his sense of deprivation is acute. Pastoral poetry proves no distraction, rather the reverse; he sees no fair love approaching through fields of flowers. He eyes his rifle, and plays with the prospect of a bullet in his brain. He makes the most of this melancholy, while it lasts. Lively airs surrender to laments upon his fiddle. Then sudden gastronomic diminuendo – not to speak of necessity, mother and father of invention in the forest – turns him to composing a plain-song score for survival. He tries to trap eels, tickle tiny native trout ashore, snare plump pigeons, forage for edible fern root. He also expends ammunition on most things that move. Success is slow to come. For the most part despair is his largest harvest as he labours from dawn to dusk; his evening meal is mostly a salad of sorrows. Since meagre diet is useful in the search for acceptance of the celibate condition, his grosser humours pass; he finds serenity catching him unaware, then a more and more constant companion as fate too becomes a collaborator, food comes his way more often, and his lean limbs begin to fatten. Summer warms the land; the sun darkens his body and fair-bearded young face. Since he doesn't see sense in burdening himself with boots, trousers, braces, shirt and cap – unless out shooting wild pig, bulky descendants of the beasts which Captain James Cook bequeathed to the country – he is more often than not as nude as the noblest savage, as self-contained as any

Crusoe. He is certainly one with the forest which unfurls around him, the gullies and ridges tangled with tree and gross vine, the thick sound of shy cicada and ebullient bird, the gentle percussion of the Porangi's currents. He finds no footprint save where he alone has walked. Earth-bound birds no longer flitter away into undergrowth as he passes; fat little fantails drift down on to his shoulder; freakishly tiny frogs sit tame on his thumbnail. He uses music to soothe the avian breast. He fiddles until the foliage around fills with curious birds: his tempo is wild, then slow. Some, growing bold, fly down to peck at his bow, presumably in hope of extending their own repertoire. Recitations are far less successful. Wordsworth wins no response. Tennyson tells them nothing. Keats' message of immortality to the nightingale is not for the birds; anyway these in ancient days were never heard by emperor or clown. Some volumes of pastoral poetry, which now seem feebly far from the point, are left out in the rain, and forgotten; they rot.

At night, on his back beside his campfire, he watches the universe arrange its nightly spectacular with much satisfaction. He doesn't feel himself diminished. Rather he delights in his microscopic role in a production so superlative, with a script so infinite; he is honoured to carry a humble spear in creation's grand parade. It would be kind to leave him content, preoccupied with his own magnificat. But the Lovelock story declines James the just peace he has won. Even in that largely pietistic publication *The Lives of Lovelock Junction*, from which it is mostly unkind to quote, the scenarist for once has it almost right: 'James, inexplicably, is reputed to have gone bush up the Porangi for a time; but his kin were evidently not of a mind to lose him forever.' Nevertheless James has a fair run before forever closes in.

Working along the riverbank with a rifle slung on his shoulder, crashing over terrain still strange, he sights smoke distantly wisping in the forest. He cannot persuade himself that it is hallucination, some consequence of his hermit condition. He approaches the source of the smoke, and possible human contact, with dry throat and quickened heart. At length he locates a fire burning outside a neat hut sited considerably higher above the river than his own. Tending the fire is an old wrinkled Maori with huge head incongruously perched on tiny body; his pure white hair falls down to his shoulders. It is of course that exiled *tohunga*, that priest and prophet of doom, of whom *rangatira* George has disparagingly spoken. This prematurely retired tragedian has a large and amiable smile for James; he is delighted, it seems, and relieved. 'Your coming was foretold all of two weeks ago,' he explains. 'When you didn't turn up, I thought I might be losing my touch.' So his welcome is warm and his laughter loud as he shares his food with James.

It seems not to distress him that in a decade he has seen no other human face; he has never, in any case, had much taste for the trivia of mortal intercourse; exile has been blessing, leaving him free to get on more intimate terms with the old gods. And that experience has never been less than instructive. Among other things he has learned, for example, that men were never meant to be. Man was created in jest, the result of a wager between one bored god and another, to prove that fools could function in the world with only five senses; the wager had never been won, the point never proved. Also this sport had produced an unedifying spectacle, like watching flies with plucked wings. With other worlds to roam, far more profitable pursuits elsewhere, the gods had largely left humans to get on with their cringing, lustreless existence. James hears this and many other humorous tales of human inadequacy during the week he camps with the top-heavy *tohunga*, whose name proves to be Upokonui. He is a blend of laughing and weeping philosopher, a brown-skinned hybrid of Democritus and Heraclitus, with a volatile joy in all mortal folly. Upokonui gives James to understand that though the visible world is but a whimsical illusion, an unsatisfactory creation of senses in short supply, it does have the virtue of not being taken seriously. The fortunate few who have been absently-mindedly allowed some scrap of sixth sense, such as Upokonui himself, have on the whole been bewildered by their gift, and done little but address confusing and often contradictory communications to mankind. They have also taken themselves too seriously, as indeed has Upokonui himself in younger and less enlightened days among the Tutaekuri. It is now his duty, it appears, to make James see the joke. Which James doesn't always, quite. Punch-lines are lacking.

Otherwise James is taken by Upokonui's talent for colouring the commonplace. There is no occasion without an anecdote, no mountain without a myth. The land around is a living, breathing, sighing thing. Legends now linger in every turn of the river. Messages rustle in every tree. Stories sing on every breeze. Portents flutter in every bird. The old man, vast head perilously wagging atop his thin neck, leaves nothing untouched or unexplained; there are now windows within creation wherever James walks.

But it seems, finally, that there is one through which all men are forbidden to look; not even Upokonui is especially privileged. This information comes to James after a question concerning one of the more remarkable features of the landscape seen from the old man's clearing in the forest. Tall on the other side of the river are two marvellously identical limestone pinnacles, delicately sculpted by wind and water, in striking silhouette against the sky. Their appearance tends to stir James singularly. Upokonui tells him that the two pinnacles were once mischievous and fatally inquisitive sisters. They had, by mischance, come upon a gateway beyond which was that knowledge men are finally forbidden. Unable to resist temptation, they journeyed through that gateway and ultimately became possessed of the knowledge they morbidly desired. This was their undoing. The instant their curiosity was gratified, they were transformed into stone portals at the gateway through which man must not travel: an example, a warning, to puny and impertinent mankind. James feels a shiver in his soul. The tohunga's tale, in the telling, has left much to the imagination. And James is not unimaginative. Nor greedy. He should just like, if possible, a small piece of the action.

Early next morning, with light still lovely on the hills, he finds occasion to desert Upokonui, who has gone into consultation with an old crony who invisibly inhabits a huge totara tree. With clothes and boots knotted about his neck, James swims across the river, dries himself and dresses again, and then climbs hand over hand up crumbling cliffs, feathered with tenacious toe toe, to the place where the two limestone sisters tower. On arrival before them he tries to collect both breath and wits; he feels in a ferment with the queer quiet of the place. No bird sings. No insect murmurs. No twig snaps underfoot. Above all nothing grows, no grass, nor even lichen, in the stony space between the pinnacles. There is no longer room for hope that James might turn back; he is about to create considerable narrative inconvenience. For he steps tentatively between the pinnacles. That does it. Now we have to hazard explanations.

On one hypothesis it might be suggested that James has happened upon a rent in the usually rational fabric of reality, a tear in the mostly impenetrable tunic of time, though he is by no means aware of this marvel yet. Consider it, perhaps, as an imperfect antipodean improvization of the Bermuda Triangle. If this fails to satisfy, do better.

James, at all events, doesn't dematerialize; he remains remarkably solid, all things considered. He gazes with amazement at a yellow signpost which says, with large black letters in the English tongue, *The Sisters*. And, underneath, in smaller script, *Estimated height 105 metres. This fascinating formation discovered in 1899*. Surprised that civilization should have travelled through the centre of the land so far and fast without his knowledge – this haste, perhaps, explaining the careless chronology, though not the rather eccentric use of metric measurement when sturdy English feet and inches should suffice – James sights still another signpost. Under an arrow this announces simply, *Central*

Wilderness Trail. Northern Route. He then observes a much-trodden path. He takes the path on the reasonable assumption that it will lead him somewhere.

After many miles, it does indeed. The forest begins to ebb fernily away from each side of the trail, and he emerges into a valley filled with vistas of pleasantly pastoral nature. Sheep and cattle graze fields solidly hedged with hawthorn and barberry; English willows green the banks of silvered streams; poplars glimmer tall on grassy hillsides. Smoke rises from a dwelling in the distance, doubtless some humble cowman's cottage. He hears the calls of thrush and blackbird. The tidily sylvan scene appears to be announcing England again, perhaps part of Devon with which he is unfamiliar, turning his past in the Pacific into a strange dream. He cannot conceive why this exquisite surprise should be sinful; he does not feel himself to be partaking of forbidden knowledge. Upokonui too has become a friend of the far past.

Just how far he has yet to discover. The trail takes him by stile to a roadside, and there he has his first shock of significance. The road is unlike any he has known. It is hard and dark, composed of some material strange to him, with white lines painted intermittently upon it. Shiny and noisy metallic machines, each with four wheels whining, surge suddenly past James. He glimpses people packaged within these machines, perhaps prisoners; the concept is dizzying. For the first time he begins to suspect that he has indeed been too long up the Porangi. He has no notion where he can walk safely in this world; the machines seem determined to destroy him should he trespass across their path.

To his fright, one stops quite near him. This machine appears to be shaking itself apart with anger; it is certainly emitting menacing clouds of smoke. A human being emerges. He is recognizably young, spectacularly hirsute, and dustily dressed in some kind of rough blue Californian cloth. Fascinated James stands trembling.

'What's your number?' asks the stranger from the machine.

James takes this, with tolerable accuracy, as an unconventional form of greeting; he is reassured. For a time, however, he finds his own voice refusing to function. 'At last count,' he replies presently, 'I was some twenty-one years. Of the legal age for all requirements.'

The stranger's face suggests, rather strongly, that this is an irrelevant response. 'I mean, man,' he says, 'are you on your way to a gig?'

'I have no gig,' James answers. 'Nor horses.'

'Cool,' the stranger says.

'Pleasantly so,' James qualifies.

The stranger seems inclined to startle easily. 'I'm getting these vibes,' he insists opaquely, 'that tell me you're on your way somewhere.'

'I'm no longer especially sure,' James has to admit. 'I have walked from the Porangi.'

'Far out.'

'It is,' James agrees, 'rather far away.'

The stranger's propensity for surprise is again apparent. 'Well?' he demands. 'You want a lift?'

'I require no immediate elevation,' James insists.

The stranger holds open a door of the machine. 'Don't fuck about,' he advises, with some astonishing insight into James's recent affairs. 'Get in.'

Indecision getting the better of him, James finds himself bundled into the back seat of the machine, which begins to travel the road again at terrifying pace; others of its kind are roaring on all sides. Companionable within are three girls with costume akin to the young man's; all rather brazenly disport an excess of beads and bangles. They are also surprisingly careless about their coiffure; their long hair streams wildly in the wind which rushes in the windows.

'So what's with you?' one asks. 'You a film extra or something?'

'Film?' James inquires. 'Extra?'

'Out of sight,' the girl laughs.

James strains to see what might be.

'Your braces are wild,' says a second girl. 'I never met anyone heavily into braces before.'

'I really relate to your cap,' sighs the third. 'How much bread would you take for it?'

'You been in some hassle, man?' asks the driver. 'I mean, like, with the fuzz?'

James judges a negative response fitting for most inquiries. Meanwhile he concludes that his companions speak an interestingly identifiable variant of his native tongue; he is not altogether lost among aliens. Nor captive, necessarily, of barbarians.

'You smoke?' says the first girl. 'We got some good green.'

'Your body language tells me you're in a very freaky mood,' says the second.

'You're so laid back,' promises the third. 'You really make your own space.' She places a hand in remarkably intimate fashion on James's tweed-trousered knee. She might, perhaps, have been more cautious had she some inkling of his late capacity for the lascivious. 'Relax, lover. Fly a little.'

Fortunately wingless James is familiar with the act of smoking; that is, with the consumption of tobacco by way of cheroot or pipe rather than chewing the substance with relish. And he wishes, on the whole, to be agreeable. What he does not expect is to find a curiously thin twist of paper pushed burning into his hand. After his endeavour to draw some smoke into his mouth, rather unpleasingly, his surprise is great when the twist of paper is rudely removed from his fingers and extended in the direction of the driver.

'Not now,' the young man announces. 'A hamburger's more my trip.'

Thereafter the girls share the fast incinerating twist of paper among themselves, and with James, who at length overcomes his compulsion to cough. On his third attempt to secure smoke, he decides the substance within the paper less unpleasant, and distinctly not tobacco. Moreover he cannot see why its nondescript hue should be considered as constituting part of the green portion of the spectrum. Green? As well call it red, yellow, or blue. When the girls rather skilfully manufacture more smoky twists of paper, and continue to insist on James sharing, he begins to feel benign about the entire experience. Life has seldom been less than intriguing anyway.

He pays much attention to the passing countryside. There is more than enough to muse on. The familiar fades. Poles and wires riot along the roadsides; they stitch together man and land most strangely. Complexes of wire attach to every farmhouse of brick or wood which speeds by. Farmers hereabout appear to hold the honest craft of the thatcher in contempt. There is never quite time enough to ponder why. The pace is paralysing, and there are other machines travelling still faster, many of quite bestial bulk. It is soon dreamily clear to him that he is in no land that he has ever known, despite surface similarities here and there, and grazing animals. He looks in vain for peaceful villages, with pleasant inns. Instead there are towns and townships, quite convulsive with moving machines, also unsightly with signs advertising bizarre products in baffling, sometimes altogether unseemly manner. Not the least extraordinary feature of such places, to his residually randy eye, are girls gaudily dressed and shamelessly showing extensive lengths of leg. In one town they stop to partake of the local fare; the place apparently has as its speciality some greenery and meat of unusual origin crushed between two halves of a very large bun.

'We're wheeling all the way to Auckland,' the driver announces. 'You want out somewhere? Or is all the way okay?'

'Auckland?' James says with wonder. And relief. He realizes he is, after all, still contained within the country in which he began this journey. He has heard of Auckland. By reputation it is quite the most unkempt corner of the colony: all muddy streets, smelly mangrove creeks, mangy dogs, melancholy drunks, failed seekers of fortune, and suicidally impoverished merchants. Not a settlement, so he has reliably been informed, destined to survive long. Nor a place to dwell without risk of spiritual desolation. Nevertheless James now sees it as a place where he might get a useful foothold on fate; the settlement might serve as a springboard for a swift plunge home to the Porangi.

'You got it,' replies the driver. 'Auckland. All the way. Right?'

'Right,' James agrees amicably.

They hurtle off again. Sometimes metal clatters off the machine as they travel, but his companions are indifferent to the loss.

'More dope?' asks a girl.

'Dope?' says James.

He discovers himself smoking again.

'Know something?' she says. 'You're beautiful.'

'Me?' James says dizzily.

'You,' she insists.

'He turns me on too,' another girl observes.

James cannot cope. Besides there are marvels too many to comprehend, especially as they approach the settlement of Auckland. The roads breed monstrously, swooping, diving, circling, living some spirited life of their own; and the world is quite mad with machines. They not only traverse the roads. They also elongate and sprout wings, most impressively, and soundlessly travel the sky. It cannot be so. It is.

Soon it seems that Auckland is far from the tiny town of ill fortune presented by presumably malicious rumour-mongers. They roar past rippling seas of rooftops in the summer sunlight. They soar over bridges and bright estuaries where the masts of hundreds of boats bristle. Then there are buildings growing bulkier by the score. Time does nothing to diminish the gross human vista. Finally, in deep disturbance, James closes his eyes. Please God, he prays, give me back the Porangi. And God, characteristically, gives him still more to manage. For when he opens his eyes the worst is extravagantly revealing itself: high tides of machines cramming streets already dense with people beyond mortal measure, and everywhere walled in by buildings higher than he dares look; the din is pulverizing.

'The weed tuning you in?' a girl asks.

'The weed?' He can hardly hear the woman.

'Our green.' She seems unaware that James has slid off the conventional spectrum. 'Does things for the world, doesn't it?'

That, so far as James is concerned, considerably understates it. He is obliged to consider the nature of the substance he has been smoking. It might explain everything. With the gypsies he heard of mushrooms which bring bliss to the mind, and sometimes bewildering visions. Is it possible, he asks himself, that there is some similar wildness in this weed? Are these streets, these machines, these buildings, all delusion?

That possibility brings James peace. So does the girl.

'Stoned is the only way I can take this,' she further informs him. 'I can see the magic.'

Her too. James knows more relief; his suspicion now appears well founded. He is, if he recalls the word right, stoned. Certainly he begins to feel as if something wondrously heavy has bruised his brain. He can therefore refuse to be impressed. Tomorrow, with his mind clear, the visions dispersed, he will tramp down Auckland's muddy main street, avoiding mangy dogs and melancholy drunks, to the settlement's desolate and doubtless dilapidated waterfront. There, perhaps at a mooring in some smelly mangrove creek, he might find the skipper of a schooner willing to risk shipping him home to the Porangi on the promise of eventual and ample payment from Herman. James might of course have problems convincing the skipper that the Tutaekuri are more placid than their reputation suggests; and that the Hau Hau, despite some excesses, have a few points in their favour. Some penniless skipper, possibly one in despair of wresting money from suicidally impoverished merchants, might well think the risk worth his while.

Visions, for the moment, part to reveal their arrival at the door of a wooden house, with wide veranda, which is in much disrepair, all peeling paint and falling timbers; it sits in an abandoned garden where tall grasses grow, and rusting rubbish of obscure origin has collected. This is far more recognizably the Auckland of which his recent intelligence tells. Even the architecture is not unfamiliar, not unlike that of the houses he has lately seen being hammered up in Hokitika. The disgraceful condition of the premises can no doubt be explained by the prevalent spiritual desolation.

'I'm all spaced out,' the driver announces. He looks at James in friendly enough fashion. 'You want a rave tonight? Or you want to split?'

'Split?' James feels he has already. As for raving, that may be only moments away.

'Of course he doesn't,' one of the girls insists, with a fond grab at James in the surprising proximity of his genitals. 'He knows where he's at. Don't you, lover?'

Still at a loss for language, James joins his companions in taking up residence in their unfortunate accommodation. He is assigned a bed, which amounts to no more than a mattress flung on an unswept floor, in a dim room much marked with damp. The day is darkening, and the girls greatly given to yawning. They complain that their journey has been considerable. 'I think we'll eat Chinese tonight,' one announces. For a chill moment James fears himself back in cannibal country again. There is more smoking, before and after meagre portions of most slippery food which is served, along with cans containing a watery beer-flavoured collection of chemicals, rather inelegantly on an oak table covered with candle grease; everything here has seen better days. James has certainly known more digestible meals. As the smoke thickens, and the night proceeds noisily and more than a little confusingly, James recalls the purity of the Porangi with nostalgia. With luck, and an impecunious enough skipper, he should surely be sailing home in the morning. One of the girls gives it to be understood that bed is now her bag. The others, not least James, who has had an unusually long day, find themselves in general agreement. The company, with a few affectionate calls of goodnight, disperses; candles are carried to the bedrooms.

With his own extinguished, James lies awake listening to his heartbeat, and then trying to locate a diminutive creature grazing upon his bare leg. On the other hand it would be unfair to his hosts to suggest that he has a comfortless night. Soon he hears soft footfalls in the passage outside his room; his door opens. He finds, of a sudden, feminine lips moist against his own. One of the girls, he doesn't know who, a matter of small moment since he will see all three that night, is saying to him, 'Know something, lover? I'd like to give you a buzz where it matters.'

James has to consider the possibility that he is being asked to participate in some ritual necessary to enliven the crude existence of Auckland's spiritually desolate settlers. So long as it is not designed to taunt and torture lonely bachelors in their loveless beds, he supposes he doesn't mind. When in Auckland, perhaps, he must do as the Aucklanders. If buzz she must, buzz she will. He hopes there is no sting. Her approach, at least, suggests some fertility rite. With fright he wonders if he is perilously near that forbidden knowledge of which Upokonui said man must never partake, on the pain of being turned into yet another limestone portal. He sees no joy in becoming The Brother forever, in the shade of The Sisters. Then he realizes that he is within easy reach of more familiar knowledge, of the commonly carnal kind, and his relief is as overwhelming as his passion to participate in the buzzing. As bees go, James is no drone. He discovers himself repeating the rite more often than he cares to count, as the girls come and go, and return again to reassure themselves. Thus one of the more piquant convolutions in the Lovelock chronicle provides for the conjecture that James might well have sired a line of long-haired Lovelocks in Auckland of the late twentieth century, a limb of the family tree still lost in the mists of the future; a prospect too irregular to be contemplated with ease.

Be that as it may, James rises brisk from his bed the next morning, before his curious companions have awoken, and strides off from their derelict dwelling. He has the appearance of a man who knows what he is about in the settlement of Auckland. That is, until other appearances begin to prevail. Daylight, after all, has not dismissed his delusions; the roads have not returned to mud, nor can he see much sign of suicidally impoverished people of the merchant class. The nightmare is intact. Mountainous buildings glitter with glass, and there are murderous ten-wheeled yellow machines hugely ready to run him down in the drumming valleys below. He has to deploy all his wit to win reprieves from death in a forest of hazards. Useless to cry for succour. People bustle and bump, no mercy in their morose faces. And the ships he finally sights, moored immensely on the waterfront, are really something more than schooners; these seagoing cities are hardly for hire. Not the least of the day's surprises is that James survives it sane. Shops are jammed with machines and more machines, some more remarkable than others, such as the boxes in which coloured pictures of people move, and even talk. Though some have large hats and horses, shooting at each other with much energy, most males and females on view are not unlike those pushing him about on the pavements. He continues to find females especially disconcerting in the immodest manner of their dress. He discovers the barely covered bulge of bosoms and buttocks leaving him quite faint with fresh lust.

In a basket evidently designed for the collection of refuse, James acquires a discarded newspaper of the day, hoping to locate some account of the outer world with which he is familiar. He would be grateful even for news of some Hau Hau horror, or perhaps of some rich new rush at Hokitika, anything to tell him all is as before; that elsewhere the country is conducting itself comprehensibly. But the most significant thing the newspaper has to say is that he is inhabiting, so help him, a November day in the year 1980. He stands stunned, at last, in the twentieth century; for the first time he confronts the sickening fact that he has wandered far from his family, perhaps far from himself; the peace of the Porangi belongs to another man, in another time. His great-grandchildren, all too conceivably, since he could at this point have conceived many potential grandparents, could be pounding grimly past him at this moment.

The rest of the day begins to disappear in delirium. He is tired, hot, hungry, and half crippled; he has no hope of finding his way home again. His unexpected transaction with time has left him totally bankrupt; he is a devalued scrap of currency in a century which makes no sense. Towards the end of that afternoon of anguish, with blisters in his boots, and worse on his soul, he sights a shop which at least purveys one familiar product. Books. True that their appearance is somewhat coarser, brighter and cheaper than those he recalls from the 1860s, but at least they remain recognizable in shape and size, an urbane oasis in a howling wilderness. He observes that a considerable number of the volumes arranged to advantage in the window have the same title: *The Lovelock Version*. A poster of rather flamboyant nature informs him that the book, written by an individual whose name means nothing, has been published that very day.

Overcome by the oddity of encountering his surname bulking so large, James enters the shop and begins inconspicuously to browse. He hopes the bookseller will not be disconcerted by his rough and increasingly desperate appearance, and rudely shove him out into the savage streets as other shopkeepers have. But the bookseller, it appears, has things other than unkempt customers on his mind at that moment. There is, most fortunately, some kind of social function in progress at the rear of the establishment; there are people in chattering clusters, with much clinking of glass and crockery as trays of food and drink are borne among them. James seems the only prospective reader in the shop as the strident voices rise and fall. It appears that the occasion is in some way connected with the volume James is seeking. For he overhears mention of its author, whom James furtively observes to be spectacled and pipe-smoking, with rather bedraggled moustache, a man very soon in the midst of making a speech about the invaluable help given him by diverse members of the Lovelock family, though he regrets that so few have seen fit to be present. James shuffles cautiously shelf by shelf toward the books on central display, pretending impartial interest in every title which presents itself to his gaze. At length he gets his hands about the book he desires; he carries it swiftly off to a quiet corner.

What he finds within the covers of the book is astonishing beyond any reasonable measure. He finds, for example, himself. And Herman. Sarah. Marie Louise. Richard. The children. All paraded, in sometimes shocking detail, on page after page. It is almost more than his mind can bear; he feels vertigo. The first chapter concerns Herman's encounter with an angel on the goldfields of Otago, which explains much that is mystifying in the now cruelly distant past. He flicks on through the book with some ferocity. Other chapters involve themselves with the alpine agonies of the Lovelocks, the events at Hokitika, the death of Sarah, often in unpleasantly plausible form. There is ever a stark account of that night he shared with Marie Louise. James wonders feverishly how he can hide all this from Herman. But he has forgotten where he is. Herman has to be dead, long dead. Marie Louise too. Richard. And, not least, himself. He, James Lovelock, is also long in the grave. That thought is especially paralysing. He cannot turn a page beyond the point where the narrative conveys the Lovelocks to the Porangi. Beyond that must be madness. He understands Upokonui's story at last. The knowledge forbidden to five-sensed man – and especially to James at this instant – is that of the exact manner and moment of his own death. It is a cross not to be carried on mortal shoulders. It is knowledge which, if Upokonui has it right, could lock his shrivelled soul within stone. It is knowledge, perhaps also, which could make each afflicted man irreverent and Godless, raging and raving, with nothing unknown or any longer to be feared up to his last earthly hour. James now has that knowledge literally in his hands. Shaken, he closes the book; it soon falls from lame fingers to the floor.

It takes him no little time to become aware again of that which surrounds him, and of the authoritative personage who has apparently been standing alongside him for minutes, regarding James with intensity and evident awe. Reluctantly, James identifies this unusually disturbed individual as responsible for his present disarray.

'So you made it,' the person is saying. 'It did happen. It is.'

James, equally slow to comprehend, wishes to flee. For conversation can only tempt him to continue dipping within the well of knowledge forbidden to man, to see his death written on the waters he draws. This person must know.

'James?' the author says anxiously. 'It is James?'

'Yes,' James allows at last. His trembling knees provide indifferent support.

'My God,' is all the man can say.

There is some silence. James looks for flight again.

'It's all right,' the man asserts. 'No one else will recognize you. People at publication parties seldom read.'

James finds this intelligence neither relevant nor comforting. He has more on his mind.

'You should,' the author adds, 'be on the Porangi.'

'Yes,' James agrees gratefully.

'And in early 1869.'

'Yes.'

'We've got to get you back there, obviously.'

James could not have hoped, on the whole, for more understanding. 'Please,' he says.

'It's not easy for either of us, of course,' the author insists.

'You must get me back there,' James pleads.

'In one sense, of course, it's academic. It's written. It's happened – by means, as I recall, too tortuous and often too tortured to relate.'

'What does that mean?'

'That it's done. And always has been. This too. There is no way out.'

Numb James has but small interest in rationalizations. Not if he never sees the Porangi again, never finds 1869.

'If you can't help me,' he appeals, 'who can?'

'First you need maps,' says the author, more practically. 'And money. So you can begin that journey back to where you began. It is something, as I remember, which you must accomplish unaided. Were it otherwise I could drive you some of the way. Unfortunately there is no provision for that in the narrative. Short-sighted, no doubt. I should have enjoyed the conversation such a journey together could produce. We should have got to know each other much better. The loss, of course, is largely mine.'

'I could tell you things,' James agrees.

'Don't. Please don't.'

'You don't know the half of it,' James persists.

'And never will. That's the real grief. Which is all written too. Things went awry.'

'Awry?'

'With the narrative. For one thing, it should have been more Herman's. Not yours, or Richard's.'

'Would you have us different?'

'Less in character, desirably.'

'Your problem,' James says definitively.

'So it would seem.'

'You can't say we're to blame.'

'Not entirely. History, perhaps.'

'Complain to Herman. Not to me. Why did you have to do it anyway?'

'Penitence, arguably. A belated attempt at repair. I can't disclose more. Not now. Once is enough.'

The author now seems in much muddle and panic; one would think, observing his agitation, that he had the world on his shoulders. He finds maps on one of the shelves in the shop, then swiftly removes money from a wallet; James becomes recipient of both maps and money, finally of more confusion. 'There. One hundred dollars. And clear directions. It's all the help the narrative permits me to give. I must add that we're due to be interrupted at any moment. By my wife, in fact. Her coming is your cue. At that point you must leave immediately.'

'Why?' asks James. 'What if I don't?'

'This all unravels. We disappear. And you never get back to the Porangi. The point is that this conversation can't be prolonged.'

'There are things about Herman,' James begins, breathless with tidings. 'About Richard too. And—'

'And you?' the author proposes.

It is unfair. And insidious. James feels terror again. Fumbling to manage maps and money, and irrelevantly wondering what happened to comprehensible English pound notes, he hears the author add, 'That, you see, is how it has to be. Which is rather more than half of it. There has to be some comfort, God knows, in a closed book.' He bends and recovers the volume which stricken James let slip to the floor. 'Don't worry. You can't take this with you. Quickly, now. It's time to leave. No need even to wish you good luck. You'll be all right; you have to be.'

James, in the circumstances, has to assume the man well informed.

A small blonde woman is advancing toward them with a smile, rather too swiftly, across the floor of the shop. 'Darling,' she is saying, 'where have you been? And who is that with you?'

James understands that to linger might be to lose 1869 and the Porangi forever; to rewrite all that which has yet to be written. He moves swiftly out of the shop, pushing past people, and is safe.

By means too tortuous and often too tortured to relate, exactly as predicted, James moves among the disconcerting creatures of the twentieth century. Consulting the maps now most conveniently made of the country, he locates the Central Wilderness Trail and at last that fascinating natural formation – one of the most conspicuous features along that taxing route – called The Sisters. It is late afternoon and he is quite at the end of his strength. He suspects he is something more than a century too late. It seems Upokonui's forbidden gate, or the Porangi Triangle, has gone into business elsewhere. For ferns and grasses now flourish between the pinnacles. Birdsong celebrates day's end. The place no longer has the bare and unnerving character James recalls. Misery springs yet another ambush. He fossicks through his apparel for some scrap of food, finds nothing, and in anger crushes maps and gives his last few futile dollars to the wind. He might as well be dead. Perhaps he is. He fights off the idea; he determines not to perish for anyone's convenience. At that moment he feels a tugging on his legs. Exploring the unseen source of this sensation, he observes first his feet, then his calves, his knees and thighs slowly disintegrating. Soon he no longer exists below the waist, a dismaying condition when his aptitude in that area is considered. Another curious thing is happening. The grass is withering, the ferns are fading; the birds are ceasing to sing. As the rising tide of nothingness takes his chest, his neck, and eddies about his chin – and James at last becomes hopeful about what is happening – he farewells the future with suddenly wistful eyes; the last thing he sees is a winged machine, silent and silver, cruising among clouds. Then, with a final gulp of twentieth-century air, he goes under.

He is lying a little way short of the pinnacles, with a heavy-breathing Upokonui hanging desperately to his legs. Morning light still embellishes the hills above the Porangi.

'Fortunately,' Upokonui is saying, 'this too was foretold. Though it was far from clear how it would end. I thought it better not to tempt fate. I just got you out of there in time. As it was, I had to take considerable risk with my own person.'

'I am in your debt,' James insists. 'Thank you.'

They rise, dusting themselves down.

'A mistake, of course, to feel obliged to tell you that story,' Upokonui adds. 'I never feel happy in the grip of events foreordained. No man should know the tale. The temptation to confirm its truth is too troubling to the soul. I shudder to think of what might have been.'

James shudders more at the thought of what has yet to be. But not for long. The Porangi's serenity still captivates. He descends in silence to the river with Upokonui, who then paddles him swiftly to the far bank in his canoe, and leads James to his hillside home.

'We are all of us fallible,' Upokonui argues over a simple lunch, 'and a little knowledge is often worse than none at all. When I reflect on that which has often been partially and imperfectly revealed to me, I sometimes wonder if I'm any better off. Does it really matter, for example, if the gods have ten senses, as some of my informants say? Or twelve, as others indicate? Yet I persist. Why? Because I must. Because someone must.' He gives a sad, stoic shake of his immense head. 'I am merely making the point, James, that it would be pointless – indeed unnecessarily frustrating – for you to aspire to my condition.'

James notes the moral implanted in this monologue. There is emphasis in the old *tohunga's* wily, lingering gaze.

'Is there anything, on second thought, you should like to tell me, James?'

James sees, then, that Upokonui is vulnerable to morbid temptation too; and covets more than James has surrendered.

'Is there?' Upokonui persists.

'No,' James decides. 'Not really.'

Upokonui's relief is profound. At least, in terms of prophecy, he will not be obliged to suffer a rival along this reach of the Porangi.

That afternoon James farewells his durably enigmatic tutor and returns to his riverside hut. He makes no attempt to move it to higher ground, despite Upokonui's stern suggestion that both hut and James would be imperilled should the *taniwha* trapped inland bestir itself, as forewarned, and launch disaster down the Porangi. A decade or two has made Upokonui appear rather vague and unreliable as forecaster of imminent doom; the wheel horses of prophecy have a thankless task. Nor does James have cause to consider Upokonui's other homilies long. In any case his encyclopedic experience of the future soon begins to seem a sad and shrivelled thing; it is more to the point that his roof is leaking, that birds and rats have plundered his kumara plot, and that his larder is bare. The future can look after itself. The present, which presumably makes it all possible, cannot. He regrets only that he has not returned with some of that wild weed in pocket; it might have given still more piquancy to his life on the Porangi, especially when solitary under the stars. Otherwise he settles for the ordinary amenities of the outcast's trade. There are times, however, when he cannot deny the lack in his life: not least because of his recent repast, albeit of forbidden fruit; must he now wait more than a century for another like feast? On occasion, with memory, he is aroused most disturbingly. The friendly birds of the forest, which can mate madly when they choose, are insensitive to his suffering. His naked plunges into the cold Porangi only serve to defer his pangs.

On one of his now regular visits to Upokonui he confides his problem over a lunch of river crayfish. Sucking at the little legs of these creatures, Upokonui meditates. Then says, 'It is, of course, a problem not impossible of solution. I have likewise had my problems – and, to be frank, temptations – in the past. Finally, however, I preferred to avoid the obvious solution.'

'Solution?' says James.

'I preferred solitude, despite the denials involved. In short, it is difficult enough getting at the gods without a demanding woman pointing out the deficiencies in one's terrestrial existence.'

'I don't understand, Upokonui. What is this solution you speak of.'

'The solution of dreaming a companion.' Upokonui appears to assume James somewhat dense. He finishes with the crayfish and licks his fingers. 'Take some of these *koura* home with you. I have never known them so abundant in the Porangi before. No doubt an omen, but I fail so far to see the significance. Sometimes, as I grow older, I suspect that such things are sent to tease us. To throw us off the scent, so to speak. Dear boy, what ails you?'

James suffers indigestion, largely due to a carelessly gulped crayfish shell. 'Dreaming a companion?' he finally gets out.

'Yes. A woman, if we must be precise.'

'I dream women anyway. Too many. Much good it does me. I'm still alone next day.'

'But,' Upokonui observes, 'at least you have a glimpse of the possibilities inherent in our dreams.'

'Glimpse is right,' says James bitterly. 'When I wake I can't even remember who they were.'

'Exactly. You are not using your dreams. You are merely allowing them to use you; you are just borne this way and that, a twig on the untidy tides of sleep. You need control. With reasonable intelligence, some sensitivity, and more than a little cunning and craft, we can command our dreams. To the point, I might add, of seeing them solidify in satisfying fashion. If it's a woman you want, for example, it's a woman you have.'

James grows thoughtful. 'Go on,' he says quickly.

'But I have a warning,' Upokonui announces gravely.

Excited James has lost appetite for crayfish. 'What warning?' he asks with impatience.

'Just this. That you may be sorry.'

'Sorry?'

'You may well manufacture a grief to haunt you for the rest of your life. That is the unavoidable risk in this business. Not to speak of the hazard in hastily producing a woman somewhat less than perfect. In which case your grief might be still larger. One way or the other, it's a perilous path. That which is dreamed cannot easily be undreamed; men of my kind have been devoured by the very monsters they have vengefully wished to loose upon others, after creating them in their dreams with care.'

James finds more to kindle his fascination and impatience. 'Life's all risk anyway,' he argues. 'What would you say, Upokonui, if I told you the future's going to have it worse?'

The *tohunga's* eyes widen. 'Is there some wisdom, James, you wish to impart to me?'

'It doesn't matter,' James replies, now regretting the provocation; Upokonui has more than enough mystery to preoccupy him. Let him dream of the trapped *taniwha*, rather than tides of murderous machines. 'I should rather you got on with imparting your wisdom to me.'

'Very well. Just remember. And prepare.'

'For what?'

'For sorrow, in whatever guise.'

Returned to his riverside dwelling, James gives himself night after night to the esoteric exercises the old *tohunga* has prescribed. These are soon taxing to the point where his daylight hours are lived in bleak exhaustion; his waking life is vague and more akin to dream than are his dreams themselves. For his dreams, as he concentrates, and learns control, take on textures he can feel and fondle with his fingertips; their touch is as authentic as that of waterside reeds and grasses, or the silver-bellied fish he flicks up on to the riverbank. Upokonui has been severe in his admonition to advance upon this shadowy terrain with care, and not to expect too much too soon. Eventually, however, after experimenting with other ephemeral creations – a small and harmless snake he is obliged to kill, an apple of rather indifferent flavour – he begins work upon a woman. Understanding that impatience could yet undo him, he settles at first for fashioning her feet. This is more difficult than it seems; time and again he finds them faulty, either too tiny or too sturdy, and altogether a test for the aspirant craftsman. With her feet finally sculpted to a perfection seldom found in this world, his confidence grows. So does more of her anatomy: the lithe delicate legs come fast, and there is inspired moulding in her tender thighs and sweet buttocks. Her back is elegantly curving and her stomach silken, but her breasts give him pause; he has to view them again and again, from many vantage points, before pronouncing them finished. He has second, third and fourth thoughts about the shaping of her shoulders; at times they tend to look awry. As always, he resists the temptation to be content with mere competence of design; he will accept nothing less than a convincing command of his medium. With her arms, and long-fingered hands, his genius reveals itself again; he has never seen lovelier limbs. The last and largest challenge is her face; it takes him two weeks of desperate and devoted dreaming. First, as he works, it seems to have something of Sarah's shy sadness. Then something of the shameless sensuality of Marie Louise. At times Ballarat Gert and California Kate peer out at him cheekily. A Tutaekuri maiden, fondly recalled, gives him a lustful wink. At length he decides it impertinent to impose himself; there will always be something of them all, however much he seeks anonymous features. The long eyelashes grow, the limpid eyes, the pert nose, the loving lips; he is attracted by the notion of tinting her a faintly olive near-gypsy colour, but at length gives her a hue between honey and gold, which will shift in shade from hour to hour. He frames her finally with long black tresses of hair. She stands at last, full length before him, in immodest glory. And Glory he names her. There is no name more fitting to crown this vision, this distillation of womanly virtue. The pity is that, at this moment, he is far from adequate to confront his creation. A Michelangelo depleted by his masterwork, he feels flesh falling away; he subsides limp into dreamless sleep.

He wakes in fright. Morning light fills the door of his hut. Glory is not languid beside him on his mattress of fern and bracken, nor anywhere to be seen. He suspects some failure of understanding, or communication; perhaps she has already fled to a more accommodating male dreamer.

He races to the door, looks out, and with a flash of delight sees all his fears as foolish. For Glory is splendidly there; she swims naked in the sunny Porangi.

'James,' she cries. 'Dear James.'

He finds it impossible to speak.

'There were times when I doubted you,' she says. 'Times when I thought it might never happen.'

'There were times when I doubted too,' he confesses.

'And now?' she says, laughing. And her laugh is pure enchantment.

'Yes,' he agrees. 'Now we're together.'

'Forever, if you will.'

'Forever,' he confirms.

She glides gracefully among the fronds of fern which overhang the riverbank. He bends to help her from the water, and her long fingers wrap gratefully about his hand. That first touch brings ecstasy. His gratitude to Upokonui can never be measured. Especially as she stands there, shaking back her long hair, with silver drops of water spilling from her honey-gold body. They are still regarding each other with much amazement, and great tenderness.

'You took so long to wake,' she observes. 'It seemed a lifetime.'

'Don't talk of lifetimes,' James says. 'One will never be enough for me now.'

He takes her hand again, to reassure himself of her substance. Glory's smile alone is sufficient to the occasion.

'But you don't understand,' she says.

'Understand what?'

'That when I say forever, I mean forever. A lifetime is too paltry to consider. In time, dearest James, I can learn to dream you too. You see? Then there are no lifetimes. There is no death for dreams. There will just be our two dreams blended perfectly, beautifully, forever.'

James is more than a little overwhelmed. Even Upokonui had not advanced so spectacular a prospectus. The old *tohunga*, compared with this artfully sculpted creature, begins to seem a man of blinkered vision.

'Come now,' she says. 'Kiss me, James. It is time.'

Her lips do not disappoint him. Nor her elegant back, which his hands slowly enfold. Her bare limbs bewitch.

There is but one imperfection in their exquisite pairing; and it is his own. Carnality has curiously, perhaps briefly, deserted him; he is not greatly distressed. He knows, though not from his own experience, that lust is easily lost in the first spiritual rapture of lovers; all literature, after all, tells that sweet if sometimes improbable tale. Upon his mattress of fern and bracken, in the cool shade of his hut, they spend delicious hours of daylight, gently fondling each other from head to toe, with lingering and most intimate kisses, and lengthening sighs of delight. It is, in fact, dusk before they know it.

James feels hunger rumble conspicuously in his empty belly; at least he hasn't lost one fleshly appetite. Of Glory's capacity to consume terrestrial food he isn't sure; he doesn't recall dreaming her internal organs, beyond her reproductive tract, rather tending to take them for granted. Diffidently he suggests a break for the partaking of food. Glory, as ever, is anxious to oblige. They toast decapitated eels, on forked sticks, over his campfire. She laughs often and mischievously. When the eels are made edible, he urges her to beware of the bones. Again she laughs. Before his marvelling eyes she slips an entire eel down her gullet without pause for breath. Then another. And another. It is as extraordinary a sight as any that day. It isn't merely her unawareness of civilized custom in the consumption of viands; it is the stunning size of that consumption. She doesn't lick her fingers between each eel, or linger long upon its flavour. She just swallows; and swallows. James can only wonder at that which his dreams have wrought. He eats pitifully little himself, finding indifference to food of any kind; the appetite he thought lost is remarkably at large in his loins again. The universe spins dizzily above his head. Then, with a leap of huge proportion, he is upon her.

'James!' she cries with surprise and delight. His name is heard uttered many times, with similar tone and inflection, all the length of that lustrous night.

He doesn't notice the unseasonably cool winds and cold rains which arrive next day. In the land of lovers it is always summer. Never less than adventurous, their exploratory lovemaking fast passes beyond the pleasantly pastoral into territory dark and tangled. There is thunder and lightning. There is avalanche and earthquake. There is flood and fire. Tempests speed them across violent seas; they soar into tender harbours. Glory she shall be forever. And forever is no mean span.

Nevertheless, after what he can only presume to be a week or two, James begins to suffer something ecstasy often heartlessly leaves in its wake, namely twinges of ennui. Man, he tells himself in a dark moment of doubt, is meant to be more than a perambulating penis. He cannot imagine Glory receptive to such a proposition. Or to the notion that there is more to life, even on the Porangi.

'You must teach me,' she says. 'You must teach me to dream you too. Then there is no death. Our dreams will blend beautifully on the Porangi forever.'

That plea is growing more persistent. Dreams, it seems, are not self-sufficient; they need instruction to better themselves, to breed their like. Not that procreation, in the usual sense of the word, is the problem. But quite suddenly James sees that it is. He cannot conceive with a dream; he cannot possess the ultimate proof of his masculinity; he can never cherish a child he calls his own. He can never see himself passing tragically, comically, heroically, humbly, ephemerally, historically, into the human ballad. Not now, nor in any perceptible forever. In the far reaches of forever he will be sundered from his kin, his kind.

Troubled in soul, the more so because he finds his flesh as fervent as ever, he leaves Glory alone for the first time in a gentle, satisfied and – he hopes – dreamless sleep; and takes himself to Upokonui. The old man, as usual, is not surprised to see him.

'I could only presume, from your lengthy absence, that your dreams did their work well,' Upokonui observes; his eyes have shrewd glitter. .

'Too well.' James, comprehending at last the extent of his exhaustion, slumps in the dust at the door of the *tohunga's* hut.

'Our desires, of course, frequently confound us in their gratification. A perplexing paradox. One on which I never cease to ponder. It makes nonsense of most of our endeavour in this existence. And demonstrates yet again the incoherence at the heart of creation. Take another example. If the brute struggle for existence ceases to be a problem, a condition to which most men aspire, what then is the problem? Why, the singularly unsatisfying nature of existence itself. That, perhaps, expresses the paradox most perfectly.'

'I just know I'm tired,' James confesses. 'And feeble.'

'That is a common condition too,' the *tohunga* tells him. 'Though I should add, in fairness, that many would envy you the cause of your complaint.'

'It's not that I don't love her.'

'Of course you do.' Upokonui is all consolation. 'I should not be so heartless as to suggest otherwise.'

'It's like nothing I've ever known,' James sighs. 'Or could ever know again. Ever.'

'Where, then, is this grief I see in you?'

'I don't see a future in it,' James admits frankly.

'Is that necessary?' Upokonui finds it difficult to conceal surprise. 'Garlands are to be gathered while the flowers are blooming. That, surely, is a universal proverb to stand you in good stead.'

'I'm strangling in garlands. Apart from which, she's offering me immortality.'

'A rare and striking gift. And you complain? A moment ago you were muttering that you didn't see a future in it.'

'I don't know that I'm up to fornicating forever. Or really want to.'

'The perversity of mankind still astounds me,' Upokonui says. 'We should all have been shaped in much more straightforward fashion.'

'I'm far from suggesting I find no delight in fornication,' James adds.

'The evidence is before my eyes. You need more flesh on your face. Delight has been taking its toll.'

'But forever?' James demands. 'Forever?'

'You are slow to the point. I find myself growing anxious to share the nature of your problem.'

'The fact is,' James explains, 'I don't want to miss out on anything.'

'And you feel you might?'

'Yes. I might. I would.'

'Death is something most of us might find desirable to do without. An encumbrance with which we are burdened from the day of our birth.'

'You don't understand,' James declares irritably.

'No?' Upokonui is as patient as ever.

'No,' James announces. 'Life is what I don't want to do without.'

Upokonui, for once, appears to have no answer.

Having spoken his heart to Upokonui, if only to cauterize a weeping wound, James returns home. Love trembles in his throat at the honey-gold sight of Glory again; lust ignites afresh in his loins. And Glory, who has been going about her business meekly, tidying his pitifully small collection of bachelor possessions, doubtless perturbed by his absence, gives him a grateful smile. 'I was worried,' she confesses, as they fondle again. 'If you had left me, what would I do? How would I survive? What happens to a forsaken dream? Where would I wander?' Such questions perish in her mouth as James penetrates her sublimely, reaping a harvest seldom found this side of heaven. But he does comprehend that Glory is dependent upon him, perhaps even more than he is upon her. At length, peaceful beside her, he startles himself with the passionate declaration, 'I'll never leave you, Glory. Never.' She weeps upon his strong shoulder.

It seems settled. Certainly their love is. Her dependence is something he has not counted on; he cannot desert this vulnerable creature of his own creation. He remembers his disloyalty, as expressed to Upokonui, with regret; it is as if he had actually been unfaithful. Unfaithful to Glory? The thought is intolerable. In any case the possibility of physical infidelity, up the lonely Porangi, is unlikely ever to present itself; their circumstances ensure serenity. They frolic through the forest; they gambol naked in God's noble world. James, despite his past and probably unreasonable reservations, begins to instruct Glory in the art of dreaming so that she, before long, will be able to manufacture a facsimile of him forever. He explains the need for care and patience; he is appalled by the possibility of a flawed James Lovelock limping eternally along the Porangi on uneven legs, or worse. There is no reason for haste anyway. The days drift; their passion never ebbs.

It might be noted that Eden too, despite most promising circumstances, and favourable situation, had an end. Otherwise this tale, like many another human narrative, need never be told. This one ends in most casual manner, not with serpent and tree, but with the sound of canoe paddles on a summer morning. James has been foraging for freshwater mussels along the riverbank; he looks up startled. A craft is coming into sight about a bend in the river. The two occupants of the craft are his brother Herman and *rangatira* George of the Tutaekuri. Herman is paddling rather ferociously; George, behind, pausing to rest his paddle often, appears to have less energy for the enterprise.

Before he can think, or hide, James cries out. He doesn't consider Glory, at that moment still asleep in their hut, perhaps practising her dreams and trying to perfect James within them. Or what that fragile creature might make of men from the outer world. The sight is too remarkable.

At the sound of his young brother's voice Herman looks up with something uncommonly like joy. He begins to paddle even more fervently, calling upon George to collaborate. Together they contrive to find several courses for the canoe before the river currents take a compassionate hand and deliver it to shore near the bare brown feet of James.

'Thank God,' Herman gasps, with uncharacteristic gratitude. 'We thought we'd never find you.'

He leaps from the canoe and, also uncharacteristically, embraces his brother. George, following wearily, is content with a handshake.

'Marie Louise has been worried out of her wits about you,' Herman explains. 'She refused to cook another meal until we came upriver to see you were still sound of mind and body. There was no arguing with the woman, in the end. So we came.'

'To take me back?' James asks in alarm.

'That might, perhaps, be a little premature,' George informs him gravely. 'I regret that memories in our tribe are long, and mostly unforgiving. With time and some indication of repentance on your part, desirably of celibacy, you may well find a welcome downriver again. Possibly not from our males. I fear to speak of our females. Meanwhile, I'm deeply sorry to say, you must remain upriver.'

James has relief too huge to express. He is safe. Glory too. Instinct, not to speak of common sense, tells him he can never return downriver with Glory. Never.

'The main thing, for the moment,' George goes on, 'is to set Marie Louise's mind at rest. She has promised *coq au vin* in return for news of pleasing nature.'

'A hell of a journey, up here,' Herman announces, emphatic about their hardship. 'Hard pulling all the way.' He looks over the thickly timbered hillsides, then up at the ranges rising blue beyond. 'But worth it for the vistas alone. It's big country. A place to plant dreams.'

Herman is unaware that he is indelicately trampling over the terrain of James with that pronouncement. James hopes his brother's loud voice doesn't disturb Glory's tender sleep. He is at a loss to think how he can introduce and explain Glory to Herman and George. Then he knows he must avoid that difficulty.

'Keep your eyes skinned for coal,' Herman adds. 'Make the most of your time up here.'

James hesitates to explain to Herman that he has been, indeed to the point some might consider surfeit. 'What news?' he asks his visitors sociably.

'The wars seem all but to have run their course,' George reveals.

'How has it ended?'

'As wars will,' George sighs, 'with disasters of diverse kind. Survivors are trickling back. Far too few for my liking. In terms of warriors, the Tutaekuri is hardly a going concern; we could barely muster enough to fight off an invasion of fleas.'

'And Richard?' James asks. 'Ira?'

'No sight of them so far,' Herman says sadly. 'Not that we've given up hope. They could still be battling their way back. They aren't, one presumes, without initiative. But what of you? What's been happening to you?'

'Too much to tell,' James replies truthfully.

'I hope you've managed yourself a rude shelter of some kind.'

'I have,' James admits with caution.

'Perhaps we might avail ourselves of your simple home comforts,' Herman suggests, 'and sample a little of such hospitality as you can offer. While we rest, that is, in preparation for return downriver as bearers of glad tidings for Marie Louise.'

James realizes that, if Glory is spied, Herman and George may well be awash with tidings. Nevertheless he sees no way out. He cannot refuse Herman and George his hut. He hopes Glory is sensitive enough to his situation to flee at the approach of alien voices.

'Well?' demands Herman. 'What's the matter?'

'Nothing,' James insists.

'It's almost as if you aren't glad to see us.'

'Forgive me, then. I'm far from accustomed to social calls.'

'I can see,' Herman concedes, 'that a man might get a little strange on his own up the Porangi. Far be it from me to suggest that your life is easy. Cultivate strength of character in this testing time. You must not succumb.'

'I shall try,' James promises warily.

He helps Herman and George haul their canoe on to safe ground. There are gifts from Marie Louise aboard, conspicuously one of her precious copper pans, intended to encourage him to prepare his lonely meals in civilized fashion. It would be ungracious to refuse such a gift, or to explain that he has, for some time, been lost to civilized fashions. He leads the intruders upon his peace through the forest, along the path his feet have daily worn, to the hut in the riverside clearing. It has never, at that moment, seemed more dear to him. But for Glory, it is all in the world he can call his own. And Glory? Is she still within? There is an anguished chafing in his chest.

Just short of the hut, he pauses; and prays.

'What now?' asks Herman, relentlessly inquisitive.

'I thought I heard something,' James fabricates. Perhaps he has. Feet in flight through the forest, desirably.

'Birds,' Herman insists. 'Just birds. What else would you expect to hear upriver? Your nervous nature might yet be your undoing; you mustn't let your imagination play tricks.'

'No,' James agrees.

He takes a deep breath, and dives into the hut with Herman and George following hard behind. He can relax at last. The mattress of fern and bracken is empty of all but blankets; Glory has tactfully gone. There is nothing to show she has ever been there, if there ever has been.

'Comfortable enough,' Herman comments.

'I manage,' James says modestly.

'The Porangi could be the making of you. I never doubted, all along, that you would survive. It was only Marie Louise who tended to get a little hysterical about the entire affair, as women are wont to do. She doesn't yet see that the Lovelocks are made of sturdier stuff than most.'

James finds a heavy brotherly hand on his shoulder. 'I shall do my best to justify your faith,' he says vaguely, mentally elsewhere with hope and certainly Glory. She may be shivering with fright somewhere out in the forest. He feels a shrinking of the heart. Then of his soul. Please God may they be gone soon.

They are not gone soon, though intentions to depart are often expressed. It becomes evident that Herman and George are less interested in contemplating the health or otherwise of his hermit state than in continuing the conversations which have taken much of the tedium from their upriver canoe journey. These conversations, so far as increasingly distracted James can comprehend them, concern the innate nature of man, and his capacity for perfectibility should circumstances be other. At least on Herman's side. On George's side there is much said about the blight which began with the trial and execution of Socrates, and the ultimate emptiness of the Hellenist world. James is more or less forgotten, other than when the rum is passed around. He sees no compelling reason why they should not continue their discourse while wending their contemplative way downriver; his longing for Glory has become a burning. The unfamiliar rum, besides, is going to his head. At length he rises giddily.

'It is past noon,' he pronounces. 'I am thinking of your journey home. You should make half the distance before dark. And be there at a comfortable hour tomorrow.'

'You have great concern for our itinerary,' Herman observes.

'My mind is with Marie Louise,' James insists.

'The woman's never out of my mind,' Herman replies. 'It's pleasant to pass a peaceful day or two with George. God knows, with her commotions, it is peace well earned.'

'She may begin to worry if your absence lengthens.'

'Women need worry to keep them happy. Peace of mind alarms them. That is something, James, which only matrimony can teach a man. I daresay you would disbelieve me if I were to suggest that your situation here has much to commend it.'

'Not necessarily,' James replies, choosing words with care.

'Men are ever hostage to circumstance. Also to women. Learn that lesson well, James.'

James, who feels sufficiently informed, helps Herman rise with difficulty. The difficulty is due to the consumption of rum. George, after several reminders of the *coq au vin* waiting downriver, is also persuaded to leave the hut in a weaving way. The riverside path, back to the canoe, is another test for patience. Haphazard human gait places both George and Herman in premature and involuntary contest with the waters of the Porangi; James conducts several rescues before the canoe is reached. At length he settles the still philosophical pair into their craft and points it downriver; he shoves it out into the current with some enthusiasm.

'God go with you,' Herman cries, flourishing a paddle. 'Remember, boy, keep your eyes skinned for coal. There might be more upriver than we know.'

'You won't be here forever,' George promises inauspiciously across the widening water.

James makes successful retreat to the riverbank, and waves farewell. With something of a lurch, the canoe is lost to sight beyond overhanging trees. Fat pigeons wing squeakily overhead. The peace passeth understanding. Seeking sobriety on his own account, James splashes water over his face extensively. Cleaner, a little clearer, though still with a faint taste of rum fouling his mouth, he goes looking for Glory.

She has made no shy return to the hut. Nor is she anywhere near it. He cries her name. Silence is the forest's answer. Apparently she has fled further than he first thought. He calls her name again, and imagines he hears faint reply. But it turns out to be birds, more birds, taking up his call as it echoes away into receding walls of wilderness. Silence again.

'Glory!' he shouts, perhaps with only heaven to hear.

Fear pushes him into the forest, faster and faster, tripping on vines, bruised and scratched by branches, all the while crying her name. Every green sanctuary is empty of Glory; the silences turn sullen. By nightfall his voice is a wilted whisper. Tears track down his torn face. Still he seeks Glory. Dark does not deter. Death itself would not.

But there is no death, not even next day, when he so much desires it. He rises from sodden undergrowth where exhaustion felled him, and recalls his unwilling flesh and bone to the quest. It turns, day after bitter day, into a dogged forced march through the forest. A penance, perhaps, or punishment, with the bayonet points of grief and disbelief pressing his body forward ever more cruelly, jabbing without mercy. One clean, fatal thrust would be kindness. No kindness is offered. The wilderness remains indifferent. His voice is a dry, cracked ghost.

Glory has gone. It takes him all of two weeks to concede to that truth. Then he limps in unconditional surrender back to his hut by the river, there perhaps to recover health and sanity, though he has no large wish for either. Mornings, when he wakes to find himself loveless and alone again, are most painful. Where has she gone? Into some forever of abandoned futures? Does she dwell among other husks of lost dreams? He does not want to think. At night, sometimes, he wakes imagining he has heard her crying in anguish across an appalling chasm never to be crossed in this lifetime or any other.

His mood takes him into the forest again; he hikes upriver to Upokonui.

'But I thought you would understand,' Upokonui says with sympathy. 'Such a dream is not to be shared. To allow it to be invaded, even by chance, is to kill it. It must, however regrettably, disappear.'

'But—'

'Remember this of me. I warned of likely sorrow.'

'Yes, but—'

'That knowledge was yours. And the choice.'

'But where is she?' James gets out at last.

Upokonui shrugs.

'She was real,' James argues. 'More real than this world.'

'Of course,' Upokonui agrees gently.

'So where has she gone?'

'There are some things, James, our meagre minds are never permitted to fathom.'

'So you don't know either,' James says bitterly.

'No,' Upokonui admits, with reluctance.

'I could have followed her. She wanted that. Now? Nothing. There is no more to my life; there can be no more.'

'You have a disagreeable tendency to overstate your case, James. Understandable, of course, but distressing to me. You could, for example, dream another woman if you wished.'

'Like Glory?'

'Perhaps not precisely. But in most relevant detail.'

'That's what I mean. It could never be the same. I've thought of it, but I could never get her right a second time. A counterfeit Glory, an unworthy imitation, seems sacrilege. Worse. Treachery.'

'There it is, then,' Upokonui concludes. 'Learn to live with your grief.' He pauses, closes his eyes briefly, and rests his heavy old head against a pole in his hut. 'Besides, James, I feel it timely to remind you that, in the not too distant past, you said to me that life was what you didn't want to do without. You spoke with some passion, as I recall. Well, you have it. It is all yours again. Life.'

'All of it,' James mourns.

Determined to distract his young friend, to give the boy's mind nourishment more material, Upokonui takes James aboard his canoe for a river journey. 'I shall give you a sight,' he promises, 'vouchsafed to none before you, and perhaps none again, as token of my sympathies. Also of my trust.'

James remains sullen in the rear of the craft as they glide upon the Porangi. Upokonui is often all promises. James has seldom, for example, seen the sad, strange spirits – of long departed, red-haired fairy people – which Upokonui claims fill these forests. Such as James has seen can be explained by river reflections, or ground mist among trees.

With a few flicks of paddle, Upokonui turns the canoe up a creek, a tributary of the Porangi James has never noticed before, which travels a tight valley. Vegetation tangles close on each side, with abundant shade; the autumn is cool about them. Then everything queerly changes. The trees become leafless and lifeless, stark and skeletal. They look like stone; they are. James reaches up to pluck a thin twig from a tree; he has to tug until it cracks. It rests shiny and silver and quite heavy in his hand. Something in the valley's soil, or simply in its unworldly atmosphere, has produced a forest of perfect fossils; flood and erosion have cleansed the trees and left a parade of glittering ghosts. James knows his first bliss in a month.

'There is more,' Upokonui says, still paddling. 'Much more.'

There is. Around a bend James feels his heart leap with fresh spectacle. Rising gaunt before them, all but filling the creek, is a vessel such as James has never seen, nor will again. A sixteenth-century Spanish frigate, once a sturdy seventy ton, and named *Santa Ysabel*, or so the corroded and barely legible name plate on its mossy hull informs James.

Though Upokonui is never to know it, and as only long research will reveal to James, this ship briefly and freakishly survived the feckless Spanish attempt to locate the fabled continent of Ophir, source of all Solomon's riches, in A.D. 1595. Among Spaniards and Portuguese the belief prevailed that Ophir lay in some unknown latitude of the Pacific, that third of the world then still abundant with mystery. The expedition's arrogant leader, an all-or-nothing gambler for gold and God's glory named Alvaro de Mendana, thought that he had glimpsed Solomon's shore as a stripling sailor some twenty-seven years earlier. Aged and greying now, made shrill by mockery and delusion, he took four ships upon the lethal Pacific again to sail by guess and by God to the beaches where nuggets shone by the golden ton. The obstinate Pacific surrendered only scurvy and scraps of tropic land: none cousin or even more remotely kin to Ophir, all poor and savage. In frustration and mad delirium Mendana stormed bloodily from island to island, harvesting death rather than riches; natives surprised by cannon and arquebus were left putrefying about Christian crosses piously erected. Soon half-decks bristled with mutiny and unsheathed swords. The Spanish vigorously fell to butchering their own kind. With some discretion, as disaster mounted, ailing Mendana gave up his own soul to merciful God. Somewhere in the human turbulence, the captain and crew of *Santa Ysabel* slipped away, likely thinking to voyage home to Peru again. Instead storm tipped them out of the tropics into cool southern waters; and they found, if not Ophir, at least a long land unmarked among the dragons and mermaids, waterspouts and whirlpools, on their parchment maps. The stricken voyagers needed nourishment. They also needed to clean and careen their rancid ship. They had the misfortune to arrive in the vicinity of the Porangi, from which point the tale is all Upokonui's.

The Tutaekuri provided their traditional welcome for the sick and dying Spaniards who sailed over their sand bar. *Santa Ysabel*, firing cannon to deter pursuit, was forced upriver, finally to take refuge in that tributary creek. There they wedged it; there the Spanish died. Or so Upokonui tells it, with a few improbabilities colouring the facts, such as that most surviving sailors were slain or enslaved by the red-haired fairies who inhabited the upriver territory. The fairies in turn perished, to the last woman and child, from a disease which reserved its worst ravages for the genitalia. On occasion the Tutaekuri searched upriver for the strange vessel which had passed over their sand bar into tribal legend. Perhaps out of respect for the miasmal and truculent fairies, none ventured far enough to find it. None until Upokonui.

James, dazed and fascinated, sees this gift of the *tohunga* as greater than gold, a miniature Ophir in itself; something at which nineteenth-century man might marvel. The timbers of the hull, a remarkable Peruvian hardwood named guatchapeli, which seems never to know decay, have weathered to a silvery-grey, perhaps petrifying like the trees along the creek. The feminine figurehead, apparently shaped from softer substance, has begun to fracture and fall, now no more than a leprous and headless torso. Breathless James swings aboard. The wilderness has done wondrous work. Saplings sprout from the deck. Ferns roost on the cabins. Creeper has replaced long rotted rigging, climbing tall to the top of the masts. Birds nest in the cross trees. The top deck is a compact conservatory, a jungle of leaf and vine. Underfoot, here and there, gruesome fragments of Spanish bone crunch in the compost which densely covers all. He kicks against something metallic and comes up with a rusty cutlass. Upokonui, far less inquisitive, does not at first board the boat with James, nor show much interest in his finds; he prefers no contact with a craft which brought so dread a disease to the Porangi's fairy people. But since James announces no urgent affliction of the genitalia, he is after a time persuaded to follow, and resumes his role as guide again. He parts foliage and reveals another miracle to James.

Behind the boat, centuries of silt and stony debris have banked up, caught in a net of tumbled trees, to form a dam; beyond the dam a vivid lake extends most of a mile back into the mountains. Mists hover soft on its shore. Shapely and colourful long-legged birds haunt the beaches and bays. Upokonui and James abandon the ship, scramble across the dam, climb a bluff, and look down on the lake. James, still skipping heartbeats, is entranced. The most seductive feature of the lake resides in its ambiguous reflections: all earth and sky mingle marvellously there, the enduring and the ephemeral, the profane and divine, the flux of time and chance. It might indeed be possible to glimpse the shifty, shifting face of God upon its waters; or maybe more gods than one, in many masks, if Upokonui has it right.

Too much for one morning. Upokonui is delighted that his secret has proved sufficient distraction for James. The boy's eyes are bright; he has glory, if not Glory, again.

They linger on the bluff, above the immaculate lake. 'All this,' James predicts, 'will bring hundreds to stare one day. Maybe thousands.'

'I am glad,' Upokonui sighs, 'that I shall not live to see it. The world deserves some secrets.'

'But still,' James insists, 'think of that ship. Men should know of its survival.'

'Maybe it might divert them for a day. Would they be any less blind on the morrow?'

'But it is history,' James pleads. 'Something of man's deeds.'

'And defeats.'

'Perhaps. But something such as that ship shows we've been here. Like a legend.'

'All the ships men launch are made to be lost. Legends are launched to live in the minds of men.'

Something gives James pause. 'I wonder,' he begins.

'Wonder what?'

'If it could be launched again. That ship.'

'There is more than enough human madness at work in the world.'

'It might be.'

Upokonui begins to fear for James. Also for this valley of fossil, vessel and lake. He uses it often for meditation. It is a useful reminder that the works of man mean nothing unless in service to the illusion of the natural world, as has perversely happened here; the place is a parable.

How more fittingly could men perish than in producing a lake so magical?

'High time to go home,' he announces.

As they descend from the bluff, James kicks something from the lakeside soil; a lump of something shiny and dark. He picks it up.

'*Waro*,' explains the *tohunga*. 'When the great *taniwha* shaped the Porangi and its tributaries, angrily blundering this way and that, its blazing breath sometimes charred the land. Leaving behind the substance you see. Interesting but useless.'

James, who suspects otherwise, pockets the lump for Herman's later consideration, and then forgets it. He has largesse more dazzling on his mind. He looks wistfully at *Santa Ysabel* as they pass it on foot, recover their canoe, and paddle away.

Upokonui finds James poor company the rest of the day. There is a lack of large conversation, and the boy's attention span is short. In the end it is a relief to be rid of him.

That night, back in his own hut, James broods. Like most men, in most times and climes, he has the misfortune to need to show something for his life. What he needs to show for his life, at this moment, is *Santa Ysabel*. More than divine discontent; divine duty. The world should share his wonder. His upriver exile need not have been for nothing. He, James Lovelock, need not have been for nothing. It might all be selfless sacrifice. But there might also be a measure of glory. More, much more, than in any mere sexual consummation, though the preliminary sensations which James is experiencing are not dissimilar.

Next morning, in dawn's glow, he paddles his own canoe up the tributary creek, rather furtively, hoping not to glimpse a suspicious Upokonui over his shoulder as he travels. Aboard he has an axe and other tools which might prove useful to his purpose. The air is chill under the reddening sky. But James is blind to the beauty of the morning, the swarms of migratory birds above the hills. The fossil forest, still more eery in the early light, gives him no pause. He has sight for nothing but *Santa Ysabel*.

It is still there. It is not, after all, a mirage of Upokonui's playful making. Water whispers about the wedged hull; there is a rustle of wings upon the verdant deck. James feels visceral awe again; he hardly dares breathe, lest all disperse. Finally, though, he climbs from his canoe and considers, as calmly as he can, the practicalities of getting *Santa Ysabel* on the move again, after near three centuries static. It is a task which, at first sight, might appear too daunting for one man. But undaunted James has never been less than an inspired lover; and there has been no love object in his life more calculated to excite inspiration than *Santa Ysabel*. He theorizes that, by doing a certain amount of damage to the dam built up behind the bulk of *Santa Ysabel*, he might release sufficient water from the lake to lift the vessel from the bed of the creek. With a shiver of expectation, he already sees the ship soaring toward some civilized harbour. Neither lack of sail nor likely disrepair of any means to manipulate the course of the craft disturbs this momentarily engulfing vision; such detail is seldom the stuff visions are made on.

The sun rises; the day warms. So does James. Teetering from log to log, he chops, chips, at the obstinate dam to which *Santa Ysabel* has given birth. The sound of his axe echoes over the lake waters behind him, and the wading birds take wing. He tosses limbs of trees aside; he hacks trunks apart; he levers rock away. As morning moves toward noon, his long labour is not without result: here and there fresh trickles of lake water are feeding the creek, though far from enough to persuade *Santa Ysabel* to rise. Sweating and aching, he pauses to consider his procedure, and at last finds the fault. He has been pitting himself against the entire dam, punching barely perceptible holes here and there. He needs to concentrate his attack, preferably at some vulnerable point: one large gap in the dam should ensure sudden and sufficient surge of water about *Santa Ysabel*, thus testing his strategy. He begins again with blistering hands. An hour later, through his sweat, he sights success: he has cut down to a soft centre, a long rotting log of considerable girth, which begins to come apart with thrilling ease. Freed water gushes about his boots. In the press of passion James doesn't much contemplate the fact that there is most of a mile of water behind him also seeking release; that it has likewise been seeking a soft centre in the dam for a century or two.

Then he is obliged to give that fact his most urgent attention. There is a creaking underfoot, a cracking, a crumbling. It is as if the dam has decided to toss him aside with contempt. When all should be sweet triumph, all is hideous with hazard. Losing his axe, he leaps for the deck of *Santa Ysabel*; foliage breaks his fall. Elsewhere almost everything is coming to pass; it is a consummation of manic dream. Logs heave up and hurtle apart; garlands of groaning water mount wildly about.

James comprehends, not before time, that he has unleashed the lake. But that begins to seem minor. With a jerk, a long rumble, and then a drunken roll of the deck, *Santa Ysabel* rises to the occasion too, if with a shade more spectacle than even James anticipated, making an impetuous leap down the creek on the back of the battling floodwaters; a vessel of Spain's heroic age is abroad again, voyaging toward the broad Porangi. Not that James Lovelock can consider himself in command;

any such claim could be dismissed as transparently ambitious and untrue. For *Santa Ysabel* has a yearning soul of its own, certainly an unfulfilled purpose. That purpose is plainly to find and explore the unknown Pacific again without undue delay, desirably to make harbour in fabled Ophir, and weight itself down with the wealth of Solomon. No matter that the dream is dead, and mad Mendana too; no matter that the game is done, no continent won, with a hundred ships as heroic gone to an ocean grave. In this first hour of freedom from a pagan prison the feeblest soul might sing afresh. History is a nonsense yet unwritten. All still seems possible as *Santa Ysabel* bursts down the creek, landscape leaping past, a sound like thunder unrolling in its wake, to surface with authority upon the Porangi.

Certainly too much appears possible to James. The Porangi does not slow the craft, nor tame the abundant waters boiling up behind. Clinging to creeper, his foothold on the deck precarious, he watches familiar and now beloved riverside reeling past; he sees the first waves of flood surge among the tall trees, tugging out the more tender growth, flinging saplings aside, beginning to gouge great holes in the banks. The sky darkens with birds in terrified flight. At last, with horror, he observes his own refuge lost: that hut built with his own hands, shared with happiness and heartache, is gulped up by the waters to disintegrate with insufferable speed; his worldly substance becomes debris on the ebullient river. He closes his eyes. 'No,' he pleads.

Santa Ysabel is indifferent. It crashes on down the Porangi, hell-bent or heaven-sent, on course for the heads and the open Pacific.

Nine

History, that promiscuous and petty-minded mother of the muses, will maintain that the collapse of the Hau Hau rebellion was heralded by the discovery of the chief Titokowaru intimate with a woman while officially consulting Jehovah and his pagan juniors in a makeshift if still sacred house of higher learning. Titokowaru may well have been with the gods, in his inquisitive way, but the fact is that the woman with whom he has been seeking revelation is no mere camp-follower; she is a woman of rank, wife of his oldest and dearest ally, the man who happens to be his host in the tribal territory where the Hau Hau have chosen to hold off the British. True that this event causes no little consternation behind the large elaborate fortifications upon which Richard, along with several hundred sweating Hau Hau, has been labouring night and day. The woman is dragged away weeping. Some local warriors demand Titokowaru's head with loud cries. Even his long loyal followers concede that Titokowaru's doings may well portend disaster. All this, however, is nothing compared to the commotion caused soon after by the doings of Ira Dix. History, happier with the prurient, will point no finger at Ira. But the disarray of revealed adultery is of small moment beside a decimated armoury on the eve of battle. Ira, craving tobacco, has been encouraged to think by certain Hau Hau companions that the dried leaves of a native thistle make an adequate substitute in times of deprivation. Packed tight in the bowl of a clay pipe, then set alight, this thistle certainly gives off a piquant aroma, if with much intensity of combustion; there seems more flame than smoke, and Ira's last respectable velveteen jacket has been considerably singed. Left alone in the armoury hut by Kimble Bent, who has been called away to silence his quarrelling wives, Ira tires of the manufacture of still more cartridges for use against the British in the morning; his mind wanders back to his roguish ways and days in the West, when all California seemed his for the conning. With a wry chuckle or two, then a sigh of regret for that rich past, he takes pipe from his pocket, and tries again to take consolation in the native thistle; sparks rise, fall, and settle on the gunpowder stored in the hut. Ira has shuffled and dealt the last of his memories. It is almost the last of Ira.

He is found flung ten yards clear of the ensuing firestorm, miraculously intact, and revived by Richard. Concussion considered, it is no surprise that Ira does not comprehend where he is. More disturbingly, he no longer knows who he is. During Richard's nightlong attempt at spiritual resuscitation, Ira takes even his name on trust, though still with some suspicion. After all, Richard is a total stranger and a queer-spoken hombre to boot. Richard grows desperate. The sky is turning pink, then the colour of blood, and there is battle to come; God alone knows the hell ahead, minus ammunition, before the day's end. 'Hokitika,' suggests Richard vainly. 'Bully Hayes. Remember Bully?' Ira answers with a slow shake of the head. Richard plays his last card to the old gambler; he mentions St Louis.

'St Louis?' Ira asks.

Richard knows all lost. So surely is the battle. At that moment British artillery opens the attack. Mortar shells begin to fall among the Hau Hau fortifications, then into the camp; there are shouts and lengthening wails. Paramena, a companion in arms, looks into the hut where Richard remains in anguished tutorial with Ira. Paramena would be a marvel in any war; he is a one-legged warrior. While prisoner in the earlier, more gentlemanly phase of the wars, and suffering a minor leg wound, Paramena was favoured by the attentions of a British surgeon with pride in his craft; the stump is neat. Paramena's service with the Hau Hau stems from disillusion with a missionary education. The missionaries, he says, were less interested in selling Christ than in buying land; the most he learned was how to make a quick penny. Now his largest complaint is that his one boot wears out too quickly on long marches. He is forced to make lone forays into the forest, stalk British sentries with his tomahawk, and return with fresh boots; these are not necessarily the right size, which can lead to blisters, further complaint and further forays. Paramena's problems with footwear are, however, far from his mind at the moment. Loss of a leg can be borne. Loss of a head, to the bounty-hunting British, is less tolerable.

'It's no use,' he announces.

'We're surrendering?' Richard asks in panic. In this battle there is no Prussian with a promise to spare him. Richard, who still feels cheated of credit rightfully his, also of promotion by way of a lissome wife, has demolished the devil and any prospect of mercy. His head is now as detachable as any other in the camp.

More mortar shells fall with emphatic sound. There is a splitting and splintering of outer defence works.

'We're evacuating,' Paramena explains. 'Clearing back into the bush. A few left behind will cover the retreat. Bent's gone already, with his wives and most of the women; he could well finish the war with a harem. As for Titokowaru, he has just judged the moment desirable to visit some cousins considerably to the north. I suggest that, cousins or no, you may well find it convenient to follow his example.'

So it happens that later in the day, and for weeks thereafter, Richard finds himself battling through bush with a one-legged Hau Hau and a mentally maimed Ira Dix. Paramena hops skilfully along on a crutch, always with a tomahawk in his free hand. Richard is Ira's crutch. The old man is increasingly confused and querulous. There are times when Richard is tempted to use Paramena's tomahawk; Ira is insensitive to the need for silence. The ruthless British patrols are never far behind; they can hear shouts, and shots. They dare not risk fires. Footprints can also be fatal. Survival is best found following streams or climbing cliffs. They chew fern, flax and particularly bitter berries for sustenance. They often pass bodies of Hau Hau perished from hunger and exhaustion in the hunt. Other corpses are bloody, often with backs blasted away and heads hacked off; there are shiny viscera and clouds of blowflies.

'Is this all there is to life?' Ira grumbles.

There are mountain ranges to cross. Beyond one mountain range there is always another.

'What was it you said we used to do?' Ira groans.

There are rivers to swim. Ira cannot swim, or has forgotten, and physically impaired Paramena is not especially capable either. It falls upon Richard to ferry them to the far bank. And often the same river has to be swum several times. If suffering purifies the soul, Richard's has never been in more wholesome condition.

'If we used to do something else before, live some other way, why aren't we still doing it?' Ira whines.

The rivers grow wider, and the ranges higher. There is storm and sleet. Sharp pellets of hail sting their faces. Sun and blood-sucking sandflies can be worse.

'Money?' Ira moans. 'What is it? Who needs it?'

Richard, it might seem, has more or less forgotten too.

There comes a day when there are no longer shouts and shots behind them. Silence is a shattering discovery. They are on a hilltop. There is wild country to the west, also to the east, north and south. It might well be concluded that they are lost. Even Paramena confesses himself puzzled. Nevertheless, he begins to hop off the hilltop, and back into the bush. He pauses only to unlace his last British boot, now a shrivelled shadow of its former self, and fling it away; he continues on one bare foot.

'Where are you going?' Richard calls.

'Home,' Paramena announces.

'Home?' Richard asks.

'To make the most of civilization. There may be something to be said for it, in a melancholy way.'

They see Paramena no more.

'Home?' says plaintive Ira. 'Where is that?'

It appears to Richard that the only possible answer is the Porangi. Home, however humble, is with Herman and the Tutaekuri. After a pause he and Ira push on, taking a different direction from Paramena, presumably or preferably toward the Porangi. Richard's war is lost; but peace, particularly with nagging Ira on his shoulder, is untraceable too. Fresh rain mingles with warm tears on his face. The rest of their journey doesn't bear recounting in a reasonable way, or so Richard's later incoherence suggests.

To Marie Louise's delight, Herman returns from his upriver excursion to report James surviving as a robust if highly strung Adam in the wilds. 'There is a God,' she says, with fresh enthusiasm. She has long imagined the bones of James picked clean by carnivorous birds. Now there seems purpose in prayer.

The miracle is compounded, within the week, by the arrival of feeble Richard and a mostly mindless Ira Dix, from God knows where, though Richard can be obscenely explicit. It is all too much for Marie Louise to understand or believe. She simply sees that the famished pair need fattening. Ira's rediscovery of civilized cuisine is sensational; he sees no point in pauses between meals, now that he comprehends there is more to the world than he suspected, and is given to displays of grief whenever exhausted Marie Louise departs the kitchen. Richard is no mealtime laggard either. In any case, if he isn't fast to the table, he is likely to find Ira forking the food off his plate. He shrinks from the prospect of explaining to Ira that man was made for more than the mere consumption of food; that he is on this earth, in fact, to make money. Life is too short to explain the other appetites. The rediscovery of sex might be rather late in the day for Ira anyway. Nevertheless, the older man sometimes tries to fit things together again, if in a wandering way.

'Tell me about California,' he asks.

For he is under the impression Richard has ridden the West, not himself. Richard is tempted to embrace that colourful past as his own. As he will later, much later, for children yet to be born. At the moment, however, Richard is unwilling to act as archaeologist of Ira's era; he has things to ask of Herman.

'What happens now?' he says.

'We wait,' Herman replies. 'These are still perilous times to be on the move.'

'I can think of better places to mark time than on the Porangi,' Richard declares.

'Fate has placed us here. Fate, in its way, may be kinder than we know.'

'All right for you to talk,' Richard says irritably. 'You weren't with the Hau Hau.' There are times when the injustice still stings.

'We must also take James into reckoning,' Herman observes. 'He can't just come downriver.'

Herman, on that count, may have cause to reconsider.

'I walked through worse,' Richard insists. 'I supped with the devil, so to speak. You'd be surprised.'

'No doubt,' Herman answers, having heard much of this before.

'Now I have life to live again. I can't just sit and wait.'

'Patience,' Herman proposes.

'For what?'

'For that which, who knows, may yet reveal itself.' Herman actually has coal in mind, but so mundane a noun might impair the felicity of his pronouncement. 'All is possible with patience.'

'On the Porangi?'

'On the Porangi.'

'Then I'll be a pig's arse,' says Richard with equally visionary conviction.

In the Tutaekuri settlement, above the Porangi's mouth, there is another man of advanced years who shares with Ira Dix the vexations of memory: he is troubled not by their lack, but by their abundance. This is George, who still ponders upon the mischance of birth which made him chief. He has done his duty by the Tutaekuri, but despite half a lifetime's labour his tribe is continuing to wilt and fade before his eyes, like a flower with frost upon it. Not for the more usual reasons: they have survived the coming of syphilis and the common cold, the Bible and British shellfire. There is no large spirit in their existence; they altogether fail to see life as worth living. George, with his nobler memories, is convinced that this is not the case. It happens that he longs to see London and Oxford again, to browse in the Bodleian, to engage in bookish debate with his peers, and to see autumnal colours woven among the willows on the banks of the Isis and Cherwell once more. All this might be possible if ever he were to get the dispirited Tutaekuri off his back. But he knows that to be the sentimental dream of a foolish old man; his destiny is surely to die here among the Tutaekuri, where the Porangi flows to the sea. Contemplating old men, and the nature of dreams in general, he recalls the unusually troubling one from which he was awoken with news of the Lovelocks' landing; it is no less troubling now. He seemed to have seen Tarawhiro, his greying father, weapons of war at the ready, most incongruously in Oxford. Was there some message in that sight? Certainly Tarawhiro, prima facie, was intent on conveying one: 'You must end it,' he said. End what, though? And how? The Lovelocks then deprived him of possible answers; not that he regrets their coming, since Herman has become so rewarding a companion, but he does wish they had shipwrecked at a more convenient hour. End what?

Then, as is often the way, the two streams of his thought converge to create a near literal river of revelation. He sits stunned; a book of rather too discursive nature, treating of the idealistic philosophy of Bishop Berkeley, falls heavily to the floor. End what? End the Tutaekuri, of course. Bankrupt, too grievously indebted to its terrible past, the tribe had to be put into receivership, and not before time. Tarawhiro, possibly suffering some uncharacteristic qualms in the afterlife, could well have been trying to convey to his son that the tribe deserved to disappear like Sodom and Gomorrah, though the Bible, as distinct from missionaries, had never been much to Tarawhiro's taste. A curse, pagan or Galilean, might explain all. To be rid of the curse, the tribe must needs be rid of itself; and George thus exquisitely left free to voyage back to England and resume that graceful life from which economic crisis and tribal duty so cruelly removed him.

Shaky with excitement at the grandeur of the concept, George takes up his book again and tries to read, as a way of settling himself to more sober and practical thought. At first the print travels as perversely as the Porangi under his gaze. He persists. Diving deep, he seems to sight treasure in the very text he is scanning. Bishop Berkeley's argument, as he divines it, is that that which is unperceived does not exist; that which is unobserved by the senses has no material existence; the world is made of mind-stuff. At other times George would have dismissed this thesis as demonstrably frivolous. Now he sees it as extremely fetching. If he ceases to perceive the Tutaekuri, the tribe will cease to trouble him further; there will be no Tutaekuri. It might merely be a matter of concentration. Of closing his eyes, blocking his ears, stuffing his nostrils, tasting no food and touching nothing tangibly of the tribe; and letting posterity make mystery of the Tutaekuri.

There follow several days of disturbance for the Lovelocks. George, never noticeably eccentric until now, closets himself in a totally dark and unfurnished room with no explanation; and declines to reappear. He fails even to be tempted out by his favourite dishes, painstakingly prepared by Marie Louise, when these are deposited outside his door. The food grows cold and is carried away to be fed to omnivorous Ira. Marie Louise takes George's rejection of her meals most personally; her hysteria is heard. 'Calm down, woman,' Herman protests. 'Don't go on. George, I venture to say, has his own good and sufficient reasons.' With his wife at last reduced to moody silence, Herman is constrained to add, 'He wouldn't do it for nothing. Would anyone?'

'So what,' she asks, 'is he trying to do?' A thought chills her. 'To die?'

'Nonsense,' Herman argues. 'There are more convenient means of embarking upon the post-mortem state.' Nevertheless his mind begins to darken too.

Herman and Marie Louise move together to George's door; and stand listening. They hear nothing.

'George?' Herman calls.

'George?' Marie Louise pleads.

No answer, no sound, not even a scuffle.

'Open the door,' Marie Louise tells Herman. 'Break it down, if necessary.'

'No,' says Herman, who does his best to respect more enigmatic Maori customs. 'We must let him be. I imagine he will allow us to understand in his own good time. Try faith, and patience.'

'My life is all faith and patience,' Marie Louise replies tartly, though with tears near.

'Let me draw your attention to your fears for James,' Herman continues. 'Faith and patience were justified to a degree.'

'But he's still alone upriver.'

'In the meantime,' Herman agrees. 'But just to keep the boy out of harm's way. The devil, in his case, finds work for idle extremities. In George's case, who knows? Faith and patience, the twin virtues, may be equally rewarding.'

He takes her fondly around the shoulder and leads her away, leaving George to his prolonged experiment in perception.

Richard is soured by the atmosphere in the dwelling. 'If it's not one old bugger driving us mad,' he announces, 'it's another. We could all finish up insane on this river; it could be an infection.'

'Sanity too can be seen as an infection,' Herman replies. 'Also reality; it drives men to drink.'

'Speaking of drink,' Richard says, 'it looks to me like you've ridden a coach and four through that rum from the schooner. We'll be dry damn soon. As if we haven't enough on our minds.'

No one, however, has more on his mind at that moment than George. Surfacing speculatively into the world of the senses again, he totters weakly from his long-shut door. The Lovelocks look upon him with alarm; he is a near ghost of himself. Herman moves forward to help. Marie Louise too. All but incorporeal George shakes them off with spiritual irritation and proceeds, with still faltering step, to his front door. There that which is customary presents itself to his gaze. That is, the entire settlement of the Tutaekuri, children playing, dogs barking, women cooking, warriors idling; strong-smelling smoke from many fires wafts up blue from the raupo-thatched whares. As mind-stuff the scene is especially potent. George utters a feeble cry of something akin to despair, staggers, and faints.

There is never any explanation, and Herman feels it indelicate to seek one. It takes three weeks, and many of Marie Louise's most inviting meals, to restore George to reasonable health. Resigned Marie Louise sees that it is her role on the Porangi, perhaps unto death, to provide nourishment for skinny males; she longs for the day when she will have depleted James at her table again. Meanwhile, she makes do with little Luke. He is now a sunny seven years old, with cheeky smile, eyes always merry with mischief; his laughter has been the music of her life since James took his fiddle upriver. If half-naked Luke is not scampering here, he is scampering there, the lucky sealer's crucifix bouncing about his neck. Or he is creeping up behind her in the kitchen to untie her apron as she cooks. Or hiding himself in the house, to her distraction; he loves her hunting him out, and hugging him with relief. Benjamin and Ernest are largely indistinguishable from the Tutaekuri children, playing martial games, listening to tribal tale-tellers, or helping fishermen haul in nets. Not little Luke. His devotion to Marie Louise often has her in tears. Unless to tantalize her, he seldom wanders far from her sight. He is never much tempted by the attentions of the Tutaekuri women who lose their tribal listlessness, delighting in his angelic nature, and give him gifts; he always runs back fast to Marie Louise, to be caught up in her arms and covered with kisses. It is her deepest grief that one day, as with every male in her experience, little Luke will no longer be little, but hairy and whiskery, smelling of sweat and likely liquor too; that he will follow females with lustful eye and hot loins, not unlike poor James, all innocence lost and Marie Louise forgotten. She fills with dread; she would like time to stand still, with Luke her angel in amber forever. That is, at her worst times. At other times she tells herself that life is conceivably for the best, though with a sigh; life is growth, and growth is life, and it would be an impertinence to propose otherwise to God in her prayers. Though she often fears for his safety, she knows little Luke more liable to be lost to her through life rather than death, a displeasing paradox; meanwhile, as appears to be God's will, she contrives to make an appetizing best of the present. The future, after all, might have something to be said for it; Luke is hostage to life's need to continue, and one day he might bring her grandchildren as lovely and loyal.

George, with his wits won back, and Bishop Berkeley dismissed as a pious hoaxer, frequently sits on his veranda, looking gloomily upon the apathetic activities of the Tutaekuri. On long reflection he finally rejects despair as unproductive and unbecoming; it is, for one thing, never going to get him aboard a boat bound for England. If his tribe is truly cursed, as he suspects, it may only be a matter of making the curse function; of giving it a nudge in the most desirable direction. If the tribe cannot be wished away, perhaps it can be persuaded. So, adjusting cravat and monocle, and locating a suitable walking stick, he begins to move among his people at measured pace.

As they gather about, he states his general theme: 'Time and chance seem to be telling us something; also, perhaps, our old gods.' George sighs; he knows that rational argument, to which he is addicted, gets nowhere in human society without the irrational baits of rhetoric. But he has never been after bigger fish. 'Time, chance, and the old gods are telling us that we are but few and weak; that evening falls on the heroic soil of the Tutaekuri. The old ways are as a torn net, useless on the shore. Our old traditions are as the fish which have swum away. What message, then, can we hear whispered on wind and wave? That we are not, perhaps, meant to be. And if that is the case then it follows, as morning the night, that we were never meant to be. That we were a mistake; a most regrettable misunderstanding from the first.'

He sees his error too late. Impatience. He should have reaped a larger harvest of imagery, and not go so soon to the nub of the matter. For there is shock in the faces around. In the appalled silence, he seeks to make some repair. Given the nature of things, that is a tremendous task; what mortal wants to see himself as a regrettable misunderstanding? He now regrets that the Galileans got nowhere with the Tutaekuri. At least the doctrine of original sin would be an adequate base on which to build his polemic.

'Take my argument,' he suggests, 'as an eel grasped in the shallows of the Porangi; it twists this way and that in the hand, slippery, assuming a hundred shapes. But when we fetch it finally to the bank of the river we find it is but one shape, proceeding perfectly from head to tail. So seek not to understand my argument too soon. See it as that eel, slippery at first, difficult to comprehend. Then see it as one, proceeding perfectly from head to tail, beginning to end.'

They seem to relax. He thinks he has them again.

'It is not we who are the mistake,' he continues. 'Not we, as separate tribesmen of the Tutaekuri. No. Never.' He pauses, clearing his throat for effect in the time-hallowed way, then suddenly and dramatically points his walking stick seaward. 'We are as but birds gathered upon a rock at the great ocean's edge, together in one resting place before storm. But the storm has passed. The sky is clear. And we still remain upon that rock.'

Perhaps there is suspicion in some eyes again; he isn't sure. He has to chance it.

'Friends,' he pleads, leaning on his stick, 'think on this. When the bird has feathers it flies away. In the dim light before storm, and within the lightning flashes of the storm itself, we have seemed to see our plumage as the same colour. Now, with the sun in the sky, we can see ourselves truly. We are in reality not of the one tribe. The blood of many, in truth, courses in our veins. There is not one of us, examining his ancestry, who can still proclaim himself pure Tutaekuri. There is always a grandparent who was some alien slave. Or some outsider who married among us to seal an alliance. We fetched many women from many tribes when such was our will in war. Let us now see that past as the ebb tide, loosing its grip on the shore, in the sunset's last light. Let us not be as miserable limpets on the uncovered stones. There is no Tutaekuri. There never has been. It was merely necessary for us and others, for a heartbeat of history, to imagine it so. Let us make peace with the past, and return to the tribes where we truly belong.'

He sees bewilderment, hears sharp intakes of breath. Time, now, to press to the particular. With a flourish of walking stick, he points one by one to the people about. To an old woman he says, 'Your grandfather was of the Ngapuhi.' To a young warrior, 'You have cousins among the Arawa.' To a venerable sage, 'Your great-grandmother was of the Rangitane.'

None can disagree.

'So what does that make you?' he demands.

'Tutaekuri,' they answer as one. There is no mistaking firmness, perhaps also subversive menace.

George backs off. A seasoned warrior knows when most tactfully to depart a battlefield with a defeat in progress. He returns to his veranda seat in the autumn sun. Herman, regretting the conversational lack, notes that George's eyes seem haunted by some far horizon. He refuses all solace.

Richard too; he remains restless. 'We are rotting here,' he announces. 'Growing old before our time, with nothing to show for our lives.' To tease Ira Dix's memory he tries to instruct the old crook in the use of a deck of cards. Ira doesn't quite see the point. Cards can't be eaten.

With poker beyond Ira's mental pale, Richard plays patience, a game in which Herman might bloody see much merit. He sometimes wonders what James may be doing in upriver exile. The furtive young sod might be discovering gold, for all Richard knows. But that thought doesn't tempt him upriver to see. The inertia of the Tutaekuri is now his too. The sun rises. The sun sets. Entire days disappear with no other significant event. The world seems to be waiting for something to happen. Richard's miseries of impatience are such that he no longer recognizes that something usually does.

What happens is his old Hau Hau comrade Paramena, hopping over the dark sand dunes on the south side of the river, pausing only to waggle his crutch in agitation and call for a canoe to carry him over to the Tutaekuri settlement; he insists on seeing Richard.

'I heard you were here,' Paramena explains.

'Unfortunately,' Richard says.

'Also with a woman, your brother's wife, and children.'

'All true.'

'Then my message is this. If you all wish a future, you must move.'

'That's an argument which fails to make much headway here. Nothing moves. Sometimes I'm not even sure of the river.'

'The Tutaekuri are ill-fated. Not to put too fine a point upon it, doomed.'

'That's no news.'

'And you with them.'

'I've said that all along.'

But Paramena has information which Richard must treat with considerable respect. Its import is such that Richard rushes Paramena to George as fast as one leg can carry him. The old *rangatira*, though disinclined to acknowledge their presence, or move his eyes from that distant shore where they now reside, at last begins to listen.

It appears wise heads have prevailed among those tribes which have backed off from the Hau Hau, or declined dealings with the Hau Hau in the first instance, even to the point of siding with the British. Certain chiefs and their counsellors have met in secret to agree that, with all the wars lost the length of the island, there is a new world in the making. If not a wholly desirable world, it may not be without consolations. Seats in Parliament and knighthoods from the British Queen are in prospect. Also some profitable land transactions on the side. Meanwhile, to encourage respectability to flourish as the flax across the land, there is some housekeeping to be done; there are things to be tidied away. The Tutaekuri top the list of things to be tidied away. The continued existence of the tribe is a reminder that there is much in the past best forgotten. No chief in the conclave saw any reasonable objection to the raising of a moderate-sized war party which might deal painlessly with the Tutaekuri problem; in fact most appeared eager to participate, to provide men and arms, with old scores to be settled. To the best of Paramena's knowledge, this war party is already gathering, if not already embarked by canoe.

George takes Paramena's breathless tale impassively. He would, of course, prefer not to believe it. Then he knows that he must. His diagnosis of his tribe's condition has not been astray; he has read the dream of his father right. But having divined a curse as the correct answer is no help now, not as its very shadow falls. He has all but failed his father. Still, he has a chance now to atone for all past deficiencies in unforgettable measure. The Tutaekuri's last stand will reverberate down the generations of men in recorded legend; a tale to make the defence of Troy seem dispirited. No matter that his imagination, given his tribe's delicate condition, is vastly outracing realities: it is a moment to make a motley world seem worthwhile.

He rises slowly from his seat in the sun; he flicks away his monocle. 'My name is no longer George,' he announces to those about him. 'I am Uretika, son of the great Tarawhiro.'

No one doubts it. Herman, for one, is alarmed by the loss of his gentle old friend. 'Consider yourself a senior warrior of the Tutaekuri,' Uretika tells him with some ferocity. 'Let us see to our defence works.'

Nor can Richard any longer complain that life is without large event. 'As a veteran campaigner,' Uretika declares, in tone distinctly final, 'you shall be my second in command.' It isn't difficult to see why Uretika has selected Richard for seniority. The tribe's remaining warriors, who have to be mustered into some sort of shape, are for the most part elderly and ailing, or juvenile and foolish. To reinforce the ranks, Uretika proclaims that all males over the age of ten years are to serve.

This includes Benjamin Lovelock. A large, lumpy and slightly dense ten-year-old, who seems due in a decade to become a large, lumpy and slightly dense twenty-year-old, Benjamin is delighted; he will long remember these as halcyon days. For he is fast learning the finer points of warfare with other uninitiated children of the Tutaekuri: how to point a musket at a man and pull the trigger, how to bash out brains with a deft swing of the club, how to use sharp instruments most effectively to split the human torso; there is soon nothing he doesn't know about killing people, and he thinks he might soon be as good at it as his envied Uncle Richard. Benjamin's enthusiasm is such that it infects his small, imaginative and extremely sensitive brother Ernest. Ernest doesn't see why he should be excluded from so vibrant a pastime simply because he is a year or two younger. His complaints are heard loudly by the other Lovelocks. In the end, to promote peace in the family, Richard promises that when war begins Ernest will be allowed a small gun of his own to kill people. Pacified, Ernest dries his tears.

Little Luke is lost and bewildered in the tumult, the stampede of tribesmen here and there, other than when gathered up and carried away by Marie Louise. 'What will become of us?' she calls to heaven when Herman isn't there to hear. 'What have we come to? Who will have mercy?'

Richard has been preoccupied with essentially the same questions, if more personally, ever since Paramena, a man with a fine instinct for coming catastrophe, passed his message and hopped homeward fast, well clear of Tutaekuri territory. Richard tells himself, and anyone else within earshot, that he didn't leave Devon to die on the bank of a bloody river called the Porangi. Nevertheless Uretika is not a chief to be disobeyed, or even mildly queried; Richard has to make the grim best of his new responsibilities. He has to decide, for example, what to do about Ira Dix. Ira, like every other adult male, even men dragged from their deathbeds, has a duty. Ira would be most happy in charge of food supplies for the Tutaekuri defenders. That, however, might well mean premature starvation for the rest. To return him to his recent profession of armourer might be more fatal. Finally Richard makes Ira his personal aide. This to ensure that, in the confusion of battle, no one inadvertently places a weapon in the hands of the forgetful old fool.

Ira, though, is the least of Richard's problems. The remainder largely concern the restoration of the *pa*, a fortified hilltop, above the Tutaekuri settlement. It is there the tribe shall shelter in the siege to come. Long disused, the place is also in great disrepair; palisades have rotted and crumbled, and need replacing; outer defensive ditches and tactical inner trenches have become slight subsidences in the earth, and need excavation; derelict shelters must be demolished and rebuilt; food and ammunition depots have to be established, and latrines organized. All this falls to Richard. Uretika sees his role as mainly one of recalling the

Tutaekuri to their terrible past, and struts among the warriors as they work to boost morale with homely tales of great battles won, great deeds done, always with much bloodshed. For that matter Herman, who has noticed circumstances uncaged and out of hand again, is little help either; he neglects his warrior's work and tends to drift in Uretika's wake, wondering at the change which has overtaken his old friend, and still optimistically hoping for the comfort of agreeably adult conversation in the clamour.

In renewing the fort Richard is seldom slow to make his frustration and fury plain; his voice is a whip on the backs of the toiling warriors, a mocking sting in their souls. His finds delight not only in the inflammatory sound of his own voice, but also in his talent for perceiving form in chaos. If Karl Marx has it right, as he muddles through manuscript, and applies pen ruthlessly to paper at this moment in his distant Hampstead house, events are the making of men, not men of events. Richard might at first seem to illustrate that thesis. He has not made this event. It is nevertheless making him. It is as if, to prove the remote prophet right again, there has been some dialectical leap from diffuse quantity of endeavour to single-minded quality, with Richard's unsuspected potential at last apparent. If not always a lovely sight, his organizational capacity commands awe; his attention to detail is maddening. Uretika himself is not taxed by any decision-making at all. Richard would now be thwarted if no day of battle dawned; his growing appetite for history is not to be denied, and is certainly something which might well give the world's first Marxist second thoughts.

With the fort refurbished soon, and women in long line carrying fresh water up the hillside, Richard concentrates on lines of fire. Most of the fort is backed by cliff too sheer to scale; the enemy must attack directly from the river. Sweating tribesmen haul the small cannon salvaged from *Lotus*, the only bonus Bully Hayes ever paid, up to the fort. There it is fixed on a platform above the palisades for point blank fire down the riverside slopes. It is loaded with sharp-edged old iron scavenged from the settlement. Richard moves about the fort to check that the loopholes are similarly aligned for withering fire.

Soon everything is ready; and everyone. People file into the fort to take their allotted places. Gates are shut and barred. 'At least James is spared,' Marie Louise observes, and then adds by way of prevision: 'He will outlive us all.' No one can find cause to contradict her. She weeps briefly, hugs little Luke, and carries him to a hut.

Richard has constructed an observation platform, a command post, with unobstructed view of the river's mouth and coast; he leaps up there nimbly, to be followed more heavily by Uretika and Herman, then

Benjamin and Ernest as runner boys, and Ira in whimpering quest for nourishment. Marie Louise remains hidden in the hut with Luke. Uretika instructs the men of the Tutaekuri to anoint themselves with canine excrement in the time-honoured way of their heroic forefathers; Richard, by way of compensation, orders an extremely moderate issue of rum.

'There will be no surrender,' Uretika announces. 'We will die as one. The tree does not grieve when the birds have flown.'

'Balls,' says Richard. 'Who's bloody dying?'

'When the frost is on the fern,' Uretika continues, 'the frond knows when to wither.'

'Those fuckers are never going to make it up here,' Richard insists.

'When the tide takes the rock, there shall be no sorrow.'

'The buggers will be sorry they ever came.'

'Better to die as the hammer-headed shark than to live as the cringing octopus.'

Tactical differences between Richard and his commander-in-chief are apparent. Uretika, arms extended, appears anxious to embrace any bullets offering. Richard realizes, with no little chagrin, that the old bastard is likely to give his all to avert a decent victory. With his longing for defeat and sublime death, Uretika is even more a liability than Ira; and God knows starving Ira is becoming a considerable pain in the arse upon the command platform. Any moment now and Herman will weigh into the chorus with an impenetrable discourse on the nature of human circumstances.

'Canoes,' shouts Benjamin, cheerfully first with fatal news.

'What's that?'

'Canoes coming. Look. Lots and lots.'

There are indeed.

'My God,' Richard says. There are more canoes travelling along the coast, toward the Porangi, than Richard desires to count; their long hulls, each holding up to a hundred warriors, make stark shadows on the sea.

'Can I have my gun now?' asks sensitive Ernest. 'Can I have my gun to kill people? Please, Uncle Richard. Please.' He begins to cry.

Uncle Richard simply doesn't hear. 'My God,' he is still saying. 'My God.' No one has ever heard Uncle Richard pray before.

Still more canoes are coming into sight along the coast. It seems few tribes have spared themselves in contributing men and craft for a brief if lively campaign against the Tutaekuri.

'They bringing food?' asks Ira with interest.

Herman is heard, if faintly, conceding that circumstances have taken a more serious turn than he supposed.

'Please let me kill people,' weeps Ernest.

'Shut up,' says Richard tragically.

Drawn by the outcry, Marie Louise leaves Luke peacefully asleep in the hut, and climbs on to the platform beside her menfolk. She has only the one observation to make. 'James,' she says with confidence, 'will see that our remains are disinterred and receive a decent Christian burial.'

Loud wails of premature mourning rise from all corners of the fort as tribesmen note the number of the enemy. For Uretika, however, proud upon the command platform, it is a sight which might be sought for a dozen lifetimes. Fate could not be collaborating more fervently to make this a deathless day, at least in legend. Let the hosts be loosed upon the shore. Let them see how tenaciously the Tutaekuri die.

As the warrior-laden canoes lift over the surf to sidle swiftly into the river, a certain old Tutaekuri woman remembers her grandfather of the Ngapuhi tribe with great affection. A young warrior recalls his endearing cousins among the Arawa. A venerable sage contemplates his descent from Rangitane. They and their many kin find a small gate near the rear of the fort conveniently easy to open. The trickle homeward to the tribes of their forefathers, through that gate, becomes an impressively quiet tide. Very soon the only Tutaekuri warriors left at large are Uretika, the Lovelocks, and Ira Dix. The fort is otherwise empty, though they are not aware of this yet; Richard isn't given to reviewing the situation on his own side, with so much on the other side demanding observation.

The canoes of the invasion fleet are beached on the south side of the river, where warriors soon darken the shore. Presumably their commanders are gathering to discuss strategy before launching their offensive across the river. It is inconceivable to Richard that there can be much in the way of tactics to discuss. Meanwhile, warriors warm the atmosphere with war chants, calling out contemptuous greetings to the Tutaekuri, proposing inventive forms of death, and baring their arses to ridicule those so soon to suffer their vengeance. These unlovely preliminaries, though useful for morale, are not of great length. In such number, who needs morale? There is work to be done. There are more loud cries as the canoes are launched again, with warriors splashing aboard in dedicated mass. The great fleet begins to proceed across the Porangi, toward the Tutaekuri fort, in lethal array. Each canoe is crowded to capacity, and bristling with weapons. Any one canoe would be enough to overwhelm the Tutaekuri, even if Richard still had an army. He has just made timely discovery that he doesn't.

Marie Louise loses all her reservations about Biblical miracles; she closes her eyes and prays that at least Luke might be saved.

Uretika's delight, on the other hand, is undiminished. 'Let us embrace in death,' he calls. 'The fish has no hope in the beak of the shag. But the fame of the brave rests on only the tallest mountains.'

He is slow to discern that he lacks a large audience.

The canoes fan out upon the river, a flight of amphibian arrows hurtling toward the Tutaekuri fort. Ira Dix is briefly aroused to the harsh nature of the non-edible world; he plucks at Herman's sleeve. 'Those buggers,' he suggests plaintively, 'aren't on a picnic, for a true fact.'

Ira cannot seem to make himself heard. For at that moment James, aboard *Santa Ysabel*, with muddy flood still in full force behind him, makes his ungentle return downriver. Not that James is conspicuous to the onlookers. He is still hidden in the tiny forest atop *Santa Ysabel*'s often oscillating deck, fighting his way fore and aft, slashing through foliage with a cutlass, trying to see where in hell the vessel is headed. As the flood meets the mouth of the Porangi, it has more room to spread itself, to give vent to pent-up pressure; tall waves soar from shore to shore.

Concentrated upon making speed to the north side of the river, there to dispatch the loathed Tutaekuri to the last woman and child, those aboard the canoes take no heed of this spectacle until they find themselves participant. Which is not to detract from *Santa Ysabel*'s appearance. Those of the war party are given little time to recall the legend of the Porangi's creation; and none, in any case, would likely have known of Upokonui's ill-received prophecy. Nevertheless, at the top of that murderous tide, nothing less than nightmare, with silvery belly and greenery streaming from its back, is unmistakably the *taniwha* of the Porangi thunderously riding a river in riot. That this vast creature appears to bear some pale and ghost-like warrior with sword only makes their last earthly vision the more dreadful.

Then all is tumult. The *taniwha* crashes over them and the flood flings up canoe after canoe in its path; the shattering craft spin high, shedding their occupants as lightly as leaves. The flood roars on with great indifference. So does *Santa Ysabel* bearing James aboard. Those watching from the fort see the battle settled within seconds. For James, however, nothing is finalized, especially his fate. In the sand bar beyond the river's mouth, the flood meets its first substantial obstacle since departing the wilderness; it swings out on each side, sending *Santa Ysabel* into another spin and at length on a course inconsistently parallel to the coast north of the Porangi. It is likely the last coast *Santa Ysabel* will ever see; it is certainly a last chance for giddy James to try his luck on land again. He regrets that he cannot keep the cutlass; he shall be more than content with his life. He leaps from *Santa Ysabel*. As the tide takes him, and tumbles him over and over, the vessel continues into the Pacific with much momentum and unslackening pace. For the next decade sightings of a floating forest aboard a Spanish hulk are to be reported by superstitious skippers, some of whom later prove insane. Then, presumably with its duty done upon the unknown ocean, this last manic vestige of Mendana's vision – and perhaps, God's mercy, of his devilishly tormented soul – departs this inexplicable plane for another, purer Pacific.

James, for his sins, is bounced brutally upon a black-sand beach. He rises, staggers a step or two, and falls. Largely in this fashion, he progresses along the coast, back to the Porangi.

While his very personal drama diminishes, those in the fort are still marvelling at the miraculous manner of their salvation. Herman feels the point sufficiently made that they have been preserved for higher things. Uretika sees that long-exiled Upokonui might, on balance, have been treated unjustly for his prophetic gift. Their deliverance is seen as an act of God, not as an act of James, and most might be irritated if informed otherwise. With so much else to see, no one has noticed him passing by aboard *Santa Ysabel*. That is, aside from Ira Dix, a demonstrably muddled man, always liable to be distracted by insignificant detail. 'There was a bugger aboard that boat,' he asserts. 'I tell you, for a true fact, he was waving a sword.'

'Nonsense,' says Herman. 'Besides, on reflection I am inclined to the belief that we might have imagined the boat. Call it hallucination, if you will. Such things are commonplace in crisis.'

'I saw it,' Benjamin argues obtusely. 'It didn't look too commonplace to me.'

'And there was a bugger aboard it,' Ira insists in his wearisome way.

Herman sees that, miracle or no miracle, he must still suffer fools.

Tribeless Uretika gives it to be understood, in most gentle voice, that he should again like to be known by the name of George.

Richard, at first as relieved as anyone, nonetheless feels some frustration at not having even one chance to test his lines of fire. He is not the only one who feels cheated. All are suddenly shaken by the crash of cannon. Marie Louise cries out with terror as old iron chews up hillside some distance down toward the river. Eight-year-old Ernest, never given a smaller gun, has just proved himself able with artillery.

'I killed them all,' he claims.

Sure that the sound must have woken Luke at last, Marie Louise hastens back to the hut where she left her child. There is a vacated bundle of blankets in the hut. No more. She is unwilling to believe it. The little scamp is surely hiding from her again, and doubtless from the commotion. 'Luke,' she calls in lighthearted tone. 'Where are you? Come here.' She darts from hut to hut, to see just where the impish boy is concealed. All are empty of Luke. The entire fort is empty of Luke. She begins to scream, and scream again. Herman is quick to her side, soon George and Richard too. 'He's gone,' she sobs. 'Gone. I prayed to God that he be spared, and God has taken him away. Perhaps because he was too beautiful for this world.' In the light of events, and in the wake of the flood, Marie Louise appears to be implying that God doesn't know what His left hand is doing while His right is at work. 'While we were up there, He answered all prayers, large and small, and took Luke away.'

'Talk sense,' Herman says sternly.

But Richard is fast to a less imaginative explanation. 'He went with the tribe,' he suggests. 'Some childless woman saw her chance and grabbed him, no doubt.'

'I'll be damned,' says Herman, with wonder.

'She will be,' Richard promises, 'if I get my hands on the bitch. Which I bloody will.' He buckles on a cartridge belt, and grabs up a carbine.

'What are you going to do?' Herman asks.

'What I must. Then bring Luke back.' His talent as tactician unproved in pitched battle, Richard now deeply desires to put more primitive skills to the test. A second bite at the apple might reveal more flavour, particularly with an efficient firearm. He sets off toward the gate through which the tribe shamelessly left.

Sobbing on Herman's shoulder, trying to comprehend that Luke might still be of this world, Marie Louise calls to Richard, 'Have mercy. Whoever stole him away must love him too. Remember that.'

Richard replies that he will keep his own counsel. Then he ducks out the gate and is gone.

Attempting to comfort Marie Louise, Herman at last becomes intimate with distinct agitation in his own tear ducts; something congeals cruelly in his chest and finds violent outlet in his throat. The echoes of that howl linger among the hills of the Porangi, seemingly in search of residence there. George and Ira shuffle about softly, baffled, in quest of the best thing to say. Benjamin and Ernest look with awe at their father and stricken stepmother, and presently begin lamenting too. They understand that little Luke is lost, perhaps forever. For the Lovelocks deliverance now seems tawdry, far from divine; all is disaster.

*

When James rejoins his kin, toward the end of that long day, he finds they have no interest in his spirited return from exile. They have ears for nothing save news of Luke. That must come, desirably along with Luke himself, upon Richard's return. But Richard doesn't return, not that day, nor the next. It seems a poor omen. Marie Louise passes beyond pain into delirium. George's house fills with desperate silences, all conversational openings stillborn. Herman sits with head buried in his helpless hands. Even Ira understands it tactful not to discuss meal times, or complain about the quality of those which James serves. James does what he must to keep the family functioning, controlling his own despair in menial tasks. Now and then, when he keeps watch by her bedside, Marie Louise reaches out for his hand. Once, in a lucid moment, her thought is his own. She says, 'Sarah.'

'Sarah?' he asks gently.

'She came to me once. Yes, from the grave. While Luke lay on my breast.'

'It's all right,' he insists. He doesn't wish more.

'She came, she said, to give me courage. Comfort and courage. I didn't understand. Now I know why.'

'Don't,' James pleads. 'Don't make it worse.'

'Nothing can make it worse,' she tells him. 'Sarah knew.'

'There are other lives to be lived,' he suggests.

'Whose?' she asks. 'Not Luke's. Not mine. I wish only to share the grave with Sarah.'

For a time that appears likely too.

In the end, which comes after a week or two, Richard arrives back on the Porangi. His face has been ravaged by the wilderness; his clothes are filthy rags. He is without Luke. Sitting on George's veranda in the weak sunlight of the season, still breathless, he tells of roaming mountain ranges into the rugged heartland of the island, of following all the tracks the onetime Tutaekuri might have taken. Their footprints, where autumn rains had not washed them away, suggested several directions; there were many small prints, indicating children of tender age, but naturally none identifiable as Luke's. Once he caught up with a couple of stragglers, old people, who even at gunpoint could tell him nothing of a Lovelock child. He had no cause to use his gun on them, on anything or anyone, unless this accursed country. Luke is lost. Lost and bloody gone. And Marie Louise, he adds, is best told now. Also told to suffer no illusion.

This isn't necessary. As he finishes, all look up to see Marie Louise feeble in the doorway behind Richard. She appears, if they read her stiffened face right, to be denying tears. 'I have the courage which Sarah gave me,' she informs them presently. 'Not my own.'

None, in the ensuing silence, can find this plausible. Herman takes his wife in his arms.

'So where's the bloody rum?' Richard asks.

Ten

Cruel winds of winter gust in from the ocean; rain seeps from surly skies. Marie Louise mystically reverts to her original proposition. God, she says, has taken little Luke away, having work for him in heaven. Herman does not contest this as a theological improbability; he offers no opinion. Nor does Richard. Having seen enough hell, he suspects hunting through heaven for Luke might be equally thankless. James, who might have had much news for all of them, though not specifically of Luke, is mostly and pensively silent; his exile upriver is of another life, perhaps even of another James Lovelock. That is, until he empties a trouser pocket and comes upon a dark and irregular lump of souvenired landscape; he drops it in Herman's palm.

Herman gazes at it with wonder. 'Coal,' he pronounces at last.

'What I thought.'

'Where?' Herman is tense.

'Upriver.'

'There's the sign,' says Herman.

'Sign?' James, at this time, can find no serviceable portent in coal.

'The sign we needed. Timber on the hills. Iron on the beaches. Now coal upriver. We were fated to finish here.'

'We damned near did,' Richard reminds him. Richard has been at work on the wreck of *Lotus*, heaved on to high ground by the flood, when winter allows him. He has the idea of sailing somewhere, if not home to Devon, then to somewhere respectably enriching. He still has much to do with his life. The rest can rot, if they wish. Not Richard. If he can float the schooner, and inculcate obedience in the craft, he already has a paying passenger to the first port; George. George sees the very name of the vessel as auspicious: didn't Iamblichus argue that the leaves and fruit of the lotus represent the motion of intellect, not least in the way the plant rises to grace from the mud of the material world?

For George has been confiding to Herman, and soon confessing to all, that his oldest and dearest ambition, especially with the chill of age in his bones, is now possible of realization. He can depart the untidy shore of his Tutaekuri ancestors. And he can revisit the charmed haunts of youth in England again. He longs to saunter through another soft English summer before he dies, to have his fill of larks and meadows and mellifluous brooks; to take Madeira in a cosy book-lined Oxford room, while burning logs aromatically crackle.

'You'll come back, though?' Herman asks.

George is vague. 'Perhaps, yes, I shall come to final rest on the Porangi. Who knows? It may be a pleasant place to retire. But meanwhile it is my experience that the spirit of inquiry is an unwanted guest in the South Sea. This is a land for rude health. For brawn, never brain. Much, I might add, to my personal regret. I must make my peace with the world elsewhere.'

Herman has cause to envy anyone's prospect of peace. There is none in Marie Louise's mourning face, and consequently little in his life. Their odyssey has become an Iliad of woe. Her sleep is restless with dreams of lost Luke; his own seldom satisfies.

'You are welcome, of course, to stay on here,' George insists. 'On the other hand, I realize the river may retain too many unhappy memories.'

Herman has been inclined to go along with this assessment of the Lovelock situation. Coal, however, gives the Porangi a different complexion. He holds it cupped in his hands like a crystal ball, in search of the future there. But black resists reflection; vision has to be of his own making. He who would eat the nut must first crack the shell.

'We are going to stay,' he announces.

'Stay?' Richard says.

'Here. Or maybe upriver. Anyway on the Porangi.'

'I might have bloody known,' Richard storms.

James, trying to look on the brighter side, which is mainly in murk, has no evident objection.

Ira is chopping wood outside. He is rapidly regaining the complex world with the discovery that wood is a prime requisite for the provision of heat and the preparation of food. Without wood there is no heat, no hot food. Work, thus, is necessary to maintain supply of wood. So a small mountain of chopped wood, with a few foothills, has risen beyond the door of Marie Louise's kitchen. Ira presumably would understand coal, probably greet it with glee, since it would free him to explore other faces of reality.

Marie Louise is last to make comment. 'If we don't stay here,' she points out, 'Luke will never know where to find us again.'

Herman is tempted to observe that if God has indeed taken Luke away, as is her current hypothesis, then He should have no problem returning Luke to any point on the planet, if such is His will. He doesn't, however, observe anything of the kind. Her argument, if not her logic, is unanswerable. Even Richard would not risk suggesting it other than conclusive. Not with Marie Louise's face haunting them all.

In losing Luke, then, they seem to have found the Porangi again.

'That settles it,' Herman points out. He looks at George. 'In this matter of land,' he begins.

'No problem,' George says. 'Take it.'

'We can't do that,' Herman says honourably.

'Most of mankind, so far as I can observe, is in the habit of grabbing land, desirably under cover of an enlightened crusade. Let us dispense with subterfuge and preliminaries; I prefer not to fight.'

'It's your land, nonetheless,' Herman persists. 'Here and upriver.'

'Technically,' George agrees.

'Traditionally,' Herman suggests.

'Tradition is the last refuge of the mental pauper,' George replies. 'Take it.'

'It's not right. Not like that.'

'Preserve us, Hermes, from Galileans afflicted with the sense that there should be rightness in the world.'

'For some it is hard-won conviction,' Herman says defensively.

'So I have, alas, observed. Far be it from me to note that the Nazarene carpenter finished on the cross. Never mind. I was young myself once. For your peace I shall retain this end of the river, and the house, for my retirement from the vexations of mental strife, if I live that long. The rest of the land, upriver to the Makutu Falls, is yours. I shall prepare a document deeding it to you in recognition of your services to the Tutaekuri.'

'But there is no Tutaekuri.'

'Exactly.'

'I must pay you something.'

'I also prefer not to be paid off.' George is revisited by the memory of Mr Thomas Pringle doing just that with bright new English banknotes. 'The giver and the taker are demeaned.'

'You may need more than a little to get along in England again. Things have changed in forty years. Prices too. You might be surprised. Nothing's the same.'

'So the freemen of Athens said after the death of Pericles. It's an old complaint.'

'You may find it more than an idle one without the wherewithal. Take our money as token.'

'Of what?'

'Services to the Lovelocks, say.'

'That is more difficult to resist,' George admits, with mellow smile. 'But I wish you a more handsome harvest on the river than the Tutaekuri. May you never become a mislaid tribe.' He pauses. 'There are times, you know, when I'm damned if I don't miss them all. The old days weren't all bad. Life sometimes had its lighter moments even if they were blurred by black hours. Doom doesn't come in a remarkable range of shades. One had to keep at it, as always, preparing for the worst and hoping for the best. And the best is an infrequent visitor to any human community. Yes, by the way, I'll take your money.'

With peace apparent upon the wintry coast, a cautious skipper manoeuvres a large trading schooner across the Porangi shoals. Conspicuous among his crew is a one-legged Maori. Paramena greets his old comrade Richard with much passion. 'I've been trying my luck here and there,' he explains. 'I even put in for a war pension.'

'Oh?'

'The government turned me down. Wrong side. So it's come to this. Commerce. Buying and selling for rather paltry profits. One can't pick and choose in peacetime. If the boot fits, wear it. Still, my position aboard is more than it seems. I'm a trade adviser. Working on commission. The skipper thinks an old Hau Hau a safe bet in the post, with the battlefields still cooling.'

Paremena is led to Herman, who arranges purchase of provisions. There is suddenly rum in abundance, and tobacco, among other appurtenances of the civilized life. Herman mentions the coal James discovered upriver.

'Fascinating,' Paramena agrees. 'I'll see the information is passed to the right quarters.'

'You mean there might be money in it?' Richard asks. His contempt for coal, perhaps, has grown from grievance with Herman.

'More than a little,' Paramena judges. 'The way things are, with settlements steaming up around the country, railways too, coal's in much demand. In places it's scarcer than gold.'

Richard finds himself, almost imperceptibly, reconciled to the Porangi.

'We may have need of it ourselves,' Herman interposes. 'I am taking into account the iron in the sand here. And the eventual prospect of smelting it for beneficially productive purpose.'

'Ambitious,' Paramena suggests.

'In the circumstances, no more than necessary. What is a new land for?'

'You have me there,' Paremena concedes. 'Last time I looked, it was old. Or moderately middle-aged. But then I lack a civilized vantage point. Meanwhile, I might point out that you have some nice lines in fine timber back in the hills. It was all wasted on the Tutaekuri.'

It is far from wasted on Ira, noisily hacking up half a tree in search of the symmetries of the world, though Marie Louise insists they have far more wood than they need for the winter.

'Timber is also within our purview, like coal and iron,' Herman says with patience. 'The significance of the three resources isn't lost on us.'

Paramena is only willing to be lost for a moment. 'All in all,' he assesses, 'I think this may have been a profitable encounter. I might be back to try my luck on the Porangi with you. Who knows? You may need someone with a head for business. I have no desire to succumb to the temptations of the pillow smoothed for the head of the perishing noble savage. And frankly I don't see a future in trading schooners.'

George, however, sees his future coming to pass with the arrival of a seaworthy schooner. He purchases a passage to the nearest port; there he should find an England-bound boat. With some remorse, soon overcome, he looks for the last time on his ancestral land; his eyes mist.

'It was ever the fate of man,' he observes to Herman, before boarding the schooner, 'to be torn between worlds. That which is here, and that which is elsewhere. Between past and future, the known and unknown. In my case it is simple enough. I am homesick here. I shall, no doubt, be homesick there. In the vast and rather laboured writings of Voltaire, you may recall, it is asked if the inhabitants of that country called New Zealand, the most barbarous of all barbarians, were baptized. The answer is that this was still unknown, but that the Jews, more barbarous in their time, had two baptisms, of justice and of domicile. Alas, that suggests the hazard in my condition. George I am and shall be. But Uretika still resides in a nostalgic corner of my heart. There is no justice. And I seem, at this poignant moment, to have no secure domicile.'

'We shall always be glad to see you back,' Herman observes practically.

From the deck of the schooner, after further lengthy leave-takings, George looks upon the Lovelocks arranged sadly on the shore. He waves with affection as they dwindle into the landscape, finally hidden by headlands and hills. Then he faces wind and sea, his long journey begun.

Most of its consequences might be left to the imagination, but nevertheless some detail is necessary in any narrative. In time, after surviving shipwreck and starvation on a sterile African shore, George does make landfall. England explodes greenly about him again. Still dazed, he makes his way through London to Oxford. But Oxford, like London, is a place of busy strangers. His favourite tavern has been invaded by a rougher breed of student than he remembers. Everything has coarser complexion than memory proposes. He inquires after his tutors. They are, without exception, long dead. With much reverence he visits their graves in mellow and shady churchyards, and conducts conversations of a one-sided nature. It proves impossible to regain a place, and a room, in his old college; people appear bewildered by his plea. The librarians of the Bodleian, caretaking the treasury of books he craves, cool to his presence. He is often seen, lips moving in silence, walking among willows on the banks of the Isis and Cherwell. It is perhaps symptomatic that passers-by and picnickers now shrug rather than stare.

With some heartburn he sees that the nineteenth century is not, at this juncture, on his side. To fight history is hopeless. The world is now well known, the improbable commonplace. He is no longer an engaging and mystical novelty from the dark side of the planet, one to whom most doors opened. Now all doors seem shut. Newspapers have no interest in him, nor the nobler families of England. His landlady in the poorer part of Oxford, not quite having caught up with history, has opened her door only on condition that he pays a month in advance and engages in no pagan practice, a rule to which he submits, even hiding his Homer; her roast beef is of inferior quality, when she serves beef at all, and there is no Madeira at table. She begrudges him the oil in his lamp when he stays awake reading long into the night, attempting to edify and instruct himself with the volumes he has purchased in abundance from booksellers who find him a most profitable customer; they alone in Oxford have a smile. But that is small comfort in a cold world. Prices are indeed higher, and even the Lovelock largesse is soon giving out. Soon there is more at ebb. He begins to recognize, with considerable grief, that there is now no news in any book. He has shared the wisdom and folly of most men, and seen and known more than but a few. Books tell him nothing with which he is not intimate. It is self-indulgence to continue confirming his despair of the human condition. When this revelation arrives, he tosses his books aside much as an adult might discard the things of infancy. Confused, he begins to wander widely, not infrequently far beyond Oxford. In exhausted and depressed condition he is found on a roadside one day by some carnival folk on their way north to keep an engagement. They are greatly and cheerfully taken by George, who in turn finds them tolerably pleasant company in the inn where they lead him. There is no harm, he concludes, in a little merriment; there might be worse fates. So it happens that the still innocent citizens of such places as Hull and Halifax soon see and hear George, often in affable mood, within a tent which outside bears the colourful legend 'The World's Last Cannibal Chief'. This is transparent untruth, as George is first to observe, but he is not one to allow fruitless hair-splitting to interfere with the natural flow of commerce, especially not if it denies people laughter, tears and mystery in their lamentably brief and bloodless lives. He discovers unsuspected authority as a thespian; there is no more distinguished performer on the carnival circuit. Nor a raconteur more rewarding. The same people crowd his tent again and again, happy, sad, or simply wild-eyed, always for more of the same: for the lyrical courage, horror and farce which compose the human lot.

In his last years, he is reported prosperously retired in a Surrey cottage just outside a village of picturesque character, with several exceedingly agreeable inns in which George is wont to be conspicuous in conversations of the rural day in public bars, as well as in deeper discourse in the saloon bars. With life now seen in greener perspective, also literature, he reconciles himself to reading again, and a large library grows about him for entertainment rather than enlightenment. He even finds, for the first time, considerable divertissement in the Judaeo-Christian chronicle, albeit in barbarous Greek. He is generously given to laughter. Why not? 'Laughter,' he tells companions in both public and saloon bars, 'is an expression of love for the world. Let us take as text for the day Proverbs 17:22. A merry heart doeth good like a medicine.' To a grieving widow, later an intimate companion, he says with good cheer, 'Consider Ecclesiastes 7:3. Sorrow is better than laughter, and by the sadness of the countenance the heart is made better.' All the same, George prefers to be a great lover of the world. To the gentle village vicar, an especial friend, he says, 'Job had it all wrong. Man's argument with God is best conducted as comedy.' To the anguished village atheist, also beloved, he asserts, 'Man is too absurd to be accidental. He must be divinely inspired.' The one remaining regret in his life before his body is put to rest amid much mourning under an oak tree in a churchyard pretty with primroses is that he has never quite made it back to the Porangi to see if the Lovelocks, for their part, have made some sense of the world. He suspects not; it is a reasonable suspicion.

The last vestige of George on the Porangi is, of course, his house. It does not outlive him. Savaged by the especially vicious winter storms of 1875, when it begins to lean in disparate directions, the house flies apart in a summer cyclone the following year. Herman, hunting through the ruins, retrieves a few undamaged books. Fearing that the worst has also befallen his old friend, he begins weeping immoderately. Then he packs the books and takes them upriver to Lovelock Junction.

But that Herman is a half-dozen years away. Lovelock Junction is far from founded yet.

It can be glimpsed, if distantly, on the day Herman decides to take James and Richard upriver to determine the existence and nature of coal deposits. He is reluctant to leave Marie Louise long, but the task is no light one, as he often makes clear. He might have been about to explore the existence and nature of one of the three proofs of Providence on the now benign Porangi. Ira is only too willing to undertake more demanding domestic tasks in their absence, provided these can be shown as contributing to the web of the world; Benjamin and Ernest are both given guns. Then Herman, James and Richard head upriver in a canoe. They make faster time than James on his dreamy pathfinding journey. Herman notes that the river is deep and everywhere navigable, even by boats of more than modest proportions. Rain falls intermittently as they paddle. In time they come to the creek James has cause to view with remorse. The marvellous fossil forest can no longer be seen; it is under debris and mud. There is nothing left to show where *Santa Ysabel* rested. The lakebed is now a drab land of silt, with a substantial stream cutting a course down its centre; nothing has yet begun to grow there. The long-legged birds have gone. All is now man's for the taking. James leads his brothers up over the bluff where he stood with Upokonui and down to the place where he remembers finding coal; there are other lumps lying on the ground. Herman sees their source is in a crumbling hillside seam. He and Richard hack for some time at this seam to determine its extent. It is not, they decide, of great extent. And there are no others to be seen. The seam appears to be a freakish outcrop.

'I might have known,' Richard says in disgust.

Rain begins to cover them finely again. The earth is soon mud underfoot.

'You must admit,' Herman insists, 'this territory has promise.'

'I'll admit only that I'm a bloody fool. There's no plus in promise. What are we doing here?'

The silence is shot through with the sibilant dripping of forest trees. Mountains crowd mute and misty on every side. It does not seem an auspicious beginning for any pioneer. The rain thickens.

Herman picks at the coal seam for a few futile moments longer. 'Who said it was going to be easy?' he asks.

'I never said any bloody thing,' Richard replies. 'I never do.'

Herman offers a plan. He and Richard will hunt for coal down the south side of the river. James, more intimate with the area, can take the canoe and explore upriver. Herman and Richard will wait for James, two days hence, on the riverside. James offers no objection. He is happy to see his two brothers feud their way off into the forest; he has a mission other than coal in mind. He paddles back to the Porangi, then upriver into Upokonui's domain.

He finds the river's last *tohunga* in feeble state. The old man is at rest, though not in repose, with eyes half shut; they do not widen when James arrives at his door. 'This too was foretold,' he says weakly. 'That I should live long enough to confront you.'

He resists James when apology is attempted. 'I suppose you think I should be grateful,' he says, 'for your apparently having made my prediction come to pass. I expected you to plead, at least, that such was your intention.'

'If you like,' James says. True that he did not feel especially in thrall to prophecy the day he let the lake loose. But it seems kinder to allow Upokonui the thought.

'Think again,' Upokonui argues. 'You call down worse. Though I shall not live to see it happen; that much is clear.'

'To see what happen?' James says, perplexed.

'All again as I said. The Porangi rising. Your work will be pitiful beside it. This will be pitiless.'

'I see.'

'You may well, before the day of your death. I do see earthly turmoil ahead for you, if not the exact nature. Never mind. Understand that disaster is necessary. Man must be tamed, trimmed, as he would the world.'

'Why do I have to know all this?' James asks.

'Because a prophet is no prophet without an audience,' Upokonui answers. 'You have to make do for mine. Now, it seems, with messages passed, I must get on with dying.'

'Now?'

'Now. You do more than make an audience. You are here to serve, by way of repentance, as digger of my grave. Make the fire larger. Warm yourself. And eat what food you find. I should not be long.'

'I'm sorry,' James says at length.

'For what?'

'For intruding here. Disturbing your world. Losing that lake. Everything.'

'Men will make many such apologies. They may sometimes mean them. And then do the same again.'

'Is that prophecy too?'

'No,' Upokonui answers. 'Common sense.'

He gets on with giving his spirit strength to fight off flesh. This happens shortly before dawn the next day. With a last sigh of consummation, spirit free, flesh slack, his monumental head lolls. James wraps the cooling body in a blanket and carries it downhill to his canoe. The sun rises weak in a watery sky; the river is dark. He paddles out of the Porangi, up the creek, with the blanketed body immobile behind him. Together they pass the burial place of the fossil forest, and arrive at the silty bed of the lake. On the scrubby bluff above, where they once kept watch, James digs a grave in stony ground and deposits the body. Then he feels deficient to the occasion; he has, it seems, no ceremony. Christian words are insufficient, anyway inappropriate, and he has no reliable knowledge of pagan ritual. For a time he stands puzzled. The sun is warmer, stippling the trees with tiny lights. Steam drifts from damp fronds of fern. Birds peal lightly. He can hear the mutter of the distant Porangi as it passes out of the mountains. He has a sense of the earth secretively about its own ceremony; he is not necessarily excluded. Words, he sees, can never be wild enough for truth. And he is merely a man, which makes the marvel all the greater. Quite suddenly he laughs, and weeps, indistinguishably. When he addresses the body in the grave, he is no longer tempted toward apology; he has no regrets at all.

'Upokonui,' he declares. 'We're all born to make old bones. This world too. Goodbye anyway. Yes, and thanks.'

He fills the grave with soil and stones, then reminds himself that he and his brothers, all three, are men with a mission. He gets on with hunting coal.

He has no luck. Next day he paddles downriver to find his brothers warming themselves before a fire under the riverside trees. Herman seems a satisfied man. Even Richard is smiling. They have, says Richard, found a hill bloody black with outcrops of coal. There is probably more, much more.

'So what did you find?' Richard demands.

'Nothing new,' James confesses serenely.

Marie Louise doesn't welcome the proposed move upriver. 'How would Luke ever find us up there?' she asks. Herman persuades her that a prominent sign, addressed specifically to Luke Lovelock, placed at the mouth of the Porangi, should be sufficient to direct him upriver to his family. Luke may not be able to read, though presumably God can.

Anyway the likelihood is that, if he ever returns, he might have a literate companion of lesser status.

There are other details to be discussed. 'I think,' announces Herman, after long consideration, 'that we should divide the resources of the river between us. The river has three resources. And we are three. That, in itself, seems a sign.'

'Of what?' Richard asks.

'Success,' Herman judges. 'You, for example, can take charge of the coal. I know you'd still prefer a hill or two of gold up there. But gold gives out in a decade. Coal could go on for centuries.'

'I won't,' Richard argues.

'Our children will,' Herman replies. 'And our children's children. The later Lovelocks. Think of them.'

'They can think for themselves. But all right. I'll take the coal. What about you?'

'As the senior of the three,' Herman says, 'I feel obliged to tax myself with the most challenging of the three resources; the one which may well demand patience, initiative, and inspiration. I mean iron.'

'I see,' says Richard. 'So that leaves James with the timber.'

At this point James feels impelled to intervene. He hesitates to disrupt the rhythm inherent in Herman's design, but he has a right to be heard. He also has, though Herman may not yet be aware of it, his own life. Timber?

'I'd rather not,' he reveals.

'Rather not?' Herman is shocked.

'No,' James confirms, less diffidently, 'I don't want to take on timber. I want to farm.'

'Farm?' Richard says. 'Up there?'

'Up there,' James agrees.

'Where?'

'That's of no great moment. But for what it's worth I do have a place in mind. I don't see why I can't. There are hungry mouths. Ours, and maybe others soon. Farming's an old and honourable occupation. We did it in Devon. People need to be fed.'

Herman, thus far, has overlooked this point, despite the visible reminder of Ira early and impatient at the dining table. He concedes that James has merit in his proposition. 'Are you sure you're up to it?' he asks.

'If I'm up to anything. I can only prove it to my satisfaction. And yours, God willing.'

James appears to have struck the note that Herman needs. The knowledge he fetched from the future, which has grown confused of late, nonetheless tells him that Herman is to be treated with patience.

'James,' Herman continues, 'does right to remind us that the founding of a fresh human community is an affair of much complexity. It is something to which, as you know, I've given no little thought. Not least as to the nature of the town we must eventually establish up there. Let us tread softly. We must see this land as a last chance for the human race. And regard the task ahead with respect, perhaps with awe.'

'I'd sooner regard it with some rum in my belly,' Richard observes. 'And, by the way, you still haven't decided about the timber.'

'You'll have to take the timber too,' Herman decides. 'I have much more to consider.'

'Too much,' suggests Richard.

'You can have Ira as deputy. He should ease the burden.'

'Ira is a bloody burden.'

'You cannot deny his enthusiasm with an axe.'

'So long as I deny him the chance of felling me. All right. I'll take timber and coal. James will farm. And you, so far as I can see, will arse about. Is that the picture?'

Though Herman is at pains to put Richard right in respect of his own commitments, James sees most things as settled now; the future is about to begin.

The trading schooner calls again, and a dinghy is rowed ashore. Richard sees Paramena approaching. He has lost his distinctive gait. He no longer hops; he hobbles. Recent profits have paid for a wooden leg.

'I promised I'd be back,' he reminds Richard. ''What news?'

'Coal. By the hill.'

'I have willing buyers. North and south.'

'Tell me more,' Richard says.

Among other things Herman purchases a large quantity of canvas, for the first upriver dwellings, from the skipper of the schooner. James makes several more modest purchases, including grass seed. The schooner departs, with Paramena paid off. He works with Richard on the restoration of *Lotus*. After a time the pair pronounce the vessel riverworthy; it can carry them all up the Porangi, with possessions. On rollers, and with blistering masculine effort, *Lotus* is persuaded to take a second chance on the Porangi; there is jubilation when it is seen not to sink. Paramena claims the capacity to sail her, with Richard as mate.

'We're in business,' says Richard, and means it. All indifference has departed. The Porangi means profit.

To James it means peace. His last act downriver is to paint the sign for Luke, should he ever pass this way. Marie Louise has entrusted

James with the task as the artistic member of the family. He does his best not to disappoint; he embellishes the written word with maps, and drawings of the Lovelock family. No one could fail to comprehend it, or their love for Luke. He makes this masterwork durable. It will stand, darkly weathering, a decade or more.

To Herman, as *Lotus* begins the upriver run on a sunny spring morning, the Porangi means most of all the prospect of human perfectibility, of which more later. With his arm about Marie Louise, who at last has a wan smile for the world, he looks down at his sons; he pronounces Benjamin and Ernest pioneers. There is a silence. Ropes and sails creak. They do not understand.

'A pioneer,' Herman explains, 'is one who prepares the way for others.'

Benjamin remains bewildered. 'What others?' he asks.

'Others of our kind,' Herman tells the boy.

'Other Lovelocks?' Ernest suggests.

'Like the Lovelocks, certainly,' Herman agrees, 'but not necessarily of the same name. People, I mean, who want to make life anew.'

Benjamin thinks he has the picture plain. 'Like Ira,' he says.

'Perhaps,' Herman concedes, though he should have liked a more suitable example of the species. 'It's true that Ira's no Lovelock. It's also true that he, in his way, is a pioneer too.'

Ira is at that moment sunning himself at the stern of the boat, largely out of harm's reach, and meditating lengthily on the ways of the Lovelock kind. He cannot comprehend the need for this journey, just when he seems to have the world in fair working order again, for a true fact.

He decides there must be more to the Lovelocks than he sees. Also more to people in general. Ira is still astonished that people flourish in such variety. Some tall, some short. Some dark, others fair. Some male, others female. He doesn't see the sense in this extraordinary disarray. He might be still more amazed to contemplate the disparate aspirations of the three Lovelock brothers upon the river this morning. Profit, peace, perfection: the Porangi shall know the perils of all three. And Ira? With misty past, and perceptibly puny future, he might well be seen at first glance as a quintessential pioneer of the Porangi. On second glance, he mightn't be seen at all.

'What happens after we're pioneers?' Benjamin asks.

'That's a big question,' Herman says. 'The biggest of all.'

'We have to be something,' Benjamin proposes. 'We have to be something after we're pioneers.'

'Indeed,' Herman agrees.

'So what are we?'

'People again,' Ernest suggests shrewdly. 'Just people.'

His father, for some reason, doesn't appear to care for that idea. 'We'll see,' Herman promises.

'What will we see?'

'Something new. With people who can do justice to the new, perhaps.'

Later, alone with Marie Louise as leafy riverside washes past, Herman offers a proposition less vague in dimension. She has been talking of Luke; he would like to think her grief largely past. 'We might yet have a child of our own,' he tells her. 'It's not too late.'

'We haven't so far,' she objects.

'Settling down, so I've heard, works wonders for fertility.'

'It might need to work a miracle, at my age.'

'I am far from suggesting that a settled life produces a child by itself. We need to work at it.'

That thought brings life to Marie Louise's tired eyes; she even smiles. 'I do believe,' she says, 'you're of a mind to get on with that work right now.'

'I can think of less genial occupations.'

'I also think, Herman Lovelock, husband, this river makes you randy. The motion of the boat, perhaps.'

'More you than the river,' he argues.

She hugs him, then saddens again. 'Another child,' she observes, 'wouldn't be Luke.'

'Of course not. A child has a right to be itself, to make its own voice heard; not that of another.'

She weeps against his shoulder, but not for long.

With tidal flush, then following wind, they make fair pace up the Porangi. Toward sunset the bulk of the land blocks the wind. With sail slack, *Lotus* drifts into a sandy bay and is moored to trees; the air is cool and the birds are loud. For a lingering moment they are less pioneers than lotophagi, those who have partaken of the lotus to forget friends and far native lands and dwell in luxurious idleness. The river carries the colours of sunset. The horizon bristles with trees in blue-black silhouette. Herman and Marie Louise sit holding each other. James, Ira and the boys light a fire on the beach; the flames flicker high. On the bow of the boat Richard and Paramena mark day's end with mugs of spiced rum. Quiet voices suggest a feeling for fresh histories in them all. After a time Marie Louise feels Herman's hand moving most intimately along her upper leg. 'A boat,' he tells her, 'is a bugger for privacy.'

*

(The archivist of *The Lives of Lovelock Junction*, with his characteristic and romantic imprecision, asserts: 'Herman Lovelock made his move upriver in defiance of the odds: it was unknown territory, remote from other European settlements, and inland was country where white men walked warily, if at all, for another decade or two. But Herman's expectations were heady; apparently every prospect pleased. His French-born wife, of whom not much is known outside family anecdote, was evidently a matriarch to match patriarch and prophet Herman. He led his little band into the wilds knowing exactly where his just city might best be founded. One imagines them armed to the teeth, seeing menace in every twig and leaf, on that tense and silent upriver journey. One also imagines Herman saw the spires and towers of his town already flashing above the forest.'

Indeed: one imagines. One can share that ambiguous problem. Is life no more than facts in cumbersome quest for truth?

In fact, not in fancy, Herman has no idea yet where to found his town; he sees no spires since he has selected no site. More to the point, with the rest bunked below, Herman and Marie Louise bed together on the cool quarter-deck of *Lotus* on that last starlit night before their tomorrows dawn.)

An hour or two after sunrise, the still breakfasting Lovelocks feel *Lotus* bump lightly against the riverbank, beneath trees lately blazed by Richard and Herman. They have arrived. Ira Dix, mostly through chance, is first ashore. Interested in the phenomenon of excitement among human beings, and intrigued to discover himself sharing it, he overbalances on the bow; and falls. Luckily he finds some land. He grapples with roots while the river laps about his ankles, then hauls himself to firm ground. He is thus well positioned to take the mooring rope which Paramena passes him, as if this has been his intention all along. Ever alert to the acquisition of fresh and useful skills, he begins to bind this rope about the trunk of the nearest tree. None can contest his competence, though Benjamin has to help with the knot.

'We ought to name this place after Ira now,' shrill Ernest calls. 'He's the first to set foot here.'

Herman, who has his own ideas, feels it decidedly premature to speak then. He leaps sturdily ashore, then helps Marie Louise more daintily across the gap. The hem of her skirt flows over coarse grass, and she has to hold it higher. She peers into the dense woodland all about. 'Here?' she asks, with reservation.

'For a start,' Herman says.

'It's so dark. We need to let light in.'

'We will,' he promises.

She laughs. 'I expect it could be worse. Though not much.'

The moist scents of the forest are garnished with another, the first of man's making, that of coffee bubbling in a billy-can over a fire which Ira organizes. His axe has begun work. The place, he tells Benjamin, as he chops more wood to feed the fire, is a bloody paradise, for a true fact. Ira has lately extended his largely functional vocabulary with Richard's principal adjective; of paradise he understands only that it is a not unpleasant place to be.

For a time, the others are content with coffee while birds bounce noisily among the branches overhead. There is much to be said, and yet not much at all. Commentary is more enlightened in feathered form, from the birds linguistically at one with this evergreen land: all bells and flutes, with imaginative discords. Silences suggest even Shakespeare's native tongue deficient to the occasion. At length Richard stands.

'There is,' he announces, with evident truth, 'a hellish lot to be done here.'

Those around become aware of their human need, of pioneer purpose; there is much to be made tolerable before nightfall. Light has to be let in, and not merely to humour Marie Louise. They need space to site their first, temporary dwellings. Some reasonably horizontal ground is located just back from the river, less thickly overgrown than most. Axes are passed from male to male, in the manner of an army about to mount attack, until all are equipped. Then the battle begins. All is sound, with much fury; a drubbing and drumming of metal upon wood; a cracking and crashing. Steel starts to flash in the sun as light is at last allowed entrance to the forest floor. Through the remainder of the morning, and much of the afternoon, they harvest the first human clearing in that wilderness. Trunks are tumbled aside. Then green debris is heaped up and fired; the flame is brisk, the smoke dark and dense. When it clears, they can be seen to have claimed the sunlit sky as roof. They pause for the hot meal of meat and beans Marie Louise apologetically provides, then proceed to erect small canvas-covered buildings, using such timber as they have seen fit to loot. These dwellings are rough, perhaps, but fast adequate. Marie Louise and the boys have begun to unload possessions and provisions from *Lotus*. All has begun.

'I still think we ought to call this place Dixtown,' cries Ernest, high and persistent. 'I'm going to anyway.'

Ira appears honoured. No one, in the heat and sweat of that afternoon, has objection. This haphazard collection of riverside huts can be Dixtown for a day or two. It isn't meant to last. Nor is Ira.

*

(According to the pedantic quill-driver of *The Lives of Lovelock Junction*, 'The lower part of the Lovelock Junction, close to mine and mill, was commonly known as Dixtown. The popular belief was that the name derived phonetically from Richard Lovelock, sometimes later known as Dick (thus Dick's Town). Certainly Richard appears to have been largely responsible for the affairs of Dixtown, which would foster the misconception. To correct the record, it must be said that the name derives, beyond doubt, from an adventurous American wanderer named Dix who at some point idealistically threw in his lot with the Lovelocks. That quarter of Lovelock Junction was plainly named after Dix in recognition of his services. It seems that he once served as a sheriff in California, and so presumably was good with a gun; certainly he appears to have been remarkably rugged pioneer material. The name of Lovelock Junction itself, however, remains altogether beyond explanation.'

Which, for one claiming to correct the record, reveals a remarkably rugged lack of research.)

Toward afternoon's end the men reward themselves with rum. Herman begins to feel something missing; liquor is no answer to his need. Then he detects it. Vision has been lost somewhere in the labours of the day; he cannot see the wood for felled trees. With survival assured, their encampment moderately neat before nightfall, he sets out on solo exploration of the area. At first he blunders among huge walls of vegetation; the trees are too tall for him to see their tops. Following an erratic course, beginning to blaze trees so he can find his way back, he observes himself slowly climbing; and he hears the Porangi again, reassuringly, not far to his right. Rocks rattle away underfoot. He skids on mounds of leaf mould. He hauls himself higher with vines. Finally he surfaces from the forest; the land levels off into a plateau of respectable proportion. The stony surface makes little provision for deep roots; it is greened largely with scrub rather than great trees. The plateau takes the lemon hue of late afternoon. Even the birds, for once, seem hushed. Herman is enthralled. More so when he sees that the plateau, in fact, resides on a dramatic bluff above the river; and commands uncommonly impressive views of the country on every side. Mountains, more mountains, and the river running below. He might well be the first man upon this plateau; doubtless there has been none with more imagination in this formidable body of wilderness. With measuring tread he moves about the periphery of the plateau, estimating at least a half score of acres, much to his satisfaction. He hears voices rising, tiny with distance, from the encampment downhill. Richard. James. Marie Louise. He sits on a rock and lights his pipe.

He might be seen as tempting celestial approval. But no angel arrives to applaud. In any case, with Herman so terrestrially haunted, who needs the transcendental?

Some time later, not long before sunset and dark, when it becomes imperative to make a move homeward, he takes up stance approximately in the centre of the plateau. His eyes wander briefly about him. Nothing is out of joint here: creation has been kindly. Earth and sky, night and day, man and God, are all well met. Light, leaf and water lovingly intertwine. Intellect and imagination enmesh. Time and truth foregather amicably. Circumstances unmistakably converge. Herman will never know a moment more replete. He gives voice to his feelings in his customary manner, and for once not out of frustration. Still, the howl is startling enough as echoes boom back off the mountains.

'Here,' he announces more quietly, not especially to himself, 'shall Lovelock Junction rise.'

Part Two

The rivers and the heights were won
To greenwoods dark we brought the sun

— Iris Lovelock

Eleven

Lovelock Junction, let it be noted now, is no small rendezvous with reality. In an anarchic universe, all symmetry is precious; but finally humankind needs more than mown lawns and well weeded flowerbeds as defence against the dark. Herman, for better and worse, has this awareness in handsome measure. At times, true, he might be seen as a man muddled by the angel's message. The problem, in short, is that there has been no fine print in the apparently celestial proposition; he has had to compose his own, and this requires large leaps of inspiration. If men must learn to live again, and there is little time to lose, someone has to get on with it. Namely Herman. And with the material on hand. Namely this country he now seems to call his own. Most might find the task traumatic. It has to be conceded that Herman has known headache and heartburn. Nevertheless he knows that New Zealand, with Lovelock Junction at its heart, must be the climactic chapter in the human story, in which it is seen that the species has the capacity to pull back from the abyss; and not another melancholy footnote on the tragedy of the times.

Thus Lovelock Junction must mean what it says on literal level too. He foresees roads and railways marching over mountains to embrace it, substantial steamships plying up the Porangi to seek it out; the world beating many paths to its door. And grown men encountering adult wisdom as they walk its wide streets.

Vision can hardly dare further. Herman, however, sees virtue in doing his best with one thing at a time.

James sees less. For a while he must forgo farming to help his brothers. Richard needs tracks cut through to the coal deposits. Herman needs a path shaped up to the plateau he has selected for the site of the permanent settlement. Days and then weeks go. Cicadas makes a dense sound in the forest with the approach of summer.

Then, it seems, James is to be left in charge of Marie Louise, Ira and the boys while Herman and Richard voyage off with Paramena in *Lotus* with diverse business in the nearest European settlement, which is known as New Plymouth. Herman is in search of an architect-builder, a man who might begin to make Lovelock Junction more tangible, and Richard and Paramena have bagged coal samples to interest merchants. Agriculture has to await their return. James protests his impatience. Herman seems deaf. And Richard has no mind, now, for anything other than coal. 'We'll be back with provisions,' they insist at different times. 'And besides we do well out of the woods. No one's going to starve.'

James has small chance to explain that food is not altogether the point; his life is the point, and the land. He tries again with Marie Louise after the others have gone.

She doesn't really understand either. 'It's going to be a lonely life for you,' she sighs. 'You need a woman, James.'

He has no observation to make. It is a sensitive subject.

'You must think about it,' she insists. 'A healthy young man can't live on dream.'

He cannot bring to himself to tell her that the warning is belated.

'If you have no wish to speak of it, I quite understand,' she continues. 'But nothing would delight me more than to see you take a young bride.'

'It is not the time, nor the place, to talk of such things,' James announces finally. He spends the rest of the day shooting plump pigeon, which are wrapped in clay and baked on their campfire that night. Later, trying to sleep on his rough bunk, he is restless. It is not indigestion. The proximity of still desirable Marie Louise, alone in the hut she usually shares with Herman, is the principal cause; there is no honourable cure for his condition. His dreams are hot, and he wakes singed with sin.

With work slack that morning, and his soul still at risk, he sees chance to make a short escape from both impure thoughts and impatience. He paddles a canoe upriver to contemplate the land where he means to plant his life. He takes with him the grass seed which he purchased from the skipper of the trading schooner. It is not a long journey. The Porangi passes. He arrives at the tributary which he decides shall be known henceforth, mysteriously to many, as Spanish Creek. Some distance up the creek he beaches his canoe and begins to walk. He notes the rocky eminence which he decides shall be known as Upokonui's Bluff. Then he treads the sandy surface the lake has left.

A century or two of rich silt shall nourish his crops and grazing grasses; he can imagine his fields yellowing in the summer sun. Above the lake bed he sees an easy knoll where his house can best be built; he can imagine poplars, and perhaps oaks, shading its lawns. He begins to tremble with anticipation. Marie Louise's nagging seems foolish and far away. A woman? But he has this land as bride. Never has there been a maiden more virgin.

He fast begins to sow his seed.

(In one of his marginally less laughable passages, the scribbler of *The Lives of Lovelock Junction* observes: 'Lovelock Junction is far from the only place name to puzzle in this vicinity. Further up the Porangi, for example, is Spanish Creek. There is no record of any Spanish settler on the Porangi. The name is possibly an obscure and poetic contrivance on the part of James Lovelock, who ran Spanish Creek farm for many years. Perhaps some early amour, in the heyday of cosmopolitan Hokitika, was of Iberian origin; and he sentimentally remembered her in this way when settling down. Who knows but that Spanish Creek may not have been named for his largest heartbreak? This is not altogether idle speculation. Some stories suggest that James was a man who could be enigmatic, at times, about his past; and his later love life was not always seen to be happy.'

Undeniably an obscure, poetic and enigmatic stance to strike when the raw material of the historian remains raw and unpalatable. And, while recalling womenfolk of Hokitika's heyday, why not California Creek?)

New Plymouth, the first collection of colonists Herman has seen in years, is conducive to melancholy. Men of his own kind, sons of Devon, have founded the town and made the name a nonsense. New? There is nothing new; in three decades the town has succumbed to premature dotage. Plymouth? It is far from Plymouth, an enfeebled counterfeit. If he had misgivings about his own recent deeds – it happens he hasn't – he would lose them here. As pioneers, its people are inconsiderable, skulking insignificantly through the streets, shadowy and transient, camped in mean houses and humble gardens; and already quite bored with the business of life in a new land. They have planted themselves on the green hem of as noble a snow-robed mountain as Herman has ever seen; they have not been ennobled. Nor even faintly edified. The heartbeat of a new world is not to be heard. The streets are mainly mud and stink of blocked drains and horse dung. Few houses have grace. The merchants, those not bankrupt, are men in depression. War's end, with the termination of profitable military custom, further confirms apathy.

Politics consists of pleas to the government, religion of pleas to God. Drink means getting drunk; the boardwalks are perilous with men struggling to set sail after browsing their jib. A stranger might never guess at the large land beyond where a man might stand untrammeled by Mammon or government, and in modest intimacy with God.

Herman's distaste for the place is such that he determines to hurry his business, and tells Richard and Paramena to speed theirs too. All, after the Porangi, is meagre of spirit. First he sets out to find an architect. This isn't easy. It seems the town even at its early burgeoning best had employment for few. At its worst, as now, the only one Herman can locate is a lean and funereal middle-aged man by name of Whisker, who is erecting a warehouse of minor dimension with his own hands, helped by a carpenter or two. His breath is pungent with whisky. 'People do for themselves here,' Whisker explains. 'They knock up a room and build on as they breed. Poor pickings for the likes of me.'

He is slow to comprehend the size of the commission Herman is offering. Also he has never heard of the Porangi; it might be on the other side of the planet, and he appears to hope it might be. When that disappointment passes, and he hears the Porangi is but a few score miles up this misbegotten shore, Whisker understands Herman to say that his first need is worthy accommodation for himself and his kin; there will be more work later as a town takes shape.

'It seems to me,' Whisker says, 'that your need can be amply filled by straightforward colonial villa. Gable roof. Fancy bargeboards. Fretwork friezes. Long veranda.'

Herman goes on to describe the site up the Porangi. More pertinently, he also indicates the money available for the project. Whisker's eyes are soon less mournful. He cannot altogether believe he hears right. He tries to control his shaky hands; his accelerated heartbeat is disturbing.

'Baronial,' he gets out at last.

'What's that?'

'Baronial. It has to be baronial.'

'I'm no baron.'

'Scottish baronial.'

'Nor a Scot.'

'It's all the rage, wherever men get rich from gold. Moreover, your site sounds perfect.'

'I'd like something new,' Herman says.

'New?'

'New.'

Whisker is stumped.

'In keeping with the country,' Herman explains. 'Also something which takes the tone of changing times.'

Whisker judges that he may have an uninformed and unfashionable fool on his hands. But a fool with finance is not to be ignored. Rather, enlightened. All his life he has dreamed of building in baronial.

'There is nothing new under the sun,' Whisker says with patience, and apparent regret.

'No?'

'No. I concede that it can be seen as distressing. Classic. Baroque. Classic revival. Baroque revival. They come and go. Trivial variations. I worked, you should know, on one of Decimus Burton's finest Gothic buildings before I left London. It was my privilege, working as draughtsman, to give him inspiration. I still prefer not to claim credit. I know my profession. Also its limitations. Much as man might want to reach for the stars, he also needs a reliable roof over his head. That's the first limitation. Much as man might want to welcome the world through his windows, he also needs four warm walls. That's the second limitation. From that point the limitations become lunatic. One is in a losing battle with the nature of man. Believe me when I say you can't do better than baronial.'

'I'd still like something new,' Herman insists.

'New?' says Whisker faintly.

'New,' agrees Herman firmly.

Whisker sees the commission in hazard. He also sees more wooden warehouses. 'I always,' he argues, 'take the client's wish into consideration.'

'Something with vision,' Herman expands.

'I could build a tower,' Whisker proposes. 'Unobstructed views on all sides.'

'And space to breathe,' Herman goes on.

'Long halls. Large rooms.'

'And dignity.'

'All you need,' Whisker promises. 'This conversation may go no further.' He sees his reputation resting on the task ahead. Between humouring Herman and pleasing himself a distinctive style might surface. On the whole, Colonial Baronial has far sturdier sound than, say, Oceanic Classic, Egalitarian Gothic, or Antipodean Baroque. Men might have good reason to remember Alfred Whisker. For near two decades, ever since he came to this country, he has been begging clients to contemplate the beauties of baronial; they have seen gleam in his eye and tended to take financial fright. Herman is plainly not one to flinch on that account. This dream client merely has to be persuaded of the durability and desirability of baronial. 'I see before me,' he goes on, 'a man of integrity, substance and spiritual stature. I should like to reflect all three qualities in my design. I trust you will permit me, at the same time, to make free with my own creative gift. And especially with my imagination. Only baronial will do.'

Herman feels helpless. In architectural matters, anyway, his knowledge is slight; in demanding the new he is in an unfairly fixed fight with history and the Alfred Whiskers of the world.

'How long?' Herman asks.

Whisker feels a joyful shiver. He does not believe time especially of the essence. 'I need carpenters. I need masons. I need materials. Given those, and a considerable advance, perhaps a year or two.'

'A year or two?'

'Or three.'

'But we're homeless now.'

'Then plainly you require something in the nature of temporary accommodation. I shall accompany you back to this river to help with that problem, and proceed with my design on the site itself. Meanwhile, I have one or two trivial debts to discharge in New Plymouth. I should be most grateful if you might see your way clear to assist.'

'How much?'

'Four hundred pounds should see me clear.' Lest the shock prove too grievous for Herman, Whisker hastily adds, 'Perhaps three at a pinch. I also, by the way, am blessed with a wife and two daughters. One of nineteen years and the other of eleven. I shall have to take them with me, of course.'

'I hope they are used to hardship,' Herman observes.

'Indeed they are,' Whisker answers with truth.

Later that day, after some search, Herman locates Richard and Paramena on the waterfront, both the worse for beer, and urinating at inordinate length into the ocean. They have been celebrating their success with merchants. Several have undertaken to receive all the coal the Porangi can provide; Richard and Paramena have quoted under the price of southern suppliers. A paddle steamer is to begin calling up the Porangi in a month to take on coal. Finally, they have recruited a half-dozen men of the tougher unemployed element in New Plymouth's taverns to help work the coal deposits.

'Already?' Herman says, in daze.

'Already,' Richard says with pride.

Herman has a vexing suspicion that, in some way, circumstances are out of hand again; he should have preferred the coal worked and sold in the fullness of time. There is iron to be taken into account. Timber too.

Concentration on coal could lead to undesirable imbalance. Not least, there is the nature of Lovelock Junction to be considered: he has been hoping its form might be found before the place is peopled. Already they have Whisker, wife and daughters, not to speak of tradesmen to come; and now Richard is recruiting willy-nilly in the taverns of the town.

He hesitates to make objection. To dampen Richard's fire is to risk being stifled in the consequent smoke. 'I feel,' he says finally, 'that some consultation with me should have been in order.'

'You gave the coal to me,' Richard reminds him.

'Gave?'

'Gave. Also the timber.'

'For communal purpose.'

'My hearing's not the best,' Richard decides.

'For the common good.'

'It's worse by the minute,' Richard adds. 'I might be deaf in a week.'

'It was, in a manner of speaking, taken for granted.'

'I don't give a fiddler's fuck for manners of speaking. I say what I mean. So should you. I have the coal. And I'm getting on with it. I can't live on air up there.'

'We lack nothing material at the moment.'

'Well, maybe I want more. Much more. A woman, for one thing. A wife. I need prospects.'

'I see,' Herman says sadly.

'You're welcome to your prospects. I need my own.'

Herman has not seen Richard's needs as abundant before. Nevertheless he now has to state his largest objection. 'To live off the labour of others,' he says, 'is no adult way to begin Lovelock Junction. You will be exploiting these men.'

'In your manner of speaking. In mine, they're getting bloody good money. Four shillings, in fact, for every ton delivered to the riverside. The way things are, they're on a good thing. I'm virtually giving the coal to them.'

'Giving?'

'Then buying it back. What could be fairer? And at four shillings a ton.'

'What do you sell it for?' Herman inquires.

'Slightly more,' Richard concedes. 'But then I have shipping costs to consider. And books to keep.'

'Profit is a form of slavery,' Herman explains. 'Most of all it enslaves the man who profits. He needs more and more.'

'In that case, life's a form of slavery too,' Richard argues. 'We all need more of it. Especially me.'

'I'm speaking of the spirit.'

'I'm speaking of my risks. They're hellish high. And my margins. They're damnably low. Coal can go up in smoke in more ways than one. Today a man, tomorrow a mouse. I may yet have to be less generous than four shillings a ton in order to compete.'

'Have you explained that to these men?'

'All in good time. When they're actually upriver they shall have a more informed view of the whole situation.'

'And a long way downriver,' Herman proposes.

'Look,' Richard says. 'A new country needs men like you, maybe, but it's made to work by men like me.'

'Alas,' Herman says, rather definitively.

It is clear that Richard's conversion to an adult conception of reality is far from imminent. Perhaps it can most peacefully wait upon release of his undoubted energies.

Lotus makes return to the Porangi with ten fresh human beings harvested for Lovelock Junction: Whisker and three disgruntled females who spend the greater part of the voyage wondering aloud, in merciless chorus, where all this will end; and Richard's first six labourers, benevolently fuelled with rum by their employer, including one who discloses to Herman that their contract has been renegotiated, on arrival at the Porangi, to three shillings a ton on coal delivered to the riverside. People, it seems, have begun to supplant the pioneers.

James manages to avoid most of the commotion which distinguishes the early years of Lovelock Junction's life. For this he often and fervently expresses gratitude to God as he ploughs his land at Spanish Creek. Before his first year is gone he has raised corn and cabbages, peas and potatoes, beans and brussel sprouts. The grass from his original scatterings of seed grows dense over the rest of the fertile lakebed; he fences it in. When he judges the time ripe, he has three cows and a bull of mediocre quality brought up the Porangi on the now regular paddle steamer, and then barged on to Spanish Creek; also a travel-weary trio of pigs, two sows and a sleepy boar, and some seasick hens indifferently attended by a rooster reluctant to herald the day. These creatures fatten fast in the enclosures he has prepared. The boar is seen to have been biding its time, the rooster regains its crow, and even the bull seems less apathetic about its prime business in the worldly scheme. There is a most satisfying proliferation of creatures. From that point James is occupied with production of butter, bacon, eggs and plucked poultry to keep malnutrition at a distance from the men, women and children of Lovelock Junction. He takes no payment for his produce, much of which is delivered to the small store which Richard and Paramena have begun to run for community convenience; James prefers to abide by Herman's founding spirit and barter his foodstuffs for those luxuries and necessities which now arrive by paddle steamer. Tools and nails are among these necessities. He soon has a comfortable hut with slab walls and corrugated iron roof; its most impressive feature is the fireplace, which takes up all of one wall, fifteen feet wide and eleven deep, with a seat around the inside. Pots hang in the centre to cook his solitary meals; damp clothes can be dried; his chill bones can be warmed in winter; he can watch dreams glow in the dying coals. Though in summer he sometimes likes to sit on Upokonui Bluff at twilight, he has no visitation from Upokonui's spirit, except once in sleep, when the old *tohunga* tells him that the next world is every bit as big and bewildering as this, perhaps even more perplexing. James has no reason to doubt the truth of this message since it has Upokonui's authentically cheerless tone. When the need for conversation overcomes him, James talks to himself, even conducting arguments so loud that the animals look askance. He is never lonely, and not for a woman; the land is still sufficient to embrace. At day's end exhaustion akin to carnal conveys him away on gentle tide. Nevertheless, approaching the task of shaping some more substantial shelter at Spanish Creek, he sees that it may well be inhabited by more than a hermit in the fullness of time. It will enclose the happiness, unhappiness and hope of other humans too. That is in the nature of things. James is not one to set himself apart from the nature of things. He wishes merely to be set apart from the uncommon confusions of Lovelock Junction as it grows, and bears ambiguous fruit. On regular visits, as the months pass, he sees more and more forest felled and then fired; and more makeshift dwellings rising in that quarter now known as Dixtown. There are rails up to the hills of coal, and wagons rattling down to the riverside, so that labourers need no longer struggle down slippery tracks with hundredweight bags of coal on their backs. There is a jetty where paddle steamers moor, and *Lotus* sags at rest, symbol of travels now terminated for the Lovelocks. James has beached at Spanish Creek; Richard's energies are harboured at Dixtown; and Herman has anchored high on Lovelock Junction proper. Upon the plateau has grown still other temporary accommodation, but of more substantial and professional nature than elsewhere, containing the Whisker family along with the Lovelocks. It is a long shingle-roof, largely dormitory dwelling with veranda and an extremely thick dividing wall at its centre. This wall separates Whiskers from Lovelocks, a modification made at Marie Louise's insistence. Two women, she says, are too many in the kitchen; Mrs Whisker, whom she thinks a toffee-nosed tart at her best, and altogether unmentionable at her worst, now cooks over her own stove.

Sybil Whisker is not appealing to James either. She is a tall, harshly handsome woman with a wintry smile when at her more agreeable. She spares herself no effort to ensure that all can recognize the elegance of a lady who has known better times; the primitive affairs of Lovelock Junction are not to her taste, and indeed she sees her foullest nightmares of life in this land given form; the Porangi is the last and least forgivable indignity inflicted by her husband. When nagging Alfred, as is her inclination whenever Alfred is within view, she does not hide her light under a bushel; her voice can be heard on most parts of the plateau. She remains bitterly unconvinced by his plea that, in consequence of his commission from Herman, the Whiskers are at last in sight of that antipodean affluence for which they set sail from England. There are, as Alfred is at pains to explain to Herman, no half measures with baronial; it has to be big. And, in most ways, the bigger the better. Herman is often hard to convince, so it is necessary for Whisker to prove the point with plan after baffling plan, until Herman reels and calls a halt. Rather than confuse himself further with the qualities inherent in baronial design, Herman gives himself to clearing and levelling the surface of the plateau, and making rough survey of the town to come, trying to envisage where other buildings might rise to advantage. In this task he is often assisted by Ira since Herman's surviving sons Benjamin and Ernest are having educational needs attended by Mrs Whisker, a one-time teacher. Though this is a most remunerative arrangement for Mrs Whisker, she finds much occasion for despair. The boys, she declares, are downright savages. Her daughter Iris, with whom the boys are obliged to endure their dull lessons, is by contrast never less than demure and obliging. When Mrs Whisker is elsewhere, having discovered urgent need to give her husband another piece of her mind, the boys delight in alarming Iris with tales of their particularly bloody deeds as Maori warriors; she wails most rewardingly. When paroled from crucifixions of arithmetic and English grammar, the two boys tend to wander away from the plateau in the direction of Dixtown. Life seems more enlightening there; it is tinctured with spurts of dark dust and the oaths of blackened men hacking sweatily into the hillsides, filling wagons of coal, or gambling rowdily outside their bachelor huts.

Ira, who once might have been seen as unofficial mayor of the quarter, is now seldom visible in Dixtown. He takes offence when Richard roars, as Richard often does, and more and more keeps Herman company on the plateau, clearing and pegging out the prospective streets of the town. To the best of his knowledge, Ira has seen neither town nor city, though Richard has told him of some place named St Louis; he finds the concept of humans grouped in bulk quite fascinating, even if he fails to see the point. For one thing, humans in number might make for scarcity of food. He has to take Herman on trust in this respect, and presume revelation forthcoming. Likewise he has to assume, for example, that there is some point in Mrs Whisker departing her abode, sometimes in daylight, sometimes in dark, to meet rather noisily in nearby scrub with Richard. On the one occasion when he raised this point with Richard, merely seeking an end to mystery, he was told to keep his bloody mouth shut. This Ira has done dutifully, even to the extent of forgoing food, but clenched teeth and tight lips in truth bring him no nearer comprehension of these encounters by day and night; he has tried to relate them to the position of sun or moon on the days and nights in question, but so far fruitlessly. Also to meal times, since they sometimes sound as if they are trying to eat each other; again there is no clear correspondence. That Herman needs a town is a true fact. That Mrs Whisker needs Richard day and night, or vice versa, is a true fact. Ira has to make do with mountains of true facts, and seldom with truth. The most attractive truth in his life is that he greatly prefers to gourmandize at Marie Louise's table rather than consume aged scrag-ends of New Plymouth mutton and scraps of salt beef boiled with potatoes down in Dixtown. Though his memory might now dwell elsewhere, God knows where in this world, Ira still has residual appetite for the finer things. Marie Louise aside, James is by far the most comprehensible of the Lovelocks. He doesn't shout inexplicably like Richard, or plod about enigmatically with pegs and plans like Herman. He produces the raw materials of meals. Ira is always delighted to see James downriver from Spanish Creek, and helps him deliver his produce. Ira observes that Marie Louise is also extraordinarily delighted when James arrives. Ira finds human happiness a most pleasing phenomenon, and on balance would like to see more of it.

On one visit, not long after carpenters and masons in abundance have arrived to begin work on the foundations of the future Lovelock residence, tripling the population on the plateau, James is told by Marie Louise, 'Life is too crowded to be comfortable. I never have time to think of Luke.'

'So much the better,' James observes.

'I just have to remember him every night in my prayers.'

'We shall have to hope they help Luke, wherever he is. And hope he is happy. Hope is all we have in that connection.'

'But he must miss us.'

'Possibly,' James concedes.

'I don't like to think.'

'Then don't,' James advises. 'Keep yourself busy.'

'That,' she sighs, 'is the least of my problems.'

She has lately been implored by Herman, for example, to participate in the naming of the streets of Lovelock Junction. It is a task to provoke argument with her husband, often of prolonged nature, when she might be more enthusiastically employed in the preparation of meals for the new arrivals on the plateau. The result is often unsatisfying compromise. That is how it happens that Circumstances Crescent, in which the Lovelock residence is about to rise baronially, is intersected exactly at its centre by Rainbow Road. There are other conjunctions as queer, but none so stark. Little Luke Lane, which is Herman's pacifying proposal, leads in beatific manner into Serenity Street, which in turn gives on to Armistice Avenue, so named to mark the termination of considerable uproar, in which Marie Louise is heard proposing an early end to her association with Herman Lovelock and indeed immediate return to Hokitika. Herman has even, rather morbidly in her view, set aside space for a cemetery; she thinks it undesirable that death should be made welcome in Lovelock Junction. Herman's response is simply that he has never seen much realism in women. If Lovelock Junction fails to provide for mortality, the living may well become indistinguishable from the dead, the town intolerably overcrowded and with no future at all. The future is where Herman dwells, for the most part. He prefers to inhabit it rather than hear Whisker daily and hoarsely telling tradesmen to get the foundations right before proceeding further. Ira, clearly the most promising candidate for pioneer residence in the cemetery, though ignorant of the true fact, is frequently to be seen sunning himself on that agreeable part of the plateau; he pronounces it restful, but cannot quite follow Herman when the latter says that the grave is the only place where men can win peace from their womenfolk. Ira has nothing against Marie Louise, her cooking considered, and fails to see why Herman should so often produce howls in her presence. Men and women, especially when he takes Richard and Mrs Whisker into account too, make for the largest marvel encountered on Ira's long mental journeys of exploration: their juxtapositions, and striking differences, take on truly alpine splendour among the tedious plains and characterless foothills of human endeavour. Ira finds himself in the greatest difficulty when trying to traverse and map the territory known as unhappiness. Most mystifying is the determination of some humans to be unhappy. Whisker, for one. The more Mrs Whisker rages at him, the more Whisker rages at his workmen. He has learned nothing; he feels obliged to spread unhappiness around. This lacks logic, and should be unlawful. Thus it is even more of a relief to see straightforward James downriver to distribute happiness along with his fare from Spanish Creek.

James is impressed and appalled by the progress whenever he returns. At the store, Paramena tells him that their transactions are now to be measured in cash, which is more convenient for book-keeping purposes. 'Richard and I know where we are,' Paramena explains. 'Barter at best is a clumsy arrangement. Someone always gets the worst of the deal. It's all right for savages. A deficit can be wiped off the books with the swing of a club. Money makes things more serene.' Richard and Paramena are incontestably more serene. At Dixtown too, the first canvas-covered dwellings have given way to sturdier confections of corrugated iron and rough-cut wood, with an air of some permanence. Smoke hovers among them and rises thin blue over the forest. There are lank women about, sometimes with infants in their arms, staring with dull eyes as James passes. There is an unhealthy smell of human refuse and excrement, also the sound of blowflies in number. Cleaner air comes when he takes the track up to the centre of Lovelock Junction. Stone, manhandled uphill with ingenuity and effort, has begun to flesh the skeletal form of Lovelock House, as Whisker's baronial masterwork is already known. There are tradesmen encamped, sometimes with wives and children; bachelors find more social joy in Dixtown. Benjamin and Ernest are more likely than not being schooled austerely by Mrs Whisker. Whisker himself, when seen, provides a passable imitation of a man in advanced stage of dementia. Otherwise – excluding the Whisker girls, especially Diana the eldest, who causes James discomfort when she crosses his line of vision – all is humanly familiar. There is Ira. Herman. Richard, sometimes. And Marie Louise. He always goes first to her.

'I have news,' she confides, in her kitchen.

'Tell me.'

'You won't believe it,' she insists shyly; she seems quite girlish again.

'Try me. I am notoriously gullible.'

'I couldn't wait till you came.'

'So I'm here. Tell me now.'

'There are miracles,' she announces.

'Of course.' It is old news to James. Then excitement arrives. 'You mean word of Luke?'

'Luke?' She becomes subdued. 'No. No word of Luke.'

James feels deflated. 'Then what?'

Her eyes brighten again. 'Herman and I have tidings.'

'I see.'

'Guess.' She is coquettishly determined not to disclose the nature of the news too soon.

'I cannot,' he says.

'I'm with child,' she reveals.

'My God.'

'Yes,' she agrees. 'Praise Him. Also Herman, of course.'

'Of course.'

'He thought it possible. I never did. He has remarkable powers of persuasion.'

'Evidently.' James remains stunned.

'Perhaps something in the air here,' she says happily, 'or of the river, who knows? He promised that a child would seal the founding of Lovelock Junction. He has made good that promise. With no little effort, I might add. Your older brother is not to be underestimated, James.'

'Apparently not.'

'It makes everything different for me. You cannot imagine.'

'I can,' he insists.

'Each new morning is a marvel. Everything is blessed. The sky seems to say rejoice. All earth too. Love for Herman makes breathing difficult. For everyone. You too.'

'Thank you,' says James.

'I even find myself more pleasant with that bitch Sybil Whisker. Not always, but sometimes. Perhaps God is telling me she is misunderstood.'

'No doubt,' James says with caution.

'As for Lovelock Junction, about which I have never hidden doubt, it is all one with the miracle. I should never have doubted Herman. He is a man who needs a larger horizon than most. His dream is bearing fruit. You are to have a niece, or a new nephew. Think of it, James.'

'I will take it in soon,' he promises.

'If a nephew,' she says, 'he is not to be thought of as a substitute for Luke. Or another Luke.'

'No,' he agrees.

'It would be unfair. There was only one Luke.'

'True.' James observes she has now moved Luke to the past tense, as if dead.

'No child could be expected to compete with Luke,' she adds. 'And none will.' Tears brim; she still smiles.

James places an affectionate arm about his sister-in-law. 'It is no time for grief,' he suggests. 'That is of another season. Rejoice. Remember? Rejoice.'

'I do,' she argues, as she laughs and weeps. 'But I do, James. I do. I do.'

James, rather helpless, begins to share both laughter and tears. Mistily he sees Herman with huge smile halted in the kitchen doorway, seeking to begin celebration with large bottles of New Plymouth ale. Also Ira behind, someone who knows happiness for a true fact, one with their mood. The old man is performing an excited and intricate dance of his own invention, all inscrutable wobbles and little leaps, but it seems to have the character of a rite, with priestly Ira inviting participation; the sunlit world hymns with him.

'Rejoice,' James repeats. 'Rejoice.' He hugs Herman and Ira too. Then Marie Louise again. Life, not death, is firstcomer to Lovelock Junction; time is about to deliver the town's first native. It is a season for celebration.

Also it is a season for fresh and furtive stirrings in the soul, and certainly the glands, of James. There is more in the bright air of Lovelock Junction than even Marie Louise might suspect. Her news makes his own need more evident; he feels insufficiency where he once knew serenity. The lack is no longer simply sexual. The spirited displays of bull, boar and rooster leave little reverberation in his own flesh, though he is far from denying certain agreeable memories. He might survive without a mate. But he cannot survive, in the most literal manner known to man, without sons and preferably daughters too. He cannot conceive with memories. He cannot make his pact with posterity; he cannot defeat death. His seed cannot become a slender lifeline spiralling across the abyss. Life is life's one durable hope and comfort. It seems, after all, that land alone makes a limp answer; it might one day be desert. No one need ever know, or care, that James Lovelock once walked this way. James, in short, discovers himself unable to defect from the long march of mankind. Almost simultaneous with this insight, to the point of being indistinguishable, familiar secretions in his flesh begin to make themselves felt.

This happens most conspicuously in the proximity of Diana Whisker, the dark-haired daughter of the architect, who is often to be seen abundantly virgin about the plateau. Now something above twenty years of age, she is altogether marriageable. Also too desirable for comfort, even when he heads home fast for Spanish Creek. She has her mother's handsome height, also an appealing pout to her lips, which she finds necessary to moisten frequently. Her shoulders appear most shapely, and nor can her garments quite conceal the promising pressure of her breasts within. Her cool blue eyes announce one disadvantage: they seldom contain more than boredom with the affairs of this world, and especially with the affairs of Lovelock Junction. James longs to give her more interest in life.

He knows he is not alone in nursing lust. He sees it in the eyes of tradesmen inattentive to their trades when Diana passes near. He sees it in the twitchy glance of his brother Richard. Small wonder that Mrs Whisker makes it her business to be protective of so marriageable a daughter in a bruising and lawless land, with God knows what next on the primeval horizon. But James has a problem larger than Mrs Whisker. It is this: surprising as it may seem at this point, James has never wooed and won a woman. The wooing, and not especially difficult winning, has all been on the other side. With one exception, on which it is undesirable to dwell, James has never made much effort with women at all. Therefore, though full of natural talent, he lacks even the more rudimentary technique of courtship; he is at a loss in making his feelings known to Diana Whisker. Besides which any approach to her on the plateau has to be a fairly public procedure, with tradesmen banging and battering, Whisker in wild sweat, Herman trying to envisage the texture of the town, Ira sunny in the cemetery, Mrs Whisker attempting to instruct Benjamin and Ernest with one steely eye to the window, and Marie Louise likely to call him into her kitchen for more conversation. He notes that Richard has no inhibitions in the matter at all; he is never reluctant to call compliments to Diana when he leaves industrious Dixtown to contemplate the untidy and undisciplined confusion of Lovelock Junction proper. Diana always looks at Richard startled, shy, not necessarily displeased. Yet it is difficult to determine what her appraisal of Richard might be; she makes no more than polite reply. Then Richard, like as not, is wont to engage in discourse with Mrs Whisker, sometimes at length, a puzzle to James since the woman is so forbidding. He arrives at the not altogether erroneous conclusion that Richard is getting at Diana by way of charming Mrs Whisker; it is not at this point plain to all that he is getting at Mrs Whisker herself in the meantime. Ira, on watch in the cemetery, has an esoteric view of the subject. The prospect that Richard may win Diana in this devious and unmanly way unhinges James sufficiently to speak to the girl when delivering produce to her door one day. Mrs Whisker is most fortunately on a natural history excursion with Benjamin, Ernest and Iris. James is for the first time obliged to look Diana directly in the eye.

'Where do you come from,' she asks in functionally interested tone, 'with all this?'

'Upriver,' he admits. 'Spanish Creek.' He is disturbed to find that thus far she has never sought explanation of his regular appearances on the plateau. In chronic indifference to the place, she may never have noticed him at all.

'Spanish Creek? That sounds romantic.'

'If you like,' he offers. He sees her eyes as a shade more alert.

'I like romantic things.'

'As do we all,' he insists.

'It sounds more interesting than here,' she adds.

'Much more,' he agrees.

'What do you do there?'

'Farm. Raise calves, pigs, and chickens. Plus all the other things I bring.'

'How lovely,' she announces.

'At times.'

'I mean I love all pretty things. Especially pretty little animals.'

'I'm sure,' he says. And, though inclined to mention mud and smells, tactfully adds, 'Me too. We are, perhaps, alike.'

She doesn't take that suggestion amiss. She smiles, then saddens. 'I wish more were pretty here. It is just people. People making ugliness and noise. Horrid. I hate horrid things.'

'Then you must come to Spanish Creek, sometime,' he argues.

'Could I?'

'Of course.' He has never hooked a fish more swiftly. 'You might find all the peace you want. Perhaps all the prettiness too. Especially when the kowhai flowers.'

'Ko-what?'

'Kowhai. A tree with graceful curved golden flower, all spring. And singing birds, feasting on the nectar, everywhere busy in its branches. There is also clematis. Cascades of bridal white through the forest. That too comes with spring. And the sun silvers the mist on the mountain-sides.'

He has never heard himself quite so lyrical before. She claps her hands. Indifference is gone.

'Wonderful,' she declares.

'All the world, if you look.'

'Except here,' she resumes. 'Here is just horrid. Worse even than New Plymouth, and my mother used to say that was the end of the world. In New Plymouth I had people to talk to. Other girls. Here I haven't anyone.'

'You have me,' he observes.

It has been far from his intention to make this point so soon. Yet it seems he has. There is a silence.

'Thank you,' she says quietly, and lowers her eyes. 'But you might discover me ever so dull.'

'Never,' he asserts.

'Nothing interesting happens to me. Nothing pretty.'

'Then we must,' he says, with certain impish invitation, and more than a modicum of confidence, 'try to remedy that.'

'If only you could.'

'I can,' James promises.

'Please,' she asks.

Long after their conversation terminates that day James feels, by and large, a very devil of a fellow again. Diana Whisker is a tonic to make any man walk inches taller. In the race for romance, he knows himself capable of giving Richard a better than even run for his money; no mistake. When James feels the spur, he doesn't just canter along with idly called compliments; he has his mind wholly on the winning post. There are horses for courses. Diana Whisker, despite first appearances, is really as willing as any woman. Poor Richard.

('Without decrying the deeds of Herman and James,' says the lyricist of *The Lives of Lovelock Junction*, 'it seems reasonable to suggest that Richard surfaced as the heroic figure in these early years. This onetime rough-riding lieutenant of the intrepid Major Gustav Von Tempsky – one of the few survivors of the affray in which the romantic major perished – now gave himself to the pioneering pursuits of the uncertain peace at the end of the wars. He mined coal in countryside where its presence had been unsuspected, and shipped it to settlements north and south; he then milled timber, and similarly marketed it widely. Lovelock Junction, then, had a sound economic base. Also, it seems, a modest prosperity. All of it apparently due to Richard's undoubted zeal.'

Apropos of this paragraph, without decrying the deeds of Richard, or denying an author undoubted zeal, it seems reasonable to suggest a few other things. Such as that the memorialist is some sentimental descendant of Richard's.)

Blessed are they who profit with pleasure, for they shall know not boredom with the bounty of this earth. Richard often regards his brothers with considerable bafflement. Herman's bullion is now burgeoning in baronial form, with the world still little the wiser for his pilgrimage to the Porangi. James is content to play humble farmer among his forested hills. They are men remote from the real world. For the real world, Richard now knows conclusively, is shit. Call it coal; call it gold-bearing gravel. It is the difference between shovelling horse shit and dog shit. The singular virtue of such shit is that it can be transformed into intriguing amounts of money. And money makes a raft on which to sail through the sewer. Richard needs a comfortable raft; one which won't rock. Given that, he can survive the stink lifelong. To Richard, the world's largest miracle is that some remain sane and still have the impertinence to smile on their deathbeds. He isn't altogether greedy; he would be happy to have Herman and James as guests at the feast; he wants little more than a lion's share of good fortune.

Mrs Whisker currently falls into the category of little more. He has no illusion about the woman. She is a taker. And he is certainly no giver. The arrangement is that their needs are mutually met. Beyond that he is no fool either. He can see Sybil Whisker may well have her eye on the main chance, namely his money. She has. Richard might be a rough diamond, uncouthly cut in civilization's absence, but he is by no means averse to linguistic improvement and demonstrably more of a man than her drunken and now frequently distraught husband. In bed and on building sites, Alfred Whisker has never erected much of account, which provides for the suspicion that he never will. Even with his hand in Herman Lovelock's till, it is unlikely that Whisker will lavish the desirable things of life upon her. His castle will surely collapse, yet another sorry chapter in the saga of Alfred Whisker. Forever denied the desirable things, she and her daughters are doomed to the lives of antipodean drudges, to the inferior quality of colonial existence. So much for feminine foreboding. Richard has energy and enterprise, not just in the vicinity of Dixtown, which she cannot but admire, and frequently does, whenever a timely and dry location presents itself; he is also not to be underestimated as a maker of money, and as a man who might with more polish be persuaded to see its value in the social scheme of things. The main chance, as it happens, makes for something of a mote in Richard's eye too. He is far from unappreciative of Sybil's sexual hospitality, albeit in the form of enlightened self-interest: a woman is a woman, and the Porangi is impoverished in this respect. But even when their intimacy is at its most unbridled he is not unaware that Sybil has a daughter named Diana. The problem is one of making progress in that direction. Sybil confuses the compass. Also she has her own map. There is one bird in the hand, and two in the bush. So much for main chances.

Elsewhere all in Richard's life is industry too. He has recognized that the surface supply of coal on the hillsides above Dixtown has a distinct limit. The real harvest, in the long term, must be within the hills. The terrain must be tunnelled. Rails must reach further. It is all taxing and at times vexing. Richard proceeds by trial and error. He makes the trials. Others, for the most part, suffer the errors. Two men with crushed legs are borne away down the Porangi by paddle steamer; they are fortunate to avoid disaster of more fatal nature in the first rockfalls. The work is seen to be dangerous. Dixtown becomes an unhappy place, with some men talking of early departure. One or two are heard to argue that Richard is a ruthless man, indifferent to sensible safety measures for his employees. This is far from fair, at least at this juncture. Richard is more reckless than ruthless. He sees no plus in playing safe. The coal is there. The coal is to be fetched and shipped swiftly and sold. He fells one of the agitators with his large fists, the other backs into the trees, and he pays them both off with a final boot in the arse as they board the paddle steamer. Nevertheless he is sufficiently sober to see that his problem is less human than formal. The temporary chaos is order unperceived. He needs patience with the petulant crafts of capitalism. As captain of industry, he is still cautious enough to hear advice from an able and loyal lieutenant.

'We need better props,' Paramena says. 'We need good timbering in the tunnels. You can't butt into a hill like a bull at a gate.'

Paramena is a partner of ingenuity, not least in matters of profit. He has observed to Richard that a disproportionate amount of Dixtown's floating money fills the pockets of New Plymouth liquor merchants, principally by way of rum shipped up the Porangi. This expenditure could be more fruitfully used to develop Dixtown. With much experiment, and after a number of disagreeable intestinal excitements, Richard and Paramena arrive at a reasonable home-grown rum distilled among other things from fusil oil, sawdust, painkiller and treacle, and bottle it under the label Dixtown Dream. Paramena retails it from unlicensed premises to the rear of their store, which is increasingly crucial to their well-being. As Paramena points out, it is only sensible that money circulates in a circle. Within a week, Richard has retrieved most of the money he has paid his men, and more so with the unveiling of Dixtown Dream. Import of New Plymouth rum is from then forbidden. There are few grumbles; Dixtown Dream is pronounced a success the first Saturday it is on sale, with the roar of the camp audible within a radius of more than a mile. The sabbath, by contrast, is one of stunned peace, truly a day of rest for the god-fearing folk of Dixtown; no priest could provoke a more thorough searching of souls. In cases of accident, Dixtown Dream is a reliable and sometimes instant anaesthetic; it does nothing, however, to dull the pained response of the men to the risk of winning coal from under the hills.

Richard, then, has reason to think on Paramena's proposition. 'All right,' he says. 'Good timber. Better timber. Let's get on with it.'

Until this point they have lived mostly laissez-faire with the forest, pilfering its product as and when needed, and felling trees when they prove impediment to the passage of coal. Richard begins to see virtue in a more systematic approach. Large trees are sought, marked, and toppled. Men are employed full-time on modest wage, pit-sawing the logs down to strong props, beams, and planks. More than enough for the need of mine tunnels. The surplus is sent experimentally down to New Plymouth, where it is sold at a price considerably undercutting northern suppliers. Richard and Paramena celebrate another success: they are now in the timber business too. The sawing-pits are roofed with corrugated iron. Bullock teams are brought in to drag logs from the forest. 'Never keep all your kumara in one kit,' Paramena says. 'If the mine gives out, we can always make do with the mill.'

While his men scratch at the last surface seams of coal, Richard begins tunnelling again, mostly solo, though sometimes with Paramena panicky at his side. Naked to the waist, caked with coal dust and sweat, a sometimes haggard and white-eyed caricature of a man, he works with a ferocity which inspires awe. This is calculated. He is determined to make the men see that their subterranean fears are nothing short of shameful. With seeming indifference to the sometimes grumbling bulk of the landscape overhead, he bangs up beams, slams props into place, in the candlelit dark. With the promise of bonuses, and gratis issues of Dixtown Dream, he finally tempts a half-dozen men to assist him. The first two tunnels strike rich seams. Rails are run in. Oil lamps make the coal faces more homely. Soon Dixtown is prospering as never before. The prosperity, however, is most evident in the case of Richard and Paramena. After months underground, Richard feels like a shit-eating troglodyte; not even Dixtown Dream, or the better quality product he and Paramena privately import, can take away the taste. He is gratified, at length, to leave a growing number of men to their labours under the hills, their ranks reinforced by men with suitably hungry look arriving upriver. He can now contemplate the impressive balances in the books Paramena keeps in finest missionary copperplate hand-writing: one for coal, one for timber; for once the flavour of shit is forgotten. And Richard sees every thing that he has made, and, behold, it is very good. And the evening and the morning are the sixth day. Surely of every tree in the garden he mayest freely eat.

On Sundays, sometimes out of accidie, more often out of carnal itch not quite assuaged by the previous evening's encounter with Sybil, he joins the improvized sabbath service of prayers, gospel readings and hymns provided for the children by the same lady, usually out of doors and always out of Herman's sight and hearing. Benjamin and Ernest are conspicuously captive there, and tradesmen's children too, along with submissive Iris. Richard, often the only adult aside from Ira, might be seen to be thinking of salvation. Or, perhaps, of Sybil Whisker. He has neither much in mind. He is mostly given to consideration of Diana Whisker, whom he often contrives to sit beside for the duration of the services. Often he can also contrive some conversation with her while Sybil delivers virtuous advice to the children for the coming week.

Diana tells him, 'I have lately encountered your brother James.'

'Oh?' He cannot regard this as significant.

'Talked with him, I mean. For the first time.'

'I see.' He wishes she would make her point.

'He is very sweet,' she announces.

Richard makes an indecipherable sound.

'Very,' she adds.

'James,' he observes, 'has all the time in the world to be sweet. He has deuced little else to be up there at Spanish Creek.'

'He has also an honest and sturdy face,' she protests.

Richard would, on the whole, prefer not to continue this conversation. It has a dangerous drift. 'You can't,' he proposes tactfully, 'always judge a book by its cover. Which is not to say that James isn't deep. Too deep for me, mostly. Practical men have to get on with things. Others can dream.'

'He is not of idle demeanour, nor nature. All the produce he brings. And the creatures he tends.'

'Maybe not,' Richard allows. Then adds with conviction, 'But there's more to life than raising beasts and churning butter.'

'That is what I mean.'

Now she is beyond him.

'He still finds time,' she explains, 'to talk of pretty things. Of his little creatures. And of flowers. And of morning mists on mountainsides.'

'Then lucky for those who find the time,' Richard says with impatience. 'Some are busy making a new land yield.'

'You mean with horrid things?'

'Necessary things.'

'But I like pretty things,' she insists. 'I like people who talk of pretty things.'

Richard senses it inappropriate to propose, for his part, the attractive balances on show in Paramena's books. Rather desperate, he discovers himself short of alternatives. He feels a dumb disgust with himself or James, perhaps both, perhaps all perverse mankind. He is conscious of the coal dust graining his hands, of callouses acquired while stacking timber for shipment. Shit-shovellers can be picturesque; they are not often pretty. Though roses bloom their best with a good mulch of compost, who is ever enraptured with the colour and texture of the compost? Richard sees it as too complex to assert that compost-makers have their place in creation's scheme of things too. Without men to shovel the shit, others would have no time for pianos, poetry, philosophy and above all prettiness; men might still be skin-clad in caves. As he has been, near enough, while making the mines workable. Now it seems he is a late starter, and heavily handicapped, in the prettiness stakes.

'To please you,' he replies, 'I shall have to talk of you.'

'Of me?'

'Why not? You wish me to talk of pretty things. You are the prettiest thing in my life.'

Diana blushes, and soon after finds occasion to flee. Richard sees Sybil advancing upon him. At least she is a woman who has prettiness in perspective.

'You have much to say to my daughter,' she notes.

'She is a pleasant girl,' Richard answers. 'Tolerably easy to talk to.'

'That is not the experience of others. They find the girl shy.'

'I must speak from my own experience,' Richard insists. 'I find her obligingly agreeable.'

'Is that all?' Sybil persists. 'Is that all you find in the girl? Let me make so bold as to suggest that you also find her feminine attractions of an enticing character.'

Richard sees difficulty rearing. He laughs without perceptible conviction. 'She is just a slip of a girl,' he asserts.

'I am her mother. I rather think her a woman.'

'Then she is a novice woman,' Richard argues. 'For myself, I recognize only real women. Like present company.' His smile has some verisimilitude.

'Men are not to be trusted, in my experience. And never in these matters. They have the morality of the barnyard. Some lust visibly for their own daughters. I am far from blind.'

The difficulty, then, remains. Richard has no wish to complicate his eminently reasonable arrangements with Sybil Whisker. A bird in the hand can bite. He reaches for diversion.

'Speaking of the barnyard,' he continues, 'I am reminded of my brother James. It rather appears Diana finds him fairest of all, if I read her eyes right.'

It is painful, all the same, for Richard to put this proposition. Present needs must.

'James?'

'Yes. My bucolic brother, no less.'

'But she has never breathed a word.'

'For her own good reasons, no doubt.'

'And I have seen nothing.'

'So much the better for young love, perhaps. It is, I am told, a tender plant. And James is of a similarly ripening age, still not much more than a boy.'

'You alarm me.'

Richard finds this satisfactory. 'I think,' he advises, 'that your mental disturbance might be premature. Their eyes are still likely filled with moondust. You would do well not to place obstacles in the path of their eventual disillusion. Of such obstacles are elopements made.'

'Elopements? Are you suggesting that things have reached this pass?'

'Never,' Richard says cheerfully. 'I am merely making a point.'

'A little too dramatically, and unnervingly, for my taste.'

'Besides,' Richard goes on, 'the Porangi offers poor prospects for eloping lovers. Where are the horses, the carriages, the cloaks and the roads running into the night? It is of other places. Civilized places.'

'On the contrary, some might think it perfect. They could hide in these wretched forests and never be found.'

'Then let me put your fears to rest. Elopement is said to be the court of last resort to lovers. It would be gross exaggeration, so far as I can see, even to call them sweethearts. I am sure no understanding exists.'

'Thank God.'

'Also James is honourable within his lights.'

'Within his lights?'

'He appears to find illumination denied the rest of us. At least that is my impression.'

'You mean he is innocent?'

'I would hesitate to go so far,' Richard says with considered understatement. And qualifies, 'He may, who knows, have sown a wild oat or two.'

'Or two?'

'I am not my brother's keeper. And I have my own oats to sow. I must confess that, in your vicinity, I find myself anxious to sow them.'

'There are people watching,' she says succinctly.

'Alas.'

'But perhaps tonight again.'

'I could ask for no more,' he observes.

'Men,' she says. 'Men are beasts.'

'They have fair competition.'

'That is no way to talk to a lady of breeding.'

'Breeding is dangerous talk.'

'I am also a woman of some maturity. If I prefer the pleasures rather than the pains of procreation, that is surely my entitlement now.' She pauses. A passing thought appears to leave her in disarray. 'I must ask one thing of you. Do you think Diana in hazard?'

'Please treat all I have said lightly,' he insists. 'She will need a rather more robust admirer than James to breach her maidenhead.'

This leads to words about Richard's choice of words. His discrimination, in Sybil's view, still leaves much to be desired.

Richard, as he tramps downhill to Dixtown, there to seek consolation in Paramena's finer rum, is vulnerable to dark thoughts. A diplomatic clipping of Sybil's wings cannot compensate for Diana still flying free in the bush. Blast James. Even rum doesn't dilute his chagrin; the dregs of each glass taste distinctly shit-flavoured.

'You don't seem yourself,' Paramena pronounces.

'I am myself today,' Richard says. 'That's the bloody point. And will be tomorrow. Maybe more so. I shall always be myself. Where does it end?'

'That is no way to talk,' Paramena argues, 'for a man fresh from sabbath ceremony. We end, as you well know, in the arms of our Maker.'

'I didn't ask to be made.'

'You go too far,' Paramena suggests. 'I ask you but one question. Would you ever say you'd sooner not have been born?'

Richard thinks. He also drinks, and at last appears to locate some real flavour in the rum.

'Never,' he replies.

Aside from tormenting Iris Whisker with a similar sporting instinct, the ways and dreams of Benjamin and Ernest have begun to diverge. Benjamin, soon tediously finishing his fourteenth year, has no ambition beyond helping Uncle Richard in mine or mill. Herman, currently locating springs and piping water to streets still unpopulated, might be mortified to know this. He might, on the other hand, be reassured to know that Benjamin wants not so much to make money as to lead a life of less distress on the Porangi. Above all he wishes to escape Mrs Whisker and her delight in baiting and bullying large lumpy boys; and whining, superior girls the like of the insidious Iris. They are not the stuff of Dixtown. He can be free in mine or mill. The Porangi offers no other places of concealment. Ernest, who finds twelve years an equally taxing age, has no such ambition; he scents hard work, and hopes to manage life without such discomfort. He likes to loiter on the Dixtown jetty, where scows take on timber and steamers collect coal. He listens to salty, sunburned men from these vessels unravel knotty yarns of distant places, other climes. Ernest finds imagination useful. He often envisages himself in distant places, other climes. He also learns to chew tobacco with some competence, spit often, and utter ferocious oaths. Unlike Benjamin, he understands that Mrs Whisker is a necessary evil; a little learning can go a long way, and a long way from the Porangi is where he would like to go. Experience is his second teacher. It tells him when in doubt to arrange lips and teeth in winning smile. In peril, he uses that smile on Mrs Whisker to considerable advantage; and soars free of her imminent wrath. Poor Benjamin, by contrast, sits petrified. He harvests it all. There is no point, Ernest sees, in pained honesty. A nonchalant dishonesty keeps others content. Appearances work many wonders.

In the matter of appearances, Sybil Whisker is an unhappy woman; she cannot maintain them. She cannot even prop up pretences. Life is still a vale of struggle. The money Alfred Whisker wins from Herman, by way of astronomic advances on the completion of Lovelock House, never finds its way upriver; it merely moves from bank to bank in New Plymouth, and then mysteriously disperses. He explains to his wife when he returns from a trip to New Plymouth, ostensibly to see to supply of building materials, that he has been investing the money soundly in the interests of their future comfort. All in all, he insists, they need never want again. Indeed they may well revel in wealth.

'What wealth?' she asks.

'Oil,' he reveals. 'The mineral of tomorrow.'

'We are living today,' she declares. 'And the girls need decent dresses.'

'What is a momentary sacrifice?'

'Life with you is an eternity of momentary sacrifices. Not to say a purgatory of penury. At last count I had suffered through a hundred lifetimes at your side.'

'You were nothing,' he reminds her, 'when I married you.'

'Now I'm less than nothing. With two daughters in threadbare condition.'

'Patience,' he urges. 'The prospects are vast.'

'Like what?'

'A veritable ocean of oil underfoot, I shouldn't wonder.'

'I should,' she disagrees, 'if you're involved. It sounds a veritable recipe for despair.'

'I'm not involved. Just our money.'

'Worse. Where fools rush in, the Whisker fortune follows.'

'Have faith,' he pleads.

'In you? That is a joke in uncommonly poor taste. As indeed you have been, for too long in my life. If God fashioned man in His own image, there is reason to suppose Him feeble-minded when I look at you. Faith? Faith in a fool?'

'In oil, then.'

'It is black. And sticky. And may well have virtues denied my faltering vision. But it does not dress my daughters. Nor find them prosperous husbands in this lonely hell. There is no gentleman within a hundred miles. Diana, for example, for want of better, appears to be greatly diverted by that dreary rustic James Lovelock. God knows where that may end. I cannot let her out of my sight. She should have been sent home to finishing school. And would have, if her father had faced up to his responsibilities. Now there is Iris. Poor sweet Iris. I fear for her future too.'

'Fear is an unhealthy emotion.'

'A reasonable one in this unhealthy place. Look at the company we keep. Marie Louise Lovelock is no better than she should be. I'll warrant her past doesn't bear close examination. If our daughters finish bad lots, you shall shoulder the blame for their degradation. For all I know, I may yet end on the street myself.'

'I promise that will not be necessary,' says Alfred Whisker mildly, a man familiar with shouldering all manner of blame; he is also familiar with women of the street, more so than with Mrs Whisker in recent years, and has no wish to see his wife unsettling a tolerably tidy profession. 'Oil,' he argues, 'shall be our salvation.'

'Last time I heard, in a past which now seems remote, it was the Lovelock mansion which was due to purchase salvation. Now, it seems, it is to be some slimy substance from the earth. We are sinking lower. Wonders never cease. Nor do salvations.'

'Wells have been sunk on the New Plymouth shore with some success. The merchants involved are made men. Our money is safe with a company prospecting a nearby piece of coast with equal promise. Patience.'

'How long, O Lord, how long?' asks Sybil Whisker. By way of postscript, she adds, 'At least you could get the Lovelock mansion finished. Is it three years now, or four? I quite understand that it pains you greatly ever to finish anything. But there are limits, even for one who likes to linger long and lovingly. That point is long past. You're indulging yourself at our expense.'

'At the Lovelock expense, rather,' he suggests.

'I think the cost to our spirit far greater,' she finishes. 'We are being pauperized, as always, in the holy name of prospects. How long, O Lord, how—?'

'It's all right, dear,' Alfred says. 'I am sure He heard you the first time.'

As if her husband doesn't make for enough hell, Sybil finds her daughter diabolically preparing a secondary inferno. Diana has begun to sulk and nag, and sullenly refuses food. Love's young dream has become feverish drama. The girl feels deprived, it appears, because Sybil will not give her permission to visit James Lovelock at Spanish Creek. She cannot see the pretty animals, the flowers, the mist on the mountainsides. Life is horrid. She wishes herself dead, and appears determined to hasten her decease. True that she seems to be thinning.

'It is out of the question,' Sybil still insists.

'Why? Why?'

'A girl alone. Good grief.'

'Where is the harm? James is gentle.'

'I should prefer not to explain. Men are not altogether to blame for their natures. There are certain biological facts of which you are not unaware. Gentleness matters not a whit when they are aroused by sight of a pretty ankle. They are all maddened animals.' She suspects relish in her tone, and tries to control herself. 'And I am a responsible mother.'

'You think me irresponsible?'

'Innocent, largely. A stolen kiss might turn your head. And end God knows where.'

'I shall never know love,' the girl announces. 'I shall die an old maid. Because of you.'

'Is it love now, is it?'

The girl refuses reply.

'Has there, perhaps, been some stolen kiss already?'

'James,' the girl declares, 'does not take advantage. Sometimes I wish he would.'

'There,' her mother says.

'There what?'

'There is the point precisely. You need protection from yourself. A mother sees these things.'

'I shall wither up,' the girl predicts. 'I shall rot away.'

'You would do that anyway, were you ever to wed the likes of James.'

'And what is wrong with James?'

'The boy is boorish. Like all the Lovelocks.'

'All?'

'All.'

'You do not,' the sly girl says, 'appear unduly distressed by conversation with Richard Lovelock.'

'We live in a hideously isolated place, in a land of great crudity. When in Rome, alas. One must at least be polite. And suppress one's instinctive, deeper feelings.'

'You seem anxious to spend much time suppressing them in his company.'

'Diana,' her mother says sharply. 'We shall have no more of this. You are verging, to say the least, on the indelicate. Richard is merely a lonely and perhaps misunderstood man who aspires, now and then, to the pleasures of civilized discourse. God knows how he must wrestle with his natural vulgarity. But he has become aware that manners maketh man. He is to be encouraged. I do my best, out of charity, not to fail him.'

Her daughter, the dense creature, appears not to have heard a word. 'Please,' she says.

'Please what?'

'Please may I, just the once, go to Spanish Creek?'

Sybil Whisker is exhausted. She sees no end to anything, except the grave. And God knows there is no guarantee that it may not all begin again. Much as she loathes compromise with hopeless husbands and difficult daughters, she also needs some measure of peace before the vexations of eternal life begin.

'Just the once?' she says wearily.

'Just the once,' Diana promises.

'I shall, of course, have to come too. You cannot be unchaperoned. I shall insist, at all times, that you behave with the greatest modesty.'

'Of course,' Diana agrees in despair. 'Do I never?'

'There is always a first time, and often likely the last, before a girl's fate is forever sealed. I must add, in fairness, that I now begin to think this visit necessary. Perhaps, all in all, it will persuade you to think the less of James. You may, just the once, see him as he is. Indeed you may. Who knows?'

'I don't know what you are talking of.'

'I am sure you shall,' Sybil Whisker promises.

'Can we have a picnic up there?'

'I see no peril in giving the occasion some degree of grace. A picnic might be pleasant. I shall endeavour to prevail upon that quite abysmal boy Benjamin to row us upriver. He looks large enough for the manual effort required; we shall have to be tolerant of his other lacks. As for Iris; I expect she may feel underprivileged if we do not take her too.'

'Must we be so many?' Diana asks, dismayed.

'There is,' her mother judges, 'safety in numbers. Take my word. There is little enough safety in anything of this world. And especially not, I suspect, of such remote places as Spartan Creek.'

'Spanish Creek,' Diana says. 'Thank you anyway. You have made me happy again.'

'Then may your happiness have a contagious quality,' Sybil says, without hope.

Benjamin is bewildered, his head quite turned, by Mrs Whisker's revealed charm; he cannot believe her the same woman who ferociously drives him into exquisite reveries of suicide while he struggles with the scansion of Keats. But it seems, for once, that she seeks less a favour from his confused mind than from his bulky body. She wants him to row her and the two Whisker girls upriver to Spanish Creek. Benjamin is fond enough of his Uncle James. Nor does he much mind Spanish Creek. If he hesitates, it is not on that account. It is rather the thought of being trapped daylong with the objectionable Iris. In the intimacy of a dinghy, then a picnic lunch, that sinister girl can only make his day a misery, with retaliation impossible in Mrs Whisker's presence. On the other hand, the miseries inflicted by Mrs Whisker might be the greater if he refuses the task. He can only agree, as amiably as foreboding will allow, to her proposition. Besides, he can always do his best to escape Iris once at Spanish Creek. There are waterfalls and pools and lonely places. He can snare eels or shoot things. He is not without solitary resource.

'You are a good boy, Benjamin,' Mrs Whisker pronounces. 'There are times, I know, when I appear to have misjudged you. But there is no denying your most obliging nature, and general goodwill; it makes me wish to forgive much. Life, as we often learn to our cost, is more than lessons. You are one, I know, who will always play God's great game fairly. And with a brave smile.'

Which really makes the woman all the more baffling. After offering as brave a smile as he can muster, Benjamin goes to Ernest in hope of persuading his younger brother to join as an ally in the journey to Spanish Creek, and help with the rowing. Ernest is far from taken with the idea of such effort. Besides, he sees enough of Mrs Whisker as things are. And of bloody Iris, he adds, experimenting with a seafarer's oath or two. 'Those sodding bitches,' he sums up, 'are all piss and wind.'

Benjamin, then, must suffer alone. They set off early one shiny midsummer morning. The Whisker womenfolk are in long flowing dresses, with wide floral hats, white gloves, and parasols. Benjamin's feet are bare and his trousers are tattered; a straw hat has been thumped low on his head, as if for disguise. The passing forest teems with birdlife and light. Diana is impulsively delighted by arboreal and ornithological panoramas on the serene river. Iris, more sensitive to her mother's mood, remains disdainful. 'Nature has no discretion here,' Mrs Whisker says, never at a loss for a lecture. 'There is no taste, tact, or delicacy. No restraint at all. It has never been shown its place in the human scheme. The effort of containing and civilizing nature of such unruly dimension can only make man more consistently vile. One must make an elegant best of so unfortunate a situation.'

Labouring Benjamin silently wishes she would keep her elegant arse still, for the sake of balance in the boat. Fantasies of vengeance flower with increasingly attractive hue: such as capsizing the dinghy where the current is swiftest, swimming for shore, and leaving the Whiskers to drown with gratifying commotion. If he doesn't, it is because of Diana. He has nothing against Diana, as distinct from his feelings about the other females, and there is something to be said for her beauty. Also Benjamin is not so obtuse as never to notice that Diana speaks often, and with affection, of his Uncle James. Otherwise he concentrates on proving his aptitude as oarsman, with eyes lowered, teeth tight, and frequent desire for deafness. His command of the river is such that even Iris, for once, cannot find anything catty to say about him. And Mrs Whisker continues unnerving him with compliments. 'My word,' she tells him, as they travel up Spanish Creek, his first trial near finished, 'I simply do not know what we should have done without you. I hope you two girls are properly appreciative of Benjamin's quite stalwart and indeed magnificent effort. Say thank you, Iris.'

'Thank you, Benjamin,' Iris says with reluctance.

'Diana?'

Diana is gazing beyond Benjamin, rather sick with desperation for first sight of James somewhere on his acres; she fears her heart is beating loudly enough for others to hear.

'Diana?'

'Thank you, Benjamin,' she says quickly. 'You really are very dear to us all.'

Iris gives herself to examining the sky with well-considered disgust.

Benjamin beaches the dinghy. Diana leaps ashore, and darts away. Mrs Whisker and Iris depart the boat with more circumspection. Benjamin struggles along behind, with the burden of the heavy picnic hamper. Dear boys, he knows, are destined to be workhorses.

Climbing a grassy ridge of land, Diana glimpses James at last, and halts; she barely contains several indiscreet cries. Shirtless, unshaven, his body bright with sweat, James pushes a plough behind a lethargic horse in a nearby field; he appears to be humming some air to himself. A plain enough prospect. Diana, however, sees profound comeliness. At length she is able to call out modestly. He looks up and sees Diana alone and abandoned on the ridge, as if in dream. A dream fast qualified by the arrival of Sybil Whisker, Iris, and finally breathless Benjamin on the ridge too; the event is credible.

He leaves his furrow unfinished, unharnesses the horse and slaps it affectionately away, and approaches the party from Lovelock Junction.

'We thought we would surprise you,' Diana explains.

'Then your surprise is a success,' he affirms. He pulls on his shirt for respectability's sake. He is aware that Sybil Whisker, for one, finds little to admire in a farmer's grubby and suntanned torso. 'I was,' he informs them, 'preparing this field for turnips.'

'Turnips?' Sybil Whisker says.

It is as if he has already breached good taste.

'For winter feed,' he adds.

'Whose winter feed?' she asks. 'Ours?'

'For the cattle,' he answers. 'Though I am partial to the taste of turnip now and again myself.'

Sybil Whisker's expression suggests that she might have known it.

'I must wash,' he says, 'and shave. You have caught me in disreputable state, up since dawn. Visitors were the last thing on my mind. I am lucky to see more than one or two a year. Today, it seems, is my lucky day.'

Diana, at least, makes it seem so. Her joy is undiminished. 'We are to have a picnic,' she reveals. 'With you.'

'Then I am honoured,' he insists, with gravity. 'Benjamin, let me help you with that hamper. You look all done in.'

James leads them to his hut, where he performs his ablutions inconspicuously at the rear, dowsing his head in a bucket, and soaping himself with enthusiasm. With razor and shard of mirror he makes his face more presentable, and finally draws on a fresh shirt. Sybil Whisker, meanwhile, has been making severe inspection of the rough hut. And of his modest bachelor belongings.

'You live like this?' she inquires, though the answer is obvious.

'For the time,' he agrees.

'The time?'

'The time it takes me to build a homestead. You can see the ground prepared for the foundations up there, above that slope. It will have a fine view down valley, and of the mountains beyond.'

'When it is built,' Sybil Whisker says.

'When it is built,' he concedes. 'I do have other demands.'

'I daresay.'

Diana stands a little distance away, fondling a small chicken she has located. Iris is evidently enraptured with a featureless patch of earth immediately before her feet. Benjamin, wondering when he might safely escape, can see no part to play in these convoluted proceedings. It is as if Uncle James has committed some crime, and Mrs Whisker is conducting investigation. He has seen constables come up the Porangi to pull fugitive criminals out of Dixtown. This is not dissimilar. He might have known Mrs Whisker would turn sour again; the sweetness was too great a strain. He feels sorry for Uncle James as a fellow-sufferer.

'It is not,' she says, 'a farm in the usual sense.'

'In the usual sense?' James gropes.

'It is not one of substance.'

'It is modest,' he allows. 'Enough for me to manage.'

'You are obliged to do all the work yourself?'

'As you see. I am happier alone, the way things have been. There is satisfaction in solitary achievement.'

'Doubtless,' observes Sybil Whisker, rather dismissively. 'But this life you lead, insofar as it presents itself to my gaze, is in no way distinguishable from that of a peasant's.'

'A peasant's?'

'Indeed. You appear to live a peasant's life. Would you not agree?'

'If you like.' James insists on remaining unruffled. 'I have no ambition to be lord and master, if that is what you mean. Not of people. Nor even of this land. I like to think, rather, that I am its servant. It was here. It was empty. And I came to help it find purpose. Not as master. As servant.'

'Less servant than slave, I think,' Sybil Whisker says, choosing words. 'You amount to little more on this land; at least that is my informed impression.'

'Perhaps. But I have a pleasing form of slavery. I wake to the birds. Each day is still new. I am answerable only to sun and rain, and things of this earth. And there is pleasure in the sunsets when the day is done.'

'That is as it may be. But where is civilization? Where is culture?'

'I plan a piano for the homestead. I have been seen to play one, on occasion. Also I have been known to draw and paint, in my spare time.'

'Of which you now have none.'

'Not much. No. But I have hopes.'

'In any case,' she goes on, successfully finding a smile to disguise her coup de grace, 'a piano-playing, painting peasant is, however quaint to contemplate, still finally a peasant. A camel cannot aspire to be a thoroughbred horse, nor a leopard lose its spots. Alas. One would that society were simpler.'

She feels satisfaction. The triumph, in a way, seems suspiciously easy; but there is, on reflection, no point which she has made imprecisely. Her day's task is done. With James Lovelock so much vulgar debris, they can now proceed with the picnic. All that remains is to keep unwavering watch on Diana until they depart.

But then she observes that her daughter, still inanely cradling a chicken in cupped hands, remains distressingly serene; the conversation has somewhere passed her by. Its essential significance will have to be underlined for the girl's enlightenment.

'May we picnic now?' Diana asks, with quite detestable poise.

'Of course,' Sybil Whisker sighs. 'That, I imagine, is necessary.'

'With all this confusion, I have forgotten to ask something,' James says. 'What news of Marie Louise?'

'It is my understanding,' Sybil Whisker answers coolly, 'that she is in her seventh month. And that a midwife is soon to come from New Plymouth to attend her.'

'I cannot wait,' Diana announces.

'For what, pray?' her mother asks.

'The baby. Babies are pretty. I want, one day soon, to have one of my own. Not just one. Lots.'

James is unable altogether to disguise interest. Sybil, for her part, winces.

'Remember yourself, girl. There are decencies.'

'There is nothing unseemly about babies,' Diana argues. 'We all begin as babies. It is a fact of life.'

'Adults are also facts of life. Which does not make them the less embarrassed, and embarrassing, under the pure gaze of God.'

Diana crouches and sets her chicken free. And promises, 'I shan't ever, ever be embarrassed about bringing babies into this world.'

'Dear God,' Sybil Whisker says to James. 'The girl, you see, is really just a child. She needs a mother's care and protection, as you cannot but fail to observe. She knows the facts of life, and none of the truth.'

'I'm hungry,' Iris moans. 'That's a fact of life.'

Benjamin, burly and bored behind them all, for once has no quarrel with Iris.

They spread a crisp cloth of Irish linen under the shade of trees in a not entirely displeasing location to which James has led them; it has clear view of pasture and forest, and a glimpse of the Porangi beyond. There are sandwiches prepared by Diana, and piquant savoury pastries Marie Louise has sent; there are also cakes, and some confections from New Plymouth to engage a sweet tooth with interest. Iris is soon happier, but

Benjamin's hunger remains impressive so long as there is food still to unveil. While others indulge, James lights a fire to produce hot tea. Conversation is largely commanded by Sybil Whisker, who is also quick to control the superfluous offerings of others. James and Diana, in any case, are more than content to look furtively, and with perceptible fondness, upon each other while Sybil Whisker's impure gaze is elsewhere. Benjamin is first to be delivered from the constraints of the occasion. He asks Uncle James if he can borrow a rifle to shoot pigeon. 'Of course,' James says. 'Provided you kill only to our need.' His nephew bounds away with great rapidity.

'Firearms I find very tedious,' Sybil Whisker observes. 'They make an extremely unwholesome sound. There is enough ugliness in this world. But I expect poor Benjamin must take his pleasures where he may. Life is one long trial for such a boy. As his teacher, I frequently feel I am both judge and jury.'

And executioner, James is inclined to add, though diplomatically silent. He shares another smile with Diana. Perhaps Richard has it right. The mother must first be wooed to win the daughter. 'It is uncommonly kind of you,' he tells Sybil Whisker, 'to think of this visit, this rare feast, and to give me some small relief from loneliness. I feel quite dizzy with it all. I should like to show my gratitude by way of a pig.'

'A pig?' she asks with alarm. 'What am I to do with a pig?'

James finds a desire to tell her exactly, but again finds silence politic. 'Not alive, nor very large. I shall kill and prepare it for you this afternoon before you leave. I have no doubt Mr Whisker would be partial to pork chops.'

'Mr Whisker, I fear, never notices that which is set before him. If I fed him potatoes alone, he would fail to lament the absence of meat. The man's mind is elsewhere. Presumably his stomach also. He is not of our commonplace plane.'

'Is his task on the Porangi nearly done?'

'It would seem so to any reasonable person. But he is forever finding flaws, and excuses to detain us interminably here.'

'I can see,' James says, with compassion for Alfred Whisker, 'that you are a woman of rare patience.'

'I regret that I must often leave that impression.'

James discovers self-control extraordinarily difficult to arrange. He daydreams of a lonely glade with Diana. Sybil Whisker is not unaware of this. She is determined James will never know more than daydreams.

Soon they hear the reverberant bang of Benjamin's first shot, followed by a long boyish whoop. He is somewhere among trees at the top of the creek. 'Much as I feared,' Sybil Whisker says. 'A truly satanic sound.'

'He seems in luck, at least,' James observes.

Iris is restless with envy. She is missing out on something. Most of her life amounts to missing out. The Benjamins of the world do not deserve the fun. But they unfairly get far more than Iris. 'May I go too?' she pleads.

'Guns are unladylike,' her mother advises.

'But I wish merely to see what he shoots.'

'He may well shoot you, I shouldn't wonder.'

'Please, mother. Please, please. May I?'

'Very well. If you must. But do be careful. And come back soon.'

'I promise,' Iris says, always obliging, and takes herself at speed toward the sound of Benjamin's shot.

'You have forgotten your gloves,' her mother cries. 'And your parasol.'

Iris doesn't find time to hear.

'I wish,' Sybil Whisker sighs, 'that the children would find themselves some harmless and more agreeable amusement.'

James fervently wishes the same of Sybil Whisker.

Iris locates Benjamin on the bank of the creek, concentrating on a fat feathered target high in the trees. Noisy Iris calls the pigeon's attention to its peril; it lifts away on loud wings. Benjamin slams a despairing shot after the bird as it disappears. Iris blocks her ears in fright. Benjamin rounds on her with disgust, 'What did you have to come for?' he demands. 'You never give me any peace. You always spoil things.'

'My mother,' she informs him, 'says you must allow me a turn with the gun.'

'A go with the gun?' He cannot trust his ears. 'You want a go with this gun?'

'Yes. Mother says I must be allowed.'

'You're mad. She is too. You're not having no go with this gun.'

'I shall tell,' she warns. 'I shall tell mother that you said she was mad. If you do not permit me use of the gun.'

'Tell her what you like,' Benjamin answers with contempt. 'See if I care. I got this gun. And you and her can go to hell.'

Iris gasps.

'To hell,' Benjamin repeats with relish. 'To bloody hell.'

His immortal soul might not be in hazard, but his mortal hide may be, if she tells. Still, the satisfaction he feels now is worth considerable suffering.

Iris, for the first time in the presence of unmistakable heresy, is impressed. 'Please, then,' she whispers at length. 'Please may I touch it?'

'Touch what?' Benjamin asks with suspicion.

'The gun. And please may I stay with you? It is really too tiresome to be with them. Your uncle and my sister are making sickly cow's eyes at each other.' To show Benjamin that she isn't incapable of dissent, perhaps even of subversion, she adds, 'And mother babbles on like a brook. About nothing, really, at all.' Her eyes moisten. 'Please, please may I stay?'

Benjamin, she is sure, is not a boy without heart in the long run.

He isn't. He is not maturing without any essential. 'All right,' he agrees gruffly. 'So long as you shut up when I say.'

'I'll shut up. I shall do whatever you say.'

Benjamin examines this proposition.

Up on the hillside, the three lingering picnickers listen for shots. There are none for a time. When a report at last echoes down the valley, Sybil Whisker expresses relief. 'I suppose if Iris were dead,' she says, 'we should have heard some small scream. Also Benjamin, by some miracle, appears not to have killed himself yet. It gives one great trust in a consummately benevolent Providence. I shall have to pray that benevolence continues to consummate and that she survives intact. Meanwhile, I suggest that we walk. After sustenance of such quantity, a small constitutional might well be beneficial.'

James has been hoping that the afternoon heat might induce Sybil Whisker to sleep in the shade. It seems not. It seems she is determined to defy both heat and heaven's intentions and remain alert the long day, lest she lose the two aspirant lovers from sight. As they gather up the picnic remains, and pack away plates and linen, James and Diana exchange adoring glances. Diana's lips pucker, behind her mother's back, into a soundless kiss floated toward James. James knows a great measure of delight, and a greater measure of frustration: he flushes.

'I shall have to think about butchering that pig soon,' he hears himself say, out of confusion.

'If you must,' Sybil Whisker says with distaste. 'Diana and I shall both, I think, remain at some distance.'

He knows, then, that the day is doomed to be altogether thwarting. He has hoped Diana might at least observe him engaged in some manly enterprise, with wonder and admiration, by way of prelude to even more manly endeavours. He is even denied that. So what is the point of their excursion to Spanish Creek? It is becoming too cruel.

They saunter, a sedate threesome with Sybil Whisker at the centre, across pastoral terrain. The nearest James can get to Diana is to assist her over a stile, for a thrilling moment or two, under her mother's chilly stare. They follow the forest's edge, over undulating ground bright with the grass James has grown, and on which his cows here and there graze. In other circumstances it might be a tolerably pleasing stroll. But circumstances are not other, and Sybil Whisker is intolerably ensuring they shall not be. The one tiny pleasure he wins from this tedious afternoon ambulation comes at the point when it is mercifully terminated. Sybil Whisker discovers herself mired in some dark sticky substance which she determines, with horror, to be fresh dung. They proceed apace back to the picnic hamper, and then make return to his hut. James serves the depleted women more tea with all the grace he can muster, albeit in old iron mugs, before retreating to dispatch the pig he has promised.

'Where on earth,' Sybil Whisker thinks to ask, 'is Iris? And Benjamin? We have surely heard no shot for an hour.'

This is a reasonably accurate estimate. Iris and Benjamin sit comfortably on the sunny bank of the creek, their bare feet dangling in the water. Iris has just been permitted to touch the rifle, with some trepidation and much delight.

'Now,' Benjamin is saying, 'if you really want a go with this gun, this is what you have to do. You have to rest yourself right back.'

'Like this?'

'Like that,' he agrees.

'Is that all?' she asks.

'Not yet. If you still want a go, you close your eyes.'

'Like this?'

'Like that.'

There is a pause.

'Then what?' she inquires.

'Then,' he says, 'you pull up your dress and pull down your drawers.'

'But I fear I cannot see what I am doing with my eyes closed.'

'You don't need to see,' he insists.

She pulls up her dress blindly. 'Must my drawers come right down?'

'Right down,' he affirms. 'That's if you want a go with this gun.'

His reminder is useful; she soon has them right down. 'What do I do now?' she asks, feeling strange.

'You open your legs wide,' he replies. 'And let me get on top of you. Like this.'

Ten to fifteen minutes later Sybil Whisker, James and Diana hear the sound of another shot. It is the first that Iris has been allowed to fire.

Benjamin has also had an afternoon of innovation. They are well placed to pity James and Diana when they see them again.

On the downriver journey, with fresh pork and pigeon piled in the bow of the dinghy, Iris is all but lost in bliss at the sight of Benjamin's strong shoulders at work on the oars. Sybil Whisker feels obliged to put the experience of Spanish Creek into some perspective, for Diana's future peace of mind. 'There,' she says. 'It was all much as I suspected. Perhaps worse, if that is possible.'

'What is?' Diana asks, with dread. 'What was?'

'My subject is this young man of whom you have seemed so unrealistically fond. I hope it has been a lesson to you. And that you will not have your head turned so easily again.'

'What are you talking of?' Diana cries.

'You surely have eyes to see now. There is no longer excuse for illusion. James Lovelock, on home ground, is no more than a yokel.'

'A what?' Diana cannot bring herself to speak the word.

'A yokel,' her mother insists. 'To call him a yeoman would be gross flattery. He is a sad yokel. A pig-killing peasant with a taste for turnips. One who is content to grub his life away on a pathetic patch of land. No more need be said.'

'You are unfair,' Diana protests.

'The world is unfair. But it is also, for better or worse, the world in which we happen to live. When you have become cognisant of this truth, you will feel happier for having put this poor wretch out of your mind. No tears, thank you.'

'Mother—'

'And no pleas. It is finished. There. Like that. God knows we are all young once. But that is no sufficient excuse for further folly. Pull yourself together, girl. Feel grateful for having the veil lifted, and not before time. You have been misled – and, most fortunately, not too far up the garden path. He is no farmer in the full and reasonable sense of that word. A peasant with pretensions, perhaps. There is no way in which he could support you worthily. Were he a large landholder, a prospering sheepman like some in this country, I might have second thoughts. But the fearful realities stifle even the notion of second thoughts; I certainly fail to find any.'

'Mother—'

'Enough,' Sybil Whisker says. 'More than enough.'

Diana gives herself to loud sobs. Benjamin, sturdily speeding the dinghy down the Porangi currents, again contemplates capsizing the craft: as justice for Mrs Whisker, mercy for Diana. He would, certainly, were it not for his beloved Iris. Her voice is next to be heard. It has a trace of smugness as she considers her grieving sister.

'I simply cannot imagine what is wrong with you,' Iris says. 'I had a perfectly jolly day.'

When James next journeys to Lovelock Junction, he meets Diana at her door. Her eyes are red from a fortnight of weeping. With his arrival her tear ducts become active again. She is slow to tell him of the cheerless aftermath of the picnic at Spanish Creek. But she does, in the end. 'So, you see,' she finishes, 'Mother says I'm not ever to see you again. Not ever. Never.'

'It is true I am no gentleman farmer,' James allows. 'But I do my best. I am my own man.'

'Tell her that. Not me.'

'Diana?' Sybil Whisker calls from within their dwelling. 'Who is that at the door?'

Diana trembles.

'Diana?'

'I must go,' she whispers to James. 'Will you talk to her, perhaps?'

'When pigs fly,' James announces. With his first and likely last kiss left compassionately on Diana's cheek, he takes himself off, in muddy boots, to more congenial doors. Mourning James gives Ira much to puzzle over on that short visit. Ira sees happiness, after all, as unreliable as summer weather; it rains for a week without pause, until the land seems awash. Dixtown floods, but those on the plateau, in Lovelock Junction proper, ride like residents of an ark above it all.

If Ira were more observant, or not so often sheltered indoors from the rain, he might have taken consolation from the discovery that happiness, like an itinerant weed, has taken root elsewhere; there is more than one sequel to the Spanish Creek excursion.

'Why do you,' asks Ernest of Benjamin, 'moon about that silly cow Iris Whisker all the sodding time?'

Ernest is not yet of an age to feel stirrings, or to find compensations in girls.

'Iris is all right,' Benjamin says defensively.

'All right?' Ernest laughs. 'You used to tell me another tale. You said as how you'd like to strangle the little bitch.'

'That was last month,' Benjamin points out.

'So what's so different about this bloody month?'

'I have got to know her,' Benjamin says, with Biblical emphasis.

In a month of many events, a lean stranger travels up the Porangi. He is in search of work, and presumably some inconspicuous residence in the world. It seems that, like many who make the upriver journey, he has a past pressing close behind, and perhaps the law. But his gaunt face and aloof manner discourage inquiries. He is a tall man, a lonely man, with an unkempt collie dog always at heel. He gives out his name as McKenzie, though most dismiss that as likely alias. But certainly he is a Scot, and he may be truthful when he says he is a sometime shepherd. There is mountain weather in his face; and he does have that dog. He has heard, he says, of a farm up the Porangi. Since he has no apparent desire to labour in Dixtown, he is sent on to Spanish Creek.

After weeks as lonely as any in his life, James sights this lanky stranger crossing his land with the dog loping behind. James prickles, sensing some apparition, perhaps fate calling to present credentials. Then he sees McKenzie as merely an old man, with loyal dog, and goes forward to greet him.

'Ye farm?' McKenzie says.

'Yes,' James says, still with pride.

McKenzie is baffled. 'I see nae sheep.'

'No,' James agrees. 'I have no sheep.'

McKenzie shakes his head sadly.

'I crop,' James goes on, though irritated at having to be apologetic. 'And keep a few cows, and pigs. But no sheep.'

McKenzie looks over the land, then up at the ranges beyond, and evidently reaches some conclusion. 'Ay,' he says. 'Brave country. And I see a braw lad. I would nae wish for more.'

'More?' James says, perplexed.

'More than is, man. Nae matter about the sheep. I can tend the taties.'

'The potatoes look after themselves, mostly,' James insists.

'The better for a little love,' McKenzie claims. 'This land needs lovers. Then its fruit will be fair.'

'I have some feeling for it, myself,' James suggests.

'Ay,' McKenzie says. 'I have eyes. But I also see sadness. A weariness with your work.'

'Sometimes lately,' James concedes. 'This rain hasn't helped. Some things washed out. And there is rot in the roots.'

'And nae lass?'

'No wife,' James says. 'No. And never likely now.' He wishes his words less bitter.

'A lone lad needs a lass,' McKenzie observes, 'and surely a son. Nae matter. For worse ye have me.'

'You?'

'Me. McKenzie.'

'Please understand. I have never had help. And I cannot pay, besides.'

'What could ye pay? Only the silver shillings of an English Queen. There is other coin more rare.'

'Like what?'

'Some call it freedom. Meaning nae to be slave.'

'What do you call it?'

'Some knowledge best has nae name. For it is coin which need never be tried with the teeth. A man who so tests it, still has the habit of slave.'

'I don't see where this gets us,' James observes, with honesty.

'To this,' McKenzie says. 'Men are of mankind. I have travelled too long and too far. I can see nae further. And a lone lad needs a mate.'

'A mate?'

'In the saying of this land. Elsewhere it may mean a woman. But where the world is new, the trees tall and mountains high, the lost sons of women look to others of their lonely kind as companion. As mate.'

'I see.'

'So here's a highland hand on it,' McKenzie says. 'To take if you will. I trust ye find it useful.'

James, after all, finds it a good hand to grip. Unexpectedly, from grief or relief, his eyes smart.

'Nae tears,' McKenzie warns. 'Men well met is better than prayer. God, they say, is seen to smile. And the devil to mourn.'

From that month, with the cruel defection of Diana, James takes McKenzie as mate. And the Porangi, for its part, flows to the sea.

Herman has his hour. So, minus a mortal minute, does Alfred Whisker. Lovelock House, or Porangi Palace as cynics soon style it, has risen to its full height upon the plateau, and can be seen in sobering silhouette for all of a mile by those approaching upriver: man could not have proclaimed his presence more intemperately on the Porangi. Within, the house has become all but habitable. The penultimate months, for there have been many, with completion again and again postponed, have not been without problems. With the shell largely shaped, and tradesmen trying to make sense of the interior, Herman detects a region of vast and inexplicable space among less unreasonably sized rooms. 'What is this to be?' he demands of Whisker.

'The ballroom,' Whisker replies.

'Ballroom?' Herman cannot contain his disbelief.

'Perfectly in keeping,' Whisker maintains. 'Besides, it gives the place proper proportion. Everything blends in perfect balance.'

'I didn't ask for a ballroom,' Herman points out. 'Who, tell me, is to have the balls?'

'There are times,' Whisker resumes, 'when an architect of vision has to observe, with regret, that the client isn't always right. Imagination is all. One must anticipate the more sublime human needs which the client overlooks in his haste for a dwelling.'

'You mean I don't know it yet, but I need a blasted ballroom.'

'In brief,' Whisker agrees, 'yes.'

'Dear God,' Herman says.

'Look at it this way,' Whisker continues mildly. 'A ballroom need not only be a ballroom. It will be admirably suited for meetings, perhaps, and certainly for concerts. I can imagine recitals of chamber music, for example, in this quite charmed setting. With the wood carving finished, it could well weave a spell of enchantment upon all who enter. I am lavishing much attention upon the acoustics. Believe me when I say I have neglected nothing. Men will marvel. True that I will receive some credit. But where, without an enlightened patron, would any masterpiece be?'

'I have been struggling for enlightenment,' Herman concedes, 'ever since you began. But it seems I am still short on illumination.'

'Now is no time to lose our nerve,' Whisker argues. 'Or to be chicken hearted. Success is in sight. Only the bold win the laurel crown. From our first meeting I knew we were fated to be brothers in triumph. Believe me when I say baronial needs a ballroom. This building is to be no meretricious imitation. No hovel huddled behind a false facade. There has to be a ballroom.'

True that this misunderstanding seems trivial when Whisker's total creation is considered. The building rears huge in grey granite, with tasteful trimmings of pale marble. Its forecourt is paved with red cobbles from Marseilles. Stone lions and eagles of mistily Scottish temper stand guard on each side of the entrance steps. There is colonial compromise and some architectural surprise in the three-sided sweep of veranda. Beyond that, the traditional is telling again. The interior staircase is a Georgian jewel in a Gothic setting. The glass is finest Venetian. The decorative wrought iron has been brought from Brussels. Medieval motifs talk in teak, oak, and mahogany. Fireplaces and bathtubs are of the best Italian marble. Room after room unrolls breathtakingly; and far too bewilderingly for Marie Louise. Herman takes her within the house, at last, near the end of her ninth month of pregnancy. 'We could lose ourselves in here,' she protests, 'and never find each other again. Where does it end?'

That is easily answered. It all terminates in the tower; the rest of the building, even at its more majestic, seems mere appendage. Were Herman and Marie Louise ever to lose themselves literally in the interior, pursuing each other through baronial canyon and cavern, they would sooner or later celebrate reunion on top of the tower. All paths point toward its winding stone stair, set centrally in the building. The breathless journey climaxes, at considerable length, in a crenellated turret open to all the world's weather. The view is too vast for immediate comprehension. The Porangi glides distant below. Hill and mountain proliferate to every horizon. The wilderness is oceanic in its astonishments; tens of thousands of trees glitter tidally, laced with currents of light and shadow. Even an atheist might fall back upon heaven to explain the handiwork implicit in this tapestry.

For Marie Louise, however, the kitchen is more to the point; she fails to find one. 'A detail,' Whisker says, and puzzles over plans. 'A mere modification of the ground floor. Or perhaps a judicious addition to the rear.' He sighs. In his experience the wives of clients, like his own wife, are impossible to please, and characteristically finding fault on principle. 'I promise your kitchen within a week.' He goes off to bark fresh orders at tradesmen. Marie Louise, meanwhile, inspects bedrooms. She finds one, on the first floor, with a quite splendid view of the river. She asks Herman to agree that it is by far the best. It is. 'Then,' she says, 'we shall keep it, and furnish it fittingly, for Luke should he ever return. Our hope shall inhabit it. As for us, we shall make do with second best. And as for the place as a whole, we shall have to suffer the pains of making it livable. Little feet may yet convince us that it is safe to call home.' Moist-eyed and huge, she hugs Herman. 'My prayer is that there shall be more to my life than housekeeping.'

The cost of Lovelock House, considerable if still short of fatal to Herman, is insignificant beside the human toll. That can best be seen in Alfred Whisker. He has aged a score of years in four. His hair has whitened, his face has withered; his eyes have retreated down dark caves. His hands quiver uncontrollably as he searches for the whisky bottles he secretes in crevices of the construction. But otherwise nothing in his demeanour demands pity. His inner content is surpassing. He has no aspiration to attempt a repeat performance; he could never be content with imitations. Like many artists exhausted at the end of a masterwork, he knows the future holds only counterfeit satisfactions. Bees have but one sting, and then die. After his similarly heroic contribution to the human hive, Alfred Whisker does not mean to die, precisely, but rather to live out his last euphoric days on the proceeds of oil exploration, in which he has invested wisely, sooner than a further struggle with the material vanities of mankind; these material vanities have become synonymous with baronial. Never again. He envisages retirement into the perspectives the great philosophers might provide, with an ample stock of finely matured malt whisky at hand.

That is why he finds Herman wholly dismaying now. Herman hasn't been idle. Not for nothing did he clear, level and peg out the plateau with Ira Dix; not for nothing did he name the streets with Marie Louise, with signposts everywhere on tasteful show, albeit on empty acres; not for nothing has he abundantly piped water from pure forest springs. He unrolls not just one plan but many; plan after plan until Whisker sags. They are all for the town to come. For some reason, he imagines Whisker is interested.

'The streets,' Herman says, 'will be wide, spacious and planted with ornamental trees. Parkland will be interspersed among the airy dwellings. The temple of learning, naturally, will sit at the centre. Children shall proceed there at the age of four. They will have practical lessons in all the manual arts valuable to man, plus exercise for the body in running and walking, along with the learning of languages and all intellectual knowledge in nature and art. Ultimately, then, our public places, which are generously planned, will be amply filled with athletic orators and poets. You may note that I have also made provision for public houses. These will provide spirituous liquors in modest quantity. The prospects are such that the tranquil atmosphere of the community will preclude the need for inebriation.'

A shaken Alfred Whisker tries to give Herman his attention. At length, in wonder, he clears his throat. 'And just how,' he asks, 'do you see the buildings?'

'In keeping,' Herman says.

'In keeping with what?' Whisker inquires with fright; he fears the answer.

'With Lovelock House, naturally.'

'In baronial?' Whisker's voice is reduced to bleak whisper.

'Perhaps less extravagantly,' Herman suggests.

'My God,' Whisker says.

'He, of course, will have His place,' Herman observes. 'You can see this large concourse before a public building, conceivably in cathedral style, where men may gather in His gaze. Less to worship in ritualized manner than to exchange revelation and knowledge of His nature, in a way befitting their adult character.'

'I need time to think about this,' Whisker pleads.

'I have not envisaged the work beginning before next month.'

'Next month?' Whisker feels faint.

'Let us see Lovelock House entirely finished first. Marie Louise is still concerned about her kitchen.'

'It's all but done,' Whisker promises.

'So much the better. You have more time to reflect.'

'I feel the need for reflection overcoming me already,' Whisker says, his mind on a bottle hidden behind a loose brick at the top of the tower; his prospects do not preclude considerable inebriation.

'Please proceed at your leisure,' Herman agrees. 'I see a man with much on his mind.'

'I'm not saying you don't tempt me,' Whisker allows, 'but it is perfectly possible that you have the wrong man.'

'I can afford to give you the benefit of the doubt.'

'I am not questioning your financial capacity to avail yourself of my services as an architect. I mean, to be frank, that I am thinking of well-earned retirement.'

'Only the dead retire. Life is challenge or nothing.'

This pronouncement of Herman's has more meaning a minute or two later when, on the move toward the whisky in the tower, Whisker is waylaid by a mail delivery from New Plymouth, just arrived aboard the steamer. Whisker has only the one communication. It is not, as he now has a natural tendency to fear, another commission. It is from his bank manager. The letter, along with several familiar complaints of a monetary nature, calls Whisker's notice to the fact that his income from Lovelock House has been invested in as sterile a shore as any known in the history of oil exploration; the director of the enterprise has been seen taking ship for parts unknown. The bank manager conveys regrets, but hopes Whisker will give his most urgent attention to the aforementioned monetary matters.

From the top of the tower Whisker gives the letter to the wind in tiny pieces; and his most urgent attention to the aforementioned whisky. Before him, indeed, looms the doom of yet another lifetime of challenge as he contemplates the plateau of Lovelock Junction. His eyes glaze; he knows something in the nature of nausea. For the first time in his life he flinches from the beauties of baronial; Lovelock Junction refuses to rise ornamentally in his imagination. What does arise less ornamentally, in the middle distance, is Mrs Whisker. She has just left the shingle-roof dwelling, divided between Whiskers and Lovelocks these last years, now commonly known as the Old House. She is walking with some evident purpose down Rainbow Road. Whisker, for want of anything better, allows his curiosity to be caught while he refurbishes his stomach warmly with whisky; where on earth is the woman wandering? It seems toward Dixtown, though the environment there is hardly to her social taste. All the more perplexing, considers Whisker, endeavouring to empty the bottle. He has, from his tower, an eminently God's-eye view of human affairs and he rather enjoys the remoteness; God Himself must often similarly meditate upon such as lonely-walking Mrs Whisker, unable to conceive for a moment what the woman has in her head. She takes leave of Rainbow Road, crosses Armistice Avenue with increasing briskness, and strides over some land Herman has designated as The Park of Sylvan Pleasures. Fortunately, this is still far from the case, the sylvan pleasures yet unplanted; the area is scantily covered with its original scrub, and Whisker has at all times a splendid view of his wife as she walks. From the tower too he has an equally splendid view of Richard Lovelock as he appears, over a ridge, from the direction of Dixtown. Richard meets Mrs Whisker. They converse. Charitably, still more mellow, Whisker supposes their meeting to be some unexpected social encounter, perhaps of mildly amicable nature; he is not one to deny his wife the small pleasures of social intercourse in her day, since by her own reckoning she has so few, and God knows it might make his evenings easier. Unable to eavesdrop on their pleasantries, Whisker has almost judged himself to have seen sufficient, and is preparing to let his attention wander more profitably elsewhere. But he cannot fail to observe that the couple have drawn uncommonly close; and that, of a sudden, they appear to be embracing with some familiarity. Indeed, not to put too fine a point upon it, since Whisker's view is panoramic, there seems to be passion at work. Richard Lovelock is hastily removing his jacket and spreading it on the ground just beyond an irritatingly opaque outcrop of rock. Mrs Whisker is as speedily discarding her dress behind a frustratingly dense veil of scrub. As belts are unbuckled, buttons undone and boots tossed aside, the intervention of the natural world in the human prospect distresses Whisker. Straining to see still more beyond rock and scrub, he rises on to the slender parapet at the top of the turret, and teeters there just in time to attain a partial view of Richard Lovelock, in particular of his sunlit buttocks, descending energetically upon prone Mrs Whisker. From that point, the precarious parapet taken into account, it is a sight to detain only the most adventurous voyeur. Whisker is not to be detained. He is suddenly and prematurely a voyager rather than a voyeur; he has eternity underfoot rather than the parapet; the smash of a bottle heralds his launching. One long and lingering cry is heard. His body strikes a steeply sloping roof, and then pitches far out into the spaces above the Porangi. Some see him suspended there, in memory, long after the river has actually received him. Then there is silence.

*

('Tradition,' says *The Lives of Lovelock Junction*, 'has many tales to tell concerning the construction of that monumental piece of architectural grotesquerie called Lovelock House. Its total cost is unknown, and presumably Herman preferred to keep it to himself. But certainly no expense seems to have been spared. The architect was one Alfred Whisker, a man who apparently pursued a distinguished career first in London, later in New Zealand, before falling in catastrophically with Herman Lovelock. Regrettably, no other examples of Whisker's work appear to have survived. We have only the Lovelock ruin as testimony to his talent, and it seems certain that in this instance he was handicapped by the eccentric, excessive and perhaps perverse wishes of his client. Why Herman should have insisted that Whisker build in baronial is beyond reasonable explanation, given Herman's generally egalitarian temper. One intriguing thought arises. His wife Marie Louise, said to be the illegitimate daughter of a French nobleman, appears to have been a mute witness to it all. Conceivably Herman was trying to provide his wife with a setting which should have been hers by birthright. That would explain the ballroom, for example. Certainly Lovelock House was a whim to which Whisker was obliged to give expression – and, in the end, with despair. For, according to one colourful story, he took his own life by leaping from the tower when the building was all but complete. If so, presumably the extremes to which Herman had driven him were his undoing. One of the few headstones still decipherable in the overgrown cemetery is Alfred Whisker's; it appears to be the earliest. And this, on the face of things, confirms the tragic tale: it records that he perished 'of an excess of sensibility' and this can well be read as a coy Victorian euphemism for suicide. Perhaps more to the point, it also conveys the impression of a lonely and sensitive artist lost in a strange and utterly bewildering land; he can, in that respect, be seen as the forerunner of many. Poor Whisker, however, unlike those to follow, made no escape from an aesthetically impoverished colony, with its slavish devotion to second hand styles, especially where money was no object, and notably money won from gold. A brave new world is not to be built in derivative baronial. Herman, even with pressures upon him taken into account, does not surface with credit from this episode in the early life of Lovelock Junction; one can indeed see its final failure writ large upon the Porangi horizon.'

Many things are writ large, especially by authors concerned to parade pet hobby-horses, make martyrs out of molehills, or a full-blown beard out of a neglected whisker, and perhaps earn an easy dollar. One contemporary chronicler, in *The Times* of London, declared that but for drink and drowning there need be no death in New Zealand. It was Alfred Whisker's pioneering accomplishment to perish of both.)

Richard and Herman row downriver in pursuit of the mortal remains of Alfred Whisker before these are borne to the sea. It is a long hunt, made the more chilling when, after a mile or two, they encounter a half-dozen coffins circling in the Porangi's current. At first sight the coffins appear to be competing for custom. After some time, and several disagreements, the brothers tow one of the coffins ashore and discover within the body of an extensively decomposed Chinaman. The other coffins are presumed to have the same contents, though neither brother is tempted to confirm this. Later they will learn of a brigantine wrecked near the Porangi mouth, with coffins Canton-bound included in its cargo; the corpses those of Chinese who have perished from blizzard, rockfall or old age in the southern goldfields, now being returned to home soil for burial. With this news will come rumour that the coffins actually contain gold, and this will lead Richard to excavate the riverbank site where he and Herman have buried the coffins with perfunctory ceremonial; and disinter only more mouldering Chinese gentlemen. Meanwhile, it merely seems that death has been trying to travel up the Porangi, on the tide, to Lovelock Junction; and has been frustrated by ebbing waters. Anyway Alfred Whisker has outwitted death's Oriental welcome party; his body is at last located another mile downriver, tangled in branches, and is rowed home by two tired men to his distraught widow and daughters. It will never be a day Herman finds it desirable to remember.

Ira Dix is not, after all, the first resident of Lovelock Junction's pristine cemetery. But after the headstone of Whisker's grave has been set in place Ira is often to be observed sitting beside it, lips moving, in earnest conversation in the autumnal sunlight. Ira is no longer without a companion in the cemetery now, for a true fact, though Whisker's responses to his lengthy queries remain unheard.

'Does this mean,' Marie Louise asks, 'that there is now a curse upon our house?'

'Nonsense,' Herman says. 'Anyone can fall.'

'That is no decent reply to a worried woman.'

'Very well. Look at it this way. It was not uncommon, in less enlightened ages, for workmen – and on occasion architects too – to be sacrificially slain and entombed within their constructions. There was thought to be fair fortune in such sacrifice. Perhaps, for lack of volunteers, Whisker felt the need to give the building his blood blessing. That's if he jumped, as some suppose. Who knows? Either way, we fail him if we decline to live there. His work would have been in vain. And, God knows, his death.'

'Are you sure?'

'Sure of everything, man might do nothing. Besides, the place cost a king's ransom, as you well know. We cannot begin again.'

'No,' Marie Louise agrees wearily. 'And I have my kitchen.'

Herman takes his bulky wife in his arms.

'Our child is kicking again,' she confides. 'The little devil is trying to kick all the doors down, and be born.'

Whisker's curse, insofar as it is most clearly discerned, falls upon his stricken widow. In a letter generally of commiseration her late husband's bank manager respectfully calls attention to certain increasingly urgent monetary matters; he encloses a copy of a letter sent to Alfred Whisker before the latter's unfortunate decease. 'We have nothing,' she tells her daughters. 'Worse than nothing. Debts too. Never mention your father to me again. Never.'

Diana and Iris, who have never much been in the custom of mentioning their father anyway, join their mother in mourning. 'What does it all mean?' Diana thinks to inquire.

'It means,' her mother answers, 'that we have no future. Also a past that is best forgotten. We must live eternally in the present.'

This is insufficiently specific for Diana. 'How?' she persists.

'I mean that we now live forever in the land of the Lovelocks and their like,' Sybil Whisker announces. 'We can never go home. Our native shore, that jewel set in sceptred seas, must fade as dream. But I promise you this. I shall still see you girls married well even if I have to take to the streets.'

Soon after, she does, at least in the more literal sense, running down Rainbow Road and across Armistice Avenue into the arms of Richard Lovelock, with whom she sobs for some time. 'Your fears are unnecessary,' he reassures her, before they proceed with the business in hand. 'I shall see you don't suffer. Nor your lovely Diana.'

'There is also Iris,' Sybil points out.

'And Iris, of course,' Richard adds.

'Thank God for a man I can trust,' she says.

'And I shall have a talk to Herman,' Richard promises.

Herman, nothing if not kind, insists that Sybil Whisker remain in occupation of the Old House; she will continue to receive income, now enlarged, as a teacher. Richard, for his part, discharges her debts, though doubtless Herman would have done so if approached; Richard sees this as giving him a firm foot in the door of the Whisker menage, with his next step primarily in Diana's direction. The largest problem, so far as his footwork is concerned, is likely to be that of tripping upon Sybil before he can see to Diana's comfort and continued well-being. It is a problem which, whenever and however he views it, gives him uncontrollable tremors of mind. Sybil Whisker may have many womanly virtues, but he cannot suppose tolerance of his intentions to be one of them. And there is no gainsaying that Diana is a pretty problem in herself.

Death may have planted itself maturely in Lovelock Junction for amiable Ira to contemplate when he ambles into the cemetery to partake of the season's cool sunlight; but life ripens too. Within a week of the move to Lovelock House, and three weeks late on nature's normal reckoning, a daughter is delivered to Herman and Marie Louise. The suspense has been huge, with the midwife hovering near Marie Louise at all times; the wait is worthwhile. The midwife is of a mind to say that never in all her years has she seen a baby more beautiful. This is no polite compliment. The child has more than passing charm. She is stunning. It is as if God, after defining limits to the loveliness of babies, has this time stretched a point. More, she is extraordinarily aware. Perhaps the late birth. Perhaps other things. Marie Louise thinks other things. But she prefers to hear Herman talk. 'Impossible,' he announces, after considering his child in the midwife's care. 'She looked at me as if she knew me. Like no baby before. And laughed. She all but talked.'

Marie Louise knows nothing impossible. She has had long labour; her smile is weak.

'Perhaps Luke is back with us,' she says finally.

'Luke?'

'In his own way. Why not? There are stranger things.'

Nevertheless their child is a daughter. With love, and happiness, they see there is only one possible name for the girl. They call her Felicity Lovelock for all the world to know.

Twelve

Biologically reliable sources say that the strongest and strangest patterns of animal behaviour have to do with perpetuation of the species behaving so strongly and strangely. Perhaps less reliably, these sources often imply that the same can be said of homo sapiens even with the magical confusions of male and female tallied. James Lovelock is not on this earth to help any hypothesis. He is at Spanish Creek to prove himself, in which he has succeeded handsomely by any reasonable measure. The problem is that some measures are unreasonable. Nevertheless he can now be seen, while his mate McKenzie harvests and fences, at work again on his homestead. A frame has risen on solid foundations. It is to be modest, but not unworthy; it will fit the landscape, never fight it. Not for James imported stone, rare timbers; his dwelling will be of the rough-sawn logs and random rocks of the land, in a native vernacular. English oaks, Californian pine and Australian gum might later give it some cosmopolitan perspective.

When he breaks from his toil to heat a billy-can of tea, he is joined by McKenzie and his dog; McKenzie is a man inclined to let his mind browse beyond the present confines of the farm, and certainly the meaner tasks in hand. He is, in short, a man averse to small talk.

'Yon hills,' he often says, 'are grand for sheep.'

'Yon hills,' James replies, mimicking his mate, 'are covered with pretty fair forest.'

'I am just saying,' McKenzie insists.

'And I hear you,' James says.

'Then I say nae more. Only that I know grand sheep country when I see it.'

'And I see beauty. A green and ferny frame about my acres. Still as fair as first seen. I hear the wind through the leaves before I sleep.'

'Then there is truly nae more to say,' McKenzie allows, with grudge.

'Why sheep?' James asks. 'You have this thing.'

'Because I know them. There is nae much I do nae know about sheep. Nor my furry lass.'

McKenzie's dog is named Sunday. Its mother had the name Saturday; it in turn was born of a bitch named Friday. Sunday is seldom excluded from conversation. And McKenzie is always patting and stroking the dog as it dozes beside him.

'Then I'm sorry about the sheep,' James says.

'In time, perhaps,' McKenzie suggests.

'In time, what?'

'In time ye will see need, I have nae doubt.'

'Need?'

'To breathe wider. Ye can nae always live like a wee crofter in a large land.'

'If I'm happy, why not?'

'Ay,' McKenzie says. 'There hangs the tale. True I see a bonny lad. But one with nae much happiness in his mien.'

'I have had my problems,' James admits.

'With a lass or two, I have nae doubt.'

'With one anyway,' James agrees.

'The grief is sad to see.'

'It is over now, mostly,' James insists.

'Yet I see ye working on yon house. More than common crofter's dwelling.'

'Maybe so. But for myself.'

'If ye say. Did this lass, maybe, see the lack?'

'And more. There was her mother. I was not seen of substance. And there's the end.'

'Ah.' McKenzie's eyes brighten. He has, after all, more or less what he wants from James. If less, it will soon be more. He is a man of patience.

They rise, dowse their fire with dregs of tea, and prepare to go about their separate tasks. McKenzie gives a last gaze to the horizon.

'There is a beauty,' he says. 'I can nae deny. And maybe, God can tell us, for the best. We are merely men.' With that, he takes long strides downhill from James, the dog Sunday panting at his side.

James is disturbed. He is often and easily disturbed. And never more than when, on his next visit to Lovelock Junction, he makes quiet visit to the Whiskers and seeks to convey condolences on the loss of their breadwinner; he is not altogether without hope that he might now be seen in a position of some advantage, in connection with Diana, though this is a card surely too insensitive to play in the circumstances. Mrs Whisker is cool, and Diana's eyes red and dead. Widowed Sybil

Whisker makes it her business to reassure James that matters might be worse; that their circumstances, by the grace of God, are tolerable. Suddenly Richard arrives jovial at the door of the Whisker dwelling, inquiring if all is well within. No mistaking the nature of Richard's presence. The space once feebly occupied by Alfred Whisker has filled stalwartly with Richard, and rather too fast to be seemly. Richard sits down, boots off and legs crossed comfortably, filling his pipe and drinking a glass of port, which is one more glass than James is offered. Transparently the Whiskers are more dependent on the grace of Richard than on the almighty. No point in James attempting to paint a picture, or even produce a swift sketch, of how things are at Spanish Creek, nor of mentioning his strange mate McKenzie.

This experience even tempers his delight in the lusty daughter born to Marie Louise and Herman; and the light surviving in the features of the parental pair. Rejoice? That light is a human incandescence he may never know. He seems everywhere a stranger in Lovelock Junction now, unless with Ira Dix.

'What I don't purely figure,' Ira says, 'is why six feet deep. That's how deep they dug him, for a true fact. I don't reckon as how I'd care for it. How about you?'

'Death demands it,' James says.

'Death? There's another thing I don't purely figure.'

'It is,' James explains, 'one of the two important things.'

'So tell me the other so I remember it right.'

'Love,' James announces.

'Love?' Ira says, with some wonder. Richard has told him money. So it seems there are three.

'And death you don't need to remember,' James adds bitterly. 'It's love that doesn't come to us all.'

James rows home to Spanish Creek to take consolation in the company of McKenzie. Spanish Creek itself now makes for queerly less. The beauty is still there, true. But he sees beauty as a burden, perhaps to the grave. Man cannot live by beauty alone.

'I dream of the dead,' McKenzie confides over breakfast one morning.

The more McKenzie talks of himself, the more James is intrigued. The Scot is no ordinary man, no common shepherd. 'What dead?'

'My dead. Ay, whose else? My own. They try to speak.'

'What were they? Who?'

'My kin, laddie. The ones who lost their lands, their crofts, when the lairds came with the clearances. Who saw their highland acres turned over to sheep, since sheep were the more profitable than people, and their dwellings blazed to make grouse shooting grounds for the gentry. I dream them. My head fills with bees. Ay.'

'They died?'

'Some slow. Some fast. Some starved of supping nae more than seaweed broth on a barren shore. Or when the blight came to take their taties. The hempen fever took those who stole sheep merciful quick. My cousin Andrew, a hungry lad, took only the two. But they had a noose the right fit for his thin neck. My grandmother, ay, was the more fortunate. She would nae give the gentry the peaceful sport they craved. So she burned up in her crofter's cottage, when the torch was put, because she said she would nae leave it never. She did nae see the darkness to follow. Were better for many had they likewise left their lives in the highlands, to save the misery to come, the clans crushed and scattered.'

'Some survived. You did.'

'Only with God. There was a matter of missing sheep, and a hemp collar ready. So I took ship to Australia. I shepherded for gentry till God sent drought enough for their flocks to perish. My master said nae more, and made mince of his brain with a shotgun. So I tried my fingers ferreting wealtl from the golden fleece. Until I had coin enough, I thought, to look for land in this country. There were empty acres in the south, some told me. Ay. Empty acres. Waiting.'

'You found some?'

'Ay. So they say.' McKenzie wipes his mouth, and casts crusts to his dog. 'Another story, laddie, in more ways than one. And too long for the telling with the day's work for the doing. A tale maybe not greatly to your taste, nor mine. There are times when I think I have lived too long. Nae matter. I am here, I breathe, and elsewhere another man by my name marches on. I can nae longer claim him as kin, though some might say he has my likeness. God is the judge. Not man, though many presume.'

McKenzie meanders enigmatically into the distance, casually about his business at Spanish Creek, with Sunday close behind. James works fitfully on his homestead. On the whole, however, he has had few days more frustrating. Sometimes he pauses, with passing thoughts of Diana melting into those of McKenzie, and looks up at his hills. They seem something less than his hills now. They are yon hills. He sees them more with McKenzie's simple eye: impersonally man's for the making.

Not until evening, with lamps lit, bellies full, and fire burning low, does McKenzie begin to make sense. For even legend, and the highlander is nothing if not legend now, has some sense as its seed. James at last comprehends that McKenzie is McKenzie, despite his denial.

McKenzie has become a name known wherever men gather to talk of great deeds in this land; a man who has passed into mountain mist, leaving lore to match the proudest peaks, now sitting grey, slow and solid, the firelight catching the corrugations in his face. Ay, says McKenzie, he came to try his luck in this land. But the gentry were first. James, with awe, and frequent need to relight his pipe, settles to listen; he has the sensation that he is back with the sage Upokonui again.

Ay, says McKenzie. The gentry had gobbled the land, where giant birds once grazed, and which Maoris found too frosty, all the way back to the mountains; they gulped plain and ridge and river, and when their pedigree guts were full, disgorged it all into tidy shapes they titled their own. They turned tides of sheep upon their acres, in bleating breakers, and built huge homesteads with wealth from wool. Outsiders were excluded, for the sake of decencies, and to keep the labouring classes useful in their place. And especially highland ruffians the unruly like of a son of the McKenzie clan, utilitarian as a warrior if persuaded to succumb to the Queen's shilling; or maybe, if careful watch were kept, as a sullen shepherd. McKenzie, persisting, at first located a little coastal land, some scrappy acres unaccountably neglected in the inland stampede to the mountains. When he tried to take title he found frustration and delay which he thought due to his difficulty with the English tongue, until at length he was told that the very land had been titled to a gentleman of repute but the previous hour. McKenzie, then, was lost in a land new in name only; the enemy was old. His money soon going, often genteelly swindled, he still had hope; he was young. And he had a dog named Friday. He had taught the bitch a highland trick or two. Sometimes it seemed they were one.

They walked, man and dog, and kept walking. Due west, into the sunsets, toward the mountains. There were days of dust, and nights of storm. They passed the point where the gentry had drawn the line, reined in their horses, and cantered back to comfort again. Beyond their boundary cairns rose the mountains. No mountains mean much to a highlander. They climbed, man and dog, and kept climbing. Blizzards blew. Lightning crackled. Thunder crashed. Snowflakes whitened them again and again as they walked. There were rivers in rampage and walls of thorn ten feet tall. Then, as McKenzie suspected, there was a diminishing in this dangerous landscape; these were not primary mountains at all. They limped on, man and dog, and at last were given their gift. The mountains moved apart. For all his optimism dour McKenzie still heard his heart hymning thanks. There, crisp under a cold sun, barricaded on all sides by bulky white peaks, was a large and empty land beyond a mere Scot's imagining. A treeless plain of three million alpine acres all told, with no footprint save that of the one man and one dog who now tramped its tawny tussock spaces. They had won a world; they commanded a kingdom. Now realist, McKenzie knew the territory safe for himself only so long as it was secret. One whisper astray, and he would be bundled aside, quite legal, while the gentry feasted afresh.

Meanwhile, his wilderness could not be left waste. He and Friday, making return over the ranges, set about stocking it. He would call at a gent's station, work a day or two for his food, and before departure show Friday a fair flock of sheep, and whisper a Gaelic word or two in the dog's ear. Overnight the flock would vanish forever. None heard Friday come. None heard Friday go. Swift and soft in the dark, Friday fastened the flock tight, and took it to waiting McKenzie. In the morning they would be marching the flock over the mountains, and soon turning them loose on the new land to graze. When fat and fit toward summer's end, the sheep were driven south by man and dog, persuaded through tight passes, swum across wide rivers, and then sold to dealers who asked no questions and paid tidy prices. Meantime, wherever gentry gathered, and whenever news printed, the matter of the missing flocks was given close attention. Who, and how, and where? None much noticed the lean Scot with little comprehensible to say, who worked for his keep, never for pay, with a queer affection for his untidy dog. Not that they were ever in sight long, McKenzie and Friday, for the keen-eyed to note.

All kingdoms fall. Even a highlander has no mandate from heaven. McKenzie and Friday took one flock too many, from a station riskily close to the ranges, and left a firm line of prints, one thousand of sheep, plus those of one man and one dog, for outraged proprietor and posse to follow. They found McKenzie camped comfortable, at the craggy door to his hidden domain, with the sheep grazing round. And Friday too, the dog some would soon denounce as witch and demand to be hanged.

There was a trial of sorts, in which much was said, though not by McKenzie, who cannily claimed inability to comprehend. He was heard, when heard at all, to be asking for his dog. The judge had no inclination to acknowledge this plea. His sentence, or so he learned by way of middling Gaelic translation, was five years' gaol. Five. He was still asking for his dog when marched away to serve his time. Some should have listened. For the thickest prison is a petty thing when intemperate love is denied. McKenzie took himself from confinement in one long stride, and began hunting through the hills for the homestead where he heard his widely-desired Friday was now lawfully employed. Police shot him twice in the back, but he plucked out the bullets like prickles and continued to run, until hounded down by horsemen, and bound with all the rope the law could locate. Back in prison he was given the darkest cell and the heaviest shackles to be had in the colony. As if these made some difference. He departed with the shackles. Hired Maoris, with horses and dogs, tracked him down. Even bloodied, black with bruises, he still seemed to have learned no lesson; he made third escape. And the crowds began to cry shame.

In virtuously Anglican Christchurch, where the wool-rich gentry were busy building old green England anew on antipodean swamp, with cathedral rising and soon cricket on the green, the lower orders were at last tending to make much of McKenzie, as even the best selected lower orders will, seeing a Scots outlaw as symbol and one of their own; they sang songs, in which his name figured, and also the word freedom, in the rougher saloons and drunkenly out in the streets. McKenzie's captors, conceivably men sometimes kindly, began suffering discomfort. Also perplexity; where in the colony could be found the prison to contain such a man? It might come to building a tomb, with walls ten feet thick, at a cost the colony could not yet contemplate; and all to confine one man called McKenzie whose Gaelic cunning, allied with love for a cur called Friday, might forever confound them. The gentry, which included judges and lawyers and sheep-farming jurors who found for the Queen, had other misgivings. God knew where the disloyal shouts in the streets might lead, perhaps to the ravings of radical Chartists and liberals who had lately given old England a bad name, and made that homeland desirable to quit. McKenzie might be their undoing. Democracy, an epidemic elsewhere, could be contagion here too.

So gentry and gaolers went to McKenzie with an interesting proposition. He was innocent, they suggested; it had all been a mistake. McKenzie, with reason, was wary. By whom, then, he asked, had the thieving been done? Who had really taken the flocks he stole? And where, by the way, was his dog Friday? Patience, they pleaded; first things first. An innocent man unjustly suffering a five year sentence should, they argued, have more on his mind than a dog. Yes, yes, if needs must the dog could be found, but let us please proceed with the matter most urgently in hand. That is, your innocence. If I am innocent, McKenzie asked, with diverse Gaelic oaths, who in hell took those damned sheep? Gentry and gaolers, men not without guile, could answer that too. It was all, they told him, the work of a vast gang, no doubt Australian, of which he had been dupe; the gang had decamped, plainly, leaving McKenzie red-handed with a thousand odd sheep. And what, demanded McKenzie, as a matter of pride, of all those other thousands I took? Unreasonable, they replied, to think that all the work of one man; the same gang had to be responsible. A right rare bloody gang, said convict McKenzie sourly; there was never nae sod to be seen when there was nocturnal shepherding to be done. Look, McKenzie, good man, they told him, we have your interests at heart; please have patience, listen, and understand. A plea for a pardon, protesting your innocence, will receive swift attention from the authorities; we can make you a free man in a month. Meantime, dear God, just don't escape again.

McKenzie began to comprehend. He stroked his beard, allowing it to be understood that he had their proposal under consideration. Yes, they added; one other thing. We should like you, when you are free, to quit the colony as quick as you can. We will pay the passage, even ensure a few pounds in your pocket. McKenzie was still further amazed to see how they feared him: there seemed no end to the bribes. And just whom were they seeking to propitiate and pacify? Why, an unlettered Scots outlaw who at home might be hung; that was who. His interests at heart? He'd see them in hell. They had their own interests hid in their thoroughbred hearts. It was no more his to wonder why. It was his to deal with the devil, and tell a plausible lie. Though tempted to spite them, and continue confessing to lifting their flocks, this meant denying his dog. Perhaps Friday, God knew, was pining loveless among strangers, whimpering through cold nights. So he had no choice; he put aside pride. He dealt with the devil, allowed the pen placed in his hand to form a shaky signature at the foot of their documents, for the sake of his dog. God might forgive a highlander who lied for love. And in a month, as promised, he was a free man with Friday. Strangers sought to shake his hand. Drunks jostled, demanding the right to purchase him ale. But in the end the crowds parted before him, for fear of witch-dog Friday's evil eye. And McKenzie, an honourable highlander, at least so long as sheep were never on show, boarded the first ship he saw; it was a vessel bound for Australia.

There McKenzie lived as merely a man by that name. For near two decades none knew him as more than simple shepherd or shearer, a man tidy enough about his tasks; never as ruler in exile from his realm. He was not so remote that rumour did nae reach him across the sea. His vast personal plain, he heard, had fast been consumed by aspirant gentry. Men with grace or gall to call the long-hid three million acres the Mackenzie Country, characteristically misspelling an honest Scot name. Soon, and here was the chief news he cherished, Englishmen began to fret with the pains of pasturing flocks in that austere wilderness; it stuck in their gullet after all, never quite digested; they died of ignorance, frostbite, avalanche, drowning and despair. So their abandoned territories, across that once solo kingdom, were taken up by tenacious highlanders denied lands elsewhere; men with names not unlike McKenzie or Mackenzie, misspelled or nae. His last laugh had bonus in his belly. He had known those acres to be for his kind, if not now for himself, as he whispered to Friday in the time she lay dying, but not before she bequeathed the world a most satisfying litter of witches, from among whom he selected the most promising pup. And likewise, before expiring under the hooves of a mad horse, Saturday bore Sunday; he enjoyed the joke of a sheepdog named for the sabbath, not least since Sunday seldom knew a day of rest. Nor he. The years were long, the work always harsh. He accepted, as most must, that he was not his own man, but beholden to masters; yet he was luckier than many, with their sullen dreams stillborn, to have the once lived luminous hours free, supping the wine of his own wilderness. But Australia became a burden on a highlander's soul. Too flat, too dry; the sun too hot, the earth too hard. He longed for mountain and moist wind. He took ship again, when he had the coin, but not home to the highlands; the past was past, his kin dead or migrated, and the Inverness police less lenient with maybe longer memories than their kind in the colonies; an old and now laughably little sheep theft might no longer mean a noose, but he'd had the once of prison to last him a life. Never nae more. But New Zealand was surely safe now. The men to whom he once gave his word were now mostly dead: who could care that McKenzie was now back in the colony? And who might McKenzie be anyway? Or such was his thought when he sighted green land again, a week out of Sydney. He could smell moistness and mist in the land, all but hear rustle of wet leaves, cool wind across rivers and lakes and lonely places. Home, or as good as for a highlander, a land in which he might more comfortably die. Even Sunday, alert on the deck, began to bristle with recognition of ancestral shore ahead; of hill and mountain her grandmother roamed, and for her obedience been denounced and all but done to death. Still, that was all near a score of years behind. Together, man and dog, they might now hope for tolerable peace. Ay. Nae more.

Ashore, walking soft soil again, revelling in gentle sun and sweet rain, McKenzie found a rift, a crevasse too wide for any mere man to bridge; he had somewhere and cruelly miscalculated. He had not counted on life. Nor on legend. The needs of men, their love of large lies for the glory of their telling, dismayed a simple Scot sheep-stealer. Everywhere he wandered and worked with Sunday, the length of the land, he discovered himself haunted and all but undone, where men took fermented fluids as their muse, by the tale of the brawny Scot outlaw, surely towering ten feet, who did down the gentry with his magical dog; a man who could outrun a horseman for all of a measured mile; a man who might fell a bullock with a flick of fist; a man with an appetite attested so huge that he needed a brace of fowls to fill his belly for breakfast; a man who prised mountains apart and pulverized prisons. A man with a dog, yes, who could near make sheep fly; and maybe the damn dog did. McKenzie, bemused, would have to sit quiet with his own tiny truth. And sometimes let Sunday sup from his ale. Often his head filled with bees and his soul with rebellion as men made free with his name. He was tempted to tell them: McKenzie is me. But who would ever believe a scant Scot, just five feet and eleven inches tall, too sober to be true? Who would believe this meek and mostly mild shepherd to be the lawless highland larrikin who brawled his way through the land's lonely places, never behaving as less than rogue bull? He longed to say, and not without love: It were not like that; I just did what I did; now, ay, let me alone. The once he confessed, because of more than enough ale, he had himself laughed out of town; with mockery his tormentors reliably informed him of McKenzie's death these many years past. Already he has been told with authority of a dozen graves in which the remains of McKenzie are unmistakably rotting, on which no grass grows, only and mysteriously Scottish heather; and where a ghostly hound is heard mourning on moonlit nights. Also, sometimes, the less chilling sound of stolen flocks passing.

'Sometimes, ay, I wish I were gone,' McKenzie tells James. 'The better I was, maybe, rather than risk the ruin of so grand a tale. It is nae without beauty. Sometimes, true, I can wish that madder McKenzie me. Other times, ay, I feel sickness in soul. Why am I here? Ay. Why? Better that I was in the beyond with Friday.' With only a few red coals left for comfort on this cooling autumn night, McKenzie rests affectionate hand on his dog.

'But Sunday,' James objects. 'You have her. And you're here. Safe from laughter. And discomfort.'

'Nae by chance,' McKenzie says.

'No?' James is surprised.

'There was, ay, despair to drive me, and maybe a wee nudge from my Maker. I looked for as lonely a river as any I could find in this land. My prayer found answer in the Porangi, a place not much marked on maps, where men are new. And my dreams, ay, dreams, delivered this place ye queerly call Spanish Creek. I saw it clear, night after night, long before I ever set foot on your soil.'

James takes this as poetic truth, though God knows he should have learned. 'I see,' he says politely.

'Only it was different, in dream,' McKenzie discloses.

'Different?'

'The lowland was the same. The crops and cows. Even the creek running bright. And, ay, I saw ye for my mate. There was nae mistaking the place when I saw it, nor ye. Dream even seemed to be saying there was love in your name. I did nae get that meaning right until I saw ye solid with your surname.'

'But what was different?' James demands, still sceptical, and impatient.

'The rest,' McKenzie says.

'The rest?'

'The hills, man. The lonely hills.'

James remains baffled.

'They were green,' McKenzie explains, 'and fair, with fine grass growing. Nae thick with trees, though some stood shady. The grass shone with dew in the morning light. And, ay, across the grass, over the hills, so far as man might see, there were white sheep grazing.'

James sighs. McKenzie, more or less as mythology has it, is not a man to leave well alone. Yet there are times when he tempts. His dream, true vision or retrospective fancy, provokes James to one of his own that night. Restless in his rough bunk, he dreams of Diana. She is clad only in white fleeces, which fall seductively from sweet flesh. Not a dream to compete with McKenzie's; or one he could confide. But its meaning, if a shade coarsely carnal, is plain.

Next day, after a breakfast of bacon and cold damper bread, he walks out into the morning with McKenzie. The crops are mostly gathered; the cows, with calf, are beginning to dry off. And the light is eloquent on the wooded hills. He remembers Upokonui, long in the grave. Penance he has done. He might need further forgiveness.

'Sheep,' James muses. 'I wonder.'

'Sheep?' McKenzie says, ever alert.

'I have been thinking. I could run a few.'

'Ay,' McKenzie agrees. 'With the hills in good grass.'

'It has not been to my taste,' James explains, 'to be a gentleman farmer. But there are times, and tides. And seasons for all things.'

'Ye talk of a lass,' McKenzie suggests.

'In a way,' James allows, 'if I am talking of sheep.'

'And a house,' McKenzie adds, 'set on large grazing land.'

'More or less,' James admits. 'The picture is plain. It seems needs must. But where to begin?'

'With the hills. Ay. Burn them off this autumn, with the weather still dry, and sparks easy spreading into tall hungry flame. The trees will take fast. There is nae pain to plants.'

James flinches. 'But the beauty,' he says.
'Think of the lass,' McKenzie advises.
'I do,' James answers. 'Alas. To my shame.'
'And your sons to be. Ay. There's little selfish in that. Man born of woman has wee time in this world. He has duty to do. There's nae shame in preparing the way for humans to come.'
'If you say,' James observes. 'But I note you have fathered none.'
'Unless a bastard or two,' McKenzie agrees. 'Though, ay, there's some say that other McKenzie spawned bundles of brats through the south. If I'd spent that time fornicating, surely those flocks would have been safe. For love of a dog much may be forgiven. There's nae been love left to spend free on a woman. So never. And never nae sons. For best I have ye.'
'Me?' James is moved.
'Ay. Ye. Times, here, I feel like a father with son to be soothed. Perhaps there is the truth I found troubling in dream. In darkness of soul I searched out a son. I could nae find one more fine. It is time for the saying. My mate is more son.'
James is embarrassed. His unfamiliar feelings are at least diversion from Diana; his moods in her connection are all too monotonous. 'I'm grateful,' he says, 'but we were talking of sheep.'
'Ay. Sheep on yon hills.'
James, now, is almost reconciled.
'When the fire's work is done,' McKenzie continues, 'ye scatter good grass seed in its shadow, through all the rich ash, with the coming of winter. In spring the first pale young blades will gather to green. Ash and earth, ay, will give the lushest of grazing. You will never know yon hills. Nae. Never.'
This is something, for the moment, James would sooner not know. 'You speak,' he says, 'as if you will not be here to share this work. Nor see its fruit.'
'Nae, lad,' McKenzie agrees. 'I'll be gone.'
'Where?' James feels panic. He now needs McKenzie. 'Gone where?'
'The burning is your task. And the sowing. Mine will be fetching the sheep.'
James does not comprehend.
'I see a long journey,' McKenzie reveals. 'But I'm of a mind, ay, for one more long drive. Maybe my last, one men may remember, if they must make still more of McKenzie. Or maybe just to show I'm not dead, for all that they say, and there's a little life yet in this lank old highland bugger.'

'You are,' James says with shock, 'talking of theft. Of going off stealing again.'

'Ay. I have, more or less, that thought in my mind.'

'No,' James says firmly. 'There's no need.'

'Need? I know what I need. There are times, ay, when my confession still shames me. The work of a gang, and me their poor fool? It were all the work of one, and my Friday, and this highland son is nae fool. They made me grovel, plead innocent, for the sake of my dog.'

'But men know that confession to be fiction. As you have said.'

'My statement is there, and signed with my hand. Nae matter that my hand was pushed. I was weak in the wit. They made me less man.'

'Guilty men plead innocent in courts every day, and kindly jurors often find them so. Where's the grief? Law is a game. I have had a lawyer tell me. He was drunk, and rich, and thought law all a matter of laughter.'

'Life is nae game for a McKenzie. And a man made less man, for love of his hound, is nae greatly given to laughter. I still have some wee pride. I may, ay, have more when this winter is finished.'

'It cannot be done,' James announces. 'I am sorry. I will not allow it.'

McKenzie, eyes bright, appears to find this of no moment. 'I have but the one fear,' he admits, 'when all truth is told.'

'What fear?' James has his own. Prison for possession of stolen sheep might not kill all dreams of Diana; it would certainly kill all hope. 'What fear is this?'

'The years have been long. The body tires sooner. But I have my bitch Sunday. As true a granddaughter as Friday could have. This will be test.'

'No,' James insists.

McKenzie acknowledges that James has inclination to protest. 'Look, lad, there is one thing ye must know. A mate is a mate.'

This is too obscure for James.

'A man,' McKenzie goes on, 'must take his mate on trust. Ye must take me as I am. Nae more. Nae less. And I promise this. Ye need only take me as I am the once.'

'All the same,' James objects, 'theft is theft. Maybe once, when this land was younger, a thief might be hero when injustice was rife. And greed. No more. The time has gone. Men must have respect for their neighbours. There is a commandment.'

'There is also a McKenzie. My kind has another commandment: He who does nae steal from the gentry, steals from his children. I would nae steal from ye, James. Never. And nae steal from the sons to be of my son.' McKenzie is vehement; it is as if James has just accused him of being light-fingered. James finds his own moral sense in much confusion. And the unfamiliar contours of McKenzie's conscience are impossible to follow. McKenzie adds, 'There let it be.'

'I cannot,' James says.

'There could be feud between us before nightfall. Between father and son.'

'Besides, there are no gentry, not in these parts. No.'

'I look further,' McKenzie says fiercely. 'Do ye have nae faith in me? There is gentry, the other side of this island, who took their lands sometimes by fair means, mostly by foul. Cousins, sometimes sons, of they who had me slander myself in the south. There is just the one account to settle. I am nae of a mind to press my claim more than is just. And they have, besides, more sheep than is good. Even a highland fool can see their large flocks turning green earth to dust. Ay.'

James, for the moment, can only marvel.

'I will see ye come spring,' McKenzie promises. 'Tomorrow I'll start.'

'Madness,' James argues. 'All madness. Not only the stealing. The other side of the island? That's hundreds of miles. There are volcanoes, deserts, vast forests. Lakes the size of seas. And Maoris still wild, who shoot white men on sight. This isn't your south. There are no empty plains. No mountains for markers. No familiar horizons to follow. Nothing. Just swampland, and swift rivers, all darkened with trees. Men have lost themselves there forever. Never again seen.'

McKenzie is indifferent. 'I take the sun as my compass. And there are stars out at night. There is also Sunday to scent peril. And I trust my own instinct's still fair.'

'God,' James says wearily, knowing defeat.

'In Him too I have more than wee trust. This highlander's nae heathen. Or nae when the going is grim.'

'Please,' James says, though now most to himself. His scruples seem puny; he has to allow that McKenzie has his own code to prove. 'All right,' he adds, compounding confusion. 'So long as you keep fair tally of all sheep you take. Maybe, when richer, I can pay compensation.'

'A theft must be theft,' McKenzie replies stern. 'A highlander's justice. Ye'll nae deny me. Never, lad, never.'

James sighs. 'Tell me no more.'

'Ay. If ye say. But we'll be back fit and bright. With a fair flock of sheep.'

Next day, with bag on his back, green staff in hand, and only a wide hat to hold off the weather, McKenzie departs Spanish Creek with his dog Sunday dawdling at heel. James watches them leave until they are lost in far trees. All is quiet, but for the birds. The hills seem the same. So do his acres. There is his old hut, and his half-finished homestead. It is just that nothing is quite real; he feels as a sleeper just awoken, unable to juggle himself free of the debris of dream.

Such a mood cannot last. Nor is it healthy with work to be done. There is forest to be fired. And grass to be sown. The autumn holds fine. Delays might mean rain. As human as he can make himself, a more or less dutiful son, he goes to his hut to fetch matches and axe. The wind is in the right quarter; the sky could not be more clear.

Later that day he sees himself less farmer than apprentice incendiarist. With chopped brushwood heaped here and there, the wind still brisk on the back of his neck, he tries to survey his preparatory labour with some satisfaction. If his calculation is correct, and he sees no reason why not, the conflagration will travel down toward the valley, taking only the trees needed. Then, please God, it will perish with a whisper when it meets his open land; there will be nothing to feed the flame further. For safety he has shifted his cows to the other side of the valley, beyond hut and embryo homestead. All is ready. There is no cause to linger. He has matches in hand. But he does linger, more and more vexingly, until by great good fortune his imagination makes free with a most intimate vision, alas not from experience, of long-limbed Diana bedded naked beside him. Ay, lad. Think of the lass. His regrets unravel; his hand doesn't hesitate. With firmly struck match, he gives himself to igniting the forest.

The bonfires blaze one by one, spilling their sparks into undergrowth; flame trickles, aimlessly at first, among fern and tree; there are short gusts of dark smoke where green foliage is caught. Like a nervous executioner, unsure of his skill on the scaffold, James is all frustration: will it never begin?

Soon he cannot complain. With hissing there, crackling there, the fire cacophonously begins to live its own life, with magical indifference to the fears and affairs of the man who fathered it. No longer in bright rivulets; in fleet rivers and glutting deltas. Flame booms tidally among the trees. All are soon torches. There is dismay; there is also glory. The heat scalds his face as he continues to back away bewildered. Further still, from a safe hilltop, he hears the first gutted trees begin to fall, sees sparks and molten debris spinning higher. The sky blackens with smoke and wind-borne cinders. And there are the birds; birds blind on the wing as their sanctuaries are cremated. Some, suffocating, fall to the flame; others fly free unsinged. He has chosen not to think of the birds, especially of those born never to fly, the wingless and weak, and of whom it is still best not to think; their demise is never in doubt. The fire? Backed by wind, it changes in nature from fluid to solid; it has the sound of an avalanche rumbling downhill, impossible to halt, difficult to see, as trees crack and crash. Daylight is turning to dusk, with red lightning flashes now and then to be glimpsed, and only unrolling thunder to be heard.

Coughing, stumbling, carrying his axe and with the last of his matches rattling in his pocket, James takes a circuitous route homeward into the valley, beyond the southern flank of the fire. At the creek, which is taking blood-coloured reflections from the glow on the hills, he attempts to wash, to cleanse himself of the smell of smoke. But the water is thick with falling ash. So, everywhere, is his land: his gardens, his fields. And his livestock, fowls, pigs, cattle, horse, all sound their distress. Perhaps, with fright, they sense the end of the world.

It is the end of his. It is Spanish Creek now in name only. He dreams of Upokonui's red-haired fairies who, or so the *tohunga* told him, had their home on his territory; their spirits are dark dressed and in considerable torment. He senses a curse. Next morning he wakes with dull dread in his body. Everything smells acridly of fire. Face, hands, hair; the blankets about him. At length, having mustered courage, he rises and looks out the door of the hut. He can note, if he cares, that as arsonist he has not been too far astray. The holocaust has left off at the edge of his fields, at the foot of the hills, though it has taken more to the westward than was his surmise. As for the hills, he can only suppose them the same. The pyrotechnics are past, revealing spiny shapes rawly sculpted, outlines and outcrops unfamiliar to his gaze; and all now a dark and still smouldering desert in which a few skeletal trees blackly crumble. The silence is startling; even the birds surviving on this safe side of the valley seem unnaturally quiet. Here and there, as on an abandoned battlefield, there are last flickers of flame, small wisps of smoke. It is not to be blinked away; his lips move with no sound. He wonders if McKenzie, surely still not too far distant as he hikes east with his dog, has looked back to see evening made red; or if those at Lovelock Junction, or even downhill at Dixtown, have been awed by a cumulus of smoke climbing the sky. Anyway the announcement must have been plain: James Lovelock is now in business at Spanish Creek. That autumn, so long as sun lasts, there are more fires lit. With winter he sows seed over the black wastes of his creation. Now and then, from conscience or compassion, he pauses to plug in slips of willow and poplar where the earth is worst blistered, also some seedlings of pine he has had sent from New Plymouth. In the same season, often under cover of canvas while the rains are heavy, he gets on with hammering up his homestead; soon it appears to be solid, though there is much work within to be done. McKenzie, mate or father, is never far from his thoughts. Diana? The Whisker household, when he visits, is as cold as the southerlies whining up from the pole. Even Diana can only manage a colourless smile, as if she has given up hope. He can only think to surprise her.

Felicity grows. She totters four tiny paces at the age of six months; she talks, quite perceptibly, in no more than another two. Herman and Marie Louise often find cause to congratulate each other on the miracle they have made. She is a rare beauty. Her colour is pale gold; her eyes large and blue. She has a light musical laugh, especially with mischief in mind. Marie Louise has to chase her child, with that tinkling chuckle, through corridor after echoing corridor of Lovelock House. 'You will make me old,' Marie Louise shouts, in an affectionate rage. To Herman, however, she argues. 'She will keep us both young. I wish she were an infant forever. When they grow, children are never the same.' Whether younger or older, or both in the one mood, Marie Louise knows one thing to be true. Felicity is the life and light of Lovelock Junction. Not only God's blessing; God's compensation too. But Luke isn't forgotten. There is never a week when Marie Louise doesn't freshen the linen on his bed. Dust never gathers, nor spiders spin webs, in that room always ready; Marie Louise regularly opens windows to welcome new air. And sometimes, at that point, she prays. God might yet have other marvels to perform, such as a lost and found Luke once more laughing at their table. If reality never quite obliges, and Luke never returns, it is not for want of prayer on Marie Louise's part. For she knows how life could be.

Herman, for his part, knows how Lovelock Junction could be, preferably with Luke, probably without. The problem is persuading others to see it; or, more precisely, to interpret his intention. Prayers, if he made them, might impress God. Mankind is more intractable. Or so Herman discovers when, seeking a substitute for now deceased Whisker, he has architect after architect, some of the colony's finest, voyage up the Porangi to stand perplexed on the plateau. All tend to arrive dishevelled, tired after travel, men made wild-eyed by the forests around; they are also, too soon, men in despair. For one thing, there is Porangi Palace, of which rumour has spread.

'So that's it,' they say, and then walk softly about Whisker's proclamation.

The phraseology of their verdict varies; but it is always, in substance, the same. Sometimes they frown. More often they smile. And one or two are heard, at least when Herman's back is turned, to snicker.

'I can't compete with that,' one says. 'Who could?'

'No town could contain it,' another observes, 'without looking askew.'

'Leave things as they are,' a third advises. 'You have something unique here. More construction would detract.'

And a fourth seems final. 'After this,' he announces, 'architecture has no more to say.'

These are contemptible excuses. For all finally confess inability to accept Herman's handsome commission on grounds of likely hardship for their wives and children up the Porangi; their womenfolk wouldn't stand for it, Dixtown is undesirably close, and where are the physicians and schools, the social conveniences? Herman, or so he is given to understand, should seek some needy architect, for whom the rigours of exile up the Porangi would be no grief. The difficulty is, they agree, that elsewhere the colony is booming with borrowed money, roads and railways being pushed through, hinterlands pioneered, towns and cities taking shape; there are no longer needy architects about of the unusual calibre of Alfred Whisker.

One architect, before departing, is more practical than most. 'If you must get on with a town,' he suggests, 'then try colonial villas. You know the kind of thing. Gable roof. Fancy bargeboards. Fretwork friezes. Long veranda.'

Herman sighs. He heard it all from Whisker before the bugger talked him into baronial.

'You don't need me,' the architect adds, before hastily boarding his boat. 'Just a reliable builder. A colonial villa is straightforward. Gable roof. Fancy bargeboards. Fretwork—'

'And good day to you too,' Herman says.

The last architect to leave the Porangi is distinctly crueller. He walks the plateau with Herman first.

'A town?' he says. 'You want a town?'

'Yes,' Herman agrees. 'Of a kind. A new kind.'

'But basically a town.'

'There is no other word for it.'

'But good God, man, you've got one.'

Herman at first does not understand. Not until the architect, after mopping his brow, points downhill. He is indicating Dixtown.

'What is that,' he asks. 'if not a town?'

There is a considerable silence. It is as if unlovely Dixtown has lurched into Herman's view for the first time. He hears the sounds of women and children, of coal wagons rumbling, and sawyers at work. Richard's domain is highly audible. It makes equally sharp assault on the sense of sight.

'I prefer,' Herman explains, 'to see that as a collection of dwellings of temporary nature.'

'Like many or most places in this country,' the architect argues. 'Or, God spare us, in America or Australia too. But they're no less towns for that. Get on with it, man. Make the best of what you have. Meanwhile, I have a steamer to catch.'

Herman takes time to recover from this encounter. One truth, however, does disclose itself among his stunned ruminations. Dixtown, almost without his noticing, that lack doubtless due to his many other preoccupations, has solidified in startling fashion. The canvas and corrugated iron of the earlier dwellings have all but gone; there are now houses, not huts. Houses of durable timber pit-sawn from the logs the bullock teams drag from the forest to feed Richard's growing mill. Inelegant, God knows, but identifiably houses; and homes. Women have planted pansies, lilies, spring bulbs and rose bushes before their front doors, and men have their tidy potato patches at the rear; there are lace curtains visible in some windows, and polished copper oil lamps. There is a pretence of footpaths, for safety from passing wagons, between buildings. There is the enlarged store which Paramena efficiently manages for Richard; and the sly grog shop inconspicuous behind. There is now a small schoolhouse of sorts, provided by Richard as concession to the unrealistic desire of his employees for social betterment of their children, where Sybil Whisker takes classes when not diverted by the more scholarly needs of Iris, Benjamin and Ernest upon the plateau. Smells have diminished; drains have been dug, cesspits improved and nightsoil collection organized since dysentery began depleting Richard's work-force. It has all, if not really overnight, happened. Even a makeshift recreation area, hardly to be graced with the name of park, on the outskirts of the settlement, where tree stumps still survive; children congregate there to kick a muddy football.

True that much is raw edged; that Dixtown is unkindly situated close to mines and mill, often shadowed by hills from winter sun, and without benefit of breeze in summer heat; that it has grown first in unkempt and then in ungainly fashion; that it is mean, mostly, and confining; that imagination has never informed it; that it just happens to have happened. Nevertheless Herman hears a treasonous inner voice echoing that last architect: What is this, if not a town? Because, good God, it is one.

Richard might at least have been content to amuse himself productively, if not altogether beneficently, with timber and coal: not to ambush his brother with an entire blasted town. Richard has long since been resident in Dixtown himself, by way of cruel emphasis, sharing quarters with his partner Paramena.

Yet Herman, as often noted, is not given easily to despair. However much detail may fail him, he still has a covenant to keep; and the trust – which God must know not wholly misplaced – which has moved him now, if dimly, for more than a decade. Dixtown can never contain virtue; the likes of that place can only pay the devil his due. It is the old world again. But how build the new?

At least not in bloody baronial. That much is clear.

To prove his thrust isn't lost, Herman takes the next boat to New Plymouth. There he finds an itinerant red-haired Irish builder by name of Barney Malone. 'It's a matter of houses,' Herman tells him. 'There's a town to begin.'

'Sure,' Malone says. 'I'll give that a go. But first I'm thinking you should tell me what you might have in mind.'

'Straightforward,' Herman explains, 'and simple. Perhaps colonial villas. Gable roof. Fancy bargeboards. And—'

'I'm with you,' Malone says.

Sybil Whisker is not without qualities. The most evident of these, from which Richard soon suffers, is an exceedingly sharp eye. It is even more than usually in evidence on a sweaty spring workday when Sybil sends him a mysterious message to please call while her girls croon over Felicity at Lovelock House. He takes the port she proffers, and sits impatient.

'You still find much to say,' she observes, not quite peripherally, 'to my daughter Diana.'

'No harm in conversation. She's a girl of some charm.'

'So I have noted.' Sybil's voice cools.

'I mean that in the best sense,' Richard hastily adds.

'I have always lived with the worst.'

'Alas,' Richard says. 'But—'

'You could turn the poor girl's head, unless you take care. She is unhappy enough. Would that she were like Iris. That dear girl is perfectly content. And much more at home here. I should prefer her less a ruffian, when she skylarks off with Benjamin, but it has to be said that she has made that boy more academic. Benjamin, in class, no longer so greatly burdens my soul.'

'All right. I will take care in conversation with Diana. Is that quite enough?'

'Not quite,' Sybil says primly.

'You want me to promise, forever, not to turn the girl's head? If she finds me attractive, what the bloody hell can I do?'

'Richard, please. You are not in the mines.'

'At the moment I wish I were in the mines. I'd know where I was.'

'You are here. Talking. And there are things to be said.'

'Then say them. I don't have all day. I'm expected down at the mill.'

'I wish your mood were more to my liking.'

'I can't help my mood. First you imply that I have designs on your daughter. Or maybe, God forbid, that the girl may be nursing designs on me. Then I'm graced with gossip. There is more to life than this. I'm a man of many affairs. There are a dozen men waiting.'

'Let them wait. I think it timely to consider the future.'

'I have no future if men stand about. And I've had to cut prices this month in New Plymouth.'

'I refer to our future.'

'Ours?'

'Ours.'

Richard has lived in large fear of this moment. 'Yes,' he says, sobered. 'I see.'

'Our association is now of some long standing. It is, perhaps, kindest to be blunt. I think you might appreciate frankness. And coming to the point.'

'Please,' he agrees quietly, with pain.

'I am approaching a subject which by its nature is delicate. And it is often thought unfitting for a woman to speak.'

'I'm not averse to trying my hand at delicate matters.' He pauses, lengthily. 'You wouldn't, perhaps, consider postponing this until I have more time?'

'No. I am afraid I cannot. I have gathered my courage. In any case I can hardly think that you mistake my meaning. It is all but said. I am talking of marriage. Does that cause you some surprise?'

'Not entirely,' Richard finds politic to say.

'Some consternation, then.'

'I wouldn't say consternation, quite.'

'What would you say? At the moment you are saying nothing of substance.'

'One thing I will say is that I'd like a touch more port. The second is that there is your husband to be considered.'

'Alfred? He's dead.'

'But hardly cold in his grave.'

'We have just survived a rigorous winter. It should, by my measure, have done much to cool him.'

'It's just a few months. The dead deserve respect.'

'He deserved little in life; and he's had his due now. I have worn widow's weeds. What more can I do? What more can we?'

'There are times,' Richard confesses, finding truth usefully elastic, 'when I am haunted by the fact of what we were about when he fell from the tower. Or jumped, as seems certain.'

'I do not know that I care to take your meaning. You mean that he knew, and we were the cause?'

'I mean that, whatever the truth, it seems an ill omen.'

'You have lived altogether too long beside Maoris, with their foul superstitions. This Paramena, for example, in whom you appear to place so much trust. You give me to understand that he was one of these murderous Hau Hau, a cannibal killer, and doubtless one with a head filled to the brim with dark beliefs. An ill omen? Indeed. Is that what he told you?'

'I am not in the habit of discussing my more intimate affairs with Paramena.'

'And I should hope not. Nevertheless this unfortunate creature seems somewhat to have infected you. What we were about, that particular day, has to my mind no more significance than what we were about on more days than is wholesome to remember. It is the way the world is. It is the way we are. I could as well have been cooking a meal, to gratify his indiscriminate appetite, the moment Alfred lost his footing on that parapet.'

'People on parapets mostly mean to lose their footing.'

'If you insist. But please put aside Paramena and pagan ill omens. We are of the civilized world. We are also, I make bold to say, talking of marriage. It would be remiss of me not to note that thus far in the conversation, unless I am very much mistaken indeed, you have neglected to smile. You have not indicated the slightest warmth toward the proposition.'

Richard attempts to smile. To indicate warmth is equally demanding.

'Or said that you love me,' she adds.

'I love you, of course,' Richard agrees.

'Much better,' she observes. 'For a moment, doubtless unjustly, I detected a faltering. I now see a gentlemanly shyness. In its way, quite attractive.'

'I wish things were simpler,' Richard argues.

'Are they not, dear heart?'

'If we were to marry, at this point, people would tend to talk.'

'Are they not talking already? For the less obtuse, surely, our affection should be plain. You are now in this house often. Conclusions can be drawn.'

'All the same,' Richard begins vainly.

'To be frank, as I must be, I see procrastination. Disrespect for the dead. Ill omens. Now fear of foolish gossip. What next?'

Diana's name teeters perilously on the tip of Richard's tongue. He swallows it fast.

'There is pressure of work to be taken into account,' he explains. 'I am expanding the mill. It is in that connection my men, at the moment, are waiting. As I earlier mentioned. You've caught me at a deuced inconvenient time.'

'Then run to your men. I may well find it inconvenient, in future, to have you share my bed.'

'Sybil,' Richard pleads.

'You have my full attention.'

'Things cannot, so swiftly, have reached this unpleasant pass.'

'You are mistaken. It is my impression they have.'

'Please understand. I have nothing in principle against marriage.'

'Most gracious. Words fail me. Doubtless there are stranger forms of courtship. Perhaps your precious cannibal companion would know.'

'Leave Paramena alone. He is a valued colleague, a trusted friend.'

'And what am I? Merely his partner's paid mistress? I don't doubt he smirks. In his savage soul he probably takes pleasure in a Christian woman's degradation.'

'You're going on.'

'Indeed I will go on. I may well have just begun. And if in consequence you feel sorry for yourself, as I fear may be the case, do not look to me for sympathy.'

Richard digs his last ditch. 'Marriage is not to be rushed into. It is an institution which needs respect.'

'You have a queer way of showing it. In the matter of adultery. I rather imagine I am far from the first.'

'Would it be so grievous to delay it a little? Hang it all, Sybil, it's a dashed awkward time.'

She remains unimpressed. Frost is perceptibly forming. 'I shall ask you just one thing,' she proposes.

'Please do.'

'Would you be seeking delay if it were, say, Diana to whom you were to be wed?' she inquires, with some sting.

'That's an impossible question. In fact quite absurd.'

'I think not. I think it places your evasions in perfect perspective. Allowing the onlooker to see how contemptible they are.'

'I don't need a girl. I want a woman.'

'But in her place. As kept concubine. I discern guilt. Also hidden desires.'

'Now you're hysteric.'

'True hysteria you may well see. So beware.'

Richard needs no warning. But if he loses Sybil Whisker, he manifestly loses Diana. Life was simpler with the Hau Hau; he looks back with longing.

'Perhaps,' she goes on, 'I can scent a sly and unsavoury plan. Such as marrying a daughter and sporting with her mother at the same time. Men never surprise me. Their lives are all lust.'

'You're beyond bloody reason,' Richard, quite forgetting himself, shouts. While the prospect of two women bedded isn't unattractive to Richard, one necessary precondition would be that neither was named Sybil Whisker. 'Give me,' he adds, more quietly, 'some little time to think.'

'A day, then. Two at most. I shall require a firm answer. Meanwhile I should appreciate it if you took no further advantage of a widow's humble and lonely circumstances; do you follow?'

'Quite clearly, my love.'

Returning to Dixtown, Richard is haunted by the sensation of distant bells tolling, though there are none on the Porangi. They are not heralding holy wedlock. They are sounding his doom. Disheartened by the more capricious qualities of his species, just when life should be replete with promise, he finds himself blindly at the mill, where he cannot quite think what to do with the dozen men who wait upon his wish. The mill must be extended. But so must imagination. He dismisses the amazed men for the day. Then he takes his perplexity to Paramena at the store. Paramena's fat and not altogether unkindly face brings some relief.

'I have problems,' Richard confesses.

'Come unto me,' Paramena says, 'all ye who are heavy laden.' Having pilfered his Biblical store, he proceeds with further spiritual solace; he uncorks a bottle and pours Richard a drink.

'You won't believe it,' Richard promises. 'I mean the dilemma I'm in.'

'Tell me more,' Paramena says, quick with Richard's refill. 'Take your time and explain.'

Most of the bottle later Richard reaches the end of his tale. 'If I'm not careful,' he concludes, 'one morning I'm going to wake up married. Not to the girl I do my balls on. To the wrong woman.'

'That's life,' Paramena sighs. 'You really want a way out?'

There is a long pause.

'Well?' Richard demands.

'Well what?'

'Don't keep it a secret. This bloody way out.'

'That's simple,' Paramena says. 'But it might not be pleasant.'

'You mean murder? That's too extreme. Besides, it seems I might have sent Alfred Whisker prematurely to glory. God forbid, for the man's peace, that his widow should follow so soon.'

'Don't panic. This is a bloodless proposal. Though I cannot quite promise that you, for example, will suffer no graze. In the short run, you may regret it. In the long run, who knows?'

'I'll try anything once,' Richard vows. 'Things couldn't be worse. Don't arse about. Give me the drum.'

'Patience,' Paramena says with sympathy. 'Don't get excited. Now, more than ever before, we need very clear vision.'

It is the warmest of Septembers; James cannot remember so balmy a spring. On hills yet unravaged there are golden cataracts of kowhai, slender waterfalls of red rata and wild clematis too; the forest mottles with fresh shades of green. Even the birds which have fled seem back in abundance; they chime him awake in the mornings. The cows are in milk again, and there are tender calves tottering on thin little legs. Also piglets in plenty, and chickens to rear. In the earth's reawakening, all fertility revealed, man remains a conspicuous defector: James, for all his ambition, is still without heir; he lacks means to make one, though he at least now has more hope. Adam, similarly situated, forfeited only a rib. James, lacking divine collaboration, has had to leave half Eden in ruin. And not only is he still far from Diana; his cindery hills are excruciatingly slow to heal. He has done his best to avert his gaze from the wasteland all winter. Now he watches with impatience, hoping each morning to see a swift garb of grass. But the seed he scattered is not, and why should it be, under compulsion to keep pace with his imagination; it germinates, as it will, with faint flutters of growth on the hillsides; it flies no vast flag. At a distance, sadly, the hills still look as dark.

Nor is there sign of McKenzie, though he has now been gone all of five months. Sometimes James imagines a sibilant Scots whisper when the wind surges through trees: Ay, lad, have patience. Ye need nae have fear. Despite such perceptions, James can also imagine his mate never back, perhaps long dead, with only legend left to raid the imaginations of men; never their sheep.

October is more generous. Rains quicken the grass. Lonely islands of green become visible, from the door of his hut, up on the hillsides; soon untidy archipelagoes swarm. Then daily he sees continents of grass conjoin over the dark sea of ash. He continues colonizing the hills with fresh sowings of seed. Nothing, however, makes sense without McKenzie. Where is his mate, and where are the sheep? When in doubt, as the lengthening days pass, he works on his homestead. He repairs to Lovelock Junction unwillingly – fearful lest McKenzie return to find no one at home – and while there, so far as he is able, remains tight-lipped about his despair. Yes, he agrees, he is growing good grass; and hopes soon for sheep. He doesn't say from where. He optimistically thinks he sees mild interest astir, if briefly, in Sybil Whisker's cool eyes; but she is fast just as remote. To Diana his information is apparently meaningless. Sheep? He might as well talk of goats. 'Is Spanish Creek still pretty?' she sighs, all too forlornly. 'I should love to see it just once more.' With this utterance, Sybil Whisker reveals herself not to be deaf; she glares. Marie Louise is far more receptive to all his recent enterprise. 'You are a marvel, James,' she declares. 'And all on your own.' He is about to remind her of McKenzie, but then Felicity falls down some stairs. Her hurt isn't fatal, but the din is impressive; James has never heard a child so skilled at producing noise of such volume from a small pair of lungs. The taming of unruly Felicity makes his own task on the hills seem slight. He makes no attempt to distract Herman with news of sheep; his brother is talking business, and interminably unrolling plans, with a red-haired builder named Barney Malone. Richard has gone to New Plymouth on some mission. There is only Ira, shambling out of the cemetery with sunny smile, ready to give James undivided attention; but the old man's world is too intricate to be befuddled further with conversation of sheep. From Ira, however, James hears one interesting rumour. Richard, it seems, is about to be wed. But to whom?

'One of them Whisker womenfolk,' Ira informs him. 'Or so I hear tell. I'm still trying to figure the plus. What purely is marriage? What does it rightfully have to do with this thing you call love?'

'Which Whisker woman?' James asks. For Richard, surely, but one prospect is possible.

'How should I know?' Ira replies. 'I just say what I hear. Now go on, son. Tell me more about love. And this custom called marriage. Does it all, for a true fact, mean the same?'

'So some might say,' James allows with gloom. 'I wouldn't know.'

He finds cause to depart, and leave Ira still baffled. On his way to the river James even passes Paramena, from whom more might have been gleaned, with the curtest of farewells. Then he jumps in his boat and battles against the current up to Spanish Creek. His hills were never more devastated. Diana is lost. It explains Sybil Whisker's vagueness. Also Diana's desire to see Spanish Creek again, before matrimony makes for a prison. At home there is still no McKenzie; there is just more life alone, and cows to be milked. Night after night he listens, always vainly, for the distant bark of the dog Sunday somewhere up valley. And McKenzie making his way home, all too late.

'God, if there is one,' James prays, now greatly in doubt, 'have mercy on sinners. And lovers too, if you have some to spare.'

November is hot, never hotter; spring has become summer surprisingly soon. The razed hills are now wholly greened, sunlit and shiny, with but a few charred phantoms of trees to tell of the forest that was; the growth is everywhere laughably lush. Who cares, now, if the hills never graze sheep? Not he, James Lovelock. Never nae more. Also there seems little profit in work on his homestead; the ghosts of a slain future can inhabit it now. So it remains no nearer completion. Not only is Diana lost; he lacks also a mate. McKenzie, for sure, will never return. His bones, and perhaps Sunday's, are now debris on the floor of some distant forest. The month marches on cruelly, the heat now quite hellish. With essential tasks done, his mood ensuring that these soon decline in number, he often slumps; and before long sleeps in afternoon shade. Dozing, twitching, he dreams mostly and mercifully of trivia until, so it would seem, he feels God's heavy hand. He has been called at last; he is being drawn on his last journey; his soul is about to float free. Then the waking world interferes. He is humanly, not divinely, being shaken from sleep. And a soft Scots voice is saying, 'Ay, lad. I'm back.'

McKenzie, having hard-earned his good name, is still gaunter; his beard grows to his waist. And considerably older, and trembling, supported by that staff still in hand. Sunday is a skinny shadow of the dog as last seen. But beyond the pair bleat a grimy flock of surely more than three hundred tired sheep; they are hungrily grazing.

'You made it,' James says in amazement.

'Ay, lad. It's nae been great bother.'

'I'd given you up.'

'Ye're a man of wee faith.'

'All the same, it's been months. Most of the year.'

'Never ye mind. McKenzie is here.'

'My God,' James says, comprehending at last. 'How did you do it?'

'Later I'll tell ye. There's muckle to say. Meanwhile some food for Sunday, and her master, would nae go amiss.'

'I should have a fatted calf to kill. Never mind. There's a pig.'

'Anything, lad,' McKenzie says. Then, with long sigh, he crumples and falls.

James, for a moment, fears the old man dead. He listens for a heartbeat, while Sunday whines around, and is soon reassured. But McKenzie can endure no more journeys; this must be his last. James gathers his mate up gently, finding him all light skin and bone, and festering grazes; and carries him quickly to the hut. Sunday limps and whimpers behind.

Restored by more than a few drams of fine whisky, McKenzie manages to keep down a light meal. His belly has shrunk, he admits, as a matter of shame; there was scant food for the finding, and first there were the sheep to sustain. He began with three thousand, a mite muckle to bring, but there were nae harm in trying; he had pilfered the best. Not all from one station; he wandered wide, often by night, and did the land service by culling gentry's flocks where he could. And then there was the journey. True it was nae always bonny. Sheep died of the bloat, of exhaustion, and oftimes of drowning; hundreds just got lost. When it seemed all might perish in foodless swamp and gloamed forest, he had to head the flock for mountaintops too cold for trees, but where good tussock grass grew. And then there were the rivers of which it is too soon to speak. Ay, he says, he has seen enough of this land now to last him his life. There were the volcanoes, the deserts, the lakes the size of seas. Though nae wild Maoris, as promised, who shoot white men on sight. Oftimes, when weaker, he would have been glad to glimpse any human creature, but there were never nae a soul the way he had come. He was nae complaining, though sorry the flock was so few.

'And the lass?' McKenzie asks. 'How does it stand?'

'Ah,' James says sadly.

'Too late have I come?' McKenzie is weary, his eyes all dismay. 'Too late is it now?'

'No matter,' James insists. 'It might be for best.'

'Ye're a brave lad. And bold, the work ye have done. I see yon hills growing the finest of grass. There's nae lass worthy, lad. There's a fair fact.'

'My brother is fairer, it seems. With his mines and his mill. I should have seen sooner. But it's water under the bridge.'

'There's always another trout to tickle, ay, when one's lost. God's a good gamekeeper, when in grander mood. Despair is the devil's temptation. Ye'll have a lass. Even if McKenzie must wander again, to find one more kind. I'll shepherd her home safe. Ye need have nae fear.'

'Never,' James smiles. 'Besides, when I think of women now, perhaps sheep make more sense.'

'I hear, lad, large bitterness talking.'

'Or pride.'

'Which is sin.'

'Only when it goeth before a fall. My fall came first. Pride coming after is pardonable sin.'

'Your theology might be bonnier with a wee bit more whisky.'

'All right,' James agrees, fetching the bottle. 'But only a little. Then you sleep well and long.'

'And what will ye do, meantime?'

'Me?'

'Ay. While I sleep.'

'I shall be making this summer's day sweeter,' James says. 'I shall be turning the sheep on the hills.'

'Not here,' Iris says. 'Not now. People might see.'

'They can't,' Benjamin promises.

With Mrs Whisker in a considerable state of distraction, they have been told to take their textbooks to some convenient shade, among scraggy trees in the Park of Sylvan Pleasures, there to consider the repellently republican nature of Oliver Cromwell and his cruel execution of King Charles. Ernest, with bloodlust soon satisfied, has sulked off toward the river and a recently arrived scow; and left the young lovers alone. Benjamin, as often, is interfering with her person; he attempts to unbutton her blouse. Iris is certain the vegetation insufficient to conceal them entirely from view.

'Besides,' she says, 'we cannot do this all the time.'

'We don't,' Benjamin observes truthfully. 'There's not always the chance.'

'It is not that I do not wish to,' Iris goes on. 'But there is a time and a place, and I do not think it here. Mother might come, and see what we are doing.'

'I bet she does it too. Often. With my Uncle Richard.'

He is down to her third button. She begins to feel loose.

'What do you know of Parliament?' she asks vainly.

'It's a place where men meet,' Benjamin answers, 'and make all the laws.'

Meanwhile, her fourth button is free.

'King Charles didn't like that,' she continues.

'I bet he liked this.' Now, almost without her noticing, he has a hand up her dress. There is some fever in her face; a familiar preliminary.

'Benjamin, please. Concentrate.'

'I'm very concentrated,' he insists.

'Another thing,' she adds. 'Men think the less of women who are easy.'

Benjamin is astounded. 'Who told you that?'

'I have heard mother say. Easy women are damaged goods; they have dented their shining shield, tarnished it forever. She should know.'

'It's not true,' he announces. 'The more I do this, the more I like you a lot. She doesn't know.'

'Anyway I should not be easy all the time. Especially when people might see. Perhaps later, after the Restoration, we might go for a walk, picking flowers.'

'The Restoration is years away,' Benjamin points out, not without knowledge. 'I can't wait that long. And pick flowers? No fear. My favourite flower's called naked lady. You'll be naked pretty soon. Then I'll pluck you.'

'You must wait,' she says severely, and slaps away his hands. She rebuttons herself; her facial fever diminishes. 'And if you wait, until we are safe, I shall tell you a secret. Is that fair?'

'Depends on the secret,' Benjamin answers moodily. 'It had better be good.'

'Promise, meanwhile, to leave me alone? While we talk about Parliament?'

'Maybe,' he allows, with grudge. 'Sod King Charles. Tell me this secret.'

'Well,' Iris finds dramatic pauses useful to cool Benjamin, though experience tells her to be sparing. 'I am not sure I should tell; I would tell only you. Mother, you see, is going to get married. And to your Uncle Richard. Next week they are travelling off to New Plymouth, to get it all done. That is why mother is all in a whirl.'

Benjamin sniffs. 'That's not news, not a real secret. I heard it this morning. From Ira. He's going too.'

'Ira? To New Plymouth?'

'Just for the ride. And because Richard wants him along. He couldn't stop babbling; he seems to think he's off to St Louis. I just got bored. Now you're boring me too.'

'I think it most exciting,' she protests. 'We shall very soon be cousins. By marriage, at least.'

'Cousins?' This thought gives Benjamin some pause; he sees shadow fall. 'Cousins?'

'If my mother marries your uncle. Of course.'

'Tell me just one thing,' Benjamin asks fearfully. 'About cousins, I mean. If we're cousins, next week, can we keep on doing what we do?'

'I expect so,' Iris says. 'Otherwise I should be ever so cross. Anyway we shall only be cousins by marriage; it is not quite the same.'

'That's all right, then. I thought there might be a law.'

'Law should remind you of Parliament. You have a promise to keep. That is, if we are ever to walk and find your favourite flower. Now, shall we proceed with what followed King Charles' execution?'

'All right,' Benjamin agrees gratefully. Near the block himself, for a sick moment, he feels quite reprieved.

Sybil Whisker is far from free of problems concerning her marriage. Richard obstinately, unreasonably – and, to be frank, piggishly – insists on a civil ceremony; he gives her to understand that he would not be seen dead in a church, and with luck not even then. It conflicts with his principles. When she observes that he has in the past shown no reluctance to sing hymns on the sabbath, he tells her that was different. 'I came,' he replies, 'to see you.' 'And, noticeably,' she adds, 'to sit beside Diana; I am not really so blind. A man with lust on his mind is not one to prate about principles.' 'All right,' he tells her. 'We'll let this thing go. If that's how you feel. It's all one to me.' That makes it too clear. By taking this stance, he is seeking to vex her, and make good his escape. He plainly doesn't count on her perspicacity. 'Very well,' she agrees. 'I shall accept a civil ceremony, if I must. Provided that you enlighten me with the precise principles at issue.' These, in essence, seem to be that he sees no profit in paying a minister to mouth words for the sake of their sound; the job can be done more cheaply, and swiftly, in a magistrate's office; God must have too much on his mind to notice the difference. 'And that is all?' Sybil asks in astonishment. 'Take it or leave it,' Richard answers. Thus the civil ceremony ceases to be an issue; Sybil refuses vexation, and Richard makes no escape. Nevertheless her suspicions are a torment. She can be sure of nothing, certainly not of Richard, until they are wed.

Then there is the matter of witnesses. Again, it might appear, Richard is deliberately tempting her to rage. Indeed no other explanation suffices.

'I am taking Paramena and Ira,' he announces.

She feels herself choke. 'A wooden-legged cannibal and a smelly old man? Our witnesses? Dear God.'

'Far be it from me to remind you, Sybil, that not too long since they were comrades in arms.'

'There are things in your past, Richard, which deserve exceedingly swift burial. As I have often had cause to remind you. Apart from which, as I have also explained, your role in that quite dreadful war – however obscure to the outsider – was perfectly understandable, not to say honourable. Some might even think it heroic. As I recall, the military sent you to spy among the Hau Hau, where you at all times conducted yourself creditably, as an Englishman should. Moreover, at considerable risk to your own person.'

'Thank God for your memory. It seems I can't trust my own.'

'So why persist in this pretence that you were really a Hau Hau?'

'Some memories,' he argues, 'have a rather rare taste.'

'And why, of all people, these two witnesses?'

'We went through war. I need them in peace. Men of trust. If you don't like my choice, you can call the thing off.'

He is all too transparent. Sybil will not be baited.

'Very well,' she concedes. 'Paramena and Ira. I hope you do not also intend to dictate the dress I shall wear.'

'You're welcome to white,' Richard informs her. 'It's no odds to me.'

In view of the likely graceless nature of the proceedings, Sybil decides against taking Diana. The girl is too tender a flower. And, God knows, her presence might tempt Richard further, make for more prevarication and procrastination. Better all is done swiftly, with minimum of stress. Three days are necessary for certification and ceremony. They are to embark on a timber scow early on the Wednesday, and return to the Junction, man and wife and two witnesses, on a Saturday steamer calling for coal. Richard has dismissed the notion of a honeymoon as highly absurd. 'Where could we go for peace?' he says. 'Another place like the Porangi? There are no quaint country inns in this country. It's all dirty beds and beer.' It is true that he may well have a point there; he certainly speaks with authority. Also, he tells her, the demands on him are considerable at the moment; he cannot be long from Dixtown; the world may be a bastard, but he didn't bloody father it. Sybil is tempted once more, not least by his language, to make some rebuke; and, just in time, she refrains. All, then, is settled; all but the austere matrimonial act.

Diana chooses not to be martyred by the news that she isn't, after all, to go to New Plymouth. Indeed Sybil's decision doesn't print itself at all perceptibly upon the girl's dreamy face. Diana is to remain at the Junction to look after Iris, and keep the Old House in order, while her mother gets on with marriage. Sybil asks Marie Louise if she might manage a watchful eye on both girls. Marie Louise, though at that time sufficiently on watch in connection with Felicity, insists that Sybil is not to worry. The girls, she assures Sybil, will come to no harm.

Thus reassured, if in other respects still uneasy, Sybil travels downriver with Richard and his witnesses on the Wednesday.

Diana travels upriver on the Thursday. Her hired chaperone and oarsman is Ernest, sworn to secrecy; he has the promise of a one pound note, ten shillings to take her, ten shillings for silence. She should have preferred Benjamin as companion but that boy, however sweet, might only babble to Iris; and Iris, as a matter of course, to her mother. With consequences unpleasant to envisage. She has told Iris and Benjamin to amuse themselves instructively with William Shakespeare while she and Ernest inspect the geographical nature of the Porangi River. Left free, Iris and Benjamin are not slow to take heart from the tale of Romeo and Juliet, even in truncated version thought proper for minors; the moral remains plain. 'They were just as young as us,' Iris proclaims. 'Does that mean we have to die?' asks Benjamin with unease. They both weep considerably at the play's climax, when the poison has worked.

Ernest does not engage Diana in light conversation as he rows her upriver to Spanish Creek; nor has he observations to make on the sylvan world shadily parading on each side of their craft. He is deep in a dream of a geographical nature. He is plying a warm lagoon, to wild waiting women, on a far tropic island; the Porangi is an indifferent substitute. 'Bloody fucking buggeration,' he shouts, when they bump on a snag. Again enslaved by reality, and remembering Diana, he adds, 'Pardon my French. We aren't going to sink. I'll get you there safe. What is it you want, exactly, with my Uncle James?' That, while the dinghy draws nearer Spanish Creek, is a question which immensely convulses Diana; she no longer quite knows, after so many bitter months, and feels rather faint. This furtive excursion might be seen by some, and especially by her mother, as prelude to elopement. It is certainly true that, in general, Diana has her deflowerment in mind; not immediately perhaps, not with Ernest around, but for preference not too distantly. She has nothing vaster or more dramatic in view. She would sooner die damaged goods than never know the strong arms of her true love. At length she manages an evasive answer for Ernest. 'I hear James has sheep,' she says. 'And perhaps pretty lambs.'

Ernest is far from fooled. He knows lambs come in the springtime. And springtime is past. He sees, however, no point in asserting his superior knowledge of animal husbandry; after a knowing look he bends again to the oars on this hot summer's day. The palm trees of the far tropics grow tall from the Porangi's banks. He can hear the sultry songs of the flowered women ashore. With one whole pound in his pocket before nightfall, he could soon stow away on scow or steamer; and make paradise real.

*

In troubled waters, as she has acutely foreseen, Sybil Whisker tries to navigate the streets of New Plymouth. There is no point pouring oil, protesting to heaven, or pleading with Richard. She has but to survive, largely in grieved silence; survive until the Saturday, when she shall have the reassurance of wedlock, and return with her groom to the homely bliss of the Porangi. New Plymouth, for the moment, brings none; it is all disagreeably drunken bedlam, wherever they move. This is mostly from public house to public house, and even murkier waterfront places. The problem, so far as she remembers, appears to have begun with Paramena. She should have known that neither Richard nor his distasteful partner could pass up the opportunity of drumming up trade on a trip to New Plymouth. So much for the sacred nature of matrimony; it has begun to seem side issue. Paramena has discerned promise of a considerable market in New Plymouth for his product, now widely famed on this coast, called Dixtown Dream; he has to make certain arrangements for its illicit distribution and sale, especially to seamen, though Paramena is confident that the labouring classes of New Plymouth will also acquire the taste if the rum is tactfully priced. These arrangements entail entertaining prospective dealers and customers in public houses and drinking dens elsewhere. Richard is not to be detached from Paramena in these unwholesome proceedings, with his cool business head; indeed he is enthusiastic participant. And Sybil, for her part, knows better than to allow herself to become detached from Richard at this time; she is familiar with far too many tales of bridegrooms who take fright and flee before the due date; it is best that Richard not be given the chance, not with Saturday near; the confusing passage of time, however, is not a little bruising to the mind and dulling to the senses. Only Ira is detached, and from them all. He is usually asleep, after his first drink, now that he is satisfied that St Louis, or such as he sees of it, is not too taxing to the imagination; he now understands for a true fact that large towns are just places where a large number of people live, for some reason, though Richard is unwilling to let him find a cemetery where he can ponder the entire problem of why people in large number must. He is impatient for return to the Porangi, and space, not to speak of Marie Louise's cooking – all he has eaten in New Plymouth have been sausages tasting like turds – and to expedite early return is perfectly willing to sign all the papers in the strange building, filled with queer-talking hombres in dark suits, where Richard, Paramena and the Whisker woman lead him. This first visit to the magistrate's office, to arrange for the certificate, takes place after champagne has been broken out, at the mere mention of impending marriage, by some of Richard's more fervently well-wishing waterfront friends. Sybil, when pressed, drinks far more than she knows to be suitable for a woman in her situation; she prays that Saturday will come soon, as the documents swim before her in that dreadfully bleak office, and people gabble incomprehensibly, but nevertheless she manages to append her signature where shown, and with dignity. Then, it appears, there is more drinking to be done. She will have some harsh things to say to Richard, with Saturday past; she walks with a wobble, if with head still high, among relatively respectable men and women of the settlement; Richard and Paramena are shamelessly riotous, and Ira Dix meanders dog-like behind. Dear God. That life in the colonies should, so soon, have come to this. She is about to give Alfred another piece of her mind, but then she recalls that he is several feet of earth distant from the sound of her voice. She also recollects that she cannot give Richard opportunity to take offence in the meantime; likewise, presumably, his unsavoury partner. That leaves but one male to whom she might express her deeper feelings. 'Hurry up,' she hisses at Ira, that appalling old man. 'Do not drag your feet.'

Diana is determined not to drag her feet. She wants to walk them quickly, and with James; she envisages their destination quite vividly. A grotto of trees is desirable, with water rippling near; but there are other locations as likely, since it is what shall transpire there that she has most in mind. The problem is that James appears intent on nursing his mate McKenzie; he is reluctant to leave his old shepherd for long. True that James has appeared delighted to see her, and indeed has rather breathlessly confessed his relief that she is not to wed Richard, as he supposed. Nevertheless the passionate nature of their reunion has been tempered by the invalid McKenzie. And Ernest, of course, is everywhere around.

Then she sees quite simple solution. She takes mercenary Ernest aside. 'Ten shillings more,' she promises, 'if you look after that old man for an hour.'

'What will you be doing?' Ernest asks with interest. 'And with my Uncle James?'

'That is our business,' she insists. 'Never you mind.'

'Another pound,' he suggests. 'Which makes two pounds in all. Or else I shall tell.'

With the price of passion established, Ernest installed by McKenzie's bed, Diana at last gets James away from the hut. He helps her over a stile; they walk a meadow bright with daisies. His pace is too moderate for her liking; they have only the hour. And his talk is filled with evasions and distractions.

'You have not noted,' he says, 'my sheep on the hills.'

'Not really,' she agrees. 'My eyes are on you.'

'Or my homestead up there. This summer might see it quite finished.'

'It looks very pretty. What more can I say?'

'That I have been far from idle. You might well tell me that.'

'Very well. You have been far from idle, James. How does that sound?'

He walks moodily.

'While working,' he confesses, 'I have thought often of you.'

Now, at least, he is less irrelevant.

'Dear James,' she informs him, 'you are a sweet man. But you must not exaggerate so prettily. I might be tempted to believe you.'

'It is true,' he insists. 'Always of you.'

They halt. Their lips, after a time, manage to meet. They walk on through the meadow. The trees on the far side take an interminable time to rise around them; the creek, exactly as she imagined, is running quite near. There is soft grass, springy moss, and birds overhead. They are safe there, quite safe, even should inquisitive Ernest gaze down from the door of the hut; and for the first time alone. Diana takes a deep breath. Then, quite shamelessly, she begins to disrobe.

James can do little other than blink. Even his more unrealistic dreams of Diana have not contained so abrupt a surprise. As her body flowers from falling garments, the wonder of the thing leaves him quite limp. She steps free from her petticoat, with arms open wide, and tries bravely to smile.

'Take me,' she says. 'Take me, dear James. Quick. No delay.'

Accustomed, though not lately, to the finer preliminaries of love-making, James fast does his best to oblige; his clothes are likewise soon shed. His breath comes in fits and starts.

'Take me,' she sighs.

That plea need hardly be made more than once. He shall have her. He may well feast forever. The problem, it seems, is persuading his body to take the same view. After they have slid to the grass, and embraced fondly for some time, Diana inquires, 'Is this all there is?'

James finds that question, for the moment, too troubling to answer.

'I mean it is lovely enough,' she explains. 'I should not complain. But I thought there was more.'

'There shall be,' he promises, through now gritted teeth. 'Men sometimes are slow.'

'I know nothing,' she whispers. 'I am all in your hands. If you only knew how I have hoped for this day. Have you prayed for it too?'

'Of course.' The thought is not helpful, perhaps the whole problem. 'You will never know how I have dreamed.'

Now sweat bursts from his brow. His performance has never been a problem in dream. Or with one. Is it the truth that, with Glory gone, he shall nevermore be roused? Is this his punishment for playing fast and loose with lust? Must his future now mean only McKenzie, and sheep? James has seldom been more deflated in spirit and flesh.

'Yes,' she urges. 'Dearest James. Please.'

He tries. God knows he tries. At the end of an hour, perhaps nearer two, his flimsy craft finally wrecks on the reef of her virtue; there is nothing to salvage. He sinks beside her, rolls over, and looks up at the trees.

'Never mind,' she says with sadness. 'We shall try again, when we can.'

There are tears.

'Perhaps I was never meant to be wicked,' she adds with a sob.

'Perhaps not,' James miserably agrees.

'So we shall have to get married,' she continues. 'The sooner the better.'

'What of your mother, though?' James asks practically. 'What will she say?'

It is something best not considered. Diana dresses, and shivers. The afternoon sun has gone from the glade.

Saturday is equally unsatisfactory from Sybil Whisker's perplexingly various points of view. For one thing it is difficult to distinguish from Wednesday, Thursday or Friday. Certainly there have been few natural divisions; they seem seldom to have slept, nor much to have eaten, since they first sighted New Plymouth, which is presumably where they still are; but at least, in this time, she has almost never lost Richard for longer than his bodily functions last beyond a closed door. He is still distinctly with her, also Paramena and Ira, and unless she is very much mistaken they are passing through the magistrate's office again, more or less together, though she again has difficulty defining the nature and texture of the vague words spoken, especially when these are directed at her; there is also vast laughter, which recedes into distance; it is all most vexingly unclear. More so when, just as she thinks she has this situation under some control, they are no longer there; they are back again in a bar, and there is deafening cannonfire of corks, followed by fountains of champagne; she is altogether gratified to discover herself the toast of the town. With wine refreshing vision, she surprises herself by giving herself to giddy waltzes with her male companions, even old Ira; Paramena shows himself capable of performing impeccably on his wooden leg. An accordion plays amid most vociferous singing. There is applause when she takes the floor. With life quite tolerable, she feels that in justice it should go on forever. Never before has she been queen for a day.

Her reign, however, falls short of the full Saturday. For shortly she gathers that they are aboard a blackened coal boat, steaming home to the Porangi. Her white dress is grubby, the waves are high and disagreeably jarring; the sea winds are sobering. Spray licks her face. She is seated, with Ira asleep near her feet, upon a covered hold in the shelter of some superstructure. Richard and Paramena appear to be entertaining the skipper, on the bridge, with their last complimentary bottle of Dixtown Dream. All, but for the condition of her dress, begins to seem as it should be; she has survived, after all, and is now travelling homeward in triumph. Hours seem mere moments. Soon they enter upon the Porangi River. The river waters on which they now plough are far more congenial to her currently frail constitution. With the wind's diminution, she opens her handbag and, helped by hand mirror, makes endeavour to repair her unfortunate facial appearance; also to curb her disarrayed hair. Deep in the handbag she discerns her prize, now in a sense to be seen as booty from the battlefield, the crisply folded marriage certificate, apparently placed there when she was unaware. With not a little delight, she removes this most reassuring testimony to her new status; and makes attempt to read it as the steamer rolls gently upriver. Upon grasping its essence, however, she gives a long and loud cry. She might have succeeded in never losing Richard from sight; but she has certainly somewhere mislaid him as husband. According to the best information available, conveyed quite coherently, she is now Mrs Ira Dix.

Up on the bridge Paramena has just been saying to Richard, 'It was a near thing. If I hadn't kept my wits, and one drink behind you, it might have been me she married.'

Ira, awoken in fright by the Whisker woman's scream, is before long given to understand himself at last a husband; and legally entitled to explore the mystery of marriage. But he does wish his wife would make less of a racket. Yelling like that she will soon wake the dead, for a true fact; even poor Whisker, long deaf in the grave.

If Richard has one relief, in the many hours of anguish immediately following, it is that Sybil doesn't believe him to have done it deliberately; not at first. It is his negligence. His obstinacy. It could never have happened in church.

'Maybe so,' Richard agrees mildly. 'But it's happened. One can't deny that.'

'I'm married off to an old man,' she goes on. It seems unlikely she will cease going on. 'Impotent, to boot.'

'We all make mistakes. And have to live with them, God knows.'

'Live with them? With him? That senile old fool?'

'Ira is by nature most obliging and pleasant. Besides, you can't disappoint him. He seems to have his heart quite set on it now.'

'Richard, you are not serious.'

'Perfectly. Why not? Given Ira's advanced age, and dilapidated condition, you won't long be a wife. Look on this as an interval between widowhood. And view Ira as lodger, if you like. Marie Louise tells me he is packing his bag; he's almost ready to move.'

'Richard, I am not sure I hear right. Is this really you?'

'I observe no one else present.'

'We can travel back to New Plymouth. Find a good lawyer. Have the whole thing annulled. Then try again, in a church of my choosing.'

'You know how things stand here. Such affairs take an age. I can't spare the time.'

'For decency?' she appeals. 'To restore my good name?'

'Let's look at it this way. We're no strangers to adultery. Nothing need change.'

'Dear God,' she prays.

'Also, as I understand it, your daughters both see some merit in their stepfather; they have both been to visit him, to convey their great pleasure. To make a change now might only confuse them, and cause them much grief. We should be selfish not to consider their feelings.'

'They thought I was marrying you.'

'Quite. All the more reason. They seem more than content to assume that there was some last minute change. And that your compassionate heart moves in inscrutable ways.'

'You are impossible. And let one thing be clear. I am not taking in Ira. On no account; never. I shall explain to the girls that it is on grounds of his health; that he would be happiest remaining with Marie Louise. And there is end to this nonsense. Mrs Dix? Very well. I shall suffer that, if I must. But I see no necessity to encumber myself with Mr Dix too.'

'Not even as lodger? I don't see the harm.'

'Never. You may move into my house in that capacity, if you care. Now that I have said it, why not? All can be arranged as before this unpleasant happening. You would certainly have more comfortable quarters with me than with that rogue Paramena; and you might smell tolerably less of muttonbird and shark. It can all be done discreetly. Next week, shall we say?'

To her acute bewilderment Richard shows distinct shock. 'That,' he points out, 'would be living in sin.'

'I am beginning to fear for my sanity,' Sybil is at length obliged to confess. 'I feel I am losing my grip on this world.'

Richard's grip is patently firmer. In stiffening voice, he continues, 'And as for Ira, I am not unmindful of my responsibilities. In the matter, I mean, of things having reached this pass. I cannot but help give thought to his situation. I can certainly not stand by and see a happy husband turned out on the streets.'

'What streets? Where? He has always had Marie Louise.'

'He has earned, God knows, some marital content at the end of his life. Such a man is not to be cruelly discarded.'

'Richard, what are you saying?'

'Much as I hesitate to remind you, Sybil, I am saying that there are, as you well know, certain monetary transactions between us. And I see no reason why this arrangement should not be subject to review. If, that is, you deny Ira a home. Indeed, if I did not take this initiative to remind you, it would rest ill on my conscience.'

'He smells,' she protests. 'He is worse than Whisker.'

'You should have thought of that.'

'How? When?'

'Before you married him,' Richard observes, with some patience. 'God forbid that you should let nervous remorse get the better of you now. It is no time for second thoughts. There is the future happiness of several people to be taken into account. Not least, Mrs Dix, that of your two lovely daughters; dare I speak of them?'

'Never,' she says bitterly. 'And especially never of Diana.'

Consequent upon this conversation, and others thematically the same, Sybil Dix's suspicions begin to grow, branch, and flower. After Ira moves into the Old House, and is icily assigned a bachelor's bedroom, Richard finds the rapidly ripened fruit of these suspicions flung in his face; it is all deuced sticky, to say the least.

'You planned it all,' she announces.

'See here, Sybil,' he says. 'See reason.'

'Nothing now escapes me, Richard. I have been a woman deluded by love, and deceived. No longer.'

'You can't believe that of me,' he protests.

'I can. I do. I believe anything of you now, Richard. Anything. Above all I believe you will stop at nothing to gain your quite bestial ends.'

'I cannot imagine to what you are referring.'

'I am referring, as you well know, to my daughter Diana. And your inherently lascivious nature. I have been a poor fool.'

'I am sorry, Sybil, but you seem to be taking leave of your senses.'

'Am I indeed? Since you lecherously desire Diana, and I stand in the way of your slaking that lust, how better a solution than to marry me off most conveniently? And to that quite grotesque old man? Well, I am far from finished, Richard. You hear?'

Richard hears. He also feels, low in his spine, a form of paralysis.

'I shall ensure, my dear Richard, that your foul aim is frustrated. Diana? You shall never have her. Never. Not so long as I live.'

'Look, Sybil, we are both rational people.'

'Agreed. I have never been more so. Doubtless because my name, not by mischance, is now Mrs Dix. Cruel reality is dawning. This fate was not written in my stars. It was written by you. I have woken to the world, and your devious nature. Diana? Please allow me to laugh in your face. You shall be sorry.'

Richard begins to feel this prediction probably accurate. Hell hath no fury. Had he and Paramena thought less in the short term, more in the long, they might have seen the snag of a scorned woman; it seems likely to sink the whole bloody boat.

'I should prefer to continue this conversation,' he says on departing, 'when you are milder of temperament. I can appreciate that you feel under some strain.'

The substance of that strain is shortly to be seen in Sybil Dix's living room. There, chatting with his rather ravishing stepdaughters, sits Mr Dix.

'Your boots,' Sybil says. 'You are tracking in dirt. Also that pipe. You might, out of consideration for others, confine that noxious habit to your own room.'

Ira shows no haste to remove his boots, nor to extinguish his pipe. He has sought advice on a husband's role from Herman and others of experience; he understands that it is best not to display weakness, and certainly never to capitulate, to a new wife. At length Sybil's uproar becomes too intense for Ira to ignore. 'Go to hell, woman,' he says, and continues with conversation.

Life, or so a near fainting Sybil begins to see, is a longer nightmare than most can envisage. Trust Whisker to see the wisdom of being quit of it first; she is tempted to follow. Especially when, within the hour, another disaster makes itself brutally explicit in her household.

'I have been waiting my chance to be alone with you,' Diana says. 'I should like a quiet word.'

'About what?' Sybil asks, busy in her kitchen. 'I am most distracted. Can it wait? Or must it be said?'

'I fear it must, Mother.'

'Very well, then. Proceed.'

But Diana stands dumb. The girl's face, for some reason, becomes quite inflamed.

'What is it, dear God?' Sybil says quickly. 'What is it, Diana?'

'I have a confession to make. One which might not be to your liking. I am not what I may seem.'

'And what is that? Be frank, girl. Haste.'

Sybil feels faint again. And Diana seems in agony.

'I am,' the girl continues, looking away, 'no longer a maiden. I have lost my honour, or so it would seem.'

Crockery crashes to the floor. 'It would *seem*?' Sybil says.

'It was so easy. I hardly noticed it go.'

There is a long silence. Out in the living room Ira can be heard telling Iris of the many human curiosities he has been collecting. Among which is love. He has a chance now, he is saying, to see how much it has to do with marriage. It is his belief, based on observation, that the two are connected.

'I cannot believe it,' Sybil says shakily. 'Is this true, Diana? How did it happen? And when?'

'When you were unaware. Naturally. Otherwise I daresay it should not have happened.'

There is more silence of substance.

'I shall kill that man,' Sybil declares. 'Believe me. I shall.'

Diana finds no reason to doubt it. Her mother has taken up a carving knife in meaningful fashion.

'I warned him,' Sybil says, 'never to speak of you. Nor will your lips be sullied with his lasciviousness, let alone his name.'

'Please understand,' Diana persists. 'It was as much my fault as his. Mine perhaps more.'

But her mother is determined to listen no longer. Much less to understand. She is undoing her apron, as if that garment might prove impediment to murder.

'You were innocent,' she shouts. 'And that devious beast took advantage.'

'Mother, we wish only to marry.'

'In hell,' Sybil says.

'And I did lead him on.'

'Then may you both burn there. Forever. You hear?' Sybil moves past Diana to exchange her knife for another more keen. 'May you both suffer eternally for a mother betrayed. Count yourself lucky that out of love I shall spare you. For that monster, believe me, there shall be no mercy.'

'Mother, you do not know what you are saying.'

'Do I not? We shall see.'

Diana observes madness in her mother's eyes. It seems, on balance, an excessive reaction; perhaps she is still overwrought by her wedding. Diana feels obliged to tempt fate, which at the moment needs some substantial incentive; she takes up a stance before the kitchen door, to prevent her lethal mother's egress.

'You shall have to slay me first,' the girl bravely announces, 'before you can touch a hair of his sweet head.'

'Stand aside,' Sybil says. The knife moves back and forward with menace before Diana's face; she hardly dares breathe. 'He has had his last day in the land of the living.'

'James,' Diana protests, 'is gentle, and kind.'

There is a pause, particularly pregnant.

'James?' Sybil says weakly.

'Yes. James. He is the sweetest of men.'

'James?' Sybil is now even more in a daze; she still cannot quite comprehend, for the life of her, just what her daughter is saying.

'I love him. Of course. There is no longer necessity to keep it a secret.'

Sybil, however, finds some necessity to slump in a chair; the knife falls with a clatter.

'James? You mean that poor peasant boy seduced you?'

'Or I him. It is difficult to say. And I cannot think that it matters. The fact is that I am now his wife in all but name. James, besides, is no more to be seen as poor peasant. Sheep graze his hills now, and he has a quaint Scottish shepherd. Before long, doubtless, he will prosper with wool.'

Diana sees her mother begin, most strangely, to laugh. This laughter, on the face of things, is an even more extreme reaction than the earlier rage. But it does bring relief. On present showing no one is likely to be disembowelled by her mother.

'James?' Sybil continues to query, also continuing to laugh. 'Dear God. James?'

'Yes,' Diana says, with anger. 'James.' Her love is no laughing matter.

Sybil buries her head; her shoulders shake. The laughs become difficult to distinguish from sobs.

'Mother, I have a most important question to ask of you. Are you listening?'

'You have my attention,' Sybil agrees, after a time.

'We should like, James and I, your permission to wed. Also your blessing.'

'And that,' asks Sybil, 'is all?'

'All.' Diana swallows. 'What more could we ask?'

'You have both,' her mother declares with dizzying speed. 'Both. Permission and blessing. Dear God you have.'

Then, to Diana's perplexity, her mother becomes quite manic with glee. She rises from her chair, embraces her daughter, and all but dances. Diana, taking fright, backs away. The miracle of her mother's blessing still has to be comprehended; it seems too easy by far.

'Just so long,' Sybil continues, 'as *he* never has you.'

'He? Who?'

'Richard,' Sybil insists.

'But what,' Diana asks, with some pertinence, 'has Richard to do with me?'

'Never mind now. To James you are welcome. Yes, James you may wed. It is short, perhaps, of the match I should have liked you to make. But it is no worse than most, I imagine. And certainly better than some I could name. And James, do you say, is now of more substance?'

'Rather. You can see for yourself.'

'That is some consolation. I may well live, much as it may seem unlikely at present, into old age. It would be to my advantage to have a dutiful daughter, with a solvent husband. One must, if you will forgive my morbidity, think of these things.'

'Naturally, Mother. I quite understand. I shall not fail you.'

'Dear Diana.' Sybil endeavours to hug her daughter again. 'We are such poor frail creatures. Worthy, God knows, of far better things. But I fear we must accept that the colonial life is now our lot. Lost here, and vulnerable, we must make the best of fate. And if for you this means some simpleton farmer like—'

'You are talking,' Diana informs her mother, 'of my husband to be.'

'—like James Lovelock,' Sybil adds, undeterred, 'then we shall have to make the best of him too. And indeed we shall, Diana. Indeed, I promise, we shall.'

'I am the one to marry him,' Diana observes, puzzled. 'Not you. Or has there been some misunderstanding?'

'Have faith,' her mother, rather darkly, goes on. 'There are trials to come, God knows. The mildest of men have a quite hellish obstinacy in their souls. As if child bearing were not enough for a woman. We are, it would seem, also destined to suffer the pathetic male ego. It demands patience, and practice, to cope. James is possibly a creature of more potential than most, still virgin soil to be tilled by an intelligent wife, even if I cannot altogether conceal my disappointment. At least there is Iris.'

Diana fails to follow. 'Iris?'

'Yes. Iris. There is still Iris, thank God. She at least will wed well, and worthily, the dear girl.'

Sybil is recipient of another ambiguous mercy at the evening meal. Before it progresses far Ira, who has been seated for safety between her daughters, finds occasion to rise abruptly; he gazes down at his meat and mashed potato in extreme agitation.

'Horse shit,' he says.

'I do beg your pardon?' Sybil inquires of her husband.

'Horse shit,' Ira insists. 'This here food is purely horse shit. It ain't got the flavour of nothing else, for a true fact.'

Herman has advised him that husbands should take a strong stance, from the beginning, in matters affecting their interests. None could quarrel with the strength of Ira's stance now, and he doesn't intend to allow his wife to bicker. Love? That problem can be left until later.

'If you have an opinion to express on the quality of my fare,' Sybil replies coolly, 'I should appreciate it expressed in more temperate tone. I see no reason why my daughters should be subject to crudities.'

Iris, with her head down, distinctly giggles. Even Diana, the dim girl, seems faintly amused. Sybil sees anarchy accumulating. Ira remains on his feet.

'I ain't expressing no opinion,' he goes on. 'I'm purely telling you. And what I'm telling you, for a true fact, is I got better things to do in my life than fill my belly with dry turds. Another thing I'm telling you, woman, is until you learn better I'm taking my meals up at the big house, with Marie Louise.'

With that, he departs. Evidently he sees his vow to eat elsewhere as a fit and proper punishment. Perhaps Sybil can hope for a promise, in the fullness of time, that he will also sleep elsewhere. A most agreeable peace follows his exit. With luck, half the battle is won.

'Stop smirking,' she tells her daughters. 'Diana? Iris? Get on with your meal. Remember, and be grateful, that God can rescue us in remarkable ways.'

'Or Marie Louise,' Iris observes succinctly.

'That will be quite enough from you,' Sybil says.

Iris sighs. 'I am really quite fond of him. I do hope he comes back.'

'That is more than enough.' Sybil takes a deep breath. 'While I think to mention it, Iris, I must note that your decorum has begun to leave much to be desired. You are no longer a child. You are, to all intents and purposes, a young lady. It is time to have done with childish things, and infantile pursuits. I mean specifically, of course, your tomboyish games with Benjamin.'

'There is nothing wrong with Benjamin,' Iris argues. 'I find him a perfectly adequate companion.'

'It is no longer, as it were, fitting. Not for a young lady. Your sister Diana may, from impetuous madness of heart, be determined to wed the first man at hand. Very well. She shall have her way. Who am I to question her choice? But I think that, as a mother, I am entitled to expect more of you. In future, Iris, you may anticipate my undivided attention to your welfare.'

With some astonishment Sybil looks at Iris. Unless she is deceived, and God knows she has suffered sufficient deception in one week, she sees tears slowly descending from her daughter's eyes. More, sniffling is to be heard.

'Oh Mother,' Iris cries. 'You are beastly.' The girl runs from the table.

'I think,' Sybil observes calmly to Diana, 'that Iris has let her curious and uncritical affection for Ira run away with her. We shall allow her a little time to recover from her distress. Meanwhile, we might give the nature of your forthcoming marriage some consideration.'

'It was your bloody idea,' Richard says, getting drunk.

'Mine?' Paramena says, with mild surprise.

'Yours.'

'I was merely trying to interpret your deepest wishes.'

'As an interpreter you make a sow's ear out of a silk purse.'

'I see few grounds for complaint. You wished not to marry. And you remain, as far as I can see, unmarried. Where is the grievance? Sybil Whisker is now Sybil Dix. I should have thought that a consummation richly to be desired. Ira's current condition suggests the likelihood of life after death. All is for the best in the worst of possible worlds.'

'Except that my bloody brother James is making off with Diana in the meantime.'

'True,' Paramena sighs. 'But you can't have everything.'

So that there shall be none of the consequences attendant upon her own recent experience of matrimony, Sybil Dix insists that James and Diana are not to wed in New Plymouth. Instead, a minister will travel expensively up the Porangi and celebrate their nuptials at Lovelock Junction. True that there is no church to contain the ceremony; but the environment of Lovelock House, in particular of Whisker's thus far unused ballroom, makes more than mean secular substitute. Marie Louise joyfully undertakes to cater. All shall be done with dignity, given the circumstances. The minor flaws in the arrangement concern smelly old men, with whom it seems Sybil is destined to be afflicted. Ira is determined to give Diana away, something undeniably his right as stepfather. Her none too bright daughter doesn't see the harm, nor the potential hazard, should champagne flow too soon; Ira, in his enthusiasm, could become a bigamist. To forestall such misadventure, Sybil arranges with Marie Louise that no liquor shall be evident in the vicinity of the Lovelock House for twenty-four hours preceding the ceremony. As if Ira were not enough, James is peculiarly insistent on his aged and barely intelligible Scottish shepherd McKenzie also being party to the proceedings; James wants him as best man. 'You could surely find someone more suitable, and more your own age,' Sybil suggests, when she visits her prospective son-in-law at Spanish Creek. She is gratified by what she sees there. She is, for one thing, sensitive to an atmosphere of impending prosperity. Sheep are now fat and woolly on the hills. And the homestead, if modestly proportioned, is approximately finished; Diana may find it in herself to give the barren interior some grace.

'There is no one more suitable than McKenzie,' James answers. 'He is my best man here, indeed my only man. He shall be my best man at the ceremony.'

'He may get drunk,' Sybil objects. 'I have had experience of Scotsmen. They need only smell the cork of a whisky bottle. Besides, he is a scarecrow, a bundle of rags.'

'I shall see to his dress,' James promises.

'What of his sheep-like smell? It is all pervasive.'

'We are amply provided with water at Spanish Creek. He can be persuaded to see virtue in soap.'

'And that dreadful dog.'

'We shall,' James allows, 'have to make provision for Sunday at the ceremony.'

'I feel distinctly that things are going to pieces,' Sybil reveals. 'I have had this foreboding before. My intuition proved all too accurate. Can you not consider someone else as best man? A brother, perhaps.'

'Richard?'

'I think not,' Sybil says quickly. 'Perhaps Herman.'

'I am sorry,' James replies. 'McKenzie it must be. I am entitled to exercise my discretion in the matter.'

'It ill becomes the seducer of my daughter to talk of discretion.'

'Are we talking of McKenzie now,' James asks, 'or of other things? If the latter, you must permit me to say that events are now taking an honourable course.'

'I have reduced my conception of honour to that apparently prevalent in the colonies,' Sybil says. 'Dear God, do not ask me to do more. One other thing. I trust that McKenzie will not, as is often the custom for a best man, be expecting to kiss the bridesmaid. My tender and innocent Iris will be filling that role. I think she might well be spared the attentions of an unlettered and unedifying old highlander, do you not think?'

'I leave that to you,' James says. 'You seem to have thought of everything.'

'If I do not, who shall?' Sybil asks.

'Don't worry,' Richard says, getting drunker. 'I'm not finished.'

'No?' Paramena says, seldom surprised.

'No. I'll have her yet. You see if I don't.'

'The way I hear it, Sybil's marriage is hanging by a thread. You could be in luck there. Ira has just discovered divorce; someone has inconsiderately planted the notion in his head. Anyway he's announced that he's moving back to Marie Louise just as soon as he's given Diana away. He doesn't trust anyone else to do it. If my information is correct, then we may safely assume that Sybil may soon be looking for a replacement lodger. Things could be worse. You don't need to complain. Not yet.'

Paramena finds nothing to suggest that Richard has heard a word.

'Wait and see,' Richard promises.

'Of course,' Paramena says.

'I'll have her.'

'Naturally. No panic. There's no horse better than a tried horse. And better an old horse than none at all.'

Richard has a lucid moment; he peers at Paramena. 'Horses?' he asks. 'Where the hell are the horses?'

'I was, if you'll forgive me, talking of one near and dear. Sybil.'

'Sybil? Who's talking of Sybil?'

'You are. Or were.'

'The hell I was. I'm talking about Diana.'

'That complicates things,' Paramena concedes.

'I'll have her yet,' Richard vows.

Richard is by no means alone with mixed feelings about the approaching marriage. There is McKenzie, who is moved by the suspicion that things may change too astringently for his taste at Spanish Creek; he could never have foreseen James burdened by a less promising mother-in-law, though he does his best to keep his distance from Sybil Dix when she visits the farm. Though he refrains from expressing his wry opinion, McKenzie also sees Diana as something short of the ideal soul mate for James, too flighty by far, muckle dainty for a reliable farm wife, and maybe a long-term menace to the boy's well-being. But his fears are well hid; he has to accept that love is an abiding affliction in the affairs of men. James is as hell-bent as any other, not least to have the entire homestead complete before bondage to woman begins. McKenzie thanks God for Sunday, who would be content with a kennel; he makes clear to James that he and Sunday will be happier not to move from the old hut; that the home of the newly and bonnily married will prosper best with privacy at its hearth. If his real reasons are other, inspired by his fears, who is James to notice? The boy has more on his mind than where McKenzie and Sunday will dwell. Meantime, while James sweats on the homestead, McKenzie keeps watch on the flock, notes that the rams are in good heart, and sees crops and cows are never neglected. After the ordeal of winter and spring, he feels life unflexing in his old limbs again. He will survive to see other seasons, and before long the lambs on the hills. He will live to see Spanish Creek more or less as he imagined, or dreamed. When all's said and done, it is land that lives; it makes mortal matters like marriage a small concern. Ay.

Included among others with mixed feelings are Iris and Benjamin. They regret that the marriage will not be their own. Their immediate climate has also been clouded by Sybil's announcement that it is time for Iris to cultivate qualities more decorous and ladylike as she matures. Indignant Iris considers herself sufficiently matured, and has a good case to argue, though not with her mother. It is too late to be ladylike. All the same, she fears her mother's austere stance in this matter may mean the loss of her loved Benjamin. At the least, it will mean seeing him less often. She is often in tears. Benjamin proves equally quick to distress. When they meet, they tend to mourn when their lovemaking is finished. The marriage of Diana and James, soon, seems to make things worse.

'We cannot,' Iris declares. 'We cannot get married. And that is that.'

'Because we're too young?'

'Of course, you silly. Why else?'

'What about Romeo and Juliet?'

'They died.'

'They found a Friar.'

'And a tomb.'

Benjamin finds that prospect unacceptable. 'There must be other ways,' he insists.

'Such as?'

'Well,' he says slowly, with brightening face, 'we could say the same words at the ceremony as Diana and James. Secretly, and quietly, so no one can see. In the eyes of God, then, we shall also be married.'

'Try explaining that to Mother,' Iris suggests.

'I don't see why we shouldn't be,' Benjamin argues obstinately. 'Not if we've said the right words. And if people don't like it, we can also elope.'

'Dear heart,' she says, and fondles his hair. 'You are so marvellously romantic. That must be why I love you. But we are both far too young for anything real.'

Some little time later, however, Iris has to qualify this assessment. The madness of marriage is everywhere at work on the plateau. Crates of champagne and fine foods have been carried uphill from the steamer to Lovelock House. A dressmaker from New Plymouth is at work fitting Diana, Iris, Sybil, Marie Louise and Felicity for the wedding. The builder Barney Malone has ceased work on his first house at Lovelock Junction to help Herman erect a marquee for the overflow of guests. Iris urgently finds herself indifferent to it all.

'We may be too young to marry,' she tells Benjamin, 'but not too young for other things. I fear, my love, that I may be with child.'

Benjamin instantly leaves off chewing a stalk of grass. He is sure he hasn't heard. 'You may be what?'

'With child.'

'How?'

'Women know these things. Even girls lacking decorum. I do not wish to confuse you. But it is very biological.'

'And you're sure?'

'Fairly, I'm afraid.'

'You can't be fairly up the duff. Either you are or you're not.'

'Then I am quite certain I am.'

With that, her stoic front springs a leak; tears trickle. 'Benjamin,' she whispers. 'Darling Benjamin. What shall we do?'

'Well, you can't tell your mother,' Benjamin says practically. 'You might finish her off. Then you'd be a pregnant orphan.'

'Don't trifle with me.'

'It's trifling with you that's got us into trouble. Now we got to trifle our way out of it. Pretty damn soon.'

'Please God,' Iris says.

'He helps those who help themselves,' Benjamin says knowledgeably.

They can hear, in the distance, Herman and Barney Malone hammering in pegs for the marquee. For the moment it might be nails in their coffin.

'Perhaps Marie Louise,' Iris suggests. 'She might know what we can do.'

'She has this wedding on her mind. And Felicity driving her bats. It's no time to talk to her.'

'Then there is no one to help,' Iris grieves.

'Not quite,' Benjamin says, thoughtful.

'If not God, or Marie Louise, then who?'

'Paramena,' Benjamin answers.

Paramena is the nearest approach to a physician in the locality of Lovelock Junction; he functions with pride within the limited range of his proficiency. He produces poultices for sprains, ancient herbal remedies for diarrhoea and falling hair, and emetics for over-indulgence in Dixtown Dream; his specific tonic for hangovers and impotence, called Dixtown Rejuvenator, has a modest sale in New Plymouth. His talent is mostly that of an apothecary. He seldom attempts diagnosis on the reasonable assumption that his task is to please the patient. If a patient insists that he is at death's door, Paramena isn't one to differ; he agrees and makes swift sale of the most approximate potion. In this respect he has a reputation for miracle cures. He also treats inquiries with discretion, if circumstances dictate. In Benjamin's, of course, circumstances do.

'Fatherhood isn't the end of the world,' he advises Benjamin. 'Many go through it, and most seem to survive.'

'But we're so young.'

'It seems a little late to plead that as excuse,' Paramena suggests in parental tone.

'And then there's her mother.'

'Ah,' Paramena agrees.

'There's no way to explain it.'

'Perhaps as an accident. A youthful prank gone amiss. No? The fact is, Benjamin, these things will happen. If they didn't, all too few of us would be here.'

Benjamin's silences become forlorn.

'But I take it,' Paramena goes on, 'that you didn't come to me for such impoverished consolation. Rather for more practical reasons; am I right? Let me reassure you. I won't bore you by listing testimonials. Your brow may be less furrowed if I tell you that pregnancy, like many other ills to which man is heir, is a far from incurable condition.'

'It isn't?' Benjamin sees hope, if dimly.

'Some have been known to make a modest living in cases of this kind. There are times when the quest for a cure, despite its distasteful aspects, is a social necessity. Such a case seems to be yours. I see the social disadvantages outweighing other considerations. Indeed I have only to place Sybil Dix on the scales to see all my scruples collapse. Social upheaval is a terrible thing to see. Especially for a pair of your tender years.'

'We haven't much money,' Benjamin points out.

'I am only too willing – indeed delighted – to take up your case on an experimental basis.'

'What does that mean?' Benjamin asks, suspicious. 'Experimental?'

'I mean free. Gratis. Also in the sense of furthering the frontiers of knowledge. I am obliged to confess, in short, that I am less than familiar with the procedures. But there is always a first time. I find instinct a reliable guide in these matters. Men tend to make mysteries of that which common sense serves best.'

'Iris won't come to harm?' Benjamin asks with agitation.

'Do I have the demeanour of one who would hurt a hair of your true love?' Paramena inquires.

'No. But—'

'My attentions, believe me, will be of the kindliest. I cannot, mark you, promise magic. If I could, I would get rid of Sybil Dix for preference. Alas, such a woman is still beyond the reach of science. No. I can but promise to test my talents to their capacity. Bring Iris to me at her earliest convenience.'

Iris's earliest convenience is breathless within ten minutes. Her mother is sufficiently distracted by Diana's pre-marital needs not to notice the disappearance of her other daughter. Paramena closes his store, gives Benjamin a spade, and hobbles ahead into the forest. At length he leads them into a riverside grove. 'This should, I think, ensure us privacy for the delicate matter in hand,' Paramena observes. To Benjamin he adds, 'Start digging here.'

'Dig what?' Benjamin asks, with dark fear. Is Paramena proposing a grave should attempts to resuscitate Iris fail?

'A pit,' Paramena says.

'For what?'

'An oven. Heat is necessary. First we light a fire in the pit. Then we heap stones from the river above. Upon the hot stones I shall then place the leaves of certain trees, and the fronds of certain ferns, I am about to retrieve from the forest. Over these leaves and fronds of proven value I shall then place a flax mat. In the course of time a medicinal steam will surface.'

'What happens to Iris?'

'We place her on top.'

'On top of the oven?'

'There will,' Paramena agrees, 'be certain discomfort. The flax mat affords some insulation.'

'She'll cook.'

'She may steam slightly. But that is the idea. Let me assure you that it is a time tested formula for all feminine problems.'

Iris is likewise aghast. 'Including babies?'

'That,' Paramena says, 'remains to be seen. In your circumstances improvization is of the essence.'

Benjamin, dutifully seeing nothing else for it, begins to dig. Paramena collects firewood and likely fronds and leaves. Iris, suffering frequent palpitations, also a sense of doom, feels she might be better off with the baby after all. Until, that is, she remembers her mother.

In an hour or two the pit is dug, the fire lit, and the river stones heated. Paramena, with a Maori incantation or two, scatters bundles of green vegetation on the stones. There is gentle hissing; soon steam becomes visible. Paramena then arranges the flax mat in place.

'I regret,' he discloses, 'a certain and unavoidable loss of dignity in this procedure. In brief, Iris, before taking your position on the mat, you are obliged to remove all undergarments. The steam must be presented with no impediment while it works into the appropriate region of your anatomy. Ours is not to reason why. Get your drawers down. Benjamin and I shall look the other way.'

'Benjamin needn't. He is familiar with that region of my anatomy. And he can console me.'

Iris soon requires extensive consolation. With her dress hoisted, as she squats on the mat, she is often lost to sight in thick steam; the heat is intense, especially about her buttocks. Her groaning grows fainter. 'How long?' she pleads.

'As long as you can stand it,' Paramena informs her. 'Another five minutes may make all the difference.'

'Five minutes?'

'Hang on,' Benjamin urges.

'You are doing magnificently,' Paramena encourages.

'I shall be a broiled bridesmaid on Saturday,' Iris moans. 'Mother promised me a bad end in the colonies if I didn't behave. Is this what she meant?'

Paramena observes to Benjamin, 'I believe she is becoming delirious. It may be a good sign.'

'What is a bad sign?'

'When boredom sets in,' Paramena judges. 'Iris still has a lively interest in affairs.'

Iris, to confirm this, begins whimpering. Benjamin, not to speak of Iris, can take no more. He pulls her fainting from the pit. Then he splashes her face, and overheated portions of her anatomy, with river water. When she has cooled sufficiently, and begun forming her first conscious syllables, he turns to Paramena. 'Is that all?' he asks.

'For today. We must now wait upon results. One of the tiresome things about medicine, I find, is the practice of patience. There is seldom immediate return for one's endeavour.'

That is on the Thursday. On the Friday morning Benjamin is obliged to report to Paramena that Iris has reason to believe that she is still with child. Paramena is undismayed. 'I have been actively bracing myself for this eventuality,' he confides, and pushes a small dark bottle into Benjamin's hands. 'Within is a most concentrated substance distilled from the root of the flax. Extremely efficacious for constipation, and conceivably also for our purpose. I must warn, however, that it is bitter in taste, and possibly toxic in immoderate quantity.'

'Toxic?' Benjamin says, with alarm.

'Too much of a good thing is often a bad thing. A little less of Iris, for example, and you would never be in your present plight.'

'That's no help now,' Benjamin says with wisdom. 'And no answer. You said toxic.'

'The best of tonics can be toxic. Good and bad you must see as two sides of the same coin. Take the berry of the karaka tree, for example.' He leads Benjamin from the store to a convenient tree. 'Eaten straight from the tree, the berry is particularly poisonous. But left in running water for a few hours it becomes admirable sustenance.'

'We're talking about the root of the flax,' Benjamin points out. 'Not the berry of the karaka tree.'

'Exactly,' Paramena says, as they return to the store.

'I don't have to place Iris in running water for a few hours?'

'I hadn't thought of that,' Paramena allows. 'But it is by no means to be rejected out of hand in the court of last resort. No, I am merely making the point that caution is necessary when dealing with potentially poisonous substances. The karaka tree being an especially potent example for clinical purposes. I have seen one recklessly hungry friend perish. Never again. When Iris finds the taste of the flax root bitter, she is not to panic. She is to persevere. She must take a filled teaspoon every three hours for the next twenty-four hours. No more, for safety's sake. And no less.' Paramena lifts a second bottle from a shelf, and presents it to Benjamin; the label describes the content as Dixtown Dream. 'This, likewise in most moderate quantity, should be sufficient to take away the taste of the tonic should it prove too distressing. No. No money. It is my pleasure and privilege. Give Iris my blessing. Tell her I am sure she shall make a beautiful bridesmaid tomorrow. But remember. Moderation.'

'I'll remember,' Benjamin promises hastily, before smuggling the bottles uphill to Iris. In a sweat, he tells her, 'You must take three filled teaspoons every hour for the next twenty-four hours. No more, for safety's sake. And no less. Then drink from this other bottle to take away the taste. All right?'

'I'm still scalded from yesterday,' she complains. 'Do you think this will work?'

'It better. Otherwise I might have to dump you in the river for a bit. How are things for the wedding?'

'Proceeding as planned,' she sighs. 'I wish I were.'

'It's a funny old world,' Paramena observes to devilishly drunken Richard that night. 'If it's not one thing, it's another. Most of the time it's everything.'

Richard, with his head on the table, doesn't stir perceptibly. The eve of the wedding is cruelly slow to pass. Paramena has been doing his best to dull Richard's consciousness of tomorrow's event, and seems in sight of success.

'Never mind,' Paramena continues, still playing verbal patience. 'It all comes out in the wash. And it's all the same in a hundred years.' He yawns, and finds bed an exceedingly comfortable prospect.

Richard, however, chooses that moment to twitch. His head rises slightly, then falls. 'Sheep,' he says.

'Sheep?'

'That's what buggered me. His bloody sheep.'

'Who, and what sheep?'

'James, you fool. James and his sheep. That was what did for me. But for those sheep I might have got bloody Diana.'

'I see,' Paramena says tranquilly.

'He can satisfy Sybil that he's got the makings of a gentleman farmer. And take off with the prize.'

'Quite,' Paramena observes. 'Life is replete with the unforeseen.'

Richard's head rises again, very slowly, until all but erect. 'What I should like to know,' he says, with some shrewdness for so late an hour, 'is where did he get them?'

'Get what?' Paramena asks, tired and slow to the point.

'The sheep. You ever see them being barged upriver?'

Paramena considers the question. 'No. Come to think, I can't say I did.'

'And they're not known to walk on water.'

'No,' Paramena agrees soberly.

'So where did they come from?'

'Look,' Paramena suggests, 'it's been a long day. There's no joy in dragging it out.'

'You want to know what I think?'

'Not much. No. By now you've told me all you can possibly think about the wedding. Speaking frankly, as a friend, enough is enough. Take my advice. Put it down to experience.'

'Hear me out. I think my virtuous bloody brother James stole those sheep. Stole them to set the scene for Diana, no less.'

'Impossible. From where? There are no sheepmen on the Porangi.'

'All the same,' insists Richard.

There is a long pause. Richard's head teeters but, to Paramena's disappointment, remains relatively upright.

'What,' Richard asks finally, 'is the name of that old Scots bugger up there at Spanish Creek?'

'McKenzie, if I remember.'

'McKenzie?'

'That's right.'

The name demands more silence; Paramena has no problem determining Richard's line of mental inquiry.

'No,' he says softly, with a low whistle.

'Yes,' Richard argues.

'It was so long ago. Some say he's dead.'

'Nevertheless,' Richard continues, 'I don't doubt the same. Two and two add up to McKenzie. Or James and his mystery sheep. Toss in that name and everything's clear. The only man, as I remember, who could make sheep migrate as cleanly as birds.'

'Life and love have the better of you. The rest is imagination.'

'We'll see.'

'I think silence on the subject preferable. At this point, by far.'

'You are looking at a desperate man.'

'I have been for some time,' Paramena notes. 'It does somewhat distress me. And I have a feeling you are about to distress me still more. I don't wish to listen.'

'Wait for tomorrow,' Richard warns.

'Please,' Paramena says. 'I don't wish to know more.'

'Tomorrow, at that ceremony, the minister is going to ask if any man present knows of an impediment to the marriage. I think I might have a small word or two to say at that point. Like asking James, And what about your bloody sheep? That should set the cat among the pigeons.'

'Or the wolf among the sheep. It would all be most unpleasant, Richard. Why can't you let other people be happy?'

'Because I aren't,' Richard explains.

Seldom in the memory of the pioneer settlers of Lovelock Junction has there been a summer day more splendid. The overnight cloud has crept quiet from the sky. There is the rustle of the river below; there is a breeze to cool anxieties; and strident birdsong abundant from dawn. Marie Louise, with Felicity scampering about her, is early at work in her vast kitchen; the clang of copper pans soon arouses others in the house. While Herman breakfasts, with Felicity on his knee, his wife confides: 'Just one thing would make this day perfect.'

'And what would that be?' Herman asks.

'If Luke came back. If he chose the wedding day of our James for his return.'

'The choice may not be his,' Herman observes, as Felicity plunders his plate; before long it is bereft of all bacon. 'And how is Luke to know, wherever he might be, that this day is different from any other?'

'You have no imagination.'

'I have. That is my curse. Don't torment yourself, woman. Take the day as it is, and be grateful.'

'I know Luke will come back,' she insists. 'The question is when. I have said several prayers for today. No one will ever deny me the hope.'

Herman has no desire to deny Marie Louise anything, least of all hope. It is too precious a human resource, and perhaps perilously close to depletion. His wish is that she should conserve it for more promising occasions.

Next to breakfast is Benjamin. He seems unnaturally solemn. He has had, of course, no contact with Iris through the night. For all he knows, he might still frighteningly soon be a father. And he has grave doubt about Paramena's potion. His sleep has been ragged. Was she to take three filled teaspoons an hour, or a filled teaspoon every three hours? His memory is a muddle. There is sweat on his face.

Ernest follows soon. He is also much taken with the embryonic potency of the day. For one thing, he has at last come to a financial arrangement with the mate of a timber scow which is to depart toward the conclusion of the festivities, or when the mate and his men are drunk enough. In all the confusion of the wedding celebration Ernest imagines his escape from Lovelock Junction will not be noted for some hours; by which time he will be launched toward large horizons, maybe with his hand on the wheel of the scow, sea winds fresh in his face. Life will be his.

Felicity helps herself to Benjamin's bacon; her brother is curiously indifferent to the theft. He sees Iris waxen in her tomb. Then Felicity moves on to Ernest's plate. He almost makes protest, but hears crack of canvas, and seabirds calling.

'I do hope,' Marie Louise says, 'that James is not late. He should be with us by now.'

'He has to milk the cows with McKenzie,' Herman points out. 'And see all is well at Spanish Creek before he leaves. Give him time. He won't fail you, even if Luke does. It is his wedding. He has the advantage of knowing.'

'I can feel God's smile,' Marie Louise says. 'It is warming us all.'

At that moment a dozen women, hired help from Dixtown, troop into the kitchen to assist Marie Louise in giving form to the ingredients of the wedding breakfast. Not even God's beneficent countenance could moderate their din. Felicity is full throated in delight. In the absence of information to the contrary, she can only assume that they are all here to indulge and entertain her. Benjamin and Ernest hasten away to don suits for the wedding and then go their different ways. Herman soon looks for a tranquillizing breath of Porangi air from the top of Whisker's tower. Against his better judgement, as just expressed, he gazes downriver for a considerable time, but observes no distant boat bringing Luke. The most conspicuous human presence on the plateau, by far, is that of Ira Dix. Darkly dressed already, he stands outside the Old House, impatient for proceedings to begin, and to deliver his stepdaughter Diana from the horrors of the woman he is about to divorce, for a true fact. Presently a dinghy can be seen arriving from upriver. James with McKenzie. Herman sighs, and taps out his pipe. There could be worse days. He would have preferred the plateau more populous by this time; but at least Barney Malone, soon yawning and stretching outside his hut, has made a reliable beginning with the first of his many planned villas; it is almost fait accompli down there in Little Luke Lane. Herman need no longer keep watch. He takes a last look downriver. There is no lost son approaching. He leaves the tower.

A swift ketch-rigged steamer brings the minister before noon. Near one in the afternoon people press into the ballroom, where seating has been arranged under the elaborate wood-carvings of vine-leaves, birds, bunches of grapes, and scenes of bacchanalian nature. Whisker's life, after all, seems not to have been whimsical waste; there could be no finer setting, at least on the Porangi, for celebration of his daughter's nuptials. In heaven, at least, his standing must now be high; celestial congratulation might appear appropriate. There is an improvized altar at one end of the ballroom. There the minister, with improvized altar boys, takes up his stance with Bible, prayerbook, and text for the ceremony. Among his conscripts, both white robed, well scrubbed and unwilling, are Ernest and baffled Benjamin. They have had some rudimentary rehearsal. They understand that their roles are not taxing; a matter mostly of fetching and carrying on cue. Herman's misgivings about ritualized religion, and the possible taint of his offspring, have as in the past been overruled by Marie Louise: 'Just for one day. They can't come to harm. Think, just think, how Luke would look in a white gown.' Some observation of his sons would reassure Herman that both Benjamin and Ernest are still remarkably free of orthodox Christian contamination; their thoughts perceptibly dwell elsewhere; they appear bored with the business, and twitchy. Ernest sees bold blue skies beyond the window of this baroque prison. Benjamin nervously examines his feet. Despite his best endeavours, he has been unable to break free and discover just how things stand with Iris; he hasn't been able to see her at all. Doubtless, if she were dead, he would be well informed by now.

Marie Louise takes her place in the front row, followed by a frilly Felicity squeaky with complaints; these largely concern lack of nutriment. Herman with firm tread brings up the rear of this party, with Sybil Dix gracious on his arm; Benjamin averts his eyes, for fear of accusation in her face. Then comes stiff Richard, pale and apparently also under strain, and limping Paramena, with an unnervingly sly sidelong smile for Benjamin. They also take the front row. For Benjamin, who feels himself unduly and unfairly exposed, they all seem to be sitting in judgement; he hopes he will not be noticed furtively mouthing marriage vows simultaneously with Iris; he has persuaded her to agree to this plan so they can consider themselves married if all else fails. All else? He wishes he knew.

There is a pause, heads turn, and then James and his best man McKenzie, hugely bearded, are seen moving up the aisle with measured tread, carnations bright in buttonholes, and altogether expertly attired and arranged by Marie Louise since early morning. A beribboned Sunday wags along behind them, with large and meaty ham bone the price of her silence. James whispers to McKenzie, 'Sybil is determined that you shall be a disgrace and ruin the ceremony. I fear she has yet more bitter disappointment to survive.'

'Look to yeself,' McKenzie whispers back. 'Ay. Ye look like a hen on a hot griddle to me.'

To Marie Louise, Sybil is saying, 'Diana looks delightful. And Iris quite divine. Wait and see.'

James and McKenzie arrive before the altar. Christ's representative on the material plane of Lovelock Junction, a man grey and impatient, adjusts spectacles and looks beyond groom and groomsman for first sight of the bride. The musician also imported from New Plymouth has begun to pump even more vehemently on her portable organ. There is a long and hot hush. James feels sweat uncomfortably trickling; his knees are giving way. McKenzie stands stern beside him, defiantly not a disgrace. Sunday relaxes and sprawls with her bone.

Benjamin is rigid. He knows what has happened. The bride cannot come. The bridesmaid is dead. It was one teaspoon every three hours. Not three every one.

Richard's wild eyes move over a matrimonial setting which should, in justice, be his. It might well be when this ship is sunk. Paramena considers how best to cope with the crisis to come. He wishes for some efficacious remedy for his desperate companion; he cannot see how to abort Richard. Then he decides on removing his wooden leg and waving it high, for diversion, if Richard insists on making himself heard.

Sybil is saying, 'I rather think that man McKenzie is intoxicated. I do believe I see the old wretch swaying. James cannot say he was unwarned. And that dog smells quite detestably in this heat.'

'Quiet,' Marie Louise says.

For the bridal party has blossomed, amid many sighs, at the far end of the ballroom. Veiled, delicate and white, Diana shimmers on the elegant arm of Ira Dix. For the first time it is plain to all that Ira is a man not unfamiliar with the finer things, for a true fact. Behind, with vast bouquet, walks Iris. Her step is slow; her eyes fierce to the front. Benjamin tries and fails to catch her gaze as the party nears the altar; he reads no message in her frozen eyes.

The minister begins. There are well-polished words. Holy wedlock is at hand. Marie Louise begins weeping. Sybil waits for smelly old men to run amok. To have both Ira and McKenzie near the altar, at this sacred time, is altogether too inflammatory. Despite her fears, however, she can still look fondly on radiant Diana and darling Iris. They make her anguished life worthwhile. She even wishes, in a weak moment, that Alfred could see them now.

Benjamin begins to feel the ceremony is forever. Ernest knows it is. Felicity, trying to scramble free of her affectionate father, is announcing her undernourished condition in a general way. Marie Louise, through tears, still looks for Luke arriving late down the aisle; it seems her prayers have again been insufficient. She finds the minister a disappointment. The man might as well be mumbling in decent Latin as in English, for all she can hear.

Richard, however, has missed no word of the ceremony. When at last he hears those words for which he has been waiting, a virtual plea for his intervention, he rises to his feet. Paramena, vainly tussling, tries to pull him down again. 'Yes,' Richard attempts to announce. 'I've got a bloody impediment to this marriage.' There is silence of a nervous nature. Sunday, sensitive to atmospheres, sees menace and gives a low growl.

In the ensuing confusion Paramena has no need, after all, to unstrap his wooden leg and wave it in a wild peacemaking effort. First Sunday leaps energetically at Richard, barking quite savagely; her teeth become intimate with his trousers; he finds it impossible to fight her away and resume proposing impediment to matrimony. Then Iris makes for an even more efficient diversion. She begins to vomit to spectacular effect, bringing much disarray to those before the altar. Diana is drenched; Ira too. The minister has never, not even in his many-coloured colonial experience, suffered such abrupt cessation of a ceremony; he senses clerical history in the making.

Richard, with Sunday still growling near, gingerly resumes his seat. Panic pours past him.

'Dear God,' Sybil shouts. She pushes toward the altar where Iris is now evidently expiring. 'What is it, girl?'

McKenzie and James are bending to Iris.

'Is she dying?' Sybil demands. 'Is she dead?'

It is all shaken Benjamin needs to hear. He knows the answer. His Juliet is pale, limp, beyond mortal care. He flees the ballroom, shedding his white robe as he disappears into the outdoors. There, in no mood to lose time, he locates one of the karaka trees about which Paramena has fortuitously warned him; he proceeds to fill his belly with its poisonous berries. 'Drugs be quick,' he whispers. 'With a kiss I die.'

Meanwhile McKenzie lifts his head from Iris's face. 'Never ye fear,' he tells Sybil.

'But, dear God, what is it? What ails the child?'

'It is nae serious,' McKenzie replies, unblinking. 'The poor wee soul's drunk.'

It takes no little time to gather in the many loose ends of the ceremony; the commonplace weave of wedlock remains, for some time, impossible to detect. The major if least conspicuous act of repair, in truth, is

Paramena's. He is swift to note that Benjamin has bolted. Fearing the worst, he follows the boy from the ballroom, and very soon finds him convulsed beneath a karaka tree. His condition can be diagnosed without need for a second opinion. In minutes Paramena is administering his most effective emetic, which Benjamin protests as worse than the poison. Paramena then persuades a deflated if still hissing Richard to carry Benjamin back to Lovelock House, and quietly upstairs to bed. Benjamin's weight taken into account, this is a task to be conjured with; Richard staggers and curses, especially when steps are encountered, but does not lack encouragement from Paramena, who sees a patient at risk, also his reputation. Upstairs they find Iris deposited, still in disgrace, upon Benjamin's bed; down in the ballroom attempts are being made to resume the ceremony with bespattered bride. On seeing Richard arrive, with Benjamin as burden, Iris utters a weak cry. 'My love,' she says. 'My dearest. It didn't work.'

'Where in hell do I dump him?' Richard asks Paramena.

'In bed beside her,' Paramena advises. 'They can't come to more harm than they have.'

'What do you mean?' Richard asks.

'I'm passing a professional opinion. They need the minister now.'

Richard and Paramena make the pale young couple comfortable and close the bedroom door as they leave. Soon after, when the ceremony downstairs has concluded to the satisfaction of some, the same door is opened by Sybil. Surprise and consternation follow. Also grief. Benjamin, under much pressure, at length sees fit to inform Sybil that she is to be a grandmother before many months pass. Sybil proves no more immune to bad news than most men and women.

Then Ira Dix, in pursuit of his wife, arrives at the door. 'See here, woman,' he tells her. 'On a day like this I don't want to see no one unhappy. I got second thoughts about divorce. I purely have. I reckon we could give marriage a second try, for a true fact.'

The reception itself, the food, the champagne and the splendour, soon makes the frothy nature of the nuptials past history. There is dancing in the red-cobbled forecourt to the unruly sound of accordionists recruited in Dixtown. Handsome James and lovely Diana lead the way; they appear entranced with each other. Ira Dix is to be seen affectionately supporting his wife through a waltz. McKenzie, partnered by Marie Louise, is prominent in a dance which might well have derived from a Scottish reel. Paramena turns the disadvantage of a wooden leg into enchanting virtue in the gavotte. Felicity befriends Sunday, and dog and golden daughter do their best to be underfoot in every location.

Herman and Barney Malone explode open a keg of the best New Plymouth ale in the marquee, and drink to a future of fine colonial villas. The minister, not averse to a tipple or two, especially after so taxing a ceremony, sees in sour Richard a man in need of religious consolations; he makes it his business to offer Richard a larger view of life, also of the life to come, though it is reasonably evident that Richard finds this one more than a match. Upstairs in the house, abandoned and forgotten by all, equally invalid Benjamin and Iris make love in enfeebled fashion. Elsewhere ignorant armies may clash by night. At Lovelock Junction, as never before, as never again, men are familiar with the harmonies of heaven, the discords of the devil.

Even for Ernest this summer day eventually progresses almost entirely as planned. Towards the afternoon's end, attracting no attention, he takes leave of Lovelock Junction forever, aboard a timber scow. True that the craft has an uncertain course downriver, on the ebb tide. Skipper and crew are drunken and soon dozing. The mate, barely upright, hangs weakly to the wheel for support. Fortunately Ernest has no doubt of the direction and is delighted, before long, to relieve the mate at the wheel. The scow isn't destined, or suitably rigged, to survive the hazards of the shoals at the Porangi mouth; nor are there seasoned hands at the helm. All are lost save one. The sole survivor is Ernest. Sobered by experience of seafaring, he is ultimately found making his abject way upriver, next morning, aboard a raft contrived from the scow's wreckage.

'I know you felt the need to go off and look for Luke,' Marie Louise says with compassion. 'But don't do it again. One lost Luke is enough. Now get off those clothes and spend all day in bed.'

Life at Lovelock Junction has begun again. Not only for Ernest.

('Festivity, of sorts, was not unknown in that odd and remote community,' says the rather joyless author of *The Lives of Lovelock Junction*. 'Some echo of it can be found, if sentimentally, in the often quaint verses of the early colonial poetess Iris Lovelock. In her slim Victorian volume "Bush Wedding and Other Verses", one finds these lines: *No nightingale in this far woodland sings / Yet merry yeomen from Old England bring / A laughing song to swell the rills and springs / That greet the bridal pair with joyous ring*. It might safely be assumed that the poem does indeed derive from some actual event at Lovelock Junction – and perhaps, who knows, from her own wedding to Benjamin, Herman's oldest son. It is followed by a poem unmistakably referring to the birth of their first child. Like many of her versifying colonial contemporaries, Iris Lovelock's forms and diction – lovingly imported, along with the best bone china – foundered on the brute fact of the landscape in which she dwelled. No nightingales? Alas. Characteristically, she neglects to name the dozens of diverse and colourful birds which *did* sing there. It suggests, at the least, that the creative imagination had a thin time of it on the Porangi. One is grateful, however, for the fugitive – if ghostly – glimpse of her girlhood at Lovelock Junction. The rest is silence; and speculation. Now the river runs quiet.'

And, in the above version, visibly shallow.)

James and Diana honeymoon simply. They leave McKenzie with the lighter tasks of summer at Spanish Creek, and take tent and provisions upriver in a dinghy; their intention is to travel as far as the Porangi allows them, perhaps to the Makutu Falls. James knows of these falls only in the legends Upokonui once told; no white man has ever seen them. It seems all too possible that they are unreliably traditional; that they exist only in mythology and imagination. If Upokonui's description is still to be believed, the place at its best is more enchanted than any other on earth: water, the *tohunga* told James, speaks there with a hundred silver tongues, defying human translation. Before mankind came to muddy the world, the gods frequented the falls as a wayside sanctuary on their journeys hither and thither. Man never marked that part of the Porangi. Most kept at a distance, believing the falls haunted by the unquiet spirits of a pair of lovers, from rival and warring tribes, who in this life found it impossible to mate; and who bonded themselves with a passionate and fatal leap into legend. These lovers, however, are still known to set the scene for soul-mates who come: to arrange all as the old gods once knew it. In theory, at least, James and Diana might find all the solitude they seek there.

For five tiring days James rows and finds no falls. For five tiring nights he voyages as vainly upon Diana's body. Her maidenhead begins to seem a citadel as remote of attainment as the falls themselves, if they exist; he begins to doubt it. The passing landscapes grow lacklustre; his mood monotone. Even the birdsong seems bleak. His manhood is an untenanted house.

On the sixth day they discover the Makutu Falls a fact. The river currents grow more convulsive about them, frightening Diana. James battles around a bend, with the dinghy dancing over fine feathers of foam, and soon they see that they have reached the upper limit of navigation on the Porangi River. James and Diana are tiny under a tall amphitheatre of limestone, everywhere veiled gently with tumbling waters in the light of late afternoon. Caves perforate the steep rock faces, their entrances greened with filmy fern; there are stark ambiguous sculptures of water-whittled limestone. There are domes and arches and arabesques. Everything that Upokonui promised, and more. Here the rococo water speaks with sonorous sound. There with classical whisper. Everywhere it seems hallucination. Echoes from the caves compound the magic. Rainbows rise and fall, flickering faintly, in sunlight and fine spray.

James moors the dinghy to the lower limb of a mammoth tree. At last ashore, they are for a time tempted not to breathe, lest they lose it all; certainly speech seems superfluous. All is too crystalline. Imagination fluently insists that a man might dwell as god here, if he dares.

'We need no tent,' James announces, and takes Diana's hand. He leads her around rocks to the very foot of the falls. Behind a thin tapestry of falling water they find a cave. Summer's thick heat is lost, and so is the sun. Within the cave it is dim, cool and quiet. Moss robs their footfalls of reverberation. Dreamily, still without speaking, Diana begins to disrobe. Soon James has shed his last garment. In the green light of the cave, a reclining Diana already and boldly awaits him; her flesh seems pearly, distinctly that of a deity, with the fruit of immortality darkly ripened between her open legs. James, quite ferocious with love and lust, falls upon her with long sigh; he feels the door burst, and his dizzy spirit longs to follow his flesh into the moist and mysterious chambers beyond. For a moment, ecstatic, he seems to be given wings by that wish; he is granted a wild and weightless ride into regions strange and remote. Then, too early by far, it appears that he and Diana are but flesh in breathless embrace upon the floor of the cave.

'Let us never leave here,' she is asking.

'Never,' he says.

'How soon,' she inquires, 'can you do that again?'

'Before long,' he promises.

'It is,' she sighs, 'quite the prettiest thing that has ever happened to me. It didn't hurt at all; it wasn't horrid. Dear James. Are you ready again yet?'

On the seventh day James and Diana indeed find it necessary to rest.

Part Three

E'en though we sometimes pained and wondered
How should we ever think that we had blundered?

— Iris Lovelock

Thirteen

The Iron Age arrives at Lovelock Junction, at least inspirationally, in the second half of the 1870s.

'We have had our first death and first birth,' Marie Louise says. 'And now our first wedding.'

Herman is reminded, though he has never quite forgotten, of another trinity now that the town is assuming statistical shape. Timber and coal are proven resources. What of iron? Something solid is needed, surely, to bond the tentative community; some major challenge met might make sense of the confusion. Until now the task of founding the town has been sufficiently and imaginatively taxing. Dixtown, true, has been an unnerving distraction at times. But with Barney Malone so reliable a builder uncomely Dixtown is destined to dwell in the shade of Lovelock Junction proper; it is merely a matter of time. Herman is relieved to see Malone as a moderately temperate man, Saturday night aside; he has no conspicuous complaint to make of the world, no idiosyncratic barrow to push; he seems content to take Lovelock Junction for granted, and get on with the job. Herman is content to let him. At first Malone lives lonely on the site, with a couple of carpenters; he gives it to be understood that he has a large family elsewhere, but is glad to be free for a time; he ships off to see them once a month, and returns to river exile with no evident remorse.

So Herman can at last contemplate iron. Huge dunes rich in that substance still rear suggestively at the mouth of the Porangi. One question to be considered is whether coal should best be carried to the iron; or iron to the coal. But that logistic decision can be left. Meantime, ironsand can be barged upriver, in small quantities, so that Herman can explore its potential for revelation. He orders texts on the subject which are for the most part recondite: the theology of the thing proves baffling. All he wants to do, after all, is persuade bona fide iron from the sands; he is asking only for mineral deliverance, not that of mankind, which should not be asking too much. Though hesitant to leave the river, and especially Marie Louise, he takes a ship north to Auckland where he can consult with chemists and others of scientific ilk; he takes several samples of Porangi sand.

Weeks pass. More weeks. Felicity feels the loss of her father most. Daily she wanders the house, calling loudly, in quest of Herman. But he is never there, not even up in the tower, considering the circumstantial promise of the Porangi. Marie Louise often finds the girl inconsolable. Letters arrive, with promises, but the boats never quite bring Herman. Without him, Lovelock Junction has no heart. Dixtown goes its way. Spanish Creek, from a distance, appears serene. But Herman?

After more than two months, nearly three, Herman comes home. He is pale, thin and exhausted. His eyes are red. He is burdened with a great many more books, further treatises on iron and its manufacture. There is conceivably now no man in the colony with wider knowledge of the subject. 'I have,' he announces to Marie Louise, 'left no stone unturned.' The fact is, however, that Herman has found nothing other than earthy under any stone. It has been considerable expense to flesh, spirit and purse. Always uncomfortably quartered in Auckland, he also found the colonial food overcooked and intolerable, constipating to boot; the merchants of the town were rascals quite as mean and grasping as rumoured; and as for the townsfolk as a whole, it was another fair demonstration of what the devil could do with antipodean hands; he had never ceased to be homesick for the Porangi while suffering the study of iron among strangers. All have found his problem perplexing. Many have found it profitable to pursue while Herman finances their research. They have sometimes confessed their fascination with the challenge. No one denies the fact, and abundance, of iron in the samples he has to show. The problem is to extract the pure iron. As Herman explains to Marie Louise, who would be content not to have the explanation, the difficulty is with the surrounding impurities. In short, which Herman isn't, the essential iron in titanomagnetite form has to be freed from its parent andesite and especially from titanium oxide; the latter is wholly thwarting by any available process. Prolonged experiment might provide useful answers. Marie Louise is happy to have Herman home in pure form. When Felicity has finished with him, she puts her husband to bed. 'You can forget about the surrounding impurities for one night,' she informs him.

These, however, have to be confronted next morning. Not only in the nature of Dixtown, busy downhill, but upon the plateau itself. In his absence four villas have been finished and a fifth is rising. Impossible to evade the fact that all four have already filled with Malones; they will surely overflow into the fifth, and God knows the sixth. Clearly Malone has been unnaturally modest about his capacity as a family man; it seems he has already bred two of substantial nature, the second after his first wife faltered and expired in her unlucky thirteenth pregnancy. His older children too have begun to breed. Bare-legged and red-haired Malone urchins dangle from windows and verandas, and battle genially in the winter mud. Within the windows crucifixes can be seen, and colourful portraits of the Virgin Mother. There are babies crying and women shouting. 'Sure,' Malone explains, 'and wouldn't it be wicked waste to leave such fine accommodations empty?'

Compassionate Herman cannot deny this. Nature abhors a vacuum. So, never to be underestimated, does humanity. Nevertheless there are questions to be asked.

'What,' he says to Malone, 'will they do here?'

'Why,' Malone answers, 'they are thinking it's unkind for their father to labour, untended, in so lonesome a place.'

'And what are you thinking?'

'I am thinking it's welcome they should be.'

'So many?'

'They are all God's gifts. I am thinking that too. The saints forbid I should be so ungrateful a father as not to want to hear their happy voices.'

The happy voices, and some less so, are momentarily deafening about them as they talk.

'But what is there here for them?' Herman is moved to protest.

'A fine town is my understanding. It would be a fearful unlucky thing for them to miss the chance. Some will be helping me in my work. And some have not been slow to seek out your brother Richard, to assure themselves of gainful employment. It's not without initiative they are.'

'I see,' Herman says, or tries to, since vision has always been the clue to Lovelock Junction, and for the most part the reality. Herman has never, in truth, quite planned how best to populate it. Dignity in itself might draw men of the right metal. Or such has been his hope. There is no denying the metal in the Malones of the world; but how win it from the parent materials, from threadbare tradition and superstition, and smelt it into orderly adult shape?

For the moment he sees the winning of ore from andesite and titanium oxide as a preferable task. Behind Lovelock House he sets up his laboratory in a lengthening shed, and also a small experimental furnace. If iron can be persuaded to announce itself purely from his endeavours, he might get a more useful grip on other matters. Titanomagnetite may yet make Lovelock Junction worth its name. Meanwhile, more villas rise; and the Malones flourish.

Benjamin and Iris are married, quickly and quietly, and as soon as legally acceptable; this is none too soon, given the proximity of parenthood. Legal acceptability is hastened by fresh birth certificates efficiently forged by Paramena in collaboration with a bribed New Plymouth printer. For Paramena himself, there is no pecuniary return; he sees his role as penitential. Having failed Benjamin and Iris in the matter of circumventing the pregnancy, and with his reputation at risk, he makes it his duty to expedite marital rapture. Iris moves up to Lovelock House, to live with her young husband and shelter, when need be, under Marie Louise's large wing. 'Felicity will have a companion,' Marie Louise declares with pleasure. 'She will no longer be the only baby in the house.' This appears an optimistic judgement; it seems certain that Felicity will have no patience with babies, and their infantile pursuits. Well before the age of two years, Felicity has the face, and almost the form, of a mature woman; there is no baby fat, despite her appetite. She struts the house as an adult in miniature, an imperious princess. She sees Benjamin and Ernest, among others, merely as retainers; their loyalty is often under test. Benjamin, besides, has aspirations toward adulthood himself; and, in enlarged Iris, also the evidence. Ernest, so far, has only grievances. He also has, when he can manage it, the company of one or other of the many Malone girls; they do not altogether compensate for the horizons cruelly lost on the Porangi shoals. Though these girls sometimes brazenly show him their navels, when alone with him in the trees, he is not tempted to make exploration of that aperture and emulate Benjamin's premature and explosive entry upon parenthood. He knows, with the wisdom of the elders to whom he has admiringly listened on the jetty, that women are in the world to tie men down; their navels are simply the snare.

In the Old House, Sybil Dix has retreated into shock with the departure first of Diana, to rusticate at Spanish Creek, and now of fecund Iris. Life, or what passes for it on the Porangi, has left her a dazed and groping stranger in the land. She has also retreated into the company of her transparently doting husband. Since she no longer has the conviction to complain about his muddy boots, no his smelly pipe, Ira is now a sight more comfortable with his wife. Moreover, he no longer takes his meals up at Lovelock House, not since Sybil suffered herself some culinary instruction from Marie Louise in order to make her evenings less lonely. To Ira's especial pleasure, Sybil joins him in exploring the complex potentials in a pack of playing cards, others not having the patience. In the colour and texture of the cards he sometimes glimpses the misty contours of another life; he is strangely exhilarated. For her part, Sybil seeks to divine God's will in the fall of the cards. She is almost invariably trumped. Their windows are often lit till late. Sometimes, and not before time, mutual laughter is heard. Sybil and Ira can also be observed tidying Alfred Whisker's grave together. There are some who say, Richard among them, that this somewhat sexless idyll cannot last. Marie Louise, with more shrewdness, notes that the feminine change of life can have beneficial effect. Much depends on the eye of the beholder. In the schoolroom – where Benjamin and Iris are still obliged to keep up the pretence of innocent pupils, along with worldly Ernest and an increasing number of volatile Malones – Sybil's tongue is considerably less cutting; even the more unruly scholars of Dixtown are not perceptibly lacerated, when she does her stint there; she is sometimes, most remarkably, seen to smile vaguely in circumstances where once sacrificial victims would have been certain; on other occasions, even more remarkably, she sobs for no evident reason at all and dismisses the class before her. In spring, girls bring her daffodils grown in the otherwise drab clay gardens of Dixtown. 'Wordsworth, where are you now?' she asks moist-eyed. Then, marginally more comprehensible to the class, she adds, 'Beauty and grace need never desert us, not even in the colonies, where there is a will and a way.'

Much may desert Richard; desire doesn't. Nor hope. As an expression of both, he surrounds himself with a dwelling of imposing dimension, his bachelor status considered. It is old lore that one must build a cage to catch a bird. Richard spares himself most of the pains attendant upon a cage-building timetable by travelling to Auckland and consulting a prosperous specialist in colonial real estate. This salesman eventually shows Richard a merchant's house which appears to lack nothing in style. Italianate, of hardwood and plastered brick, it has an Ionic portico, curving verandas, parquet floors of oak, and smoking and billiard rooms of generous capacity. The price is six thousand pounds. Richard, rather than haggle, buys for four. 'When do you want to move in?' the salesman asks. 'Never,' Richard explains. 'I'm moving it out.' Within the month, it has risen on an elevated site between Dixtown and Lovelock Junction proper, not quite of either, and complete with large bay windows.

'Why do you need it?' Paramena asks.

'Independence,' Richard answers. 'First I lived with my family. Then with you. I need space to think my own thoughts.'

'Space? All that?'

'They chase each other. Thoughts do.'

'There's more to it,' Paramena suggests.

'All right. Maybe.'

'Only a woman would make sense of it.'

Richard is not disposed to confirm this.

'Come on,' Paremena urges. 'Confession is good for the soul.'

'Not mine,' Richard insists, with some self-knowledge.

'Ah. So there is someone in mind. Someone special. Not one of your Dixtown women.'

'Guess away. Think what you like. It's all one to me.'

Dixtown now has sufficient population to sustain a respectable race meeting, on a track roughly shaped around the recreation ground at the edge of the settlement. Richard's colours tend to fly past the winning post more often than is fair. Paramena, doing service to the community as bookmaker, is frequently out of pocket. 'You could tell your riders to slow down a little,' he advises Richard. 'And make it more of a race.'

'And not win?' Richard says, amazed.

'We have to keep a sense of proportion.'

'I'm in this to win. Who loves losers?'

'Winners can likewise pose problems for the affections. At the moment, old friend, you are testing mine.'

'You're telling me not to win,' Richard protests.

'Just a little less. In moderation. Otherwise I'm with you all the way.'

'Last time I was moderate, I was pipped at the post by sheep. Never again.'

Paramena sighs. It seems he is likely never to hear the last of it. Richard's grievances prosper best with regular airings.

'You're talking of the larger world. I'm talking of providing Dixtown with wholesome entertainment. And certainly with more congenial odds.'

They arrive at a compromise: handicap races. Richard often rides himself, distrusting others, and ruthless with the whip; none would ever suspect him of pulling his mount. He never does. If he still wins, it is within reason. As bookmaker Paramena at last struggles out of the red. Before long Richard is also conspicuous at New Plymouth picnic race meetings; Dixtown has become too small an arena.

'It makes sheep look sick,' Richard says, on return to the river with a large silver cup. A remark which Paremena, on the whole, finds puzzling; even Richard can't win them all.

*

Iris gives birth to Benjamin's son on a cool spring day after a sluggish winter. The event is preceded by much consternation on the part of Marie Louise. Iris seems too slight for childbirth; it may kill her. The girl confounds these dark expectations by shedding her son within five minutes of her waters breaking; no one has seen anything more painless. Iris is soon sitting up bright and bird-like in bed, baby at breast, showing competence in every maternal capacity. Benjamin is awed, and ashamed that his role remains so minuscule; he seems altogether unnecessary now. While Marie Louise and Sybil and the midwife flutter, and jealous Felicity piercingly demands that her needs also be noted, Benjamin seeks relief in a long row upriver to bear the news to Spanish Creek. While ferny banks pass, he perceives injustice; he begins to see that fatherhood is honoured largely in the breach.

This reservation about the experience is, however, diminished by his reception at Spanish Creek. In the absence of Iris and the child, he becomes the centre of celebration.

'To ye, lad,' McKenzie toasts, with whisky.

In recognition of his new status, Benjamin also has a handsomely filled mug; for the first time in his life he is more than a boy.

'And may there be many,' James adds, quite as delighted, slapping Benjamin's shoulder.

Diana finds a modest sherry more suitable for celebration. She sips delicately; her eyes are slightly vague. 'And the baby,' she asks, 'is it pretty?'

'Very,' Benjamin answers, with pride. His pride increases in proportion to the warming whisky consumed. 'When,' he inquires pertinently, 'will you have yours?'

'Ah,' McKenzie says. 'There's a bonny question.'

'Soon,' James suggests.

'No doubt,' Diana agrees.

Silence then cushions the subject. Despite the whisky colouring the world afresh, Benjamin sees it best to be discreet; he observes shadow in the eyes of James, and some shyness in Diana. He asks, not altogether tactfully, after the lambing on the farm. The flock has swollen. Hardly a ewe has failed to deliver a healthy lamb; twins have not been uncommon. This summer will see the first large shipment of wool downriver. The climate at Spanish Creek, all round, seems to be sunny; there is only the one cloud. And Benjamin doesn't consider procreation an especial problem. If the worst comes to the worst, he can always tell Uncle James how.

Benjamin soon races home to wife and son. He leaves behind an atmosphere.

'You do not forgive me, do you?' Diana says to James.

'For what?'

'For not being with child yet. You envy Benjamin's son.'

'It's true that I should be grateful for a child. But all things in good time. I am patient. The fault could as well be mine.'

'But you do not really believe that. You believe it must be me.'

'I don't really believe anything. There is no sure knowledge on which to build belief.'

'I can tell. I can tell you are blaming me.'

'There is no blame attaching to anyone,' James argues, more harshly than he means. 'There is just life.'

Diana begins to weep. 'I try to be a good wife,' she pleads. 'I try to keep things pretty for you.'

'Of course,' he agrees.

'The rest is in the hands of God,' she says. 'Perhaps He has made some judgement on us.'

'Nonsense,' James insists. 'Come now. It's time for bed.'

'Our barren bed. Perhaps I was wicked in some past life. And am paying now. Do you think that might be it?'

'It is no occasion for hysteria. We are not even a year married. Many wait longer.'

He tries to take his wife gently by the shoulders. She shakes free.

'You are so good,' she goes on. 'And I am just a lost, wicked soul wandering this world.'

'Excellent,' he observes, snuffing out the lamps in the living room. 'So come to bed and be wicked with me.'

There are satisfactions in the bedroom. Not solutions. Diana's larger demands are now elsewhere, and mostly concerned with making the homestead still more handsome. It is no effort for James to concede that its interior is now less bleak to the eye. Silverware soon dignifies their dining table, and silver candlesticks in keeping; then his original scrubbed table must of necessity be replaced with one of the best English oak, with graceful sideboards to match. There is lace; there is fine linen. They eat off the best Wedgwood china. Carpets, homely floral or exotic Persian, have begun creeping thickly across bare floorboards. Lamps with fragile and fancy shades mushroom in corners on unfamiliar tiny tables. Their feather mattress is the finest to be found in New Plymouth, also their polished brass bed. Tasteful reproductions of paintings by the more distinguished English landscape artists make wall space less monotonous. 'We are really,' Diana pronounces, 'becoming quite remarkably civilized.' James is also quite remarkably in debt. There is a bank manager to placate. His first money from wool makes little impression.

In late summer, with shearing done, work slack, McKenzie finds James alone, and with skyward stare. 'Ay, lad,' he says. 'Ye're thinking.'

'True.'

'I see ye looking at yon eastern hills; the ones ye left alone. Is it more burning on mind, maybe?'

'Maybe,' James allows. 'I need more land. More sheep.'

'I see the lack,' McKenzie observes. 'Also need to keep the lass happy.'

'And myself,' James adds, without conviction.

'So?' McKenzie asks.

'So we burn again,' James sighs.

Through late summer and early autumn Diana is given to lengthy complaints about the cinders invading the homestead through door and window. She also declares the smoke often too stifling to tolerate. Her largest strictures concern her blackened, sweaty husband himself. 'I hardly recognize you,' she says. 'You have begun to look like nothing more or less than a negro. Even with soap and water, you still reek unmentionably of smoke.' To emphasize her displeasure, as more fire races through the forests, she journeys down to Lovelock Junction to visit her mother and sister, and once or twice still further, to New Plymouth, to shop for necessities of the civilized life.

'I saw Richard in the town,' she announces after one of these excursions, returned with a new hat, a new dress, and accessories. 'He was in great good humour. It seems a thoroughbred horse he has purchased had just won the New Plymouth Guineas. He was celebrating with champagne.'

'Good for Richard,' James says. 'I trust you offered our congratulations.'

'I took a glass or two with him. It seemed only fitting.'

'Of course,' James agrees gently. 'Well, you shall be relieved, no doubt, to know that the burning is done. The rains have arrived; the forest is too saturated for more.'

'I am certainly glad to have the man I married again. Not to speak of clean air. I cannot help but feel that with this manic endeavour you have been losing life's larger perspectives.'

'What does that mean?'

'I mean, and please do not be cross, that it is time for a little more elegance in your life.'

'You have bought me a suit,' he guesses, dreading the bill.

'I have been rather more thoughtful than that. I remembered your desire to instal a piano in the homestead, and I took it upon myself to investigate suitable instruments. Most, I fear, were rather cheap and horrid, not to be suffered. So now we have a grand.'

'A grand?' James says, with disbelief.

'A very grand piano, if I may say so. It will look most pretty in the living room. And our evenings no doubt will now be less empty. Grace can be cultivated.'

James, whose present concern is with cultivation of grass, cannot quite see how he will ever keep pace; he may have to burn and sow clear across the country and back again to make peace with creditors.

'Talking of grace,' she goes on, 'reminds me of a minor matter. I have been reluctant to take it up with you before, but there is no time like the present. One sees things with fresh eyes after a welcome break from the workaday tedium of the farm. One also, I fear, sees the flaws in the life.'

'What are you talking about? Grace? Flaws?'

'I am talking of your man. McKenzie.'

'What of him?'

'I think it reasonable to suggest that we see a little less of him in this house. I know that it has been your custom to treat the man as an equal, to the extent of bidding him enter whenever he appears at our door.'

'Naturally. As my mate. We have been through much together.'

'That is as may be. But there are times, mistakenly no doubt, when I have the impression that I am married to him also. Or that you expect me to be. I regret to say, James, that you are stretching my tolerance in this matter. It cannot go on.'

'What cannot?' Perhaps she is pregnant. He has heard women with child become irritable, and have to be humoured.

'McKenzie. And his dog. They have much in common; they are both full of fleas. They may come to our door, but no further. In any case, there is enough talk of sheep in this house. There is more to life.'

'No doubt,' James says, though too tired to see.

'You must make separation between your life and your work.'

'I have always seen them as one.'

'God knows I must suffer the smell. But not the infinite talk of sheep, sheep, sheep.'

'We are only doing our best by the wisdom of Solomon. Be thou diligent, he said, to know the state of thy flocks. For riches are not forever, and the lambs are for thy clothing.'

'Are you mocking me?'

'I am not,' James sighs. With more reason than ever for hope about her condition, he sees it as necessary to pacify her, for a time. If irritability is indication, her pregnancy may be well advanced. 'All right,' he agrees with reluctance. 'I will do my best not to invite McKenzie in, if such is your wish. The wish of the lady of the house is law, I am told.'

'It is my wish,' Diana says firmly.

'Nae matter,' McKenzie says, later, when James explains the position. 'Nae matter, lad. Women are queer. And, ay, old men untidy.'

'I'm sorry, all the same,' James confides helplessly.

'Regret, lad, is hindrance to clear vision. Get on with your life. I'm nae sorry for mine. Make the lass happy. Grief enough grows in this world. If your dwelling is forbid me, my door is always open to ye. I can find a bottle filled with consolation, and fling the cork far.'

Another month demonstrates that Diana is not with child. To save embarrassment, McKenzie no longer approaches the homestead, unless with firewood. Lonely within, too often for comfort, and sometimes a stranger under his own roof, James engages himself with the grand piano. Seldom with satisfaction. His fingers have stiffened; he lacks lightness of touch. Also the music he makes seems at odds with his hills. They are still there, obstinate, at the end. And the sheep. The music? Lost; a world away. More often than not he finishes taking pipe and tobacco down to McKenzie's hut, still bachelor terrain. There is always a black billy can of tea brewing; and an uncorked bottle, as promised. There is also more convincing melody in the cadences of McKenzie's life and times than in any composition he attempts upon the piano. And there is peace.

'Look there, lad,' McKenzie now often says, drawing James to the door of the hut. 'There never were hills more fair. Nae. Never. All as I dreamed. All green with the finest grass growing. The poplars shady, the willows too. And across the grass, over the hills, white sheep grazing.'

'Yes,' James agrees. 'A good sight to see.'

'Maybe,' McKenzie says, 'I was dreaming of death, when I dreamed these hills.'

'Death?'

'My death. Ay.'

'Don't say that,' James protests.

Benjamin comes upriver more often, bringing Iris and their baby son. Iris is soon fattening with a second child, which does little for James's morale.

'I have responsibilities,' Benjamin explains earnestly. 'I have to think of the future.'

'Indeed,' James agrees. 'At this rate.'

'One of the things I have been thinking,' Benjamin goes on, 'is that I should like to throw in my lot with you.'

'With me? What of your father? Herman is not to be forgotten. Nor his feelings.'

'He is too much involved with the problem of freeing iron ore from its parental materials. Too much, that is, to converse sensibly on any other subject.'

'But when he has freed the metal? What then? He will notice your loss. He will need you.'

'Time enough, then,' Benjamin suggests. 'He will not have to search far for me, if I'm at Spanish Creek. Meantime, I want to make more of my life. I need independence. I could do worse than make myself a farmer. Iris would be near her sister. And your sheeplands, I notice, are much enlarged. You must need more help. McKenzie is old.'

'I'll think on it,' James promises.

He does not have to think long. That winter rain and biting gales from the west turn the lower pastures into dank puddles, and all tracks to deep mud. The misery colours man. McKenzie weakens in a fever; Sunday whimpers by his bed. In the end only one act is possible. James wraps McKenzie in a warm blanket and bears him uphill to the homestead. There, whatever the welcome, his mate can get the nursing he needs. The old shepherd's lean body, wasting, is leaner still; he can be carried with comfort through the slush.

Diana is within view of the door when he arrives with his melancholy burden. 'And what,' she asks, 'is this?'

'A sick man,' James answers. 'Also old, and maybe mortally tired.'

'That much I can see. And are we to have him here?'

Pools of muddy rainwater are forming, where he stands with McKenzie, on the polished floor. And Sunday, following close, has left conspicuous paw-marks.

'Where else?' James demands. 'I shall put him in the guest room, and light a fire.'

'And is this to be the custom, whenever it is your whim? And whenever winter severe?'

'A Christian custom, perhaps,' James replies shortly.

'I believe you have long been looking for an excuse to get that old ruffian into the house. And that now the excuse is conveniently at hand.'

'If it is necessary for you to believe that, it would be kindness not to contradict you.'

That said, he pushes past Diana, dripping his way into the guest bedroom.

She makes last appeal. 'Don't you know what you are doing?'

'I know what he is. I know what I am. No more.'

'Such knowledge must be of great consolation, not to speak of convenience, to you. Where is my convenience? Where is my consolation, castaway here among these hills? Who am I any longer? Tell me. Pray do.'

'You are,' James says firmly, for the first time, 'my wife. Fetch fresh linen. And extra blankets.'

A day or two later, when the weather clears briefly, Diana finds it convenient to have James row her downriver to Lovelock Junction where, after seeing her mother, she thinks she might well catch a steamer to New Plymouth, and there seek some relief from the rural winter. James isn't inclined to take issue. Alarmed to have left McKenzie so long, he rows home against the current to Spanish Creek, his arms fast aching. Dark cloud drifts low again, with rain soon merciless on his face. He runs from the landing to the homestead. With relief he hears the Scots voice, quite coherent again, from the bedroom.

'Ay,' McKenzie is saying. 'There's the wee lass. Ye go. I'll follow.'

But James, at last at the bedside, sees the old shepherd is in delirium. He is hearty and young among high hills again, and maybe white mountains. And talking to Sunday. Or, more likely, to Friday.

'There, lass,' McKenzie continues, each breath coming hard. 'There. Just as I told ye. A muckle hole in the mountains. And look ye now. More. Land, lass. More than ye ever saw. All ours, lass. We can see forever. Was there ever so fair a sight?'

A breath or two later McKenzie is dead and Sunday strident with grief.

Next day James buries the highlander far from home, from glen and croft, alongside the cairn under which Upokonui rests. Bareheaded in cruel rain, James finds Christian words perfectly suited. But when the grave is filled, Sunday refuses to leave it. The dog sprawls on the sticky clay.

'Come, lass,' James pleads.

The dog only whines. Four days later she is still there, growing skeletal and feeble, though James offers food. Within the week he has another, if shallower, grave to dig.

When Diana returns, James simply says, 'McKenzie will vex you no more. He has gone.'

'Gone?' she says blankly.

'Perhaps because he no longer felt welcome in this life. Sunday too. So there's the end to it.'

He is reluctant to hear intelligence of New Plymouth, even of Lovelock Junction. He leaves the homestead, saddles a horse, and takes a considerable ride across his land.

('Sometimes,' types the tireless scrivener of *The Lives of Lovelock Junction*, 'it would seem that the inhabitants of the place had little better to do with themselves than invent traditions to tease the twentieth century. Some of these suspect tales have survived. Let us take just one. The hills and mountains to the west of Spanish Creek are clearly marked on maps as the McKenzie Range, doubtless the whim of some early surveyor whose name may well have been McKenzie, or one of whose workmates might have been of that name. From this grain has grown the pearl of a proposition that the name actually derives from the most notorious McKenzie anywhere in the New World record – the Scot who made an epic of sheep-stealing far to the south of the Porangi and whose name, albeit misspelled, remains indelible on alpine high country to this day. (The solo highlander was credited with theft of tens of thousands of sheep, and discovery of three million unknown acres. Recent research argues that he was really not much of a rustler, nor much of an explorer, but never mind.) Tradition – or the rags and tatters of Lovelock family legend – says that McKenzie later found sanctuary, for a time, with James Lovelock at Spanish Creek; and died there. Nothing reliable in the written record confirms this. There is, however, a suggestion that an obscure Scot did reside as farmhand at Spanish Creek for a time, and possibly later at Dixtown; there one finds, certainly, such names as McDonald and McDuff among men employed by Richard Lovelock. All the McDonalds and McDuffs in the world – and all the plausible tales of the Porangi – cannot make the connection convincing. One dislikes interring colourful tradition, even the transparently spurious, but it seems time this one was sanely laid to rest. The original McKenzie, after his demonstrably inept days as an outlaw, and a pardon on grounds of mistrial, went off to Australia and perhaps home to perish in Scotland; there is nothing to suggest he was ever seen in New Zealand again.'

It also seems time the transparently spurious sanity of the twentieth century was laid to rest. For one thing, it can't leave well alone; it has to shrink all in the past, especially people, to puny shape. One can see why, of course; the moral is plain. But to pass this way without protest is to be equally culpable.)

*

The return of summer softens Diana. Benjamin and Iris have moved up to Spanish Creek, and Benjamin builds a house while helping James on the farm. In the meantime, such is their need for independence, the young couple have taken McKenzie's hut after smoking out the fleas; they would sooner marital privacy than the comforts of the homestead. Nevertheless, their presence qualifies Diana's loneliness. She also aspires to set an example, as pioneer wife, to Iris. She is less voluble about her discontents, and only audible to James. Need to trip down to Lovelock Junction, or travel on to New Plymouth, has apparently passed for a time. Actually Iris wants no example. She is energetic about her daily tasks, despite the distractions of her baby and her second advanced pregnancy; she churns butter proficiently, carries curd to the pigs, and feeds the fowls; her soda bread, cooked on an open fire, is as fine as any on the Porangi. The truth is actually that Iris distinctly makes the pace for Diana. In the matter of maternity, anyway, she has clearly outdistanced her sister. James often visits the hut to observe her baby son. His eyes are wistful. The impregnation of Diana has begun to seem an impossible task; he will never see a child. It will never, however, be for want of trying. Not on his part. Diana has more delicacy in the business; and certainly, from time to time, less enthusiasm.

'I think you still mope for McKenzie,' she observes.

'Now and then,' he agrees. 'He taught me much of what I know. There is reason for regret. For better or worse, he was a father to me.'

'Mostly for worse, I fear. I cannot fail to note the level of the whisky bottle after you have been acquainting yourself with its contents.'

'That,' James insists, 'is not McKenzie's doing. There are times when a man needs to think.'

'Thoughts you cannot share?'

'Not entirely. No.'

'You make me feel an inadequate wife.'

'Then I am sorry. What can I say?'

'That you love me, for example.'

'That is the least of my problems; my love can be taken for granted.'

'And me?' she demands. 'Am I also to be taken for granted?'

'Of course not. It is just that you appear to find talk of sheep, and things of the land, exceedingly tiresome. So I avoid it, where possible. Alas, there is then little left in my day upon which I can sensibly converse. I have no large excitements, like Richard with his winning horses. Mine are small, and perhaps too commonplace. To help a distressed ewe bring a lamb into the world can be a tender triumph, but who wants to hear?'

'I detect criticism,' Diana says.

'Unintended. I was seeking to explain my silences.'

'And the whisky. Are you also endeavouring to explain that?'

'If you like.'

'I should sooner see you playing the piano. You are very dear to me then. More the man I remember.'

'Maybe so. But the music seems to mock me. It calls me away. And I am not to be called. I am earthbound. More, perhaps, is the pity. I cannot change what is.'

'You laugh less often. Sometimes you become a stranger to me. What ails your soul? Is it me? I feel some evil fairy in your life. Perhaps, in truth, I am.'

'That is absurd. Without you I should be poorer, in the most literal way. With love as spur, I now farm eight thousand acres, more each year, and with half as many sheep. What reasonable man could complain?'

'You were happier with less.'

James shrugs. 'Any unhappiness I have now is doubtless in the nature of things.'

'Richard is not slow to take pleasure in material advantage. Why must you fret?'

'Perhaps because I am not Richard.'

'Would that sometimes you were. More like, I mean.'

'In that case, I can but apologize.'

'Dear heart. I was only teasing.'

'I heard some undertone of conviction.'

'Richard is nothing to me, and never has been. True that, when encountered, he can prove an entertaining companion, with a fund of lively anecdote about races won, or other men's horses gone lame. But no more than that. He can also, often, be boorish in the extreme when he talks of business matters, of profit and loss, in order to make himself the more impressive in the eyes of others. I am not deceived. It is not a pretty thing to see.'

'Yet nor am I, evidently.'

'You are my husband; my love. I never forget it. I am merely distressed that you are not yourself.'

'To the best of my knowledge, I am still James Lovelock. Who else might I be?'

'The father of a fine son,' she suggests. 'I well know that lack to be one of your griefs. Your eyes conceal little.'

'Maybe so. But the world is not perceptibly ending on that count.'

'I pray,' she says. 'I pray daily.'

James, though never doubting the efficacy of prayer, nevertheless knows from experience of animal husbandry that the problem must be approached practically; and also daily, for preference. That eve, at least, the desire is granted. Bedded with Diana, gently one with his wife, he hears her faint whisper. 'Do you remember,' she asks, 'our honeymoon? And those enchanting falls?'

'Would I be one to forget?'

'Sometimes I wonder. Summer after summer has begun to slip past. And we have never gone back. Yet you promised we would. Indeed once there, I recall, you vowed we should never leave. Quite reasonably, I took that vow as belonging to the domain of the spirit. We were obliged to make material return to the world. Alas, I think our bedraggled spirits – left without sustenance there – have followed us home.'

'I am failing, perhaps, to make your meaning.'

She sighs. 'Never mind. I am simply saying that we have never gone back, despite your fervent promises.'

'It is a considerable journey. And a long time to leave the farm neglected.'

'Of course,' she sighs again. 'How dare I forget? The farm. Your precious farm.'

James, incommoded by the deflating tone of the talk, at length makes a manful revival; and gets on with giving petulant Diana something more substantial to sigh about.

Three or four dozen villas now stud the plateau. The more Malones, the faster they rise; and the faster they fill. Some have come from as far as Ireland or Liverpool, anxious to be in at the beginning. Lovelock Junction is like a log or rock rolling downhill of its own accord. It is certainly true that most of the inhabitants of these houses flow down to Dixtown for employment. There is nothing profitable or productive on the plateau other than, of course, the making of the town itself; this can only keep some in pocket. In rising to the sun, a plant reveals its purpose. Lovelock Junction, despite Herman's hopes, appears hostage to the shade of Dixtown. This gives yet more urgency to his quest for pure iron, essentially a one-man preoccupation, though he tries to interest Ernest in the possibilities. But finally Ernest too finds the downhill tide irresistible. Having followed Benjamin and Iris to freedom, and finished with schoolbooks, he fails to discern a future in fetching and carrying for his father, or in Herman's blackening furnace, where ironsand resolutely remains itself. 'Uncle Richard has offered me a job,' he announces to Herman. 'In a year or two I could be his deputy. It is an opportunity not to be missed.'

'Perhaps you should travel first,' Herman suggests astutely.

'Travel?' Ernest is surprised his secret is out.

'Some opportunities are best missed. Travel can be conducive to the health of vision.'

'It isn't conducive to the health of my stomach. The sea, I mean. I need more money in my pocket.'

'How so?'

'I mean money I can call my own. Then I can travel in comfort, and style. Not in the first boat to come along. By the time I have the money steamers may be bigger, and safer; no real risk at all.'

'I see.'

'So right now I want to take my chances with Richard. He seems to think I will prove useful. I have a good head for figures. I can relieve him, he thinks, in many day to day details. So long as mines and mill run smooth, and money comes in, he can give more attention to his horses.'

'What of the people he employs? I'm minded to think they need more attention.'

'Horses seem more to his taste. My employer's preferences are not my problem.'

'No doubt,' Herman says, with an irony which escapes Ernest. 'All right then. Do what you must.'

But irony does not make iron. Nothing does. Not even the most determined explosions, in the furnace, liberate the metal from its impurities; these detonations, which often shake the plateau, sometimes even bring Dixtown to awed standstill. They are followed by a distinct human howl, indicating that Herman has again survived, but which nonetheless leaves reverberation in the spines of the listeners. Felicity screams. Marie Louise comes running to see her man has lost no limb. He is seldom more than scorched, though sometimes bruised by falling bricks. He is soon to be seen rebuilding the furnace with infinite patience. Also experimenting with fresh substances, sent from Sydney and other peripheral parts of the planet, which can conceivably unlock iron. Many show promise at first. But all fall victim, even if they survive the parental ambush of andesite, to diabolic titanium oxide. Necessity may well be the mother of invention; but who, Herman asks himself, is the blasted father? No mortal has aspired to mate with necessity more piously than Herman. With chemistry proving inadequate to the Porangi sands, he begins to contemplate alchemy.

And there are the Malones. They are everywhere brawling, breeding, and handsomely housed, perceptibly indifferent to the chemistry of the Porangi, the alchemy of vision. Women, despite the airy advantages of the plateau, lament that they have a long walk to Paramena's store.

Men audibly regret the lack of a corner public house in which they can win relief from the tongues of their womenfolk, as is only decent. They see Paramena's place of business as a poor substitute; it is a difficult steep journey home from Dixtown besides, and many on Saturday night never make it; there are alarms, and panicky search parties. Herman is not prepared to complicate life prematurely with commerce of a conventional nature on the plateau; he would prefer the place left pristine, so far as merchants and Mammon are concerned, until in the fullness of time some fresh form for necessary human transactions offers itself to his gaze. In the meantime he has an equally intractable problem with the impurities in the Porangi sands. All the same, something has to be done about the Malones; Marie Louise, in particular, points out that there are more than enough. 'In all fairness,' she argues, 'a stop has to be called. We are overrun. Ira and Sybil call frequently to complain about the noise at nights; they say they find it difficult to concentrate on their card evenings together. They have my sympathy. You have your town, or near enough. It is filling with people keen to make the most of your kindness, to say the least. Be content. If this goes on, we could finish with a metropolis. There is no sense in building for the sake of building – and in the end to save Richard the inconvenience of providing suitable quarters for his workmen. You get no thanks. Besides, I have begun to doubt whether some of these newcomers are Malones. Some are blackhaired.'

Confronted with this claim, Barney Malone is unabashed. 'There is a Protestant side to the family,' he concedes. 'Sure, and you wouldn't be wanting us to be intolerant?'

'Of course not,' Herman says, in defeat.

Soon after, he notes some males in a family or two whose hair colour is largely concealed by black skull caps in apparent celebration of a Saturday sabbath.

'Are you telling me there's a Jewish side to the family too?' he asks.

'By marriage,' Malone agrees, 'now you mention it. I got nothing against the Jews. Aren't they all good Christian folk at heart? I'll not hear any blackguard tell me different.'

Herman is not prepared to.

'In the matter of faith,' Malone goes on, 'there's one suggestion I'm of a mind to make. I'm in the way of thinking a church would be a fine thing.'

'A church?'

'Of small nature. There's a priest on the coast, a fine fellow of a man, who would be happy to come and conduct masses here, and give the devil a fright from these pagan parts.'

'You're talking of a conventional institution,' Herman objects.

'What kind of faith is that?' Malone asks, suspicious. 'I never heard the like of that one. Is it some heresy, maybe?'

'Conventional faith is the great heresy,' Herman explains. 'It keeps the minds of men in bondage to rigid ritual. God goes out the window.'

'Then we want no part of that,' Malone agrees. 'We just want a church to call our own. These are perilous times for Christian men. In some Protestant parts, I hear told, there are swine allowed to argue that man was of the monkeys. The fellow who told me swore to the fact. With that kind of libel at large in the world, God might be of a mind to give us up, unless we ask the Holy Mother different.'

'In a church?'

'Of small nature. Where men can make their Hail Marys heard.'

'What of revelation?' Herman demands.

'Of what?'

'Personal revelation. What of that?'

'I'm thinking we've got nothing the like of that in our family. The saints forbid. The measles at most.'

'The fact is,' Herman is at pains to explain, 'I feel the town has gone as far as it can tidily go. For the time being. Finish the houses begun. But no more. I daresay most out of work can find employment in Dixtown.'

'You're saying, unless I'm mistaken, no church?'

Herman hesitates. 'Perhaps, at most, a hall of modest proportion and plain nature where men can foregather amicably, with respect for each other, and their individual beliefs. And testify, if they must, to their love and concern for God's world.'

'Fair enough,' Malone says with relief. 'For one moment there I thought you was saying we couldn't run to a church.'

Later that day another explosion is heard from Herman's furnace. The howl following is particularly impressive. Aspiring to algebra, Herman still finds himself infuriated by arithmetic. He hobbles home unaided, with tearful Marie Louise and sobbing Felicity at his side. Then Sybil comes running.

'Dear God,' she says. 'It's Ira.'

'Ira?'

'He fell to the floor in his fright. He was holding three aces. But the worst thing is that he hurt his head and seemed to suffer some change in disposition. He glared at me in a most unnatural and unloving way. Then he shuffled and dealt the cards again, insisting we continue as if nothing had happened. He said there was just one thing he wanted to know. He wanted to know, if you'll forgive the phrase, what the hell happened to Hokitika?'

'A harmless question,' Herman observes.

'Not in the manner of his utterance. He slammed the table and said he could have bought and sold Hokitika once. He appeared to be attributing some blame to me. He is altogether so fierce and frightening I felt obliged to flee. I should be most grateful if you discover what ails him.'

'Of course,' Marie Louise says, disturbed.

They tramp to the Old House, and find Ira within. At first sight Sybil appears to have been embroidering his condition. Ira's face isn't fierce; there is, if anything, a measure of bliss. This in part is no doubt due to his success in dealing himself three aces again, spades, diamonds, and clubs. He has certainly contrived to continue the game with Sybil as if nothing has happened, with one variant. When Herman takes his shoulder to awaken him from apparent trance, the ace of hearts flutters from a sleeve. Ira doesn't awaken. His head falls forward on the table. What ails Ira is death. When Marie Louise has removed devastated Sybil from the room, Herman makes Ira presentable on a couch, closes his eyes with coins, then as afterthought gathers up all four aces and folds them into the old gambler's fist. There seems no reason why Ira shouldn't have them as guarantee against losing the next game.

Ira himself looks on. He has given up the attempt to resume tenancy of his derelict body. But at least he has death purely figured, at last. He notes with approval that his grave is being dug next to Whisker's; he examines with interest the coffin Paramena is crafting with care, and no little love. But before his burial begins he finds he has more urgent things on his mind. He is now free, for a true fact, to explore the finer things of death. He regrets that Sybil sees fit to grieve so. Then he departs.

Twice widowed within a decade, Sybil Dix is a lost woman. Iris and Diana take her upriver to Spanish Creek for a time, to recover, but she is drawn back to Lovelock Junction; she appears determined to dwell where her husbands are buried. Seldom a day passes when she doesn't pick flowers to garland their gravestones. For reasons of economy, to save paying Sybil's salary, Richard has arranged for a teacher in government employ to take over Dixtown school. He has an alternative proposition for Sybil. 'I need a housekeeper,' he explains.

'Good God. Who do you think I am?'

'Still a sturdy enough woman, so far as I see.'

'You wish me to scrub your floors in return for the favour of sharing your bedroom. Is that it?'

'I should prefer the transaction on a purely financial footing.'

'There is a word for it. Prostitution.'

'I said nothing of my bedroom. You shall have your own. And your privacy, let me insist, shall at all times be respected.'

'In your character, Richard, I detect the need to humiliate women. You wish me to cook your meals, and polish your boots, for some pittance. Is that the proposition?'

'It is more than menial. I need standards set in my household. I have business friends I need to entertain when they visit the Porangi. Also companions of the turf. I had a Malone girl for a time. She had no idea of how to set a table. And her cuisine was all boiled potatoes and burned mutton.'

'Very distressing. I feel tears forming.'

'Your sarcasm is misplaced. If needs must, I am self sufficient.'

'So you think you are doing me a favour?'

'I should not care to push the argument.'

'What you need, Richard, is a wife to relieve you of disagreeable domestic detail. A legal slave, in short. It mystifies me that you have failed to make the most of the many opportunities which have doubtless come your way.'

'That is my business,' he insists.

'Needless to say, I no longer aspire to that role. Your character considered, I feel my escape to have been fortunate. I thank God also for the safety of my daughters, now both beyond your reach. Once again, true, you see a vulnerable woman. But you will not have the advantage of me on that account. I should sooner find rest beside my husbands.'

'I would make it more than worth your while,' he promises. 'Also I would provide you with a handsome household budget out of which you could employ one or two domestics to relieve your daily burden. Your life would still be your own.'

'I sense desperation,' she observes. 'More yours, now, than mine. What game is this?'

'Some might call it respectability. It is true I have appearances to keep up.'

'Your honesty is numbing.'

'Shall we say three hundred pounds a year?'

'Also your generosity. I think, for my pains, something in the vicinity of five hundred a year a more agreeable figure.'

'Four.'

'I should prefer you to let the full five fall reluctantly from your lips. I might then be able to deceive myself that you need and indeed value my services, for some reason.'

'Your living quarters will be ample. I shall provide a largish sum for you to furnish the house in the best of taste. You will be welcome to call my home your own, and have your own guests. Your daughters, for example, should they desire to visit you.'

'My daughters?'

'Yes. Your daughters will always be welcome in this house.'

'I see.'

'And your personal expenses, in this situation, would be few.'

'Five,' she suggests.

'Many of excellent education and background in this colony make only half that figure.'

'Precisely,' she says. 'That is why the sum so much intrigues me.'

'All right. Five hundred.'

'It is certainly food for thought.'

'What does that mean? Yes or no?'

'It means, Richard, that in all fairness I should point out that it would be far cheaper to marry; I cannot but wonder at your intentions.'

'All in good time. I am greatly preoccupied with horseflesh.'

'You have never conspicuously lacked interest in womenflesh.'

'Maybe so. But there's a time and place.'

'For what?'

'The right woman.'

'And is she to have no choice in the matter of time and place? Must it be at your convenience?'

'Desirably. Though I shall doubtless do my best to be accommodating in other respects.'

'I feel some chill in my soul,' she says.

'You haven't,' he points out with impatience, 'made clear answer to my proposition.'

'I rather think I need a period for prolonged contemplation.'

'Six hundred,' he says.

'Dear God. I fear adequate answer still fails me. It seems I am belatedly discovering my true worth in this world.'

'Seven,' he offers. 'I cannot do better. And, to set your mind at rest, I am sure I shall find you worth every penny.'

'Curiosity now has the better of me,' Sybil confesses. 'Not the money. I seem, in this very instant, to have succumbed.'

Richard has the appearance of a man well satisfied; not of one who has come off worst in the bargaining.

While still reeling from this encounter, and trying to comprehend the essence of Richard's proposition, Sybil is approached by Herman and Marie Louise with another. Felicity, five years old, needs a tutor to encourage her remarkable talents; she already reads and writes with skill and intelligence. She is also plainly of artistic temper. As an aspirant actress, she has always had the techniques to confect drama from the commonplace. Lately, with a paintbox, she has begun to articulate surprisingly gaudy perceptions of her environment. She also hums strange tunes which she insists she hears in her head, and often clambers on to the piano stool in quest of tunes trapped in the keyboard. Such energy has to be channelled, for the sake of sanity; the girl is everywhere at once, and everything, all the time; she needs restraint, and more direction. And Herman and Marie Louise, above all, need more peace. Though fearful of Felicity herself, Sybil agrees to help as best she can, in the circumstances.

'Unfortunately my first commitment is now to Richard's household,' she explains. 'But if I understand the situation aright, the domestic situation is not as demanding as it might be. I will have free time to give to Felicity. But please understand. I cannot promise miracles.'

'We want no more of those,' Marie Louise sighs. 'Felicity is enough to manage. It's only now I understand God may arrange them to test us. At the moment it seems more affliction than test.'

'In short,' Sybil says, 'you need succour.'

'Now and then,' Marie Louise agrees.

'And some quiet,' Herman adds. 'A man cannot think with Felicity at large.'

'Very well,' Sybil says. 'I shall not shirk the challenge. It is possibly superfluous to suggest that Felicity is not destined to be a modest young lady. Our problem is to discover a seemly alternative. We must pray that the discovery is not displeasing. Felicity is a flower not easily to be nipped in the bud.'

Felicity, who has been listening from a doorway, now announces herself stridently, and with a considerable clatter of feet.

'How can a flower be nipped in the bud,' she asks pertinently, 'if it is already blooming?'

It seems the adults have no answer. The nonsense they talk. They never get anything right. They seem to need more nursing through life than Felicity suspected.

With Sybil seeing coolly to his household, Ernest efficient in the office and soon relieving Paramena of bookkeeping problems, Richard has more opportunity to hunt for horseflesh of quality. He travels to every corner of the colony, neglecting no breeder, making the acquaintance of men who know the best bloodlines. At length he finds a filly which fulfils every expectation. From late imported English thoroughbred stock, she is a descendant of the distinguished stallion The Libel by way of the equally stunning sire Traducer; the sons and daughters of Traducer are seen to be taking rich purses on every racetrack in the colony, and in Australia too. This nervy filly seems likely to be no exception. He doesn't trust anyone else to train her. Only unqualified devotion will do; he brings her back to the river with a groom. The awed workmen of Dixtown, along with Ernest and Paramena, watch the filly led delicately off the steamer and to the new stables near the town track. Her name, Richard gives it to be understood, is Porangi Belle. 'The whole colony will know it soon,' Richard predicts. 'Maybe the world.'

'Whoa,' Paramena pleads. 'It's only a horse.'

On the other hand Paramena is relieved to see Richard, in the not uncommon and altogether human manner, has begun to find means more absorbing than ends. It is certainly true that as he works Porangi Belle out on the track in the mists of morning, and then watches his groom rub down her steaming flanks, Richard has little passion left over for people; and in particular for his sister-in-law Diana should she be spending a night or two with her mother under his roof. Though as a guest she has been earnestly desired, and expensively arranged, even Diana can often be a distraction. It is more than pride of possession. Porangi Belle has become the point of his life; the filly is proof that something precious can flower from all the shit he has shovelled. Others can make what they will of poetry, music, and the like. The crisp sound of her hooves makes Richard's existence worthwhile. Sometimes at midnight or still later, before he retires, he strides down to the stables to see she is content; he sometimes remains with her an hour, his head against hers. As for Diana, he tries to kill two birds with one stone by taking her to the track where she can make free with superlatives directed at Porangi Belle which can be translated as tributes to Richard's prowess as trainer. The filly provides seemly if often muddy ground on which they can meet. Diana, infected by Richard's ardour, feels a muscular world in motion, a sensation denied her among Spanish Creek's soft acres. And Porangi Belle is an undeniably pretty creature too. Yet at the dining table, in her mother's presence, she remains as demure as a visiting sister-in-law should be, and as discreet. Thus, away from the filly, her relationship with Richard is inconclusive. Sybil Dix, who now isn't without some affection for her reliable son-in-law James, ensures that the relationship remains inconclusive. When Diana is staying, Sybil leaves her own bedroom door ajar, to make stealthy movements in the house the more conspicuous to her ear; she sometimes hears Richard taking a nocturnal stroll to the stables, but no more. It is small penance to observe, her salary considered: if Richard thinks he has hired her to pick daisies, while he turns Diana's silly head, he shall find himself very much mistaken.

When Porangi Belle is a lithe two years old, Richard begins to race her gently. He is in no haste; he knows the richest prizes remain for the taking. He ships out with Porangi Belle, and Paramena, to meetings at New Plymouth, Wanganui, Nelson, and smaller southern places on the New Zealand coast. Ernest, conveniently, is now of an age to manage most affairs of Dixtown, especially financial, in their absence; Sybil keeps Richard's house orderly and aired for his return. The lessening of domestic demands allows Sybil to pursue the business of channelling Felicity's energies constructively. Though excavating such channels leaves her exhausted, Sybil sees in that remarkable child a girl – unlike her own Diana and Iris – who is destined never to disappoint; and never to accept the Porangi as a prison. Sybil is more than willing to cast her bread upon the turbulent waters of Felicity's imagination; to tease Felicity with the arcane and lyrical, and complex compositions for the piano; the returns are always spectacular.

Richard's, meantime, are more erratic. At her best, though not yet tried against the toughest competition, Porangi Belle is a credit to her gentleman trainer. She can make moderately mediocre opposition appear altogether abysmal. She leaps lengths ahead of her rivals, and seldom works up a lather to win most races. But there are other races lost. She is seen distinctly to slow in the last furlong, with the way to the winning post clear, and allow the rest of the field through. Richard is accused, more than once, of having his horse pulled to lengthen future odds; but investigation clears him and the jockeys he employs. The explanation is distressingly simple.

'Wind,' announces a veteran jockey.

'Wind?' Richard says.

'That's right. Horses have to fart too. Most have the decency to abstain in a race. But there's always the odd one out.'

'Why me?' Richard asks. 'Why her?'

The jockey shrugs.

'And why with the race all but won?'

'Nerves, maybe. She's a sensitive girl.'

'What of my nerves? It's getting so I can't watch the last lap.'

'She may be sharing your panic.'

'My stomach's not even rumbling,' Richard protests.

'If she has the need,' the jockey insists, 'who's to deny her? Nothing I can do. It's like a small earthquake. And by then it's too late anyway. She's lost concentration, even with the whip working. She has the fart more on her mind than a fast last furlong.'

'What can I do?' Richard demands.

'Calm down,' the jockey suggests. 'Try faith.'

'Jesus,' Richard replies.

'That's the idea,' the jockey agrees.

Later, to Paramena, Richard declares, 'I'm not going to be felled by a farting horse. Never.'

'Be reasonable,' Paramena proposes. 'You're not facing ruin. She wins beautifully, most of the time. She should be allowed to gratify a modest physical need on other occasions. No one's perfect. Look on it as God's tiny flaw. Something fashioned to remind us that we are still, alas, of the flesh; even exquisitely fast four-legged creatures.'

'She might as well be running on three, for all the difference, when she has this problem.'

'Believe me, it may come from trying to win for you. Even if she does offer the illusion of travelling backward. Think on that. Your relationship with this horse, I fear, is too intense. Too spiritual, Richard. Indeed I would go so far as to suggest that it is the fart in itself which offends you, not the loss of a race. You see her as less than divine.'

'You're getting personal,' Richard says with anger.

'I am seeking to remind you, old friend, that she is only a horse. And that a race, after all, is only a race. Lost or won.'

'But better for winning,' Richard observes.

'Agreed,' Paramena sighs.

Whatever his spiritual relationship with his filly, from now on Richard does not neglect Porangi Belle's physical nature. He takes specialist advice in the matter of her diet. She is pastured only on clover, and fed only the finest quality oats, and no rubbish; she is given no excuse for wind. But the problem persists, perhaps one race in three, too often for Richard's comfort, and certainly for hers. Her deflation, as she runs against stiffer competition, can be even more devastating in the last furlong. Again there are official inquiries; again Richard is fast acquitted, with sympathies expressed. Sailing so close to the wind, Richard finds his heartburn chronic. The best of wins can leave him uneasy, with the certainty that intestinal lightning is soon again to strike.

'What about your Maori medicine?' he at last asks Paramena.

'What about it?'

'There must be something you can do. Some potion. Some brew. To keep her on the straight and even.'

'You mean to win all the time?'

'The races that count.'

'Which races don't?'

Richard finds it difficult to be specific.

'I should like to propose some sure remedy,' Paramena goes on. 'In honesty I can't. My herbal treatments are intended for alleviation of human afflictions; not those of horses. Horses are a white man's hobby, but an entertaining adjunct to civilization as I see it. In any case farting is no large human affliction. Most see it as a sign of good health. Better out than in.'

'Don't trifle. You must have something to settle a nervous stomach. In the last resort, that seems the problem. Not the wind itself.'

'I'll think about it,' Paramena promises.

'Don't think,' Richard insists. 'Get on with it. She's near three years old now. At that age she should be taking every big race in the colony. After she's taken the Dunedin Cup in the south, we'll pick up the New Zealand Cup in Christchurch. Then the Wellington Cup on the way north. We'll crown it all with the Auckland Cup. After that, nothing will stop us; we'll clean up in Australia too.'

'I hate to sully your vision,' Paramena says. 'But you may have to forgo a cup or two. The fact remains that she farts.'

'We are not,' Richard decides, 'going to be beaten by a bit of foul air. Use your native ingenuity.'

Paramena experiments. From trees fringing a racetrack he gathers the leaves and roots of the kawakawa, a good all-purpose stomach curative, and foliage from the korokio, also with an impressive reputation for calming colonic disorders. After stewing these for some hours, he spices the concoction with seaweed and finally adds the fleshy petals of the tutu berry; the latter is a calculated risk. In immoderate quantity, the tutu is conducive to visions, transporting men and cattle from all terrestrial care, sometimes past the point of no return. A reasonable amount might put Porangi Belle in mildly luminous mood, and relax her digestive tract. In short, it should clear the air.

In her next race, consequent upon this medication, Porangi Belle certainly suffers no loss of power in the last furlong. On the other hand she does not display much power either. She finishes a dreamy third.

'Marvellous,' Richard says. 'Now she's a reliable also-ran.'

Paramena is cruelly hurt by Richard's otherwise excessive reaction; it seems their long-standing partnership may be at breaking point, because of the tutu. 'You might have poisoned her forever,' Richard says starkly. 'You can fiddle with fate up to a point. But some things are sacred.'

'I can see that,' Paramena concedes.

'She's not to be put at risk again. Ever.'

'Give me another chance,' Paramena pleads.

'For more bloody black magic? Never.'

'No potion. I promise. I should like to attempt making good the damage I might have done. In brief, I would like to have a minute or two entirely alone with her, largely for the purpose of meditation, rather than medication, immediately before she races.'

'What for? Some pagan incantation?'

'Never mind. Just trust me.'

Richard agrees, if with lingering reluctance. At the next race meeting he farewells Porangi Belle prematurely and takes his place in the stand with other owners and trainers. Paramena, left alone, diligently adventures. He knows from experience that if a problem cannot be controlled at its source, a direct assault on the symptom can have spectacular short-term result. Horse races, even at their lengthiest, are highly short-term affairs. Instead of herbs, this time he has gathered an assortment of vegetables of promising shape and size: carrots, kumara, parsnips, small turnips and potatoes. These are not for Porangi Belle's consumption. In a sense, quite the reverse.

'Easy now,' he whispers.

Without giving her time to protest, he attempts to find the vegetable best tailored to the task in hand. Carrot, turnip, kumara and parsnip find no firm residence within Porangi Belle's rectum. But the potato fits perfectly. She does no more than whinny. There is a long silence which might be construed as a period of mutual meditation. She does not try to expel the potato; she seems quite resigned.

'Good girl,' he says happily. 'I think we can safely give pagan incantations a miss.'

She wins that day; her hooves seldom seem to touch earth. She also wins, with no protest, no apparent discomfort, her next six races. Richard is beside himself. 'You've done it,' he declares. Paramena doesn't dare research further. No one argues with success. And what Richard doesn't know won't make him disagreeable. Paramena now never travels to a racetrack without a well-chosen potato in pocket. Queried once by Richard about the conspicuous bulge in his apparel, he explains, 'A good luck charm. One which best never sees the light of day.'

'I'll take your word for it,' Richard says.

'You'd better,' Paramena suggests darkly.

Richard's remote successes seem to seed Diana's fresh discontents with Spanish Creek.

'Nothing ever happens here,' she announces.

James remains silent. They are at breakfast. He has just observed, while shaving, his first grey hairs. He is tempted to tell his wife of the triumphs to which his discolouring hair, and hardened hands, are testimony. But he tactfully refrains from reminding her. It has all been said before, and to no purpose. A substantial sheep station, with six thousand sheep still proliferating, has happened. Even more substantial wool cheques are a regular happening. What still hasn't happened, on the debit side, is a son. It has to be conceded that this, at worst, suggests all has been vanity. Sometimes, from the homestead, he sees his hills as a green desert, with a poignant oasis of forest here and there which fire failed to take; at other times, in still bleaker mood, he sees his distant sheep as maggots making the most of a grassy carcass, sacrificially slain. The native birds which once announced dawn have departed. Blackbird and thrush sing thin on his lawns. He once saw himself as servant here. A servant? He has made himself master. Other than, of course, in his own house. He is more comfortable in Benjamin's dwelling, with his nephew's children, than at his own hearth with Diana. In practical and prodigally maternal Iris, James sees a mate who might have made his life, and conscience, lighter. Iris doesn't cultivate discontent with Spanish Creek; she cultivates her muse, when motherhood allows, in celebration of colonial virtue, and the pioneer Porangi. Her verses are now prominent on literary pages the length of the colony. Her spirit is enviable:

Land of noble mind and deed
Where Beauty stalks the verdant glade,
Where Man is free from grief and greed
And Faith shines bright and unafraid,
Where children sport the glorious day,
Fresh of face and lithe of limb,
Where Hope and Love hold radiant sway
And virgin Dream is there to win.

The substance of her Lovelockian optimism is visible about her, in griefless and greedless Benjamin, and children fresh of face and lithe of limb. Still, James is not one to begrudge Benjamin his bright-eyed spouse; the boy is a good companion, and reliable mate, when they shear or boundary-ride together. Benjamin and Iris together make Spanish Creek more tolerable than it might lately have been. They save James from the temptation, sometimes encountered, of saddling a horse, riding into the sun, and settling into the solitude of some other valley; and leaving life with the loveliest lady on the Porangi some distance behind.

'Are you listening to me?' Diana demands. 'I said nothing ever happens here.'

'I heard you,' James sighs. 'So what do you want?'

'A little excitement,' she says. 'Some prettiness, perhaps. I think we have earned it, with our hardships here.'

James is unwilling to remind her that the hardships have largely been his; that he has been careful to keep her at a distance from things manual. 'I am not inclined,' he points out, 'to purchase a thoroughbred horse, in imitation of Richard, and complicate my life unduly. I have sufficient excitement in a bad season. It is all short of glamour, perhaps. But then I have no wish for other worlds.'

'Exactly,' she says. 'You have little imagination. Less and less, as the years go by. How long is it since I have seen you at the piano? Or at work on a watercolour?'

'Those things may be luxuries for those who come later,' he oberves. 'For such as Iris, perhaps, and her children. Or ours, God willing.'

'God is not particularly willing. That much is clear. Perhaps the message is that the time for some luxury – at least some diversion – is now. Not later. Life is for the living. Not for slow dying.'

'If it's diversion you wish, then I have made clear that you are more than welcome to join, with your mother, in one of Richard's equine expeditions. It is my understanding that Richard has again issued such an invitation.'

'Mother prefers to be preoccupied with Felicity. I cannot imagine why. She is a wretchedly knowing child. At all events the invitation cannot be taken up. I cannot go alone. It would not be seemly. Unless, of course, you were to accompany me.'

'Racetracks are not to my taste. Nor the people.'

'Some of the finest families in the colony are to be found there.'

'That's as may be. One representative of the Lovelock family is enough. I see no glory in whipping poor beasts pointlessly around a track.'

'It is far from pointless. There are handsome purses.'

'More is the shame.'

'You are cruel to sheep. With your shears and, worse, with your butchering knife.'

'That is from human need. For warmth and food. I might wish it other. But I have to assume that God knows His own business best.'

'It ill becomes you to pose as the final authority on human need. Is food and warmth the be-all and end-all of man? There are other needs.'

'Of course,' James concedes. 'Love, to name but one.'

A delicate subject. Diana seems inclined to dismiss it.

'What of challenge beyond the commonplace?' she asks. 'Is that to be denied?'

'Love is abundant with challenge. Like the climbing of tall mountains, with terrible crevasses below. It is remote from the sickness of soul which leads men to gather and gamble at racetracks. But perhaps I lack vision.'

'Indeed,' Diana agrees.

'Then go off with Richard and have your fill of excitement,' James says, at last angry. 'I shall see Sybil myself, and prevail upon her to go too, if in truth you need some chaperone. I don't doubt that, when I have furnished you with sufficient money, you shall cut a fashionable figure on the racetracks of this colony. And Richard, I imagine, will make free with champagne and oysters.'

'You are being cruel,' Diana says.

'To myself, perhaps. In the form of kindness.'

He saddles his horse and is seen no more that day.

A fortnight later Diana and Sybil travel south with Richard to see Porangi Belle take the Dunedin Cup, and one thousand pounds in prize money. The performance is soon repeated in Canterbury's premier race, the New Zealand Cup, which Diana and Sybil are also present to observe. The conquest of the South Island is complete. In the elegant and gentlemanly sporting community of Christchurch, Richard is no longer a graceless outsider; his rougher qualities seem of small moment beside his successes; he is considerably feted, at function after function, with his retinue. Diana, naturally enough, is often taken to be his wife, though Sybil, if present, is swift to correct the mistaken impression. She is not always present. Often an excess of champagne sends her early to bed, and once a bad oyster leaves her indisposed for three days; she has to ask Paramena to act as chaperone. Paramena's disadvantage, in this respect, is that he sleeps nightly in Porangi Belle's stall, to save her being nobbled or lamed with malice aforethought by some rival owner or trainer. Thus Richard and Diana, flushed with forthcoming triumphs, are enabled to spend many pleasing evening hours together, quite free of surveillance. There is, however, less to this than might meet the eye, give or take a goodnight kiss. Richard, with Porangi Belle his primary obsession, coolly prefers to be clear of complications, and certainly scandal, until non-adulterous needs are gratified. Which isn't to say that he is ungrateful for a decorative companion to grip his arm fervently in the lucrative excitement of the last furlong. Fornication, by contrast, seems a paltry affair, something best left to fallen women whose ministrations can be hired quickly in the vicinity of any reasonably appointed racetrack. His pleasure in Diana's company stems precisely from the fact that she is demonstrably not a fallen woman, though it would take only a faint shaking of the tree. Diana, with strange shivers of the soul, remains perplexingly and precariously a prisoner of virtue's realm: specifically of that part of the Porangi called Spanish Creek.

There, Benjamin sees grass-widower James as a man of troubled mind. In short, James is moping. Magically, considering the silences of the recent past, he is heard at the piano offering Chopin to a summer evening; these pieces, however, tend to taper off into an alarming crash of chords. Less magically, he also breaks windows with flung and presumably emptied whisky bottles. Next morning his eyes are heavy-lidded with hangover. The confused symptoms of his uncle's decline at length embolden Benjamin to speak.

'You should have gone off too,' he suggests. 'A holiday from this place is what you need.'

'Holiday?' James says, baffled.

'From Spanish Creek. It's all become too much.'

'Or much less,' James observes opaquely.

Benjamin is undeterred. 'To be frank, Iris and I are concerned about your condition. We should like to see you free of the farm for a few days. In New Plymouth, perhaps. Or further south, where Richard is racing.'

'There is nothing there for me,' James insists. 'My life is here. And one day, no doubt, my death. I must take care to make myself available at the appointed hour.'

This is too sepulchral for Benjamin. 'It is impossible,' he goes on, 'for us not to note that your marriage is in some disrepair. It grieves us both. We are only trying to help. We would like to see you in more relaxed mind when Diana returns. Otherwise we fear the worst.'

'And what is that?' James asks. 'The worst?'

Benjamin is reluctant to say.

Nevertheless, upon reflection, James takes up Benjamin's generously intended offer of freedom from the farm. He doesn't, however, travel downriver and take a steamship to civilization. He labours upriver, into the silences and shadows of the land; it is the first time he has pushed a dinghy up the Porangi since his marriage. Perhaps his quest is for peace; perhaps he yearns for his youth on the river again. He isn't sure. He wishes only to keep rowing, on a river which never ends; never again to stop, against the current all the way. His contest is no longer with the wilderness which ripples moist about him, but rather with his stony inner landscape. It is there he travels while the hypnotic rhythm of rowing frees him of flesh; it is there, eventually, he finds some serenity. But not on the Porangi. With a lurch of current and spirit he confronts the Makutu Falls again, where he honeymooned with Diana. Seen with less longing, the falls are less haunting. All is visibly shrunken. Much has literally crumbled and collapsed, with fissures and fractures everywhere evident in the limestone. Caves have closed with rockfall. Fountains of mellifluous water have become feeble trickles. The river has carved more functional routes. Perhaps the place never was as it seemed, other than in legend, and when lovers were so minded. At all events James has gone as far as he can go. He drifts downriver again, sleeping under the stars and awakening early to see the thin white light on the river; in four days he is home again at Spanish Creek.

'You are looking better,' Benjamin argues, having ridden down to the landing to greet his uncle.

'Maybe so,' taciturn James says. 'My journey seemed lighter on return. Doubtless with the current on my side, and some baggage unloaded on the way.'

'Baggage?' Benjamin inquires, puzzled.

'Of a mental nature. Illusions, if you like.'

Spanish Creek, at least, hasn't shrunken in his absence. On the contrary, his acres seem even more immense. The grassed hills glitter vast in the sun.

'I have good news,' Benjamin declares. 'Diana is back. She awaits you up at the homestead.'

It is not news that James especially desires at this moment. But he must, it seems, make the best of it; and of his wife.

'She cut short her southern tour,' Benjamin explains. 'And came home with Sybil. It seems she was worried about you. She was quite dismayed to find you absent on her return.' Benjamin hesitates shyly, then adds, 'I cannot say she is the happiest of women.'

This, sooner than he might prefer, James has a chance to observe for himself. In his kitchen he finds clean clothes warming, hot food, and an anxious wife. 'So what has happened to all the excitement?' he asks.

'Please do not be cruel.'

'It is not my intention. I am merely curious.'

'I cannot complain that I haven't had my fill. Far from it. But, if truth be told, I grew suddenly frightened.'

'Frightened?'

She throws herself into his arms, abandoned and distraught.

'Frightened?' James persists, beginning to fondle her. 'Of what?'

'Of myself. Dear James. Dear, good James. My husband. Take me to our bed.'

Nine months later, or near enough, their son is born.

Alchemy of more literal nature is now at work downriver. Having tracked down every tome on the subject in the colony, and sent to Sydney for others, Herman contemplates the extraordinary lives and writings of such as Agrippa, Paracelsus, Helvetius, James Price and Alexander Seton. Most of these primitive pre-chemists aspired ambitiously to manufacture noble metals from base. Herman is not ambitious. He would be content with a clue to suggest how he might claim as base a metal as any from the prehistoric sands of the Porangi; an aspiration to manufacture iron is not immodestly patrician. Reading Paracelsus with a powerful thrill, as dust drifts from the pages, Herman learns that man's spirit is an entire star, out of which he is built. If therefore a man is perfect of heart, nothing in the whole light of nature is hidden from him. All can be won from the inner and outer universe by means of the imagination. Titanium oxide should prove but a pitiful obstacle.

Retorts no longer bubble in his laboratory. His furnace cools. There are no more commotions, or explosions, to disturb Lovelock Junction as Herman concentrates. Nor is his howl heard for months. Rather, the calm is remarkable. Marie Louise has to make the best of a husband who refuses argument or even mild irritation, no matter what the provocation of the outer universe. Even Felicity, for once, fails to infuriate him. His frustrations with Lovelock Junction seem forgotten. He ceases lecturing the stunned people of the plateau, as has been his need, on the desirability of waging war on human circumstances in order that a new world might be won on the Porangi, a happy colony free of the deformities which abound in older, darker lands; the small plain building provided for adult purpose is now almost exclusively used by priests, and sometimes Protestant clergy, who minister to the needs of the Malones, also to many now confessing to other names, and who for the most part reconcile their flock to the imperfectibility of human circumstance. Marie Louise, not one to let opportunity slip, takes advantage of Herman's pacific mood to attend a mass or two; in any case she has never seen harm in a few Hail Marys. But she does fear that Herman is sickening for something. 'What is it?' she asks finally. 'Why this silence?'

Herman looks up at her amiably. It is quite unnerving.

'I am seeking,' he explains, 'perfection of heart. One must begin within oneself.'

Marie Louise cannot suggest this endeavour as other than admirable, no matter how maritally dismaying.

'The world,' she suggests, 'seems to be passing you by.'

'Exactly,' he agrees.

'And what is the point of this perfection of heart?'

'You shall see,' he predicts serenely, 'soon enough. Nothing in nature shall be hidden.'

'It might be more to the point,' she argues, 'if you could see what is hidden in Felicity.'

'Felicity?'

'Your daughter, unless I'm much mistaken. I have no memory of her conception as other than carnal. The Holy Ghost has not, these two thousand years past, made a habit of usurping conjugal rights.'

'What is it with Felicity now?'

'I hardly know where to begin. She is out of control. Already, not ten years old, quite beyond managing. Sybil has lately confessed to me, quite tearfully, that she can do no more with the child. In the matter of her education, she is always a textbook or two ahead of Sybil. Having mastered Latin and Greek, our daughter is intolerant of her tutor's clumsy attempts to cope with the grammar. Sybil now feels that she, not Felicity, is the pupil.'

'So send her to me,' Herman proposes. 'I daresay I can find employment for her active mind. Meanwhile, it seems clear that another tutor will have to be found for Felicity.'

'What of her wild ways? Who is to curb them? And before all is lost? It seems we need more a prison warder than a tutor.'

Herman takes Felicity in hand, nonetheless, and into his confidence. His extraordinary daughter is at first impatient with his lengthy explanations of alchemical achievements, in centuries past, and cannot quite see the relevance to the ironsands of the Porangi. Soon, however, she begins to feed upon the dilapidated books with an intensity which stuns Herman; she claims to hear the music of the world within them. She trips through far firmaments of the imagination. All this is splendid, in its way; Herman has to hobble after her, footsore among the same firmaments, with wonder at his child. Sometimes she appears to go into trance, eventually emerging to announce that nothing in the world is as it seems. This is no news to Herman. More to the point, titanium oxide is still as it seems; iron in titanomagnetite form is unwilling to be wished free by the purest of hearts, however much Herman and Felicity give of their spirit.

Marie Louise is gratified to find Felicity at least more tractable. After expensive and extensive advertising, throughout the colony, a tutor is employed to further her musical education. It seems agreed that the remainder of Felicity's education can be furthered only at peril. The tutor's name is Sylvester Spring, a thin tragic young man, English educated, of southern gentry stock. His philandering sheepfarmer father, after sending Sylvester to England, sold up his station and decamped to Canada with a scullery maid, leaving wife and children, and conspicuously Sylvester, quite penniless. Curly blond Sylvester has had to forgo promising prospects as a musician and voyage home to the hellish crudities of colonial life. It is his first post as tutor. The salary appears sufficient to support his bereft mother, who now irons the shirts of Christchurch gentlemen, and his threadbare brothers and sisters; his own needs are few, and mostly aesthetic. The Porangi, however, is paralysing on first impression; he all but whimpers with fright as the steamer bears him upriver. Then, at the end, he is given sight of Felicity. Though still technically a child, Felicity has the features of an altogether bewitching woman; and before long the figure. Sylvester is bewitched. Felicity at last has her slave. And in Felicity he at last sees his fate. Their vocal duets are something on which all of Lovelock Junction can feast; sometimes melodic scraps from the table fall as far as Dixtown.

'Tell me just one thing,' Marie Louise says to Sylvester. 'Does the child have a future?'

'Madam,' Sylvester replies, 'I am surprised you need ask. The world, I shouldn't wonder, shall soon be at her feet.'

'At her feet?' Marie Louise fears for the world.

'The girl is remarkable. She has perfect pitch. To discern the difference between C major and E major is nothing to her. As for her inherent vocal quality, I have heard nothing to compare.'

Before farewelling alchemy, and committing herself to the music of the material universe, Felicity attempts one favour for her father. She recalls from the writing of Helvetius that the philosopher's stone is of yellowish colour. Some of the substance of this stone, used by Helvetius after its acquisition from a passing stranger, transmuted old lead into new gold. Felicity does not have the advantage of a passing stranger; but she does have knowledge of a distinctly yellowish substance, in coarse powdery form, hidden in a large and tightly fastened bag at the back of her mother's wardrobe. Younger, exploring with intent to mischief, Felicity emptied the contents of this bag on her parents' bedroom floor. This produced many satisfying shrieks from Marie Louise, who then hastily swept the yellow substance back into the bag, and made Felicity vow never to breathe a word to her father. This caused Felicity much curiosity about the substance contained in the bag: plainly precious, but for what purpose? Felicity is not to know that, these many years, Marie Louise has continued to mistrust the human institution of money, especially in the form of banknotes; that she has continued to carry, though never to hatch, a golden nest-egg from Hokitika's heyday; that out of respect for Herman's feelings, particularly concerning the degraded and degrading nature of gold, it has to be kept well hidden. Felicity is thus enabled to theorize that the yellow substance, akin to the colour of the philosopher's stone, could contain a property congenial to Herman in his pursuit of humanly useful metal. She burns a coal fire in Herman's furnace, while he is otherwise engaged with alchemical tracts, and fills a small crucible with Porangi sand and a generous quantity of the yellowish material filched from her mother's wardrobe. The crucible goes into the fire. Soon there is a crackling, a hissing and bubbling. The contents of the crucible begin to glow red and then solidify. Delighted Felicity, lifting the crucible from the flame with gloved hands, sees that the tedious parental andesite and devilish titanium oxide have both clearly capitulated. She calls her parents.

'There,' she says. 'Iron.'

Undeniable that there is something to her claim. The cooling content of the crucible certainly has the appearance of iron, if errantly streaked here and there.

'Genius,' Herman says, and sighs.

Marie Louise is more observant; she sees the emptied bag from her wardrobe trodden on the floor.

'My gold,' she says, faintly.

Herman, unable to express himself with less coherence, howls.

Felicity has, in fact, smelted the most precious base ore in the history of metallurgy. Impossible to persuade her parents to see the humour of the thing. In this matter as in others they lack, all too plainly, perfect pitch. From that day Sylvester Spring is instructed that, so far as is possible, Felicity is not to wander further than the firmaments of the human voice. It pleases Sylvester to have his pupil so wholly to himself. Concerned equally for her physical safety and her musical future, he accompanies her everywhere she walks, even to disagreeably muddy games of football in which her half-brother Ernest now cuts a wiry and elusive figure. In recent time the round ball, which men and boys did no more than kick, has vanished from the playing fields of Lovelock Junction and Dixtown; there is now an oval ball not merely for kicking, but also for passing from hand to hand, and which has to be sought, for the most part, at the centre of bruising and frequently bloody encounters of masculine flesh. In this taxing game, or imitation massacre, there is none more fleet of foot, or more adept at evasion of unpleasant physical contact, than diminutive Ernest Lovelock. With the ball taken tight into his arms, he swerves and side-steps trickily through the most brutish melee, leaving his muscular opponents lurching baffled after him; there are times when his limbs seem to float free of terra firma. And indeed Ernest often desires never to stop; never to pause to dab the ball down fastidiously under the opposition goalposts; to soar beyond the shouting, the tackling, the thudding feet. Only reality restrains him. All too soon he is earthbound again, in muddied boots, under the hills of the Porangi; the cries of the crowd are no consolation.

'Ernest,' Felicity observes to Sylvester, 'never looks pleased with himself.'

The truth is that Ernest's gratification is elsewhere. He now has money he can call his own. He has Richard's money he can call his own. His evasive quality on the football field is exactly matched by his inventive method of accountancy, which Richard tends to overlook while pursuing his travels with Porangi Belle. When Ernest has diverted sufficient of Richard's money for lifelong comfort, and desirably lifelong luxury, reality should become no more than an occasional irritant; in the meantime he concentrates on perfecting a facsimile of Richard's signature, which is useful for many purposes, not least that of mortgaging mines and mill while Porangi Belle distracts Richard on the racetracks of the North Island, completing her invincible progress through the colony. Before Richard returns, Ernest should have side-stepped out of the Porangi, and quite out of the country, in some more than passably comfortable passenger steamer.

After anguished labour, Diana begins to give birth. Sybil and Marie Louise have travelled upriver to help Iris and the New Plymouth midwife through this critical time. James is a man deranged by his own futility. Benjamin attempts to console and divert him as the hours of crisis pass.

'You will look back on all this and laugh,' Benjamin promises.

James thinks this unlikely. He braces himself as Diana screams from the bedroom again.

'If everything were easy,' Benjamin proposes, 'we should take life for granted. The way things are, we must be grateful for the gift.'

Benjamin seldom excursions so far into philosophy. But the occasion demands. He fears for his quivering uncle's sanity should the night be too long. Whisky is inadequate as anaesthetic. James has known no sleep for three days. Toward dawn, however, he begins to doze. Relieved Benjamin, soon after, notes a change in the density of sound issuing from the bedroom. Diana no longer screams, but whimpers; there is also a confusion of feminine voices, then significant sighs and silences. Finally he hears a small and faltering cry, unmistakably that of a fresh Lovelock in the world.

Benjamin shakes James awake. 'I think it is over,' he announces.

As James teeters to his feet, Marie Louise enters the living room with sombre face.

'You have your heir,' she tells James.

Benjamin continues to hold James upright.

'And Diana?' James breathes, at length.

'Well,' Marie Louise says shortly.

'Well?'

'In a day or two she shall doubtless be herself again.'

'Then what is wrong?'

'Sit down,' Marie Louise says.

'Where is my son?'

'You will see him soon. You must not be shocked.'

'Shocked? What are you saying?'

Sybil follows Marie Louise into the living room, drying her hands on a towel, and also unsmiling. She undertakes the task Marie Louise has been attempting.

'We are trying to say, James,' Sybil begins, 'that your son has been born with a blemish.'

'My God. Does he lack some limb?'

'Mercifully not. The disfigurement is merely in the matter of appearances. And unfortunately of a facial nature. It is most commonly known as a birthmark.'

James feels relief. 'A birthmark? Why talk of something so trivial?'

'Sit down,' Sybil advises.

'Will people stop telling me to sit down?' James protests. 'My feet are perfectly reliable. Where is my child?'

'We are only trying to prepare you,' Sybil continues. 'Diana has already endured sufficient distress, through prematurely insisting she see her child. Indeed, poor girl, she fainted away.'

'Because of a birthmark?'

'It is, we must warn you, of regrettably substantial nature. Blue and vivid to a degree. In fact, to be brief, it covers one entire side of his face. One cannot help but be optimistic and hope that it is a temporary discolouration. The effect is curious, not to say disturbing. It is as if one half of his face is in the light, and the other half in shadow.'

'Let me see my son,' James demands.

*

With but one large race left to win in the colony, Richard and Paramena take Porangi Belle to Auckland, where she is quartered comfortably and placed under hired guard. Collecting the Auckland Cup, and the thousand guinea stake, already appears a formality. No lower odds have ever been offered on any horse, where bookmakers can be found willing. Even that once profitable favourite of the colony's race-tracks, Crimson King, has few backers, though bookmakers seeking to cover themselves are now despondently offering twenty to one, and higher.

The night before the race, the pair walk gaslit streets, passing noisy public houses. They have already imbibed in many, and been toasted in most; they take a hazardous course across Queen Street, and survive several menacing hansom cabs.

'Where now?' Paramena asks.

'Home,' Richard says. 'To the hotel.'

'You mistake my meaning. After tomorrow, where?'

'Australia,' Richard says. 'The world.'

'No thanks.'

Richard stops, stunned, and swaying slightly. 'What do you mean?'

'It's a long time since the last laugh.'

'A queer complaint from a man who has been filling his pockets fast. I have registered certain smiles of satisfaction.'

'But it's not the same,' Paramena argues. 'Not any more. It's the monotony of the thing.'

'Of what?'

'Of winning. We've forgotten what it's like to lose. There's no flavour.'

'You're a romantic,' Richard insists. 'Romantics are in love with losing. Either that, or you're lily livered.'

'Careful,' Paramena warns. 'I'd most like to hear you suggest that we're heading home to the Porangi after tomorrow.'

'Not immediately. In a week or two. I've notified Ernest that we'll be back after all arrangements have been made for the Australian trip. With those out of the way, we can see how things prosper back on the river. To tell the truth, I have unfinished business of an intimate kind back there. With tomorrow's race won, I can give my mind to it in more depth.'

'You're talking, I take it, of Diana.'

'Who else?'

'Past history. You've left your run too late. The way we've heard it, she's back happily with James, and with child. Maybe a blissful mother already.'

'She may well find more bliss in the prospect of Australia. And, who knows, of the United States.'

'What of the child?'

'A nurse can be engaged. She need not find motherhood overly demanding as we travel.'

'My God. You think of everything. Except one thing, perhaps. James. Your brother.'

'That has, on occasion, caused me some distress. But James, as we well know, is not quite of our world.'

'What world is that?'

'The winning world. To the victors the spoils.'

'And, like I said, no laughs. It might be a cruel life, but I lack the taste for making it crueller. All things considered, friend, I think our ways might well part here.'

'Might what?' Richard says, with disbelief.

'Part here,' Paramena hiccups. 'Now.'

They are in an intricate contest with a street corner; horses and carriages racket past. At length Paramena hobbles away.

'What the hell would you do without me?' Richard demands. 'Cultivate some poor bloody kumara patch?'

'I find potatoes more profitable,' Paramena answers, reminded of something; he begins to reach into a pocket.

'Lily livered,' Richard taunts. 'Chicken hearted.'

Further imprecations are checked by a tuber lofted in his direction.

'There,' Paramena says. 'Fame and fortune may have been founded on less. But I doubt it. Try that for size tomorrow.'

Richard picks up the potato. 'Tomorrow? What for?'

'I don't know why I bother. Porangi Belle.'

'Porangi Belle?' Richard says blankly. 'This? A bloody potato? Go to hell.'

'Then,' Paramena sums up angrily, 'I give you two guesses where you can stick it.'

Richard makes the wrong guess, and doesn't comply. He attempts to decipher the potato, with much perplexity, as Paramena disappears down the city street; he cannot read any message in the vegetable beyond its edibility. Later, sobering in his hotel room, he arrives at the quite reasonable conclusion that, all along, his devious partner has been making a monkey of him. Pagan potions? Pagan incantations? A potato, pure and simple, has been the secret of Porangi Belle's prolonged success.

Paramena, meanwhile, suffers some sentimental remorse at not having given his longtime partner more precise instructions concerning the potato; but he falls in with agreeable company in several saloon bars, and wakes late next morning in an unfamiliar house, evidently of poor repute, without his wooden leg; this necessitates a prolonged room to room search of the dwelling, made the more dramatic by many feminine screams. Soon it is clear that some prankster, in the evening just lost, has souvenired his leg. Time is passing. The racetrack is the better part of ten miles out of town. With a broom as crutch, a slow moving horse tram, and a growing sense of panic, Paramena reaches Queen Street and searches out a shop specializing in surgical appliances. After an unnerving length of time a reasonably fitting leg is located; he sets out, despite his better judgement, to save Richard from himself.

The racetrack is all crowds and commotion. The beer tents are busy. Rival wild men from Borneo ferociously try to tempt customers; likewise the Floating Lady, with promise of miraculous ascents, in another carnival tent. Monkeys prance on barrel organs; punters test their less intuitive skills in Skittle Alley. In the boxing booth, Slogger Sam from Sydney is offering two pounds a round to any man who will take the ring with him. Remote from the more mercenary mob, crinolined ladies and morning-suited escorts parade fashionably on the lawns before the members' stand. Naturally Paramena is not to be distracted. He barges a way among clamorous bookmakers, and reaches the birdcage. The candidates for the Auckland Cup are already on show, mounted by jockeys in their colourful silks. Paramena sights Richard among the watching trainers; at length he grabs Richard's shoulder.

'The potato,' he whispers.

'It's all right,' Richard answers coolly.

'Thank God. No trouble?'

'Not when I peeled it, cut it into small portions, and coated it with sugar. She found it most acceptable.'

'I see,' Paramena says at length, and quite calmly.

'I confess,' Richard goes on, 'that I'm surprised to see your face at all. It was my understanding, forgive me if I'm wrong, that we were finished. That the joy had gone out of things.'

'I find my interest in life reviving,' Paramena explains.

'How so?'

'I have a pleasing sense of the random at work in the universe again. Excuse me a moment, old friend.'

'Where the hell are you going?' Richard demands.

'To answer a call of nature, in one sense,' Paramena replies.

In fact, Paramena shuffles away to answer a call of fate in the conspicuous last-minute cry of one of Auckland's better-known bookmakers; Crimson King, now despairingly on offer at forty to one, and perhaps with persuasion at fifty, appears an enchanting bargain. If the dice are still loaded, so be it. Porangi Belle's potato certainly isn't. And there are doubtless worse times and places for honourable retirement from the sport of kings. Empty in pocket, lighter in heart, Paramena finds Richard again; they move to the members' stand, running a gauntlet of preliminary congratulations.

The crowd is quite as restive as the horses. The three preceding events of the day's card have had unsatisfactory features. The first, spectacularly won by a hitherto indolent hack, has left lively suspicion of a ring-in. The second was marked by considerable interference, leaving two jockeys blinded by rival whips, and many lamenting. In the third a belated no-start was declared by stewards, but not before most of the field, including the favourite, completed the course; in the re-run the exhausted favourite finished near the rear of the field. Stewards have been placed under police protection for the remainder of the day. The beer tents fuel the sensitive feelings of several thousand gamblers. Surfacing into the hot sunlight to observe the race of the year, they tend to express themselves flamboyantly on the subject of the largesse which has not come their way.

This time, at least, they cannot complain about a no-start. The horses explode cleanly from the barrier. Before the first bend, Porangi Belle has broken from the bunch, and slipped comfortably behind Crimson King on the rails. She seems not in the slightest extended; she makes the first mile more a country canter. Soon after the second has begun, her jockey nudges her wide ahead of Crimson King, and offers her an entirely unobstructed track.

'I told him,' Richard says, unblinking, 'to show us just what she could do today.'

She pulls away from Crimson King, length after length, with magical energy.

'There,' Richard says, with satisfaction. 'She has space to express herself at last.'

She has. Especially in the breathtaking final furlong. Ninety seconds later, or roughly a minute after the chestnut Crimson King and two extremely dark horses have passed the winning post, the great Auckland Cup riot of 1884 begins.

No one is more prepared than Paramena. While riderless horses scatter about the track, and their riders are left in disrepair, Paramena with much presence of mind shepherds dazed Richard into the boxing booth, offering him stripped as a challenger to Slogger Sam of Sydney. This is to spare Richard the more indiscriminate and mindless violence in progress outside the tent. Slogger Sam is impressed by the punishment Richard is prepared to take. He is still on his feet, if increasingly frail, at the end of the third round. Meanwhile, having hired the unloveliest of the two wild men from Borneo as bodyguard, Paramena locates the bookmaker of his choice before that businessman of the turf departs the track; and collects on Crimson King without prolonged verbal persuasion. More monetary inducement, to the Floating Lady, provides the pair with feminine attire in which to get clear of the course; rumour already says that a shady associate of Porangi Belle's owner has bet heavily on Crimson King.

Some hours later Richard and Paramena share a rural hilltop. The silence is splendid. They have pleasantly pastoral prospects to the west, also to the east, north and south. There are roads in the distance, townships, farmhouses with smoky chimneys; there is even a railway track upon which a locomotive is plodding. Cattle low. Sheep bleat. Feminine attire is scattered about them; they are again in masculine garb.

'What of Porangi Belle?' Paramena is at length disposed to ask.

'She can go out to grass, I expect.'

'And you?'

'I could do worse.'

'On the Porangi?'

'Where else?'

'Good luck,' Paramena says, and sighs.

'You're not coming back with me?'

'You get the point, old friend. I have this deep craving to catch myself a fish again. And watch it cook on my campfire. Life's short.'

'You're still a bloody savage at heart.'

'Maybe. I don't doubt that civilization has something to be said for it. And I don't deny that I enjoyed the ride while it lasted.'

He rises, shakes Richard's hand with some courtesy, and then begins to retire from the hilltop.

'Where now?' Richard calls.

'Home,' Paramena explains. 'Where the heart is, I hear.'

('Unlikely though it may seem now,' insists the publicist of *The Lives of Lovelock Junction*, 'the settlement was once celebrated for equestrian reasons, largely because of its reputation as home turf of Porangi Lady, one of the most electrifying horses on antipodean racetracks in the late nineteenth century. Richard Lovelock raised and trained her. In her brief – indeed mysteriously short-lived – career, this mare won virtually all the colony's major races. The exception was the Auckland Cup, in which she was a controversial also-ran. The circumstances clouding her failure led to racetrack turmoil, to Richard Lovelock being disbarred from the colony's racetracks for life, and to Porangi Lady being sold off as brood mare at her supposed peak. The adventure cost Richard dear in other respects also: his enterprises on the Porangi, during his prolonged absences, were evidently mismanaged by Ernest Lovelock, Herman's son. To the end of his life Richard protested his innocence of racetrack malpractice. There does indeed appear to be some substance to the belief that he was, in fact, victim of a cunning fraud perpetrated by a close business partner. The details are obscure, but it is a matter of record that this partner never returned to the Porangi with Richard after the Auckland fiasco; he was never heard of again.'

More characteristically careless research. Other records show that Paramena perished, much mourned in his native village, and still prosperous, celebrated as one of the last living Hau Hau, in his eighty-ninth year; his death was presumed after he failed to return from a lengthy solo fishing trip in a leaky dinghy. Long search disclosed a wooden leg washed up on a beach; never a body. This was finally interred with the ceremony due to a complete corpse. For some years a one-legged spectre was reported in the vicinity; it was reasonably supposed to be that of Paramena in quest of his lost extremity. Little was done about it as the spectre, when it appeared, had a useful gift for predicting the names of winning racehorses, thus bringing prosperity to Paramena's former tribe. But after a decade in which the issue was much debated, and children and pregnant women much disturbed, the surviving leg was disinterred and launched upon the sea again. The spectre made no further appearance. The spirit of Paramena, it was said, had honourably earned its peace.)

In making his premature and inconspicuous return to the Porangi, Richard has ample time for reflection upon his affairs aboard the slow and strong-smelling cattle boat which carries him to New Plymouth. There, with a day in hand before a coal steamer departs for the river, he is given still more on which to reflect by his bank manager, on paying that gentleman a notionally social call.

Ernest, the afternoon of Richard's unexpected return, is engaged in a vigorous game of rugby football; it is a practice game for the forthcoming season, a season in which Ernest will not participate, since he will be somewhere beyond Sydney, but he sees no reason not to keep up appearances, especially not when there is money to be milked to the last moment. A ruck has formed among the forwards; the ball is loose on the ground, and heeled back by Ernest's team-mates. It is passed to Ernest. At the moment he feels the leather in his hands, and begins to take flight, he sees surprising reinforcement among the opposition backs moving to tackle him. They have been joined by Richard and his New Plymouth bank manager, advancing with apparent intent to injure. Ernest senses an unmistakable finality in the nature of the game now being played. His farewell appearance on the football field will be one long remembered. Technique does not desert him. He twists out of tackles, swerves, jinks, dummies and side-steps; no one brings him to ground. Richard's frantic face floats past, also the bank manager's. Hands reach out and fall away. He fends off a burly forward to quite fracturing effect. Soon Ernest is in the clear, with only the full-back to beat; a dazzling change of pace and direction leaves that last human obstacle sprawled ineffectually on the ground. Ernest doesn't neglect to touch the ball down over the goal-line as a demonstration of his infallible capacity to score. Then he keeps on running until lost to sight. Also lost to sight, for the most part, is Richard's realized capital worth.

James tries to persuade Diana to see her son. One attempt is enough.

'Take him away,' she screams.

Later, sobbing, she explains, 'I wanted a pretty baby.'

'Of course,' James says, still consolatory.

'He isn't pretty. He is horrid.'

'But he is ours. For better or worse.'

'It is the devil's mark,' she argues. 'It is my wickedness bearing fruit. He is the devil's child. Not ours.'

'This is foolishness,' James answers. 'He is a small innocent human creature, like any other. What, in truth, would you have me do? Kill him? That is where your logic is cruelly leading you.'

'I no longer know,' she weeps. 'I only know I cannot see him without revulsion. Please bear with me, and understand.'

'I am trying,' James persists. 'I am also endeavouring to remind you that you are now a mother. And that you have a son. I propose to call him David.'

'David?' she says blankly.

'It is a strong name, reminiscent of great deeds. Perhaps our son too.'

'You are trying to win me around to him. To reconcile me.'

'Perhaps. I am sure your shock cannot endure. You are not the first mother to suffer grief of this kind. Nor, I daresay, the last. Please see him again. You will find your natural tenderness rising. Believe me.'

'I find blackness rising. Muddy. Oily. Evil. I find only hate in my heart.'

'For what?'

'For him. I could not be trusted alone with that child. It is my own darkness of soul which discolours his face. I have dealt with the devil. Now I read the message that the full price has yet to be paid.'

'Price? Paid? What are you talking of?'

'I have almost betrayed you, James,' she explains. 'All but. I have been an adulteress in my innermost self.'

It is not fresh intelligence to James; he accepts this with calm. 'The past is best past,' he suggests. 'No grudge need be borne. I would be disturbed only if you were to say my son is not mine, but Richard's.'

'Would that he were,' she says. 'And this life less torment. He could go to Richard. Perhaps, in natural justice, he should.'

'Talk sense, woman,' James replies sternly. 'Make a beginning. Make the best of what is. See David again.'

'Never,' she vows.

'Diana. Please.'

'If you wish me for wife, keep that child from sight.'

In attempting to manage Diana, Sybil and Marie Louise are equally helpless. Iris, more practically, sees to the sustenance of the blemished son born to Diana and James; she takes him maternally into her own household so that his cries need not disturb Diana. Shaken James comes frequently to fondle the boy, and to be reassured by Benjamin that Diana's condition is surely temporary; that time will heal. It is the best that Benjamin, or anyone, can say; it is the only hope James himself has. But time's medication, as days pass, does no more to transform Diana into a willing mother than the most urgent verbal persuasion. Risen from her bed, her eyes hot and strange, she wanders the homestead.

'Where have you hidden him?' she demands.

'David is with Iris. For the moment.'

'For what moment? How long a moment?'

'Until you are yourself again. Until you are, perhaps, disposed to embrace your son.'

She shudders. 'Then you misjudge the nature of this moment. You are speaking of eternity. Look upon me, James. Look well. I am myself. The mother of a monster.'

'You befoul your mouth. You are speaking of our child.'

Soon after, Diana attacks herself with a sharp knife. Sybil, Marie Louse and James have to wrestle her back to bed. The wound proves superficial, but there is blood in abundance. James now knows things cannot last, because he cannot last. The madness must be contagious. For in fantasy he sees himself finishing the task which Diana began with the knife. He is but a twitch or two from being a murderer. He can no longer be trusted alone with his wife; no more than she with her son. He is quite indistinguishable, a citzen of hell.

News arrives of Richard's return to the Porangi, and of his misfortunes. Porangi Belle abandoned and sold. Paramena's apparent defection. Ernest's embezzlement and presumed departure from the Porangi. Sybil leaves her duties to Marie Louise and hastens downriver to put Richard's house in order; at least he will have some domestic comfort.

'Where is she?' Diana asks vaguely, next day.

'Who?' James says, affecting ignorance.

'My mother. Where has she gone?'

'Downriver, I understand. To attend to certain pressing matters.'

'You mean,' Diana says shrewdly, 'that Richard is back.'

'That may well be the case,' James agrees.

'Is he or isn't he?'

'It would appear so,' James confesses with reluctance.

'Why should you be so slow to tell me?'

'Because it is not of great relevance,' he claims. 'Other matters have priority in this household. The recent birth of a child, for example.'

'Don't,' she says, blocking her ears. 'Never tell me again.'

James observes redness colouring his vision; he longs to twist her white neck with his hard hands. He retreats outside, just in time, leaving Marie Louise to attend Diana. He sits shivering on the stump of a tree. Eventually Benjamin locates James there. Benjamin can find little useful to say. So he shares the stump and places a comforting arm about his uncle. The two men remain seated on that stump long after dusk.

Next day, Diana's bed is found empty. A dinghy has gone from the farm landing. There is a note, quite short.

Dearest husband, it says. *Please take this as my farewell to Spanish Creek. It is for your serenity, and that of your son, that I must now go to discharge my debt. Forgive me all, dear God. May you now be happy. David too. There. I have at last brought myself to acknowledge his name, to utter it for the first and last time. Please, I pray you, expect no more of me as wife. There is no more of me. Say to yourself: Diana is dead. You will thus be able to phrase the same function for your son.*

It is smudged and stained, presumably with tears, and in part near illegible.

James cannot deny relief welling, like a pure spring, in the toxic waste of his anguish. What has been, cannot be again. He has, moreover, been saved from himself; he will not hang for murder, and leave David unloved. His flesh and spirit are no longer shredded between wife and son.

Later that day, to spare James further mutilation, Benjamin rows downriver to ascertain that Diana is indeed now in residence with Richard; a distressed Sybil is attempting to attend to her needs. Sybil instructs Benjamin to report that her heart is heavy with shame on behalf of her daughter.

James hears this in silence. After a significant lapse of time, in which all is apparently digested, he requests his son from Iris. He takes David in his arms and conveys him slowly uphill to their homestead. Benjamin and Iris watch from their door. Moved by the unknown, and afraid, they hold tight to each other.

Though none can know it yet, and as even Sylvester Spring can only suspect, it will be Felicity who immortalizes the months to come on the Porangi: her interpretation of her roles as Violetta and Lucia, Mimi and Marguerite, Gilda and Gioconda, and many other similarly stricken heroines of grand opera, will owe much to personal observation; and to her childhood on the Porangi. For the greater part of her career she will be in debt to Diana. Indeed, Diana, or some costumed approximation of her, will live and die luminously, year after year, around the world; often in the presence of crowned heads. No life is waste.

To the victors the spoils. To the losers, the spoiled. Richard is not the first to discover that that which he most desires has been corroded by time and circumstance; and is no longer desirable. Romance, let alone lust at last consummated, has an alien hue. His predicaments are many, and of a monetary nature. He has to begin again; his debts, all round, are close to catastrophic. Worse, he can no longer trust anyone. There is no one, no Paramena, no Ernest, to whom he dare delegate responsibility. He is on his own. When he has finished supervising his labour force for the day, he sweats over his accounts in the light of a late-burning lamp. As if that isn't enough, there is still Diana in his bedroom with burning eyes.

'Here I am,' she says. 'Take me to your need.'

It could be seen as compensation. It isn't. His sexuality has never been slighter.

'I am yours,' she adds.

She seems some jerky and mocking marionette, a caricature of the delicate woman he once aspired to wed. She is coarse and unbuttoned; her greasy hair drifts over her eyes. He cannot understand what he ever saw in this creature; he can only and profitlessly surmise.

'Go to your room,' he often suggests. 'There is nothing between us which cannot be left until a more convenient hour.'

'You wanted me,' she observes.

'True,' he acknowledges, in despair. 'Once.'

Qualifications escape her. 'Having me, then, cannot be left until a convenient hour. I am yours now, Richard. Now.'

Useless for Richard to explain his depleted condition; she has no ears for news of his reduced circumstances; material things are now beyond her. Their lovemaking, at best, becomes a disagreeable obligation for Richard. The price of her silence; but a price his flesh is less and less willing to pay.

'Save me,' he pleads to Sybil.

Her laugh is bitter. 'As you sow,' she answers, 'so shall you reap.'

'Your daughter,' he asserts, 'is all but undone.'

'It is your undoing. On your account she has surrendered husband and child. Might I suggest, now, that in charity you offer her more of your time, and some tenderness?'

'I have no time,' he argues. 'And as for tenderness, that is something not easily manufactured.'

'To be frank, I find it impertinent that you look to me for succour.'

'You run my household. I pay you well. More, in truth, than I can presently afford.'

'It was never my understanding that I am paid to tidy away your personal follies. And conceal the fruits of your lechery from sight.'

'Diana, besides, is your daughter.'

'I regret to inform you that she is a stranger to me now. And equally a stranger to her responsibilities at Spanish Creek – to James, in short, and her child. I have tried to reconcile her. To no avail. There are times when I fear she fails even to understand her native English tongue. When near lucid, which is seldom, she prefers to employ some argot of her own. Felicity, who appears to follow Diana about a great deal, and sometimes helps her pick flowers, may well understand her. I can no longer pretend to.'

'You give me no choice,' Richard announces finally. 'From this moment consider yourself discharged from my employment. I should be grateful if you could vacate this house before midnight. I should also be grateful if you could remove your daughter with the remainder of your possessions.'

'This is not unexpected,' Sybil replies with calm. 'I must confess my relief. But as for your last request, you seem to be labouring under some misapprehension. I should dearly like to oblige you by removing Diana, for her own sake, not yours. But she is not my possession. Flesh and spirit she is now your property. Surely you cannot mistake the quality of her devotion to you?'

'You are trying to take advantage of my better nature.'

'The revelation of your better nature is one I must await with great interest.'

'Get her out of here,' he says.

'By force?' she asks.

'Anyhow you choose.'

'Forcible removal is out of the question. I am a relatively feeble woman of middle years. Diana is young and still strong. A limpet on a rock. You are the rock.'

'A split rock. Increasingly so.'

'Nevertheless,' Sybil argues.

'Then, God damn it, take my house. Take her. I shall dwell elsewhere until some sanity begins to prevail.'

He dashes a brandy glass against a wall and slams out. That night he does not return to the bed which Diana is determined to share; he toils over his accounts, and at length sleeps on his desk. Next morning he wakes to commotion. Search parties, it seems, are setting out to recover Diana from the Porangi; all is hysterical clamour, orchestrated by Sybil, with much shouting and launching of boats. Not long before noon a dinghy returns with Diana's naked body, made partially modest by a cover of masculine garments, draped in its stern. Sybil wades into the river, to the dinghy, and with huge effort gathers up her daughter; she refuses helping hands from the men about, and apparently prefers Diana uncovered. Then she stumbles toward Richard, and drops Diana at his feet. 'There,' the stricken woman says. 'She is yours forever now.'

It is like a curse. Richard sees some of his oldest and most valued employees backing away. Marie Louise, lately returned from Spanish Creek, leads Sybil off to Lovelock House, sharing her grief. Soon no one remains near Richard apart from his niece Felicity, who seems to see all, know all, though Sylvester Spring is trying to coax her elsewhere.

'Go away,' Richard tells Felicity. 'It is not a fitting sight.'

'For whom?' she inquires, perhaps pertinently.

'For anyone. Go away.'

'You're not a very fitting sight either,' she observes. 'If I were you, I'd do something about it.'

'You are not me.'

'I shouldn't be too sure about that either,' Felicity answers. She seems, rather frostily, to be gazing into his soul.

'Get her the hell out of here,' Richard shouts.

What Richard does, since there is little else to be done, is wait upon James to arrive from Spanish Creek to claim the sodden corpse of his wife. No words pass between the two brothers. There is no more to be said, possibly not if they live another hundred years.

After Diana has been buried with subdued ceremony beside her father, under a clear winter sky, James makes return to Spanish Creek with Iris, who carries the infant David in her arms. Benjamin has remained on the farm with the other children.

At the landing, James moors the dinghy. 'Here,' he says to Iris. 'I can make him my own now.'

She surrenders David, and James bears his son home. Benjamin makes opportune arrival; he assists his weeping wife to her children.

In the homestead, James settles his son, and lights a large fire. 'There,' he tells the sleeping boy. 'We have to make the best of things now, you and I. If there is lack, it will not be of love.'

Then James finds himself empty of courage. He is soon on his knees, in front of the fire, heat on the hands covering his face, and beginning to pray. At first his prayer is confused, and perhaps selfish in nature. He asks for strength to survive known perils and those more mysterious; he asks forgiveness for failures. Then he comprehends that he is no longer pleading for himself, but for Diana. He asks that her soul be brought home from the great darkness in which it must dwell; he asks that she be allowed light everlasting. Finally he prays for their child: he wishes David strong, sensitive, with a natural nobility. He confides his desire to have his child grow with the grace of a willow to the sun, rooted deep in the earth; to have him unsullied by large or mean sin, a miracle of love.

When he finishes, the fire is low, his knees are stiff, the homestead dark. And his son awake, with a hungry whimper. James lights a lamp and carries it to the child's cot. There is something unfamiliar. It takes time to place it. Then he does. The blue birthmark on the boy's face has grown as pale as a passing shadow. It might have been ebbing for moments, minutes, hours, perhaps days: it might be that James has simply not noticed. No matter. Debts can be discharged. Compassionate prayers might have answer. He moves through the house, lighting lamp after lamp, and then warms milk for his son.

Fourteen

Herman's affairs need not elude us, though they have begun to elude most on the Porangi. Chemistry and alchemy have proved craven allies in the quest for iron. He seeks a reliable pact with electricity. It appears to have much in its favour. For one thing, it works invisibly. The impurities in the Porangi sands, which refuse to release their grip on the iron, are likewise largely invisible to the human eye. Fire has to be fought with fire; the invisible with the invisible. He is given to understand that electricity is a new power source destined to transform the entire nature of things; it has its own laws, its own whims, and most fortunately is not dependent upon perfection of the human heart. Coils of copper wire, magnets, dynamos and a small generator make their appearance up the Porangi. Herman conjectures that a sufficiently large voltage sent surging through the Porangi sands might purge all parent materials, all impurities, and leave the iron visibly free. For months Herman is seldom seen. Marie Louise tends to suspect electricity as a hazardous new offshoot of mysticism; she is not comfortable with the subject, nor with Herman's talk of immense floating palaces which will soon sail the sea, powered by this magical substance which normally cannot be seen, smelled, heard, touched or tasted. 'If it is so wonderful,' she declares, 'why can't you use it to fetch up a new wife for James?'

'There are limitations,' he insists.

'Or send it in search of Luke?'

'I cannot wire up the past. Electricity cannot go back seventeen years.'

She is even more unimpressed. It saddens him to have a wife so single-minded. With Benjamin all but buried beneath his own offspring, Ernest likely engaged in putting Richard's money profitably to use elsewhere in the world, and her own Felicity now Sylvester's perplexingly melodious cuckoo in the Lovelock nest, Marie Louise has begun to mourn anew for Luke. And with Herman now mostly enmeshed in glittering galleries of wire, she becomes still lonelier. Though she travels upriver often enough, to see Sybil, Iris, Benjamin, James and above all baby David at Spanish Creek, her discontent grows. She says she often dreams of Luke still alive, somewhere in the country, though these dreams never place him precisely.

When Herman has rigged enough wire through numerous junctions to diverse terminals, he fires his generator with coal and invites Marie Louise to participate in the adventure. Samples of ironsand are ready to be shocked into a different order of things. All Marie Louise is obliged to do, so as to observe the beneficial and entirely rational nature of electricity, is throw certain switches at Herman's command. The first switch is no problem; she hears, however, an unearthly humming. 'There,' he says. 'It is becoming audible.' The second switch produces crackling sparks and tiny threads of lightning through a series of coils. 'Now it is visible,' he announces. 'Throw the third that all may reveal itself.' Hesitant Marie Louise finally does as instructed. There is a vast flash. Engulfed, she touches, tastes and smells the marvel of electricity in the moment she disappears into a different order of things. When she revives, Herman is dragging her clear of his workshop.

'How long have I been away?' she asks him with wonder; he is surprised to find her taking so charitable a view of events.

'Away?' he says.

'Away from you. And Lovelock Junction.'

'I don't understand,' he insists. 'A few seconds ago we had a small setback in our experiment with electricity.'

'I must be ten years older,' she claims.

'You are a little singed,' he argues. 'You will soon, no doubt, collect your wits.'

Marie Louise indignantly takes issue. 'I have never been more calm,' she tells him. 'Nor sane.'

'Very well,' he says tolerantly.

'Moreover, I found Luke.'

'Luke?'

'It was a long journey. Years in all. I often tired. But I found him. Yes.'

Herman finally sees no reason not to humour her. 'And where,' he asks, 'did you find him?'

'In a native village. By a lake, with a bold mountain beyond. He was dwelling in a landscape of many lakes. There were also warm pools in which people bathe. And boiling pools in which they cook. There were fountains of steam rising pale around. He laughed when he saw me, and kissed me, and took my hand. He was about to lead me lovingly into his world. But then you pulled me back into this one.'

She appears to be implying that Lovelock Junction is a poor second best.

'An interesting dream,' Herman observes.

'It was no dream. Unless this also is dream. I was there. I saw Luke.'

'You were also here. In a faint.'

'I cannot account for that,' Marie Louise says dismissively. 'Let me tell you one other thing, to convince you.'

'Please do.'

'He still wore, about his neck, that crucifix. That old crucifix you said was found in a sealers' camp in the south. He still wore it.'

'Remarkable,' Herman agrees. 'And how old was he?'

That question gives Marie Louise pause.

'Was he bearded, for example?' Herman persists.

'No. Not bearded.'

'Did he appear capable, perhaps, of growing a beard?'

'It is difficult to say. His face glowed.'

'Damn it, woman, I am asking a straightforward question. Was he still a child?'

'Still our child. Yes. Still our loving Luke.'

'There. Luke is – would be – a young man by more than a score of years. You have been suffering delirium.'

'Never,' Marie Louise asserts. 'I know what I saw. I know where I have been.'

From an upper floor of Lovelock House, Felicity's voice, backed by Sylvester Spring's piano accompaniment, floats out upon the sunny afternoon; it descends in a poignant spiral, and Marie Louise is disinclined to resist tears. Herman helps her into the house, seats her in the kitchen, and tries to reconcile her to the visible world with a large cognac.

'I know this too,' Marie Louise adds. 'Luke is in danger. That was why I had to travel so far, and long, to find him.'

'What manner of danger?' Herman asks gently.

She shakes her head, and weeps again. 'I cannot remember. I only recall that the nature of my mission was urgent.'

'I don't doubt that you have had some distressing experience,' Herman says at length. 'But we must attribute it to electricity. You have had what is known as an electrical shock. The electrical current, as I see it, capriciously found its way through you instead of the ironsand. Doubtless a fault in my wiring somewhere, producing what is most commonly called a short circuit.'

'Then short circuit me again,' she pleads. 'I must get back to Luke and warn him.'

'Of what?'

'I shall know when I see him.'

'Impossible. Such electrical shocks can, I understand, be fatal.'

'What of Luke? His danger may be mortal. It would be worth my risk.'

'I'm sorry,' Herman says. 'It cannot be countenanced. I am not willing yet to be a widower. Besides, it is perfectly understandable that your alarm should set free certain morbid imaginings. In danger yourself, you dream everyone else must be.'

'Not everyone else. Just Luke. And it was no dream.'

Herman is irritatingly determined to believe otherwise; his rationalizations at length become intolerable, and lead to prolonged commotion, first in the kitchen, and then along several corridors, and in and out of a number of rooms. Herman takes to the tower for peace. Eventually Marie Louise conveys her troubling experience upriver to James. He hears her out with more apparent patience; he bounces two-year-old David on his knee, to keep the boy pacified, as he listens unsmiling to the account of Marie Louise's electrical excursion.

'I know he is there,' she finishes. 'Just as I have described. And in danger.'

'I see,' James says coolly. He sets David free, to scamper outside, and lights his pipe.

'Well?' she asks. 'What do you think?'

'There are but two possibilities. You are right. Or you are wrong. It is more comfortable, of course, to believe the latter.'

'So?' she demands.

'I confess myself uncomfortable.'

Marie Louise sighs. She has an ally.

'He must be found,' she argues.

'Indeed,' James agrees. 'But where? Inland, there are conceivably many places which could conform to your description. A mountain? A lake? Hot springs?'

'I recall the mountain best. It was rugged, without singular shape, rising sheer from the water. Of uncommonly dark tinge.'

'There might be many such,' James observes.

'Wait,' Marie Louise says.

James waits.

'I remember more. There were others. Other people. Not native. People of our own complexion and clothing. They came and went in small boats. Visitors, perhaps.'

'That may mean something,' James concedes.
'You could find him,' she says.
'Me?'
'You. Only one who believes me can find him. Others might falter.'
'I am in no position to travel,' he objects, 'nor so much as to leave the farm. I am not alone in this life. I have David to think of at all times now.'
'I am not blind. I see your devotion. But I also observe three other adults resident at Spanish Creek. Sybil, his grandmother. Also Iris and Benjamin. David will lack for nothing in your absence.'
'Other than a father's love. He has no mother, handicap enough for any child. Thus he depends on me more than is perhaps natural.'
'I am far from blind to that either. But think of Luke.'
'Luke?'
'Of Luke in danger.'
'Your intuition is inexact in that respect.'
'You must believe me; I know.'
Her vehemence is extraordinary. In the end James capitulates; Marie Louise has had an experience too compelling for rational detail to coarsen their discussion.

This is in the middle of May, 1886. Shearing is long done for the year, winter evident, and lambing three months away. Tasks at Spanish Creek are mostly trivial, and easily entrusted to Benjamin. Less easily, David can be left with Sybil and Iris. James realizes that his fears are for himself, not his son. Without David he feels vulnerable to the darkness at work in the world. Within a week, nevertheless, James has ridden off into the wilderness at the centre of the island, saddle bags bulging with provisions to sustain him on his strange journey; none but Marie Louise altogether comprehends the nature and urgency of his quest. It is less perilous than it might have been a decade earlier; the warring tribesmen of the interior have been bribed with booze and other component paraphernalia of civilization to keep the peace and part with their lands; even the most shamelessly murderous have been royally pardoned so that railway construction can proceed with convenience. The menace inland, thus, is not from man. It is inherent in the terrain; and in the absence of man. A fall from his horse, a broken leg, and James might never be seen again.
James determines to be seen again. He has but to think of David. For the most part he leads his horse. Rivers saturate. Mountains impede. The damp forest clings. There is bitter rain, then thick frost, finally

snow. On an especially comfortless day, just when he has begun to contemplate retreat to the Porangi, vegetation begins to offer less obstruction. He arrives on volcanic plain, mostly sandy desert, with tussock sprouting thinly here and there, and untidy drifts of snow. The volcanoes themselves, with icy flanks, stand smoky off to the east. It is the first day of June. He can orient himself at last. He travels north, pausing only to rest his horse, or pitch his tent, upon this lunar territory. There is no man to accost him, or ask his business. The crust of the earth is sometimes thin, and he steers his horse around sibilant fissures which feed scalding steam into the frosty air. He glimpses great inland waters stippled with sunlight. Toward the end of June's first week he sights something approximating civilization; a road considerably rutted by the carriages of travellers. He follows the road, and westering sun, and in late afternoon enters a settlement, mainly Maori, but with a European hotel, and stables. Around the settlement rises the steam of hot pools and geysers. With his horse fed and watered, a warm bed in prospect, and rum mellow in his belly, he tests the hotel proprietor's geographical knowledge; he describes that which Marie Louise suggests she has seen. 'It sounds to me like some place north of here,' the proprietor answers. 'Ohinemutu, maybe.' He shrugs. 'I'm the wrong man to ask; I'm new.'

'We all are,' James observes.

Next day James rides north, on a pale highway of crisp pumice, across treeless plains. Oily pools of hot mud begin to sputter near the roadside. As he nears Ohinemutu toward dusk, smells sulphur, and sees the lights of solid hotels in the steamy lakeside village, he knows this is not the place, not yet; it lacks Marie Louise's uncommonly dark mountain rising sheer from the water. James bathes his saddlesore body in a warm pool hired out to visitors by Maoris. Over a pint of ale, in a nearby bar, he resumes his quest. 'Sounds like you're looking for Lake Tarawera,' the barman declares. 'It could be Tarawera mountain you're talking about. There's three villages around the lake. Te Wairoa. Te Ariki. Moura. Might be one of them you're looking for. Try Te Wairoa first. It's on a coach road, ten miles out. There's a good hotel. Joe McRae's. A braw liar of a Scot; he'll see you right.'

'Who goes there?' James asks.

'People. Tourists. Englishmen. Americans. Australians. Te Wairoa's where you take the boat for the Pink and White Terraces. Don't tell me you never heard of them.'

'No,' James confesses.

'A wonder of the world, some say. Stairways to heaven, others tell. All queer and crystal, made by the mineral in geysers, climbing toward the sky. There's nothing the like anywhere else on earth.'

'And people go there by boat,' James says, indifferent to other detail.

'By the hundred,' the barman assures him.

It is all James needs to know; stairways to heaven are superfluous. Luke, if found, will be the largest wonder in the Lovelock world. It is too late, too dark, to push on; anyway he is tempted to make the most of civilization's amenities in this sulphurous region. He books into an hotel, stables his horse, and discovers a well-appointed dining room, French wine, and feminine company at his table. Feminine company comes in the hearty form of a Miss Hilda Lavender. Miss Lavender is companion and apparent amanuensis to her aged English author father, Augustus Lavender, who is presently compiling an account of his fearless travels in the South Sea, though he looks too senile by far. It is all of four decades since his *Polynesian Odyssey*, a startling autobiographic narrative of young manhood misspent among feckless Tahitians and ferocious Maoris, made him celebrated in London's literary salons; his publishers, possibly in despair of his sales since, hope for a repeat performance. Athletic Miss Lavender is perhaps forty years old, near enough in age to James, but distinctly not old maidish; nor, for that matter, maidenly. She has a bold eye, and a laugh in keeping.

'You don't,' she observes, during dessert, 'look in the least like an antipodean sheep farmer to me. More like a poet, perhaps.'

'That,' James replies, in good humour, 'may be my problem.'

'What's that?' Augustus Lavender asks, cupping a hand about his ear. 'What's that you say?'

'I was saying,' Hilda tells him, loudly and slowly, 'that Mr Lovelock looks too sensitive to be a sheep farmer.'

'Embalmer?'

'Farmer.'

'Embalming,' Augustus states with authority, 'is not a Polynesian practice. They often hang their dead in the trees until they make old bones.'

'We are not,' Hilda attempts to explain, 'talking of Polynesian ways.'

'The old days?' Augustus says with satisfaction. 'I can tell you things about Tahiti in the old days. Met Melville here. Got the rogue out of prison. Things aren't the same. Nor the women. The place is poxed.'

'This journey has been a strain on father,' Hilda informs James. 'His faculties are incommoded by the fact that we sailed from Tahiti more than a month ago. He remains there in spirit. I have the hope that prolonged immersion in the spa pools here will restore his cognitive powers. Otherwise, alas, I may be obliged to compose the New Zealand portion of his new chronicle myself. Thus far, I fear, we have encountered little or no excitement for the purpose. It is too quiet a country, without upheaval to generate necessary narrative interest. Maoris no longer make war, the gold rushes have gone. The romance of pioneering has faded. Where is there adventure enough to make flesh and spirit tingle? What can one say?'

James is at a loss for suggestions. He is less at a loss, however, in dealing with Miss Lavender's ankle, which is intermittently inclined to brush his beneath the dining table; he responds pleasantly to the pressure. Miss Lavender makes him aware that three years of celibacy have not especially suited his nature. So does the fine wine. She is increasingly congenial company. And a most worldly woman.

'And what, pray, brings you roaming this infernal region?' she asks.

'A quest, of sorts,' he explains.

'Ah. Mystery.'

'In a sense.' He is reticent.

'To be frank, and I must be, I see you as something more than the common run of tourist. You shall disappoint me utterly if you suggest that it is anything less than a search for the meaning of life.'

'A vain search,' James proposes. 'I now find the meaning of death a subject of more fascination.'

'How so?' she asks, surprised.

'Without death, life has no meaning. But to make sense of death, I fear, one must become its intimate.'

'A morbid view.'

'Perhaps,' James allows.

'Melville wrote *Typee*, you know,' Augustus interposes. 'Confounded fellow. Made a fortune. All a pack of lies. The wretch has written since about whales, I believe.'

'I suspect you have seen tragedy,' Hilda says.

'It is true I am a widower. But I have a small son to claim my affections. I cannot complain. All is not black. I would not wish the past away. For I should also be wishing away my son.'

'D'you know,' Augustus roars, 'what Charlie Dickens said to me after *Polynesian Odyssey*? Go back, he said, and do it all again. So I'm here. I'm at last taking Charlie's advice. The hell I am. Better late than never.'

'Bravo,' Hilda says. To James, sotto voce, she goes on, 'You move me strangely. Men with inner content are few.'

'Content is merely an absence of restlessness,' James qualifies. 'Not necessarily happiness.'

'That much I observe. Your eyes have some sadness.'

'Tennyson took it upon himself to write to me,' Augustus informs them. 'D'you know what dear Freddie said? He said my book made the world dew-fresh for him. Dew-fresh. What d'you say to that?'

'Bravo,' Hilda says. She tells James, 'Father's glories, I fear, become the more precious with the passing of the years. I shall have him safely off to his bed soon. Would you consider it altogether too brazen if I were to suggest we partake of brandy together after he retires? I should like to think our intercourse might strike less philosophical notes.'

'Indeed,' James agrees.

'Come, father,' Hilda says. She shepherds Augustus from the dining room with no more than token protests, thunderously conveyed. Hilda is not long detained by the bedding of her father. She returns soon to find James in the hotel smoking room, the brandy already ordered. He has been trying to remind himself, without success, that he needs an early night to be on the road to Te Wairoa by first light in the morning. He may, God willing, be only hours from discovering Luke.

'There,' Hilda says, on her third brandy. 'That is a considerable improvement on the earlier state of affairs. Your eyes are perceptibly less sad. I even see, perhaps faintly, a modicum of boyish mischief resident within them. Dare I flatter myself by suggesting that my company might be the cause?'

'I should be churlish to disagree,' James answers, beckoning the waiter, and drawing attention to glasses made empty.

'There is a formidably bright moon tonight, I understand,' Hilda tells him.

James requires no further information on the subject. After their fourth brandy, soon finished, they stand outside the hotel. The winter air is cool, tempered with gusts of warm steam from the thermal pools. Moonlight is bright upon the waters of the lake.

Hilda shivers. James, gentlemanly, removes his jacket and drapes it over her shoulders. They walk together.

'I still tend to forget,' she tells him, 'that this is the southern hemisphere, and that June is an inclement month.'

Moonlight presently reveals to them a warm pool of modest size. It is deserted and secluded. Hilda stoops and tests the temperature with her hand. It appears to her satisfaction.

'Do we dare?' she asks.

'Dare?'

'To spurn so agreeable a gift of God's world?'

'It is difficult other than to succumb,' James concedes.

'Done,' she announces.

They disrobe, a discreet distance apart, and before long sit nakedly immersed to their necks in the pool.

'There,' Hilda sighs. 'The chill of the world is well lost. I cannot but feel that there is something magical in our meeting, in this lonely outpost, and particularly in our present situation. Some decree of fate, perhaps.'

'It could well seem so,' James says amiably.

'The magical, of course, isn't magical unless rooted in the mundane.'

'I am not sure that I take your meaning.'

'Then I must be more explicit. I trust you will not think it immodest of me if I mention something apropos of our situation at present. In consulting the available literature of this region, I made the intriguing discovery that the natives of this place consider these pools to have, let us say, an aphrodisiac quality.'

'Fascinating,' James says. He is slightly out of breath.

'It is doubtless rumour. Or ill-founded mythology. One cannot imagine science lending credence to the tale.'

'Indeed not,' James agrees.

'All the same,' she says.

'Yes?' James says. 'All the same?'

'It is really quite remarkable.'

'Quite.'

'And astonishing.'

'Altogether.'

There is a pause as the pool gives the lie to science.

'Dear James – do you mind if I call you James?'

'Of course not.'

'Dear James.'

There is another pause.

'Dear Hilda.'

'Dear God,' she says.

Toward first light next morning, as their exertions wane, they rise from the pool and make furtive return to their hotel rooms; they kiss upon parting. 'That,' Hilda whispers, 'is a night never to be forgotten.'

'Never,' James concurs, weak in the knees.

'I feel a sated guest at Aphrodite's feast. Would it be unforgivably ambitious to propose that we might, perhaps, meet again tonight?'

'I have, alas, a quest to resume,' James reminds her. 'I must ride to Te Wairoa.'

Hilda's distress is considerable. Eventually he enters his bedroom dazed, and more than a little internally dehydrated by the thermal waters and Miss Lavender; he gulps an entire jug of drinking water, and drops upon his bed.

He wakes to loud knocking on his door; it is a maid. 'Mr Lovelock,' she is saying, 'we thought you was riding to Te Wairoa today.' His timepiece tells him that it is appallingly near noon; he should have been swiftly on his way hours ago. He rises in panic, trying to piece himself together. Guilt grates in his head. How could he have wandered so far from his mission, and Luke? Within half an hour he has departed Ohinemutu in haste; and without his promised farewell to Hilda.

The winding road to Te Wairoa, though picturesque, tests his patience. His travel-weary horse is unwilling to be persuaded into more than a vague trot; and has to be rested even on gentle rises. Forest and lake pass. Up in the hills frost still lingers under the fern. He is grateful to leave the smell of sulphur behind. Finally he descends into a green pastoral valley; there are English trees flecked with the last rusty leaves of autumn. He rides into a tolerably pleasing village, with a church, a schoolhouse, a mill, a store or two, cottages and gardens and Maori dwellings set high above the shore of a large blue lake. The mountain beyond is unmistakable. It is rugged, without singular shape, rising sheer from the water. And of the uncommonly dark tinge which Marie Louise also proposed. Please, he prays, let Luke be here. With a shiver of anticipation, he reins in at McRae's hotel. It is a prosperous and imposing two-storey affair, assertive of solidity with the best native woods. McRae himself surfaces soon enough. A bearded tidy-talking man, with the deeply fissured forehead of a onetime seaman, he fails at first to understand James.

'Slow down,' he pleads.

James begins again. 'I am looking for a young man. A relative. One lost many years ago, kidnapped by Maoris. I have reason to believe that he may be dwelling among them in this vicinity.'

'A queer story,' McRae observes. He adds suddenly, 'My God, man. You must be talking of Ruke.'

James is quite faint. 'Luke,' he says. 'You know him?'

'Ay. Blue-eyed Ruke. His native name. I know the lad.'

'And he's here?'

'Near enough. He's across the water. The other side of the lake, under the mountain. He's been living there, with his people, as long as I've been here.'

'With his people?'

'The people of Te Ariki village. His kin.'

'He has other kin.'

'Not the way I heard it from Ruke himself. To people made curious by the colour of his skin he says he was made orphan in some distant tragedy. And then adopted and cared for by people who came to Te Ariki from the west; he has never had wish to leave them, though some have tried to persuade him to seek his fortune in the white world. He's too happy a lad to care greatly for fortune-seeking.'

'One detail,' James says, breathless. 'Does he wear, about his neck, a large old crucifix?'

McRae thinks. 'Ay. He does.'

'He is my nephew, then,' James declares. 'I have come to take him home to his father, still living, and his stepmother, both of whom grieve for him greatly. I am here in consequence of a long search, spurred by his stepmother's notion that he is alive, after all, and in danger.'

'Danger?' McRae says shortly.

'So she would have it.'

'We like no loose talk of that nature in these parts. It can cost us custom.'

'I'm sorry,' James says diplomatically.

'To my taste,' aggrieved McRae says, 'there has been too much of it in recent days.'

'What do you mean?'

'I mean there is no hazard here. See for yourself. The place is all peace. The tourists come to wonder at the great terraces. Ruke – or Luke, if you like – and his people prosper by selling them fruit and cooked crayfish when they cross the lake.'

'I should like to venture across the lake to find him,' James says. 'As soon as possible.'

'You'll not get a boatman to take you across the lake now.'

'Why not?'

'Too late in the day.'

'It is hours until dark,' James protests.

'You should have been here this morning to join the tourists on the regular voyage.'

'I should pay well for the inconvenience.'

McRae is uncomfortable. 'Listen. Wait for tomorrow. Take the tourist craft.'

'But why cannot I hire some Maori boatman now?'

'Because you will not find one willing. Take my word. Most mornings, now, men have to be argued and bribed into taking the tourist craft.'

'But why?' James persists.

'In my experience,' McRae replies, 'there is no accounting for human superstition. Now, do you want a bed for the night or no?'

'Thank you,' James says finally.

'You'll find your kinsman tomorrow,' McRae promises.

Impatient James finds only one fellow guest in the hotel; the others are across the lake partaking of that apparently celestial experience called the Pink and White Terraces, and having their photographs taken as proof. This guest, Edwin Bainbridge, a gentle moon-faced young man lately out from England, has done his sightseeing. Earthbound again, after his exhilaratingly heavenward climb, he has been hunting pheasant, and is now cleaning his gun on the hotel veranda. To Bainbridge James confides his frustration. 'What is wrong here?' he asks. 'And why McRae so surly?'

'He has difficulties.'

'No doubt. So have we all.'

'His are of unusual nature. Did he not tell you?'

'He seemed averse to telling me anything. Other than that I could not cross the lake this afternoon.'

'Perhaps I should not disconcert you either. But I daresay you will hear it whispered soon enough.'

'What might I hear whispered?'

'The tale of the canoe. A few days ago, before I arrived here, some tourists on the lake, and their Maori guides, had an experience of an unsettling kind. There was a priest in the party, I understand, and a doctor; most sober and reliable people. Shortly after their excursion began they sighted, on the lake waters, a large Maori war canoe.'

'Well? Why should that so unsettle them?'

'No such large canoe has been seen on the lake in the memory of any man living. It travelled silently through the winter mist. Some of the occupants were paddling. Others were standing wrapped in flaxen robes. Their heads were lowered, and their hair plumed with the feathers of rare birds. They made no acknowledgement of the tourist vessel when hailed. Finally it was understood that all in the canoe were not of this world; they were dead.'

James is silent.

'I am sorry,' Bainbridge says. 'I find it displeasing to talk further of this. It is a melancholy subject, best left in the mists. I venture this account only to explain McRae's present state. Such phantoms can be interpreted as omens, and are not conducive to commercial success here. The Maoris, as is their nature, have made the most of the affair; an aged tribal priest has been prophesying doom. McRae thus far has failed to buy him into silence. More and more monetary inducements are necessary to get Maori guides to travel the lake. McRae is at his wits' end.'

'No doubt,' James says. 'So am I. To be so near my goal, and now stranded so trivially.' He pauses. 'And what do you believe?'

'Me? I believe something not easily explicable has been seen. That much is apparent. I have talked to witnesses.'

'And you think it may be an omen?'

Bainbridge shrugs. 'Possibly.'

'Of doom?'

'I cannot presume to say.'

'You linger here. Why?'

'There is good hunting.'

'There is good hunting elsewhere, in regions less disposed to harbour phantoms and omens.'

'I do not take issue with Providence,' Bainbridge insists. 'If all is provided for, who am I to argue?' Bainbridge renews the cleaning of his gun with great concentration. 'I am by no means averse to reunion with my loved ones.'

'Who isn't?' James says, though thinking of incarnate Luke.

'My father died when I was but seven. My mother followed soon after. Last year my brother Cuthbert perished from a gunshot wound, it would seem self-inflicted. My one sister May fell into a rare fatal illness. That left me alone. I was prompted to travel to the ends of the earth. I seem to have found peace almost at its brink. I have never felt more at home. If my restlessness has gone, along with my grief, why should I move?'

Having accomplished his task, Bainbridge peers down the barrels of his shotgun, and appears altogether satisfied. Disquieted James is soon relieved to see other faces. First, sightseers back from their expedition across the lake, with scarce a crease in their elegant attire; they appear quite unhaunted by the experience, with no intelligence of phantom canoes abroad, merely of the delight inherent in taking their first tentative steps up the exquisitely glittering path to paradise; they are alight with the seductive nature of their day. Then a carriage comes bearing more guests from Ohinemutu, to travel the lake next morning. Not the least of these arrivals are Augustus and Hilda Lavender, to remind James of his recent and now regretted delinquency. Had it not been for Hilda, he might now be across the lake, in joyful reunion with Luke, and persuading his nephew home to the Porangi. It appears, however, that he has a carnal gauntlet of immodest proportion to run again. Yet an evening with Hilda must be immensely preferred to one with, say, the melancholy Bainbridge and the moody McRae. There is no point, as Bainbridge suggests, in taking ungracious issue with Providence.

'An agreeable surprise,' James says.

'I felt need to see you again,' Hilda explains. 'All day I have been thinking of nothing else. It is fortunate you informed me of where you were bound. Father, you remember Mr Lovelock, don't you?'

'Peacock?' Augustus says. 'Thomas Love Peacock? A fancy sort of poet. Fact is, I could never stomach the damn fellow. All words.'

'No, Father. Mr Lovelock.'

'Lovelace?'

'Lovelock.'

'Hilda, I can assure you Lovelace did not write *Rape of the Lock*. After his time. Pope wrote it, girl. Pope.'

'I hoped,' Hilda confides, 'that the carriage ride might jog father into fuller possession of his faculties. Alas; it seems further to have confused him. Father, come along now. We must feed you and get you to bed. An early night would be in your interests.' To James she adds shamelessly, 'And ours. We shall be together again soon.'

She speaks with great conviction. While the Lavenders are ushered to their rooms by McRae, James avoids conversation with the earnest Bainbridge, now sitting idle with the gun across his knee, by taking a walk through the village and down the dusty track to the lake. All is quiet again. The carriage has departed for Ohinemutu with that day's sightseers. He watches the early winter sunset colouring lake and mountain. Birds farewell the last of the light. There is no wind; the lake is calm. James tells himself, with some passion, that tomorrow he will be crossing the lake to find Luke; that Marie Louise's fancy is now only hours from accomplished fact. Before long serene lake and mountain dim and disappear; he walks back to the hotel in the chilly dark. McRae has large log fires burning in dining room and drawing room. No accommodation could be warmer or more amiable. Bainbridge, the Lavenders and McRae are already dining; there are only one or two other guests. It is the winter season, McRae explains. Trade is slack. So also is conversation at the table, though it is now and then filled out by Augustus Lavender, who feels impelled to discuss the demerits and unkempt personal lives of certain dear deceased literary friends and acquaintances. Hilda's eyes rest steadily upon James; he finds this disconcerting.

'For those who may be interested,' McRae says, 'there is an occultation of the moon tonight.'

'Of what nature?' James asks.

'At twenty minutes past ten, Mars will move close to the moon, disappear for a time, and emerge on the other side.'

'I fear I shall be abed by then,' Hilda informs the company. 'I confess to no great fascination with the movement of heavenly bodies.'

Her sly sidelong glance at James, together with a suggestive twitch of lips, makes it apparent that she anticipates greater interest in bodily movements more terrestrial. He feels a flinching of the spirit. One night never to be forgotten is enough; his energy is still at ebb.

'I shall share the experience with you,' Bainbridge tells McRae. 'I lose no opportunity to witness the handiwork of God. Praise Him.'

'Amen,' James says. 'But I regret that I need to be fresh for tomorrow's travelling.'

'What's that?' Augustus demands of his daughter.

'We are talking of Mars, Father,' Hilda shouts. 'And the moon.'

'*The Moonstone*,' Augustus asserts, 'is a damn fine book. I told Wilkie so.'

'No, Father. We are talking of an occulation.'

'The occult? Many's the time I sat with Betty Barrett Browning watching Dan Douglas Home move furniture around like matchsticks. Damned if I don't think it was real. I saw a piano float clear across a room, and two chairs jump on top of it. Then Dan himself drifted up to the ceiling. I had to grab his legs before the spirits flew him out a window. Don't talk to me about the occult, girl. I've seen it all.'

'Of course, Father.'

'Bob Browning, you know, was infernally jealous. He called Dan Home Mr Sludge the fake. Exceptionally nasty poem. Fake? Never. I'm more inclined to agree with Hawthorne in that area. Nat said it was all a bit of a bore. When you've seen one ghost, you've seen them all.'

McRae, presumably perturbed by thought of phantom canoes, is uncomfortable with the turn the conversation is taking; his guests are steered toward the fire in the drawing room, and Hilda removes Augustus to his room for the night. She then reappears in the drawing room with the clear intention of similarly removing James as soon as discretion permits. McRae is liberal with brandy for his guests, but Bainbridge temperately declines all alcohol; he asks instead for tea, which is ordered from the kitchen. This leads to consternation on the part of the cook. He arrives from the kitchen to announce that the kettle will not boil.

'Use your wits,' McRae says. 'Build the fire bigger.'

'I've done that,' the cook insists. 'It still won't boil. It must be something in the air.'

'Nonsense,' McRae says.

'It's a fact. See for yourself.'

'Thank you, Mr McRae,' Bainbridge says, to keep the peace, 'but I shall do without tea.'

Hilda rises. 'Alas,' she says, 'but I cannot do without bed.'
'Nor I,' James adds after a suitable interval.
'Whoever heard of a kettle that won't boil?' McRae is still muttering as James departs the drawing room.
In his cold bedroom, James lights his lamp and moves to the window. The countryside beyond is calm and slowly silvering. In the distance, a dog howls at the rising moon; soon others take up that mournful canine cry. Beginning to shiver, for reasons beyond his control, he is suddenly glad of the soft knock on his door and Hilda's warm arrival in his arms. 'Dearest James,' she says. 'You are so chill. Never fear; something in the air tells me I shall bring you fast to the boil. You have a woman burning bright with the fire of love.'
This cannot fairly be denied. And he finds, after all, no infirmity of flesh. He is soon as Mars to her moon. Hilda's mouth is awash with tender obscenities. At some point past midnight, with James proceeding into his third or perhaps fourth occultation, their mutual animation apparently begins to produce extraordinary phenomena, worthy of Daniel Douglas Home himself. A wardrobe detaches itself from the floor and starts wandering about the room. The oil lamp, long extinguished, floats briefly in the air and shatters against a wall. Curtains swell and flutter free of the windows. Finally the room fills with strange lights, 'My God,' ecstatic Hilda cries, 'we are taking the world with us.'
Past ecstasy, however, the hotel continues to reverberate; to shake itself apart with creaking, cracking sounds. The bed, no longer agitated by their endeavours, continues to heave of its own accord. Hilda's heartfelt sighs cease abruptly.
'James,' she says in panic.
'I know,' he answers.
There is a low, growing roar beneath them.
'This is bigger than us,' she is obliged to say.
'It seems so,' he confesses.
The room is determined to develop a sideways tilt.
'No,' Hilda says.
'Yes,' he announces.
'It is out of hand.'
James is silent.
'Say something, dearest.'
McRae says it. He is calling down the corridor. 'All downstairs. No need for alarm. It is just another earthquake.'
James falls back upon his pillow with a large expression of relief; all else is surely anti-climax. Hilda, with feminine expressions of alarm, is less philosophical. She pushes him out of bed.

They are soon dressed and downstairs with sleepy Augustus, who declines to be removed from nightshirt and nightcap. Bainbridge already stands stiff in the drawing room, Bible in hand. McRae is fetching servant girls and other guests. The hotel windows flicker with something akin to lightning. The roaring outside does not diminish.

James opens the front door and takes a speculative step into the night. He is all but gusted off his feet by a giant wind. Trees are clashing and crashing in a gale. At first he cannot comprehend the cause. Then he does. The mountain is a thing of many lights; the sky is inflamed.

He returns to tell those assembled in the drawing room, 'It is no earthquake. It is the mountain.'

'The mountain?'

'In eruption,' he explains.

McRae, just back with the servant girls, is inclined to argue. 'That mountain is no volcano, man.'

'Nevertheless,' James says, 'it is under that impression now. And, I should hazard, not easily to be disabused of its current identity.'

In confirmation there is another jolt, and still louder roaring underfoot. This even penetrates the deafness of Augustus.

'Russian cannon,' he claims. 'Into the valley of death rode the six hundred.'

'We are not in the Crimea, Father,' Hilda reveals. 'We are in New Zealand.'

'New Zealand?'

'Yes.'

'Damn me, girl, why didn't you say so?'

McRae staggers outside with James. The mountain, in moments, becomes even more impressive. Fire now soars skyward from several vents. And the lights are no less spectacular; the Milky Way appears to be drifting earthward. Terrified Maori villagers are running to take refuge in the hotel. It seems they have long known of a giant lizard locked in the mountain; they presume it to be indicating its displeasure at human indifference.

Hilda arrives outside with James, and holds his arm. 'It is a splendid sight,' she says calmly. 'Are we to die?'

'I think not,' McRae announces optimistically. 'It is a good ten miles away.'

'But the people on the other side of the lake,' James says. 'What of them?'

'They will doubtless be taking shelter,' McRae assures him.

'I should like to launch a boat and get across there.'

'At night? Madness, man.'

'This night is turning to day,' James observes. It is true. Hills and trees are reddening as if in vivid dawn.

'Besides,' McRae adds, 'the journey would take you beneath the mountain. Into the vicinity of the eruption.'

'All the same,' James says.

'Time enough for the journey when the mountain quietens,' McRae argues. 'None would keep you company now.'

'Then I shall go by myself.' James disengages from Hilda.

'James,' she says. 'Please.'

'Wait,' McRae shouts.

James soon hears neither; he runs down the steep track to the lake, skidding, falling, but on his way to Luke. Trees tumble about him. In the glow of the mountain he sees several boats on the shore, with oars neatly shipped. He selects the smallest, and pushes it down a sandy slope. The lake rises to meet him, with the blood-coloured waves growing large. He flings himself aboard, falls breathless at the bottom of the boat, and fights upward to gain the oars and some grip on the lake. It is drunkenly intent on hurling him back to shore again, or worse. The volcano, at which he prefers not to look, offers still more bruising cacophony to his brain. The boat begins to spin, the oars are torn from his grasp like twigs; the entire lake lifts, quite mountainously, and he is no longer in the boat, but human debris strung in the branches of a cliffside tree. The shore of the lake, beneath, is ceasing to exist. The first fireballs are falling.

Perhaps an hour later, through ash and falling stones, across shattered trees, and among dwellings ablaze, James makes sufficient sense of the reeling terrain to find his way back to those still huddled in the hotel. Pale Hilda embraces him with relief. Most are given to prayers and hymns. Bainbridge, in a seeming transport of joy, locates apt Biblical consolation. 'Whosoever shall seek to save his life, shall lose it,' he reads. 'Whosoever shall lose his life shall preserve it.' Augustus aside, Bainbridge has an attentive audience. Augustus has recalled the natives of New Zealand as always unnecessarily excitable, not to say damn irritating, and resumed his disturbed night's sleep after consumption of most of the available brandy.

'God be with us now,' Bainbridge says. 'Our lives are in thy hands. Have mercy and forgive. Lead us on the straightest road to Heaven.'

James now understands that Bainbridge, in pursuit of his deceased loved ones, has travelled to earth's end to set foot, at last, on that road; he seems determined not to miss a moment of his extinction.

To Hilda, James is gently mocking. 'I trust you have your necessary narrative interest now,' he says. 'Is there upheaval enough to leave flesh and spirit tingling?'

'It is, of course, the end,' she replies. 'We are to perish as the people of Pompeii.'

This prediction is given some emphasis as the roof of the hotel discloses its frail nature; it collapses under the bombardment of rock. The upper story is crushed. The staircase disappears; there is much dust. Mud begins to drip through the perforated ceiling. An insidious excrement, reeking of the earth's hot bowels.

'We are besieged,' McRae says.

'By God,' Bainbridge announces. 'Bid him enter your hearts.'

'The hell with this,' James tells Hilda. 'We are waiting to die.' He takes her hand firmly. 'We must look for some safer construction, elsewhere in the village.'

'But Father?'

'We will come back for him. And the others.'

'We will wait,' McRae agrees. 'If you cannot return, we will take our own chances.'

Outside there are the descending fireballs again, and trees and houses alight. James and Hilda cover their heads with a blanket. But stones nevertheless strike them to dazing effect. And the thickening mud drags at their feet. Presently they blunder against a building; a Maori cottage, abandoned. It seems solid, still undamaged; it is certainly a temporary shelter. James drags Hilda within. 'Hold me,' she asks. 'If we are discovered in death, let our bodies be entwined.' While James finds this prospect of severance from flesh preferable to Bainbridge's passivity, it is short of acceptable. Nevertheless he holds Hilda tight, to calm her, as rocks crash upon the iron roof. 'I must go back,' he argues presently. 'And fetch the others.'

But when he tries the door again, it will not give. Striking a match, he sees that it has been made inert by the pressure of the mud, and is even beginning to bulge inward; likewise the walls of the cottage. The windows are too tiny for escape. They are quite trapped.

'So hold me,' Hilda says again. 'Let our last minute make a legend, at least.'

James moves toward her at the moment the cottage crumples. They are thrown to the floor as the roof descends. James tries to rise. He cannot. They are both pinned by a beam. Above the beam is iron. And above the iron mud and rock still mount. He has just one arm free. 'Hilda,' he says, and hears her sigh. She is alive, if altogether confined by the beam across her shoulders; he feels her face and then, with horror, the mud rising around. He seems to be saved from the same peril by a table tilted above his head; he can breathe. Upon Hilda the mud falls in sputtering cataract. He tries to pull her toward him. She is not to be moved.

'James,' she says.

'Yes?' He pushes mud clear of her face.

'Let us live while there is time.'

'Of course,' he agrees.

'Take me home with you. To your farm. As your love. Your bride.'

'Now?'

'Now. Take me.'

James takes her. His verbal voyage, at first hesitant, soon lacks nothing in intensity, or colour. He rows her up the Porangi and delivers her to the landing at Spanish Creek. She is enthused by the spectacle, by the promise implicit in their journey. He does his fervent best to confirm her first impression that he is more poet than farmer. Together they walk his green acres. It is spring. The sky is blue. Lambs bleat, and bound over the grass. Then there is the homestead, and the marriage bed. Years pass pastorally, and blissfully. There is never an ill word spoken. Hilda has happiness. So has James. Their lives fill with light.

All the while, never flagging, he tries with his free hand to clear the cruel mud so that Hilda can continue to breathe.

'Go on,' she whispers. 'Quickly. Please.'

They age. James is white-haired, and Hilda gently greying. David is now of sufficient maturity to take upon himself most large tasks of the farm. James and Hilda can devote themselves to that which gives them most pleasure, now in the realm of spirit rather than flesh. They share their thoughts, making their peace with the past, while watching the sunsets; they see out their contest with time. They laugh at the antics of animals, ponder the more capricious qualities of the passing seasons.

'And we die,' Hilda says.

'We die,' James agrees.

The foul slime is now beginning to cover her mouth, despite his best efforts. His hand is cramping; his fingers refusing to contain the mud.

'I rather think I die in your arms,' she manages to say, 'at the age of eighty-seven years. You, in grief, survive me but a month or two.'

'No more,' he affirms. 'I have not the heart left for life upon your passing.'

'There,' she says. 'I cannot complain.'

'Nor I.'

'And then?' she asks.

'Then?'

'Beyond death. What then?'

'Ah,' James says, and swiftly and passionately fixes a kiss upon her forehead with the strength which remains in his fingers. In moments there is only mud to feel; Hilda has gone.

Fifteen hours later James sees light in irregular form. It has been shaped by the shovels of a search party. Understanding this at length, he cries out. 'There's a live one here,' someone shouts. He is soon dragged clear of the sticky debris by McRae, among others. McRae pronounces that James has no bones broken; he produces brandy. Meanwhile, Maoris dig out Hilda's corpse.

'What of the rest?' James asks.

'Augustus is safe,' McRae assures him. 'And on his way to hospital. We took shelter, finally, in a smaller dwelling, like yourselves, and propped the beams with our bodies. I lost only one other guest.'

'Bainbridge?'

'He has met his Maker. Along with many here less willing.'

'And across the lake? The other villages?'

'No news.' McRae is sombre. He makes some effort to clean James, with a bucket of murky water.

'None at all?'

'None. And the lake is still too poisonous to make a crossing. But my God, man, what has happened to you?'

'To me? Nothing. I live, as you see.'

'But your hair.'

'What of my hair?'

'White, man. Pure white.'

James watches as the human form of Hilda is carried clear of the cottage, wrapped in a blanket, and borne away to rest beside other bodies collected in the village.

'You look a score of years older,' McRae persists.

'Perhaps,' James says with indifference.

He cannot recognize his surroundings; they are beyond recognition. The village has gone but for a few rooftops and treetops. Hills and valley are under a bleak cover of blue mud. There are shapes identifiable as dead cattle and pigs. Blind and bewildered birds and slimy rats stagger across the terrain. Humans are few, and mostly grieving Maoris in search parties. The mountain still smokes.

'I must get across the lake,' James insists.

'In good time,' McRae proposes. 'Think yourself lucky you did not get across yesterday.'

'In that case,' James says, 'it seems I have a guardian angel to thank for my survival. One who detained and delayed me. It seems, for once, I might have misconstrued the nature of carnality. Beyond it was grace.'

'What are you talking of, man?' McRae plainly fears delirium.

'Of my bride,' James says, to confuse McRae further. 'My lost bride, it would seem. Perhaps she understood I was not free to follow her to the grave.'

'Come on, man. Lean on my shoulder. You've had enough. As for your nephew—'

'Yes?'

'Trust in God.'

'It would be charitable to believe He has no part in this.'

'In His mercy, then.'

'It is, at this moment, impossible to discern,' James says, as he limps past an untidy pile of excavated bodies, stifled Hilda now conspicuous among them. He is impelled to pause, and take her hand for the last time. Her hand is cold. So are her lips, when he finds them.

'We must believe,' McRae says, kindly.

'I am willing to hear one convincing word in His favour,' James replies. 'Thus far, I fear, He has to be found guilty.'

It is two days before a fit search party can be mustered, and a whale boat brought overland, for the crossing of the lake. At first there is no place for James in the party. But a government geologist, who has hastened to the region on horseback, declines to board the boat. 'It is death out there,' he announces. James is then allowed to join with those prepared to risk renewed eruption and toxic gases. Out on the lake, as they row, the fumes are strong. They shred shirts to cover mouth and nostrils with cotton. The surface of the lake is often semi-solid with ash, debris, torn trees. The mountain smokes blackly above them.

Before long the worst fears for the remaining lakeside villagers are confirmed. Moura is under perhaps one hundred feet of still steaming mud. Te Ariki, where Luke lived, is even more immensely lost. When they attempt to set foot ashore, they are driven back to the boat by the heat, and mud moving in avalanche. Ash falls lightly on their faces. The Maoris in the party give out sounds of mourning; their relatives, taken by death in terrible form, will never be seen again. James is not heard to speak during the entire expedition. Finally, it seems, the paradisial Pink and White Terraces, every shiny silica stair, every precious particle, have likewise forever been lost to sight of man. There is just a landscape of hell, all brimstone and boiling streams; and the suffocating mud of the underworld. They turn back.

*

At Lovelock Junction the eruption manifests as earthquake; Marie Louise is woken in the night by the crashing of copper pans in her kitchen, and after much effort manages to call Herman's attention to the phenomenon. Felicity runs down the corridor, crying out operatically, in her nightgown. Sylvester Spring blearily follows soon. He has been shaken from a dream of leading his pupil on to the stage of La Scala for her first audition. Now he finds a performance in progress. All race outside. Soon they hear, seemingly, the sound of gunfire inland. Before dawn there is perceptible glow in the sky; it is too malevolent to be seen as the sun. Marie Louise, who alone knows where James has gone, remains mute for days after, as the skies darken with ash. Herman, investigating the effects of earthquake, finds cracks in Lovelock House, none sufficiently serious to warrant alarm, though the tower – on second thought – seems slightly out of true and is perhaps best climbed with caution.

At the end of a week, the earthquakes diminish. The skies clear. The ash melts away; mornings are bright with clean frost. The crew of a steamer brings news of the devastation in the hot heart of the country, and of many lives lost. Marie Louise is still not audible. Her lips, nevertheless, are often seen moving. Even the Malones stop gossiping to marvel when, still in disarray, she passes silently down Little Luke Lane on her way to Dixtown and the jetty in hope of overhearing more news of the disaster. There is no more; not until the land surrenders James alive. He arrives lonely and weak back on the Porangi, a far from familiar figure. It is not merely his white hair; his frame is gaunt, his face the colour of a corpse, and his eyes seem bruised. His voice has become that of a stranger.

'Luke is not to be found,' he tells her with authority. Lest she quibble, he adds, 'Luke is never to be found. Never. There is no place conforming to your description in the interior. You were wrong. My journey was fruitless, and near fatal. Ask no more of me.'

He refuses to celebrate his survival. He returns swiftly to Spanish Creek, to his son David, and is not seen again for many months. Even Benjamin is never burdened by knowledge of where James has been, or what he has witnessed. Though tempted to ask, Benjamin knows the meaning of discretion. Iris agrees. 'It is enough that he is back with us,' she says. 'Be thankful for that, for David's sake too.' She has reason to say so. There has never been more impassioned a father, or farmer, than James Lovelock. But there will always be mystery. Older, David asks, 'Who is Hilda? And why do you call her name in the night?'

His father is not disposed to make satisfying answer.

*

('After the tragic accidental drowning of his wife while visiting her mother,' alleges the romancer of *The Lives of Lovelock Junction*, 'James was apparently compelled to travel by way of losing his grief. Perhaps the Porangi suffered him too many reminders of marital happiness. This explains his presence in the vicinity of the Tarawera eruption in 1886, when a great part of the interior of the North Island was laid waste, and the entire country clouded with volcanic debris. He was among the last to glimpse the fabled Pink and White Terraces, virtually in the shadow of Mount Tarawera, before their destruction. He was also considered somewhat fortunate to have lived through the eruption, his proximity considered. On the other hand, an author, seeking out survivors in later years, is known to have travelled up the Porangi to question James; in a footnote the author records an inexplicable rebuff, with the near libellous inference that some might have reason to recall their part in the affair with shame. In the most vivid contemporary account, *Polynesia Regained*, by the English author Augustus Lavender – who was also in the vicinity, and whose daughter perished – James Lovelock is not mentioned at all. Much of Lavender's moving narrative concerns the valiant attempt of a young English tourist, a buoyant bon vivant named Edwin Bainbridge, to preserve his daughter's life; Bainbridge was to perish too while proving his British grit. At all events James remains a perhaps decently obscure participant. Further speculation seems superfluous.'

So too, on second thought, is commentary.)

James is not alone in finding the Porangi a refuge. Richard, after his more metaphoric scorching in the outside world, has a sanctuary too; his house is a place of astringent silences, punctuated by the clinking of bottle and glass, with accompanying obscenities. Also, sometimes, there is randomly directed gunfire to make for curiosity among the inhabitants of Dixtown; and, afterwards, walls and windows to be repaired. His dreams are often terrifying. He does not attempt to locate substitutes for Ernest and Paramena; to trust others again would be to prolong the agony. He is back to shovelling shit, if mostly at second hand. In pursuit of better quality coal, his mines must be pushed deeper into the hills. There are accidents, fatalities, irritating stoppages of output. He mills further into the forests, over steeper land, for profitable lines of timber; production is slower, and prices poorer. He cuts wages when inclined, and he is frequently inclined, given his desire to do better than balance his books. The fact is, the Porangi has been creamed; skimmed milk is meagre sustenance. Nor is a diet of Spanish Creek mutton alone satisfying fare.

Socially, Dixtown does not quite do without him. Alcoholic occasions aside, there are rowdy Saturday night dances at which Richard sometimes makes himself visible, especially when lack of female company begins to seem significant. Sometimes too there are concerts from touring parties impoverished enough to risk the journey to the isolated community in hope of a paying audience. On one occasion, drawn by sight of a strangely promising woman arriving on the jetty, Richard purchases a ticket for a performance by an acrobatic troupe called The Flying Flynns. The woman, whose spangled costume reveals her as even more shapely than Richard first supposed, is part of this troupe; she is bounced and spun about the platform by four muscular brothers, and later does a dizzying solo turn on trapeze. Richard finds desire reaching intense proportions. Nor is it to be denied. He makes it his business to entertain the troupe in his house, with the best booze available. The woman's name is Nancy. She is, with her brothers, from Sydney; they have been travelling small antipodean towns for longer than anyone cares to recall. These are depressed times. It shows in their faces. Close, Nancy's lips have a hard line; she also has a hard laugh. Richard is not disconcerted. His preference is for substance in a woman. Her brothers are a surly crew, clearly suspicious of Richard's hospitality; his attention to Nancy does nothing to dispel their surliness. Eventually, after whispering among themselves, they make moves to leave; they indicate that Nancy's departure is also expected.

'Go to hell,' she tells them, accepting another drink from Richard. 'I have my own life.'

Though apparently unwilling to accept this, the four male acrobats nevertheless file out into the night, leaving Nancy alone with Richard. 'I don't wish to make for family feud,' he says, though without large conviction.

'Forget it,' she says. 'They aren't really my brothers anyway. They are just a drear lot of smellers it is my misfortune to be lumbered with. I used to work with my husband. He got killed on the trapeze. I had no other business. I been on the road with them ever since.'

'A hard life,' Richard suggests.

'It gets no easier,' she admits. 'Look, you want to sleep with me?'

Richard is not accustomed to such conversation turning to intimacy so soon; on the other hand he is by no means averse to speeding preliminaries. Before he can convey interest, she adds, 'If you do, there's no time like the present. They'll be back soon. Those four.'

'What for?'

'Me,' she says. 'But mostly you. They aren't dainty.'

'I don't follow.'

'Their strong arms aren't just for the stage. When pickings are lean, they can always cut up rough, in their brotherly way, about finding me in someone's bed. Like yours. And leave town with their pockets better padded.'

'You're talking about blackmail. Or money with menaces.'

She is indifferent to his definitions. 'It's a good act,' she observes. 'Four furious brothers.'

'Why tell me?'

'Because I'm getting fed up to the back teeth with the buggers, the way they use me. Besides, I like the look of you.'

'Take that as mutual,' he tells her.

'Good,' she says. 'That's always a help.' She pauses. 'I can go.'

'No,' he insists.

'So where's your bed?'

He leads her. 'Just one thing,' he asks. 'Why me?'

'Because I need something for myself for once. Not them. That's why you. It's time to get off. Come on. They generally need all of an hour or two to fill themselves with enough outrage, and gin.'

Later, after justice has been done to Richard's bed, he and Nancy dress and return to the living room. Richard is unusually satisfied by the experience. There is a vicious quality in her lovemaking which he finds fulfilling. Moreover, he feels far from sated. Her strong and supple body might have more to tell him. 'What now?' he asks.

'I leave,' she proposes. 'Before they arrive.'

'The hell with that. Why should you?'

'You could be sorry.'

'They might be more so.' He takes a revolver from a drawer, and checks the contents of its chamber. 'This is my house. My territory.'

'I can see a real man,' she announces. 'But thanks all the same. I'll leave quick and quiet.'

'Do you want to?'

'Now you mention it, no. But the fact is those four are my bread and butter. I got no one else.'

'Stay,' he argues.

'It's not worth it. Fists. A gun. I'm worse off.'

'I mean stay with me here. On the river.'

'Is this a proposal,' she asks, astonished, 'or a paying proposition?'

'Suit yourself. It's all one to me.'

'You do want me bad, don't you?'

Richard takes this as read. 'Well?'

'Sorry. Those buggers would give me no peace. They'd be back. I'm all they have too.'

'I see,' Richard says. 'So it's like that.'

'So to speak,' she agrees. 'I can't say it isn't satisfying, for a woman. One man tires faster than four.'

'No doubt.' Richard is bitter.

'You had your fun. Don't go on. Put the gun away.' She rises. 'I know what the end of the road looks like; I been there and back. It's not the end of this river. I can't see myself here.'

'I would,' he vows, pouring more brandy, 'make it well worth your while.'

'I've heard drunken promises before.'

'I mean it. Sit down.'

She continues to stand. In consequence Richard is obliged to present the revolver in her direction. She sits, rather breathless. She also, after a pause, takes the brimming glass Richard pushes across the table with his free hand.

'My God,' she says at last, with some awe.

They wait, mainly in silence, with more brandy consumed, until violent knocking on his door. The four spurious brothers stand there. They find Richard not in post-coital disarray, hair untidy and shirt hanging out, but cool and dressed, revolver in hand. Nevertheless they keep meticulously to their script. 'You have been,' claims the foremost, 'seducing our sister.' 'Where's our Nancy?' demands another. By way of answer, Richard fires a shot over their heads. 'Piss off,' he instructs them, with some scorn. They decline to take him with the gravity which might appear appropriate to their situation; they are, perhaps, too intimate with danger. They continue to advance brawnily upon Richard, familiarity with their role breeding contempt, and then considerably more. Backing off, Richard fires two shots into the faces of the brothers most immediately menacing. They collapse bloodily to the floor. The remaining two brothers flee. It is plain they cannot be left to live. He shoots them both down before they have travelled five yards from his door. One needs a second shot to the head. Soon none stirs.

'No,' Nancy whispers.

'Yes,' he insists.

She gives off a whining sound. 'Not me too?'

'Never,' he promises.

He drags the outdoor bodies back to the house. There are still lights visible in Dixtown. A few; not many. There are fewer still after the gunfire.

'What now?' she breathes.

'Wire,' he says, 'and old iron.'

'Wire?' Her voice is faint. 'Old iron?'

'To sink them fast.'

In shock, she is inclined to be retrospective. 'Did you have to?' she asks.

'I meant only to maim. But they forced the issue. Self-defence. You saw that.'

'Is that what I have to tell the police?'

'Not with those four in the river. No. I'll manage the police.'

'Why the river?'

'Cleaner. The bloody police pester. Give them four bodies, and gunshot wounds, and they'll make a murderer of a man.'

'The police will still want to know where they went.'

'No doubt. The buggers like to pry.'

'So?'

'So we shall have to sweeten their drear lives with a different tale.'

Some time later, after the lengthy matter of wiring the bodies durably to available old iron, and sinking them in a sufficiently deep part of the Porangi, Richard launches a dinghy into the river and overturns it. Then he casts a couple of oars upon the dark water.

'I don't doubt,' he says to Nancy, 'that you recall how we argued against it.'

'Against what?'

'Against their drunken determination to take a midnight jaunt on the river. Alas, they were too fired with brandy and bravado to listen.'

'But the shots?'

'I daresay no one in Dixtown heard any shots,' Richard says with confidence. 'Not to speak of.'

'The bodies?'

'Swept out to sea, I don't doubt.'

When the police arrive a week later, on receipt of information from Richard, they are provided with a cautionary tale on the perils of the Porangi. The riverbanks are searched. Guns are fired to help the bodies rise. They never do. Questions are addressed respectfully to Richard, less so to the surviving member of the troupe, a woman commonly known as Nancy Flynn whom their files reveal to have several convictions recorded against her, largely minor frauds. They are not altogether satisfied by her answers; there are several discrepancies in her account and Richard's as given to the inquest summarily convened at Dixtown. On instructions, the police make a second visit to the Porangi, and they discover it is now pointless pursuing discrepancies;

the woman commonly known as Nancy Flynn is now Mrs Richard Lovelock, suspicious enough, but in the circumstances nothing can be done; a wife cannot be obliged to testify against her husband. Or, for that matter, a husband against a wife. And there are clearly no other material witnesses to the possible events of that curious night when the male members of the Flying Flynns flew this life as one. None in Dixtown can be persuaded to say he or she heard or saw anything of unusual nature.

In the course of questioning, however, the otherwise frustrated police locate a distillery of elaborate construction, the discovery of which justifies their journeys up the Porangi, and makes for much needed distraction from the untimely deaths of the acrobats. Richard demonstrates his capacity for outrage when the matter is brought to his attention; two of his more senior employees are later prosecuted and imprisoned for sly-grogging offences. A handful of long-wanted men are also picked up and taken shackled to New Plymouth in the course of the investigation. It is concluded that the Porangi is territory in which law and order might profitably be pioneered; a constable is thereafter stationed upriver. Dixtown, older identities soon say, isn't the same. With the loss of Paramena's long established distillery, nor is Dixtown Dream; it is now contrived in cruder versions in portable plants at a distance from the settlement, and on the whole less economically from Richard's point of view; distribution is also more difficult until Nancy, now more than a sleeping partner in his life, points out that the constable is doubtless ill-paid and might well be appreciative of a regular monetary sum to ease his plight. The constable, by name of Stubbs, soon enthusiastically proves the beneficial effects of law and order by destroying a rival and rather amateurish still worked furtively in the forest by some miners dissatisfied with the current quality and price of Dixtown Dream; the men are discharged from Richard's employment, and taken downriver. 'It could have been going on for years,' he tells Nancy. 'It probably was,' she answers. 'You see? You need me.' Richard seldom has to be reminded. Though a mix of alcohol and memory compassionately tends to confuse some of the more critical facts in their relationship, especially of its birth and convulsive baptism, it has never quite succeeded in placing the hot revolver convincingly in Nancy's hand; nor has there been need to, in the last resort. No bodies rise to flaw the tranquil flow of the Porangi. Indeed, rather than engendering ghosts and guilts, such memory as remains coherent lends an abundance to their lovemaking, an agreeable excitement, a sometimes exhilarating sense of forbidden fruit, which is pleasingly slow to pass; not least in the area of Nancy's natural facility for cruelty in the act, which Richard continues to crave. Omens were never more auspicious. Some marriages might be made in heaven. Those arranged elsewhere can be equally sustaining.

('Among the many odd tales of the Porangi,' says the prose minstrel of *The Lives of Lovelock Junction*, 'there is none more odd, nor more capable of confirmation, than – as newspaper headlines of the day neatly summarized it – The Mystery of the Missing Acrobats. In essence, the story is that four men in an acrobatic troupe of five vanished without trace after a performance in the settlement of Dixtown. The fifth, a woman, evidently gave a distressed and confused account of events preceding their disappearance. This account, though largely confirmed by Richard Lovelock, tended to arouse police suspicions, and resulted in a prolonged inquiry. It was said that the four, in the course of a boisterous and apparently all night party, launched a dinghy upon the river. Why? Perhaps to win a wager, said the woman when pressed. A wager with whom, since all four were in the same boat? Plainly with Richard Lovelock. But in his own statement Richard insisted that he had tried to talk the doomed four out of their hazardous and somewhat inexplicable excursion on the river, hardly the act of a gambler; and he made no mention of a wager. He pleaded that his memory was blurred by alcoholic indulgence on the night in question. The river was searched without result, apart from retrieval of an empty dinghy and an oar. Suspicion fell on the unfortunate and now unemployed survivor of the troupe and, even more surprisingly, on Richard Lovelock himself. There might have been some motive for the woman – the troupe was known as a quarrelsome and quick-tempered crew and had run foul of the law on more than one occasion – but there was none in evidence for Richard. Many theories were canvassed and rejected. In a heart-warming sequel to the tragedy, Richard took pity on the woman – who presumably had nowhere to go, and no future without her four partners – and married her. Their first child was born within two years. The mystery, however, was slow to die. It was revived in a journal of sensational reputation in following years. A onetime inhabitant of Dixtown claimed, in an interview, that several shots had been heard on the fatal night. There had also been some unusual outdoor activity, with lanterns seen moving about Richard's house and later in the vicinity of the river. The purveyor of this account, however, proved to be a convicted bootlegger, one who had been discharged from Richard's employ at some time after the affair; there was good reason to presume the man was speaking from malice. Also he had no opportunity to repeat the tale to the police. He was found with smashed head in a back alley of a New Plymouth public house, after an apparent fall from an upper-story veranda; death by misadventure was recorded.'

It might also be recorded that the public house in question was often frequented by seamen and others who had business on the Porangi, specifically with Richard. This could, of course, be coincidence. God knows hearts need warming in a cold world.)

The third proof of collaborative Providence on the Porangi resists verification. Titanomagnetite iron, in the embrace of parental impurities, chooses to remain insensible to the prolonged assault of electrical current, though Herman shares with Marie Louise the experience of being left insensible by explosive short circuits. Rather than leap free, to know itself naked in the world, the metal cantankerously clings to the womb and spits flame in his face. But all need not be lost. There is still the generator. If electrical current cannot prise iron from the Porangi's sands, it might yet reveal the metal in man; it can illuminate the lives of Lovelock Junction. Even the most recalcitrant Malone might be transfigured. Cables are strung across the plateau. Homes are wired, often after protest, and evacuation of the inhabitants to Dixtown. In each home a bulb is enshrined conspicuously. Marie Louise is prominent among those on the plateau who want no part of this demonology. She will not have a wire invading Lovelock House. The next thing, God forbid, there will be a bulb in her kitchen. Herman wins a hard fought compromise. He is permitted to run a cable across the roof, and wire a bulb to the top of the tower; there, perhaps, it will serve as a symbol of a different order of things coming to pass; it can also, parenthetically, act as beacon for vessels abroad on the Porangi in winter dusk. Herman labours with desperation, and mostly alone, to get the electrical current equitably distributed; at heart he knows he has his last chance to demonstrate the unworthiness of Dixtown; Lovelock Junction will shine out upon the world. Circumstances Crescent, fittingly, is chosen for his first experiment in street lighting; Rainbow Road and the like can be left until later, when success is visible. As an afterthought, he attaches a bulb to a post at the cemetery gate; even the dead are entitled to some light shed upon their condition. One task gives him particular satisfaction: the wiring of the meeting hall. If conventional faith of priest or Protestant cannot survive illumination, so much the better. Men might comprehend that they are of this world, with duties accordingly, and make themselves worthy. Soon all is ready. It only remains for the generator to be fired, switches to be thrown, and

God's will to be made familiar without self-serving interpreter; all shall have the potential of personal revelation.

When Marie Louise declines participation in the accompanying ceremony, and announces her intention to leave for Spanish Creek, Herman turns to Felicity. His daughter is now a slender and most comely sixteen years of age. In pleasing contrast to her mother, Felicity is fascinated, eager for new experience, especially for the opportunity of throwing the master switch, to set light in motion. She sees this, as Sylvester Spring unimaginatively does not, as an occasion of pure theatre. Sylvester has to be bullied into approval and into complementing her role. He is fearful of the possibility of his pupil's voice coming to grief, and thus their mutual future, if Herman's wiring is inefficient. Felicity is the point of Sylvester's life. He can no longer recall having any other. Their relationship has become more than musical. It is now several months since Felicity, one memorable afternoon, seduced him. In the physical sense, at least, she has turned into his tutor. Sylvester suffers no further doubts about his sexual nature; his love is of a kind which, in due course, can dare speak its name.

It is inarguable that, Herman and Felicity aside, there is a sullen mood infesting the people of the plateau that early autumn evening. Malones and their cousins, in groups of a dozen or more, stand outside their dwellings – often with cases packed, and untidy collections of furniture, if permanent migration from the plateau proves advisable – and look up toward Lovelock House. Marie Louise's absence has enabled Herman to set the master switch in a temporary frame on the front steps, between stone lions apparently ready to roar and motionless eagles evidently eager to take wing. At the top of the steps Sylvester sits at a grand piano, which has been manhandled there for the ceremony. In the distance, as dusk thickens, people from Dixtown can be seen cautiously rising upon the rim of the plateau, carrying lanterns; they prefer not to advance far. Mustering such volume of voice as he can command, Herman sets the ceremony moving with many well-chosen words, largely to the effect that darkness will nevermore be sufficient excuse for man to mistake the nature of reality; electrical current will henceforth be seen as harbinger of new man in a new world, where night and day shall be indistinguishable with the painless manipulation of a small switch. There are harbingers of exhausted patience toward the end of the speech, though mercifully remote, and inaudible to Herman. He delegates proceedings to Felicity; she glides to the switch.

'Let there be light,' she says in resonant syllables.

There is light. First a bright star is born on the summit of Lovelock House. Incandescence of no lesser intensity unravels, from source after source, the length of Circumstances Crescent; then it threads through the town, zig-zagging from window to window, before bringing dawn to the cemetery gate. All of Lovelock Junction glitters. There are no fatalities. Nor are the dead raised prematurely. The ensuing silence is brief. Sylvester, in a cold sweat of relief, strikes blindly at the piano, offering the opening chords of the Donizetti cabaletta *Quando rapito in estasi*, his tempo calculated to unlock the gold and silver resident in Felicity's lungs, larynx and pharynx; it is her first public performance, and quite literally electrifying. Before she claims her high D, in unerring fashion, even the more articulately mutinous inhabitants of Lovelock Junction have made their peace with God's new gift, or Herman's; they gather at their glowing windows to marvel. Evacuees soon return from Dixtown. Children chase each other up Circumstances Crescent before being called home to bed. Furniture is carried into houses proved uninflammable; doors are shut again, and curtains drawn. The last sightseers from Dixtown disperse. History, presumably just made, is uncommonly shy about showing itself; revelation has somewhere short-circuited, leaving human metal still comfortably one with parental impurities. Some luminescence aside, Lovelock Junction remains much as before. Before Herman himself retires to meditate on this, he sees a solitary figure approaching. It is Richard, with congratulations. 'I'll have to do the same for Dixtown,' he tells Herman. Soon after Richard's departure, Herman's howl – not in evidence for some time – is in atmospheric pursuit of Felicity's high D.

(A typically tired and impoverished passage in *The Lives of Lovelock Junction* records: 'Remote though it may have been, the Porangi made progress welcome. Lovelock Junction and Dixtown were lit by electricity at the beginning of the last decade of the nineteenth century, well ahead of many more substantial centres and indeed many cities in the southern hemisphere. The responsibility may be presumed to rest with the energetic Richard Lovelock. Herman seems to have had less heart for the enterprise. Only one street in Lovelock Junction proper was ever wholly lit, for example; the rest remain unwired. Indeed, with his failure to find a suitable process for extraction of iron from the river sands, some apathy seems to have overtaken Herman at the beginning of this decade. But that is another story.'

Which is, for example, one way of not telling it.)

Herman and Marie Louise agree in one area: they are older than they were. Their sixtieth birthdays have long gone. They never cease to reflect on their good fortune in finding a tutor as attentive to Felicity's needs as Sylvester Spring. Sylvester has likely added years to their lives. Marie Louise has no problem in making the most of these bonus years, with her regular visits upriver to Spanish Creek, the excitements of being with Benjamin's children, recalling the Porangi's past with Sybil, or sharing with James the joys of his tall son David. Herman, on the other hand, has less content. 'It is time to slow down,' Marie Louise tells him. 'Time to take stock.'

Stocktaking dispirits. Herman sees himself, rather starkly, as the ageing proprietor of a pointless and unprofitable community which at best and worst serves to sustain Dixtown. Iron might have made things otherwise. But he even begins to doubt this once firm article of faith. Grown men decline to live in an adult way wherever his gaze wanders. In disillusion, which time cannot but augment, it becomes clear to Herman that the human race is a hang-dog affair. More, the world as a whole is unsatisfactory. From this thought, which he might once have dismissed as huge heresy, it is a short step to the notion that the world needs to be invented all over again. In that way, and perhaps that way only, can a brave beginning be made. An alternative society requires alternative people. Much as it is to be regretted, men are something short of brothers: they are often less than second cousins, as the Malones make clear. The raw material is deficient. Likewise a new world cannot arise from a transaction with the old. In reinventing the world, the critical problem is the past. But the past, after all, is only what people choose to remember and record of the past. Why should it not – and here Herman does not wholly comprehend how vast a problem he now truly has in hand – be remembered and recorded as other?

Thereupon Herman's stocktaking takes on new and remarkable dimension. First bundles of books begin to arrive up the Porangi, then giant bales of printed matter; Lovelock House takes on the appearance of a metropolitan library as bookshelves rise from floor to baroque ceiling, in room after room, in an attempt to contain the erudite avalanche. Revisionists need first to know the wily face of the enemy. Herman's enemy is all mankind's knowledge of its nature, no less. If men can be persuaded to see themselves as other, they will surely incline, perhaps with enthusiasm, to be other. One clear difficulty is where to draw the line; has the tide of history instantly to be turned back all the way to Adam and Eve at the foot of the tree, the fruit whereof they did not eat, with Cain and Abel making merry, like all sons of man since, in the groves of Eden? God knows that has its temptations; Herman sees the plausibility of that portrait subverted by certain temporal limitations. Best to stalk his way back there step by soft step, in the manner of a guerilla fighter, rather than call out the cavalry to ride ruthless over current and faulty human perception. Man's perception of himself is, after all, the point; suggestion and not aggression is the way to win the battle. In time, reality will be revealed as altogether inspirational. Meanwhile, Herman has a great deal to master. Marie Louise learns not to trespass idly upon the terrain where Herman is fixing his bayonet beyond a diversionary screen of tobacco smoke. Unnoticed by newly bibliophile Herman, Lovelock Junction begins to empty of people. House after house is vacated, and left to spiders and mice, as the Malones and many others make their way downhill toward the social, commercial, physical and cultural advantages of Dixtown.

James has the sensation of the century closing down with unnatural haste; an extended season is beyond the capacity of the performers. He is also, for the first time, feeling his age, though still short of his fiftieth birthday. If he has one answer to life, in the form of Spanish Creek, he has forgotten the question. Perhaps it is the theme of things that men must pass the question to their sons. David is a strong and thoughtful son, still an answer to prayer. They ride together; they hunt together; they read together. Stripped to the waist, the boy soon shears beside his father and Uncle Benjamin, and Benjamin's sons. His grandmother Sybil has his education in hand. 'There is no doubt about it,' she tells James. 'The boy will go far.'

'Far?' James says, with concern. 'Where?'

'That is for the future; his brilliant future. The fact is that his intelligence cannot and should not be confined to this farm. The land may be sufficient for the likes of Daniel. Not for David.'

Benjamin's eldest son Daniel, now eighteen years old, seems a younger and more muscular version of his father; he asks few questions, and is reliable with sheep. A suntanned, graceless boy, and exceedingly good-natured.

'David is different,' Sybil insists. 'You must face the fact.'

'When I come to it,' James says warily. 'It is not yet an issue.'

'It will be,' Sybil warns.

He finds cause to reflect on this conversation. He cannot yet contemplate his son's loss. Spanish Creek seems to lose purpose. So does James. He conveys to his son, when expedient, the pleasures and pains of early days on the Porangi, though editing the account here and there; he makes the boy see that their existence there is no accident, but a thing of hope and sacrifice; also that there is worse to the world beyond. David does not appear unreceptive. If the boy has one large question to ask, it is in the area of maternity; he remains curious about the nature of his mother.

'She suffered a melancholia,' James explains shortly. 'She no longer felt of this world. It is not unknown in women after the birth of children. Most recover. Your mother, sadly, did not; there is no more I can say.'

There is no more James will be persuaded to say. His son's eyes, in any case, are soon visibly less inquiring; he has distractions.

James has fewer. In the summer of his son's thirteenth year, with the shearing done, the wool shipped south, David is taken pig-hunting by his cousin Daniel, with whom his kinship seems closer, and Benjamin's other boys; James is left alone in his homestead for the first time since David was born. Sybil comes often; likewise Benjamin and Iris. They evidently fear for James lonely. James prefers to be, as test for himself, a tentative survey of the future. News upriver from Lovelock Junction is not reassuring. There, it seems, Herman and Marie Louise are under pressure from Sylvester Spring. Sylvester argues that it is time for Felicity's vocal chords to give their all to the world. Delay might be damaging. It is clear that Herman and Marie Louise cannot do other than capitulate. The first-born Lovelock on the Porangi is about to flee; who will follow? David, surely, if omens are to be read. *Lotus* is long at the bottom of the river, but the Lovelock voyaging is far from done.

In vexed mood James rides his farm. In late afternoon, near sunset, he reins in on Upokonui Bluff. The cairn upon the *tohunga*'s grave is still being fashioned by the elements, durable nonetheless. And McKenzie's grave, like Sunday's, is greened with the Scots heather James has planted to give legend its due. He often finds peace there, unlike the cemetery at Lovelock Junction where Diana rests, and which is conducive to turbulence of soul. He dismounts, allows his horse to graze, and waits upon serenity of mind. He smokes his pipe, listens to water, wind, birds; and sleeps.

He dreams, it seems, of that which will be. And, more, of those still to be. These faceless inhabitants of the future refuse to know or understand. They live for their minute, no more. Life is a laugh; death calls for derision. When James moves among them, merely to make himself known, they endeavour to drag him kicking back to his grave. 'Listen,' he cries. They will not listen. 'Believe,' he protests. They will not believe. They push him into his grave; they shovel earth upon him. Yet he still allows them no peace; he shouts and shouts again through the tumbling clods. Until, yes, he knows himself heard. There is silence. The clods cease to fall.

When James wakes, his back against Upokonui's cairn, he finds a lizard crawling up his trouser leg; it is already dusk. His horse has wandered. He sees light glimmering in his homestead up valley. David is back. So too, for the moment, is peace of mind. He sheds his confused nightmare, retrieves his horse, and rides home to his son.

Fifteen

Trade unions, of embryonic nature, begin to make Richard's existence irksome in the last decade of the century. More so after a run of fatalities in his mines, and conspicuously a disaster which alone leaves ten corpses entombed. He has reason for complaint about the quality of his workmen, their careless approach to production of coal. This, however, doesn't prevent him awarding widows any back pay owed their deceased husbands; in some circumstances Richard has even been known to provide bereaved families with steamer fares downriver to the town or city of their choice. It is the men arriving upriver, looking for work, he now has to watch. In the past troublemakers were easier to pick. On the whole, they have been men with too much to say for themselves; also men with unsufficient respect for their employer. Richard has preferred to engage men fresh from distant and impoverished climes who still have some sense of the fitness of things, hesitate to quibble if their pay is a few farthings short, and are decently grateful for any job offering. But men of that nature, inclined to tip their caps as Richard passes, are fewer in number now. Many have been spoiled by insipid employers elsewhere. Others have known no recent employer, having left goldfield, gumfield or failed farms, and still seem to think themselves independent. There are always those who imagine the world, and especially Richard, owes them a living. Most now have more to say for themselves than is desirable. Richard suspects grudges and incipient disloyalty. To Nancy he often expresses regret that the old days on the river are gone; life was simpler in the seventies. He even goes so far as to suggest that money is the source of the rebellious evil abroad in the land. Given more, men want more. There is virtue in resisting the tide.

'I don't follow,' Nancy protests. 'Are you trying to tell me you shouldn't pay the buggers at all?'

'I am talking of greed,' Richard answers. 'An honest word. In the mouths of agitators it becomes justice.'

'I'll tell you what I think,' Nancy says. 'Money is here to stay.'

'Alas,' Richard agrees.

'And I don't notice you in a hurry to give yours away.'

'To what end? I provide society with a service. I provide men with employment. It is all a grim grind, God knows why. I have never noticed, to be frank, money making for happiness.'

'More fool you,' Nancy observes.

There is seldom a day when he doesn't count himself fortunate to have Nancy; she remains earthy in life's more perplexing extremities.

The first unionist to make himself detectable in the settlement, with conspiratorial gatherings in his dwelling, is no problem. Property, a collection of Nancy's jewellery, is found to be missing from Richard's household. As a result of information received, Constable Stubbs locates the stolen property beneath a floorboard in the agitator's dwelling; the man, still protesting his innocence with some determination, is taken downriver for trial. Those seen farewelling him on the jetty, with bitter fervour, are dismissed from Richard's employ. There is no more talk of trade unionism in Dixtown for a time. The outside world may be a sour sea of labour dissidence; the Porangi is unpolluted.

'It seems I have you to thank,' Richard admits to Nancy. 'A bastard like that would have wanted to get down on your jewellery anyway. Envy. Greed. It was just a matter of speeding things up.'

'If you say so,' Nancy agrees.

'Anyway I'm damn grateful.'

'Show me,' she suggests.

Richard, when that call comes, has no hesitation. His endeavours upon Nancy's body are extraordinarily fruitful. Six children, four sons and two daughters, are born so fast that he often has difficulty remembering their names.

Perhaps domesticity relaxes his vigilance. His troubles arrive fully armed. It is true that there has been hint of restlessness, of coming and going, mostly of going, among his workforce. Attributing this accurately to the fact that men have been tempted by better wages and conditions surrendered by employers embattled elsewhere, Richard with ill grace does his best to stabilize Dixtown's population by raising wages within reason, and offering a half-day holiday on Saturday; he points out to his employees that this near suicidal generosity could well be reciprocated by increased output; and observes that more concessions might only lead to closure of mines and mill, with shipping costs so prohibitive, and markets fluctuating. His men, for the most part, appear suitably impressed. But perhaps, as it turns out, they are less impressed by the quality of Richard's sacrifice than by the revelation that he is as human an employer as any other; he cannot do without them. Revolution, as is well known, seldom comes from men ground underfoot; it comes from those given their first glimpse of light between the clay of a careless tyrant's toes.

At all events Richard wakes one weekday morning to find Dixtown silent. No rumbling wagons, and the steam-saws quiet in the mill. Imagining an accident, he dresses quickly. From his front veranda he takes in an unfamiliar scene. His immediate foreground is filling with many, perhaps most, of his men. Possibly two hundred are taking up stance on his lawn. Some few dozen stand at more discreet distance.

'What is this?' he demands.

They are unnervingly slow to tell him. Some shuffle. Some look with concentration at the ground.

'Come on, now,' Richard says, more amiably. 'What have I here?'

There are mutters, but one word is audible. What Richard has, it seems, is a strike.

'Nonsense,' he tells them.

They are silent.

'So let's go back to work,' he suggests, encouraged.

They make no move.

'There are,' Richard informs them, 'no strikes here.'

He examines faces. Few are strange. There are a number of reliable Malones, among others. Also foremen who should know better, and will.

'I'm prepared to forget this,' he offers, 'if you do. We can call it a misunderstanding.'

'Call it what you like, Mr Lovelock,' one emboldened voice says. 'We still call it a strike.'

'Ah,' Richard says. 'A spokesman.'

This is a gaunt awkward young man, with untidy crop of hair, whom Richard has never really had cause to notice before. Now, however, Richard sees the hot eyes of a malcontent undisguised. How in damnation had he got into Dixtown? Perhaps when Richard's guard was down; perhaps when Richard was less able to pick and choose. He cannot even recall the bugger's name. Not a formidable adversary anyway. Still wet behind the ears, he wouldn't know his arse from his elbow.

'Do me the favour,' Richard proposes, 'of telling me what this is all about.'

The young man steps forward. Trembling in his hand is a long sheet of paper; a list of demands.

'Your name?' Richard asks.

'Finn,' the young man replies at length.

'I'll remember it,' Richard promises. 'Also your face. You look so full of shit your eyes are brown.'

Nevertheless Richard accepts the list of demands. They are much as might be expected. There is conspicuous concern with money, and hours of employment; there are grievances concerning safety. And there is much verbiage about natural justice. Enough, in fact, for Richard to find his patience fraying; he crumples the list. To further indicate his feelings, his fists are most useful.

Finn, whoever he is, is soon on the ground; his mouth is bleeding; he spits out a tooth.

'Anyone for more?' Richard asks.

There are no volunteers.

'Right,' Richard says with confidence. 'The fun's over. Let's get back to work.'

Two men help shaky Finn to his feet. The others reveal no immediate interest in Richard's proposition.

'I represent the union,' Finn protests thickly.

'You are mistaken,' Richard answers. 'There is no union. Not now. Not ever. Get your arse out of here.'

'You'll see me again,' Finn suggests.

'In hell,' Richard warns.

The men, Finn supported among them, before long disperse; Richard is left looking at his trampled lawn, then at Nancy, arrived silently at his side. 'Those sods,' he tells her with amazement, 'seem to have forgotten who's boss.'

'Never,' she says, with sympathy.

'They are actually,' he goes on, now with as much rage as amazement, 'trying to tell me my business.'

'Piss on them,' she says.

Richard does not discard the advice as impractical. 'Don't worry,' he argues. 'I know my men. Creatures of habit. They'll be back to work before noon. Just give them time to cool. Then they'll crave their jobs back. You see.'

He is, for some reason, wrong. There is no resumption of work before noon. Nor that afternoon. Nor the next day. He refuses to express curiosity in the affairs of Dixtown, and its rebellious inhabitants; he remains with Nancy in his house, declining even the walk downhill to his office, which is a temptation. His high-pitched children would put even the most temperate housebound spouse on test. But some sacrifice must be made; he has to show his contempt.

'They shall soon,' he promises Nancy, 'be as bored with the business as I am.'

Two days later, however, the boredom of his employees has still failed to demonstrate itself satisfyingly; no wagons rumble, no saws whine.

'You must face facts,' Nancy says at length. 'You have a strike on your hands.'

'There are no strikes here,' Richard insists.

'I think you deceive yourself,' Nancy proposes.

'Are you against me too?'

'You know better than that. You also know that, unless you do something, they have you by the short hairs.'

Richard is not easily to be inconvenienced by truth. 'Do something?' he asks finally. 'Speak plainly, woman.'

'It can't go on. Otherwise, where's the profit?'

She might well ask. Richard prefers not. A steamer and a scow have already returned empty downriver, their skippers having waited vainly for cargo.

'What do you want me to do?' he demands.

'Make sense of things as they are.'

'You mean come to terms? Negotiate?'

'If you like,' she agrees.

'I'm not sure I hear right,' he tells her. 'Unless I'm mistaken, you appear to be addressing yourself to some dim-witted weakling.'

'I observe a practical, rational man. No more.'

'Besides,' he says, 'negotiate with whom?'

'There was mention of a union, as I understand it.'

'There is no union,' he tells her. 'Not on the Porangi.'

'Your men appear insistent on having another view of the matter.'

'One of the buggers,' he allows. 'And he'll never make old bones.'

'Nevertheless,' she begins.

'Nevertheless, nothing. I have done my negotiating with him. With more mercy, perhaps, than he deserved. Aside from which, he has no future on the Porangi. He is in no position to speak for anyone.'

'Again, Richard, your men may have a different view. Loyalty is a word you might not care to hear. But it does have a hypnotic effect on some.'

'You look after your kitchen. I'll look after the likes of Finn.'

'Am I allowed no word, then?'

'I have no objection to communications of a moderate nature.'

'The world has changed. Things are not as they were. Especially not in this country. That is all I am intent on telling you.'

'I am aware, woman, that your sex is now possessed of the right to vote, for reasons which thus far escape me. Understandable only as a means by which our simpering colonial politicians can hide beyond the skirts of womenfolk and, God knows, perhaps even wear them. Doubtless also to purchase peace from prattling wives. I am unaware, on the other hand, that legislation has likewise been passed entitling female intervention in matters concerning masters and men. Or am I to be enlightened still further?'

'I speak only as wife. With respect.'

Richard, if grudgingly, is pacified. 'So what would you have me do?' he asks.

'Clear your mind of obstinacy. And allow realism to enter. There is a strike. Also, it seems, a union. Start again from there.'

Richard takes time to consider this. 'All right,' he announces finally.

'All right, what?'

'There is a strike. I'll go that far. No further.'

'No union?'

'No union. You think I'm a fool?'

'As you please.' She hesitates. 'I hate to risk your wrath again, but it leaves one suggestion unanswered.'

'Like what?' He has begun to find this conversation too taxing. Human beings, not least Nancy, tend to play havoc with his peace of mind; and make him feel, among other things, older than he should. Physical and mental reminders of his approaching sixtieth birthday are not to be countenanced. Alert Nancy seems yet again a leap ahead. 'Like what?' he repeats.

'Like what, exactly, you intend to do about it. If, that is, you now concede that you have this profitless problem. This strike.'

'Easy,' he declares.

'Oh?'

'Why women were given the vote will remain beyond me. They've no sense of history; of tried and true tradition. We starve the buggers back.'

'But the union?'

'There will be no union. You can't eat a union card. Finn's arse, on the other hand, might be more nourishing. When they've finished roasting the fucker.'

'And what of us?' Nancy ventures. 'While you starve them back?'

'We trim our sails. Ride out the storm.'

'And that's your last word?'

'The skipper always has the last word. I run a tight ship.'

'I heard you,' she sighs.

That day Richard hammers nails into the door of the store, shutting it for the duration of the current disturbance. Upon the door he affixes an announcement that the store will be reopened when his employees find themselves unanimously of the opinion that no union is known on the Porangi; and that they likewise know nothing of a malingering miner commonly known as Finn. He instructs Constable Stubbs, that frail and often unsteady local limb of the law, to give attention to matters pertaining to the keeping of the peace. 'We want no disorders here,' Richard explains, after ensuring that justice is sufficiently provisioned to see out the siege.

'There'll be no nonsense here,' Stubbs promises. 'I'll see to that.'

'And while you're at it,' Richard says, 'it might be worth your while to find out if anything's known elsewhere of this bastard named Finn.'

'First name?'

'It's your inquiry,' Richard proposes. 'Get on with the job. Finn might be an alias anyway. Give out a description. The man must be known. I shouldn't be surprised if you find cause to make an arrest.'

'I'll see what can be arranged,' Stubbs agrees. 'But understand that these things have to be done legal. They sometimes take time.'

'And money,' Richard suggests.

'Now you mention it,' Stubbs says.

A month later no one in Dixtown appears perilously undernourished. Daily there are parties of hunters out in the hills; the small streets fill with the smell of wild pork and pigeon roasting; the produce of vegetable gardens can be supplemented by that which is edible in the forest. Dixtown appears festive rather than famished; more so when Richard shuts down the school, also supply of electricity. Lamps twinkle about communal bonfires, and pigs turn on spits; children racket about the settlement from dawn to dusk, or fish in the river. Worse, Constable Stubbs, though diligent in research, can find nothing known of Finn or anyone answering his description. Not in the Maritime Strike of 1890, or in lesser strife since. It has been Richard's hope that Finn is wanted elsewhere in the colony, preferably on a charge of seditious utterance; there isn't even the mildest of obscenities noted against the man. For all police purposes, he doesn't exist. This mystery, this void, appears to make Finn even more a menace to Richard's future well-being; he seems to have been shaped specifically to persecute Richard, perhaps to the grave, a vengeful phantom bred from Porangi forest and mist. Richard dreams badly. He shouts in his sleep.

Meanwhile, insofar as their view is detectable, his workmen appear unanimously of the opinion that a union exists; and that one by the name of Finn is popularly resident among them.

Richard is tempted to take a gun into town and let some daylight into Finn. But that might pose even Stubbs an impossible problem. Given that garrulous swine's concern for his career, large monetary inducement might not produce sufficiently credible perjury. In any case Stubbs, for his own selfish reasons, would not be slow to desert a suspect ship. All the finesse of the law might not be enough to acquit Richard of Finn's manslaughter, however justifiable. There could also be prejudicial memories aroused in the matter of the missing acrobats.

Nancy is no help. 'What of your contracts?' she asks. 'These merchants you supply.'

'They can bloody wait,' he tells her.

'Or go elsewhere,' she suggests.

'What are you trying to tell me?'

'Nothing you don't really know,' she assures him.

Nancy has twisted too long on trapezes, walked too many high wires, and seen one husband shatter himself with contempt for the odds; she has a survivor's instinct for hazard. She sees hazard shaping now. And not even the most diminutive safety net in evidence. Minus mines and mill, Richard's future is unthinkable. So is hers. Rather than think the unthinkable Nancy takes it upon herself to negotiate. By way of an anonymous note, promising an encounter to his advantage, she makes a rendezvous with Finn, who as a result is far from clear whom he is about to meet, or why, among the thickets and weeds to the west of the riverside dump. The malodorous nature of the place ensures privacy. Finn is stunned by Nancy's appearance there. This should perhaps give her tactical advantage. It doesn't. She is equally stunned by Finn. She has envisaged, from Richard's description, some manly hell-raiser. Instead she has no more than this lanky, visibly trembling young man who has barely begun to shave. No real antagonist for Richard at all. Where, then, does his threat reside? She would wager he has never seen a female in so intimate a situation. This, at least, she can use; she has not been forty years a woman for nothing.

'Let's talk,' she proposes briskly.

'Talk?' he repeats, still unnerved.

'Of matters to mutual advantage.'

'I fail to take your meaning. I cannot imagine such matters.'

'Then your memory, perhaps, needs some titillation. Your name is Finn, unless I'm much mistaken. And, unless I'm even more grievously in error, there is a strike in progress.'

'What can I say?' he shrugs, warily.

'That you aren't deaf. That my facts are not too far astray. That you are Finn.'

'I'm Finn,' he agrees with caution.

'Thank God,' she sighs. 'All is not lost. Might you have more to say?'

'Only that I'm not fomenting any strike. I merely make myself available. As a medium through which the inarticulate can speak. And make grievances known.'

His voice, at least, has found more audible level.

'Such nobility,' Nancy says.

'I am used to sneers,' he answers.

'It is clear you never suffer them in silence.'

'Justice is a fresh tide in the affairs of men. It is washing strong on the shores of this country. Though some would play Canute.'

'You speak of my husband.'

'The water is up to his knees. It might soon reach his neck.'

'To what end? If he goes, so will your jobs; the jobs of many.'

'That is a chance which needs must be taken. Truth, as Marx says, is the recognition of necessity.'

'Who is Marx? Another of your ilk?'

'A German philosopher of Jewish extraction. Lately deceased.'

'I fail to see why the name of some dead Yid needs utterance by the Dixtown rubbish dump in connection with my husband. I am here, to be frank, just to speak of this strike. It can't go on.'

'Your husband has but to settle. Without victimization. And recognition of the union.'

'You ask much. Too much.'

'We could ask more. All in good time.'

'That is my husband's fear. Where will it end?'

'Some might say in a just society. Where no man exploits another. Where there is no want, no war.'

'A pretty thought.'

'History is on its side,' Finn announces.

'And this history of yours is hungry for sacrificial victims such as my husband?'

'That is to put it brutally.'

'What did he do to hurt anyone?'

'I prefer to ask: What did he ever do to help anyone?'

'He is just a man. Possessed of the ordinary passions.'

'Particularly in matters of profitability, and his own comfort.'

'How else would you have him?'

'More reasonable.'

'He might well ask the same of you. I see greed against greed. Pride against pride. It doesn't become one so young to succumb to the deadlier sins. I see you as someone with a future, given the right path. Nor without an education, unless I'm wrong. Someone who could better himself with ease, other than on the Porangi.'

Finn quietens. 'Is this it, then?' he asks. 'Do you come bearing a bribe?'

'Unofficially. My husband, in the wrong mood, might initially be averse to the notion. But in time he might be persuaded to part with, let us say, five hundred pounds, in denominations of your choosing.'

'Silver is customary. In multiples of thirty.'

'Think what you could make of yourself. This country goes begging for young men of imagination with capital. You could travel far.'

'There are other journeys. Ones which involve no betrayal, nor a sore conscience. Ones which make life, and the living of it, worthwhile.'

'You are obstinate. And doubtless, in your own eyes, admirable. But your courage, if that is what it is, places you in some peril.'

'How so?'

'I could cry rape. Here. Now. Rend my dress. Muddy my face. Your word against mine. And your word would count little with the law, as a man of no substance, and troublemaker to boot.'

Finn backs away. 'First bribe. Now threat. It is an old story. Take my head, though, and another grows. Justice is a hydra with a hundred heads. Seed has been sown here; your husband might have a crueller harvest.'

'Perhaps. Or most might take fright. And settle for less.'

Finn continues to back away.

'Don't panic,' she pleads. 'The fact is I find you, after all, more agreeable than I suspected. In your curious way, you are far from without charm.'

This gives Finn pause.

'I see a young man of much energy,' she goes on. 'And also with imagination to burn. One who, without other opportunities, feels impelled to expend both in perverse and unproductive ways. No. Don't trouble to contradict me. We need no longer feud. Our negotiation, if it is worth that name, is done. My interest now is you. In what makes you work.'

'I have,' Finn says, though with some tremble, 'revealed myself fairly.'

'There has been some baring of soul,' she agrees. 'But I have still not altogether seen you as naked as I might wish.'

'I fail to follow,' he confesses.

'Touch my face,' she suggests. 'Come now. Don't take fright again.

Just a gentle hand.' At length she is obliged to guide his reluctant hand to the desired situation. 'There,' she adds, 'surely that isn't so bad. I am seldom known to bite, other than in passion's play. What do you feel? Tell me the truth.'

'Your face,' he admits. 'That of a woman.'

'No more? Come, now.'

He is all twitches; a quivering chaos which needs calling to order.

'You are making mock,' he proposes.

'I might be making more,' she says. 'I might, by some miracle, be making your manhood accessible. What do you say? Or, rather, what do you feel?'

'Discomfort,' he argues. He tries to pull his hand away; she clamps it to her face. 'Great discomfort.'

'But of an uncommonly interesting nature. Dare you admit it?'

'What is your game?' he demands.

'The oldest,' she says.

'Why me?'

'That is the essence of the game. The mystery. Never ask questions.'

Nancy, in truth, is now sufficiently enthralled on her own account. Husbands notwithstanding, a woman needs some continuing conviction of her power over men. And vexatious Richard has lately been beyond her. In short, for the story is long, he has grown casual about claiming his conjugal rights.

'I'm sorry,' Finn protests.

'Listen to your flesh,' she urges. 'It has its own history. Its own song to sing. Your eyes tell all.'

Lowered, Finn's eyes tell still more.

'Kiss me,' she says. 'The once should do.'

'Please.'

'Courtesy is unnecessary. And at this point impolite. The proposition has been made. Perhaps I could put it in a manner more attractive to you. You wish, or so it would seem, nothing more than my husband's hide. You could settle, at least for the moment, for a little less; but a shade more satisfying. His wife.'

Still not without agony, Finn at length ventures his dry lips upon hers. She distinctly doesn't cry rape, though she emits a number of other words as provocative. Finn, among the thickets and upon the weeds, in unpleasant approximation to unkempt mankind's refuse, is lurchingly persuaded to settle for a concession won, so to speak, from the womb of capitalism, and not in the short term displeasing. In the longer term, their transactions take on more colour and nuance as the strike continues elsewhere. Finn is as much drugged by Nancy's needs as by his murky recognition of other necessities; he is afflicted by unreality in its most pernicious and feverish manifestation. Nancy, for her part, retains a more acute grip on the nature of things. It is her frustration, though in the event a minor one, that she fails to pacify and perhaps neutralize Finn; that the best she can make of him is a muddled malcontent, a marginally less efficient troublemaker. Grief is superfluous. There are compensations. She has always delighted in the revelation of lust. Finn, for all his skinny frame, can unleash more than enough. And his endearments, at times, can be phrased very sweetly.

David and Daniel, back from hunting, are first with the news, and small carcasses. Fresh creatures for the table are at large about Spanish Creek. Uninvited, but all the same welcome.

'Rabbits,' James says, with surprise.

'Up the valley,' David tells him. 'We could have shot a score.'

'I have always been partial to roast rabbit,' James discloses. 'Rabbit pie, even more.'

That night they feast on the gift. Nature seems kind. Though James, while indulging, is tempted to reflect; to ask a pertinent question.

'Where,' he wonders, 'have they come from?'

'Downriver,' David suggests. 'Perhaps escaped from Dixtown, who knows?'

'Or cares,' James says with digestive complacency. 'The fact is that they're here. Good English rabbits, no less. They don't appear uncomfortable in a new country. Their taste isn't impaired. Rather the reverse. There is a certain succulence, perhaps from their grazing here, I cannot recall.'

In enthusiasm David and Daniel set out with their guns and return with more rabbits next day.

'All we want,' they announce. 'Whenever we need them.'

The abundance becomes embarrassment. Grandmother Sybil is pushed to find sufficient recipes to vary cuisine: boiled rabbit, curried rabbit, fried rabbit, rabbit stewed with lard or milk. Marie Louise, upriver for a visit, makes further suggestions: rabbit ragout, rabbit à la minute, rabbit au gratin. She takes some home to Herman with the hope that they might prove to have restorative virtue; he has lately lost his appetite, and Marie Louise has been losing heart.

Otherwise rabbit makes welcome change from Spanish Creek's dour mutton; at least when some equilibrium is again established in their diet. There are complaints from Benjamin's children, in the lower homestead, that rabbit is running out of their ears. 'Enough is enough,' David agrees. 'We shall begin to look like rabbits at this rate.'

He and Daniel confine their excursions up valley to one day a week, or less frequently if larders are still full. In any case wild pigs make for far more satisfying pursuit, in the sunless depths of the forest. Flutters of fur on Spanish Creek's steeper hills are a contemptible sort of target; no trophy, no tusks. Wild pigs are devious, menacing, and must often be dispatched intimately with a knife, while dogs bay around. The two earn torn flesh and grazes, honourable wounds, and blood to their elbows.

'What will you do with your life?' David asks his relative.

'Live it,' Daniel says with confidence, as they sit on a rocky hill. He is past dreamy adolescence, though still tolerant of David's.

'Is that all?' David inquires.

'What more can you want?' Daniel answers. 'Life is life. A good place to be.'

'Some say it has purpose,' David ventures, 'as an arena for the testing of souls.'

'I'm buggered if I know,' Daniel replies, 'about that sort of stuff. As for souls, I have heard that no surgeon can find one. That's good enough for me. They're men who know best.'

'And God?'

'Maybe he's up there. Maybe he's not. The same either way, it seems to me. I don't lose a moment's sleep, to tell you the truth.'

'In dreams, though, do you never make strange journeys?'

'Never,' Daniel affirms. 'I have enough bloody trouble getting things done in daylight. I'm too shagged to travel by night.' He is curious about David, nonetheless. 'Journeys? Where the hell do you go?'

David is reticent. 'It's difficult to say. There are unfamiliar places. Not to speak of unfamiliar people. Sometimes—' He pauses.

'Sometimes?' Daniel encourages.

'Well, sometimes there is a woman.'

Daniel laughs. 'What you're telling me, then, is that you have these wet dreams. I remember my first. I thought my balls had sprung a leak. It's just something that happens, when you get to an age. Don't be embarrassed. Girls get worse; they spout gore on their sheets. Just make your bed quick.'

'They are not dreams of that nature,' David insists.

'No?' Daniel says, with some disbelief. 'Then what of this woman?'

'She is gentle. All peace.'

'And doesn't play with your tool, like the ones in my dreams?'

'No,' David says quietly. 'I sometimes think she might be my mother.'

'I see.' Daniel is sobered. 'Well, I wouldn't know too much about that. And it might be best if you didn't either.'

'She's always there, at the worst, when my dreams turn bad.'

'Bad? How bad?'

'There is horror. And slaughter. And men torn apart much as we take apart pigs. She is there with a smile. And saying not to fear; that seems most of her message.'

David is too shy to say more.

'Come on,' Daniel prompts. 'You must tell me the rest. You leave my flesh crawling.'

David perseveres with reluctance. 'I am hung painfully by my arms, with my feet bound, in the manner of our saviour. More than that is not plain. It is all cruel, but for that one sweet face.'

'My God,' Daniel cries. 'That's a nightmare and a half. I can see what you mean. Take my advice. Don't listen so much to Grandmother Sybil. She's a proper old fart when she gets on to God. Religion's all rubbish. Take the world as it comes.'

'I try,' David argues.

'Think of Christ a bit less, and pussy a bit more, if you want dreams with more flavour.'

'Pussy?'

'There's nothing nicer to talk of. You won't be long seeing. Perhaps next summer you might make it, when the shearers are upriver with their daughters. There's quite a few turn it up. And more than one I can recommend. I'll tell them you're modest; you'll soon get the knack.'

'I'm in no hurry,' David suggests.

'You should be. With nightmares like that. You are too much with your father, alone. You need more clean living.'

Which Daniel then demonstrates, as a rabbit bobs below them, by lifting his rifle and loosing a swift shot; the creature arches into the air, all life extended, and falls shrivelled to earth.

'Make the most of our manhood,' Daniel adds; he is protective of David, and feels fonder of him than of his own self-sufficient brothers. 'We're not given long.'

They gather the small corpse with their haunches of pork and continue riding downhill. Spanish Creek station is splendid below them in the late afternoon light, with gorges beyond, unconquered fortresses of forest, and silverings of the Porangi's flow. Both may have reason to recall that panorama, especially of their own pastoral valley, on that immaculate afternoon. It is a sight not to be seen beyond this decade, though who would doubt its durability now? Not Daniel. And not David, not even in uglier dreams. This valley breeds all sons as brothers; it is theirs to inherit and harvest its wool; this century, thanks to the exertions of fathers, can teem with content. Though others, at this moment, can be sullen about having the Porangi as heritage.

'What word of the fair Felicity?' Daniel asks, when they rein in again. The homesteads are now visible, among trees. 'Is our shrill relative still causing right fucking commotions about her future?'

'She is leaving,' David tells him. 'At last. My understanding is that Uncle Herman and Marie Louise are agreed that the agony cannot be prolonged. If go she will, go she must. That seems the verdict. She leaves within the month, with her sweet Sylvester as chaperone, and blessings from all concerned. I daresay some relief will be felt; certainly some silence.'

'Marie Louise will grieve.'

'In her way. But she still has your father and us, even if only by marriage. And Felicity, besides, has been a lost cause as a daughter, as Marie Louise herself often confides. Nevertheless, we shall all have to do our best to cheer her when Felicity departs. And who knows? There may be consolations if Felicity, as predicted, makes her mark.'

'On who?' Daniel asks.

David takes the point. 'I should not care,' he agrees, 'to find myself presenting some impediment on her path to triumph, and find myself trampled, like a poor bug.'

'It takes all sorts,' Daniel says. 'Take, for example, you and me. We're not alike. More like our fathers maybe. Felicity is like no one.'

'We have to be charitable to Felicity,' David suggests. 'Much as I find it difficult, myself.'

'Charitable?' Daniel finds the proposition too comprehensive by far.

'We have to see her as one cursed, or blessed, with an artistic temperament. Or so I believe.'

'Artistic my arse.'

'She is sensitive, I mean, and may suffer more. And one cannot deny her beauty.'

'Speaking for myself,' Daniel observes, 'I'd sooner fuck an old boot.'

There is a farewell party, of a sober sort, for Felicity and Sylvester at Lovelock House the following week. Most at Spanish Creek travel downriver for the occasion, with Benjamin and Iris all but driving Daniel with a whip; James and son David are present, and naturally Sybil. Faint-hearted Marie Louise makes a formal attempt to conjure up regret and remorse among her guests at this moment of her daughter's departure; at best she wins general goodwill. There are toasts to Felicity's future success, and also to that of her dutiful tutor; together, it is said, they make a team which cannot be denied by the obstinate aristocracy of the musical world; all walls will fall.

'I believe,' Sylvester says, rising to reply, 'that we are privileged. Few can say that they have been at the beginning. At the birth of a legend.'

Marie Louise, beginning quietly to sob, recalls Felicity's long gestation and difficult arrival; memory can be cruel. James, seeing pain, takes her hand.

'I shall never forget you all,' Felicity promises. 'Whatever I do, wherever I go, my thoughts will be here.' Her eyes dramatically moisten; nor are her outstretched hands given to understatement.

She is beyond Herman. But for Herman most humans are. He is no longer to be diverted by the gaudier details of mankind's condition; his daughter, so far as he is able to see, is but another creature of fictitious circumstance. Grief is out of order in so narrow a spectrum. Time is much more dismaying. With so little left of the century to run its course, the twentieth century needs urgently to be given the amnesiac chance to change for the better. Tactful erasures of the record, and some inspired substitutions, might yet make men work the marvels they must; and at last walk adult on the earth. The problem is getting started: how, when, where? Felicity's absence may make him less liable to distraction; and perfectly pitched disturbance. There is that to be said.

'Where's Richard?' he finally thinks to inquire of the assembled company. 'Why isn't he here?'

The answer appears to be that Richard is preoccupied with labour problems, and in consequence not leaving his house until his employees return abjectly to work. Such has been the situation for a considerable time. Nancy has sent apologies to Marie Louise, with the explanation that she dislikes leaving her husband's side in the crisis, lest he take reckless action alone.

James sits quiet while this information is conveyed in interminable detail. He has not sat at the same table as Richard in fifteen years or more. His brother's absence is a relief. Diana's grave is between them, still open, an abyss. David sometimes wonders at his father's stricken face.

Felicity brings herself to kiss all at the table. Only Daniel, whose feelings have no disguise, visibly winces.

'I shall be back,' she promises, or threatens. 'Whatever I am, or will be, belongs here.'

There is a launch waiting in the river for Sylvester and her to embark; it has had to be ordered upriver especially, because of the strike and lack of regular ships.

Marie Louise insists on a last undertaking. 'While you're out in the world,' she asks of Felicity, 'you must keep an eye open for the others. For Luke, first of all. And, naturally, unfortunate Ernest. God knows where both boys may be. Just make sure that they know of our love, and that they are never forgotten. Especially for Ernest, forgiveness is here.'

'I think forgiveness is a matter best raised with Richard,' Benjamin points out, largely unheard.

'I shall write from London,' Felicity calls, as the launch begins noisily to move. 'Or perhaps from Paris. You shall have all my news.'

Sylvester, blond curls tossed by the wind, supports her with apparent affection as their figures dwindle on the downriver launch.

'God go with them,' Marie Louise cries. 'Someone must.'

They are gone. Soon too are most of the tears. The Porangi is poorer in some way yet to be determined. Felicity, for all her conspicuous demerits, has at least been distinctive. The hills and valleys about will no longer quiver with the piquance of exotic coloratura, and are again of unhaunted native hue. The legends which once gave grace to the river are lifeless; the Lovelocks are left with their own, most still unborn, or melancholy miscarriages. Felicity, for one.

('Some mention must of course be made,' Shadbolt suggests somewhat timidly in *The Lives of Lovelock Junction*, 'of Felicity Lovelock, a kind of comet across the operatic sky of Europe and the Americas in the early twentieth century – indeed, to push metaphor further, her high point coincided almost exactly with Halley's heavenly body of 1910. Though the connection is not often made – she appears to have been diffident about defining her origins too precisely – the fact is that the people of the Porangi were first to hear her remarkable voice. One which left "globes of light lingering in the auditorium" according to *New York Times* critic George B. Lancaster Jnr, discussing the way she, as love-luminous Mimi, departed the stage at the end of *La Bohème*'s Act 1. No account of the pioneering Porangi can afford to forget that she *was* a Lovelock – indeed daughter of founders Herman and Marie Louise, though some writers have confused or made mystery of her parentage, some supposing her to be a waif, others speculating that she may have been residue of a noted Italian tenor's antipodean sexual exploits. Was Lovelock Junction, in some way, the sylvan seedbed of her success? We shall never know. Certainly Europe found her fully armed and formidable. Much is usually made of her tempestuous love life, theatrical temperament, her rages, and especially her bitter rivalry with fellow antipodean Dame Nellie Melba, in whose footsteps she was long – perhaps too long for her peace of mind – obliged to follow; she never forgave Melba, for example, for being first to win Puccini's heart with her Mimi; she was never consoled by the fact that some critics thought her superior. "This other angel from the bush is even better," exulted one. The two prima donnas never met, though opportunities were offering; and identical lovers apparently passed through their hands. And more fascination resides in the terminus of her career than in her beginnings in obscure and ill-named Lovelock Junction. Among the many romantic rumours available, one has it that she entered a convent late in World War I, following the cruel and still inexplicable loss of her voice, perhaps forced too far and ruthlessly in that contest with ageing and unsinkable Melba. She never, alas, unlike Melba, became Dame Felicity. She can be glimpsed as a doomed minor character – dismissed within pages – in a best-selling Michael Arlen novel of the 1920s. Naturally one is tempted to make more of her story here; perhaps even to give credence to reports of her return to the Porangi. To be fair, though, Felicity only confuses the entire picture. She was lost to Lovelock Junction the day she sailed downriver. To reclaim her for that community, and make more than genetic connection, is an uphill task for the casual chronicler.'

Some chronicles are less uphill than others. Even a casual climber might find himself, without too large a loss of breath, making a memorial – from the crumbling rock closest to hand – to someone called Sylvester Spring. With, perhaps, a prayer and a sigh. One can give credence to anything. Even to a Felicity Lovelock fully armed.)

Upriver again, James and Benjamin, along with their sons, receive the first of their shocks; their vegetable gardens have been ravaged, beans and peas nibbled to nothing, cabbages left but a few inedible shreds. The damage has demonstrably not been done by cattle or sheep; fences are intact, and hedgerows unholed. Short of God's withering finger, however, the cause can only be attributed to one of His creatures.

'Rabbits,' James says, with disgust.

'They must have moved down the valley,' Benjamin observes.

'The buggers,' James adds. 'As if we haven't enough on our minds. Wool prices down. And the warm rain bringing out eczema.'

'Easy fixed,' Daniel announces with optimism. 'We build better fences. Davie and I will get it done.'

'Our gardens must have been temptation,' David points out. 'A paradise of plenty. You really can't blame them. They're here; we have to learn to live with them now.'

His father, uncle and cousins have less compassion.

'It's time to take them serious,' Benjamin declares, 'and blast them to blazes. And we can, besides, turn a profit on the skins.'

Next day the first shots in anger are fired. It is the start of the war. David remains slower than most to comprehend the gravity inherent in the thing; he fails to see mammals so tiny and tender as more than a passing and trivial menace. With the grazing lands of Spanish Creek so spacious, why cannot the rabbits be given fair share with sheep?

James, who has begun to give the matter serious study, produces succinct answer. 'There is no wild predator in this country to keep them in check,' he says. 'Nothing to curtail the size of their colonies.'

'So man must become predator?'

James sighs, perhaps with thought of his life. 'When is man not?'

David does not reply; the subject needs thought.

'Look to your Bible, if you must,' James adds. 'There you will see, when the Creator is done with the setting of scene, that the creature fashioned after His own likeness is given dominion over things of fur and feather; the right to rule.'

'If earned, I should have thought.'

'Ours is not to question. Though the temptations are plain. Ours, for the most part, is to survive.'

'For what?'

'Ah,' James says. 'Better to ask later, with a warm meal in your belly.'

'Which means to ask not at all.'

'We do have that choice.'

David is ferocious with adolescent virtue. 'There must be more, surely, than animal content.'

'If you insist,' James says wearily. 'But it might be more to the point if you got our firewood chopped. The fowls also need feeding.'

David, especially at this point, is not to be deflected. 'There is cruelty in this world,' he observes. 'Something not easily contemplated.'

'All tooth and claw,' James agrees. 'Not least among men, when warfare prevails. Why, one might well ask, should animals know more mercy?'

'That is something else I cannot understand,' David goes on, 'though it seems remote here. Why men savage at the throats of others, sometimes for sport? Some of Uncle Benjamin's sons ache for the chance to travel the seas and shoot at the Boers – of whom they have heard, and know next to nothing.'

James, at the least, is gratified to find his son unattracted by the allure of elsewhere; Felicity's departure has left him with new foreboding of the boy's eventual defection. 'There is no accounting for a sense of adventure,' James explains. 'In my late experience, it is best left to others. Meanwhile, what of that wood? And those fowls still unfed?'

'In good time,' David insists. 'But I am interested in truth.'

'Who isn't?'

'Some seem to care less than they might.'

'And some find their souls too taxed, and tired, to do more than accept. Truth becomes that which they prefer to believe; that which makes for least effort.'

'You describe the coward's calling.'

'Or the realist's. Truth is still there for the taking. In an honest axe, for example, and a log of unsplit wood.'

There is a silence, not without pain, between father and son.

'I'm sorry,' David hazards, at length.

'I rather think rabbits have run away with us,' James argues, though not with conviction. 'Their nuisance here – no more – hardly justifies our entering so treacherous a region, and finding ourselves strangers. Understand this. I am not without grief, wonder, or despairs of my own. Would that you were protected from the worst of our lot. I accept, as Sybil insists, that I am blessed with a sensitive son. A prayer fulfilled is sometimes a sorrow.' His arm becomes harbour for David's young shoulders. 'Need I say more?'

David doesn't pull away; not for a time.

'I will cut that wood,' he promises. 'And feed those fowls. And tomorrow Daniel and I will have secure fences to show.'

'That's my boy,' James says, unwilling to wonder.

The campaign against the rabbit soon lacks nothing in vehemence. The mischievous trespassers are driven from the vicinity of the two homesteads. Toward dusk, for some weeks, there is the sound of measured gunfire across the near fields, followed by methodical oaths, and still later the snap of steel traps. The farm dogs fatten with the abundance of flesh; fences are garlanded with skins hung to cure. Beyond new defences, vegetable gardens begin to green again, corn to grow tall, palpable indication of success. Random patrols are now thought sufficient to keep the rabbit curse in check; and the traps are sometimes empty of all but a few recalcitrant stragglers. Rabbit no longer figures much on the menu at Spanish Creek. The menfolk complain of the monotonous taste, even with ingenious disguise; the hottest curry cannot quite kill it. The boys propose to sell off the skins, turning the slaughter to profit. Daniel, for one, would like a fine horse. If he has an ambition larger, it is to ride against the Boers in southern Africa.

'Or perish of enteric fever,' David suggests, literate enough to consider the casualty lists in the newspapers which, sometimes months late, make their way up the Porangi.

'That's as may bloody be,' Daniel answers. 'But there's still some will survive.'

'What for?'

'For the hell of it; why not?'

'And a few more dead Boers.'

'The fuckers ask the world for a fight. It would be unfair to deny them.'

Perhaps fortunately for the Boers, though frustratingly for Daniel, there is another war, likewise unfinished, and far closer to hand. David and Daniel, boundary-riding together, looking for slack fences and lost sheep, comprehend that the first battle with the interlopers has been but a skirmish; the rabbits are not beaten at all. They have intelligently taken the hint that they are unwelcome down valley; that humans are murderous. The astute among them have claimed as terrain the more remote hilltops, tunnelling for safety, and bountiful breeding; it looks for all the world like a network of fortresses, tactically and swiftly fashioned. Everywhere excesses are visible. There are rocks between which hardly a blade of good grass now grows; the hooves of the horses kick up a fine dust where once was firm grazing. Sheep are not conspicuous; they have evidently surrendered their right to browse on the heights, and some look listless already. 'Sweet Jesus,' Daniel says, dismounting, unsheathing his rifle, and steadying it for his first shot. 'The buggers are everywhere. They got us by the balls.'

He is not long taking sight, and squeezing his trigger. The landscape up there, with the wind whining about, is alive with the enemy, scorning concealment, indifferent to man. One rabbit crumples; another falls to the shot following. A half hundred others scatter, showing at least some formal concern.

Even once compassionate David now has to allow that pestilence is upon them; that no quarter can be shown. He grabs up his own rifle, slaps away his horse, and takes stance beside Daniel. Together they move grimly over the perforated ground, unleashing shot after shot. For every dead rabbit left cooling in their wake, five others are seen flaunting life, and at most minor wounds. By the afternoon's end their rifles are hot and their ammunition expended. Hawks wheel overhead, waiting to feed. Daniel and David are too tired even to salvage the skins; they recover their horses, leaving the landscape much as they found it, and ride home with news impossible to construe as anything but bitter. James and Benjamin hear their sons out with some disbelief; next day they are saddling their horses and riding out to see for themselves, with rifles too, and more ammunition.

When all the surveys are done, and boundaries ridden, the picture is one of brutal dimension. The rabbits are taking and holding the heights, turning useful hilltops to desert, and working greedily down to grasses still choicer. The sheep suffer the loss of their grazing, and move elsewhere. Man is not one to accept plague so tranquilly; but where to begin? Until now it has been a hot and slack summer, especially since the shearing gangers departed with their pay packets and willing womenfolk, though not with young David's cherry, to Daniel's regret. Even the sturdiest of the visiting trollops failed to persuade him to part with it, despite bawdy taunts, and a bold pair who tumbled him into the greasier wool; David appears determined to save the substance of his manhood for another season, or at least for his sheets. Now the high times and sweats of shearing seem trivia. Now all is alarm. Spanish Creek is in siege.

So too is Richard, in his congested way, not more than a few miles distant. The hot weather, continuing even as summer subsides, has not been conducive to mellowness of temper, nor helped his marriage, though Nancy has some mysteriously quiet moments, almost as if with thoughts of her own; in addition the din of his offspring, as he stalks his own house, is often insufferable. Nevertheless his determination not to concede sovereignty on the Porangi, certainly in the environs of Dixtown, is undiminished. True that starvation has proved a poor tactic. The men he could once call his own can fend for themselves effectively in the wilderness. Worse, what they lack – especially that for which money is normally necessary – is made good by malcontents raising funds and food supplies elsewhere in the country, presumably friends of Finns', men hell-bent on undermining masters, and the time-tested natural order of things; they send their aid stealthily upriver, sometimes in small boats under cover of dark, distinctly with no other purpose than the thwarting of Richard. Doubtless they see the standstill on the Porangi as a symbol; some last bastion to fall so that trade unionists, and others of similarly unkempt ilk, can begin to use the world, and those who create wealth, to their will. If so, they reckon without Richard. He is not in the mood to make himself a doormat for the muddy-booted of the earth. If everyman becomes master, all will be anarchy, freedom a farce; men will be undisciplined slaves to their own selfish appetites. Richard's moral stiffening has come late; one could say it well earned.

Law and order has begun to seem a shifty ally, certainly in the fat and sweaty shape of Constable Stubbs. There have been marches through Dixtown, within view of Richard's windows, and banners brazenly displayed, slogans shouted uphill. Stubbs, more and more typically, does nothing. 'I have to live with these people,' he explains to Richard. 'They're my kind, you know.'

'That's an interestingly recent discovery,' Richard is obliged to observe.

'What do you expect me to do?' Stubbs demands. 'Stand there, alone in the street, and provoke a disorder?'

'You could do worse,' Richard suggests. 'And then call in reinforcements.'

'It's my head gets bashed in,' Stubbs laments. 'I'm not such a fool. It's not as if I've done nothing for you. I did my best to get something on Finn. It's hardly my fault that the bugger's unblemished.'

'Look at the sods,' Richard points out. 'They're all bloody Finns; I can't tell the difference. Even most Malones look the same to me now.'

'That's your problem,' Stubbs argues, 'with things going so far. You could have given an inch.'

'Of the first mile. Along which I dance to their tune. I pay the piper. And, I might remind you, the taxes out of which the government, for some reason, employs such as yourself.'

'Things aren't so simple,' Stubbs pleads. 'There are some men in government, and I'd soon as not mention their names, who argue that working men have rights. Doubtless the sods are after working men's votes. But that's not here nor there. A fact is a fact.'

'Piss off,' Richard says, lately inclined to find facts mentally and intestinally fettering.

Stubbs leaves without even his customary sampling of Richard's best whisky; he has reason to think the master of Dixtown might be over the hill. Stubbs might have to consider covering his own tracks, lest he soon follow Richard.

Richard, incarcerated in his own house, and soon with sunless pallor, has but one sure retreat when he sees fit to brood; the billiard room. It is not of concern that he lacks an opponent. He can play ingeniously against himself; and otherwise concentrate on perfection of shots. The longer the strike lasts, the easier it becomes to sink any ball at will. Even those in the most immobile situations, apparently safe in a cluster of balls dissimilarly coloured, are ambushed by Richard's skill in selecting surprise angles; and are plucked free of their fellows to soar into a pocket of his choosing. Here, at least, he has the world in control. Even a demonstration outside, the most raucous of shouting from strikers, does not distract him. He can find something akin to happiness for a few hours. The sound of his cue is just that for Nancy; she can take it that Richard is preoccupied, and that she is thus available for Finn, even if at short notice. Her signal is efficient; a pair of lace drawers arranged to air on the sill of an upstairs window. Finn, even if speaking to a crowd, in the middle of an outdoor meeting, discovers his ardour as strike leader impaired; and excuses himself to find his way to the west of the rubbish tip. Though homely, this site has as virtue no likely onlookers; among his fellows his defection across the no man's land of class warfare is unsuspected; they merely assume that Finn, a scholarly sort, requires seclusion to think out future strategy. To be fair, his connection with Nancy involves no gross betrayal; he believes he turns their association to ideological advantage. There is more to it than sex undiluted, though certainly the act of copulation, especially now he has the hang of it, can take some time. He can win from Nancy some intelligence of the enemy. Airing knickers can in themselves tell of Richard Lovelock's increasing desperation, a boss with his back to the wall, and yet another working-class victory in view. Nancy likes to share confidences; not all their love-talk is of idle or inflammatory nature.

'The bugger would sooner ruin himself, and us all, than give in,' she has occasion to tell Finn. 'His mental condition is poor.'

This appears to give Finn a much-needed clue. 'Could some way be found, perhaps, to confine him?' he asks. 'Perhaps some medical examination might be arranged.'

'He doesn't have dealings with doctors. The buggers meddle, he says, and bury their mistakes. If indisposed, or constipated as now, he uses herbs familiar to the Maoris of which he also has knowledge.'

'I see,' Finn says sadly.

'Anyway,' she asks, 'where would that get us?'

'It came to me that, if proven currently unstable of mind, and confined, his affairs would be taken from his hands. You, for instance, might take over. And settle.'

'With you? With the union?'

'Naturally. And full recognition.'

'A dream,' she argues. 'Though I don't say it isn't pleasant to contemplate.'

'In dreams are our beginnings,' Finn proposes; he has always found poetic utterance useful in swaying a crowd. And, more recently, in causing Nancy some sensual agitation; he has given her a feeling for words.

'All very bloody well,' she replies. 'But what when Richard came back – if this ever happened – and found what had been done in his absence? There could be unfortunate consequences. Murder, for one.'

'I've accepted greater risks. Don't fear for my safety.'

'I'm talking of mine.'

'Let's forget it, then,' Finn agrees, and tries to, until further thought makes him articulate. He never lacks prose when poetry has steamed to the end of the line. 'These herbs you mention, used for his constipation. If he never leaves the house, who gathers them now?'

'I do, of course,' she answers. 'I have to roam far and bloody wide;

there's no one else he can trust. If it weren't for the gathering of herbs as excuse, I might have less time with you.'

'Why can't he trust others?' Finn queries. 'Why only you?'

'Because I know the right herbs from bitter experience,' she tells him. 'In confusion, once, I picked the damn flower of the tutu. It roused him to considerable rage. He mentioned once almost losing a racehorse; anyway a race. It can cause delusions. And, in some cases, death.'

'I've heard that,' he says.

'So I've learned better; he knows my choice safe.'

Finn grows quite thoughtful. And Nancy alarmed.

'No,' she says.

'Yes.'

'You're asking me to poison the bugger.'

'In moderation. Only to make his mental condition more apparent. You could notify his brothers; they would have to take him in hand.'

'Quiet. I don't wish to hear more. What must you think of me?'

'That's a difficult question to answer, at times. Only in your arms is there some certainty. For the rest, I'm confused. Something must happen, for better or worse. The slightest straw is worth clutching.'

'Straw isn't poisonous. You're talking of tutu.'

'Well, yes,' Finn concedes. 'And of the care, and confinement, which your husband much needs. We're talking of mercy. A charitable act.'

'Your tongue could tame a tiger. I'm not bloody deceived. You want your strike won.'

'I'm not averse to discussing ends and means, if under protest. It is a useful philosophical bone for a quiet hour. But words never substitute for action, the only practical test.'

'Now that you mention it,' she says, prone beside him, 'this is becoming all words, with bugger all action.'

Finn, as reliable as usual, gives her no further cause for complaint. Fortunately youth is on his side, as it certainly isn't on her husband's. As for Finn, though their satisfaction is mutual, he is now aware that on balance Nancy is the more needy. Pride in his honest masculine craftsmanship, hard earned in the thickets, is tempered with an affectionate cunning. It is a day with bonus for both. A soft word can subvert a hard world. His last soft word to Nancy, who now seems much less inclined to take fright, is tutu. He might well have sown seed in more ways than one. Truth to tell, he will likely be sorry to see the end of the strike. He knows, as a matter of faith, that the masses become educated in the struggle for better conditions, as witness the battle beside the Porangi, a perfect example of men made militant where once most were sheep. He has never quite counted on himself being beneficiary too; it is all most informative.

Within a day or two, trembling Nancy begins to embrace her task. Richard, at breakfast, after the children are banished, reports his constipation still chronic, doubtless due to his surfeit of seclusion.

'You don't need to coop yourself up here,' Nancy tells him, not for the first time. 'You could take a stroll in the evenings. It's all your own choice.'

She hopes he will hear. She would still sooner not venture upon perilous measures. The man, would he but see it, is determined to place temptation in her path; and specifically tutu.

'Damn you, woman,' he answers; he has never been one to dissimulate anger. 'I don't need a lecture. When I want your advice, I'll ask for it. I've merely seen fit to mention my bowels.'

'Which could use an airing to advantage. That's all I've said.'

'And I've bloody well heard you. Don't go on more. My life is my own business. Likewise my bowels.'

'You make them mine too, whenever they prove to lack enterprise. It is not the most tasteful of subjects at breakfast.' Nancy, since marrying Richard, and bearing his children, is sensitive to her role as lady of the house, an arbiter of civilized custom, perhaps more so because of her boisterous and on the whole unmentionable past; she believes in at least a minimum of decorum, though Richard in this area would drive a saint to sinful utterance. I've come to suspect that the source of your problem is less in your bowels than in your confused brain. Your inner obstinacy may well be because you can no longer see reason.'

It is, however much Richard may decline to recognize it, a last despairing appeal. She is asking Richard to save her from herself; and thus himself too.

She has no choice. Within the hour she is out on hillsides above the river, gathering herbs. She snatches at the forbidden flower after no little hesitation, and with a faint heart; and then dizzily closes her eyes. She would prefer not to examine the essence of the journey on which she has embarked. On the practical side, however, she sees no difficulty in disguising it, well crushed, among the other herbs Richard needs to enlighten his bowels; a few grains of sugar will work wonders with the taste. She senses fate vastly and invisibly tugging her on; she feels herself tiny in a tempestuous wind. Rather than give that sensation a chance to undo her, and fail not only Finn but herself, she hurries weakly homeward to Richard. Before very long, in only the time it takes her to confect it, her husband is consuming a watery mish-mash of herbs, followed by a tumbler of rum, with his usual satisfaction. 'You can't beat it,' he says, and grows sentimental. 'The Maoris mightn't have known how to make the most of this country,' he informs her, 'but in other ways they weren't slouches. Not when it came to giving the guts a good sluice.'

'If you say so,' she replies, now as submissive a wife as Richard might desire. She is watching his eyes lest they grow prematurely wild, perhaps even turn inward; God knows the horror which may be in store. Meanwhile, she hopes he cannot hear her heart beating. There is already a symptom, conceivably, in his abnormally amiable mood.

'While this stuff's working,' he tells her, 'I think I'll bash a few balls around the table. There's nothing better than billiards while awaiting the call.'

'Of course,' she says, 'but do take it easy.'

'Easy?' he demands.

She panics. Is he suspicious? 'I mean you're still a man under strain. This strike gets you down.'

His next and last word is perhaps meant to relax her. But it rather dismays.

'Never,' he answers.

With that, he retires to the billiard room. She hears a rattle of balls on the table as he shapes them up for a game. Then there is silence, an unusually long pause before the first click of his cue. She listens, unable to interest herself in domestic affairs, or to make her feet move.

Nancy's concern, not to say fear, is unnecessary. Richard is in the grip of a vision quite dazzling in nature; and attributing it, if attribution is needed, wrongly to the tumbler of rum. He sees, as no man has, the coloured balls all arranged in mystical conjunction; they make even tarot cards seem silly. They offer a message. Then he understands what it is. The meaning has to do with his mastery. They are suggesting their disposal, from pocket to pocket, right down the table, all in one swift and shrewd shot; something no man has ever attempted, nor even contemplated, with a billiard cue gripped in his hand. The concept is breathtaking, but Richard finds himself blessed, at this moment, with an abundance of breath. Of the ten billion neurons known in the average human brain, most of Richard's might be presumed to be excessively active. Even a growing rumble in his lower bowel leaves him unmoved. Only his nostrils quiver, and then but faintly, as he leans feline over the table, eyes flickering from ball to ball, ascertaining all the available angles, most unrevealed to man until now; indeed he crouches quite as a cat over a multi-coloured colony of mice. He checks, and rechecks; he finds no calculation in error. History is his. 'Now,' he whispers. He steadies himself coolly; he shoots. The result, even if arranged, all quite foreseen, nevertheless remains astounding; he has but to stand back, and let it all happen. Balls riot and richochet the length of the table, briefly protesting personalities of their own, despite Richard's intricate manipulation. Confusion soon clarifies. There is just one end for all. Some balls sprint to the pocket; others glide with great calm. A few find argument with each other, before spinning off into pre-selected oblivion. No matter how tenaciously they try to cling to the table, they have no real chance; they have never had choice. Of the final half-dozen left contesting this truth, five soon locate their abyss, and fade from the table. At length just one ball, red in hue, is left rolling. There is no mistaking the symbol. 'That's fucking Finn,' Richard shouts. 'Damn you to hell.' The ball, nothing if not obedient, in a faltering way, points itself toward a pocket, travels the last few inches; and then teeters. 'Drop,' Richard commands, a hangman in haste. 'Drop, you red bastard, drop.' He no longer sees point in subterfuge; he is God. Then, to prove it, the great game is over. The red ball gently, and gratifyingly, falls; there is just a faint clatter as it joins with its fellows. The table is clear.

So is Richard's mind, most impressively, as his wife Nancy is soon first to see. He bursts from the billiard room, doors banging behind him; he has never stood taller, with eyes so incendiary.

'Is it your bowels?' she asks with alarm.

'Don't talk of trivia,' he answers. 'I've much more to put right.'

'Much more?' she says weakly.

'The world,' he discloses. 'It's all bloody awry.'

'No doubt,' she tries to say calmly. 'But are you sure you're up to this task?'

'You've no bloody faith. Not when my chips are down.'

'But where,' she pleads, 'to begin?'

'Here. Now. With this pitiful strike. There'll be no more nonsense. Never.'

'You mean you'll settle?'

'Settle?'

'With your men.'

'Exactly,' he says. 'I'll give them one sack of shit.'

Richard is suffered a reminder of his acute internal condition. He takes himself with speed to the privy, there proving the efficacy of the herbs in which he has trust. For the rest, or for the one herb in which he doesn't, shaken Nancy can only ask herself: Dear God in heaven, if You're up there, what damage have I done?

Aside from certain distant sounds of satisfaction on the part of her husband, she has silence for answer; and stands quite in trance.

Richard returns, if not with the settlement he is disposed to make with his men, at least with fresh vocal vigour. 'Get moving,' he orders. And further instructs her, 'Fetch up my clothes. Pack me a bag.'

'Why?' she says, with wonder. 'Where are you going?'

'To a city,' he says, brisk. 'It doesn't matter which one. Not for the transactions I have in mind.'

'There's no steamer,' she points out practically. 'They've almost stopped calling. How can you get there?'

'I'll row myself down to the coast. And find some fast ship. North, south, it doesn't matter a fuck. I'll bloody walk if I must. And I promise you this. Every blister I get will be paid for, in full, and with considerable interest.'

Now Nancy does have great fear. 'What are you planning?' she asks, through a thick throat.

'What you don't know won't hurt you.'

Nancy feels this unlikely. For one thing, intuition tells her that Finn's prospects are unpromising. And, in addition, her own. Trysts near the rubbish tip, and Finn's sexual vivacity, could soon be a thing of the past. She has never seen her husband so pure in menace.

'You could,' she suggests tentatively, 'allow me one tiny hint.'

'It's no time to procrastinate. Or pass idle words. Get on with preparing my bag. And, while you're at it, pack my revolver. I might need it damn soon.'

Nancy does know the worst. The rest is mere detail.

Before Richard departs, on his still cloudy mission, he calls Constable Stubbs up to the house. 'I could convey a message to your superiors,' he tells Stubbs, 'concerning the rumours that are rife here.'

'Rumours?' Stubbs asks.

'Of violence in the offing. Plans to loot the store, and leave mines and mill blazing.'

'News to me,' Stubbs says blankly. 'I've never known things more quiet.'

'Before the storm,' Richard observes, 'things usually are.'

Stubbs displays early symptoms of palsy. 'So what are you getting at?' he finally asks.

'The need for strong police reinforcement. No more. You can't control things alone. Surely that's clear.'

'My God,' Stubbs says, more distinctly. 'You sure about this? You wouldn't be making me look a panicky fool?'

'I admire your raw courage,' Richard says, not without charm. 'But you must heed the risk. There's more to life than being a dead hero, and earning some posthumous police decoration.'

Stubbs, with speed, produces a lengthy report for Richard to convey. On the whole it sums up Richard's suggestions precisely; he couldn't have composed better himself. Stubbs, by way of precaution, the more entirely to satisfy his superiors, has embellished the communication with urgent fancies of his own; nor has he failed, for example, to draw attention to the precarious and unloved lot of a solitary constable on the Porangi.

That accomplished and sealed, Richard rows off downriver with gusto, not content to ride the current, and favourable tide. Heartsick Nancy watches him vanish, hangs lace drawers to air from the upstairs window, and sets out to meet Finn. 'Crisis is coming,' she warns.

'Not unexpectedly,' he says with assurance. 'We were never in doubt that his nerves would one day crack.'

'I'm thinking of skulls being cracked. Yours among others.'

'Your concern touches me,' he admits. 'But we're ready. And can't lose. History is on our side.'

'You might be a bloody sight better off contemplating geography,' Nancy suggests. 'Men can get away with murder on the Porangi. Believe me. I know.'

She can hardly say more; not as an accessory. But Finn is unaware of her approximate confession. His hands grope, rather feverishly, deep into her garments. Nancy isn't inclined to be obstructive, or to dampen boyish enthusiasm; she is disarmed, and quite soon undressed. Lovers and lunatics have something in common. They imagine the world beyond themselves barely exists.

In that world, which has a prima facie existence, Richard makes his way fast to a city. In the nature of things, and certainly of human society, his task takes some time. Monday is the day for his major enterprise; the rest of the week is for the most part waste. On Monday the stone city prison releases inmates who have served their full sentence, and done for a time with the breaking of rock. Outside the prison, just beyond the steel gate, an affable Richard sits upon a large dray drawn by four horses. For the least attractive convicts, particularly those most parched, and of no fixed abode other than prison, Richard has a tempting package to offer. Immediately, full board and booze, followed by a short coastal journey; and finally permanent employment in a place where they can, God willing, make more of their lives. Richard chooses not to confuse with fine detail. It is enough to suggest that there are others, selfish in character, dogs in the manger, who would deprive his listeners of his well-intentioned offer; and who might, at most, create peripheral disturbance. As for the rest, he points out that his audience has little to lose; and that the job is best suited to men of generous muscle. If they have friends fitting this description, and who might be considered trustworthy, so much the better. The more the merrier, in truth.

Three such Mondays, with discreet expenditure of oratory, are sufficient for Richard to gather a large, fresh and altogether willing labour force – though again in the nature of things, often to be found in emptying bottles, some run foul of the law again and are lost before he can get them aboard ship. The trip, given good weather, takes only two days. As the vessel steams up the Porangi, Richard addresses his prospective employees – some still seasick, and some even sober – on the subject of their rehabilitation in the workaday world; he is at pains, as is fair, not to promise too much in the way of immediate advancement; he contents himself with the observation that, in matters of virtue, nothing need stand in the way of the human will. He then draws their gaze to many lengths of knotty black wood arranged on the deck. These, he says, might well be useful in establishing their credentials ashore; and may even be necessary if minor difficulties are encountered. Desirably, each man should attend to his own needs in respect of accommodation, with roofs plentiful in Dixtown; it might be noted that winter is near, and the nights growing colder. In due course – perhaps tomorrow – they can get mines and mill working again. Richard only shows impatience when questions are asked concerning the further availability of alcohol. All in good time, he argues; he promises, when pressed yet again, a large issue of liquid refreshment that night. By way of afterthought, he announces that no one is to be alarmed by the sight of police in number ashore. Some aboard, given unfortunate experience, might see human beings in uniform as habitually enemy. Not so. In this instance, the police are to be counted as friends; they will be present only for the protection of his employees, certainly of his mines and mill. This announcement causes some stir, but no listener is slow to make a selection from the batons Richard has also humanely provided.

The end of the often high-spirited voyage is near. First Herman's tower, then the bulk of Lovelock House itself, rise on the river horizon. There is an animated oath or two. Conversation as such ceases. A last bottle splashes into the river. The steamer rides under the extremities of Lovelock Junction's plateau, and shortly berths at the Dixtown jetty. Stubbs is soon aboard, with a senior police sergeant. Richard makes it his business to give both a full briefing. There is no reason, he insists, why the affair should not pass off peacefully. He is perfectly prepared to give the strikers time to evacuate Dixtown. Also more than prepared to provide them with passage downriver at no cost to themselves. Given all the circumstances, he suggests, this is eminently fair. Neither Stubbs nor the police sergeant appears to cavil, other than in matters of detail; it seems, in any case, that their attention is more taken by familiar faces among Richard's fresh and muscular work force. 'It looks like you'll be doing us a favour,' the city sergeant says warmly, 'if you can keep this lot upriver, and out of harm's way.' Stubbs shows less enthusiasm for the citizens in his future care. He finds himself contemplating early retirement, a quiet garden somewhere, a view of the sea.

'There could be some difficulties,' the sergeant observes.

'Undeniably,' Richard agrees. 'We're not unprepared.'

'I mean for us. In keeping the peace.'

'God knows,' Richard says with sympathy, 'it's always unpleasant.'

Difficulties visibly arrange themselves ashore. There are demonstrators, more by the moment, not only strikers but their womenfolk too. They unfurl their already frayed banners, shout their now pointless slogans, and in general defy Richard to do his worst. He vows not to disappoint them, and in particular Finn, conspicuously rousing his rabble. Between demonstrators and the steamer's restive criminal cargo there stand a few constables, rather less than a score. Most have been bored by inactivity on the Porangi. Today, at least, they can have no complaint. There is point to their lives. All carry batons.

'Right,' Richard proposes to the sergeant and Stubbs, 'it's time to get on with the job. Let's get it over and done.'

The sergeant, with tiresome formality, insists on a speech first; an address to the strikers. Taking up stance on the jetty, he appeals to them to keep their heads, and make their departure, with their families, from the Porangi in orderly fashion. The strike is over. Work must proceed. The rule of the law has to prevail on the Porangi as elsewhere. Otherwise neither he nor his men can be held responsible for the consequences.

'It's not quite the riot act,' Stubbs murmurs to Richard. 'But it might do the trick.'

Stubbs, always an optimist, is out of tune with events. And a coward to boot, as Richard well knows; the bugger's face is all sweat.

From the strikers and their women, the sergeant's over-long speech draws diverse expressions of contempt. 'You're helping your class enemy,' Finn informs the sergeant. 'Shame,' a woman cries. 'Does your mother know you do this?'

The sergeant, old enough to be motherless, is not seen discomforted. To Richard he says, 'Things may not go well.'

It is no surprise to Richard. He simply reassures himself that his revolver, belted under his jacket, doesn't make far too suspect a bulge. If the rule of law isn't sufficient, there is always a court of last resort; not necessarily lethal. Gunfire in his experience can work many charms, and be immensely persuasive. Even police inclined to indolence suddenly keep up to the mark. Especially if it is unclear who is firing, in times of confusion.

'I can only suggest,' the sergeant adds, 'that you lead your men ashore. While mine stand by to keep public order.'

'Stand by?' Richard asks. 'Is this what you're paid for?'

'We're obliged to keep things as calm as we can.'

'No more,' the craven Stubbs agrees. 'As the sergeant can doubtless explain, we can't go beyond our brief. If resistance is offered to you, or impediment placed in your path, we may be obliged to take requisite action.'

'May be?' Richard queries. 'You bloody well will be. It's time to point out that we are the innocent parties. Those sods up on the riverbank are making the trouble. Not us; not me.'

'Don't tell me my job,' the sergeant replies. 'I'll give the orders. At this moment it's entirely over to you. Are you going ashore?'

In even poorer humour, not least with police, Richard is left with no option; he endeavours to rally his men, most of whom have been overawed by the presence of enforcers of law. Richard finds obscenities useful in making clear where they all stand, and in helping them feel more at home here; the law for now can be ignored.

He advances along the jetty toward dry land and demonstrators; there is an untidy tramp of feet behind him as his men leave the boat. A sound on the whole satisfying. His men may not be especially palatable company. But at their best, with batons, they are not bloody cowards.

'Scabs,' the people of Dixtown call. 'Blacklegs. Furry tails. Scum. Go home.'

This suits Richard. His men need to be put in candid mood. He reaches the bank beyond the jetty, beginning to cross ground gritty with coal. He doesn't pause. Despite their abuse, he continues marching directly toward the strikers. If men wish to see who is master, he will give value for money. It might also favourably impress the police; those bastards only back winners. Impediment, however, is placed in his path by a rock of some substance. It strikes him in the approximate centre of his face, momentarily blinding, certainly stunning. He seems to be trying to rise from the ground. Another stone hits the side of his head, proving the first to have been no ill-tempered and solitary mistake. Euphoria quite gone, he looks back for his men. They are likewise battling against objects flung by the demonstrators: not only stones, but large nuts and bolts, broken bricks, and particularly damaging lengths of timber tossed like a Scots caber; the immediate horizon has palpably darkened with debris made airborne. From his men, some pinned down, some barely conscious, there are acute sounds of dismay. They had bargained for resistance of reasonable nature, not beyond normal tenacity. The police, living up to expectations, and contrary to their extensive vocabulary concerning public order, seem to have no great interest in playing a part in this scene. For one thing, they are few.

The problem is still Richard's. And patently it is no time to shrink from showing his power to command, his knowledge of what makes men work best. 'Take the buggers,' he shouts. 'Five pounds bonus – better still, ten – for everyone who helps me clear this whole bloody town.'

The offer is imposing, and made at a good moment. Perhaps with useful missiles few to hand, there is diminution in the bombardment contrived by the strikers; some of the sods are perceptibly backing away. Still more begin to defect when Richard, loud on his feet again, urges his men forward. 'Clear the town,' he repeats. 'From now on it's yours. Bash the bastards from arseholes to breakfast time.'

A baton, even in skilled hands, lacks the precision of a billiard cue; nevertheless the effect can equally astonish. Richard's men, bruised and bribed, are soon working among the foremost of the strikers with intelligence and energy. There is blood; there are men fallen; there are boots when batons alone fail to gratify. It is far from one-sided; there are strikers sufficiently foolish to fight back. But the attack is stiffened pleasingly by police reinforcement; even Stubbs can be seen trying to make himself functional. They drive on into the centre of Dixtown. There are moments when everything seems much as Richard first saw it in vision: in place of pockets about an agreeably clearing billiard table, there are dwellings into which strikers flee, presumably to skulk safe with their womenfolk. Most are soon enough dragged out again and dispensed solid medicine. Richard nevertheless wishes things to shape with more speed; he would also like bloody Finn to reveal himself in all this confusion. Women screaming, children crying, only add to his irritation; there are too many irrelevant human beings underfoot, and about. He begins to find much of the fighting peripheral, lacking real piquance. Just one man matters now. That man is Finn. So where the hell is he?

Then Richard sees the skinny blowhard, streaming blood, in a large brawl; Stubbs is there too, for all that he matters, clumsily trying to club his way out of the scrum. Richard cannot but succumb to temptation; he braces himself against the quiet side of a house, with luck unobserved, and hunts out the revolver under his jacket. He takes a quick sight. Finn's head is quite clear, if ducking and diving; Richard needs merely to anticipate where it will move. He fires just the once. And it seems, in a moment, that once is enough. Panic spreads, with men briefly frozen, as the sound of the shot reverberates back from the hills. Even that vigorous brawl on which Richard has concentrated seems to lose heart. But when figures separate in shock, it is not Finn who falls. It is Constable Stubbs.

Richard pockets the revolver rather than test his luck twice. Fate must stand uncorrected. Serious things are shaping, demanding quick wit; he races into the clamour, aiming fists and distinctively foul language at Finn. 'I saw you,' he shouts. And to others, 'I saw the shit do it.'

Stubbs is not dead, nor even dying, though giving fair imitation. He bleeds and groans in the dirt. Nearby, while most are distracted, and Finn flees, Richard locates a revolver on the ground; he shows those who gather a single round missing from the chamber. 'This is it,' he announces. 'This is the gun I saw in bloody Finn's hand.'

One or two others, men who might well make useful witnesses, find the authenticity of Richard's account quite captivating; they begin to recall the gun in Finn's hand too. Stubbs himself is not neglected. The bleeding in his shoulder is staunched, though there remains a bullet to be extracted. Fellow constables carry him away.

Meanwhile, the fight ebbs away to the remoter edges of Dixtown. The streets crowd with strikers and families now finding it practical to depart. Some of Richard's former employees pass him in police custody; most have been arrested on charges of resisting arrest. Heads need bandaging; there are broken limbs to be set. Many of Dixtown's older identities are moving toward the plateau, others toward the steamer, or perhaps just a spare dinghy. For Richard, all an intoxicating sight; it only needs Finn's arrest to make it perfect. Vision allows for no less.

Unwilling to fit into Richard's final mosaic, and all blood and blackening bruises, Finn gropes blindly among his belongings in a bachelor hut near the north end of the town; he grabs up books and a few bits of clothing. He has no time for more. Outside again, sobbing and gasping, he takes to the trees. Richard's day is left with a flaw. But triumph tempered by regret is still better than none.

Later Richard carries his news uphill to Nancy. She has seen and heard most from the house, though there were times when she didn't dare look, and once when she covered her head with a blanket. She wishes to ask Richard about Finn. She cannot.

'Things were due for a change here,' he tells her. 'They couldn't go on.'

He glows. She has to look at him a second time, then a third, and a fourth. He seems to have shed a decade. Her mouth turns quite dry. No more lacklustre, he is unmistakably her husband, and a man of some substance; also one who can cringe rather marvellously to her carnal whim.

'Then there's the matter,' he goes on, 'of that bastard Finn. He took a cowardly shot at a copper – poor bloody Stubbs, to tell you the truth. Then turned tail and ran for his miserable life. It's all over for him and his kind on the Porangi. You can't turn a gun on the law and get away with it. The police are bloody particular about offences like that. Doubtless they'll bring him in soon.'

Nancy, after all, finds small cause to grieve. Finn, or so it would seem, no longer much matters.

'Doubtless they will,' she agrees.

Marie Louise anxiously takes it upon herself to interrupt Herman, a matter not light, not with the human condition in flux. He looks up from his current text, *The Age of Reason*, from which he has been taking copious notes when able to get the better of his irritation. He is exploring the probably temporary hypothesis that man cannot, and can never by nature, be entrusted with reason; a pessimistic view perhaps, but Herman believes in building from rock bottom. There is another, if marginal prospect: Was the discovery of reason, albeit delusion, the original sin? This might be worthy of experimental provenance; it could cause many towers to topple; the consequent rubble could be a base quite as reliable as rock. Then comes the infernal interruption; reality crowds in his damn door; there is nothing hypothetical about Marie Louise. 'You'd better come quick,' she tells him, altogether breathless. 'You'd never believe it.'

'Believe what?' He knows from hard-earned experience the woman will believe anything. Give her a penny, and fancy will print her a pound.

'What's happening out there. God in heaven, half the population of Dixtown's coming over the hill.'

Faced with this claim, from a wife who treats truth with extravagance, Herman is tactically cool rather than cantankerous. 'Be precise,' he urges. 'And concise, if it's not too exhausting.'

'I swear it. See for yourself.'

With reluctance Herman finally sees it desirable to answer her plea. Further argument with the woman will only take precious time. Anything to amuse her and get back to work. The twentieth century, too close at hand, is already and unseasonably sending out feelers, fine tendrils and buds; the bloody blossoms might be falling around him before he can get its embryonic fruit fertilized. News has reached him of rowdy conveyances abroad called horseless carriages. There are some, possibly not fools, who talk of soon flying. If men cannot get themselves right now, what hope have they of hearing in the din of tomorrow? Worse, he has a suspicion that he will shortly be seventy. Three score years and ten now seems something less than a prize. Not with life still to elucidate.

Time winged at his heels, then, Herman begins to take himself toward the top of his tower. Marie Louise, less used to the stairs, and fast out of wind, follows some distance behind. Herman warns her to watch for bricks loose or falling; also not to clutch the rail too tight, lest she pull away portions of the tower. 'You're telling me it's unsafe,' she declares, with her customary overstatement. 'It might creak a bit,' Herman answers, 'but then so do we.' He then prophesies with remarkable accuracy, 'It will see out my life. There's no cause to panic.'

At the top Herman, still feeling harried, and hopeful of giving his wife acerbic rebuttal, finds himself blinking, and not just because of bright sunlight. There are times when he feels his eyesight has been weakened by long hours of work. This is not one of those times. Below, right across the plateau, he sees people in number quite distinctly, all presumably in search of safety and shelter. Their distress is apparent; fresh bloodstains too, and worldly goods crudely gathered. Marie Louise, for once in her life, and God knows by what miracle, has actually minimized the position. Wherever he looks, and his field of vision is ample, there are still more refugees from Dixtown rising upon the plateau; many Malones and other old faces.

In years past, he would have welcomed this sight; he would not have been slow to identify the event as heralding the death of Dixtown, not before time, and the rejuvenation of Lovelock Junction's real centre; he would have seen it all, with justice, as triumph. Now, with the best will in the world, he cannot deceive himself. Triumph is arriving too late. Youth has gone, also brute energy, and prospect of iron. The earliest houses, conspicuously those in Little Luke Lane, have too long been abandoned, though even in disrepair they may afford a few a temporary roof. The hall, built to hold questions of human import, is all broken windows. The Old House, in the wake of gales, has all but given up the ghost. Begin again? The thought appals. There are no useful second chances. The first chance is life. The second is death, which resists all improvement. Moreover, he has unfinished business, and of more global scale; a mere town seems a toy. And giving it point appears rather a hobby when set against the opportunity of presenting humanity with a new grammar; he has, after all, only to sort out the spelling, a task not impossible with patience, and time.

Which is demonstrably denied him. Perversely, as usual, humanity now chooses to press itself upon him; and before he has a hope in hell of getting things right. Useless to plead that he is placed in an embarrassing position; that a few years' postponement might serve matters best. Yet again he will have the problem of finding the wood among the trees.

The plateau, of a sudden, swarms with migrant trees. A God's-eye view will no longer suffice.

'We've got to get down there,' Herman announces, 'and do what we can.'

For one thing he has observed wretches with batons driving people the last few steps up the track from Dixtown. This enables him to make sense of the scene. It is Richard again; Richard trying to tame people to his purpose, or profit, and obstinately missing the point. People, and even eventually hirelings with clubs, finally live for themselves: they cannot live for the infinite convenience of others. Not for Richard's convenience. Nor even for Herman's. There are times when Richard might have tempted Herman's brotherly sympathy; they might have commiserated together. Given other circumstances, that is, and conceivably another Richard. Other circumstances are seldom the case; they are certainly not now. And Richard himself can apparently become only more so. Time inflates rather than remodels, to Herman's despair.

He and Marie Louise hasten down from the tower. Their incautious descent shakes a brick loose, and sets off some structural grumbling, but this is ignored. Marie Louise hunts out bandages and bedding. Herman fetches his best shotgun. With this he patrols the plateau, giving the new people protection, and turning back Richard's thugs with extensive advice. They take fright at Herman's appearance, menaced by his loquacity; no one has warned them, or even hinted, of a mad gunman abroad in this rum bloody wilderness. Meanwhile, Lovelock House, under Marie Louise's command, most resembles a casualty clearing station behind battle lines. There are bitter men groaning as Marie Louise cleans out their head wounds; there are women and children camped through the corridors, and in every available room. Little Luke's included; it provides for five children. Even Herman's personal study, though Marie Louise hesitates, finally has to be commandeered. Herman does not show undue disturbance. He has to concede that his research into reason still leaves much to be desired; it has lately, in fact, lacked first-hand inspiration. Now he has this reminder that the human condition is inhumane, even more than he thought; he is not ungrateful. Nor for his outing with the shotgun, which on the whole has made him feel healthier than a day given to books written by men often unworldly and overwrought. If there is virtue in Richard, it must surely and solely reside in his capacity to clarify issues. The world might be poorer, and even more confused, without such as he. It can thus reasonably be supposed that Richard's existence, and that of those like him, is part of some great plan. A supposition worth further exploration, when he can reclaim his study from those wounded and weeping. As things stand, however, Lovelock House has never had more meaning; even Whisker's bloody ballroom, where dozens are bedded, makes far more sense. Herman stalks through the house, with intentions for the most part seen as kindly, though Marie Louise sometimes has to ask him to keep out of her way. She eventually gives him one useful function. He is sent to boil water while a premature baby is born. He accomplishes this task with his customary efficiency, suffering only the one scald. As for the baby, it bursts into the world with great agitation; and is seen to be male.

'We shall call him Herman,' the shy and grateful mother decides. 'Herman Lovelock Malone.'

Herman senior could ask for no more. To help his cup brimmeth, he brings up a barrel of brandy from the cellar, aided by several willing menfolk. The women who demur, when offered a drink, are persuaded to see the contents of the barrel as much-needed medicine. This is in a sense true. Shock passes; and tears. After a time, ragged outbursts of singing rise here and there. There is a recital of Irish rebel verse from Barney Malone, now ageing and patriarchal among his huge tribe. Lovelock House becomes peaceful, with adults deeply sleeping, and but a few children fretful, in the latter part of the night.

Marie Louise is up early, and fast to her kitchen, to begin yet again feeding the host. And yet again, though she does tolerate some helping hands, she makes the miracle of the loaves and fishes appear puny. Herman, rising later, with no more than mild hangover, still feels fulfilled; he sees no cause to regret the loss of his study. Indeed he is disappointed when he hears talk of the refugees wanting to put the Porangi behind them; and then observes some packing to leave, the best way they can, and as soon. 'Must you?' he pleads.

'There's no point in staying,' he is told. 'Not to put a fine point on it, your brother has buggered us. We'll have to try elsewhere to get this union thing right. Don't think we're ungrateful. You've done what you could. But we must make a move, and look for fresh jobs. There's more new country out there. And men still needed to build roads and railways and all.'

Herman, with a twinge, remembers his hope that roads and railways, marching across mountain and river, would seek Lovelock Junction; and wisdom. They will never come now. Another message is clear. These people will never be back. Not even the new Herman, whose parents are among the last to move out. Within a fortnight, in fact, Herman is back with his books, alone again with Marie Louise; there are soon times when he marvels that he was ever able to manage more of humanity.

Every gun must be made useful, and every male who can hold one, even Benjamin's more diminutive sons. Gunfire now doesn't merely punctuate the life of Spanish Creek; it becomes of its essence, so that all can survive, and perhaps peace return. The heights are contested again and again; the release of bullets and pellets makes for a sometimes seamless pattern of detonations over the hills, with echoes roaring around. For a time they gather the corpses; then skins become too abundant to take. The creatures are left where they fall, giving off stench, and luminescent fox-fire of decay in the early dusk. Then there is more. Hill pastures have to be cleared of sheep so that traps can be set and poison baits placed. No means of extermination can be neglected. David dreams badly, sometimes crying for mercy, and then as a man gets on with the job. When shot, steel jaws and strychnine have made their point, fresh carnage begins. Fire flushes rabbits from their intricate tunnels, in the form of blazing oil-soaked rags on long sticks, with a smoke black and suffocating. The creatures are shot as they surface, or killed quickly with clubs. Spades do the rest. Infant rabbits are uncovered, often new-born and blind, still huddled with mothers; they are bashed, or simply chopped to pieces, with the implements in hand. The burrows become a large graveyard. The rest, in hundreds and then thousands, blacken with odour even thicker in the warm autumn sun; David wonders whether he will ever be rid of that smell. As the season cools, and Porangi mists rise up the hills, he is relieved to hear his father at last announcing, 'One way and another, I think we have things under control.'

'They'll be back,' Benjamin warns. 'Things can't be the same.'

'When are they ever?' James asks.

'I'm only saying,' Benjamin protests.

'And I hear you,' James insists.

David has never seen his white-haired father looking older. Nor, for that matter, more weary. But then neither condition is news. His own nausea with the weeks of massacre now seems selfish indulgence. For his father, if just to spare him, he would do it again. The two walk homeward together. A fine rain falls. 'A fire would be cheerful tonight,' David decides. 'You just get yourself a whisky. I'll cook the meal.'

Next day, when he sets out with Daniel, just the pair of them hunting, the first winter storm beats them off the hills; they end their search for rabbits surviving. Those skins salvaged and cured are packed for dispatch down the river. The sheep can be let loose upon the hills again, if not upon plentiful grazing; their lives will be thinner this winter, and their wool.

'Know something?' Daniel says. 'I think I'll give the bloody Boers a miss. I hate arriving late. If you want a decent war you've got to be there, boots and all, right from the start.'

David is silent, with thoughts of his own.

'One thing about the world,' Daniel goes on, 'it's never short of a war. There's always a next time.'

'No doubt,' David says.

He encounters Grandmother Sybil, whom he often guiltily tries to avoid; at least when alone, and more vulnerable. 'You have to be fair to yourself, child,' she tells him. 'And do justice to your gifts.'

'I do my best,' he asserts.

'I'm talking of your education. And its furthering. I mean, to be frank, that you can't linger here. Not in all fairness. You need university. A time of calm contemplation, and study, to make a career of your own.'

'I have a career,' David proposes. 'I am a sheep farmer.'

'Never,' Sybil answers with shock. He has never seen fit to say this before. She then adds sadly, 'I see. So I've lost.'

He doesn't care to see her distress. 'It's not a matter of winning or losing,' he explains. 'It's just an impossible problem.'

'What is, child?'

'Being both fair to myself and fair to my father. Who gets it right in this world? Or elsewhere? Even in the gospels you read us, God and his Son seemed to have some misunderstanding. Christ asked on the cross why he had been forsaken, after all he had done.'

'You take the world, and not just the gospels, most literally,' Sybil observes.

'I don't see much choice,' David declares. 'There is too much pain for it not to be treasured.'

'I begin to think,' Sybil says finally, 'that you are not just a loss to yourself, remaining here, but a loss to the world.'

'That's as may be,' David replies. 'Now I must put these sheep through that gate.'

Winter brings high wind and rain, often sharp frost; snow even falls on hill pasture, most unusual, remaining for days. James and David find affairs of the farm contested by matters more domestic. Things go missing, with no explanation; particularly food. Sliced ham fresh from their smokehouse; a small leg of hogget, cooked and gone cold; a day-old loaf of Aunt Iris's bread, and seemingly butter. James notes sudden shortage of whisky; he is concerned that it may be his own rate of consumption, though it plainly cannot. All most perplexing. They frequently allow for their own absent-minded behaviour, but still the things go. At pace, as winter continues, and with no precedent in their experience. It cannot be vermin. It has to be human. Confirmed when David discerns blankets flown from the spare bedroom.

'But whom?' he demands.

James shakes his head. At first inclined to suspect Benjamin's children, practical joking, he sees no humour in the thing now.

'We'll have to lock doors,' David says. 'Bolt windows. And keep better watch. I don't mean to be unkind, or unfair. We have things in plenty. And no need to begrudge strangers. But there is mystery here. It must be cleared up.'

James could not have summed up the position more exactly himself. Often it seems the pair speak with one voice on anything of moment.

'We could leave a note outside,' he suggests, 'to make our attitude clear. And asking, perhaps, for elucidation.'

'That could cause panic,' David points out. 'Perhaps flight. Better we know. We would be left wondering.'

His father judges this true.

They fix locks, bolt windows, keep better watch. Benjamin and Iris – who never know where food goes anyway, with so many children – are told to take similar precautions. The prescription, however, is literally negative in result. Their food is unplundered; the mystery remains large. Until apparent deprivation and desperation produce a clue. There is a nocturnal, and ineffectual, attempt to force a window, and footprints left in the frost. These leave an unmistakable trail up the valley, to a dusky triangle of forest still virgin between the smooth flanks of two hills. David knows from childhood that a cave exists there; he often tried to terrify himself with its clammy secrets, and sometimes succeeded. On horseback he follows the trail, with three dogs behind, before the sun takes the frost. He has no rifle; he carries a knife only of necessity. The footprints begin to wander, the sign of a creature confused, and certainly no danger; there are marks where the stranger has evidently fallen in the forming frost, and crawled for a time. David, in pity, now regrets the locking of doors and bolting of windows; too cruel a means to earn an end to the mystery.

This isn't long coming. David dismounts. His dogs bay ahead, thrilled by some scent, into dense bush. David, less agile, and wishing no hurt to a human, blunders behind; and tries vainly to call them to heel. Creeper slows him, and slippery ground. The dogs ahead clamour; his own breath is quick. Then the bush thins, with the trunks of aged trees fallen, a small creek trickling, and a cave beyond low fern. At the mouth of the cave his dogs are defiant. He calls them off sternly. With a tremor, perhaps childhood's, he at last looks into the cave.

An old man squats there, long-haired and untidily bearded, shivering fragile under a soiled blanket. His eyes are huge with appeal. His filthy skin is hard pressed to cover his skull.

'Who are you?' David asks gently. He cannot demand.

'Me?' The creature looks about wildly, seemingly at a loss. He might be a lunatic. Perhaps something more; David indulges a superstitious dread. Then tells himself ghosts are gone from this valley, and besides are not known to leave footprints in frost.

'Yes. You. Who are you?'

'If you must know,' the stranger says, after some pause, 'my name is Finn.'

The name means nothing to David. Nor much of what follows.

'Why is it necessary?' he inquires. 'Your living like this?'

'Because necessity is recognized. It is simple as that. I live a life of pure truth.'

'Truth?' David shakes his head. 'I'm sorry.'

'Theory and practice must be seen as inseparably twin. Apart, each is worthless; both blind alleys. If theory dictates this for me, leaving no choice, practice must follow: which isn't to say that they cannot act upon each other, and produce other possibilities, to that point unseen. This is, or has been, a life of some virtue.'

David suspects sanity lacking; he holds tight to his own. 'But you've been thieving,' he observes bluntly.

'Regrettably. True. Though some would argue that theft is a form of proletarian protest. I wouldn't agree. It reeks of adventurism. The fact is, however, that I had to. Apologies all round. It isn't the first time I've had problem with principles; I fear Marx might not have allowed sufficiently for animal appetites.' Finn sighs, and rises shakily. 'Now get on with it. Do what you must.'

'What I must? Me? You seem the issue.'

Communication seems all but prostrate.

'Don't toy with me,' Finn asks, not without dignity. 'You know perfectly well that I'm a man on the run.'

'On the run? You? Where from, or to?'

'I've had much time to think. Some must be martyrs. I'm prepared for my vocation. And, of course, for my speech at the trial.'

'Trial?' David feels giddy. 'Whose? Yours? And what for?'

'Murder,' Finn says. And then adds with conviction, 'I didn't do it, of course.'

'How many years ago?' David asks. 'Most must have forgotten.'

'Not years. A matter of months, though I confess my sense of time vague.' Finn falters, and goes on, 'I suppose it's pointless protesting my innocence.'

'Not at all. But it might be more to the point if you had some good food.'

'For one thing, I've never in my life carried a firearm. For another, I'm not a believer in anarchism.'

'Anarchism?' David asks.

'Or necessarily even in armed insurrection. Violence can beget more intensive repression. On the other hand, I stop well short of pacifism.'

'Pacifism?' David asks.

'It is in the nature of capitalism to put up a fight, to turn vicious when its foundations are shaken. Indeed that's how I'm here. Reaction is not to be underestimated. The path to socialism is bound to be thorny.'

'Socialism?' David asks.

'I can see you need enlightenment on several subjects,' Finn concedes. 'Much as I should like to, I shan't dwell on them now. You did mention food.'

David gives Finn the horse, upon which he sags pitifully. He also carries Finn's things, mostly books and handwritten papers, bundled into a blanket. At the homestead his father is equally bemused by their prowler made captive. 'You must be talking of that affair down at Dixtown,' James concludes. 'That strike. And my brother Richard.' He still likes to keep utterance of that name to a minimum.

'That's right,' Finn says gratefully, all but extending his hands for the shackles. 'You know it all now, I fear.'

'I did hear of a shot fired. But not of a fatality. The constable wounded made recovery in pretty quick time, as I understand it, and has retired from the force on a pension plus a certificate for bravery. It's all over now.'

'Not for me,' Finn insists. 'I'm surely still wanted. If not for murder, then for grievous bodily harm, malicious wounding, presenting a firearm, and a dozen other charges they can doubtless manufacture with ease.'

'Very likely,' James has to allow, while Finn gulps down cold mutton and a great many potatoes. 'But there are such things as courtrooms, where justice is done. A man honest should have nothing to fear; you are innocent until found guilty.'

Finn, bolting a lumpy mouthful, manages to laugh harshly. 'But what of the lackeys of capitalism, and their lies? What of the judges who serve the interests of monopolist masters? And hireling lawyers, puppets and clowns? And juries hand-picked from the craven middle classes? Where's justice to be found there?'

James is unable, and unwilling, to make answer; every challenge of Finn's is a minefield where an isolated river-dweller must walk ill at ease. He would, for the most part, prefer not to hear.

'I'll tell you,' Finn says. 'There is no justice for me. The system cannot allow it.'

'I'm not up to such matters,' James confesses. 'I have to take things on trust.'

'Trust me, then,' Finn argues. 'Believe me when I say I used no firearm in defending working-class rights. If explanation of that shot must be searched for, then I believe it may well be found – if you'll forgive me – with your brother Richard. Not that he'll ever be called to account.'

James is inclined, Richard considered, to believe Finn's story. Meanwhile, there is the unfortunate Finn himself, insofar as he remains physically of this world. Though a bit on the garrulous side, he plainly means no great harm. Also, in his present condition, he needs help and care. If he is destined for prison, long years lonely in a stone cell, he can at least be made fit to survive that ordeal.

'You could stay on here,' James suggests.

'At your risk,' Finn says, with surprise at the offer. 'In the eyes of the law, you'd be harbouring a wanted criminal. And likewise found guilty. I must make the facts plain.'

'I see no criminal,' James says, mildly passing verdict. To his son he adds, 'David, look about the house. And see if we harbour something, or someone, hitherto unseen.'

'Please believe me,' Finn says. 'You place yourself in a most precarious position.'

'That shall be my business,' James determines. 'What else would you have me do? Give you up to the law?'

Finn considers. And appears to arrive, rather slowly, at certain self-knowledge. Martyrdom, after all, is not to be taken lightly; it needs a firm sense of mission.

'Perhaps not,' he agrees.

'So it's settled, then,' James says with satisfaction. His main fear is of further ideological challenge. He would sooner not allow David to see that he cannot quite cope. The boy is all ears. To Finn he continues, 'Feel at your ease. David will make your bed and boil up some bath-water. I shall have words with my nephew Benjamin, asking that he and his family try to take your presence for granted. And be careful to whom they speak. I hope you shall find, as we do, that Spanish Creek offers some peace.'

'I'm sure,' Finn replies, all hesitancy lost. 'Perhaps I could help with some jobs.'

'Time to talk of that later. At the moment you would be useful only as garden scarecrow, to keep off the birds. The problem is that our sheep might also take fright, and our fowls cease to lay eggs.'

'I'm sorry,' Finn says humbly. 'I feel I have forced myself upon you.'

'We are all of us forced upon each other,' James answers, 'from the time we are born. And obliged to act fairly.'

'You have a socialist's belief,' Finn claims.

'A Christian's,' James protests. 'Though I prefer to think my faith largely my own. Christ I understand. God, never.' He rises swiftly from the table, attempting to disengage from perilous debate. 'I must leave you to David, and get about quelling curiosity elsewhere on this farm. I think you will find my son attentive to your needs, if not to your philosophy.'

'I've found that already,' Finn says. 'As for my philosophy, do not regard it as infection. It is simply a scientific approach to fundamental social reality.'

'My fundamental social reality is this farm,' James asserts, 'and all which goes with it. Besides, I have no need of science to instruct me that you are now most in need of warmth, a bath, and sound sleep.'

'Thank you,' Finn says.

With food in his belly, soap, razor, scissors, and considerable sleep, Finn's years drop away with extraordinary speed. David sees a young man climb from an unkempt chrysalis; and one, after all, not so much older. David's clothes fit Finn more or less. In the end their guest wants for nothing, though he talks wistfully of class struggle proceeding elsewhere, of humanity marching toward a new dawn. Meanwhile, he must make do with David; his audience, if diminished, is nonetheless sensitive. 'About capitalism,' he explains. 'Every stage of history contains the germs of its own destruction. Capitalism created the working class. Thesis. Antithesis. The synthesis of opposites can only result in a classless society.'

'I see,' David says, though not altogether.

'Anarchism?' Finn says. 'Simple, really. It's really a question of individual action rather than that of people en masse. The deed is seen as more crucial than that of more sluggish collective endeavour. It is the gospel of the impatient and desperate.'

They ride the farm together. Finn proves himself eager for competence when lambing begins. 'Birth is a fascinating process,' he concludes. 'A perfect illustration of Marx's dialectical leap. Slow quantitative change as the ewe fattens. Then sudden quality; the first breath of life. Marvellous to see. Above all, I note that it is not without struggle.'

Sturdy Daniel has less patience with Finn. 'I don't know what you see in the bugger,' he tells David. 'I don't bloody like the cut of his jib. He spouts all this rubbish from morning to night.'

David defends Finn quietly. 'He has interesting things to tell of the world. Of how things are wrong, and might be made better.'

'There's nothing wrong with the world,' Daniel maintains, 'that a good fuck can't cure. Take my word, Dave. Don't miss the boat.'

Daniel appears to resent being superseded as David's companion, and instructor in social affairs. He begins to give Finn wide berth, and thus David too.

'About pacifism,' Finn says. 'It's basically a belief that all violence is evil, even in defence of the self. To turn the other cheek, as the Bible commands, is a most pleasant notion. But where does it leave us? With things as they are.'

'But there is the example,' David protests, now growing bolder in dispute. 'I mean, if I can mention it, for the good of men's souls.'

'I'm not unaware of spiritual matters,' Finn then confides. 'To tell you the truth, I trained as a priest. In the seminary I bled from Christ's crown of thorns. I prostrated myself, and prayed nightlong, on the stone floor of my cell. In the end to no purpose. I saw too many priests worldly and well-fed, while their flock went without. I could never be one of their kind. In the world again, I became a Knight of Labour, tilting here and there with my lance. All pinpricks. Pennies and pounds. And merchants and bankers, surrendering a pittance only for peace, still quite unscathed. Far from enough. Then I found Marx. He offered clear formulation. And a sound plan.'

'For what?'

'The Kingdom of Man.'

It sounds stirring. David finds it is, in the end.

'About socialism,' Finn continues. 'It is quite straightforward. From each according to his ability. To each according to his need. What could be simpler? I mean, in short, all men become brothers. As we are, all of us, under the skin. Would you deny it?'

David cannot, though his silence is cautious.

'And no greed,' Finn adds. 'No capitalism. No nations. No war.'

Having made free with negatives, Finn seems content, but David remains wary. 'Is that all?'

'I find brevity best. If you wish casuistry, I remind you of my training as priest. I could count how many proletarian angels dance on the head of a pin. To what purpose? To muddy a clear stream?'

'One thing isn't clear,' David suggests. 'You take no account of man's soul.'

'No need. The concept of soul is a residue of religion. One French thinker, whose argument I like, offers anatomical definition. The soul, he says, is the sum of the functions of the neck and the spinal column. And, physiologically, the sum of the functions of the power of perception in the human brain. We have science on our side. And no need for nonsense.'

'But what,' David asks, 'if we feel things beyond the power of physical perception? Not only feel. Also know.'

'We all have strange thoughts,' Finn answers. 'And passing fancies. But no real cause to make them into a fad. I'd be the last to deny that life is like the ocean, with some hidden depths. But that doesn't stop us sailing its expanses. Man would have done nothing. No Athens. No Rome. No socialism to be.'

There is a pause. Despite brevity, Finn often becomes breathless. David's imagination, a quick magpie, picks up things shining to bear to its nest; in bed he dreams still more wildly of things both socialist and sexual, the two quite confused. Also once he nightmarishly sees Marx on the cross, twisting with agony, a vision daylight fails to sustain: all quite absurd. Finn informs him that the old fellow failed only of age, though he worked on the theory of surplus value right to the last. 'What is the theory of surplus value?' David has to inquire. 'Knowledge,' Finn replies. 'A tool for changing the world.' From which assertion David deduces that Finn is vague too, and in some ways quite human.

This is made more clear with spring. In that season rabbits rear out of the hillsides again, undeterred by autumn's slaughter, and transparently asking for more. The spring grass is thin; they leave the growth still thinner. Some hilltops have none, all weathered rock and patches of desert. So fresh destruction begins. Finn, though useless beyond short range with a rifle, keeps David company. 'I appreciate the need of your father,' he declares, 'to preserve his property as an economic unit.

Production might soon be outstripped by consumption – not least that of the rabbit, if I may be forgiven the joke.' When he again gravely approaches materialist analysis, at dinner that night, James suffers in silence and soon rises from the table, leaving David alone to debate if he chooses. David doesn't. Alarmed by the fear he sees in his father, he wishes for some way to ease it. He cannot see one, unless down the sight of his rifle, with still another rabbit left skidding lifeless.

Until an early summer day it seems Finn might be with them forever. He walks high on the hills with David, the valley sunlit below. They detect movement. A small boat is about to berth at the distant farm landing. There isn't one expected. 'Who?' David wonders aloud. 'Why?' The answer to the first question is fast seen. A party of police. They move up the valley, jogging and shouting, and several of them armed. The second question is answered by implication. They have come to fetch Finn. They soon surround the two homesteads. And before long can be observed in consultation with Benjamin and James.

'I expect it's up to me,' Finn announces, in sweat.

David has to agree. They are flat on the ground together, offering no silhouette to the intruders down valley.

'I detest decisions being pressed upon me,' Finn continues, 'before a period sufficient for contemplation. It's all quite unfair.'

David wonders what brought the police, or who. They look like men in a hurry. Also reasonably informed. He tries to suppress a risen suspicion, but cannot with ease.

'To be frank, David,' Finn says, 'I don't feel I'm up to it. Not any more.'

'Running?' David asks.

'Staying. Those men down there look unnecessarily agitated. Also the fact is I've grown fond of freedom. It is no longer a concept so abstract. Which way should I go?'

'North,' David suggests. 'Then east. Follow noon sun first. Then locate sunrise. Sooner or later you should find a farm.' He pauses. 'But what,' he adds, 'of your speech to the court?'

'It needs more rehearsal. At the moment words fail me. Please give my best wishes to your father, and thank him for all he has done. Tell him I'll never forget.'

'And what,' David asks, 'of all your books and papers?'

'Keep them,' Finn proposes quickly. 'Consider yourself keeper, in fact, of my socialist conscience.' He offers a handshake as binding. 'Don't forget me either. We'll meet again.'

David doesn't reject this as improbable, however inclined. He is more concerned about ensuring Finn's safe passage. 'Follow ridges around the farm,' he instructs, 'and keep to the treeline. Avoid open ground. Make use of rocks too. Very shortly, I'll become visible toward the top of the valley. That should distract them, at least for a time.'

Finn summons up breath. Then he runs, never again to be seen near the Porangi. David has a last view of Finn tobogganing on his backside down an abrasive slope. All grows silent, but for faint wind. With gun slung from a shoulder, David at length reveals himself on the skyline, no doubt tantalizingly to those on watch below. Then he moves on with measured if shaky tread. He doesn't look down valley, nor turn a head to the shouting, soon very near.

There is gunshot. Two blasts, and bullets unnervingly near overhead. He flinches, and freezes, as echoes disperse among the hills. At last he allows himself to see the ragged line of uniformed men toiling toward him. Most are unfit, and convey a sense of their condition with the liveliest language at their command. At their sour instruction he drops his own gun. Then they are all about him, and bruising.

'Finn, isn't it?' they ask.

'David Lovelock,' he answers, though for a moment in doubt. In a sense he is indeed also Finn, in flight over the hills, perhaps into the future.

The present, however, requires extensive clarification. At length the day's commotion subsides, and the disgruntled police make their departure. It seems no charges will be pressed against James and his son, pig-ignorant farmers, or Benjamin as accessory. They are clearly men insensitive to political matters, to issues burning elsewhere, and best left alone. They plead that they saw Finn only as a human in need. Twelve jurors might well be goats enough to believe them; these rustics are not of the stuff from which examples can be made. 'Nevertheless,' a tall and austere inspector with military moustache warns disagreeably, 'we won't forget you up here. Not from now on.'

They also make it known, so there need be no misunderstanding, that they have come to Spanish Creek as a result of information received, now proven reliable; they are not to be mistaken for fools, though Finn might have outfoxed them again.

David continues to experiment with suspicion. But it is days, nearly a week, before he can approach Daniel, and have his worst fear made flesh.

'I might have,' Daniel agrees, and then laughs.

'Might have? You must know if you did.'

'I mean I might have mentioned him to the skipper of the last steamer to make it upriver. When you've got booze in your belly, you forget what you say. All right, so I might have mentioned the bugger. It would be hard bloody not to.'

'I see,' David says.

'Forget it,' Daniel insists. 'He was always, for my money, something crept from under a stone.'

'He was a friend,' David replies.

'That makes it worse. He was fucking you up. With all those big words. Where do words get you? They don't shear no sheep.'

'You don't want to know, do you?' Dave says; he feels unmanly tears too close for comfort, and is biting his lip.

'Know what?' Daniel is made uneasy by such apparent distress.

'Just what you've done.'

'If Finn's had his arse kicked off here, it's not before bloody time. There's a kind of bugger goes looking for trouble. He can't complain if he finds it.'

Daniel, in common with Finn, then finds it too. His young cousin's fist catches him across the right eye. He rolls with the blow, and doesn't hit back. 'Shit,' he says. 'Did you have to do that?'

'Not especially,' David answers. 'But I'd do it again.'

No more words pass between them. Not for a month. If men are brothers, and David believes that truly, then his kinsman carries, quite unmistakably, the old mark of Cain.

Meanwhile, he finds a Russian writer, by name of Tolstoy, who makes quite tolerable reading. It is a pamphlet which Grandmother Sybil felt might be spiritually instructive. As against Finn's books, arranged above his bed, the pamphlet doubtless lacks science. But it does protest love, in a way most subversive, certainly of David.

There are worse in the world than Daniel. And few easier to forgive.

Up the valley, after they have ridden together in silence, David reins in his horse, and puts out a hand. Brothers must be forgiven. They know not what they do, and Daniel was drunk.

'All right, Dave?'

'All right.'

'I'm sorry too. Especially about Finn.'

'You don't have to say things you don't mean.'

'But I do. It was just that something about him gave me the pricker. Maybe you too. You becoming a stranger, after all we've bloody shared.'

'You don't need to go on,' David argues. 'It's all over now.'

It is, for the most part. And when it isn't, it can be made to seem so. Love, it appears, sometimes needs an ally in guile; no heart is quite pure.

Dixtown is industrious again. Prosperity should follow. Made eager by bonuses and booze, unencumbered by unionism, Richard's new men begin building mountains of coal, towers of sawn timber. Though clumsy at first, sometimes crushed under coal wagons or toppling trees, they soon get the hang. Richard, as boss, again proves his ability to get the best from his workmen; he labours alongside them to share hardship and shit, as in the old days, though past sixty and now and then showing his age. Especially in the evenings, when he gets home to Nancy. He is sometimes asleep, and quite soundly, before she can get a meal on the table. As for other marital matters, the prospect of revival, there are some things best left unsaid. Otherwise Richard, if briefly, appears much as he was: he has won power again, certainly the wealth of the land; it is only a question, as ever, of shaping shit into money. It might be noted that the power and wealth of fabled Croesus failed to stop his dethronement by Cyrus of Persia, leaving Lydia and such as Aesop bereft. Richard, on admittedly lesser scale, and without the myth-making wisdom of a slave to console him, finds difficulty too; the malcontent Finns and treacherous Malones of the world are still at work to usurp him. He discovers this from the skipper of the next steamer calling upriver.

'I've brought in supplies,' this skipper says. 'As for your coal, I'm sorry. I can't take it on. My men won't have it aboard.'

'Why not?' Richard asks, with some irritation.

'They say it's black.'

'Of course it's bloody black. What other colour is coal?'

'I mean, old shipmate, that it's called black by the unions,' the skipper continues with patience.

'Let them call it blue if they like. Or red if they must. It's all one to me.'

'Black is their symbol; I daresay they style your timber the same. Produced, as the stubborn buggers would have it, by non-union scab labour. And not to be touched by my men, among others. They're union, you see.'

'The answer to that's simple,' Richard suggests. 'Just let them hear the whip whistle. Tell your men their jobs are now on the line. Show them who's boss. In the end, take it from me, you'll earn their respect. Firm words, well chosen, can work like a charm.'

'Sorry. More than life's worth. I get on with my men. I need to. I can't afford strife, or anyone sulky when storm's blowing up. Also my head office doesn't fancy long hold-ups. Not when there is other cargo to be profitably taken. Yours, to be blunt, is expendable now. There's better business to be done all up and down this coast. That's the story, in short. I could make it longer.'

'No thanks,' Richard says. He neglects to produce whisky for the skipper, or to relax in discussion of other news of the day. 'I see where I stand. And where you don't.'

'After all,' the skipper says, with some resignation, 'it was only a matter of allowing a union in here. It couldn't have done that much damage if you'd conceded the point. Much less than you've suffered.'

'There we go again,' Richard shouts, and with anger still visibly rising. 'Every other bastard seems to know my business best. If you've no other gutless advice, why don't you fuck off? I've work to be done.'

'Good luck, then.' The skipper stands. Richard has no inclination to shake the man's offered hand. The steamer, with incoming goods unloaded, leaves Dixtown's new mountain range of black coal quite unexplored. The skipper proves not to have been colour-blind. Timber scows, despite Richard's urgent communications, do not even trouble to call. The sawn wood grows slimy with rain, and warps in the sun. Shit remains shit, quite untranslated, and Richard contemplates things cruelly monetary. He suspects, for one thing, that his men might not find an I.O.U. acceptable in place of a weekly pay packet. Taking things further to heart, not least the parting words of the skipper, Richard arrives at the point of seeing virtue in indulging the world beyond Dixtown. This after lengthy self-scrutiny, sustained by much whisky. He has been an excessive sentimentalist, too obstinate a dreamer. It is time now for realism, reason, and modest compromise.

'All right,' he roars, baring his conscience, and alarming Nancy at breakfast. 'They shall have it. They shall have their trade union.'

'They shall what?' Nancy fears his choking on toast; unmasticated fragments fly from his mouth.

'I shall take a close interest in the matter myself,' he informs her. 'There is no reason why these things cannot be done in orderly fashion, with a minimum of upheaval and distress. Let it never be said that I stand in the way of social advance, as some style it. I shall present the bloody union to them, as it were, on a plate.'

There are times when Nancy sees that, some appearances perhaps to the contrary, Richard needs her no less. No one else, for example, would ever understand him. In offering her these confidences, he is revealing himself as appreciative of the fact. It is his form of love play, not to be denied or diminished.

At his earliest opportunity, or within the hour that same morning, he calls together his labour force, and climbs a stepladder. From that eminence he looks out over the formless ranks of his now often endearingly faithful recruits, and outlines the advantages of responsible trade unionism; it is a subject on which there have been social misunderstandings, but these need be no more. His speech becomes still more persuasive as the stalwart faces before him grow still more puzzled; he stresses, more lengthily than he would like, the downright desirability of trade unions as a moderating factor in the minor disputes which arise from time to time between masters and men. Some would argue, God knows, that trade unionism is a fact of modern life. The Porangi is no place set apart. Facts have to be lived with. He finishes. There is silence. No applause, and no more than a few baffled whispers. He realizes that there may have been partial obscurities, here and there, in his speech. They seem not to know what to do next. He has to make the point plain.

'I suggest,' he shouts, into a chill wind, 'that you get on with making a union, here, and right now.'

'Us?' a voice says.

'You. For your own good.'

'Bugger me days,' another says, amazed. 'Are we Arthur or Martha?'

'Take a vote,' Richard prompts. 'Get the bloody thing done.' He despairs of mankind. Just so many sheep to be led. 'I should warn, in advance, that I will find only one resolution acceptable. That is, in brief, immediate formation of a trade union here.'

'Let's call it done,' urges a huge individual with crossed eyes and exceptionally razor-slashed face in the front row. 'We're wasting good time. Do we get paid for this?'

'There shall be no deductions for time lost,' Richard promises. Then, 'Do I hear any dissent?'

He gathers there is none. A union exists. Some of its perplexed membership have begun to squat wearily on the damp ground.

'Then,' he goes on, 'we must proceed with the election of officers. President, secretary, and committee. I have to know with whom I am dealing. And you must exercise your democratic right of choice. The matter cannot be left.'

Again there is silence.

'Can I have volunteers for office?' Richard asks. 'Did I hear someone back there?'

He heard a whisper. It ceases.

'Perhaps I should clarify the nature of the posts,' Richard continues. 'President first. He chairs meetings, keeps order, and handles general affairs. For argument's sake, he might well make it his business to pacify men who feel in some trivial way aggrieved. The secretary's tasks are more specific. He, for example, looks after the funds. You might argue that there are no such funds in existence at the moment. I should like to reveal, now, that I intend making a donation of handsome nature to get a trade union off the ground here.'

Several fast volunteer for the post of secretary. On a voice vote, complicated by challenges and resonant dissension, the scarred and cross-eyed giant in the front row, by name of Crabb, wins the job. His talent for terrifying invective is never in doubt; his fiscal skills as secretary remain to be seen.

'President, then,' Richard says briskly. 'Key posts cannot be left in abeyance. Such a man must be firm and fair handed, popular with all, tactful, unselfishly willing to give of his time to his fellows, and above all discreet and sensitive to compromise.'

No one presents himself as candidate. Nor does any face of conspicuous virtue meet Richard's questioning eye. Many men discover their feet a fascinating sight.

'Come on,' Richard pleads. 'I need only one name to put to the vote.'

'Then make it yours,' the hulking Crabb suggests. 'Seems to me you fit the bloody bill best. You know more about trade unions than we do. They don't have none in the jug. For another thing, it would save all this arsing about. I'll select a committee. I reckon that between you and me we can keep this town tidy. That's what you want, right?'

'In a sense,' Richard agrees. 'But as your employer I must decline the nomination, with respect. My being president could, in the eyes of others, be construed as an irregular arrangement.'

'What others?' Crabb demands.

'Other trade unionists. Elsewhere. The malicious among them might allege conflict of interest. They might also claim, unjustly, that your union isn't genuine.'

'So who's running this place? And this union? Aren't we?'

Crabb calls up considerable and defiant agreement. Richard's message, especially that concerning democratic right of choice, has not been quite lost; he falls victim to his own gift of persuasion. In all the commotion Crabb claims the stepladder from Richard and addresses the crowd. 'Do I need to put Dick Lovelock's name to the vote?' he asks, and then answers, 'Not on your sweet fucking Nelly. He's thought this thing through. He knows this union thing best.'

Richard tries gracefully to acknowledge the compliment. But he cannot make himself heard.

'The bloody question is,' Crabb continues, 'whether we run this show for ourselves. Or for other buggers elsewhere. If it's not our own union, there's no fucking point. Anyone argue with Dick for president? Or with me, for that matter?' As orator, Crabb is pure and undisguised energy. What he may lack in thematic variety he makes good by vivid quality of exposition. The onlooker is aware of bulky fists and bruised knuckles. Richard's lone voice of protest makes no impression upon the din of response. Men wish it understood that they want no argument with

Crabb. 'Right,' he announces to Richard. 'That's it. Consider yourself president. Unanimous vote.'

'Shit a bloody brick,' Richard says, turning away. 'Forget the whole bloody thing.' He is chilled, not just by the wind and ball-freezing winter; his frigid face is that of a man who has seldom known larger despair, one who might one day embrace death as a friend. To Nancy, later, he says, 'I tried. God knows I tried. I almost, damn it, got a union off the ground. But they couldn't get the idea. And a dumb sod named Crabb, then finally the lot, killed the whole thing stone dead.'

'What now?' Nancy asks.

'A good question,' Richard observes.

'That coal. That timber. It's earning us nothing.'

'The fact has impinged upon my attention,' Richard replies coldly.

'Well? What happens?'

'Unless there's a miracle,' he proposes, 'we wait for the end.'

'Your men. What will happen to them?'

'I'll break the news to them, naturally. As I pay them all off.'

'They won't be too happy.'

'What do you want me to do? Cry?'

To Nancy's consternation, he then does. She has never thought her husband capable of tears; it is quite as frightening as his visionary consumption of tutu. His sobs shake the house. Her thoughts turn to widowhood, reasonably young.

Next morning Dixtown is still. He knows of no funeral. It seems his men have the message. He walks out into black frost, to be confronted by Crabb. 'Fuck me hooray,' the brute says with glee. 'You wouldn't believe it. It really has happened.'

'What has?' Richard asks. He feels certain indifference.

'The strike,' Crabb explains. 'It really has happened.'

'The what?' His own voice seems remote.

'The strike.' Crabb's grin wanders into his razor-slashes. 'I'm here for the union.'

'The game's up,' Richard announces. 'The whistle's just blown.'

Crabb, undeterred, presses on with irrelevance. 'Look, it's like this. Me and the boys, we got together. Since you lost interest, we thought we might have a bash at giving this union thing a go by ourselves. I mean take the thing really to heart. Just to show we're right with you. Only one way to prove it. A strike. This morning we're out one hundred per cent. That should please you.'

As it happens, this does; on that day of all, Richard could have no better news. If not of a kind to make his heart leap, and in truth little could, it at least suggests an end to the problem of paying his men.

'Keep up the good work,' he urges Crabb. 'For my money, you can strike as long as you like.'

Crabb asks for elucidation, and doesn't take the news kindly. 'You're not getting off as easy as this. You can't treat us like you treated your last lot. No bloody fear.'

'Suit yourself,' Richard says, with some unconcern.

'You ought to need no reminding there's some hard doers among us. Men who would have worn a hempen cravat if they hadn't been lucky.'

Richard, who could tell a similar tale, judges the moment inopportune. 'Unless I'm much mistaken,' he observes, 'you're uttering threats.'

'My fucking oath.' Crabb, after putting an anatomically implausible proposition to Richard, then removes himself with further picturesque language relayed back over his shoulder. Soon, down near the jetty, he gathers a crowd. The information he imparts to his fellows is plainly not of a kind to make Richard popular. There is, before long, an increasingly audible volley of threats. Some with enough menace to make even Crabb seem a moderate. Richard finds it possible to regret the loss of the Malones, perhaps even of Finn. At all events he sees no advantage in braving the black frost further; he retreats homeward to check out his guns.

Norse legend tells of the Fimbul Winter, a season of horror such as had never been known, lasting three years with never a summer to lessen its cruel impact; men and their handiwork perished by way of clearing the ground for Ragnarok, the great day of doom. Beyond Ragnarok, beyond doom only, there was prospect of peace and man's regeneration. While events of that winter at Dixtown are less cosmic and less lethal, lasting something closer to three weeks than three years, there is impressive similarity. Richard and Nancy share watches, never a bed, with guns at their windows, likewise their senior sons. They suffer numb fingers through the cold nights. Daylight, when at last arriving, is mostly feeble under a dense mist. The sun seldom shines. Few shots are fired. The men loose in Dixtown present untidy targets; they taunt from a distance, and provide themselves with warmth and illumination by burning down dwellings. They also provide themselves with food by looting the store, and with liquor by locating Richard's underground deposits of new-distilled rum. His bullock teams are slain, one by one, and beasts in prime condition are barbecued nightly. While fire makes the most felicitous source of entertainment, explosives, while stock lasts, also prove a congenial antidote to boredom. Coal dust storms down valley as fresh tunnels are blown; soon, so far as Richard can judge, the mines are no more. Wagons roll down the tracks into the river. Then attention turns to the mill. Gelignite, fuelled with sawdust and oil, produces imposing flashes of flame; corrugated iron, and less identifiable debris, flutter high above the forest. Exactly the prospect, in fact, which Richard fluently invented for Stubbs; it has all come to pass. Not that Stubbs, even with reinforcement, could have been other than powerless this time; nor his replacement, if ever the sod arrives, which he hasn't, and now needn't. There is precious little left to police. Dixtown, as dwellings burn, shrinks fast. The long nights are lit red. The destruction cannot last. It doesn't; even the Fimbul Winter had to finish. A supply steamer arrives upriver, fortunately timed, to offer Crabb and his companions distraction. They fall upon the supplies. Then they commandeer the vessel itself. In their enthusiasm for this enterprise, however, they do not neglect to fire the last of Dixtown, nor the riverside ranges of coal, kindled with stacks of sawn timber; the smoke is dark and thick, quite engulfing as they depart. Eyes watering, poisonous fumes filling his lungs, Richard coughs his way across the smouldering residue of Dixtown; he can but confirm entire extinction. If not quite Ragnarok, the climactic day of doom, it is a near flawless facsimile.

Yet he is not, after all, much in dismay. Resurrection of Dixtown may be out of the question. Not regeneration of man. The miracle has happened, and not material in nature. In the reaches of the night, in icy silences of his heart, Richard has located the truth that things of this earth are transitory. The ordeal has not been for nothing; he stands reborn among the ruins. All about others may be losing their faith, making disbelief the new doctrine for the ten pristine decades which eternity is now urgently pressing upon mankind. So not before time, in the last score of weeks left to his native century, Richard has, in fact, found God.

(In that confused catalogue called *The Lives of Lovelock Junction*, the scribe's version runs thus: 'There were few years richer in event for the people of the Porangi than 1899; certainly life took a fresh turn. The central figure, as so often, was Richard Lovelock. This rugged pioneer entrepreneur – and that noun seems to serve this flamboyantly theatrical quality well – resisted the upriver intrusion of trade unions, well entrenched elsewhere in the then colony, and so set the scene for a savage and extended labour dispute which left many reverberations. In view of the grievous cost to himself, and taking his later life into account, it might safely be presumed that his stance was that of a stern moralist's. He certainly appears to have believed in individual self-improvement and redemption; and not, apparently, in the illusory shelter offered by secular institutions of man's shaping. Indeed no other hypothesis covers his obstinate and costly hostility to trade unions, nor his curious consequent behaviour.

'Strategist of the strike which shook Richard, challenging his fundamental beliefs, was one Thomas Finn – who as Tom Finn, workingman's champion, made his mark later on the nation's political life as a colourful Parliamentary character, never at a loss for iridescent and humorous invective. Friend and foe alike were to mourn his passing. There was little humour, though, in the long struggle on the Porangi. Finn's still unpublished memoirs, composed late in life, record that Richard Lovelock consistently refused to meet with him and negotiate. This too suggests Richard was more than the simplistic and caricature rogue capitalist which Finn tries to portray; the latter does not seem capable of recalling at least one old foe in tranquillity. Though Finn does have a generous word or two for Richard's wife Nancy: "A most humane and misunderstood woman," he writes. "Not above giving succour, on the quiet, to a striker in need."

'Richard Lovelock travelled to the city to recruit able-bodied and non-union men willing to try their luck on the Porangi in place of the strikers. "Human vermin," Finn claims, and then in interesting reversion to his former Marxist vocabulary adds, "Lumpen proletarian of the worst kind." The bitterness of the struggle transparently coloured Finn's memories five decades later: at a time, incidentally, when the then aged Parliamentarian was styling class struggle as "a dead Red duck", Marxism as "an atheistic fad for fools", Communists as "red herrings with yellow bellies", and denouncing militant unionists as morons whom he wouldn't employ "to build a lavatory for a grasshopper".

'Richard brought in his new men under police protection. Things took a turn predictably ugly. There was a brief and bloody struggle, rather sensationally capped by the shooting and wounding of Dixtown's much-loved local constable. Finn was held responsible, several on the spot claiming to have seen him with a revolver, but the quick and wiry young union organizer eluded police capture. "I ran for my life," Finn writes, "and lived off the land. Some were amazed by my survival in landscape so forbidding. They should not have been. A man ablaze with the dream of social justice – a dream now come to pass – isn't to be blocked by mountains, rivers and forest. I learned my own strength. I became beholden to none. Bliss was it in that dawn to be alive."

'Peace returned, if evidently not to Richard Lovelock. For from that point conventionally mean motives simply do not make sense of his behaviour. In an apparent fit of remorse after the affray, and to ensure that such brutal scenes need never be repeated, he demanded – despite himself, and doubtless with anguish of conscience – that his strike-breaking workmen form a union. The cost of this move was considerable. It proved no tame company union, as a cynic might surmise, but one of genuine mettle. In a period of economic stress, soon after, Richard found himself facing another trial of strength with labour. Disorder prevailed; indeed riot. And Dixtown was left literally destroyed.

'Nor does the story – and Richard's erratic behaviour – quite stop there. The following year, Tom Finn was apprehended by police – while peacefully working on a remote farm far to the north-east of the Porangi region – and brought to trial. The first jury disagreed; so did a second. Finally the grave charges against Finn were pressed no further, though suspicion remained. His memoirs do not entirely dispel it: though he maintains that he possessed no gun, it is always possible that some other striker might have passed him one in the heat of the moment; the intensity of his feelings, near a half century on, suggest that he would have liked to shoot Richard Lovelock, at least.

'The courtroom confusion was understandable. Richard – described as still pale and shaken, also extremely low-voiced, by one journalist present – was brought to give evidence against Finn. Such as he gave was often at odds with his earlier firm statements to police; he grew vague where precision was crucial, and proved far from impressive under cross examination, sometimes altogether lapsing into strange silences until called to order by the judge. Two other witnesses could not be found; they were in legal difficulty themselves, and were being sought unsuccessfully in Sydney. A fourth, a junior constable, began badly by asserting that he saw a revolver in Finn's right hand. The defence produced proof that Finn was left-handed. In sum the prosecution case was left weakened; most of all by Richard Lovelock's testimony. Asked after the second trial if he had comment to offer, he answered enigmatically: "Forgive thine enemies. If thy right eye offends thee, pluck it out." Legal authorities appeared to agree; there was no third trial. *Fiat*, perhaps, *justitia*.'

Or *fiasco justitia*. Enough, yet again, is enough. By way of querulous postscript, it might be added that Richard's right eye remained enigmatically unplucked.)

Of the last days of the century, little is left to be said. Life, for some, is still best lived at a distance from the Porangi. Felicity's, for example. Her letters are few, brief, and many months old by the time they arrive. Marie Louise and Herman make what they can of them. Some clues to her condition can be easily deciphered. She tells of life in London and Paris, of literally singing for her supper in noisy public houses and smoky cafés; of eating kippers cooked over a gas flame, or stale croissants retrieved from restaurant garbage; of dank basements and draughty attics, and landlords in unfeeling pursuit. With such anecdotes out of the way, pleas for money give her correspondence consistency of character. It appears the original dowry Herman gave her as bride to her art hasn't gone far. Consummation has still to be effected, though conspiring Sylvester argues that the triumphant union is any day due. 'Art is long and life is short,' Felicity pens from her cold nuptial couch. 'I'm quite philosophical and patient – so long as it doesn't go on. I remember reading, in one of Father's dreary old tomes, about how when Virgil wished to be a poet he beguiled the Devil into a bottle and kept him there until he had all the tricks he needed to make his name known in the world. If I had that chance, I wouldn't let the Devil out of the bottle again. I'd keep him as pet.' Meanwhile she plainly has Sylvester as less awesome substitute. 'He is so faithful he's preposterous,' she confides. 'Quite like a cuddly little old dog. There are times when I'm tempted to purchase him a collar. He keeps saying he loves me. I imagine he does.' This intelligence leaves Marie Louise uneasy. On the other hand, if Felicity has succumbed to Sylvester, her virginity is many months lost; there is nothing, across time and oceans, an alert and troubled mother can do. Sylvester, so far as masculinity is concerned, isn't crème de la crème by her measure. Despite all, Marie Louise still wishes the best for her daughter.

'Who is this man Wilde?' she asks Herman, while perusing a letter.

'Who?' He is fresh from a bruising battle with Montesquieu, fought to draw in his study, and needs peace of mind.

'Oscar Wilde,' Marie Louise goes on. 'It seems they met this man in a café, and he took a great shine to Sylvester. He also borrowed a few francs from them. Felicity says that, given his present condition, she fears this Wilde can be of no use in furthering her career.'

'I can't see it either,' Herman agrees. 'I'd give the cadging sod, whoever he is, bloody short shrift. How much does she want this time?'

'She doesn't quite say. Just enough, she says, for bare essentials. They must entertain, and good wine isn't cheap. They were, when she wrote, on the way back to London. Sylvester hopes to arrange a small concert, in a grand house, especially for a musical critic called George Something Shaw. Felicity feels it's a faint hope, the Shaw man's a lecherous fool. She says if the worst comes to the worst, she can always try vaudeville. She's so bored with waiting she'd be glad of an audition with a white slaver.'

Marie Louise, while Herman spars upstairs, often sits weeping for children. But there is one for whom she evidently need have no fear. The information is contained in a letter from Felicity in London, along with news of her debut in the Covent Garden chorus. At the stage door afterwards, quite dapper, with a bouquet of white roses, stood one Ernest Lovelock, apparently in pursuit of a new mistress, a part which from his box at the opera he had selected anonymous Felicity to fill. Upon their stage door encounter the coincidence of their mutual surname was remarked. Then, in astonishment, they fell upon each other with tears. 'He's really quite handsome,' Felicity assures them, 'and not only that. Quite devilish rich. He dashes hither and thither across the Atlantic, sometimes even to Russia, to keep up with all his concerns. He took Sylvester and I off in his cab, still in great good humour about his near incestuous mistake, and entertained us to supper at the Cafe Royal, no less, regaling us with anecdotes of his experiences in far foreign parts, and of great names he had met. Waiters tumbled over themselves to serve at our table, and of the wine list Ernest would have only the best. Now for the splendid news. Ernest says he will stop at nothing, expense no objection, to see the world gives me my due. He will hire halls and impress maestros. He says some critics can be bought for a song. An odd way to put it, I thought, but with my voice I shall certainly be attempting to purchase their affections. Ernest says he has been looking for a hobby, to give his life larger zest, and sees no harm – indeed much spiritual profit – in allying his career with my own. Sylvester is silent on this proposition, much to my impatience. He tends to get moody and – dare I say – jealous. He declares suspicion of Ernest. Family is family, I explain to Sylvester. What are brothers for?'

This question, in truth, is one to which Herman has never had satisfying answer; it has been provoked more often by Richard than James. The recent incandescence of Dixtown has not been lost upon Herman. Nor the mercantile detumescence of once virile Richard. A penitent and salvation-seeking Richard, often damn near cringing, is still less to Herman's taste. Also, Richard is determined to distract Herman with tidings mostly of a New Testament nature; he needs someone to share. Herman has often to lead his urgently communicative brother downstairs, and at length firmly push him out the front door. Even then, back in his study and trying to concentrate, Herman can hear Richard beyond the window, promising resurrection and light.

'The bugger hasn't got God,' Herman pronounces. 'He's just got religion.'

Brothers are there, in brief, to get in the way.

'Did you hear what I said?' he inquires of Marie Louise. The point may need clarification before further commentary. Apart from which he suspects the woman is deaf, growing worse with the years.

'You were splitting hairs again,' she asserts. 'In connection with Richard. I understand you find his conversion inconsiderately timed. But beggars can't be choosers.'

'I called him a bugger,' Herman insists, 'not a beggar. It's always the same. You never hear one bloody word.'

'I was thinking of Luke again,' she pleads. 'If only we knew.'

'Luke?' The name still makes Herman falter. Few other things do.

'We no longer have to wonder about Ernest,' she explains. 'And Felicity's success seems assured. Dear reliable Benjamin is still just upriver with James. All that makes it worse. What of Luke?'

'There,' Herman says, as her commotion grows more intense. 'Try to look at it, if you can, in some other way. What you don't know can't hurt you. As I've told you too often, he might long be dead. Those whom the gods most love die young, or so the ancients believed.'

'Those whom I love,' Marie Louise claims fiercely, among sobs, 'aren't going to die.'

'So tell Richard,' Herman suggests. 'I'd sooner he curried your favour, at the moment, than Christ's. If he were less concerned with his impending decease, and the hot fires of hell licking his arse, I might well get more work done.'

'That's all you think of,' she accuses. 'Your work.'

Herman feels it relevant to state his position. 'It's time things were faced,' he argues. 'A new century is at hand. Luke is of that past we should put behind us. Mourn if you must. But forget if you can. Our century will soon be no more.'

'Nor will we,' she proposes. 'Perhaps it is mercy.'

Herman would sooner not be suffered this reminder. He hastens upstairs to resume a prolonged bout with the tricky and fast-moving Rousseau. In Herman's experience the realm of the everyday is queerly resistant to truth; it never allows itself, he notes, to be confused with knowledge. He is also taken by the notion that as superfluous qualities and faculties fall away, with human ageing, pure wisdom remains. Marie Louise, of course, is the exception which proves the rule. Herman sighs, and then discovers Rousseau reluctant to leave his corner for the fifty-first round. Herman compassionately decides not to pursue the matter; he goes into training for Malthus and Machiavelli. Man is ever in a graceless scramble with mortality.

Part Four

I pray some unborn bard in future times
May find our hopes and loves mean more than rhymes,
For should he raise again my pen from rest
He will but echo songs which we knew best.

—Iris Lovelock

Sixteen

If our two million evolutionary years tell us something, it is that reality is too contrived to be taken literally; that life is too improbable not to mean something.

The Lovelocks? Well, yes. Alas. They all die, sooner or later, despite Marie Louise. Mostly later. Death seems to grow less predatory on the Porangi with the passage of years.

At first sight January 1, 1900, might be mistaken for a summer day much like any other. There is a cool dawn, with sweet bursts of birdsong. Then a warm sun rises above tall hills and river. By ten it is hot. On the upper Porangi all routes soon propose a path to Marie Louise's New Century dinner. This nomenclature for the banquet is her one concession to Herman, who otherwise might not be persuaded to attend with good grace. For herself, she sees no point in making more of passing time than need be. New Year dinners are more than enough, dear God. On the other hand, New Century dinners are not to be repeated; nor can comparisons with others be suffered, and changes in menu remarked. For the first time in years, and indeed for the last time, the disparate Lovelocks shall be as one; it might also be seen as significant that Lovelock is virtually the only name left on the river, all others dead or departed. Sybil Dix remains as lonely exception, and now as good as a Lovelock, for better or worse. Even James and Richard, as bedevilled as any two brothers have been, have consented to sit at the same table on each side of Herman, who of course shall preside. Womenfolk will be interpersed among children. Iris, Nancy and Sybil are to sit among Lovelocks bred for the new century, large and sometimes still small. Of this unruly tribe – and only tables placed end to end down the long ballroom can contain them – David and Daniel, the two most responsible, are to be tactfully placed to keep order. At the far end, directly facing Herman, and perhaps at a fortunate distance, Marie Louise will dwell, with Benjamin on her right. On her left, and that much closer to her heart, a chair shall remain vacant. No one need ask questions; all know for whom. Other absentees will be remembered less physically. Toasts are planned for distant Felicity and Ernest, though Richard might find difficulty raising his glass for the second. The graves of such as Alfred Whisker and Ira Dix, names now near majestic of the irrecoverable past, will be bedecked with huge bouquets of flowers which Sybil has prepared especially for deceased spouses. In the course of this ceremony, their graves may well be watered with tears, and God knows no little spilled liquor. If insufficient for their resurrection, mineral content might make memory and grass greener. Nor shall one other dead spouse be forgotten. James and David have their own ferny wreath of red roses for Diana, more sober than Sybil's tribute of Star of Bethlehem entwined with forget-me-nots. Richard, desirably, will remain at a distance. Though not averse to making his views known on the Kingdom of Heaven, and particularly to recitation of the twenty-third psalm, he should be prevailed upon to see that there is a time and a place; that even a new century might ask more than mere contrition of self-confessed sinners.

For a time, all goes as foreseen. Undeterred by the hot weather, Marie Louise produces steaming tureens of her best onion soup, followed by frogs' legs and escargot exquisitely sauced, and four kinds of pâté with long crisp loaves of French bread. The children, who have been gathering the frogs and the snails, now feel much as the inhabitants of Spanish Creek do about rabbits; grumbles are heard. David and Daniel hiss for silence. Then come truffles imported at no small cost, and trout cooked in almonds, all by way of preliminary. There is poulet in five versions, and beef in the form of chateaubriand, pigeon in herbs, pork with pistachio, spring lamb in garlic, and rabbit à la Porangi for those unafflicted by surfeit. With some cosseting and coaxing, Marie Louise has everywhere improved not only on nature, but also on abjectly orthodox human cuisine, often to the point of revelation; it is also a meal made memorable by no lack of good wine. Herman at length discovers his feet. He suffers even abstemious Richard to fill his glass for a toast to the twentieth century. It is for James to propose that all rise to drink to the future health of the clan. In a speech conspicuous for its understatements, he recalls the pains of the past and the pleasures. At the far end of the table Marie Louise finds the time opportune to rise. 'For the women,' she proposes, 'who have put up with them all.' None drinks to this more devoutly than Nancy. Iris, by contrast, looks at her faithful Benjamin; and tries to hide tears. She makes a mental endeavour to fashion some lines of celebratory verse, rather fastidiously, but doesn't quite succeed in persuading them to scan; she is distracted by a hiccup, then by quarrelling children. Sybil, growing sleepy, seems to be slipping away under the table. Daniel uncaps bottles of beer, more to his taste when there is real drinking to be done, and more filling besides; he needs no glass, swigging straight from the bottle, and then pushing it in David's direction. 'Wrap your laughing gear around that,' he urges. 'Wine's a woman's drink. Take it from me.' Further along the table, convivial Herman insists that Richard should drink more; no man, he argues, should inhabit the first hours of the new century sober and sour. He also draws Richard's attention to the Biblical injunction on the value of wine as an aid to the digestive process, advice to be neglected at peril. While Richard contemplates this literalist interpretation, James remains silent; he feels qualified melancholy the mood most useful for the occasion. The din grows considerable. Now and then Marie Louise can be overheard telling Iris and Nancy that she hasn't had communication from Felicity since Ernest's timely offer to manage her finances; nevertheless she hopes news will come soon. Meanwhile, the ballroom fills with confusion and the smoke of pipes and cigars. Pet dogs bark, and munch on bones; children play postman's knock or hide-and-seek, depending on age, under the long arrangement of tables.

The noise is no less when the strangers arrive. At first, in fact, they pass unnoticed. Soon silence finds token footing in the ballroom, here and there thwarted by the shouts of children determined not to let the new century become boring. Most prominent among the strangers, distinctly a family group, is a lean and mature man of perhaps forty years; his handsome face has seen most kinds of weather and doubtless much hardship, and is quite darkly tanned, almost to the point of being native in hue. The woman beside him, presumably his wife, is unmistakably Maori. Motherhood evidently hasn't weighed too heavily upon her, though there are a half-dozen children gathered attractive about her. Lithe, of some grace, she has strangely confident poise.

'Welcome,' Herman says, rising, never at a loss as a host. 'We've still plenty for all. If you don't mind me asking, what brought you?'

'A canoe brought us,' the seemingly taciturn man informs those before him. 'We just paddled upriver, as we were told.'

Herman finds this reply short of satisfying. 'If you'll forgive a personal question,' he continues, 'who might you be, exactly?'

The stranger apparently needs time to be exact. He looks first at his wife, who has a shy smile, and then at the assembly; all are impatient to hear.

'I seem to be your son,' he tells Herman.

'My what?'

'Your son. I have reason to think my full name is Luke Lovelock.'

From Marie Louise there is a remote cry. Sybil, for even she is awakened, moves fast to her side. Other adults rearrange themselves with caution. Benjamin has long ceased to believe in his brother, or even to conjecture; his imagination works energetically to encompass the event. James cannot utter a word. Alone in the room he knows a ghost when he sees one. He farewelled Luke fourteen years before, in that malign landscape of volcanic mud still steaming. This counterfeit Luke, like the phantom canoe preceding the catastrophe, perhaps foretells doom for the Lovelocks.

'Luke?' Herman says, slow to the point.

'Luke,' Luke insists. 'I have no wish to upset you. But I thought it better I came.'

'My son,' Herman says softly.

'The same.'

Three decades shrivel. In the stranger they hear Luke's laugh.

'He can only be Lucifer's,' mesmerised Richard is heard saying. 'Begone from this place. In the bowels of Christ I beseech thee.'

James, who has risen, watches his glass fall to the floor from a paralysed hand.

Herman can be seen as an old, trembling man. His mouth opens and closes. No words escape.

In the end Benjamin demonstrates what best to do. He guides feeble Marie Louise almost the length of the ballroom toward the new Lovelocks, and finally to Luke. 'My boy,' she is saying.

Luke peers into her face. 'Mother?' he asks.

She appears to be shaking apart. With a disjointed leap and a queer moan, she leaves Benjamin's arm and rips open the newcomer's shirt to reveal an old crucifix plain on a chest rather hairy. Then she engulfs Luke like a great breaking wave. He sinks from sight, and Benjamin can soon be observed trying to extricate his brother from the undertow and spray. Marie Louise is not easily to be deprived. She fights off the faithless, those grown too tired to believe, and particularly Herman, who considers he has some paternal right to enter this fray. 'Your turn can come later,' she announces. 'My boy has come home. His room is still ready.'

Stunned Luke surfaces to say, 'This is my wife. And these are my children.' All quite superfluously. It has been the one reasonable conclusion in a spectacle lacking much reason, but not short of love.

Herman, still frustrated, unable thus far even to shake his son's hand, decides it not inappropriate to get on with proceedings; he calls for fresh chairs to be fetched, and yet more wine for the charging of glasses. Marie Louise retreats to her end of the table with Luke and his family gathered tight about her. From his end, his voice again usefully commanding, Herman indicates that he should like to say a few words further on the nature of the new century. There might be some, he suggests, who prematurely think it a rum sort of affair, really no different from the last. He asks them to take no heed of the slight and indeed altogether insubstantial quality of the evidence so far available. What they have witnessed is no more than unfinished business. If not chickens coming home to roost, then certainly a son and his brood.

The eyes of his listeners have, however, no chance to glaze. Something dictates a brake on Herman's verbal journey; there is reason, for a moment, to suppose him suffering failure of heart. He stands swaying. The words will not come. Tears make themselves visible. A howl rises. Silence quivers. 'Bring Luke to me,' he pleads. 'Bring me my son.'

It takes several days, nearly a week, for all to become clear. Truth doesn't put history out of countenance. Nor can it quite win a smile. True, for example, that Luke lived more than a decade in that doomed village on the lake where James all but found him. Of his original kin he knew only that they were deceased and better forgotten. It was never anything to query, or contest; his adoptive parents were more than adequate to the everyday, and never more so than when love was needed. In the village he wooed many girls, as a young tribesman should, and finally carried off the most coveted of all maidens; they married in a missionary church. By the time they begat children, Luke was quite prosperous and respected, a tribal orator of note. Then he suffered mysterious affliction. One day, while out gathering crayfish, he fell into a trance before fellow tribesmen; some thought him dead. He became possessed of a most urgent vision. A woman, elderly and European, yet not quite a stranger, was trying to indicate some sort of summons. Largely incomprehensible, she did convey the word peril. He and those whom he most loved were at risk; they must flee.

Awoken, Luke repeated this message to those gathered about him. He was mocked, as who wouldn't be, when he suggested calamity impending. At a tribal meeting, called to quell panic, he heard himself denounced as a mercenary undercover representative of unscrupulous white land-dealers, men who craved the village site to build a fine tourist hotel. Luke again proved the maxim that men born white could never be trusted. In support, Biblical texts were quoted selectively, and to sustain the mockery. Did Luke think himself Moses, perhaps, proposing to lead the Israelites across the Red Sea? No reference could have been more ill chosen. Luke, in the light of later events, with lakes dividing much as the sea opened before Moses, might have been proposing just that. Now alien among his people, suspect even to his parents, cruelly hurt Luke gathered his few belongings, his wife and infant children, and moved on. His wife had relatives among another tribe distant on the coast to the east. Not long after they left, while still rafting across lake and toiling over mountain, they saw the disaster begin behind them: the torrent of fire, the dark days to follow, while their campsites creaked and the ash fell dense.

By the time they reached shelter with relatives, in a small coastal village, Luke was a prophet of proven quality; but one, alas, who would henceforth have to live off his reputation, with no further trances or visions to frighten. Nevertheless people felt safe with Luke near as mascot, or talisman; he was especially welcome aboard the many-oared longboats when whale herds seasonally crossed the horizon. With Luke as harpooner, who could be hurt? To preserve his reputation – if not to extend it – Luke became exceptionally precise, often quite fearless, with the harpoon; he would leave his lethal strike always until the last moment, despite the danger of some maddened bull running amok and sinking his boat. Always a man among men, Luke soon controlled the whaling with spirit and grace, down to last details, the flensing of the great carcasses, the boiling down of blubber in the black tri-pots on the beach. With no labour making for waste, the annual harvest was huge. And with Luke dwelling among them the villagers felt indeed blessed with luck.

There was no real change until last summer. For then Luke and his still lovely wife sentimentally chose to revisit scenes of their youth in the land's steamy interior; they lingered on unrecognizable lakeside where they once courted, giggled among reeds, or pursued each other among hot pools, and found only sadness and silence. No new village had risen, nor even a white man's hotel, though ferns and tender trees had begun greening the new sombre hills fashioned by the eruption. In retreat, before they terminated their pilgrimage, they decided to spoil themselves with some civilization. This decision led them by road to the tiny town of Rotorua, garlanded with geysers of amiable proportion, where men might again delude themselves they were masters of nature; and treat themselves to safe thermal sideshow. Here they met an aged publican by name of Joseph McRae, no stranger to Luke, though not seen since the many-omened event which singed their lives mutually. In conversation, while arranging the past to their need with McRae, they learned for the first time of a highly strung stranger maybe called

Lovesomething – James Lovesomething, to the best of McRae's unsteady recollection – who on the fatal eve had come looking for Luke; and who, unless memory played McRae false, had damn near perished himself, with a woman who did.

From the moment he heard this tale Luke had been as a man haunted, sleepless at night. If he still had kin, where were they now? And who? There were false leads near and far. He found families called Love, Loveday, Loveless, Lovelady and even Lovemerry. None of them kin. Finally, a few days earlier, in some proximity to the Porangi, wandering Luke and his family heard the name Lovelock float musically toward them, and news of three brothers called Herman, Richard and James. They even encountered rumours which tended to agree that Herman had a son kidnapped by Maoris in the region's misty past; the mourning of the child's stepmother was already a small legend. From then Luke never knew doubt. He pressed on to the Porangi, and finally upriver, clearly not before time, or so Herman has lately been heard observing.

For his part, Luke confesses that his life, and most certainly his reputation, now make more sense. The woman he saw, while in trance, was beyond doubt Marie Louise, warning him to flee fire and hot flood.

Marie Louise, in fairness, points out that Herman's contribution is not to be discounted. Without his electricity, nuisance as it may have been, she might not have reached Luke. Never had its generation been more auspicious, nor had more purpose, than saving a lost son.

Naturally, more tears are shed. Luke cannot be taken for granted.

'You won't go back whaling?' she asks, with anxiety.

'Probably not,' Luke allows. 'The harpoon is for men younger, less rusty than me. Anyway the great herds are going, with the hunt so ruthless elsewhere. For us it was more a profitable challenge, something to make life more keen, and the world more precious.'

'I see,' Marie Louise says, and doesn't. She still needs Little Luke, eyes all mischief; she prefers no appearances to the contrary if they can be avoided. Not that she overlooks Luke's wife and children; they can be included in Marie Louise's world view as in the nature of miracle's bonus, accumulated interest on the investment of faith, and above all as piquant sauce on the love-feast. For all the meals she serves now are such feasts, in impressive procession; the original banquet, presumably because Luke came belated, appears likely to last many months, conceivably until the end of the current century; anyway there are more than thirty years of missed meals to make good. 'Please,' Luke often protests, on behalf of himself and his family, 'we'll fatten like pigs.' These pleas go unheard. Herman is at pains to advise his new-found son that it is profitless to quibble; that in his experience argument only provokes the confounded woman to feats more spectacular, and there could be grievous consequences for all if these continue to be culinary.

Meanwhile, more has to be considered, and most of all the future. Luke now sees that his fate, as revealed, is to share with his family, for better or worse, perhaps by bringing new blood; why else, he asks, should his life have been preserved? His earthly purpose has become plain: to see out his parents, and persuade them of happiness, on the last of their mortal journey. Who is he to argue? He does not; he accepts. He seems as a prisoner recalled from parole to serve his natural sentence. True that the Porangi no longer has prospects for the young and ambitious; that its economic progress has, so to speak, been grossly uneven. But Luke is no longer young, and still a stranger to ambition. For the moment he and his own have a roof overhead, if often in much need of maintenance. There is the river; there are his parents; there is peace. If his children want more, as most children will, then let them look elsewhere. If they go, he will of course grieve, but without grief what is the point of parenthood? His own life is instructive testimony. For it isn't just reason – or firm belief in fate – which makes him complacently at home on the Porangi. In recent years he has suffered greatly from savage and inexplicable pains of the back. At first he took it to be some consequence of whaling: damage done in the long hours alert with harpoon, often in wild weather, the sea always jarring. Once he rode eighty-six miles to the nearest physician, who failed to find anything organically wrong. The pain has come and gone, near crippling, crushing him to the ground as if under rocks and old iron. Now he understands these cruel symptoms to have been the weight of Marie Louise's grief. The pain is gone, quite gone; he knows it will never return.

'Yes,' he informs Marie Louise. 'Of course we're staying here with you. Where else could I go?'

She weeps for all of two days.

Luke digs and plants a large garden for his parents, fetches and carries, and effects repairs to Lovelock House where he can. The condition of the tower, however, defeats him; he forbids the children to climb it, and tries to persuade Herman to at least use it less. His wife Tui, no longer as shy as the songbird for which she was named, likewise helps in the house where she can, sweeping and laundering, though she finds it impossible to ease Marie Louise from the kitchen; that kingdom, for the moment, cannot be claimed. As for Herman, it has to be said that the new century, while not a disappointment, has thus far cost him much in equilibrium, with children again clamorous in the corridors, shouting down cavernous stairwells, hammering Felicity's grand piano to hell, and joy not infrequently getting quite out of perspective. There are times now when such as Plato can sneak a punch past his guard; and others, alas, when he reels dizzy on the ropes. Or simply, in exhaustion, collapses asleep on his desk.

The annual mountains of rabbit corpses appear insufficient propitiation. Alarms and excursions at Spanish Creek do not cease with the new century. More sacrifice must be made, and not just in sweat. The first winter gives the warning; the still heavier rains of the second bring confirmation. The rabbits have worked like termites into the upper terrain, leaving scarce a good root of grass, and the surface everywhere undermined. When gusts of rain rip into the hills, excavating rivulets, the soil begins to surrender and move away gently as silt; then entire sectors of hillside sag and slump. This erosion seems infectious. Indeed, from a distance, it resembles disease: sunlight shows it as yellow weeping ulcers, with no scar tissue forming; and certainly no grass. Just sticky clay, corrugated, sometimes shaped into crevasse. The fine net of forest roots has long perished; there is nothing to hold the hills together other than prayer. Of which there is much, often profane in expression, but never lacking in fervour. Too much good grazing has gone. The second summer of the century sees James and Benjamin barging a thousand ewes downriver for slaughter, and town-dwellers' cheap mutton. 'It won't hurt to trim the flocks down,' James says, with optimism. 'Nature appears to be giving us some message.'

Benjamin is silent. He knows this cannot go on. On the other hand he feels it undesirable, perhaps disloyal, to afflict James with the truth. To Iris he confides, 'The future, so far as I see it, is bleak. Spanish Creek may soon no longer be able to support all of us here. I am thinking, of course, of our immediate family.'

'Just what are you saying?' Iris asks.

'I suppose I am saying that, sooner or later, we may have to move. You and I and the children. And Sybil, of course.'

'Leave Spanish Creek? Leave all the Porangi?' She has just published, in fact, her fifth book, *Poems From a Lost River*. That title now appears disturbingly prophetic. 'Is that what you're saying?'

'Roughly,' Benjamin agrees. 'You and I, we still aren't too old. We could cope with a fresh start, for the sake of our children. Better sooner than later, when I come to think.'

'What of James?' she inquires.

'James and David, I don't doubt, will be competent to manage the land and sheep left.'

'Could he not construe our role as that of rats taking leave of a sinking ship?'

'In a sense,' Benjamin concedes. 'In another sense, his voyage may be made lighter. Our sons grow no smaller, nor our daughters in truth. I fear we might all fast become burden. More than the land can carry.'

'You diminish yourself. And Daniel. The other boys too. You have always given of yourselves heart and soul here.'

'You needn't go on. I have regret too.'

Benjamin postpones making announcement. Perhaps nature's perversity will pass. About this time the people of the Porangi cease to be Victorians, becoming instead Edwardians, though they learn the news a month or two late. The passing of a Queen is much like the quitting of the last century; it makes no perceptible difference, though it inspires Iris to a poem. She places the deceased monarch, now in no position to protest, within a context of brave pioneers felling great trees; her stanzas are elegant and wistful, with a slow dying fall. An era to be cherished, she suggests, in which men won new worlds; its virtue is not lightly to be surrendered. In this respect, if no other, she is right; it will not.

Benjamin, meanwhile, has an obligation to appraise the new world, or what passes for it on the Porangi, with realism. Not least when another thousand sheep are barged downriver. All look lean; they will not fetch much. McKenzie would weep. Also the annual wool cheque, when it arrives, is not something to celebrate. Nor is the money for rabbit skins, now collected and cured with more system, great recompense. Fact has to be looked in its uncompromising face. Benjamin labours reluctantly uphill toward this confrontation; at length he hears himself speaking to James.

'Go?' James says, bitterly shaken.

'For a new start,' Benjamin explains. 'While there is still time. I'm thinking not only of Daniel, but of my other boys too. I'd like to see them set up, all safe, before I pass in my hand. There's no safety here. And bugger all future. I'm sorry. It's time to be frank.'

'If you must be,' James allows. 'My problem, perhaps, has always been seeing all points of view. Sometimes this makes for blindness. I imagine you are not to be persuaded otherwise. For my part, I have little to say. Except good luck. And to express my gratitude, which you might take as read. I have always regarded you as equal partner in this venture – or adventure, which it was once. My grief is that, in the end, you go with so little asset. Not even your own home. Nothing for all the years you have slaved.'

'Those years are my asset,' Benjamin asserts, perhaps astutely borrowing from Iris. 'They are not to be forgotten. Nor ever to come again. Yet they still give me strength. I have only to look, for example, at my sons. There is asset too. There is nothing more tangible.'

James finds his dismay not to be swiftly subdued; he takes it to David. Over their evening meal, he says. 'So it's over to us, now. You and me. No more.'

'What about Daniel? Can't even he stay on?'

'In essence,' his father explains patiently, 'Benjamin is right. Our circumstances are reduced. It seems that it is in the nature of circumstances to shrink. Likewise man's expectations. There is a closing of doors, and at length just one left ajar.' James pauses. He has no desire to be specific; he is too close to sixty. 'As for Daniel, it isn't for us to detain him. He must have the chance to spread his wings wider. Perhaps the Porangi, in its way, must be seen as a nest. I am aware of the bruising of your affections; I know that you and Daniel have been close.'

David leaves the table in haste, lest tears be seen; they are very near, but saved for his pillow.

Dry-eyed next day, he rides alongside Daniel. All is now known. They have nothing to say. They follow a steep line of ridge, relatively uncrumbled; they have sun and stiff breeze in their faces. Daniel halts unexpectedly on a summit. Startlingly, he takes a knife from his belt and slashes a thumb. Before time for protest, he has grabbed David's hand and is doing the same. The two spurting thumbs are fast pressed together. 'There,' Daniel says. 'How's that? We're more than just cousins now. We're brothers in blood. And we're not to forget it, wherever we go. Whatever we do. Right?'

'Right,' David agrees. All the same, he wishes that the ceremony had more conviction. He sees it as something perfunctory, arranged for his consolation. Which isn't to detract from Daniel's well-meaning words. But Daniel, in spirit, is riding other skylines already.

Nor is his flesh far behind. He goes, with all his family, before the year's end.

The quiet of Spanish Creek now has curious, quite unfamiliar texture. Even the rowdy shearing gangs, coming and going, leave it unbreached, though one of their women does persuade David to part, if rather convulsively, with his virginity. Then David begins to understand the silence surrounding. The land has too soon become haunted. A gross thought, and unsettling to grasp. He shrinks humanly into the life formed by the farm, his books, and his father.

'You see?' James often announces. 'We survive, you and me. You couldn't ask more.'

'No,' David agrees, with less and less difficulty.

* * *

('Of Spanish Creek,' says the librettist of *The Lives of Lovelock Junction*, 'there is little to be said in connection with the last decade of the nineteenth century and the first of the twentieth. Life doubtless had a pleasing rural rhythm. None of the drama attendant upon events at Dixtown and Lovelock Junction proper – violent labour struggles, the rediscovery of Herman's lost son – appears to have had counterpart here. We have only Iris Lovelock's verse to tell of affection apparently felt for this passionless part of the Porangi; and it is true that under her Victorian bric-a-brac some genuine pulse of feeling is evident. On the other hand it might be suggested that, like other pioneers, those at Spanish Creek simply used the land ruthlessly, plundering it for immediate purpose, rather than farming it for posterity. Iris and her husband Benjamin, for example, appear to have departed it about the end of 1902. The cause isn't clear. Perhaps there were now better pickings elsewhere. Or was there some feud with James? It is hardly conceivable that the peripheral problems of Spanish Creek – the rabbit pest, say, or possibly ubiquitous hill country erosion – might have caused family tempers to fray. Mystery remains.'

It might also be said that many authors use their material ruthlessly, plundering it for immediate purpose rather than farming it for posterity. The cause isn't clear. Mystery remains.)

Migration from the Porangi, for a time, seems to shape as stampede. Next to leave is Nancy, together with sons and daughters. A departure not unforeseen; in fact, so far as Nancy has been concerned, it has been coming for years. Not to gild a limp lily, Richard has become a miserly drag. Bad enough that he has been hobbled by the destruction of Dixtown; does he have to be in harness to heaven too? He lacks the compassion to understand that others might take offence at his impecunious condition, and particularly Nancy. If Richard isn't willing to keep her in the manner to which she has grown accustomed, then at least in the city she can send her sons to work; there is also still a fair prospect that she might find a new man. Before she departs, she patiently strips the house of all articles of value. To express her feelings still further, she kicks out a few windows, and hurls articles largely worthless at walls. Richard fails to see much of significance in these acts, try as he might. Earthly existence has become more and more a mystery; Nancy appears to be confirming it merely as a squalid affair, and unnecessarily noisy. He can take it all gratefully as a dramatized sermon. On the other hand his gratitude is all the greater when Nancy has gone. He has never heard quiet to compete.

Richard has one large problem left in his lifetime. This is also financial. For some time it has been his custom to employ a preacher, of unqualified fundamentalist faith, to make a monthly journey up the Porangi, and conduct services in his house; in the recent past Nancy and the children have been press-ganged into attendance. Now the preacher's congregation is one. Much as Richard detests bankrolling religion, especially on dwindling funds, salvation seems a most reliable investment. Praying solitary before the preacher, he grows certain of God's consummate attention. The hotter the hellfire offering, the more he revels. The preacher is not slow to discern that he has a man on his hands with contempt for sugared placebos; he has one who needs larger and larger dosages of the real thing. Also the more scalding the sermon, the more chance of a modest bonus from his employer; he is thus not above embellishing the wages of sin. On the return journey downriver, after doing his duty by Richard, he is often perilously exhausted, and not beyond sharing a soothing cigarette and hip-flask of brandy with the overly conversational Papist who sometimes calls up the Porangi to hear Marie Louise's confession. This priest – who to spare Herman's feelings must come clad in the disguise of a traveller in fine foodstuffs – has confided that he learns more from Marie Louise in one sitting than in seven years in a seminary. He also, after breaking bread at Marie Louise's table, and invigorating debate with Herman, leaves the impression of a man unfairly replete. The preacher, insofar as his own client is concerned, has to be content with cold mutton and monotonous expressions of piety; he sometimes has the sense of a mislaid vocation. Were it not for the money, he might well be glad to leave Richard tormented with damnation; and so avoid being depressed by this well-fed priest who has the impertinence to take spiritual pleasure from a Porangi voyage.

Richard, at worst, suspects his comforter might be a mercenary poseur. Also at worst he fears that his funds, though long and well hidden from prying eyes in an obscure bank, may not last his life. If he cannot pay for a preacher, or arrange for visits on a purely complimentary basis, what then? It is unthinkable. For the most part, he attempts not to think; there is no point in exhibiting withdrawal symptoms prematurely, nor in nursing unnecessary fear, when the likelihood is that Jesus will first come to claim him.

Perhaps a year or two after Nancy's departure, perhaps more, a matter of indifference with his life so largely fulfilled, Richard hears one morning a bang on his door. There has been no steamer; it cannot be the preacher. It has to be Luke, who calls regularly to see that his Uncle Richard remains in tolerable health, and is not short of vegetables.

Richard unburdens his knees of a particularly heavy and large-type Bible, rises arthritically, and answers the continuing summons. It isn't Luke at the door. It is someone, so help him, Richard would prefer forgotten; or dead. The bulky and razor-slashed renegade by name of Crabb stands there with idiot smile. Richard sees, in a moment of illumination, just how his own life is due to end. Here, or very near. Now, or quite soon. Strangled or struck down by this heavy-breathing monster who has come to exact final revenge. Richard isn't to be deceived by that sly smile; the man bulges with menace. With a deep breath, and much internal agitation, Richard prepares to embrace fate, the more so to let his soul soar. May Crabb be mercifully swift.

Crabb isn't. His great fists twist into each other, all knuckle; his arms and huge shoulders are flexing with preliminary emotion. Nor are his bright crossed eyes, eerily wandering at odds with each other, much reassuring in respect of mercy. If not quite Satan himself, at least as Richard pictures him, Crabb qualifies as an eminently lifelike Beelzebub, next in power and next in crime.

The grotesque creature feels, for some reason, impelled to speak. 'I suppose you thought you seen the bloody last of me,' he says.

Richard agrees that this has been the case.

It seems to give Crabb considerable pleasure. 'Well, I'm back,' he announces superfluously. 'See? I'm back.'

Richard agrees that this also appears to be the case. He inches backward. Crabb inches forward.

'Things aren't the same here,' Crabb suggests.

Richard agrees that no, they are not.

'And you're alone?'

The fiend is plainly not averse to ensuring there are no witnesses to make his task lengthier, and perhaps still more murderous. 'Up to a point,' Richard agrees evasively. 'I'm only alone up to a point.'

'What point?' Crabb asks, puzzled. 'Who in hell do you mean?'

'I speak of my saviour,' Richard explains, 'with whose grace I reside.'

'Who the fuck's he? And is Grace his sister, or wife?'

Richard cannot but be conscious of his frail spinal column, especially in the vicinity of his neck, of vertebrae all too easily displaced. His skull, far too thin a shield for the brain, doesn't bear thinking about at all. Nevertheless he persists with explanations which might pacify Crabb, or God knows distract him. But he has a strong sense of the Christian message falling as seed on devastated ground.

'Well, I'm damned,' Crabb says.

'Exactly,' Richard proceeds.

Before long, however, Crabb feels compelled to come to the point of his mission; there are apparently things still unsaid. 'You and me had our differences,' he tells Richard.

Richard finds that a fair statement of the position.

'You know I been breaking rocks for the past seven years?'

Richard says he imagines Crabb might well have been. Indeed, for Richard, the thought has been of considerable comfort, if not at the moment.

'On account of that steamer we took. I got to admit that was our one big mistake. I got attempted piracy, grievous bodily harm, wounding with intent to injure. Six charges in all. I turned Queen's evidence on two. Otherwise I'd still be inside; some poor buggers got more. I also got a few years off for informing. In the jug, a man can go out of his mind if he don't have an interest. The prison governor reckoned a lenient view could be taken of my sentence.'

Richard agrees that this was long-sighted and considerate of the authorities.

'But I haven't come to bloody bore you with this,' Crabb says.

Richard argues that no, whatever else he may be, Crabb isn't boring; he would really be quite interested in learning more of Crabb's recent life history.

'No,' Crabb sums up. 'I'm here to talk about us. About you and me. You see what I mean?'

Richard doesn't, quite; or refuses to. Anything to lengthen his last hour. For one thing, his freed soul might suffer less shock on its journey.

'In fact, I'm here to settle things, like,' Crabb confesses. 'I don't mind telling you I done some fucking hard thinking.'

He pauses, quite unnecessarily, for effect. Richard is thus obliged to allow that Crabb is clearly a man who gives matters much thought. Might he, perhaps, care to take tea?

'Tea?' Crabb says, with some awe.

'Tea,' Richard repeats. 'I'm fresh out of cocoa. The boat's yet to call.'

'Look,' Crabb says, 'there's something you ought to know. Right here and now.'

Richard waits. 'I might find some medicinal brandy,' he suggests. Anything as bribe; Crabb is visibly a man not quite in control, especially of emotion. He continues heaving and sighing, and twisting those great fists. Not even to be distracted by the likelihood of hard liquor.

'I just want you to know – well, how can I fucking put it – that I don't bear you no grudge.'

'*You* don't?' Richard says, quite amazed.

'No,' Crabb says charitably. 'I've forgot all our differences. To make no bones, it's all in the past. That's why I'm here.'

Richard sees Dixtown burning again, then finds elsewhere to look. His knees are numb with relief; his head starts to reel. 'I need to sit down,' he admits.

'By all means,' Crabb says with concern. 'Can I get you that tea?' He sighs. 'Then we can talk.'

Crabb, conceivably because of solitary confinements, the unenviable fate of prison informers, proves to be a man of extensive conversational capacity. Tea, or perhaps even a sociable glass of water, is more than sufficient stimulus. He doesn't wish to deprive Richard of the meanest of autobiographic detail. It appears, for example, that he survived all manner of hazards in returning to the Porangi afoot. When he tried sleeping under a hedge, police persuaded him to heave his arse out of town. Had it not been for an obliging grocer, who chanced to leave a side window unlocked, Crabb might even have starved. As for actually making his way upriver, minus a craft, that was all misery too. He crashed through bush. He swam. Nothing deterred him. Not even the Porangi currents. 'A man born to hang doesn't drown,' he assures Richard. 'I always been told I got a gallows complexion.'

Richard does not dispute this. Crabb's facial revisions cannot be called cosmetic advance; his colour remains that of a man bred for the rope. There is, however, more which should be made known. 'Why?' he asks Crabb. 'Why did you do it? Why did you come?'

There is a prolonged pause. For a time Richard despairs of an answer. Then tears seep from the bloodshot eyes, drip down the blue scars.

'Because,' Crabb confesses, 'this is the only place where I ever been happy.'

'No,' Richard prays.

Nor has Crabb quite finished. He is a man possessed with vision of the future.

'We could get things going again here,' he discloses. 'I mean you and me.'

'I fear that I'm past it,' Richard protests. 'In a very short time, I must tell you, I'll be three score and ten.'

'Think of the good times,' Crabb urges.

Richard finds this difficult.

'They could all come again,' Crabb promises.

'No,' Richard says firmly. 'There's nothing more tedious, it is said, than a twice told tale. To err is human. To forgive, divine. To err again might be a tempting of fate. Certainly of divine intolerance. In that respect, I feel I've had more than my share.'

'You've lost me,' still tearful Crabb says.

'I'm saying no,' Richard explains.

'Then I'll get things going again by myself,' Crabb offers. 'You don't need to do nothing. Take my word. Man to man.'

'No,' Richard shouts, to his own consternation.

'And I'll look after you here,' Crabb proposes. 'You won't have no worries. I tell you for a fact I got a lot on my conscience. I'd just as soon not go to the gallows with the thought of you ruined. Even the quicklime wouldn't give me mercy. Nor all the worms in the world.' Crabb dries his eyes on the soiled sleeve of his shirt. 'More tea?' he suggests.

Richard lifts his eyes heavenward, but finds no revelation. 'If I may make so bold to say,' he suggests, very slowly, 'the best thing you can do is head off downriver again.'

Crabb cannot conceal hurt. 'Are you threatening?' he inquires.

'Not at all,' Richard says, reasonably.

'Turning me out, then?'

'In a sense,' Richard allows.

'You can't do that to me,' Crabb argues, with some subterranean aggression.

'Of course not,' Richard discovers himself agreeing.

'That's all right, then. You gave me a bad moment. The last thing I want is to be turned loose on the world again. You get what I mean?'

Richard's comprehension is quick to the mark. The world, for its own dark reasons, has turned Crabb loose on Richard. And the monster, perhaps by way of earthly retribution, may well have to be suffered for the soul's purity. 'Of course,' he listens to himself declaring. 'Your meaning is, I find, quite unmistakable.'

'You didn't say whether you wanted more tea,' Crabb observes amiably. 'Yours must have got cold. Don't get up. Just sit there. I'll boil up the kettle again.'

'Thank you,' Richard says weakly.

'And did I hear some mention of food? I got the appetite of an elephant.'

'In the larder,' Richard points out.

'Good,' Crabb says. 'There's no place like home.'

That night Crabb appears at pains to dispel Richard's last vestige of loneliness. He spends all his sleeping hours walking his hog to market; the snores shake the house. Richard, two rooms distant, watches dawn on his ceiling. Crabb doesn't waste his waking hours either. Soon after an ample breakfast, he stalks among the ruins of Dixtown, in places greenly overgrown, and tosses aside huge pieces of charred timber obstructing his path. He locates wagon tracks under fern, and finds his way up to the demolished mines; he also patiently assesses the prospects of salvaging the mill.

'Nothing to it,' he diagnoses. 'I can get things going again, even if it takes me ten years. Where there's a will there's a way.' For emphasis he feels obliged to thump Richard on the shoulder, presumably so the latter is left in no doubt of his willpower. Richard, as it happens, isn't. He stumbles away dizzily, and falls. 'You're right,' Crabb concedes. 'You are getting old. Take it from me. You got nothing to worry you no more. Leave everything to yours truly.'

This coincides with Richard's deepest desire. Crabb's enthusiasm for life back on the Porangi, though far from infectious, never wanes; his impact on Dixtown is much less perceptible. True that as weeks pass, then months, the place becomes a marginally tidier collection of ruins. Crabb's exertions, in the nature of things, are mostly on the margin; it is too much for one man, even for so muscular a ghoul. Stripped to the waist, heaving and sweating, Crabb appears even more evil; tattooed snakes undulate all over his torso. When restoration of dwellings defeats him, for lack of surviving timber, he turns his bulk loose upon first things. Rockfalls, when he attempts to reopen mines, prove indifferent to willpower, near lethally. Likewise more than willpower is needed to piece together the rusty and scattered machinery of the mill. Nevertheless Crabb has no problem persuading himself that the future is coming to pass; he continues to potter with visible satisfaction. Richard would be the last to deny him happiness, as earlier noted; nor would he now deprive Crabb of the spiritual companionship the poor creature so much craves. Crabb, despite first appearances, is also possessed of a soul; he shows a childish excitement in the sharing of Richard's interests, which have become almost exclusively religious in nature. Though unlettered, he is not slow to get the gist of the Lord's Prayer, if not its entire message, and can say grace competently before consuming most of the food on the table. If he has any remaining weakness, it resides in his dilution of tea with the medicinal brandy. Yet even this act has virtue; it stops his stomach rumbling too audibly. One thing, however, perplexes him: the visits of the preacher.

'You pay him?' Crabb asks.

'Expenses,' Richard says. 'The man must eat too.'

Crabb is prepared to allow any man his appetite, provided it suffers his own no impediment, but all the same finds ten pounds too high; he gives a low whistle. 'Ten nicker a time? For that price he ought to produce all of St Peter's keys. Not to speak of a few pearls off of them gates.'

'I'm afraid I don't follow,' Richard says.

'Ten nicker's too high. That's what I'm saying. I could do it all for you. No charge at all.'

Though at first tempted to spurn the offer, Richard is overcome by Crabb's fresh dedication. Crabb explores the alphabet, lips moving, getting the hang; before long he travels across entire words, and embarks upon Genesis. When the preacher visits, Crabb listens with unfeigned interest, alert to those nuances which most affect Richard. He sees the need, for example, to improvize on Biblical passages perhaps too pacific in tone; and then, by way of acute contrast, to pull out the plug and let Satan and sin flow away fast; a pure and radiant Jesus at last waits upon Richard. He also notes the advantage in giving a sermon its head, to allow it to canter across the danker marshes of human existence, then suddenly to surface in sunlight and salvation; Richard is best ambushed by Christ.

'Right,' Crabb says, after some months. 'I think I got it all now. Next time round, you can boot that preacher's bum downriver. You don't need him no more. I'll do his job.'

'But,' Richard protests, 'you don't look the part.'

'Just give me an old suit, and a back to front collar. Then see how I go. I'll wager you now you'll never see no bloody difference.'

Richard, though stiffly declining to wager, is persuaded, nonetheless, to see economic advantage in the arrangement. Though Crabb's theology brushes the unorthodox, if still on the safe side of heresy, it has to be conceded that the growth of a beard gives him far greater presence. For one thing, his hideous scars are largely concealed. Tattooed serpents might writhe beneath clean white shirt and reversed collar; no one would know. Beelzebub never had better disguise.

There is another advantage, far from mundane. Monthly visits from a preacher were always a test to the patience; Richard would tend to be twitchy after three weeks. Crabb, for all his faults, and these can be seen as sins of omission, is always on tap. Richard can now arrange for sermons nightly, if necessary. Always obliging as a religious raconteur, Crabb never finds donning of clerical garb a great pain. As for the atmosphere of the household, it could not be more congenial; divine grace glows through their days, the devil quite banished. The regular preacher, who now seems a man of impoverished imagination, finds his employment terminated upriver; Richard tips him a last sovereign, and tells him not to come back. God's irregular, the ex-convict named Crabb, has things quite in control. Still more so with time. His vocal range is not inconsiderable. Nor his skills as narrator. God can become a battering barrage, a ten-day thunderstorm, a deluge drowning all the known and loveless landscapes of Richard's long life. By contrast he can also be manifest in the wistfully sweet visage, framed by gold locks, of the young Jesus-child. Naturally, given choices of images, Richard prefers to settle for the second; Crabb's portrait of the tender infant Christ pleading, and no Michelangelo did better, can reduce a strong man to tears. The storm has passed over. There the child stands. Who could wish more? Richard falls to his knees, his adoration implicit. Crabb is never at a loss in exploiting iconographic riches; and certainly no miniaturist. His inventive realization of the Jesus-child proves a lode of pure gold. From it Crabb excavates a shining cell, and shapes gleaming chains. Richard is utterly incarcerated, a joyous prisoner of Jesus. This narrative, in fact, need follow Richard no further. To pursue him might be interpreted as invasion of privacy.

About this time the Lovelocks cease to be colonials, and become instead citizens of a young nation, but the brave news never quite reaches upriver; nor the drumbeats, bugles, and carnival buskers entwined with this event. Likewise the information that they live in the new century's social laboratory fails to make significant impression, though it is attested by Americans, Frenchmen, one or two Britons, and a Fabian named George Bernard Shaw; there is even a scholarly treatise in Russian which an exile in Zurich pseudonymously styled Lenin is angrily annotating to the effect that antipodean reform might place world revolution in hazard. Iris, who at least kept the river-bound Lovelocks lyrically informed of contemporary affairs, has years gone. She and Benjamin, failing to find another farm, not for love nor money, and especially money, have settled for life in a city; Benjamin works eight dusty hours a day, six drab days a week, as a customs clerk. Iris, to make their money go further, actively pens ever lengthening contributions to literary pages; one of her reviews, which causes no little stir, is a denunciation of the disagreeable sexuality to be found in the work of a compatriot, another lady of letters called Katherine Mansfield. Daniel, unable to shake off old habits, has gone wandering as itinerant shepherd and shearer; he never quite makes it back to the Porangi, however, possibly because of the chronic shortage of girls on the river, and certainly because of the many public houses to be encountered on any return route. Letters from Iris and Benjamin are markedly less informative as time and urban living corrode, though one reveals with sadness the sudden death of Sybil. She died in mid-sentence, so to speak, in full conversational flow, while explaining that the quainter customs of life in the colonies – Sybil also being too old to adjust to the first ebb of the imperial tide – were still utterly beyond her comprehension; death put an end to her lifelong perplexity. Marie Louise feels it unfair that the Porangi should have preserved Sybil for just another grave in a city cemetery, so far from her two heroic husbands. On the other hand Sybil, young again, and verbally undiminished, may be causing Alfred Whisker and Ira Dix both swiftly to seek refuge in some remote colonial outpost of the beyond.

From Felicity communications are few and still terser, often just postcards revealing triumphs and travels with Ernest; some are even written and signed by her personal secretary. Yet again there is a sadness, made more poignant with brevity. Sylvester Spring, it seems, cut his throat messily in a Florentine hotel, or so Felicity has heard. She observes that Sylvester was never quite able to cope with success, and never really much more than a poor man's Svengali. While she hesitates to attribute his fatal condition to envy of Ernest, a man of far greater substance, she supposes facts must be faced. Marie Louise, who for herself found Sylvester a life-giver, and also deserving of a more than casual place in Felicity's affections, is grieved; then aggrieved. And who, she writes to Felicity, is this Svengali? Even Herman, who makes it his business to be on speaking terms with most names worth knowing, cannot supply an identity. It suggests unpleasantness anyway, making dead Sylvester seem sinister, when the reverse was demonstrably true. He might be seen – though Marie Louise doesn't go so far as saying this in her letter – as a good man fallen victim to Felicity's follies. At all events much remains enigma; Felicity doesn't see fit to enlighten her mother further about Sylvester's demise. For the most part the river still efficiently keeps death remote; perhaps there are too few people left to make a visit profitable, with custom so abundant elsewhere.

No one makes more use of this apparent reprieve than Herman. In 1906 he allows it to be known that, with all research done, the past reconsidered, he has begun compilation of his collected works in twenty-four volumes. It is to be his testament to the condition of humankind, with certain autobiographic interpolations to illustrate – and desirably illuminate – major points at issue. By 1909, the year of his eightieth birthday, the first five volumes stand bound and sealed on his shelves. The pace picks up thereafter, with his mind concentrated marvellously, and by the time Halley's Comet has passed he is within sight of finishing the tenth. True that there are times when he appears a trifle wild-eyed about this project, no doubt in despair of ever getting it done. Groans, not infrequently climaxed by a great howl, indicate to the other inhabitants of Lovelock House that Herman's industry does not diminish with age, which transparently does not weary him, even if the years condemn; the project is infinite, in truth, and Herman is finite, this consideration causing him to specify only twenty-four volumes. It will be for some mute, still inglorious and perhaps unborn Herman to continue the chronicle; it is too much for one man alone. None of this should suggest that life is static in Lovelock House, though it may pass soft-footed beyond Herman's locked door. Marie Louise still finds much to celebrate in Luke's return, not least his continuing company, and that of his wife; she crams four decades of love into one, with Luke then no less than fifty and grey. Luke's children grow taller and leave, some for the city, some for old tribal lands; he is soon several times a grandfather himself. Marie Louise, though taking vague cognizance, appears to consider this inadmissible evidence; she has far more telling testimony that Luke is still the Luke she lost. Luke discovers no difficulty in playing this role, not merely to humour his stepmother, but as proof of his affections. The truth is that Marie Louise is tiring, and Tui has begun cautiously to take over the kitchen; Marie Louise retains, as it were, a watching brief. With luck and love, however, she is determined to outlast Herman, since she suspects with reasonable cause that no successor would find him tolerable, or have sufficient patience with his history-shaping endeavours and remodelling of man. Luke cannot provide luck; he can supply love, and never sees need to be sparing.

Spanish Creek's condition has begun to seem stable again, within limits. Those limits do not include most of the hills. The high country has largely been left to erosion, rabbits, and aspirant scrub. Dwindled flocks graze the low country in comfort. Truce has been struck. James, in his sixties, is grateful at least that boundary riding is a less bruising affair. Nor is lambing, with once extensive hunts through the hills, anywhere near such a seasonal depletion of strength. David too has more freedom, which he uses to pursue his bookish interests, travelling thorny paths James for the most part cannot follow. It has begun to appear that hermithood is an inherited vocation, along with the land. David indicates no large desire for feminine company, unless by convenient chance, with summer and shearers, or very rare sorties with Luke's sons downriver; he apparently has no temptation to marry. James thus at times wonders if he has really done his best by his son. He tries to suppress such doubts when encountered, particularly on the keyboard of the grand piano, lately rediscovered. Many notes, naturally, have aged impurely. On the other hand a sonata or sonatina can now seem less in conflict with his hills, and certainly his life. Savage breasts are long soothed; music, at last, need be no more than itself. For James, unlike his niece Felicity, it is not a vehicle to be driven. Reports suggest that she remains in fine voice, and moreover in passionate heart; ambition's grip on the wheel hasn't slackened. But where is she hurtling? What of the future?

If James has one furtive ambition left, it is that of seeing the future – or some modest part of it – come to pass. Its present wearisome unravelling, all fits and starts, plays havoc with his patience; he begins to believe it may never happen at all. To hasten its passage and reassure himself of sanity he imports a species of internal combustion engine to Spanish Creek, of the kind commonly used by horseless carriages elsewhere. Also he buys in light wood, wire, canvas, wheels, and material more esoteric and perhaps desirable for the construction of a heavier-than-air craft.

More than most men of his time, James knows what is possible; until now he has never felt need to take advantage of the fact. The problem, then, is not one of precognitive capacity; it is one of coming up with an adequate design, of feeling his way round the stresses and strains likely to be encountered in conquest of air currents. David is astonished by his father's belated interest in the dubious possibilities of aerial engineering; he suspects senility. To confound him, a cumbersome craft rises in a large shed which James has lately shaped as a workshop; there is a thunderous engine, two sputtering propellers, and four long wings which flap in the commotion. James beadily gives himself to study of birds as they swoop, glide and soar; creation's designs are never less than enlightening, and often lead to approximate imitations as his aircraft erratically finds form. It fattens, then thins; lengthens, then shortens. It depends, that is, on the bird currently under consideration. Avian forms are notoriously diverse. Canvas can never do the work of feathers, God knows, but James explores the potential of synthetic material. And one day, to David's horror, two horses are dragging his father's manic creation downhill; he comprehends that the situation may be mortally serious. It is.

James has mown a path through a steep-sloping field with a modest cliff at its edge. He shrewdly proposes to use gravity in order to defy it: the impetus of the slope will toss the craft over the cliff, from which point westerly wind will pluck it up and bear it away as it becomes buoyant with its own combustive energy. Indifferent to David's pleadings, James fastens on goggles, takes a shaky seat, and gives himself to manipulation of levers which provide for wings rising and falling in a manner pronounced satisfactory; he instructs David to shove heartily upon a word of command. It is also indicated that a son should have more faith in his father; the likes of David would have man earthbound forever. Increasingly distraught, David does as told; he becomes mute witness to the unfolding horror. First with the engine, smoky, and briefly flaming: sheep in panic flow away fast. As the craft creeps forward, all impediment removed, David is tempted to pull rather than push; but moments later the matter is quite out of his hands; he trips, tumbles, and feels hot exhaust in his face. His suicidal father speeds down the slope.

James feels earth bump away beneath him, tilting faster and faster; the hills see-saw ahead. There is a last terrestrial lurch, an exhilarating quiver of canvas, and then the world is all air. The cliff gone, he climbs. He cannot doubt that every horizon is now his. The foliage of the forest streams luminously below; the sunlit river unwinds under his wings. And still he climbs. The largest trees begin to look more like lichen; the silver river shrinks to a thread. It is beyond all expectations; he becomes a joyous beachcomber plucking gems from the wilder shores of awe. One problem stubbornly persists. The machine has no wish to respond to the controls he has contrived for its guidance; it proposes a route straight into the sun. James fights for breath, also for vision. Hot and huge, the sun sucks him in; he is dazzled, then deafened, by sight and sound of that vast furnace. Finally, and rather perplexingly, he appears to be no more; he is at one, and floating in peace, with the primary light of the world.

Near asphyxiated David, earthbound and bruised, has a less elevated view of the event; he sees a shorter-lived Icarus. He rises just in time to see the improbable machine take the cliff in its stride. For one moment it is undeniably, and majestically, airborne. Then it stutters, spits, farts and falls. He is denied sight of the crash then ensuing, though the impact is quite audible, followed by a small tower of dust mixed with smoke. All within David's expectations, but for one detail. When he scrambles down the cliff he doesn't, after all, find his father dead in the aeronautical ruin; he is for the most part intact, if difficult of access, in the branches of a tree, and at some risk of being barbecued by diverse fires burning below. Understandably, there will be discrepancies in tales told thereafter; only God is really fitted to judge their respective authenticity. For James, though, one thing is plain. Man has no need to fear death. Give or take a formal funeral, he has been there and back. Mortality is but a skin to be shed. He is not tempted to make himself experimentally hostage again, or to put further pressure on the future. When news of the Wright brothers reaches the Porangi, two years or more after their Kittyhawk triumph, James feels entirely justified and relieved; the future can now be left to look after itself. In 1909, the year Bleriot outwits the breezes of the English Channel, James happens upon rusted and rotting remnants of his own enterprise at the foot of the cliff; he surveys them with nostalgia, which is the most painless way of paying history its due, and moves on to rescue a cast sheep.

(With its usual lax reliance on second-hand sources, *The Lives of Lovelock Junction* gives up the sad ghost at this point: 'Another odd tradition persists that the Porangi was venue for one of the world's first heavier-than-air flights – perhaps even the first. The early atmospheric voyager was supposedly James Lovelock at Spanish Creek. The author Gordon Ogilvie, in his *Early Antipodean Aviators*, finds the tradition too thin to take seriously. Ogilvie examines the proposition that not one, but two New Zealand back-country farmers – Richard Pearse in the south, James Lovelock in the north – in fact flew before the Wright brothers. In support, he has excavated material remains at the Pearse farm, near Temuka in the South Island, and at Spanish Creek on the Porangi. He is firmly of the view that the eccentric and inventive Pearse, later to die frustrated and forgotten in a lunatic asylum, possibly did precede the Wright brothers in powered flight, albeit by a month or two. But the wreckage of the Lovelock plane, Ogilvie considers, offers nothing significant to the history of aviation. Nor need we linger on so quaint a claim here.'

Again the point is quaintly missed. James Lovelock, God rest his perplexed soul, had no designs on the history of aviation; his concerns were elsewhere, and he didn't die mad. But who needs to hear?)

Followers of Felicity Lovelock's vivid career suffer some frustration in the year 1911. The prima donna's disappearance makes for mystery, and many headlines. Last seen in New York and Chicago, and in both cities feted, she cancels engagements at Covent Garden and La Scala by unusually cryptic letter. Rumour places her once in San Francisco. There is talk of breakdown, vocal loss, alcohol, drugs, nymphomania, a Rockefeller and a Bulgarian prince. Sufficient to say that in the same event-filled year Luke Lovelock, while digging up potatoes, sees an unscheduled steamer arriving upriver. He takes his wonder down to the jetty. From the steamer a fine lady, resonant with jewels, and in wrap of white fur, is alighting. She is accompanied by a man, cloaked and top-hatted, plainly of substance. A confused retinue follows them both ashore. Luke, though working from photographs rather than first-hand experience, quickly assesses the significance of the scene. His half-forgotten brother Ernest and never-seen sister Felicity have come home. His delight isn't reciprocated as much as it might be, presumably because travel has left the pair lacklustre; Luke's grey and grimy presence is rather taken for granted. Indeed they all but brush him aside in their haste to get uphill to Marie Louise. In the instance of Ernest, this may have something to do with the proximity of his Uncle Richard's dwelling, and old scores unsettled; he isn't to know that Richard is wholly occupied in morning prayer with the Reverend Crabb, being not led into temptation and delivered from evil, though Ernest if seen could conceivably leave prospects of the divine kingdom crashing.

'Not a word,' Felicity warns Luke. 'All are sworn to secrecy, everyone with us. This isn't happening.' Breathless Luke, struggling to keep pace, inclines to wish it were not. It is too much for the senses. Not only for sight and hearing. Felicity leaves a dense French-scented atmosphere in her wake; Ernest, for his part, appears to need large quantities of eau de cologne to make ship travel tolerable. He takes a lordly view of Lovelock Junction when obliged to pause for breath. 'I'm surprised, damn it, to find anyone still here,' he declares, and shivers. 'This place is pure death to the finer feelings. Thank God I got out. How could anyone of sensibility survive?' True that Luke, who once slew and beached whales, and is now content to harvest potatoes, doesn't make a point of parading sensibility. Finer feelings can be a luxury when life has to be lived, children prepared for the world, and parents protected from time and each other. Nevertheless he sees no reason not to ask his brother, 'So why have you come? What is it?' Ernest grunts unintelligibly; Felicity has a frosty stare. 'Come on,' Luke persists, with continuing lack of sensibility, 'tell me why you're here.' He receives unexpected answer. He hears, behind him, a faint cry. More than baggage is being manoeuvred uphill by the grand couple's attendants. They are also burdened by twin babies. A girl in silky pink; a boy baby in blue.

It takes time to put explanation entirely together, at least for Luke, who might seem slow-witted. Those offered by Ernest and Felicity, to Marie Louise among others, are to be taken at considerably more than face value. Earthy Luke, who likes adding up, knows that one and one are necessary to make two. Felicity remains conspicuously unmarried, thirty-seven years old, with her aspirations at peak. To be cruelly cut down by pregnancy has not been on her schedule. Not just one bastard but two might mean death to her career; she would be unfit, at a gala, to stand in a royal receiving line. So far, so sad. Felicity puts her own case with poignancy. All the same, these children, these innocents, have a right to a reasonable life, at a discreet remove from their mother. And where more discreet than on the Porangi, with Marie Louise? Later, in retirement, Felicity will return to collect them, of course. Meantime the children will be well financially endowed, thanks in the main to the generosity of Ernest. Aside from the fact that Marie Louise is shaky and past eighty, it is an altogether plausible plan. Luke, however, still finds the arithmetic awry. Much as she might like to have it so, Felicity is no solitary procreator. Moreover, Luke suspects that a modicum of money might purchase discretion with convenience elsewhere in the world. Why home so far to the Porangi, and anyway who is the father? Luke doesn't smell a rat precisely. He smells Ernest's eau de cologne. Luke then sees that Felicity has considerably understated the potential for scandal. He keeps the knowledge to himself; no one need know. He has lived long enough to be aware that human passion doesn't confine itself to conventional channels; sometimes flood breaks the banks, though it is difficult to imagine Ernest's passion as more than a sly trickle. But who is Luke to judge his brother and sister? Incest, he concludes, isn't the end of the world. More to the point, what of their children?

'I'll take them as mine,' Luke proposes. 'Ours have all grown.'

'I shouldn't like to put you to trouble,' Felicity answers, with no great warmth.

'There would be less to me,' Luke observes, 'than to our mutual mother. She is far from immortal, besides.'

Marie Louise, in her deafness, has missed most of this. Indeed thus far she hasn't quite comprehended that Felicity has returned bearing gifts. 'Their names?' she is asking. 'What are their names?'

'We haven't quite decided,' Felicity sighs. 'I find choices so difficult. They are still not baptized.'

Having received this message at least, Marie Louise apparently prefers the condition of deafness. Herman is likewise bemused, having been torn from his thirteenth volume, still painfully far from his goal. Worse, he has been contemplating revision, beginning all over again. He cannot deny that he is glad to see his children. But they still, as when young, tend to carry on so.

Ernest slaps Luke on the shoulder and pours his brother a large cognac. 'Let me be first to say,' he announces, 'that you're really quite a fine fellow. One right out of the box.'

Luke wishes to return this compliment. Finally, however, he finds it impossible to oblige. He simply sips cognac, but even that kindles no warmth.

'I think Sybil,' Marie Louise says at length. 'Sybil and Sylvester. There are two honest names for your children. Your tutors, besides. Let those names be their memorial.'

Felicity shows some discomfort, but makes no explicit objection. 'Splendid,' Ernest intervenes, brotherly on her behalf. 'They sound just the job.'

'They shall be baptized,' Luke promises. 'Also well fed and clothed. As for their education, I can at least ensure that they will not be lacking in knowledge of this world. When you return, as you say, I trust you shall not find Sybil and Sylvester a disappointment, or unworthy of you.'

Felicity begins delicately to weep. 'I don't know that I can do it,' she grieves. 'I don't know that I can leave them.'

Ernest appears to know, if anyone does, that this protestation is perfunctory; more in the nature of a brief recitative before the aria of renunciation. 'We all understand,' he tells her. 'Motherhood, as we well know, is a highly emotional affair. But you must think of the future happiness of your children. Also, of course, of your career.'

Felicity, nevertheless, is not to be denied. She falls upon startled Marie Louise, then in turn upon helpless Sybil and Sylvester, hugging them all with phosphorescent high notes heard among moans. This performance past, tears dried, everything is settled; Sybil and Sylvester shall be Luke's at least in spirit, and still Lovelocks by name, as is doubly their due.

'You'll be here for a few weeks?' Marie Louise asks Felicity and Ernest, with visible hope.

'For just one or two days,' Felicity explains. 'More's the pity. I have a season to confirm in Vienna. And Ernest has large contracts hanging fire in France.'

'Arms,' Ernest amiably informs Luke. 'These days there's no swifter return on one's capital. A honest penny can become two in the space of a German politician's pronouncement. Not to speak of that of some bellicose Briton. One doesn't really need war to turn a tidy profit. A warmongering mood is lucrative enough. Of course, if one comes, I shall have even less cause for complaint. Naturally, like any man of liberal instinct, I believe basically in peace, within reason. Arms dealers aren't really the frothing monsters we're pictured to be. So long as men find slaughter a social necessity, we do our best to provide goods and services, as someone must, as efficiently and humanely as possible. It is not a profession for amateurs.'

Luke finds himself unable to deliver any comment of a constructive nature; he tries to keep his mind on Sybil and Sylvester. Tui, no amateur in the profession of parenthood, has already efficiently fed them; and is humanely preparing them for sleep. Luke helps her carry them upstairs.

'Life must go on,' Felicity discloses. 'Though at times it seems too great a cross to bear.'

She and Ernest, perceptibly unburdened, depart the Porangi within their allotted two days. So it happens that the population of Lovelock Junction fails to suffer the anticipated decrease. Death ignores its prime competitor, shows no haste at all. By 1914 anyway, when Sybil and Sylvester are at large in Lovelock House, lustily toddling the corridors and plunging downstairs, there is a harvest of more substance ripe for reaping elsewhere. Herman, in his eighty-sixth year, has his seventeenth volume well in hand, with twelve now wholly revised. The twins often have to be persuaded that their grandfather needs no assistance in this task; they are not easily convinced. Marie Louise has at last succumbed to a wheelchair for motion around the ground floor; and has to be helped upstairs. Luke and Tui, tossed back and forward between senior and junior generations, suffer some strain; but they never have cause to doubt that there is point in their existence. An assassination of an archduke in Sarajevo makes no large impression on this household; nor the consequent upsurge in diplomacy by other means. Speaking yet again of death, which never brooks indefinite postponement, it falls unfairly on Daniel and David to become intimate with it before time.

Seventeen

Daniel, in a noisy public house far from the Porangi, and at a late hour, hears the call first; he doesn't allow it to interfere with his beer, nor with the bedding of a lively barmaid, not after a day sorting dirty sheep through a race. But at nine next morning he is in an office enlisting, and swearing an oath of allegiance, since this appears a necessary preliminary. He finds more satisfaction, soon after, in a lemon-squeezer hat on his head, and khaki puttees bound tight to his knees; on the whole his private's uniform fits well, and might even have been tailored. Delays in the procedure grow irritating. No one really needs to tell him what to do with a rifle. Nor can he see point in forming fours, still less in learning to salute officers. That demonstrably isn't getting the war won. But boredom has further refinements. Aboard ship he has to make the best of battling with seasickness, and in Egypt with heat, flies, and hangovers after wog beer. For a time it seems his lot is to be sand and pyramids. Any fool knows the fighting is in France. What in hell is he doing here? Then some fancy pain in the arse of a pouf English officer mounts a platform to inform Daniel, and thirty thousand companions in arms, that in all confidence battle is about to begin. They are off to fight Turks, and not Huns. Turks, of whom Daniel knows nothing, appear a poor substitute. As for Turkey, whose existence he ascertains, it is a long way from France and the Hun. It seems politicians and generals exist to muddy a clear stream; in this instance because some blowhard by name of Churchill thinks the Dardanelles should be taken. For Daniel, again in difficulties with geography, the Dardanelles sound more like a disease, or maybe some medicine, much like the clap acquired from a Cairo brothel or the consequent mercury cure. He learns, not too late, that the Dardanelles amount to no more than a thin strip of sea, with land leaning close on each side. On the one side is some tumbledown town called Troy. On the other, hills and coves hide their prickly bushel under the name of Gallipoli. It has all been used as battlefield before, God knows for what reason, again something doubtless arranged by idiot generals; and with bloody miserable consequences for a couple of customers named Achilles and Hector, not to mention a great many others. Daniel gleans at least this much, really more than he needs, from a fellow private as the invasion fleet moves across the moonlit Aegean; two hundred other craft drum shadowy on each side of their ship. This fellow private is a scholarly character named Peach, who wears spectacles when reading, which he does too much for his health. Some sort of student before he enlisted, he quivers with the romance of the coming encounter; and even confides that he has written a poem.

'It's too much to believe,' he tells Daniel. 'More like a dream. Sailing like this, I mean, over Homer's wine-dark sea.'

'It doesn't even have the colour of bad beer,' Daniel objects.

Peach doesn't allow leavening. 'I could never have imagined fate so miraculously kind. We shall actually do battle where Hero awaited her beloved Leander. And then march on to claim Constantinople again for all Christendom.'

'I thought we were here to kill these mug Turks,' Daniel answers. 'Tell me if I got it all wrong.'

'That too,' Peach agrees. 'But where better to win glory as a warrior?'

'Anywhere for a fight,' Daniel insists, 'is all right by me. Glory sounds like too much farting about.'

This, more or less, especially after meat and beans, continues to be their misfortune. As the hour of dawn nears, and dark heights bulk ahead, they are not sent ashore in pinnaces with the first of the invasion force; they are held in reserve, cramped and sticky, on a ship static at anchor. Ashore, searchlights flash; and sometimes a flare. The Turks appear to be wilier buggers than first thought; they are entrenched on the peninsula, and waiting. A rocket rises. Then another. The first shot sounds thin, like a pebble dislodged; then there is the rumble of cordite avalanche. The first pinnaces have beached. Those still at sea observe only vivid flashes, and hear the vague thump of artillery. Sunrise, which comes slowly, reveals terrain twitching with injurious human activity: distant men rising and falling over ridges and gullies, trying to battle up into a stark maze of which no one has warned them; smoke spurts, and drifts, from shells thickly falling. The day is already awry. The troops were promised level landing on a long beach. Instead, they have often sheer cliffs to climb.

Worse still, at least for those condemned to watch the disaster across the water, there is another British officer piped aboard. Their dainty commanding general, no less, with words of good cheer; he hopes every man will do his duty and die well today. 'Let me tell you,' he goes on, from his beribboned eminence on the bridge of the ship, his back to the battle, 'that it is my belief that every so often a mysterious wish for war must pass through people. It must be taken as instinct natural to man. It is time to be quite frank with you. I have given this subject much study. I now know that only by intense suffering can humanity grow. There is no other way. God has begun his celestial spring cleaning, and our star is to be scrubbed bright with the blood of our bravest and our best. He will be a keen witness to your behaviour today. It is for you not to fail Him. I am sure you will not. I see men before me who have been worth His making. Men who fight for love – all the way from the lands of the Southern Cross to put the unspeakable Turk in his place. Not only that. To make Constantinople congenial for Christians again.'

After placing the day in historical and metaphysical perspective, General Sir Ian Hamilton, Commander-in-Chief, scholar and poet, intimate of Churchill and beloved colleague of Lord Kitchener, elegantly returns to his flagship to confide the same sentiments to his diary, lest they be lost to posterity, which otherwise might take a cooler view of proceedings ashore.

Daniel and Peach shuffle together along the ship's gangway, queuing for the rope ladders down which they can scramble to pinnaces; the gunfire has become densely staccato ashore. Peach has no observation to offer. He has grown quite pale; his military webbing has tangled, and his fingers are refusing their function. Daniel does his best to make his mate suitable for the occasion. Glory is no longer quite as Peach has seen it. Not under Turk shot and shell.

'Don't worry,' Daniel assures him. 'Just stay by me. I'll see you through.'

Their boats clumsily beach on a stony bay already spring-cleaned with gore. Valour doesn't stand on ceremony here; it is often horizontal. Some corpses turn slowly in the Aegean current. Others are stacked untidily on the stained shore; there are ranks of stretchers with wounded and dying, more by the minute. Shrapnel sings overhead. Bullets ricochet off rocks, pluck at sand and soil, and sometimes strike down stretcher bearers. There is nowhere to hide, nor to pause. On the other hand there is nowhere particular to go. Nevertheless officers, as muddled as men, order advance. They shout, sometimes curse, and have persuasive revolvers on show. Some men oblige for a few paces before falling, often remaining quite still. The rest, among them Daniel and Peach, are impeded by a near perpendicular slope of land, all thorn bush and scrub; they clutch at roots, kick footholes, and climb. Peach, heavily breathing, is far from having firm grip on his Homeric hillside, which is crumbled in places and innocent of relics other than military effects that morning discarded. Daniel often has to haul Peach higher, if not to safety, at least nearer to God bearing keen witness above. Their fellow warriors thin out on each side. Some tumble away into gullies. Others, without even a cry, roll back toward the shore. A few, cast like sheep, simply cling to the cliff and wait for the worst as a Turk machine-gunner searches out fresh targets. Daniel preserves Peach from such fatal paralysis.

As the climb continues, with one cliff giving way to another, and the beds of dried-up creeks never making for more than scant shelter, Daniel discovers that he and Peach have the war mostly to themselves, but for one irritant Turk sniper, more and more precise; he has certainly taken uncomfortable fancy to Daniel and Peach. Daniel eventually determines that the bugger is dug in among scrub and rock to their right. A bullet chips into the earth beside them. Yet another punctures and drains Daniel's water canister. This loss, of filched naval rum, is really too much. Daniel pushes Peach behind a boulder of modest proportion. 'Lie flat,' he advises, 'and just fire off the odd shot. Don't show your head. The sod needs something to think about while I work my way around that ridge.' 'What for?' Peach asks in panic. He clearly dislikes Daniel leaving. 'At this rate my bayonet's getting rusty,' Daniel says. 'You just stay here.' Soon after, though not without effort, the sniper is induced to fall silent. The Turk makes a wild boar seem tame, but when perforated enough is really most harmless. Daniel hears for the first time the sucking sound produced by a bayonet departing a body; he has never contemplated a human being holding so much blood. He skids back to Peach and advises that they are enabled to proceed. 'Where did you say we were headed?' he asks.

'Constantinople,' Peach replies weakly. 'I mean, in due course.'

'So get your arse into gear,' Daniel suggests.

'We should wait,' Peach protests. 'We need further orders. There must be a plan.'

'I've just made it,' Daniel insists.

Terra firma populated with Turks, as if the thorns weren't enough, soon slows them to a crawl on their bellies; their mouths foul with dust in the din of a mortar barrage, plainly intended to deter any stray crusaders still with designs on Constantinople. Easing their way up to a summit, some sort of plateau, they find an oasis of Christendom surviving among the hellfire of Allah's cruel hills. There is a ragged officer and the few men left of his platoon; the remainder have been shaped into a protective parapet of bodies, in death still doing their duty. 'We were going quite well,' the officer grieves, though glad of fresh faces. 'Then the Turk chose to mount a counter-attack.' Still indignant, he makes the counter-attack seem incontestable proof of Turk treachery; the enemy cannot be trusted to fall back with grace.

'We can't just stay here,' Daniel argues with authority rather in excess of his rank. 'They'll pick us off like rabbits.' He unpins a grenade and lofts it downhill, agitating the huntsmen gathering on one flank.

'What,' the weary officer asks, 'would you do now?'

'Anything,' Daniel urges. 'Except staying here. Back there it's bloody murder. We have to go forward. We might meet up with more of our men.'

'Admirable spirit,' the officer says. 'I take it, then, that you're volunteering for a solo patrol?'

'I'll take my mate along too; he needs looking after. Just tell us where we are, which way to go. I didn't notice any bloody signposts the way we just come.'

The officer unfolds a map. He turns it this way and that with puzzled expression; it is suddenly flawed by a bullet-hole just short of his thumb. 'All quite simple,' he proposes at length. 'The secret, if any, is in taking possession of those heights ahead. The Sari Bair range. Unless I'm mistaken that's the principal height directly before us. Chunuk Bair.'

'Height?' Daniel says. 'That's just a miserable tit of a hill.'

'Nevertheless,' the officer maintains, considering Chunuk Bair with binoculars, 'could we but get our guns into place up there, we could command the entire Dardanelles. And have the Turk on the run. If this map is to be believed, the summit must offer an excellent view. Virtually all the way to the Sea of Marmara.'

They are shaken from the prospect of sightseeing by mortar shells falling a fraction off target. 'Meanwhile,' the officer continues, 'we must hold this hill. To the last man, if necessary.'

'I wouldn't be surprised,' Daniel observes, 'if men have won the Victoria Cross for much less. And had their hands shaken by the King. Or anyway their widows'.'

'You might say that,' the officer concedes, as two more men die.

'Right,' Daniel says. 'I think it's time Peachy and me took a quick stroll. If we get to Chunuk Bair before dark, we'll give you a shout.'

With a machine-gunner providing some scrappy cover, Daniel and Peach roll swiftly off the plateau and into a ravine. For a time they remain there, indistinguishable from a great many fresh corpses. 'It's like this,' Daniel explains. 'I didn't see no future back there. One thing you want to get clear in your mind, Peachy old son. War's about not losing your balls, and keeping out of the way of mad sods who fall in love with getting themselves killed.' This is confirmed by explosions and shouting, also some whimpering, on the plateau they have just vacated. Before long, after a Turk bayonet charge, there is an emphatic silence. 'If we're not going to make it to Constantinople today,' Daniel adds, 'we could always go have a gander at Chunuk Bair, while we're here. We can always tell our grandkids we seen it.'

Peach still imitates a corpse with determination. On the other hand, when Daniel begins scrambling away, he finds resurrection expedient. 'Wait,' he whispers, with sweat. Every crevice and corrugation in this coarse countryside, where even insects are denied more than lean living, can conceal friend or foe seeking someone to kill; there is no front line, and no rear, which makes all bullets intrinsically unfriendly. Travel is mostly a matter of keeping your arse down, not to speak of your head. An hour or two later, in hot afternoon sun, they part scrub near the base of Chunuk Bair, and gaze upward; it isn't a hill to offer Daniel much more than a healthy half-hour hike. He isn't tempted to take it, not even to view the Sea of Marmara. Too many Turks. 'Time for a smoke,' he tells Peach with professional judgement. 'I could do with a beer. Soon we better get back to the beach. They'll be taking us off in barges before tomorrow, you bet. There's no war to be won here. In France they got things better organized; you know where you are. This is the world's arsehole. It's not worth a fight.'

He and Peach then meet a fate worse than a Turkish battalion. Another of their own lunatic officers, in fact; he falls panting beside them. 'I see you men have established a forward post here,' he tells them, to their own fascination. 'Fine work. I'll see you're both mentioned in dispatches. I'll take command now. I've orders straight from General Sir Ian Hamilton himself. He says no evacuation, and asks for supreme effort. He instructs you to dig, dig, dig.'

'Here?' Daniel asks. Chunuk Bair shrugs itself taller above.

'Here,' the officer orders.

'And what bloody with?'

'Unfortunately trenching tools are still out at sea. You must make do with bayonets. Dig, dig, dig.'

Howitzers become industrious high on Chunuk Bair; it is soon surprising how much Turkish earth can be shifted with bayonets. By morning, which does come, they have a quite tidy trench, with even a telegraph wire installed so that the general staff can be apprised immediately of mass Turkish advance. Their vista of Chunuk Bair is widely held to be unsurpassed, though officers begin to find a periscope preferable to showing their heads. The dead are best built into the proliferating earthworks; it is easier than carrying sandbags up from the shore, and soldiers of Allah or Christ are equally insulating. Peach's Post, as it is commonly called, Daniel Lovelock having intemperately declined the honour for the sake of his loyal old comrade, is not a tour of duty keenly sought; it becomes even less popular when Turkish trenches unwind magically down Chunuk Bair to within ten yards of their own. On the other hand, grenades grow increasingly pointless as missiles; they are too soon returned. Cans of bully beef flung with precision can win a volley of grapes, sweetmeats, or even Turkish Delight. Pork proves a riskier gift; the men of Mohammed, made unclean, surge from their subterranean world with fixed bayonets. On bad days, when boredom gets the better of a man, the war can be enlivened by reducing it to a duel between two, though this is best done by prior arrangement insofar as linguistics allow; one man on each side shows his head and each then seeks to demonstrate his great efficiency as marksman, with intervention by any third party understood to be unsporting. Similar camaraderie prevails when an armistice is called for the burial of corpses which have begun to make no-man's-land not only unpalatable but impassable even by the least squeamish of scouts. Turkish cigarettes, stronger and coarser, are demonstrably better than British in anaesthetizing the nostrils. For the rest, on the floor of a trench, or deep in a dug-out, scorpions and centipedes can be trained to battle each other; bets can be laid, also, on the capacity of any given ant-lion to suck the life from humanly supplied beetles. Daniel manages this enterprise, with Peach as accountant; Turkish mortars can be intolerable diversion.

Daniel, for three months and then more, particularly on moonlight patrols, has abundant views of Chunuk Bair from everywhere but the summit. He doesn't feel deprived; it is now known that the ruthless Mustafa Kemal dwells up there, directing the Turks from underground headquarters, saving his country for a better tomorrow, and inconsiderate with prisoners when he needs questions answered. Daniel would like to ask a few himself, and especially of General Sir Ian Hamilton, but that gentleman remains mostly elusive, preferring to praise his front-line troops lyrically from afar; he notes thrilling vigour, tallness and majestic simplicity of line, rose-brown flesh burnt by the sun and purged of all grossness, Ajax or Diomed in antipodean reincarnation. Daniel would like to express himself on the subject, largely by telling the old bugger to go bite his bum. In this connection Peach is more fortunate; he at least survives a personal encounter virgo intacta. Returned from a beach hospital, with a shrapnel-graze treated, he reports sympathy and congratulations from the commander-in-chief himself, genteelly browsing by bedsides. 'I mean he was quite interesting,' Peach insists, 'from his point of view. He explained to me that there are poets and writers who short-sightedly see nothing in war but carrion, filth, savagery and horror. Not heroism, radiant devotion to duty, moral triumph over death, and above all five minutes filled with more life than five years elsewhere.' Peach pauses. 'You know, for five minutes there I almost bloody believed him.'

Daniel is pleased with Peach and his progress; he should make a soldier any day now. Together they have outlived most of ten platoons, five captains, and several lieutenants radiantly devoted to duty; not without luck, which cannot be counted to last, nor without shrewd effort. Daniel has made some progress himself. On his shirt, when he wears one, are the three stripes of a sergeant, other than when he is demoted for disciplinary reasons; the stripes are returned when he has to lead a patrol and probe Chunuk Bair. On the whole, though, he prefers peril alone, so he can contrive his own odds, rather than with men in the mass; and persuades Peach to take the same view. Since liquor is unavailable, intoxication can be sought by drinking in Turkish defences. Thyme, poppy and oleander bloom on the slopes, to be shorn by shrapnel or to wilt and die fast in the thick summer heat. Lice prosper and show tactical initiative; they madden more than bullets. Dysentery trickles through the trenches; bluebottle flies, fattened on the piquant spoils of no-man's-land, foul bully beef as soon as cans open. Daniel takes this personally; the entire bloody war now seems directed at giving him the shits. Peach suffers too. He needs more than General Sir Ian's persuasion to see his anguished bowels as merely symptomatic of moral triumph over death.

'Anything would be better than this,' Daniel argues.

Everything is what he is offered. Chunuk Bair, more or less. The whole hill, perhaps the whole war. The proposition is placed before him by a rather tense Lieutenant-Colonel, whom Daniel feels no compulsion to salute, still more so when he learns they may have the Porangi in common; the man seems to be another Malone, son of Dixtown Malones, one who took up soldiering as a trade when his parents were driven downriver at the end of the strike. He arrives at Peach's Post in tattered condition after making his way through trenches and tunnels up Shrapnel Gully; a sniper has parted his hair and singed his tunic, and one shoulder flash hangs by a thread. From Daniel he receives no condolences. From Peach he gets a mug of tepid tea.

To Daniel he says, 'I believe there's no man alive knows Chunuk Bair better.'

'All the others are dead,' Daniel agrees.

'I mean the disposition of the Turk defences. Their system of trenches. Also possible places of access, their weak points.'

'If there weren't any weak points,' Daniel observes, 'I wouldn't be here.'

'Point taken. Perhaps you can give some examples.'

'Precipices. They think precipices, up there, can be left to look after themselves.'

'And you find your way round them?'

'And up them. There's sometimes an odd sentry. I always carry a knife.'

'Good fellow. Now I think we might talk business. Perhaps I should say, first of all, that our situation is serious.'

'I wouldn't know,' Daniel replies. 'I only work here. No one tells me a thing.'

'Nearly four months now, and what have we won? A mere scrap of land. Four hundred paltry acres we've managed to make into a fortress. No more.'

'Don't blame me. I was told to dig, and I dug.'

'The Turk still confines us. We've got to break out. It may be our last chance. Every vital crest remains theirs. It's time to contest their supremacy in force, and by surprise. Much may depend on it. Perhaps the entire war. If we can make captive those summits, the Dardanelles are ours. Beyond that, Constantinople is powerless, defenceless, ripe to fall. Within weeks we could bring relief to Russia, and the Czar, turn the tide on that front. Germany would be mortally weakened. Their armies would crumble on the western front. The war could be all over before 1916. France free of the Hun, the Czar safe, and the Kaiser sent packing. And the world at peace as before. You may not realize it, Lovelock, but there's a chance for you to write history here.'

'Me?' Daniel asks, with mild environmental scepticism. There is a thud on the roof of their dug-out. They duck. Some dirt descends.

'Among others, of course.'

Daniel is relieved. 'I don't mind killing the odd Turk if I have to. Don't ask for more. Anyway soldiers don't get into the books.'

'That's as may be. But the fact is that much depends on you now. Remember the proverb. But for want of a nail, the war was lost. If Chunuk Bair can be taken, the rest must follow. There's no man more crucial to that enterprise. Not even General Sir Ian himself.'

'I get the picture. I'm just the nail in a horseshoe. He rides the fucking horse.'

'History humbles us all. Even such as Sir Ian. Destiny makes all men equal.'

'Demotion helps too,' Daniel suggests. 'For my money, it's a bloody marvel he's hung on to his job.'

'That's sedition,' Malone notes, with pain.

'Just for starters. I could go on.'

'I shall overlook it for now,' Malone answers tersely. 'Perhaps I could familiarize you, first, with the entire position. I'm commanding a night attack on Chunuk Bair. The prime aim is taking the summit. Bearding the lion in his den, so to speak. Dislodging Kemal and his men. We won't be without support. Every available naval gun will soften the hill before we begin. On our right flank, from Lone Pine, the Australians will be launching a diversionary offensive. On our left, there will be twenty-five thousand new British soldiers put ashore at Suvla Bay, working their way toward us along the Sari Bair range. By dawn, at the centre, in all the confusion, we should be taking and holding the summit. Mustafa Kemal, if lucky, might be made prisoner. All Chunuk Bair should be ours. Then the Dardanelles, Constantinople, the war.'

'Just like that.'

'Like that,' Malone agrees. 'And you lead the way.'

'I thought there was some catch in it,' Daniel reveals. 'I had a feeling, from the first, that bloody hill was going to mean trouble.'

'This is, of course, in the nature of an order.'

'Don't worry,' Daniel says. 'I wouldn't miss the view up there for the world.'

'Good man. You shall have it. All the Dardanelles at your feet. Not only that. The Turk, and then the Hun, in total flight.'

'Just one thing I wonder. Where's General Sir fucking Ian Hamilton while I'm winning the war?'

'At sea, naturally, aboard his flagship.'

'Naturally. You mean out of the way?'

'Not at all. He shall be acting in his normal supervisory capacity. Directing naval salvoes on to the Turkish heights, for example. And above all giving particular attention to the success of the Suvla Bay landing, and the relief of our left flank.'

'Shit,' Daniel says, at length.

'What's wrong?'

'Nothing. I just knew it was too good to be true.'

Asked by Peach later what he is about, in the glow of a shy candle, Daniel answers, 'Writing a letter or two home. Months since I did. You'd best do the same. And, while you're at it, pack up any special possessions.'

'What's on?'

'Just another stroll up Chunuk Bair, old son, by the light of the moon.'

'Another patrol?'

'This time we're taking a few thousand others.'

Peach also sits to compose letters.

The moon, in its last quarter, rises just before 10.30 p.m. That at least goes according to plan. The Australians are already brawling up a ridge to their right, mostly with bayonet, boot and rifle butt, since firearms as such are useless in the tight Turkish trenches. The enemy, according to a message, appears reluctant to concede more than two hundred yards. Yet it might be presumed that with this diversion Chunuk Bair's immediate defenders are thinning. Naval searchlights fasten on the summit; the slopes shake with salvo. Daniel and Peach guide Malone and his long clumsy column through familiar gullies and around goat-tracks also intimately known. Then they arrive at a precipice they particularly favour. 'Up there?' Malone asks, with dismay. 'Up there,' Daniel assures him. 'My God,' Malone says. Nor do the men banking up behind seem in the mood for mountaineering; the column halts, with mutters becoming more audible. 'There must be some easier way,' Malone proposes. 'If you don't mind Turks,' Daniel agrees, 'there are a dozen other ways to go. All fairly fatal.'

Malone, after much indecision, pronounces his men too diminished by dysentery to attempt the ascent, also too burdened. 'I shall take responsibility for the change in route,' he declares.

'I was hoping you'd say that,' Daniel answers. 'It takes a lot off my mind. I can't see Peachy and me being in shape for a court martial.' Some hours and several dead ends later, in a ravine filled with loose rock, they are reduced to painful shuffle, and worse. Men, having stumbled and fallen, remain asleep on the ground. Some are not even to be woken by the Turkish machine-gunner who begins work above; others tumble beside them in sleep even more soundless. Clear that Chunuk Bair's Turks, despite theoretical depletion, can mount a convincing night shift.

Malone spins from a shot in the shoulder. Miracle keeps him erect, and then Daniel's secular support. Too late. Some hundreds of men, and before long most of the column, deploy themselves in a downhill direction. Others, in the dark, find themselves continuing to blunder into battle, behind Malone and his guides. Dawn, which is reached with difficulties, most of them deadly, shows them to be on an easy ridge just below Chunuk Bair's confused and indented summit. They breathe with pain; they bleed. There is cool breeze off the Aegean. Flat on stony ground, they observe Turkish tunnels and trenches. Cooking fires burn.

A few Turks, visibly tired and bruised, drag themselves about their duties, or defecate into convenient craters; some are plainly sleeping off the long night's bombardment. Some distance downhill, on the right flank, the Australians can still be heard competing for Turkish attention in the vicinity of Lone Pine: all dust, smoke, blast, and carnivorous cries.

'I'll be damned,' Malone says, still viewing the summit with some disbelief. 'We've made it. I do believe we can take it. All according to plan.' With one hand,he holds his ruptured shoulder together; with the other he awkwardly unsheathes his pistol. 'Fix bayonets. Charge when I fire. Lovelock, I want you to see no Turk's left alive. We can't afford mercy. We'll have to hold the summit until we've got relief from our flanks. We need every man fit to fight.' The sound of Malone's shot is crisp across the morning; so is the work to which it is cue. This is mostly a matter of stabbing, hacking and chopping at every Turk showing his face on the summit. Then of grenading out those still underground. The few who emerge and try to take flight are efficiently shot down. No rifle plucks more from their feet than Daniel's hot Lee-Enfield; nor, for that matter, is any bayonet more often cleaned. Malone's trust isn't misplaced; no prisoners are taken, or wounded left suffering. The earth underfoot becomes slimy with the residue of slaughter; the trenches reek sourly of spilled viscera. Daniel soon feels free to take a larger view of the event. 'Sweet Jesus,' he says to Peach. 'Just take a look down there.'

For it is all before them, and abundant. The Dardanelle narrows seem, at their feet, just an incandescent river in the dawn; beyond burgeon Asian hills and blue Trojan plain. Peach contemplates their prize with wonder, and a grounding in classics, lately of little use in surviving this war. 'Down there,' he says, never in despair of enlightening Daniel, 'Xerxes built his bridge of boats to bring his army into Europe. It must still look much the same.'

'Xerxes? Who's he?'

'A Persian general.'

'Another mad bugger. Like General Sir Ian.'

'A man of humanity, some say. When Xerxes watched his troops marching over the water down there, he wept. Of this multitude, he said, how many will ever return?'

'He didn't tell them to stop and come home?'

'Not exactly. No.'

'That's what I said. Another General Sir Ian.'

Damaged Malone having tallied his own dead, rises bitterly alongside them. The war hasn't melted away and history is refusing to reconsider; the Turkish hordes are not conspicuously in flight toward Constantinople, and further; the Czar remains embattled and insecure to the north. On Chunuk Bair's summit they stand quite alone; their immediate environment is still untamed and Turkish. Mustafa Kemal, not found resident in his den, must be off countering the offensive elsewhere. More to the point, he is bound to be back; he needs Chunuk Bair as base for his brave new Turkey, and will be all tooth and claw for impertinent trespassers. Malone sees no relief arriving from left flank or right. The Dardanelles thus do not impress him as much as they might; he is more concerned with the view to their rear. Not with Imbros and Samothrace floating distantly upon the Aegean, or even the misty glimpse of Greek mainland. Rather with their own naval vessels nearer at hand; and above all with the British troops landed at Suvla Bay who by now should be trekking through the foothills of the Sari Bair range to rescue those occupying this desirable summit. They are not. As the sun rises hotter, the thousands of troops delivered to Suvla appear more entranced with the attractive shoreline, and vast sandy beach, than with battling inland. Through Malone's binoculars, some can distinctly be seen sunbathing and swimming, making the most of a superb summer day. General Sir Ian Hamilton, whatever his virtues may be, especially as martial bellettrist and philosopher of carnage, is signally not giving due attention to the success of the Suvla Bay landing, as promised; on the other hand he might still be recording, in his lengthening diary, his astonishment and pride that his fresh troops have been set ashore virtually without loss; so clean a sheet could yet impress his anxious superiors, not to say the entire British Cabinet. From the vantage point of Chunuk Bair's summit no enthusiasm for warfare at all becomes visible. And certainly no British columns bringing relief on the left flank. To the right, and still too far downhill, the Australians are contriving to fill their nation's largest war cemetery. Malone orders his survivors to clear the Turk trenches of dead, and dig in still deeper. They have a day of strategic interest ahead.

By noon Turkish gunners have found more accurate range; their shelling grows selective as afternoon moves on. Emboldened machine-gunners surround the summit, and infantry thickens behind shrubbery and rock. For every Turk to fall, there are always three more. Malone still hopes for relief, but is prepared to be patient. 'If we can hang on till tomorrow,' he insists, 'we won't be alone.' He is distracted by flashes of fire from the warships in the bay far below. The British navy is at work, even if the army is not. A moment or two later the shells fall among them. Trenches cave in, and dug-outs explode; the cries of men limbless are lost in the roar. Their own guns, with the Commander-in-Chief's usual attention to detail, are now making good the deficiencies of the Turkish artillery.

'Thank you, Sir Ian,' Daniel observes. 'Just what we needed. Bang goes the bloody war. I thought for a moment we'd won. Bugger the Dardanelles, fuck Constantinople, and shit on the Czar.'

Peach is also intact, but Malone has a fresh wound, this time to the head. Chunuk Bair's summit is largely colonized by the dead and the dying.

In the afternoon heat, it only remains for Mustafa Kemal to make star appearance. This he does not long before dusk, after urgent engagements by popular demand elsewhere in his line. As indication of contempt both for his cowardly colleagues and those still clinging to the summit, he doesn't attempt to conceal himself; he stalks uphill with raised whip, cracking it for encouragement, while his men race ahead with the bayonet, and shooting at will. Malone, with one wound too many, dies with no complaint heard. 'There's a hero,' Peach whispers, with awe.

'Dead men look all the same to me,' Daniel answers, clipping a fresh magazine to his gun. 'Very damn dead.'

He experiments with a parting shot at Mustafa Kemal, but the man seems indifferent. The watch on his whip-hand shatters and falls in fragments to the ground, and he keeps coming on, the Turkish lion reclaiming his lair. 'That's it,' Daniel suggests. 'Always leave a party when the host cuts up rough.'

He grabs Peach by the collar, then pushes him back through the trenches; a few other refugees follow. There is a fifteen feet drop down an escarpment, and rocks jagged below; necks might be broken, but losers can't be choosers, and there is always a chance of a decomposed cadaver to soften the fall. Daniel, taking leave of Chunuk Bair's summit, suffers no more than severe jolt, his arm twisting under him; Peach, though bruised, likewise survives. A handful of others drop after them; two or three are shot down as they jump. A slope of scrub has to be gained, but not before Kemal's men have manoeuvred a machine-gun into place, with a clear field of fire from the summit. Bullets catch most of those fleeing in the back. Some succumb quickly. A few, Peach among them, stagger weak into the scrub and collapse. A half-dozen. No more.

Daniel appears the only one more or less exempt from disaster, though this remains to be proved. He cannot crawl to examine Peach close. It is risk even to lift his head and cry comfort; the machine-gun still works too intensely over the scrub. Peach appears immune to inspiration, and possibly past saving; he groans. Then the machine-gun, singeing the dry scrub, also sets it alight; breeze fans the flame. They are all due to die, if not by bullet then by fire. Nightfall can no longer be counted as ally; they will never see it arrive. 'Go,' Peach calls to Daniel. 'While you've still got the chance. But for God's sake don't leave us like this.' His meaning is plain, but Daniel refuses to apprehend it, at least for a time. 'Please,' Peach says. 'I can't move. Do it. Do it now.' Flame unfurls closer; there is a cry as the first man incinerates. Daniel takes a huge breath, and presents the muzzle of his rifle toward Peach; this act requires effort, and his arms suffer cramp. The range is two yards. 'Christ forgive me,' he gets out at last, and presses the trigger. Peach's face flies apart. Beginning to crawl back and forward through the scrub, the fire now useful camouflage, Daniel performs the same function for four other companions. The machine-gun has ceased; the Turks must assume his shots to be ammunition exploding in their localized inferno. Beyond the blazing scrub, tumbling, skidding, Daniel finds darkness; and by morning, still dazed, his own trenches.

For three days he is moody and largely left alone, with sympathies expressed; he is deaf to any call of duty, certainly to orders. Finally an officer prevails upon him to report for medical parade, helped by the two largest medical corpsmen available; they deliver him down Shrapnel Gully to a tent hospital on the beach. As precautionary measure, in view of his repeated desire to have the guts and hide of General Sir Ian Hamilton, he is also disarmed; and his sergeant's stripes stripped.

'All right,' the doctor says. 'Tell me what's wrong.'

Daniel considers first causes. He finds them unutterable. But it is clear he must humour the man.

'I might still have a little problem with dysentery,' he allows.

After lengthy examination, sometimes quite painful, and excessively personal, the doctor says soothingly, 'I can set your mind at rest on one score. You're all clear of dysentery.'

So much for the miracles of medicine. Daniel concedes a sound of relief which might be mistaken as mere obscenity.

'There is, however,' the doctor continues, 'the matter of two bullets in your thigh, another which appears to have punctured both liver and diaphragm, and finally your fractured left arm. No need to panic. There's nothing we can't mend.'

'Then go up Chunuk Bair,' Daniel urges, 'and fix my mate Peach.'

For the sake of his survival, also for the security of General Sir Ian, Daniel is shipped soon to Imbros, and at length to Egypt for specialist attention. As for the rest of the battle, in which he expresses small interest, it seems there is no defeat which winter can't cure.

Hospital beds about him fill with the frostbitten; he listens unwillingly to anecdotes of death by drowning in the trenches, of sentries frozen solid, and of the final evacuation of the Gallipoli peninsula, judged a triumph for military precision by journalists on hand; others have difficulty in respecting his desire for silence.

Nor does he take kindly to questions concerning his wounds, or current condition. His most frequently expressed wish is for others to piss off, and leave him alone.

Nevertheless doctors feel it their duty to persist. In the fullness of time they pronounce him in a fine state of repair, and moreover ready to be returned to the war. This time to France, and a front called the Somme. 'The real thing,' he is reliably informed. 'So far you've seen only a sideshow.'

David's call comes later, in the form of conscription papers, which he burns. In response to a further request he announces himself unavailable for war, unwilling to kill. Then the call comes in force, with fifteen policemen fanning out beneath the homestead, and fast closing in. It all seems to have happened before. It has. Even down to the austere police inspector with martial moustache who once came to arrest Finn, and left in frustration. The prospective arrest, if sixteen years late, gives the greying inspector much satisfaction in the settling of old scores; he makes the most of memory.

'I'm not surprised to be back,' he reveals. 'I might have known a place like this would be a refuge for a coward. A man too craven to do his duty.'

'My son is no coward,' James objects. He doesn't pretend to understand David, but this much is clear.

'Shut up, you old bastard,' the inspector replies. 'Or I'll have you under arrest smartly too.'

'Why so many to arrest me?' David inquires.

'To prevent violent resistance. Why else?'

'There would be no point in my pacifism,' David proposes, 'if I resisted anyone violently.'

'That's enough from you,' the inspector insists. 'I know your kind. All talk and no guts. I'll soon give you less to smile about. A month or two of decent discipline is a quick cure for fancy talkers like you.'

James, who has been ailing, trembles for his child. 'You could still change your mind,' he suggests to David.

'I'm sorry,' David answers. 'I must go my own way.' He has already rejected his father's proposition that he take to the hills for the length of the war; he says he must face things. James thus has reason for fear.

'They could shut you away in a cell,' he argues now, 'and batter the life out of you. And no one would know.'

The inspector doesn't contradict James. He has David handcuffed. 'You'll soon see how you feel about fighting your country's enemies,' he promises.

'I have no enemies,' David says. 'There is no mortal man against whom I have grudge. I believe in loving my neighbour, as the Bible instructs, because every man is my brother. It is little enough to believe, in one way. In another, too much.'

'I am not here to listen to speeches,' the inspector announces. 'Just to get a sanitary job done. Someone has to cleanse the country of treasonous vermin.' He adds, 'Like your son.'

Hands fastened before him, David is hurried away downhill.

'Am I not allowed to say goodbye to my boy?' James asks.

The inspector seems not to hear. To a constable he says, 'Watch that old bugger. He might go for his gun.'

James, under restraint, watches David borne away. Then all the police leave; their boat too, with David densely surrounded on deck, presumably to prevent him from further subverting the interests of his country by indifference to war. Desolate James finds himself alone at Spanish Creek for the first time in near fifty years.

On the way to the city David suffers some jostling and bumping, with the police not particular about where they leave bruises. But that prelude begins to appear frivolous by contrast with that which follows. He is marched through the streets, along with others of his kind lately arrested, between troops with fixed bayonets. Elderly ladies spit, and offer white feathers.

In the guardroom of the army barracks, locked up with drunks and deserters, David becomes recipient of well-meant arithmetic from the sergeant in charge. 'I have been making calculations,' this sergeant says, 'about the risk of being killed in war. It's not nearly as high as you'd think. Maybe one in one hundred. I'd think that over, if I were you. Apart from anything else, I suspect we may have to shoot you, unless you submit.'

He then orders David to accept his military kitbag and don the uniform within. David, still apparently unconvinced by statistics, has to refuse; he is shoved into a small solitary cell. Soon after, a soldier sloshes a bucket of dirty water through the bars. His clothes drip; the floor floods. He cannot sit down. He has no bed, no stool. When tired, he must lean against the cell wall. Forty-eight hours later the sergeant again orders him to accept his military kit. This time a saturated cell is considered an insufficiently salutary warning. A colonel finds him guilty of disobeying a military order and sentences him to a month's detention on bread and water, with one blanket and no mattress. 'In France you'd be shot,' the colonel informs him. 'I'll tell you one thing. I'd volunteer for the firing squad; my finger wouldn't falter on the trigger.'

The mood does not vary significantly elsewhere. When he develops rheumatism on the moist floor of his cell, a doctor denies the condition's existence; apparently the Hippocratic oath has been suspended for the sake of winning the war against the bestial Hun, certainly for those who would give the enemy aid and comfort. 'You deserve all you get,' the doctor declares. 'Nothing would give me more pleasure than pronouncing your life extinct, at the end of a rope.'

A guard kindlier than most slips cold potatoes through the bars. 'Give up,' this man advises. 'There's no end to this, you know.' A full court martial, in the meantime, may provide final solution; evidence is offered that David Lovelock has offended consistently, and with aforethought, against the discipline of a military barracks. Three months in a civilian prison is judged adequate sentence. 'We'll see how long you last,' the colonel says, 'among common criminals. Where scum like you best belong. I promise you this. We shall have you crying mercy. I'm surprised you can still look your fellow men in the face. A socialist, aren't you? One of these confounded politicals.'

'A believer in brotherhood,' David tells him. 'Such a belief, in these times, is doubtless political. Nevertheless I am what I am. As you are what you are. Both of us kin.'

The colonel, unfulfilled by the formal nature of the court martial, strikes David down. He then instructs guards in the use of the boot. 'Don't forget the other cheek,' he orders.

Prison garments are coarse and poor fitting, marked with broad arrows. If they have any virtue, and this must be sought, it is that they are not military. No man can ask him to murder. His dark cell, where light enters weakly even at noon, has been selected to separate him from other politicals, lest ideology or obstinacy infect him. Other infection, however, is rife; his blankets are foul, filled with lice, and he soon has a fever. The prison doctor, a man of many pressing affairs, declines to attend any prisoner with supposedly and spuriously principled objection to war. After all, this man of medicine points out, he has principles too. David becomes crippled with back pains, unable to rise; his urine darkens with blood. Warders report him for refusing to work, ensuring his diet is restricted, and finally drag him from his cell to polish and re-polish, as many times as requested, the steel of a long prison stairway. His fever abates. Other things, never. The nights are thick with human sound. Men howl rage and fear in nightmare, and others just weep. No night is noisier than that of one before a hanging, until the condemned man drops, an event promoting considerable quiet. It seems understood then that men are brothers in hell; there is but one release, and not necessarily to heaven.

On a day otherwise undistinguishable from any, David on his bunk hears his cell door opening; a visitor is announced. Finn stands in the door, with Homburg hat set back jaunty on his head, stylish moustache, dotted bow tie, and a cane. Sixteen years on, Finn cuts a lively figure in Parliament, though he hasn't before made use of his political privilege to enter and leave any prison at will, as a free man.

'Don't stand up for me,' he tells David. To emphasize egalitarianism Finn seats himself on a meagre prison stool. 'Your father wrote. It seems he is concerned for your health, and denied opportunity to visit you here. He asked me to come. And I came.'

He appears to be inviting David to consider the significance of this, also the possible risk to a political career.

'So tell me,' Finn goes on. 'What's this all about?'

'I should think it is clear.'

'You tempt tragedy,' Finn suggests.

'Of a paltry personal kind. Yes, perhaps. It seems to me that tragedy has less trivial temptations elsewhere, when I consider the casualty lists. I shall never be humiliated by anyone asking what I did in the war. I shall simply say I tried to stop it.'

Finn laughs. 'By yourself?'

'Yes. By example. By calling no man my enemy.'

'The Goliath of war isn't to be felled by so feeble a slingshot. Still, your optimism begs admiration. The pity is that you perform for the deaf and the blind. I see no crowds of sympathizers awaiting your release beyond these prison walls.'

'You seem to argue for the madness.'

'For realism. Fact.'

'Or surrender to evil. It sounds far from the Tom Finn I once knew, and who gave me to think on these things.'

'You are not of the world. A politician's trade is with fact. Truth, alas, must often be left for later. It carries some risks, as you yourself must have lately observed. War is fact. Disagreeable, no doubt, but to be lived with. It is even possible, given a cool eye, to see positive advantages. War weakens capitalism. The great monoliths totter. With the system in such disarray, social change can be speeded. Something new can rise from the ruins.'

'Will these social changes also provide for millions to rise from their graves?'

'Fortunately, arrogant idealism is not unfamiliar to me. I am merely making the point that I have placed myself in a position of advantage, to seize upon opportunities to make useful reforms.'

'Abolition of war might be seen as useful legislation.'

'Your sarcasm misfires. You know well that no man spoke with more vehemence against the machinations of the international financiers who made for this war.'

'That makes your silence, now, merely more stunning.'

'On the contrary. A question of tactics in a time of hysteria.'

'Or you might otherwise be here, in this prison, with some of your stubborn colleagues. And me.'

'Socialists too can have differences of opinion. Sad the day when our movement cannot provide for purists. Practical men must get on with the job.'

'I know little of politics. And begin to care less. But I do believe in principles. And, for that matter, in a certain commandment now thought tactless in the pulpit.'

'Exactly my point, David. A time of pestilence, or plague. Believe me. We can live through it. And we shall.'

'I can see you will,' David agrees.

'You ascribe mean motives,' Finn says, with irritation. 'I am trying to tell you that capitalism can be hoist with its own petard. Hung as high as Haman, on the fifty cubit gallows he prepared for another.'

'I know only that sick earth must produce sick harvest. I cannot see that your socialism can make for much that is healthier.'

'I suspect I still hear Christ in your stance, David.'

'Perhaps. Among many others. Even if this world were all there is – even if God is a nonsense, and our prayers pass into void – the teachings of such as Christ would still give our history some meaning; man might be redeemed by the knowledge that his nature can be more than that of a beast. With love.'

'Love is difficult to define in legislation,' Finn sighs, tugging at his watch-chain, and then examining the hour. 'I must come to the point, David. Which is, of course, your well-being. I am not without influence. I have already had words, on your behalf, with certain authorities. The fact is that I am now in a position to make you a reasonable offer. No further prison, and no more court martials, if you accept non-combatant military duties of extremely modest nature. What could be fairer?'

Finn waits for reply.

'You could be out of here tomorrow,' he adds. 'Perhaps even tonight.'

David allows temptation to drain from his bowels. Spirit must speak. Never his flesh.

'No,' he says finally. 'I am sorry. I am grateful for your concern, and for your attempt to spare my father. But I will not, by accepting non-combatant duty, release another to kill. I would be denying my life. And my purpose on earth. You are still offering a deal with the devil. And asking submission.'

'Conscience is, of course, a pretty thing,' Finn observes at length, and rises. 'I have done what I can. It is all on your head.'

'Yes,' David agrees.

There is a pause. Finn holds out his hand. 'Would that I could save you,' he says, 'from that which is to come.'

David feels himself shake. 'What do you mean?'

'Take courage. You will need it all. And goodbye.'

It could be the eve of execution, and a death cell. David soon sees what Finn means. True that next morning he is not on the gallows; he stands at the prison gate, and back in his own clothes. But there are troops again, with fixed bayonets, and a half-dozen men as bleak as himself. The troops march their prisoners down to the docks, along a route designed to make the most of a spectacle so shameful; military boots bruising their heels serve as a spur. The half-dozen are herded up the gangway of a rusty vessel lately commandeered for the transport of troops, of whom there are already ample aboard. Moorings are cast off; the ship soon pitches in swell. No need to ask where they are going. They are all bound for France. The clink contains David and his equally mutinous companions. They are not men made for fame, nor likely to be much missed; that may be the point. Examples have been selected on an experimental basis, it seems. If martyrs they must be, they can perish unseen. 'You'll fight in France,' an officer promises, 'or face five loaded rifles.' And who could care if Corrigan, the intractable Irish rebel, never comes back? Cullen, the quiet Catholic pacifist? Falloon, the gentle socialist bootmaker? Lovelock, the Tolstoyan farmer, is a name no less obscure.

First, of course, they have to be encouraged to wear military uniform. Soldiers confiscate civilian clothes. Then hose them down, naked, with cold salt water, hilarity not always held in check. When the captives shiver satisfactorily, an officer tosses military kitbags one by one into the cells. One by one they are tossed out. Defeat of temporary nature is acknowledged. Strategy then dictates that the recalcitrants be paraded naked on the deck, skinny and blue, before several hundred troops. A gramophone with blunt needle renders 'Onward Christian Soldiers,

Marching as to War' to set the scene for derision. There is laughter and jeering, but soon quieter and encouraging calls. Muscular Corrigan cries in vain: 'Is there no one here man enough to shoot me?'

For uniforms again, not guns, arrive. Three men forcibly dress each of the prisoners. A fist can work wonders in establishing the right fitting; they are soon in the most serviceable khaki. They find their hair cropped short, no effort spared with the clippers, before being returned to the clink for security's sake. Sometimes fruit, chocolate and cigarettes fall down the ventilator shaft from the soldiers above.

In England, a land first sighted in grey winter drizzle, they appear unwanted. 'What are you lot doing here?' a captain complains. 'We've enough of our own.' Consigned soon to France, they are granted separate interviews with a colonel who dwells at length on the atrocities of the Hun, then on the efficacy of martial discipline. This officer makes some impression on quiet Cullen. Eyes lowered, before he passes on into the trenches, he confesses: 'No use. I know I can't hold out. Not against all they've in store for us. You'd best do the same. If you don't, God save you. God save us all anyway.'

David is next. 'I'll make myself plain,' the colonel says. 'You are now in the war. Civilian niceties are no longer observed. Should you refuse further to serve, it is our intention, in brief, to make your life hell.'

'You can make me suffer,' David concedes. 'Human flesh makes that task no great feat. But as for making my life hell, I think not. That is with me.'

'Handcuffs,' the colonel orders. 'Get this one out.'

In his cell, later, David is beaten from wall to wall, apparently from martial necessity, while he staggers in handcuffs. When he bleeds enough, he is kicked to the floor. 'Nothing personal, you understand,' explains the sergeant in charge of this assignment. 'In many ways I'm sympathetic with fellows like you. War, who wants it? I once shot sixty Hun prisoners because of an order. There they all were, dead, in their own shit and blood. I wasn't allowed to think what it was for. Orders are orders. We just do our best.'

Softer persuasion comes from a specialist padre, who suggests David see the spiritual blessings which can flow from this time of trouble and sacrifice, which he has a duty to share with his fellows. There also arrives a lieutenant, much decorated and on leave from the front, who proves of stuff less stern. After several minutes, and an attempt to make plain the meaning of valour, he begins to shiver and weep. 'You know from the start,' he whispers to David, 'what it has taken me two years to learn. For God's sake, don't give up. I need to know there's some decency left. They may shoot you, of course.'

The man seems to be proposing that David die for him, personally. 'Yes,' David allows. 'I'm aware of that chance. If it helps you at all, I intend seeing it through.'

'Even shooting can be a mercy,' the lieutenant asserts. 'I've seen what happens, up there at the front.' He drops to his knees, most embarrassingly, before David. 'Pray for me,' he pleads. 'I go from here to Ypres, to begin butchering again.'

Finally an elegant and monocled major appears to think that fondling David might help. 'Is there anything you want?' he asks. 'Just say the word. Only too glad. You could serve as my batman. I'll keep you out of harm's way.' At length David has to protest, through the bars of his cell, at the continued interference with his person, punishment not normally prescribed by courts martial. The guards, who show no haste to arrive, and perhaps have been bribed, appear to regard the major as a convivial sort of character.

David's companions at last shrink to two; the others have defected and embraced rifles. Corrigan still has contempt for the beatings; he has known worse in street brawls. And Falloon still has his faith that the workers of the world will yet find fault with their military masters, fling down guns and gas-masks, and join as friend and not foe. They have to be manacled together, the three, and railed by cattle truck to Belgium, and the front. German aircraft drift across the cool winter sky. There is the thump and puff of guns at work, and more frequent craters. And a truck, seen passing, with a cargo of corpses, all bagged and tagged, or at least the remains recognizable. A muddy column of German prisoners, freed from the front, appears remarkably cheerful; the men sing and joke, and really need no guards. Outside a farmhouse, and near a suggestive stone wall, officers again attempt to make the three a gift of rifles, which they reject. They are then invited to inspect a list of men lately sentenced to death for dereliction of duty, and asked especially to note the sentences carried out. Rifles are offered again, and refused. The firing squad, nevertheless, still fails to arrive. First, it seems, there must be the formality of yet another court martial. And another colonel presiding, one quite as concerned with the virtues of discipline, if more amicably. Before proceedings begin, he takes David aside. 'Look,' he argues, 'be a good chap. You must know by now that you're making yourself a confounded nuisance to us all. All we want to do, after all, is get on with the war. A fellow like you gets in the way. You could do something useful like grow cabbages. Or help in the cookhouse. Would that really hurt?'

'I'm sorry,' David says.

'You're going to be sorrier. The fact is, old man, we're obliged to break you. Which we will, believe me, sooner or later. So give it away now.'

'What use would I be to you, or anyone, if I'm broken?'

'That's of no great concern. It's your submission we want, Lovelock, not your services.'

'I must still say no, to any military request. As a matter of principle.'

'I'm a man of some principle myself. All the same I must put it to you, as fairly as possible, that you will never leave this front alive. Your story will never be known, and your resistance here made futile. You will be reported dead, in the usual way, as a serving soldier. Could the picture be plainer?'

The last brush-strokes are provided, economically enough, within the court martial's khaki frame. The colonel, perhaps from compassion, sentences David not to be shot, but to fourteen days' number one field punishment, this punishment to be administered as close to the front line trenches as convenient. It is time, the colonel feels, for David to be given authentic taste of the war, rather than the theory; it may make him a man. The colonel instructs a doctor to pronounce the prisoner fit. The brief consequent examination enables David to inquire into the exact nature of the field punishment styled number one. 'It was, and sometimes still is, known as the crucifixion,' the doctor explains. 'That was from earlier in the war, when I'm afraid it was a more primitive proceeding. Men were spread-eagled and lashed to gun carriages. The symbolism was, I fear, distasteful. Let me set your mind at rest. It's done with much more science and humanity now. For example, this medical examination, beforehand, was once unknown; it was often left to the last, by which time the prisoner was dead, or as good as. It makes the whole affair cleaner, wouldn't you agree?'

The colonel considers it expedient to treat with one man at a time; Corrigan and Falloon, receiving similar sentences, then have them suspended. David, it is felt, should set sufficiently encouraging example. Wastage of military manpower, in the process of punishment, is thus also avoided.

Military police march David solitary toward the front, in formation larger than a party of German prisoners would require; he can take this as tribute, or triumph. It may be his last. Artillery batteries manned by busy gunners roar all around. Here and there retaliatory shells fall and flash. Barbed wire and bogged trucks line the swampy road; there are railway lines shattered, gutted farmhouses and giant craters brimming with rain. Nearer the line, the pale faces of soldiers surface from mud like maggots from slime. All look taut, tired and wasted. He feels pity, which proves mutual. They fail to see David as danger to the prosecution of the war. In the front line, all men are prisoners, and hostage to death; they attempt to press chocolates and cigarettes upon him as he is marched past, and here even his guards often relent. The serpentine trenches unfold, filled with troops all but submerged in the marsh; slippery duckboards allow a precarious footing. The firing grows quieter. 'We're not inhumane,' the sergeant of guard says. 'We're taking you to a sector where things aren't so frantic, and German shells don't often fall. Things could be worse.'

It is difficult to see it, when the rites of punishment are at last divulged. His guards lift him from a trench to a relatively solid spit of earth, where he can look out upon the dun swampland of war, and even discern corpses, dark scarecrows hanging in wire, where some offensive has failed. A willow stump, twice his height, is dug deep into the ground. When satisfied this is rooted strongly, the sergeant, with the expertise born of a long war, begins to arrange David. He binds his prisoner to the stump first by the ankles, then by knees and wrists. The sergeant knows exactly where to pull and strain so that the ropes cut into flesh and achieve desirable effect in the stoppage of circulation. Also important, apparently, to have the toes lower than the heels so that the captive's feet get no grip on the ground, thus helping the torso sag forward, placing additional pressure on the roped wrists. The willow stump has been set at slight incline so that human muscles, cramping and straining, can find no natural position. The prisoner has to be virtually hanging, and altogether quite helpless. If an aesthetic improvement on the gun carriage method, certainly in refinement of the principles involved, it remains a tolerable replica of the crucifixion, still worth the name. David tries not to groan. The first minute is murder. He has fourteen days more. The punishment squad removes itself to the trenches, also their sergeant, when it becomes clear that David can now contemplate war to the full. He is free to groan, with no captor in hearing, no colonel to defy. It takes time to appreciate the privilege of being displayed on a quiet sector of the front. Germans, surveying him from their trenches, on the low ridge across no-man's-land, may well decide that a bullet would be waste.

Agony, after a time, seems to cancel itself out in accumulation; his mind, apparently paroled, wanders the numb terrain of his flesh. He finds himself indifferent to cold rain, and sour wind; he can fall into a dream, and a doze. The sergeant judges six hours sufficient on that first day. When untied, and allowed back to the trenches, David discovers himself unable to walk; he has to be carried to a moderately dry dug-out in the mud. This he shares with several soldiers. His captors have dwindled to two, and the sergeant. The rest, front line regulars, shamelessly reveal sympathy; they offer hot tea, and hard military biscuits. They also furtively slip portions of cheese into his mouth, since his official punishment diet precludes surplus protein. 'We're socialists ourselves,' says a soldier with Scots accent, a Clydesider named Harry. 'We know why you're doing it. Would to God we had the guts. Don't worry. We'll do our best to see you don't suffer. Some day we'll make the capitalist class answer for this.' He carries David to a rough bunk, and covers him with a blanket. The sergeant of the guard makes no protest at this subversive expression of concern; men in the front line, like the Scot, have idiosyncracies and besides seldom live long. David doesn't hear argument, anything; he soon sleeps.

On the second day his limbs have stiffened enough to need no setting on the ropes and lone willow stump; he has, it would seem, been sculpted for suffering. His hands, grown black with congealed blood, suggest some argument with the raw material. The miracle is that his mind navigates back to the riverside in childhood, to pasture and trees, homestead and hills. Some might call this delirium. David knows it is not. He has never in his life travelled landscape more real. He feels cheated when his guards take him down. For then he is pure and painful flesh again, and has nowhere to hide.

On the third day, despite promises, three or four German shells crash quite near; shrapnel whines distinctly around him. No more than a distraction, in the end. He is done no real damage.

The fourth day brings blizzard. He feels snow on his face, sees it form drifts at his feet. His vision, when focussed still further, persuades him that even the constituency of the malevolent cannot quite disenfranchise beauty; the hoarsest of man's sounds are quite muted; no-man's-land is lost, the mud too, and the dead. The smoke of far shellfire is but an ephemeral blemish. It has become God's world again, one and white; it argues that man's tenancy might soon be terminated.

Clydesider Harry creeps out from the trenches, ignoring the instruction never to disturb David when bound, and does his best to cover the captive with an army greatcoat, also to force warm food between chattering teeth. 'Dear God,' Harry says, and sobs. 'Even Christ himself wasn't crucified so long. Can you stay alive, boy, and beat them?'

'I can,' David says. 'I must.'

'Must?'

'Must. Otherwise, what is life worth?'

The fifth day and sixth, then the seventh and eighth, form patterns too remote to be clearly discerned. There is receding resonance of sound, and soon arabesques of dissonance. This might be explained sometimes by stray German shells detonating near. But David inclines to see the shape of some message. The white world appears destined to remain so. To avert a Clydeside mutiny in the trenches, the sergeant now permits David a greatcoat while out on punishment. This privilege leaves him, for the most part, indifferent. If anything, the coat tends to make his body hang heavier, with the ropes cutting deeper into his raw wrists, and knees.

Between the ninth day and twelfth, perhaps the eleventh, the snow melts away, with just dimming streaks of white left across mud and ruin. His body, however, refuses the thaw; it has never been more solid, or accounted for less of himself. People sometimes pass; one seems to be a captain on a tour of inspection, who finds the offensive against David Lovelock worthy of notice on this part of the front. Another officer pleads: 'Does this have to go on? The man is near dead. I'm afraid my men won't take it much more.' The captain suggests hard discipline, perhaps even shooting for front line impertinence. War cannot be prosecuted successfully without cowards on show. Hopeful of proving this point, the captain prods David with his baton, asking him to indicate whether he has suffered change of heart about serving as soldier. David, when prodded again, indicates that he hasn't. 'I am of the same mind as ever,' he utters, when he locates tongue and lips to form words.

On the thirteenth day and fourteenth he begins to take leave of his body. A radiance, pure and strange, passes over the world. No-man's-land is lit with green trees, bright birds, and soon children singing; he becomes eavesdropper on eternity. He knows death no disaster, perhaps even the blessing that corrupt padre promised, if something hard earned. For he partakes of more; he sees something of God. Not His face; it is hidden by coarse countryman's hands, corroded with infinite labour, and now most useful for concealing despair. 'Son, son,' He is grieving, 'why hast thou forsaken me?' David, who better, tries to console.

At the end of his last day soldiers unbind him limp from the willow and lift him into a stretcher. Then carry him clumsily along through the trenches. David floats above. He watches troops sob and sidle forward to touch his slack flesh as the stretcher passes their way. For rumour has spread. Not of a miracle; of a man. Too late, he sees Clydesider Harry feed his rifle's muzzle into his mouth, and then jerk back with the bullet. Most of a platoon rises in strength, defying officers, shedding guns, to go over the top, through sandbag and barbed wire, to make no-man's-land humanly habitable once more. Since the Germans mistake their intention, they die too, but not in defeat. David begins to know his own death redundant. As his body is conveyed into an ambulance, and before a last door shuts him out, he makes his return; he forces himself back into his flesh, which is unwilling. Then feels the pain.

There is a hospital, daffodils in an English garden, woods not far across a sunlit meadow. And Corrigan, dying, two beds away. After failure with David, those administering military justice felt improvization necessary. Corrigan was bound under the armpits with wire, and dragged over duckboards, through miles of trenches, until his tunic tore away, and much of his torso; he has blood poisoning, and pneumonia is taking him. Falloon's fate remains mystery. It cannot be worse. Scales say David's weight now under seven stone. Once, on horseback, it was nearer thirteen. The hospital window may offer vistas pastoral and horticultural. Within, the flower of fighting men are rancid petals. There are those who have blasted their own feet away. Or simply reaped madness from France, and now rave nightlong. Many are unsuccessfully restrained from cutting their throats; they finally win by attrition, and there is broken glass and another corpse in the bathroom. This belated pacifism proves impervious to medical science. Doctors despair, visibly affected by long hours and liquor. Corrigan dies with David holding his hand, having honourably quit his last brawl; it took an entire war to quell him. 'Take it gentle,' he tells David. 'You too,' David says.

A ship towers above, perhaps at Southampton; no one quite tells him the port. But it is, so he hears, bound for the Pacific. And filling with soldiers of no further use at the front. For one thing, many lack limbs. Others are as shrivelled as David, as prematurely aged. An officer in shiny riding boots, fresh from a desk, supervises the embarkation. 'Name, rank, and regimental number?' he asks David.

'Lovelock,' David answers. 'No more.'

'Come on, man. I'm busy.'

'I serve with mankind. Perhaps God knows my number, but not as a general. My understanding is that He has been reduced to the ranks for the duration. Doubtless with cause.'

'You bastard,' the officer says, at last comprehending. 'What is your kind doing here? Why weren't you shot?'

Not having a pistol for embarkation procedures, he flings away his pen and uses his fist, presumably to demonstrate David morally as well as physically feeble. In the second endeavour, he enjoys swift success; David falls stunned at the foot of the gangway. Retribution appears in khaki. The officer is flung aside by a maimed soldier who needs only his one arm. Where the other should be is just a limp sleeve. Weightless David finds himself helped back to his feet.

'Let no bugger touch him again,' a loud voice is saying. 'This man is my brother.'

Daniel and David embrace.

Eighteen

War needs but one postscript, so far as the Porangi is concerned. A fatality must be recorded, if far removed. This is of Ernest, about transatlantic business aboard the *Lusitania*, sunk by a moderately humane German torpedo, one derived from a design he marketed with no small success. The last report of his life has him rushing an overloaded lifeboat, thrusting women and children aside; his old suspicion of sea travel is generously vindicated. Soon after this incident, Felicity Lovelock is reported in total retreat, and one day goes missing from the Bournemouth seaside hotel where she has been sequestered. Some suggest suicide, as is natural, but it is also said that she has lost her Top C and is now singing in American musical comedy under an assumed name. Opera, newspapers say, virtually by way of obituary, cannot be the same again; she was, perhaps, a prima donna born to be legend; in these dark days of war let her light be remembered.

Armistice makes no large impression upriver. For all practical purpose, the region has always been at peace anyway. All the same, something has been lost. If not innocence, then the sense of a place set apart, and preserved. Emaciated David and mutilated Daniel, who arrive to relieve lonely James at Spanish Creek, are but symptoms. Silences flourish. There is now a flaw in the fabric, a rift through which death can force entry. No point in composing a miserable litany. In any case, the facts fail to sustain it. Take any three brothers. They all have to die. Marie Louise too is as mortal as any woman born to suffer the male sex. Perhaps her death should be treated first, since it is painless, and by far the least perplexing. When her flesh fails in her ninety-first year, and she is obliged to leave Luke to look after Herman, perhaps through to his century, she feels fewer qualms than she surmised. One day, in a wheelchair, she looks long at Luke, and then with effort gathers Sybil and Sylvester to her bosom; they become unusually subdued, perhaps with sense of occasion, and observe their grandmother's sight slowly going; she closes her eyes and surrenders all things of this world. If more needs to be known, one has only to look into God's kitchen.

Richard makes for more of a problem. His preoccupation, in his last years, is with the risk that the faithful Crabb may predecease him; he becomes haunted by the idea of travelling into the dark without clerical consolation. Fortunately, this isn't the case. Perhaps because Richard becomes even more attentive to Crabb's welfare than to his own, in matters of diet especially, the latter lives loyally on to Richard's last breath. Which is actually more in the nature of a hiccup, given Crabb's propensity, whenever Richard is fading to revive him with brandy as well as the Bible. (Crabb has his own fear: that with Richard gone, he may yet cry cockles on a gallows, as his complexion foretells.) This time, however, Richard lurches off on his own. He is faintly alarmed by mist, and grass and fern underfoot. He has to conclude with some sourness that Crabb, the sanctimonious sod, has finally deserted him. The earth beneath him becomes less uneven; the mist begins to disperse. He happens, without warning, on a remarkable scene; the colours are so fresh all could just have been painted. There is a green field before him and, in the distance, dark woods. Crabb still fails to put in an appearance. But the Jesus-child does. And in this bucolic composition just as Crabb has always portrayed him, golden locks, innocent eyes, tender face filled with virtue, and little arms lifting for Richard's embrace; a sight to take a strong man by storm, and Richard's eyes certainly rain tears as he looks upon that child, in that field. In consequence, he is slow to note the men and horses waiting off to his right. The faces are all familiar. Burgess and Kelly, the cut-throat bushrangers. Bully Hayes with piratical wink. Von Tempsky, moustached and unsmiling, as erect in the saddle as any Prussian yet seen. Cannibal chief Titokowaru still minus an eye, which suggests that some things are slow to improve. Finally, God help them, in this collection of villains, Paramena and Ira Dix, holding a horse vacant between them. This sleek nervy creature has to be, and is, Porangi Belle.

For a moment, not really much more, Richard sways back and forward. The Jesus-child mutely pleads, implicitly promising a place ready for Richard in a house of many mansions. By contrast the men on horseback shout rather coarsely. They appear in haste to head off into the dark woods in the distance; they have the hounds of God on their heels. Richard seems to have little choice left. He isn't there to be bored. Besides, as is well known, the devil finds work for idle hands; heaven could be a disaster greater than Dixtown. With never a look over his shoulder, he begins to run, lest they leave him behind. He swings his light limbs over the saddle, feels Porangi Belle powerful beneath him, and urges her into a gallop. The hoofbeats about him, as they all gather pace, are quite thunderous; the dark woods rise ahead. Before they ride into refuge, he does bring himself to look back: the field is empty, the Jesus-child gone, and Porangi Belle, as reliable as ever on the last furlong, chooses that moment to fart. She also halts and whinnies, celestially perplexed by the absence of a rectal potato. His companions pay no heed; they thud away into the trees. To his panic, he can persuade Porangi Belle into no more than a most grudging canter. Worse, when they arrive at the woods, the overhanging limb of a tree cruelly fells him; he topples from the saddle and Porangi Belle, beginning to gambol, leaves him behind. Silence heals around him. He rests exposed and alone at the edge of the woods. Night is close. It is cold. He hears the hounds of God baying.

Herman is something of a headache too. He doesn't see out his century, though he has the heart for it, and all other pre-mortem indications are equally auspicious. Circumstances, in short, dictate otherwise. Or, more to the point, Alfred Whisker's workmanship. In his ninety-sixth year Herman completes his superhuman task. Twenty-four volumes – 28,564 pages – and all extensively revised. Toward the end, in truth, his revolutionary revisions tend to follow conception and creation by an ephemeral paragraph or two; and at the end the two acts are indistinguishable, since he is of the one mind. He seals the last volume and sets it on a shelf. He has already instructed Luke, as his executor, in the matter of their eventual disposal. Seeking to celebrate, Herman decides on taking pipe and tobacco to the top of the tower, and there surveying the Porangi at sunset. The climb is no longer easy, and the climber no longer young. Fifteen minutes are needed as against five in the past. But the view from the top still steals his breath more than the ascent. The wilderness whispers; he sees a flight of birds float upon a molten horizon. As for smoking his pipe, of that he is cheated. It falls from his hand when he comprehends, at length, that he has company. His companion up there, if not unwelcome, is anyway unnerving. He looks with alarm at the angel he thought six decades gone from his life. The creature, observed close, is in even worse repair. Indeed distinctly tatty. His wings shed feathers; the halo above his head appears uncommonly counterfeit; his face is haggard, perhaps haunted.

'Thank God I've found you,' this individual says. 'I've been looking for years. And I've made it just in time, it would appear.'

'What the hell is this?' Herman asks, not unreasonably. 'What on earth do you want me for now?'

'My apology,' the angel answers. 'I hope you won't take it amiss.'

'We'll see about that when I've heard it. Meantime, say your piece. I can't stay up here all night.'

'Indeed,' the angel says. 'I'm keenly aware of that fact. Time presses. Very well. Let me say, so that there need be no misunderstanding, that the last time I spoke to you it was in the nature of a speculative venture.'

'Speculative what?'

'Venture. On my part. Alone. To put it more bluntly still, I was acting in an unofficial capacity. Free-lancing, if you like. I don't wish to tug at your heartstrings, but I should explain that I had once been on the regular staff, and in an extremely senior position too, I might add. There's more to it all than being a virtuoso harpist. I don't want to list all the difficulties entailed, nor tell you of all the parchment work involved. It was not inconsiderable. My responsibilities were infinite. In brief, I was without even prospects of a pension.'

'The point, man,' Herman suggests. 'I haven't all night.'

'Very well. The unpleasant truth is that there was a purge. Our superior, and who can quarrel with Him, argued that there had been a hardening of bureaucratic arteries in the beyond. There was a regrading of staff, and quite a few cutbacks. And, to be quite frank, the axe fell on me. I was demoted. I lost my seniority, my fringe benefits, and most of my comfort. In fact, I found myself merely third assistant gatekeeper, a most menial role, in charge of the spare set of keys.'

'I don't see what this has to do with me,' Herman notes with rising impatience.

'But it has,' the angel insists. 'I took advantage of my position, and the keys, for an unscheduled flight. I thought that perhaps if I pulled off a coup I might win back my seniority. You can hardly blame me for trying.'

'No,' Herman sighs. 'Have I heard it all now?'

'You fail to take my meaning. My coup was to be you.'

'Me?'

'You. A nudge is as good as a wink, they say. But better a divine nudge; a wink might be mistaken for a change in the weather. I hoped that, with a little encouragement, you could make more sense of things here; indeed make it a success. I can assure you that similar enterprises elsewhere have been far more rewarding. This earth is a neglected corner of the kingdom. Some even call it a slum and suggest total clearance. So much the more credit for me if I pulled the coup off.'

Herman discovers anger at last. 'Hell's teeth,' he demands, 'why pick on me?'

'You seemed as reliable an earthly prospect as any. And in an advantageous position, in a new land. I'm sorry. I went far beyond my brief. If the truth be told, and I'm afraid it must, I spoke with no authority at all. I've suffered for my unauthorized tampering, I might add, with further demotion. You may be aware of the damnable fate reserved for fallen angels. I've only just been permitted out on parole, following my plea that I be allowed to attempt making good the damage I've done.'

'You're years late,' Herman declares.

'Do you think I didn't try to tell them that? But the request had to go through proper channels, in fact right to the top, to get a decision on your rather exceptional case. Then it had to wander all the way back through the same channels again. I don't mind telling you it can take an eternity. I had to point out that you didn't have all the time in the world either. There. See what I mean?'

For the tower has begun to tumble. First in small fragments, then in larger, with loud shudders; the brickwork underfoot ceases to exist. In one sense, so does Herman. In another, he does not. For all mortal purposes he descends, with a last and vast howl, under the dust and falling bricks; and requires considerable excavation. He is also, however, aloft in the angel's arms. Wings whirr. Feathers, rather disconcertingly, are still being shed. And bad breath, given Herman's unnatural intimacy with the creature, also contributes to his discomfort. They rise higher. 'There's no point in dwelling on disaster,' the angel advises. 'Don't look down. People who get into a morbid cast of mind find it difficult to make a fresh start. Apart from anything else, I've something to show you.'

This proves to be no more than the truth. They are shortly walking an impressive avenue, passing parks and particularly pleasant squares, with buildings of modified baronial style rising everywhere around. Fountains play; trees rustle; songbirds flit overhead. And Alfred Whisker, looking not a year older, and conspicuously more sober, shamelessly waits to serve Herman as guide. Herman has no chance at all to express an opinion on the spectacular manner of his decease, all due to Whisker.

'Here I must leave you,' the angel announces. 'As you'll see, I've done all I can. I must warn you, however, that old grievances are best left behind. Before I depart I'd like to see you both shake hands.'

Herman obliges, though still with some grudge. The angel's wings shadow them briefly; their sound soon fades, and a last feather drifts down.

'I only just made it,' Whisker explains. 'In the terms of my contract, they gave me damn little time.'

Herman keeps his silence, and refuses all sympathy. Nevertheless he allows Whisker to lead him.

'You'll note,' Whisker says, 'the colleges with conservatories, workshops, swimming baths, riding schools. Also the terrestrial and celestial maps as you proposed. Over there, you might observe the groves embodying history, the muses, and mythology. I've had to function, I don't mind telling you, as nurseryman too. To our left, coming up now, are the manufactories which provide a most congenial environment for men at peaceful, productive and socially beneficial labour; you'll see that the public horticultural garden and arboretum are placed discreetly with this end in view. I don't think there's any score on which I've failed you. Right down to the public houses which preclude the prospects of inebriation; I have a former brewer and distiller working on that very problem. In view of their desirability, from the viewpoint of social intercourse, the public houses have been frequently and tactfully placed. I haven't forgotten the culinary craft either. That large building to our right is the college of cuisine. There are little cafes arranged outdoors where the work of the pupils can be perused for comparative purposes. I am hopeful that Marie Louise might be allowed to work here in at least an advisory capacity, despite the extraordinary demands on her elsewhere.'

This calls Herman's attention to a lack. 'Where are the people?' he asks.

'Populating the city,' Whisker apologizes, 'wasn't within the terms of my contract. But I gather there have been a great many applications. From my widow, Sybil, unfortunately for one. The name Malone also seems to come up again and again. Oddly enough, my foreman-in-chief, a Barney Malone, was of that family; I had to talk him out of a suburb solely constituted of colonial villas, but otherwise he brought things in on time. No; I'm sorry. I'm afraid that part of it – the people – is all over to you.'

'God damn it,' Herman says, now with more authority, sagging into a seat in Whisker's artfully landscaped Park of Sylvan Pleasures. If this one is flawed in conception, it may be because there is no view of a cemetery; and, worse, no prospect of one. 'It can't be. No. Not all over again.'

Whisker, sitting down too, provides sympathy. Also one of several bottles which, by good fortune, he has secreted under that very park bench. Even more fortunately, the contents of these bottles represent a failed experiment on the part of his still baffled brewer and distiller; inebriation is guaranteed.

After the burial, in which the Reverend Crabb has been eager to officiate – he feels all too alone in Richard's dwelling, and even more fearful of the quicklime and unhallowed earth to which a hangman might deliver him at the end of his solitary future – Luke unlocks Herman's study, sends Sybil and Sylvester downstairs, and settles to his task as executor. He feels Herman not to be far, perhaps even looking over his shoulder; he also finds much awe in that quiet room long reserved to his father. The mountains and ravines of books; the dust drifting as thickly as snow; the smell of Herman's pipe, perhaps even a lingering tendril or two of smoke toward the ceiling, as if after a volcanic eruption. The volcano is extinct. The cooled lava has been contained in twenty-four sealed volumes. Luke lifts down the first, finding it no mean burden for a man of sixty-one years, and carries it to the desk. He strikes off the seal; the pages spill apart. Luke begins to contemplate his discovery.

How to describe it? It has first to be said that Herman toward the end, conceivably in senile despair, conceivably in wisdom, began to believe book worship idolatrous, something which benumbed, bewitched and besotted the reasoning faculties; and made for no more than a Babylon of folly and confusion. He knew the true face of the enemy at last. If not Caxton and his kind, then the first man to make a mark on a clay tablet. (He was not slow to take heart from Socrates who, doubtless sensing this, shrewdly left no written word, thereby bequeathing his pupil Plato a profitable and misbegotten vocation. Told by the Delphic oracle that he was wisest in Greece, Socrates replied, it might be recalled, that this must be because he alone of all Greeks knew that he knew nothing.) Luke now incredulously considers the result, the long maturing fruit of his father's labour in the vineyard of man. Herman's twenty-four volumes do not quite constitute a Cabbala, reconciling the finite and the infinite, a revealing of God's great plan, yet can be taken as something more profound still. Each of the wholly revised volumes is unblemished by verbiage; Herman's last word to the world comes in 28,564 entirely blank pages.

Easy, of course, to dismiss this as black jest. Or as an old man's contempt. Luke sees it as neither. Intimate with his father's intention for too many years, an all-purpose confidant, Luke knows what has been there, and now what is not. Though Herman's ingenious formal solution surprises, Luke also understands that in the end life is lived between the lines, and that this is Herman's monumental way of making the point, Herman merely provides a frame within which the individual imagination can move, unfettered by history, unhindered by language: a window on the terrestrial, in which all might be seen. For Luke, then, volume after volume swarms with visions. Men grope from dark swamp, fashion weapons, fell beasts. Hunters descend from the hills to become herdsmen, and harvest corn in the valleys. Men mine and smelt the first metals. Slaves put together pyramids; the people of Pericles offer posterity the Parthenon. The Great Wall of China rises on the blood of its builders. Mayan places of worship grow tall in the jungles. The Vikings soar over the North Sea. The Polynesians voyage the Pacific. The Aztecs sacrifice men to the sun. Temples rise and totter; dynasties tremble and fall. Marco Polo arrives in Peking. Michelangelo paints the Sistine Chapel. Da Vinci tries to fly. Columbus sights the green leaves of a new world. Shakespeare composes his sonnets. Christopher Wren builds St Paul's. Heretics blaze at the stake. Kings are beheaded; republicans are crowned. Over all is the colour of miracle. No man in his right mind would believe it, but Herman makes it seem altogether possible. He rids human eyes of linguistic dust, to let everyman make his own legend.

Luke is entranced. No volume moves him more than the twenty-fourth, in which the Lovelocks at last make their appearance. All is as Luke knows it to have been. Inevitably, the saga presses on to the present: it is not to be ignored, especially not by Tui, to whom Luke has to listen. Facts are facts. Luke, in Herman's study, has been neglecting the garden. The future is nil. Lovelock House has proven collapsible; the fallen tower, so fatal to Herman, surely portends troubles to come. Then too Sybil and Sylvester have to be considered; they have a right to a reasonable education elsewhere, of more conventional kind. Since Ernest's lamented death, and Felicity's disappearance, no money comes in; not that it is particularly needed. They have endowment and affluence enough, the twins, in their two loving parents, Luke and Tui; they have never known other, nor ever will now.

'All right,' Luke agrees. 'We must go.' He sees that, in any case, he has done his job here. He need feel no guilt at the graves of his parents. He has seen them through to safety; God can take over now.

All the same their departure, their last day at Lovelock Junction, isn't without sadness. Especially in respect of the Reverend Crabb. Quite adamant, he refuses to leave Richard's dwelling; he declines to age piously in Luke and Tui's care. 'I must stay,' he argues, 'where I've been happy. Besides, I know the world out there. It's just waiting to pounce. I can't take the risk. There are times when I wake from nightmare, still seeing the noose.'

'Nonsense,' Tui says. 'Who doesn't have bad dreams?'

'Thanks for your kind offer,' Crabb says. 'But you go. I'll stay. It might be comfort for poor Richard to know I'm still here, trying to get Dixtown going again.'

Farewells must be made at Spanish Creek too. Luke embraces his

Uncle James, always much loved, but has no fear for his future; not with David and Daniel as two gentle guardians. Luke shakes hands with his cousin and nephew and wishes them well. These two scarred and weathered bachelors, with sheep seemingly all they want of the world now, are certain to be the last Lovelocks left on the Porangi, aside from the dead. Daniel can even shoot one-armed from the saddle, but only for food. Between them, in any case, are three good arms to attend to their flocks; they sometimes seem the one person, and perhaps are, in their way. Doubtless they would find women welcome, though some females might interfere.

There are tears, not least from Tui. 'I found a family,' she mourns, 'and now I've lost it again.'

'You have Sybil and Sylvester,' Luke points out. 'They're more than small mercies. We can be grateful for them. The Lovelocks go on.'

'All the same,' she says.

'I know,' Luke agrees.

Back at Lovelock Junction they walk the plateau for the last time, Rainbow Road, Circumstances Crescent, and Little Luke Lane. Foundations, ruins, are bright with fresh greenery. Sybil and Sylvester follow slowly behind. A handsome pair, which proves nothing about incest, but perhaps something of the hope inherent in the human species; they are pleased to be making a move, looking forward to a larger share in worldly affairs. At length the four stand on a rock overlooking the river.

'Who will know,' Sylvester asks, 'that we've ever been here?'

'And who will care?' Sybil inquires.

'We will,' Luke proposes. 'And God. Who can ask more?'

In testimony to this belief, in a way, Luke has a final job as his father's literary executor. Herman's written instructions are his least ambiguous legacy. A bonfire must be built of all his twenty-four volumes. Luke comprehends why this is necessary. Not to preserve Herman's life work from misunderstanding and mockery. It is more in the nature of a tribute to Luke himself. He has, in spirit, been made Herman's sole heir.

Nevertheless, he postpones the task until it can no longer be left, until they have trundled down to jetty and steamer the last of their possessions and Marie Louise's more portable bric a brac; her copper pans too will find a place in their new home. Herman's memory will be less material. Luke returns alone to the plateau, to perform his last duty, and kindles 28,564 pages to flame between the discoloured stone lions and eagles still guarding Lovelock House's front steps. Then he hurries to join wife and children and yet again shake the hand of disconsolate

Crabb, who waves alone on the jetty. As the steamer slides down the Porangi, the smoke of the pyre can be seen tinging the sky. 'Well, that's it,' Luke tells the three who mean most to him in this world. 'We're on our own now.'

James? Death finally arrives to claim its full quota. But he does see the future come almost to pass. In the year of his dying, and not too far from the hour, he observes a lost aviator circling his craft, with wings dipping low, no less than three times over Spanish Creek. Then, apparently making certain calculations on his compass, this airman flies north over the trees.

James, when he begins to shrug off his flesh, in a long coma, is even slower to get his bearings; he whispers sometimes, for David to hear, but on the whole prefers to investigate his dying in silence. Daniel keeps Spanish Creek working, in a left-handed way, while David nurses his father; James isn't alone at the end.

Nor is he post mortem. Vague shapes solidify; glimpses grow to full vision. No mistaking his situation now; he is not in the slightest off course. *Santa Ysabel* stands before him, quite virginal, at the foot of the lake. Spanish Creek, all around, is again spectacular with forest and bird. But the vessel itself astonishes more. The decks are no longer a verdant picture of neglect; they are scrubbed bright, and the cannon all polished; the timber of the seaworthy hull is unflecked with moss. Rigging has been restored, with the voluptuous feminine figurehead intact again and bright painted. Large square sails with the cross of Christ, unfurled white in the sunlight, give off a crackle as breeze begins to balloon them. Moorings have been cast off; the ship goes through the first motions of the voyage impending. Crew appear to be no more than three, and mixed in their gender. Strong and hirsute McKenzie and venerable if still wiry Upokonui busily give themselves to the duties of life under sail. At the helm Glory laughs, waves, commands James to leap aboard quickly. He rises and drifts down into her arms. With passionate reunion past, they take charge of the wheel as *Santa Ysabel* starts to soar like a dream. 'There's something I must tell you, beloved,' Glory begins.

She has no need to say more. Passengers have begun to surface slow from their cabins, and move generally in the direction of James. And not a male among them. All are there, and not to be outshone by Glory. Diana, of course, who has to be. Hilda Lavender too. California Kate and Ballarat Gert. A considerable number of Turaekuri maidens personally deflowered, not to speak of widows whose grief he once eased. Others, too many to count, whom he but faintly recalls, other than by way of brief fleshly thrill. They gather silent, with some sense of expectation.

Glory sees fit to promise, 'It's going to be a long voyage, my dearest. It's my duty to see that you shall never be bored.'

After they have delivered James to his grave – sited as specified, and as might be supposed, on the bluff beside Upokonui and McKenzie – David and Daniel share several melancholy bottles of beer and, from time to time, their less confused thoughts.

At length David, who is troubled, makes a confession. 'The old boy came out with a queer thing or two, you know, before he died.'

'Oh?'

'One thing he said I'll always remember. In fact, it must have been damn near his last.'

'What was that, then?'

David hesitates. 'He said, well, would you believe it, "I have seen glory".'

'Seen what?'

'Glory.'

'My God.'

'Yes, I know. That's the way I felt too.'

Next morning they roll a large rock upon James, and David with inspiration roughly cuts an epitaph beneath his father's name, age, and date of death. The lines are ones he remembers from *Lear*. Shakespeare might have crafted the words for his father, and for all founding Lovelocks. *Speak what we feel*, the inscription asserts, *not what we ought to say . . . We that are young shall never see so much nor live so long.*

The year after James Lovelock's death still more of the future comes to pass, though in this instance it is Upokonui's old prophecy partially proven. If not an angered and desperate *taniwha*, a dragon trapped deep in the terrain, something of substance does bestir itself inland; certainly it seems more than mere earthquake. Tall hills teeter; narrow ravines shake themselves wider; high ridges fall. Floodwater, grabbing up trees of the forest, stampedes down the Porangi with unprecedented ferocity. Hardly anyone, and here might be seen irony, since no prophet is perfect, is left to be drowned. Disaster resides in the debris strewn the length of the river. Rock, root and branch – everywhere dense – are ready to snag the misguided voyager. The Porangi, in short, is no longer navigable. In places there is just enough depth for a dinghy; barely enough breadth for a moderate punt. At Spanish Creek David and Daniel have lost their one link with the world. So, downriver, has

Crabb, who couldn't care less, and inclines to celebration; he sees no hope for the hangman now. For Spanish Creek, however, it is death sentence. David and Daniel have no way of barging wool downriver, or selling off sheep; no way, any more, of making the farm work. Miles inland there may be now roads, of course, but with trackless mountain and unbridged river between. When they tire of the taste of their own mutton, they arrive at the only reasonable conclusion, both being reasonable rather than romantic; they ride about Spanish Creek, making farewells, recalling the past, and on occasion concealing moist eyes from each other. Then they fill dinghies with all they can salvage, including themselves, and set off downriver, on their way to a city; there, perhaps, to take their appointed place among their fellow men. (Daniel weds a widow, fathers three sons, and despite his specific wish has a funeral with full military honours, even rifles fired in salute over his grave. David finds comfort in the arms of a like-minded school-mistress, whom he survives, and technically dies without issue, though among many of the secular and dissident young revered as a paternal saint.) The last Lovelocks have left.

Crabb remains alone on the Porangi. The river still needs a romantic.

Those who feel contempt for the storyteller's trivial calling need dismay themselves no further. While they amble to the liquor cabinet, turn on television, or contemplate topics more sober, the rest of us are freed to pursue the few perplexing loose ends. Certainly something can still be found in the fainter shapes of legend. Let us suppose that on a sunny summer morning in 1932 – or a warm winter afternoon in 1933 for that matter – a woman in late middle age, and plainly once a fine figure, though facially rather a ruin, arrives upriver with a hired and bored boatman as guide; her lips are painted blue-red, her hair is a yellowy blonde, an indifferent triumph for peroxide, and she is clad in now crumpled crêpe-de-chine dress under a floppy straw hat graced with flowers of an artificial kind which are proving as perishable as real. She speaks, when she brings herself to, in an imperious English voice, if sometimes flawed by American vowels. The outboard motor cuts out; the dinghy drifts against a skeletal stump of jetty, and is moored. 'Here?' she asks, with disbelief.

'Here,' he assures her. 'I can't take you no further. Not for the money agreed.'

'This is Lovelock Junction?'

'That's right. Where it was once.'

'Once?'

'A few years back. I'm new on this coast. No one really comes up here, not any more. Fishing's all to hell; lines get too tangled. There's sometimes an odd hunter. I brought one up last year. Interesting chap. Name of Herman Malone. Told me this yarn about how he was the last child born here.'

'The last?'

'I expect the first would be dead.'

'No doubt,' she agrees.

'There's still a hermit around. No one's ever seen him much. He takes to the hills when he hears a boat.'

The woman shivers. The sun is quite hot. The boatman rolls and smokes a slow cigarette.

'I must go ashore,' she tells him, or herself. 'I can't put it off.'

'All the same to me,' the boatman observes. 'I thought it was what you paid for anyway. You want me along?'

'I can manage,' she argues.

Felicity, for it has to be she, launches herself delicately barefoot into the riverside mud. On dry land she sits down to fit lizardskin shoes on her feet. She begins to walk though tall weeds, wild gorse, and bracken. Presently the one-time home of her Uncle Richard offers itself to view on a slope, above gross blackberry, and among aged apple trees. Paint peels; windows are broken. Curiosity diverts her; she circles the house, kicking against cans, crunching over glass, and takes a tentative step through a wide open door. This proves a mistake. Partly because frightened birds, perhaps disturbed in their nesting, flutter into her face; and deposit something unmentionable down the back of her dress as they escape. But principally because, prominent in the kitchen, the decayed corpse of what must recently have been an ugly old man hangs from a beam. 'Dear God,' she says, shaken and awed, and crosses herself. Since Ernest's death she has found Catholicism convenient. With her flight so precipitate, she sees nothing of the satisfaction of a man who, with health failing, still has the strength to cheat the hangman of an honest day's pay. And the vermin-ravaged Bible on the table, had she but noticed, is open at the chronicle of Christ's death between two criminals on Calvary Hill; this story never failed to move Crabb, and never more than at the last. Neatly placed beside the Bible is the clergyman's collar he exchanged for another.

Trembling, still sickened, Felicity moves swiftly up to the plateau. Weeds and wilful saplings command here too. Honeysuckle swarms over the ragged ruin of Lovelock House; hardly a wall still stands intact. Her feet find a path through the rubble, and up the steps to the arch of the front entrance, still obstinately aloft. One stone lion has toppled; the other is leaning. The eagles are headless, presumably decapitated by those hunting souvenirs. Soon, with a sigh, she has seen more than enough. She crosses faded cobbles softened with a rich crop of grass.

Until lately still cleared and tended by Crabb, the cemetery is not too difficult to locate. Here her heart beats uncomfortably; she can fancy its echo heard all through the hills. She moves from gravestone to gravestone, sometimes peering close and picking off lichen to decipher names. Her eyes – though the bright sun must be taken into account – begin smarting quite cruelly. Herman is here. Marie Louise. Aunt Diana. Uncle Richard. But there is no Lovelock interred here by name of Sybil or Sylvester; it is all she needs to know, and perhaps all she need ever. The chances seem fair that they are still alive, and desirably prospering, if somewhere lost in this land. An incomprehensible panic overtakes her; possibly best explained by deprivation, a sense of pasts unknown, kingdoms perished, and perils to come. She runs through abrasive bracken, breathing with difficulty, downhill to her boatman. For one moment he has the impression that she is about to fling herself into the river. At length she consents to be helped aboard.

'All right, lady?' he asks.

Her hat is askew. And she has somewhere lost a silk scarf. But she is more concerned with locating a silver flask in her handbag; she seems determined to drain it of the last drop of liquor.

'Perfectly,' she answers. 'I've never been better. But there's a dead man up there.'

'Dead?'

'For some time, I should say.'

'That's something best left for the police,' the boatman finally judges. Then he gives himself to an issue more pressing. 'I've just worked it out. I've seen you before. And not around here.'

'Possibly,' she concedes.

'In the movies, maybe. With John Gilbert, wasn't it, or Valentino? I can't just get my tongue round your name.'

'Fay Love.'

'That's it. Fay Love. Should have known from the start. Must tell my wife. She'll never believe it. We haven't seen you for years. What the hell happened?'

'The talkies happened,' she replies coolly.

'The talkies?'

'My voice, in the opinion of some, didn't seem to suit. Too squeaky, said one. Too brassy, said another. Any excuse. Anyway there were no silent roles left, not for one of my stature. And a scrap of a girl named Garbo was making herself felt, and grabbing my roles.'

'Hard luck.'

'On the contrary, a relief. I fancy I made a more graceful retirement than most. I have my memories to live with. Not to speak of money invested wisely, unlike some. If the truth be told, and I see no reason not to tell it, I could buy and sell a city or two now.'

'You're joking.'

'Not at all. That was another complaint. That I had no sense of humour.'

The boatman, in the end, does not contest this verdict. 'Right,' he says. 'Where can I take you now? If you want to see more of the river, I could take you on to Spanish Creek for another two pounds.'

'No. Take me home.'

'Home? Where is that?'

'St Louis,' she says.

Nineteen

All earthly horizons have been harvested; and now some of Mars and the moon. Yet the past, like death, is still a lost land. In legend's light there is no shadow, no shading; the divine and demonic dwell where only virtue and sin were seen. Heroic ages – and God knows nations still seem to need them – tell of the times when the sons of the gods mated with the daughters of men, at length to sire something more sober than mythology. History – the rot, that is, which set in with Herodotus – is the name of the dull-witted substitute ensuing. It is the depopulated Porgani's good fortune to be spared such diminution. Made to serve myth, it still does its duty, with no history worth more than a cryptic guidebook paragraph or two. Trendy citizens of the global village speed past its mouth, over a quite modern bridge, in something less than a minute; most feel no compulsion to look upriver or ponder on what they have missed.

The point of this preliminary, to be taken with salt and preferably also with pepper, is that the later Lovelocks, unlike the river, must settle for less; they have to make do with history, like most sons and daughters of men, and there is no future in that.

Less? They become butchers, bakers, and crooked lawyers. Tinkers, tailors and posturing television personalities. Soldiers, sailors and airline stewardesses. Rich men, poor men and moderately middle-class. Beggarmen, thieves and advertising executives. Undertakers and accountants. Plumbers and dentists. Used car salesmen and literary critics. Publicans and baffled bureaucrats. Professors and jockeys. They perform heart surgery, and run quite reputable brothels. They fight wars and more wars and, like most men, find greater profit in peace. They become protesters and politicians, fanatical freethinkers and Jesus-freaks. They die decorously virgin and desperately alcoholic. In affairs of football, they rumble across the rugby fields of the world with all the finesse of fire, flood or avalanche. They gather Olympic laurels, not least in middle distances, and barge their way up the planet's tallest peaks. From social fracas and economic fiasco they shape a society no worse than most, and better than some, in which the rich get richer and the poor get placated. Who shall sing of their little lives, make golden their lacklustre times? It is plain someone must. If we hear Homer clear, he is telling us that the deeds of men are destined for dust unless enshrined in the song of a poet. Fortunately there is a later Lovelock to fill that lack too. True that his song may not be altogether imperishable, but then the same might also be said of our species. Given an encounter with a sufficiently large comet, let alone a holocaust of our own incompetent making, humankind itself may leave at best a faint yawn in some corner of the cold cosmos.

Anyway that leaves us with Hillary Lovelock. No further need to roll drums; he is quite capable of contriving his own resonant entrance to this tale. In a land where the prose of existence has been primary, the pose of a poet is startling. No one – not even in the lands where language was born – believes much in poets any more. In poetry, perhaps. Not in poets, men who live and die by their lines. Such poets, to be frank, are a pain. They lack all perspective; they think everything matters. And commuter trains cannot be caught on time if one is overly concerned with a small sparrow's fall.

Great-grandson of Herman, by way of Benjamin and Iris, Hillary Lovelock grows tall and athletic, a gifted and graceful Apollo, whose largest handicap in life – and gravest embarrassment – is no more than his grandmother's sentimental pioneer verses, often still prospering in print, in sweeter-natured if minor anthologies. These seem hard to live down, especially if one has inherited the same trait, and trade. Otherwise, in fairness, Hillary loves being seen as a man of many parts: a once champion swimmer and swift rugby winger, he plays a mean game of tennis, and is quite a good golfer; as a gardener he can talk with authority on the virtues of compost, and as citizen advance fluent political views; he is far from averse to playing the fool, to appropriate audiences, particularly to students, possibly by way of proving that poets are human. Living such a life isn't effortless, not least for those bewildered wives and mistresses who find themselves sharing its less lyrical pains.

His poems? Well, yes. They might be called great shouts (here he may owe something to great-grandfather Herman's howls rather than to his grandmother's genteel emissions); shouts which he whittles sensitively down to whispers as he works, always in search of the less tangible meanings beyond the familiar syllables of human sound. For some, too intimate a whisper. Ladies, the young no less than the old, find it sexy; they confess to feeling randy at his public readings, which are many and mostly profitable; not a few find themselves privileged with a private reading, in hotels or wherever Hillary is lodged for the night, and in this respect too he is never in the red. He writes of lovers in lonely windswept places; of wise hermits, noble savages and children of nature in heavens of solitude; of haunted wanderers, men seeking some grail, in harsh and Godless wilderness. This is, of course, to simplify unpardonably. It merely helps make the point that on the whole he prefers lovemaking in a soft double bed, finds solitude soon boring, and keeps watch on the wilderness from the window of a fast-travelling car. He isn't to be dismissed as hypocritical; rather as one of ourselves writ large. The poet would fail us if he gave our equivocal aspirations no tongue. So much for subject matter. Well, not quite. For immediate purposes it should also be noted that Hillary, though making something of his pioneer origins, tends to do so ironically and allusively; one can fancy that, even in middle age, he remains determined not to be confused with his grandmother. In fact, not in fancy, he knows little in detail of those origins, finding the broader brush-stroke sufficient; and next to nothing, say, of the Porangi River. He is content to encounter it, if at all, as an obscure and remote name on a map: territory still too tainted by his grandmother, though the anthologies are by now long out of print, and her verses forgotten by all but a few.

To the point also that in a late middle-aged crisis – and in justice it must be said that none seem to suffer such crises more severely than poets, with the sins of man on their shoulders – Hillary, following a painful divorce and the still crueller departure of a mistress, finds himself emptying his soul for inspection, also the contents of a great many bottles. The locks of Apollo are grey and perceptibly thinning; his tennis forehand is shaky; his back garden has gone to hell; he has lately begun to decline opportunities to lecture, and read. Worse, he finds writing no solace. That is, when he can. It isn't that a poem no longer arrives on demand. He cannot content himself with manufacturing more of the same. It has to be harder. He has always believed, if largely in theory, that the practice of poetry involves damnation; he has only to consider some of his more distinguished predecessors in this field (Rimbaud, Crane, Thomas *et al*); their lives make for a litany of suicide, insanity, dipsomania and squalor. He has also always been aware, without pursuing the knowledge further than necessary, that it is the destiny of the poet to chance madness, despair and death for the possibility that man's existence might be redeemed by the word. With some reluctance, Hillary now admits himself unwilling to make common cause with so brave and embattled a band. For one thing, it seems a still futile gamble. He fails to see any words yet written which quite redeem man – merely many which do no more than make the commonplace momentarily tolerable – and with the best will in the world doesn't see himself bringing off that coup. Aside from which, he is also perilously outliving them all; great poets seldom make grandfathers. Shrinking from words, he contemplates deeds. Not as diversion, nor as vehicles for despair; rather as means of making words flesh. His words, his life. Both might have less empty sound.

Not too far from this station, still staggering with anguish under a cross of his own carpentering, his eye alights at last on the disaffected young of his time, rootless, repudiating the past, and in search of renewal, though their quest tends to terminate in unkempt rooms reeking with pot and cacophonous with music. Hillary lacks a war, which is the Byronic solution for a poet in his condition. But he does see an army. He isn't unknown to the young. He has been another boring name in their school textbooks. On the other hand some among them are academic defectors who recall him as a gymnast lecturer, bawdy within bounds, who shamelessly uses whisky-laced water to moisten his throat; also one notably lucid to female students in the nearest pub afterwards. As a freaky sort of cat, one with no little cool, his credentials as guru appear impeccable. They are prepared to listen, and turn him on with a joint, if not always to turn down their immoderate music. If pressed to make his message more explicit, and certainly more audible, Hillary indicates that his main concern is that they effectively channel their energy and idealism, not let it dribble away into drugs and unconventional sexual activity. A new world waits to be born, one loving and tolerant, but city back streets are more congenial for abortionists than midwives. They are delivering themselves into a dead end; they must turn elsewhere for a new and true beginning.

This is to precis. Hillary, with a fund of confessional anecdote, and often penitent about his middle-class past, hasn't lost his gift for fashioning vivid phrases, now often salted with argot derived from rock music. Clearly he has to be taken as more than a man just back from a bad trip. If pressed still further as an ageing oracle – and at this point even the priestess at Delphi had her difficulties – Hillary cannot freshmint a prospective future; his prescription, most humanly, partakes of the past. Those who know no history may be doomed to repeat it; but so, as distressingly, are those who do. The phantom wing of an angel might just have brushed Hillary's shoulder; but let us, in charity, put that thought aside. Hillary removes not feathers, but a strand or two of fallen grey hair. His progress has been faltering, but it should by now be clear where he is proceeding. Given a mental corner or two yet, and some spiritual signposts, he is on his way home to the Porangi. He has to concede – to himself, privately – that it has all been secreted in his verse anyway; it is time to take himself literally, to launch himself on his own lines. For Hillary no longer finds affliction in the thought that he may yet prove his grandmother's heir; the gusto with which he inhabits the crash-pads of the young distinctly suggests otherwise. Of his great-grandfather Herman he knows much less, which may at this point be mercy. Enough to know that he has Utopia in his genes. To the young, then, he hears himself extolling the rediscovery of essential pioneer virtue, and from there it is but a short leap to the Porangi River, and the prospects thereof for a commune. If one is to begin anew, and yet again, where better? The marvel is merely that it has taken him so long to see the Porangi plain. (He has only seen it in his mind's eye thus far, but no matter.) Isolation should in itself make for a self-sufficient, self-respecting community conducting itself on organic principles, always guided by collective debate, and with love and concern for things of this earth. An example, in fact; a deed to shine out upon a naughty world, perhaps even lending his murkier poems lustre.

Pied Pipers traditionally tend to generate publicity, not all of it unwanted, but much of it unfair. Only to be expected, perhaps, that one bitter ex-wife should suggest that he is going bush, and playing pioneer pauper, to duck maintenance payments. There are also parents pronouncing in the newspapers on his corruption of their innocent young, and his taking unfair advantage of their difficulties with drugs and social adjustment. Socrates had it worse. Hillary cannot be requested to drain the last drop of hemlock. The truth is that the law can't lay a hand on him, though he does, before leaving the city, start to duck photographers and television cameras.

Neither can be avoided, of course, when the actual journey upriver begins. Hillary, reverting to the river's Polynesian past, judges canoes – at least in the contemporary form of kayaks – the most suitable means of negotiating the now snag-ridden Porangi. Cameras whirr and click as the mini-armada prepares to set off; there are hoarse last-minute interviews suggestive of a manned shot into space, or polar exploration. Hillary's command canoe takes to the river first, dragging a second low in the water with supplies; he looks back once and waves, smiling most memorably, to well-wishers and cameras. Somewhere between fifty and a hundred kayaks soon follow.

Primevally, at least, the Porangi can hardly fail to live up to expectations. When not swerving about bleached carcasses of great trees, or ducking under menacing branches and root systems in the river, Hillary tries to see it all as his ancestors might have just one century earlier. This isn't difficult – since mountain and forest are for the most part as left on the last day of creation – but the hazards do prove distracting, not something his forebears faced. Five kayaks, in inexperienced hands, hole and sink on the first stretch of river; no amount of marijuana will keep their occupants buoyant. Survivors have to be brought ashore, consoled and dried down, and supplies stored on the riverside for recovery later. Arguments develop, accusations abound, and Hillary has to make extensive use of his verbal powers to win peace and progress again. By nightfall six more kayaks are lost, or all but irreparably damaged. Three others are found beached some distance downriver, their occupants asleep on the bank, or in hallucogenic daze. More supplies have to be abandoned, to make way for people in those craft still intact; it becomes a logistical tango, with Hillary's choreography under stern test. Fortunately for all, however, it is a warm summer night; no tents are needed, guitars proliferate in the firelight, the moon is romantic, and even predatory insects seem to succumb to the benign atmospheric conditions.

Next morning, however, romance wilts again; most are unwilling to be woken. When shaken, they rise with diverse grudges. They complain loudly, and mutinously, of stiffening limbs. None appears ready to contemplate the preparation of breakfast; Hillary has to organize sustenance himself. There are also suggestions that the flotilla proceed no further upriver; why can't they stay here? Hillary, at pains, points out that there is little level land on this stretch of the river, and such as there is unsuitable for agricultural purposes. They must move on. In truth, of course, Hillary has a hankering for precedent: he has already selected his site; superfluous to add, except for readers who may have come late to this narrative, that he has Lovelock Junction in mind. His supplications have no success for the greater part of the morning. Not until near noon can a start be made. Once again incidents intrude upon peaceful progress; the avant garde of the future remains formless, with drenchings and near drownings even more commonplace. Intimations of famine also arrive; an unscheduled stop has to be made for consumption of substantial quantities of food, thus providing even more room in those kayaks designated to carry supplies. Vegetarians grieve at having meat forced upon them, and those less herbivorous mourn that the canned stew is lukewarm. Hillary also has to face the undesirable fact of defection for the first time: a kayak, carrying two, furtively heads downriver; his plea to return, to carry on with the quest, echoes emptily back from the hills. An untidy resumption of the voyage is made; stiffened limbs are even more difficult to flex, after a large lunch, and the sun is too bloody hot. Tin containers and a few last crumpled cartons of yogurt litter the riverside.

Dusk again denies Hillary his goal. He gathers in stragglers; a camp is made among trees. Sour notes strike, though Hillary attempts harmony. Life in the wilderness now evidently leaves something to be desired. Sanitary arrangements are perfunctory, and Hillary finds shit on his shoes. Songsters thin in number and strum guitars sadly; the moon becomes elusive beyond thickening cloud. Longings are expressed for king-sized hamburgers, even for old-fashioned fish and chips; there appears to be regret that the Porangi can provide neither, with not even a Coca-Cola outlet around the next corner. The night turns out to be restless, often sleepless; several girls are in near hysteria with the attentions of mosquitoes, and equally disturbed by undefined noises in the forest. Morning reveals even more nightmare. Biorhythm charts, brought by some, proclaim emotional, intellectual and physical cycles entirely at odds for the day. Adventurers in astrology discover it suggestive that Hillary is a Scorpio, with his planets in unpromising juxtaposition. Finally, after some dispute, the *I Ching* has to be consulted, to see if the present moment is propitious for the crossing of the great water. Tossed coins, in the absence of yarrow stalks, produce contrary verdicts; a third throw still leaves the matter in doubt. It is, however, at last regarded as significant that the oracle recommends respect for the teaching of the master. This may safely be presumed to mean Hillary, who has tired of telling his companions that they must make use of the day. None now contests this profundity. Enlightenment is theirs; the great water presents no peril. Kayaks are again carried to the river, and the conquest of the Porangi proceeds, if not at great pace.

By late afternoon they arrive, unmistakably, at their last stop. A few slimy sticks of jetty; the bones of some old boat cast up on the bank. Here, Hillary announces; here their community shall take root, on pioneer soil. Tempted toward some rather secular service of thanksgiving, to crown the occasion, he fears that Buddhist marginalia might make for confusion, also for intolerable delays. Beyond the riverside the wilderness now expresses itself fairly impenetrably, but Hillary sees this as no cause for premature despair. A few bolder spirits launch themselves inland and return to report the wreck of a house, some ruins, and graves; the consensus appears to be that the place is pretty damn spooky. Hillary, who has been supervising unloading of supplies and construction of temporary canvas-covered shelters, deploying the little labour available for these tasks, wearily rouses himself to personal exploration; he leaves instructions behind, making clear that an evening meal and shelter for the night are both necessary, crashes solitary into undergrowth and overgrowth, and after some bruising struggle surfaces on the plateau. It requires much mental and spiritual inquiry, given his depleted condition, to see this as territory sacred to the Lovelocks; also difficult to see it, despite its aesthetic advantages, these being principally panoramic, as more than another large and melancholy lump of rock above a river. The ruins of Lovelock House are already anonymous, time and inquisitive vandals having trimmed most eccentricity and excrescence, and now appear to testify to nothing in particular, everything in general.

Gravestones, when he locates them, prove far more inspirational. Not least because the name Lovelock recurs with some frequency; Hillary at last feels a pioneer pull. These lives cannot, must not, have been lived in vain. Refreshed, somewhat renewed, he descends to the riverside. In his absence, all is at standstill, no further work done; most of his fellow pilgrims find prone positions congenial. Moreover, they feel that a democratic decision should be made on the selection of a site for the commune. This place, to be frank, which more and more are, looks like a bummer; it isn't their bag. The girls especially are getting bad vibes. If Hillary were more aware of the abandoned acres at Spanish Creek, that region celebrated by his grandmother and not too far removed upriver, he might have pulled off quick coup with a substitute site, and suffered less heartburn. As things are, however, he offers no option. He has to stand or fall by their present location; Lovelock Junction, even in the heyday of Herman, has never had more articulate or visionary defender. Nor is he without guile. He observes that democratic decisions are all very well, in the right time and place, but the fact is Rome wasn't built in a day and night is damn near; they have to settle down somewhere. Morning may make mature consideration possible. Partly because of Hillary's gift for telling detail, partly because of a fresh supply of mind-enhancing substance recovered from a leaky kayak and fast dried out over a fire, the general mood becomes more pacific. It is agreed, at least, that they shall all crash there for the night. Transcendental meditation, cultivation of mantras and yoga exercises soon prevail.

Morning presents its usual complications. But disagreement over the selection of site seems to have vanished overnight, perhaps due to particularly sound sleep, some sexual congress, a certain amount of amnesia, and the sunlight dispersing extreme vibes. On the other hand, before noon, four or five kayaks – it is now difficult to tally – have also vanished gently downriver, with twice that number of occupants, toward the familiar conveniences of twentieth century civilization. Some of his band, to Hillary's relief, already show themselves pioneers of conviction. He finds them, on their own initiative, clearing ground for cultivation, digging it over, and sowing their first seeds. But it seems, upon inquiry, that they believe the riverside silt promises a rich crop of cannabis; by summer's end they should be harvesting a fair-sized plantation. Lettuces, cabbages and carrots can be left till later. Besides, as one lucid agriculturist observes, they may need a cash crop; they mightn't be into subsistence before winter.

Elsewhere more lethargic trail-blazers are into providing themselves with further home comfort in the form of rock music dispensed by battery-powered tape recorders. Too much for Hillary to hope that the sound will soon weaken, at the current rate of battery usage; there are bound to be more in reserve, or parties dispatched to buy more down-river. He has his first twitch of despair. But he really has more cause for it when he attempts to arouse interest in the erection of substantial and durable shelters, a proposition conducive to prolonged argument. Some find pyramidally shaped dwellings pleasing to contemplate, since these best contain the life force and spiritual tranquillity; others feel geodesic domes desirable, and also argue their cause with impressive if still notional energy. While striving to explain the need for more immediately functional forms, Hillary sees the sky darkly clouding, and feels brisk wind from the west; within the hour their first rain falls. The efficacy of the few small shelters so far constructed is soon under test. For one thing, they cannot contain crowds with comfort. Some collapse. Some simply flood. Several despairing souls make a move, willing to race through the vindictive rain, to the one remaining roof – once Richard Lovelock's – in the vicinity. Though the roof leaks, secondary shelter can be taken beneath a derelict billiard table. The rain lasts a week, by the end of which Hillary – taking temporary leave of the collective – has contrived a personal refuge some distance inland, in the shallow mouth of a collapsed coal mine. This has its discomforts, but the silence is agreeable, and he has a book or two and several cans of baked beans. Thoreau, however, proves to be pessimistic reading; Hillary has the impression that all the world is turning to Walden pond beyond the mouth of the mine. The rain is unresponsive to his fears. An Ark might have more utilitarian virtue than pyramidal shapes or geodesic domes.

Nevertheless, he rides out the storm. When he makes his way back to the riverside it has to be noted that the prospective refurbishers of Lovelock Junction have further dwindled in number. Advantage has fast been taken of the approach of sunshine; the risk of bouncing in a kayak down the flooded river is preferable to that of remaining. Malnutrition is apparent among the saturated survivors, also some grief.

Rain has played havoc with their project to make the Porangi rejoice and blossom as the rose; the seeds so far sown have all been washed out. Hillary's plea for patience goes largely unheard; he finds indifference to his assertion that they have passed their first test, that now they must learn to live with the whims of the natural world.

The whims of the human world become apparent next day with the arrival of two jet-boats bearing uniformed members of a police vice squad. There have been rumours of drugs, orgies, and minors involved. Putting paid to these pernicious and malicious suggestions robs Hillary of more precious pioneering hours. Among his companions, in the course of the police inquiry, there is a general move toward the trees; they are slow to return and participate in the preparation of the evening meal. As before, this task falls for the most part to Hillary. Later he hears many complaints, sometimes loud, and all ungracious, about the meagre portions of rice and beans handed around. Exhausted and diminished, no doubt much as his ancestors were at similar stages, he finds himself unable to participate usefully or amiably in campfire conversation. He settles for a drug-based orgy of his own; the base in this case being a personal and carefully preserved bottle of the best malt Scotch whisky. With this tight under one arm, he takes a torch and battles his way up to the privacy of the plateau. Arriving at the ruins, he no longer needs his torch; all is astral under the moon. Athens, Carthage or Constantinople could produce no more bewitching rubble; the night seems filled with ancestral whispers, or possibly opossums, and he hears the river sibilant below. The night is mild, really quite humid, and he has never seen stars more abundant. He prefers not to damage the whisky by dilution with water; its warmth powerfully repels melancholia; the ruins of Lovelock House splendidly silver by the minute as he sits on the topmost of the surviving entrance steps and, as might be imagined, meditates. There is much in this world, often a surfeit, on which a man can meditate to spiritual profit; and Hillary has, at this moment, more than fair share. He is sufficiently diverted not to notice the diminution of the whisky; his optimism as latter-day pioneer, also as one heir to the Lovelock heartbeat, increases in approximately reverse proportion; he knows he will not be shaken again by little local difficulties. Nor, if he can help it, by familiar human imperfections. These, for Hillary, are most healing hours. His one problem is that when he attempts to rise from the ruins, a phoenix now rediscovering the capacity for flight, the world momentarily and perhaps malevolently pilfers his equilibrium. After a time he reconsiders his position, which is horizontal at the foot of the steps, and decides it as being on balance more comfortable than exploration of the vegetable world on the way back to the riverside camp. He sighs several times, and then sleeps.

With daylight, the sun already pitiless, Hillary unfurls slowly and cautiously from the past's irregular shadows; and confronts the present when able to establish its exact nature, and his current location. Reassured, he experiments with his pedestrian competence, presently finding secure foothold on the terrain, and begins in rather somnambulist fashion to progress downhill to the riverside. At length, his largest hindrance appears to be a headache; he also has a decidedly dry throat. But as he covers the last few yards he is met by no welcome smell of coffee warming over a campfire; he is met by nothing, and no one, at all. The silence, if not welcoming, inspires awe. The camp is quite empty. Every kayak has gone. A few discarded batteries testify to recent human occupation. Otherwise an archaeologist would have extremely poor pickings. A midden of cans, perhaps; and a pair of torn jeans.

Hillary tries to assess the situation; he has to concede subversive relief. Before noon, sustained by coffee, quantities of river water, some of a second bottle of whisky, and such food as he finds still fit for human consumption, Hillary is almost himself again. Certainly lyricism, no mean ally, has been swift to his rescue, and now helps him hold the fort against peril within and without. He refuses to be seen as one abandoned to disillusion, or as a bitter castaway up the Porangi without a paddle, and kayak for that matter. The prescience resident in his poetry cannot be denied; he partakes of the tree of knowledge, the fruit of prophecy, with no serpent in sight.

Forest, river and sky form his captive audience. 'I am,' he announces, 'the world's last free man.'

Six weeks later he is found, feeble and skeletal, attempting to pole a raft of rather inept construction down the Porangi. No cameras, since fortune can sometimes play fair, are on hand to freeze this event for the record. Some years elapse before publication of Hillary's next volume of verse. It is notably spare, sober and cryptic; he treats of his Porangi period in a manner critics are pleased to call astringently confessional. 'Lovelock,' claims one transparently partisan reviewer, 'has clearly scaled his literary Everest. While he braves the rarefied air, the remainder of us gasp humbly at his base camp.' Words may involve a poet in despair and damnation; so evidently do deeds. Hillary Lovelock, conspicuously supported by his new spouse, seems more than content with his former station in life. One fan letter especially surprises. Written in shaky hand, forty pages long, it comes from an elderly gentleman who identifies himself as one Herman Lovelock Malone, the last child born at Lovelock Junction and hence named for its founder.

He has reservations about Hillary's vocabulary. He hopes Hillary might be persuaded to take a second look at the Porangi and perhaps see the bright side.

Wait. The Lovelocks have not finished with the Porangi, nor vice versa. One other tale has to be told if this version of events is ever to be called complete. (God knows it is not, but there is no point in engaging in that One-sided argument.) Enter Frank Lovelock.

Great-grandson of Richard and Nancy, and never known by either, Frank might at first be mistaken for one of the less distinguished members of the Lovelock line. Some, true, see him as a skeleton in the cupboard; they deny all relationship, even immediate kin. Understandable, and to be explained by Frank's notoriety. He is less to be seen as a chip off the old block, like Hillary, than as particularly bruised fruit from the family tree.

The city suburb, where he grows, never quite contains him: he views the houses in his street as so many well-tended kennels where people quietly and colourlessly go mad, if sometimes with canine whimpers and cries: this despite the advantage of three meals a day, many modern conveniences, perhaps a pleasure launch or a yacht, and motor vehicles with automatic transmissions. In his own house there seems more excuse for madness, with lack of all luxuries and indeed of much money, due in great part to his father's drinking habits, which in turn are consequence of his mother's prolonged infidelities. Aware of cause and effect unnaturally early, Frank suffers paternal beatings and maternal neglect with patience and stoicism, but only up to a point. When that point comes, he flees home and school and takes roads which, because of police intervention, never lead anywhere. He is always brought back, though social workers sometimes talk of a juvenile home. Life seems less a trap when he masters motor vehicles left with keys in the ignition. Never a gang member, or altogether orthodox in delinquency, Frank's crimes are solo, and those of spiritual need rather than physical greed; there is a high-speed crash or two, then tedious courtroom talk, initially lenient magistrates, and later the first of many confinements.

Frank's maiden escape is not especially inventive. He simply eludes two warders on a prison farm reserved for youthful offenders; and leaps hedges and fences which present any obstacle. The need to place distance between himself and his pursuers again makes motor vehicles desirable; the more, in many ways, the better. His other criminal acts – food thefts here, shopkeepers' takings there – stem largely from the requirement to keep four wheels fast on available highways. Road blocks need not a prison make; Frank crashes through them when possible, with much damage to metal, and evades them where essential. Given time and an empty gasoline tank, he finds himself serving a larger sentence in a considerably smaller cell, one with barred windows. The bars offer little resistance to human tenacity; Frank is on the run again. His sentences lengthen, his prisons grow more austere; there are higher walls, armed guards, and much stronger bars. This merely gives Frank further opportunity to excel. Some of his feats, particularly those involving walls, have acrobatic ingenuity; he is not Nancy's great-grandson for nothing, and would have admirably suited her doomed travelling troupe. Others, and here perhaps he leans toward great-grandfather Richard, involve diverse subterfuge; and prison laundry baskets, for example.

Technical minutiae, which authorities are anyway reluctant to release, need not detain us; Frank never is. Enough to say that his enterprise is never in doubt; he is seldom a year out of the headlines, sometimes for months at one time, until he is yet again caught. The cost to the public purse prompts the speedier completion of an all-electronic top security prison to ensure he serves his accumulating sentences, now more than terminal, longer than any conceivable natural life. Frank feels all the more obliged to escape. His tally of convictions – for escapes, car thefts and trifling burglaries – approaches the round thousand. Crowds, sensing injustice in Frank's current situation, gather to hiss and jeer at the police whenever they make him captive again; by contrast Frank receives fervent cheers. *Free Frank Lovelock* T-shirts are marketed with huge success. Rock groups compose boisterous authority-taunting ballads; folk-singers interpret his tale more wistfully, as emblematic of man's eternal longing for freedom.

Frank, to be fair, can't make much sense of this. He just wants to steal cars. He is aware of his public status as hero mainly in passing. He discovers notes left on the doors of holiday cottages instructing him not to break in, but to locate the key under the front door mat; also informing him where to find food. He makes a point of washing up the dishes before he departs – which makes more sense than leaving them dirty as clue to the police – but this only serves to enhance him as folk hero; he appears to be considerate and gentlemanly too. He is given credit for a sense of the comic, in some part deserved. Up a tree for some hours – like his great-grandfather Richard again, he often finds treetops convenient – he observes a pursuing constable taking time off from the hunt, and removing his boots before a short sleep. Frank descends, souvenirs the boots, and exits with speed. He leaves the police-issue footwear, along with a signed note drawing attention to deficiencies, at the door of the nearest shoe-repair shop. Anecdotes have him sending flowers to carless old ladies, conveying his regrets, though such incidents might best be attributed to pranksters making free with his name. Certainly true that he lets loose some hundreds of battery hens, from their tiny cells in a vast and sunless shed, but not as a compassionate lark; rather, practically and tactically, to cause confusion among his pursuers, more so when an aggrieved factory-farmer appears discharging a shotgun at random.

Frank's intoxicating career, in common with most, takes a less frivolous turn. Often, while on the run, he becomes bewildered by entire strangers pressing hospitality upon him, and sullen if refused. For a long time he can never quite see the bloody hell why. When he does, it comes as a shock. He comprehends that people need him, and not merely those attempting to administer justice. The law needs him in. People need him out. Imprisoned in tiny and trivial worlds – serving time in jobs, mortgaged homes, and especially marriages – they applaud a man who can show a clean pair of heels to it all; they can believe Frank's freedom their own. He is their daydream made flesh; they can live larger than life with Frank loose. Thus the hissing, jeering and cheering. Thus the singers, rock and folk. Thus the notes on the door and food thoughtfully provided. Thus the offers, wherever he is recognized, of a bed for the night, or a friendly bottle of beer. It all adds up; there is no way he, Frank Lovelock, can be subtracted. The responsibilities of his role – of his inadvertent mission to his fellow men – begin to overwhelm him. The fun goes out of it; this in turn leads to critical loss of confidence. His flights, when in uncomfortable proximity to the police, begin to seem a bleak formality; the theft of a car a joyless and functional act. He wants nothing more than to hide. The fact is that Frank too, more or less, is on his way home to the Porangi. And the Porangi, more or less, presents itself at an opportune moment.

Up to that point he has possibly survived a half-dozen chases past the mouth of the Porangi without the river's name impinging especially on his mind; he has been more concerned with clearing the approach to the bridge at high speed, and bracing himself for a likely road block on the other side. On the occasion in question he idles along the coast warily, with no apparent pursuers, in a large and comfortable vehicle recently converted to his purpose. His currently restive mood is accelerated by the discovery that the vehicle is plainly the legal property of some medical man, possibly a professor. Opening the glove box in search of cigarettes, his eyes still on the winding road ahead, he encounters instead something cold and unfamiliar under his hand, and tugs it out for visual inspection. With horror, then dread, he looks directly into the eye sockets of a human skull. In consequence he barely escapes collision with an oncoming car, and skids perilously close to the edge of a cliff. The skull swiftly goes over the cliff. His fear of an omen, however, fails to make a similar journey. Life, he begins to see, is a dead end. Especially his life. It has become lethal habit. He has been given few chances to stop, look, and see what the hell it is all about. Too often, when he has, there have been uniformed humans in number upon his immediate horizon. Also he realizes that he has increasingly become indistinguishable from his responsibilities to the rest of mankind; he is fatally trapped in a script not his own, but collectively composed. His heart still thudding, all faith in his future ebbing, he drives on with caution; he uses the brake far more than is his custom, and even reads roadside warning signs with new respect. There are more perils on the highway than he has ever previously supposed. Worse, the world begins to teem with intimations of mortality; every town, township and even meagre hamlet seems possessed of a considerable cemetery. Solitary country churches, for this newly attentive sightseer, appear to exist only for their decor of gravestones. In truth, he has never seen death as so bloody rampant before. Surfeit arrives when he sights a cemetery, with lonely gravedigger turning the first sod, above a blind corner; Frank finds it impossible to persuade feet and hands to propel the vehicle further. He slides the car to the edge of the road, and emerges with relief; he has a sense of escaping his imminent coffin, and even prison is preferable, a trivial risk against the vague chance of resurrection. Nerveless Frank walks. Inconceivable as it might seem to his many admirers, Frank Lovelock has just called quits to crime.

Fortunately, fellow travellers on that coastal road are few, and even more fortunately none of these pause to pick him up; they might have been bemused and indeed physically stunned by his reaction if so. They leave him hiking lonely, and not altogether unpleasantly. Within the same hour he reaches the Porangi; he looks over the river's wide mouth with a sting of revelation. The name on the bridge is unmistakable; he remembers it as figuring in his father's drunken anecdotes about the feats and faded glories of the Lovelock clan. According to Frank's old man, in his cups and out, the tragedy of the Lovelocks, the original sin, was that of departing the Porangi; the Lovelocks were no longer real men, but faces lost in the crowd. Strictly speaking, this can be put down as sentimental invention; the fact is that Frank's father never knew the Porangi either; by his time the river had become inherited rumour. But now this muddied heirloom flows real. Frank has never felt much of a Lovelock before. Now he is inclined to see his surname in a new light. He bloody well belongs here, perhaps. So much for fate; there is more.

Sitting on grassy riverside, watching the water dawdle down to the sea, he has yet another encounter with one of his fans and aspirant sponsors. This one an old man, and lame, who doesn't ask for an autograph. Frank simply agrees with some resignation that, yes, his name is Frank Lovelock, for whatever that is now worth. From that point Frank asks the questions. The old man is a retired fisherman of the mostly holiday community – with farms north and south – grown around the river's mouth. Like most, he has never been far upriver. What, Frank asks, is up there? Nothing, the old man answers. No one. Unless you count trees. All most informative; Frank perseveres. What, he inquires, could a man do up there? The old man is at a loss; he first proposes the pursuit of madness as a possibility. Then his talk turns to opossums. Australian opossums, and there is no more destructive an imported pest for coastal farmers and fruit-growers, have become a considerable presence up the Porangi in the past three decades; they also play foul with the forest itself, stripping bark, killing trees, and consuming seedlings. There is a bounty paid on their killing. Moreover, their skins fetch a pretty fair price. Yes, a man could make a mint from opossums. Provided, that is, he could put up with the Porangi; the place has driven men to drink. This isn't news to Frank. He is more interested in the manifest vistas of peaceful enterprise on the Porangi; at the moment they shape as a matter of life over death. He can abscond from his role with a rifle. In this connection he puts a proposition to the old man concerning collection of bounties and sale of opossum skins. In remarkably short time they have become business partners. Their arrangement ensures Frank of a reliable dinghy, a Remington .22, a quantity of ammunition, opossum traps, and sustenance for a month. Before dark he is rowing upriver.

Little new can be said about Frank's life on the Porangi for the next two or three years; it has all been lived, more or less, by Lovelocks before him. But seldom with satisfaction so large. The hue and cry of his hunters becomes more akin to surly mutters; the headlines shrink, with a reflexive twitch of type now and then, when theories are advanced that Frank has perished obscurely, perhaps suicidally, making his last escape by walking into wild ocean. (A car has been found, with his fingerprints, abandoned on lonely coast; that appears to prove it, and a psychiatrist suggests Frank a longtime sufferer of paranoid delusions. True enough. Paranoia is an occupational hazard of prison escapers.) Frank's deep feeling for the river derives in great part from the reasonable notion that he has never had it so bloody good. The notion might be seen as irresponsible by his eulogistic and hero-worshipping fellow men, the majority of whom are frustrated by his disappearance; a relatively tidy minority concern him on the downriver voyage, when he delivers his skins. This because his business partner, the old bugger, cannot keep silence. Frank finds himself dragged to the pub, where the name Lovelock is often toasted too lavishly, by new friends in uncomfortable number. All insist it unfair that he should be expected to serve his many sentences; all assure him that his secret, his Porangi hideout, will never be revealed, not by them; all buy him more drinks. Celebrity, so far as Frank is concerned, is shit street; he can't stand all this pissing in his pocket. Nothing gladdens him more than to escape the fawning, and continue rehabilitating himself upriver. From his remote eyrie on the Porangi, mankind seems but an unholy and boozy babble; human society all squealing brakes and crumpling car metal. Sometimes he would sooner not have to sell off his skins. But he does need tobacco and beer.

He doesn't lack much else, as the months pass. For shelter, he restores his great-grandfather's long dilapidated habitation efficiently enough, one room at a time; he even contrives to make the mildewed and moth-eaten billiard table more functional. Fruit trees, peach, plum, crab-apple, begin to flower and fruit. He has a vegetable garden sufficient to his solitary condition. Opossum stew can be tedious, but there is always wild pig, also eels from the river. Outside the house he builds racks for the curing of skins. As for the rest of Lovelock Junction, he considers it best to leave well alone. Ruins are ruins. Frank has never found respect for history any advantage to a man on the run. Nor, more to the point, do ancestral graves have large appeal. He would prefer to ignore them, if the cemetery were not a site much favoured by opossums. As things stand, he has a trap set on Herman's grave, another on Richard's. He feels more superstitious about the final resting place of Marie Louise; she sounds like a witch with more yet to say. Working by torchlight, freezing the tiny beasts in a beam, he shoots many opossums off a stone erected to the memory of one Ira Dix, and another to someone called Whisker. These shots call up no disturbed shades. He can convince himself that the dead are immaterial to his current concern. That is, to make life seem less manically ephemeral. The longueurs of the Porangi go far to creating a contrary impression.

As for paranoia, already conceded, the Porangi also goes far toward providing a tolerable cure. Paranoia is ill-suited to survive the punitive conditions of uninhabited forest and unvisited river. Frank has men off his back, for the most part. For the lesser part, however, he longs for a woman. Like any Lovelock, and let the name be legion from this point on, Frank is capable of being felled by man's most modish flaw; the reproductive urge rides again on the Porangi. Which isn't to suggest that Frank wants an heir. He just wants a mate. Or, to be more Frank, a fuck. Stone walls, in Frank's unlettered experience, do a sexual prison make; and iron bars a carnal cage. And life on the fly has left little time for other than couplings of great brevity, often to the disappointment of smitten and ambitious girl Fridays; Frank has always decamped before Saturday dawns. The Porangi's eternities, if desirable in one sense, do have the disadvantage of allowing the subject to be considered and reconsidered.

James dreamed Glory. Frank meets Shirl, which is short for Shirlene. Dreams depend much on the eye of the dreamer; and on the fevers inherent in sleeping alone. Shirl may not be everyman's dream, even with certain native contours in her favour. But from Frank's point of view she will handsomely pass.

She is small and plump and blonde, in the pub on his monthly visit, and making it known that she is on long vacation from a lover in the city; in fact she never wants to see the bastard again. After the customary vow of secrecy, given to all in the bar, she loudly refuses to believe that Frank is indeed Frank Lovelock. Frank bloody Lovelock? Here? Never, she says. Everyone knows, she goes on, that the cool bugger's dead; even the police seem at last to have got it into their thick heads. Finally convinced, and again vowing silence, she glows with more than gin and tonic from a glass frequently topped up; her ample flesh tends to encompass Frank as their drinking proceeds and the evening prolongs; he knows a camp follower when he sees one, and possibly a camp cook; the purpose of his stay downriver becomes physical rather than fiscal, with Shirl his material accomplice, in tall riverside grass. Noon locates them well up the Porangi, with the wilderness welcoming; next day Lovelock Junction's population has doubled. Shirl assures Frank that no one will miss her much; not even the aged uncle at the Porangi's mouth with whom she stays most conveniently when lovers have to be lost. She has left this uncle an explanatory note, circumspect but suggestive, about her departure.

A little femininity goes a long way in Frank's life. His bed is now graced by sheets as well as blankets; and moreover clean. Shirl insists also on washing his underwear at least once a week. Bread bakes aromatically in a wood-fired oven. Meals can be uncomfortably filling. He no longer plays lonely and near schizophrenic games of billiards; she makes it a contest, and can play some cruel shots. She holds the torch when he shoots opossums by night; and helps him cure skins. When beer begins to run short weeks earlier than usual, this due to their custom of drinking their way off to bed, Shirl doesn't let impending adversity precipitate a thirsty trip down the Porangi; instead she brews a fine drop of cider from an abundant crab-apple crop, and ferments a potent blackberry wine from the berries which grow wild to their back door. She sings through her day, energetic in bed and out. Often Frank is disinclined to get out. The killing and skinning of opossums has lost much incentive. When bedded with Shirl between warm and clean sheets, the freedom of the great outdoors, which Frank has had reason to prize, can likewise lose flavour.

The regaining of paradise is not a realistic prospect, especially not on the Porangi, or so one might imagine. Frank, however, indicates that it remains possible to get Eden in working order again. With cider and blackberry wine on tap, not to speak of Shirl, Frank has something perilously close to happiness, a subject of which it is all but obscene to speak in any twentieth-century narrative; but who is to deny any era its useful inhibitions? Frank doesn't find the proximity of happiness in the least incommoding. The Porangi is again instinct with human promise. Every panorama pleases. Even hills darkened with rain. That means a day entirely devoted to Shirl. A life given to crime, and the compulsive acquisition of vehicles, merely seems quaint; he seems to have been missing the point of the business for too bloody long.

Call it compassion, or plain sentimentality, but there is at this point a certain temptation to tamper with truth, and allow Frank to tamper timelessly with Shirl on the verdant slopes of the Porangi. So easy, in truth; a slip or two of the pen, and neither Shakespeare nor Homer might long hesitate. On the other hand, who wishes to contribute to the harsh sum of human discontent, and cause mass and likely profitless migration to the Porangi? Fortunately for our peace of mind, though unfortunately for Frank, the facts dictate otherwise; it is too premature for the wishful thinking of literature and legend. Frank can live outside the law, but not outside life. In Shirl, he has embraced more than he supposed.

His first news of this comes in the form of a police boot early on a bright summer morning, with Frank still abed. This boot is planted firmly on his chest. Frank blinks; Shirl screams. Two other policemen engage with his arms. It has to be nightmare. Nevertheless, it goes on. Their bedroom, a lovenest so recently and florally curtained by Shirl, fills noisily with uniformed police and plain-clothes detectives. One of the latter smiles with especial satisfaction, and addresses Shirl in intimate and unloving terms. Shirl has unaccountably neglected to tell Frank that the lover she was actively losing, when they first met, was a diligent employee of the Criminal Investigation Bureau, already awarded two certificates for zeal. Frank knows from experience that a good detective never gets lost; he would have placed some distance between himself and Shirl, fast given her the shove, had he known. This smug bugger tracked clues to Shirl up the coast, as far as her aged uncle, and from that point found prospects of promotion of far more interest than the rekindling of Shirl's sexual fire; long-hunted Frank Lovelock, for this vocational Galahad, is as good as the grail. Frank is handcuffed twice over, to the heaviest constables present. Other uniformed men begin to lead grieving Shirl away; she is allowed, since even the law can be human, to kiss her Frank first.

'You won't ever forget, will you?' she pleads.

'No,' Frank promises, with feeling. 'Never. Don't bloody worry.'

So it is that Frank Lovelock – though now in an all-electronic prison, the best public money can buy – still lives in Lovelock Junction for twenty-four hours of his day. About him rises reinforced concrete, toughened steel, and bulletproof glass; there are no glimpses of green, and even sight of sky has intentionally been made scarce. Beyond bars and more bars there are watchtowers manned by warders with sharp-shooting skills, spiked moats, infinite walls of impenetrable wire mesh, wandering Alsatian dogs and searchlights. Precautions have been taken to ensure helicopters pluck no captive away; the exercise yard, within which Frank walks for sixty minutes daily, and sometimes sees sun, has been roofed with a fine metal web. (Once, by miracle, wind bears in a green leaf. Frank consumes it with relish, to the surprise of some prisoners.) It would take more than a small army to excavate Frank from this ingenious crypt. Gates open and close reverberantly with no apparent human intervention; orders arrive via a faultless public address system, or personal intercom units in every cell; computers programme Frank's day. Warders at complex control panels, with red buttons to sound sirens, monitor his every twitch on television screens. No matter. Frank remains indifferent. His eyes are remote. He dwells upriver with Shirl. His accumulated sentences, unless some future parole board relents, still add up to more than normal life span. Safe enough to say, then, that no Lovelock living or dead has had more permanent tenure on the Porangi; Lovelock Junction has never had so eternal an inhabitant.

Postscripts, in some circumstances, can be seen as lacking in taste. This appears to be more than true now. Nevertheless this narrative must push on distastefully to its dying gasp. Which should shape itself as a question.

Natural history never goes amiss when homo sapiens is the issue. The vegetable realm holds few mysteries greater than two kinds of bamboo, categorized for convenience as the umbrella and fountain. Their precise genus remains undefined, for the very good reason that no man alive has observed either bamboo flowering – no flower, no genus – and their blossoming comes but once in a century. When that time comes, and it is due any day now, botanists may cease to be baffled, but shall have no second chance to view the event. The parent plants, once flowered, will perish. Yet here and there, germinating and taking root, young umbrella bamboo will begin to give shade and shelter, and fountain bamboo leafily to play. With no haste; they have a century's vegetating ahead. Let no one deny, though, that these seemingly colourless plants, technically just a tall version of common grass, do have their day.

Lovelock Junction can be left to legend now; and the Porangi, perhaps, to the itinerant ecologist. Sun shines. Rain falls. There is still the sound of wind and river. Take almost any day of more than three hundred and three score in any one year. No one comes. No one at all. The Lovelocks and their like, genus still undefined, have strutted and fretted their little hour upon this obscure stage. As props, ruin and river no longer have purpose; the human adventure has ceased. Sooner or later, and preferably later, the same shall also be true of all earth. There is no point in premature grief. Whether as protective umbrella or inspirational fountain, and heaven knows sometimes as satanic mutant or benign hybrid, we have an abundance of unfinished business to consider.

Existence, clearly, is more than the sum of its parts. On the other hand life can be construed as subversive of God. Art might be seen as a plea of extenuation, an always imperfect excuse. But this still begs the question; it has to be asked. Who but He holds the key to unfasten the Lovelocks of this life? Who?